DARKMANS
Nicola Barker

HARPER PERENNIAL
London, New York, Toronto and Sydney

Harper Perennial
An imprint of HarperCollins*Publishers*
77–85 Fulham Palace Road
Hammersmith
London W6 8JB

www.harperperennial.co.uk
Visit our authors' blog at www.fifthestate.co.uk

This edition published by Harper Perennial 2008
4

First published in Great Britain by Fourth Estate in 2007

A catalogue record for this book is available from the British Library

ISBN 978-0-00-719363-9

Typeset in Postscript Linotype Frutiger light, Post Antiqua bold and
Avant Garde extra light by Palimpsest Book Production Limited,
Grangemouth, Stirlingshire

Mixed Sources
Product group from well-managed
forests and other controlled sources
www.fsc.org Cert no. SW-COC-1806
© 1996 Forest Stewardship Council
FSC

FSC is a non-profit international organisation established to promote
the responsible management of the world's forests. Products carrying
the FSC label are independently certified to assure consumers that
they come from forests that are managed to meet the social,
economic and ecological needs of present and future generations.

Find out more about HarperCollins and the environment at
www.harpercollins.co.uk/green

For **Scott Ehrig-Burgess** in Del Mar,
who filled out that comment card

'These demanders for glimmer be for the most part women; for glimmer, in their language, is *fire*.'

Thomas Harman – *A Caveat for Common Cursitors* 1567

PART ONE

ONE

Kane dealt prescription drugs in Ashford; the Gateway to Europe. His main supplier was Anthony Shilling, a Waste Management Co-ordinator at the Frances Fairfax. Shilling was a quiet, Jamaican gentleman (caucasian – his family originally plantation owners) who came to England in the early seventies, settled in Dalston, London, and fell in love with a woman called Mercy, whose own family hailed from The Dominican Republic.

Mercy was British born. Anthony and Mercy moved to South Kent in 1976, where they settled and raised four daughters, one of whom was a professor of Political Sciences at Leeds University and had written a book called *Culture Clashes: Protest Songs and The Yardies (1977–1999).*

Kane was waiting for Anthony at the French Connection; a vulgar, graceless, licensed 'family restaurant' (a mammoth, prefabricated hut, inside of which a broad American roadhouse mentality rubbed up against all that was most intimate and accessible in Swiss chalet-style decor) on the fringes of the Orbital Park, one of Ashford's three largest – and most recent – greenfield industrial development sites.

The restaurant had been thoughtfully constructed to service the adjacent Travel Inn, which had, in turn, been thoughtfully constructed to service the through-traffic from the Channel Tunnel, much of which still roared carelessly past, just beyond the car park, the giant, plastic, fort-themed children's play area, the slight man-made bank and the formless, aimless tufts of old meadow and marshland with which the Bad Munstereifel Road (named after Ashford's delightful, medieval German twin) was neatly – if inconclusively – hemmed.

It was still too early for lunch on a Tuesday morning, and Kane (who hadn't been to bed yet) was slouched back in a heavily varnished pine chair, sucking ruminatively on a fresh Marlboro, and staring quizzi-cally across the table at Beede, his father.

Beede also worked at the Frances Fairfax, where he ran the laundry with an almost mythical efficiency. Beede was his surname. His first

3

name – his Christian name – was actually Daniel. But people knew him as Beede and it suited him well because he was small, and hard, and unquestionably venerable (in precisely the manner of his legendarily bookish eighth-century precursor).

Beede knew all about Kane's business dealings, and didn't actually seem to give a damn that his only son was cheerfully participating in acts of both a legally and ethically questionable nature. Yet Anthony Shilling's involvement was – in Beede's opinion – an altogether different matter. He just couldn't understand it. It deeply perplexed him. He had liked and admired both Tony and Mercy for many years. He considered them 'rounded'; a respectable, comfortable, functional couple. Mercy had been a friend of Kane's mother, Heather (now deceased – she and Beede had separated when Kane was still a toddler). Beede struggled to comprehend Tony's motivation. He knew that it wasn't just a question of money. But that was all he knew, and he didn't dare (or care) to enquire any further.

'Beede.' Kane suddenly spoke. Beede glanced up from his second-hand Penguin orange-spine with a quick frown. Kane took a long drag on his cigarette.

'Well?'

Beede was irritable.

Kane exhaled at his leisure.

'What the fuck are you doing?'

Kane's tone was not aggressive, more lackadaisical, and leavened by its trademark tinge of gentle mockery.

Beede continued to scowl. 'What does it look like?'

He shook the book at Kane – by way of an answer – then returned to it, huffily.

Kane wasn't in the slightest bit dismayed by the sharpness of Beede's response.

'But why the fuck,' he said, 'are you doing it *here*?'

Beede didn't even look up this time, just indicated, boredly, towards his coffee cup. 'Should I draw you a picture?'

Kane smiled.

He and Beede were not close. And they were not similar, either. They were different in almost every conceivable way. Beede was lithe, dark, strong-jawed, slate-haired and heavily bespectacled. He seemed like the kind of man who could deal with almost any kind of physical or intellectual challenge –

It's the radiator. If you want to try and limp back home with it, I'll need a tub of margarine, a litre of water and a packet of Stimorol; but I won't make you any promises . . .

Ned Kelly's last ever words? Spoken as he stood on the scaffold: 'Such is life.'

You're saying you've never used a traditional loom before? Well it's pretty straightforward . . .

Yes, I do believe the earwig is the only insect which actually suckles its young.

No. Nietzsche didn't hate humanity. That's far too simplistic. What Nietzsche actually said was, 'Man is something which must be overcome.'

To all intents and purposes Daniel Beede was a model citizen. So much so, in fact, that in 1983 he'd been awarded the Freedom of the Borough as a direct consequence of his tireless work in charitable and community projects during the previous two decades.

He was Ashford born and bred; a true denizen of a town which had always – but especially in recent years – been a landmark in social and physical re-invention. Ashford was a through-town, an ancient turnpike (to Maidstone, to Hythe, to Faversham, to Romney, to Canterbury), a geographical plughole; a place of passing and fording (Ash-*ford*, formerly *Essetesford*, the Eshe being a tributary of the River Stour).

Yet in recent years Beede had been in the unenviable position of finding his own home increasingly unrecognisable to him (*Change*; My *God*! He woke up, deep in the night, and could no longer locate himself. Even the blankets felt different – the quality of light through his window – the *air*). Worse still, Beede currently considered himself to be one of the few individuals in this now flourishing 'Borough of Opportunity' (current population c.102,000) to have been washed up and spat out by the recent boom.

Prior to his time (why not call it a Life Sentence?) in the hospital laundry, Beede had worked – initially at ground level (exploiting his naval training), then later, in a much loftier capacity – for Sealink (the ferry people), and had subsequently become a significant figure at

Mid-Kent Water plc; suppliers of over 36 million gallons of H2O, daily, to an area of almost 800 square miles.

If you wanted to get specific about it (and Beede always got specific) his life and his career had been irreparably blighted by the arrival of the Channel Tunnel; more specifically, by the eleventh-hour re-routing of the new Folkestone Terminal's access road from the north to the south of the tiny, nondescript Kentish village of Newington (where Beede's maternal grandmother had once lived) in 1986.

Rather surprisingly, the Chunnel hadn't initially been Beede's political *bête noire*. He'd always been studiously phlegmatic about its imminence. The prospect of its arrival had informed (and seasoned) his own child-hood in much the same way that it had informed both his parents' and his grandparents' before them (as early as the brief Peace of Amiens, Napoleon was approached by Albert Mathieu Favier – a mining engin-eer from Northern France – who planned to dig out two paved and vaulted passages between Folkestone and Cap Gris-Nez; the first, a road tunnel, lit by oil lamps and ventilated by iron chimneys, the second, to run underneath it, for drainage. This was way back in 1802. The subse-quent story of the tunnel had been a long and emotionally exhausting tale spanning two centuries and several generations; an epic narrative with countless dead-ends, low-points, disasters and casualties. Daniel Beede – and he was more than happy to admit as much – was merely one of these).

Politically, *ideologically*, Beede had generally been of a moderate bent, but at heart he was still basically progressive. And he'd always believed in the philosophy of 'a little and often', which – by and large – had worked well for him.

Yes, of course – on the environmental brief – he'd been passingly concerned about the loss of the rare Spider Orchid (the site of the proposed Folkestone Terminal was one of the few places it flourished, nationally), and not forgetting the currently endangered great crested newt, which Beede remembered catching as a boy in local cuts and streams with his simple but robust combination of a small mesh net and marmalade-jar.

And yes, he was well aware – more, perhaps, than anybody – of what the true (and potentially devastating) implications of a Channel link would be on the Kentish shipping industry (a loss of around 20,000 jobs was, at that time, the popular estimate).

And yes, *yes*, he had even harboured serious fears – and quite correctly, as it later transpired – that many of the employment opportunities on the project would pass over local people (at that point Ashford had one of the highest unemployment rates in the country) to benefit non-indigens, outside investors and foreign businesses.

It went without saying that the Chunnel (now a source of such unalloyed national complacency and pride) had caused huge headaches – and terrible heartache – in East Kent, but Beede's greatest betrayal had been on a much smaller, more informal, more *abstract* level.

Beede's maternal grandmother's home had been a neat, quaint, unpretentious little cottage (pottery sink, tile floors, outside lavvy) in the middle of a symmetrical facade of five known as Church Cottages. They were located at the conjunction of the old School Road and Newington's main, central thoroughfare The Street (no shop, no pub, twenty-five houses, at a push).

Much as their name implies, Church Cottages enjoyed a close physical proximity with Newington's twelfth-century church and its similarly ancient – and much-feted – graveyard Yew.

Beede's paternal grandparents (to whom he was slightly less close) also lived locally – several hundred yards north up the aforementioned Street – in the neighbouring village of Peene. Just so long as any inhabitant of either of these two tiny Kentish villages could remember, they had considered themselves a single community.

When the developer's plans for the new Folkestone Terminal were initially proposed, however, it quickly became apparent that all this was soon about to change. Several farms and properties (not least, the many charming, if ramshackle homes in the idiosyncratic Kentish hamlet of Danton Pinch) were to be sacrificed to the terminal approach and concourse, not to mention over 500 acres of prime farmland and woodland, as well as all remaining evidence of the old Elham Valley Railway (built in 1884, disused since 1947). But worse still, the access road from the terminal to the M20 was due to cut a wide path straight between Newington and Peene, thereby cruelly separating them, forever.

Beede's maternal grandmother and paternal grandparents were now long gone. Beede's mother had died of breast cancer in 1982. His part-senile father now lived with Beede's older brother on the south coast, just outside Hastings.

Beede's parents had moved to the heart of Ashford (14 miles away) two years before he was even conceived, but Beede maintained a lively interest in their old stamping ground; still visited it regularly, had many contacts among the local Rotary and Cricket Clubs (the cricket grounds were yet another Chunnel casualty), friends and relatives in both of the affected villages, and a strong sense – however fallacious – that the union of these two places (like the union of his two parents) was a critical – almost a *physical* – part of his own identity.

They could not be divided.

It was early in the spring of 1984 when he first became aware of Eurotunnel's plans. Beede was a well-seasoned campaigner and local prime mover. His involvement was significant. His opinions mattered. And he was by no means the only dynamic party with a keen interest in this affair. There were countless others who felt equally strongly, not least (it soon transpired) Shepway's District Council. On closer inspection of the proposed scheme, the Council had become alarmed by the idea that this divisive 'Northern Access Route' might actively discourage disembarking Chunnel traffic from travelling to Dover, Folkestone or Hythe (Shepway's business heartland) by feeding it straight on to the M20 (and subsequently straight on to London). The ramifications of this decision were perceived as being potentially catastrophic for local businesses and the tourist trade.

A complaint was duly lodged. The relevant government committee (where the buck ultimately stopped) weighed up the various options on offer and then quietly turned a blind eye to them. But the fight was by no means over. In response, the Council, Beede, and many residents of Newington and Peene got together and threatened a concerted policy of non-cooperation with Eurotunnel if a newly posited scheme known as 'The Shepway Alternative' (a scheme still very much in its infancy) wasn't to be considered as a serious contender.

In the face of such widespread opposition the committee reassessed the facts and – in a glorious blaze of publicity – backed down. The decision was overturned, and the new Southern Access Route became a reality.

This small but hard-won victory might've been an end to the Newington story. But it wasn't. Because now (it suddenly transpired) there were to be *other* casualties, directly as a consequence of this hard-won Alternative. And they would be rather more severe and destructive than had been initially apprehended.

To keep their villages unified, Newington and Peene had sacrificed a clutch of beautiful, ancient properties (hitherto unaffected by the terminal scheme) which stood directly in the path of the newly proposed Southern Link with the A20 and the terminal. One of these was the grand Victorian vicarage, known as The Grange, with its adjacent Coach House (now an independent dwelling). Another, the magnificent, mid-sixteenth-century farmhouse known as Stone Farm. Yet another, the historic water mill (now non-functioning, but recently renovated and lovingly inhabited, with its own stable block) known as Mill House.

Beede wasn't naive. He knew only too well how the end of one drama could sometimes feed directly into the start of another. And so it was with the advent of what soon became known as 'The Newington Hit List'.

Oh the uproar! The sense of local betrayal! The media posturing and ranting! The archaeological *chaos* engendered by this eleventh-hour re-routing! And Beede (who hadn't, quite frankly, really considered all of these lesser implications – Mid-Kent Water plc didn't run itself, after all) found himself involved (didn't he owe the condemned properties that much, at least?) in a crazy miasma of high-level negotiations, conservation plans, archaeological investigations and restoration schemes, in a last-ditch attempt to rectify the environmental devastation which (let's face it) he himself had partially engendered.

Eurotunnel had promised to dismantle and re-erect any property (or part of a property) that was considered to be of real historical significance. The Old Grange and its Coach House were not 'historical' enough for inclusion in this scheme and were duly bulldozed. Thankfully some of the other properties did meet Eurotunnel's high specifications. Beede's particular involvement was with Mill House, which – it soon transpired – had been mentioned in the Domesday Book and had a precious, eighteenth-century timber frame.

The time for talking was over. Beede put his money where his mouth was. He shut up and pulled on his overalls. And it was hard graft: dirty, heavy, time-consuming work (every tile numbered and categorised, every brick, every beam), but this didn't weaken Beede's resolve (Beede's resolve was legendary. He gave definition to the phrase 'a stickler').

Beede was committed. And he was not a quitter. Early mornings, evenings, weekends, he toiled tirelessly alongside a group of other volunteers (many of them from Canterbury's Archaeological Trust) slowly, painstakingly, stripping away the mill's modern exterior, and (like a deathly coven of master pathologists), uncovering its ancient skeleton below.

It wasn't all plain sailing. At some point (and who could remember when, exactly?) it became distressingly apparent that recent 'improvements' to the newer parts of Mill House had seriously endangered the older structure's integrity –

Now hang on –
Just . . . just back up a second –
What are you saying here, exactly?

The worst-case scenario? That the old mill might never be able to function independently in its eighteenth-century guise; like a conjoined twin, it might only really be able to exist as a small part of its former whole.

But the life support on the newer part had already been switched off (they'd turned it off themselves, hadn't they? And with such care, such tenderness), so gradually – as the weeks passed, the months – the team found themselves in the unenviable position of standing helplessly by and watching – with a mounting sense of desolation – as the older part's heartbeat grew steadily weaker and weaker. Until one day, finally, it just stopped.

They had all worked so hard, and with such pride and enthusiasm. But for what? An exhausted Beede staggered back from the dirt and the rubble (a little later than the others, perhaps; his legendary resolve still inappropriately firm), shaking his head, barely comprehending, wiping a red-dust-engrained hand across a moist, over-exerted face. Marking himself. But there was no point in his war-painting. He was alone. The fight was over. It was lost.

And the worst part? He now knew the internal mechanisms of that old mill as well as he knew the undulations of his own ribcage. He had crushed his face into its dirty crevices. He had filled his nails with its sawdust. He had pushed his ear up against the past and had sensed the ancient breath held within it. He had gripped the liver of history and had felt it squelching in his hand –

Expanding –
Struggling –

So what now? What now? What to tell the others? How to make sense of it all? How to rationalise? Worse still, how to face the hordes of encroaching construction workers in their bright yellow TML uniforms, with their big schemes and tons of concrete, with their impatient cranes and their diggers?

Beede had given plenty in his forty-odd years. But now (he pinched himself. *Shit*. He felt *nothing*) he had given too much. He had found his limit. He had reached it and he had over-stepped it. He was engulfed by disappointment. Slam-dunked by it. He could hardly *breathe*, he felt it so strongly. His whole body ached with the pain of it. He was so stressed – felt so *invested* in his thwarted physicality – that he actually thought he might be developing some kind of fatal disease. Pieces of him stopped functioning. He was *broken*.

And then, just when things seemed like they couldn't get any worse –

Oh God!
The day the bulldozers came . . .

(He'd skipped work. They'd tried to keep him off-site. There was an ugly scuffle. But he saw it! He stood and watched – three men struggling to restrain him – he stood and he watched – jaw slack, mouth wide, *gasping* – as History was unceremoniously gutted and then steam-rollered. He saw History *die* –

NO!
You're killing History!
STOP!)

– just when things seemed like they were hitting rock bottom ('You need a holiday. A good rest. You're absolutely exhausted – *dangerously* exhausted; mentally, physically . . .') things took one further, inexorable, downward spiral.

The salvageable parts of the mill had been taken into storage by Eurotunnel. One of the most valuable parts being its ancient Kent Peg Tiles –

Ah yes
Those beautiful tiles . . .

Then one day they simply disappeared.

They had been preserved. They had been maintained. They had been entrusted. They had been *lost*.

BUT WHERE THE HELL ARE THEY?
WHERE DID THEY GO?
WHERE?
WHERE?!

It had all been in vain. And nobody really cared (it later transpired, or if they did, they stopped caring, eventually – they *had* to, to survive it), except for Beede – who hadn't really cared that much in the first place – but who had done something bold, something decisive, something out of the ordinary; *Beede* – who had committed himself, had become embroiled, then engrossed, then utterly preoccupied, then thoroughly—

Irredeemably

– fucked up and casually (like the past itself) discarded.

And no, in the great scheme of things, it didn't amount to very much. Just some old beams, some rotten masonry, some traditional tiles. But Beede suddenly found that he'd lost not only those tiles, but his own rudimentary supports. His *faith*. The roof of Beede's confidence had been lifted and had blown clean away. His optimism. He had lost it. It just *went*.

And nothing – *nothing* – had felt the same, afterwards. Nothing had felt comfortable. Nothing fitted. A full fifteen years had passed, and yet – and at complete variance with the cliché – for Beede time had been anything but a great healer.

Progress, *modernity* (all now dirty words in Beede's vocabulary) had kicked him squarely in the balls. I mean he hadn't asked for much, had he? He'd sacrificed the Spider Orchid, hadn't he? A familiar geography? He'd only wanted, out of *respect*, to salvage . . . to salvage . . .

What?

A semblance of what had been? Or was it just a question of . . . was it just a matter of . . . of *form*? Something as silly and apparently insignificant as . . . as *good manners*?

There had been one too many compromises. He knew that much for certain. The buck had needed to stop and it never had. It'd never stopped. So Beede had put on his own brakes and he had stopped. The compromise culture became his anathema. He had shed his former skin (*Mr Moderate, Mr Handy, Mr Reasonable*) and had blossomed into an absolutist. But on his own terms. And in the daintiest of ways. And very quietly –

Shhh!

Oh no, no, *no*, the war wasn't over –

Shhh!

Beede was still fighting (mainly in whispers), it was just that – by and large – they were battles that nobody else knew about. Only Beede. Only he knew. But it was a hard campaign; a fierce, long, difficult campaign. And as with all major military strategies, there were gains and there were losses.

Beede was now sixty-one years of age, and he was his own walking wounded. He was a shadow of his former self. His past idealism had deserted him. And somehow – along the way – he had lost interest in almost everything (in work, in family), but he had maintained an interest in one thing: he had maintained an interest in that old mill.

He had become a detective. A bloodhound. He had sniffed out clues. He had discovered things; stories, alibis, weaknesses; inconsistencies. He had weighed up the facts and drawn his conclusions. But he had bided his time (time was the one thing he had plenty of – no *rush*; that was the modern disease – no *need* to rush).

Then finally (at last) he had apportioned blame. With no apparent emotion, he had put names to faces (hunting, finding, assessing, gauging). And like Death he had lifted his scythe, and had kept it lifted; waiting for his own judgement to fall; holding his breath – like an ancient yogi or a Pacific pearl diver; like the still before the storm, like a suspended wave: freeze-framed, *poised*. He held and he held. He even (and this was the wonderful, the crazy, the hideous part) found a terrible *equilibrium* in holding.

Beede was the vengeful tsunami of history.

But even the venerable could not hold indefinitely.

'You know what?' Kane suddenly spoke, as if waking from a dream. 'I'd *like* that.'

Beede didn't stir from his book.

'I'd actually *like* it if you drew me a picture. Do you have a pencil?'

Kane was twenty-six years old and magnificently quiescent. He was a floater; as buoyant and slippery as a dinghy set adrift on a choppy sea. He was loose and unapologetically light-weight (being light-weight was the only thing he ever really took seriously). He was so light-weight, in fact, that sometimes (when the wind gusted his way) he might fly into total indolence and do nothing for three whole days but read sci-fi, devour fried onion rings and drink tequilla in front of a muted-out backdrop of MTV.

Kane knew what he liked (knowing what you liked was, he felt, one of the most important characteristics of a modern life well lived). He knew what he wanted and, better yet, what he needed. He was easy as a greased nipple (and pretty much as moral). He was tall (6' 3", on a good day), a mousy blond, rubber-faced, blue-eyed, with a full, cruel mouth. Almost handsome. He dressed without any particular kind of distinction. Slightly scruffy. Tending towards plumpness, but still too young for the fat to have taken any kind of permanent hold on him. He had a slight American accent. As a kid he'd lived for seven years with his mother in the Arizona desert and had opted to keep the vocal cadences of that region as a souvenir.

'Come to think of it, I believe I may actually . . .'

Kane busily inspected his own trouser pockets, then swore under his breath, sat up and glanced around him. A waitress was carrying a tray of clean glasses from somewhere to somewhere else.

'Excuse me . . .' Kane waved at her, 'would you happen to have a pencil on you?'

The waitress walked over. She was young and pretty with a mass of short, unruly blonde hair pinned back from her neat forehead by a series of precarious-looking, brightly coloured kirby grips.

'I might have one in my . . . *uh* . . .'

She slid the tray of glasses on to the table. Kane helpfully rearranged his large Pepsi and his cherry danish (currently untouched) to make room for it. Maude (the strangely old-fashioned name was emblazoned on her badge) smiled her thanks and slid her hand into the pocket of her apron. She removed a tiny pencil stub.

'It's very small,' she said.

Kane took the pencil and inspected it. It was minuscule.

'It's an HB,' he said, carefully reading its chewed tip, then glancing over at Beede. 'Is an HB okay? Is it soft enough?'

Beede did not look up.

Kane turned back to the waitress, who was just preparing to grapple with the tray of glasses again.

'Before you pick that up, Maude,' Kane said, balancing his cigarette on the edge of his plate, 'you wouldn't happen to have a piece of *paper* somewhere, would you?'

'Uh . . .'

The waitress pushed her hand back into her apron and removed her notepad. She bit her lip. 'I have a pad but I'm not really . . .'

Kane put out his hand and took the pad from her. He flipped though it.

'The paper's kind of thin,' he said. 'What I'm actually looking for is some sort of . . .'

He mused for a moment. 'Like an *artist's* pad. Like a *Daler* pad. I don't know if you've heard of that brand name before? It's like an *art* brand . . .'

The waitress shook her head. A kirby grip flew off. She quickly bent down and grabbed it.

'Oh. Well that's a shame . . .'

The waitress straightened up again, clutching the grip.

Kane grinned at her. It was an appealing grin. Her cheeks reddened.

'Here . . .' Kane said, 'let me . . .'

He leaned forward, removed the kirby grip from her grasp, popped it expertly open, beckoned her to lean down towards him, then applied it, carefully, to a loose section of her fringe.

'There . . .'

He drew back and casually appraised his handiwork. 'Good as new.'

'Thanks.' She slowly straightened up again. She looked befuddled. Kane took a quick drag on his cigarette. The waitress – observing this breach – laced her fingers together and frowned slightly (as if sternly reacquainting her girlish self with all the basic rules of restaurant etiquette). '*Um* . . . I'm afraid you're not really . . .' she muttered, peeking nervously over her shoulder.

'What?'

Kane gazed at her. His blue eyes held hers, boldly. '*What*?'

She winced. 'Smoke . . . you're not really meant to . . . not in the restaurant.'

'Oh . . . *yeah*,' Kane nodded emphatically, 'I know that.'

She nodded herself, in automatic response, then grew uncertain again. He passed her the pad. She took it and slid it into her apron. 'Can I hold on to this pencil?' Kane asked, suspending it, in its entirety, between his first finger and his thumb. 'As a keepsake?'

The waitress shot an anxious, side-long glance towards Beede (still reading). 'Of course,' she said.

She grabbed her tray again.

'Thank you,' Kane murmured, 'that's very generous. You've been really . . .' he paused, weighing her up, appreciatively '. . . *sweet*.'

The waitress – plainly disconcerted by Kane's intense scrutiny – took a rapid step away from him, managing, in the process, to incline her tray slightly. The glasses slid around a little. She paused, with a gasp, and clumsily readjusted her grip.

'Bye then,' Kane said (not even a suggestion of laughter in his voice). She glanced up, thoroughly flustered. '*Yes*,' she said, 'of course. Thank you. *Bye* . . .'

Then she ducked her head down, grimacing, and fled.

Beede continued reading. It was as if the entire episode with the waitress had completely eluded him.

Kane gently placed the pencil next to Beede's coffee cup, then picked up his danish and took a large bite of it. He winced as his tooth hit down hard on a stray cherry stone.

'*Shit.*'

He spat the offending mouthful into a napkin – silently denouncing all foodstuffs of a natural origin – then carefully explored the afflicted tooth with his tongue. While he did so, he gazed idly over towards the large picture window to his right, and out into the half-empty car park beyond.

'Expecting someone?' Beede asked, quick as a shot.

Kane took a second (rather more cautious) bite of the danish. 'Yup,' he said, unabashedly, 'Anthony Shilling.'

'*What?!*'

Beede glanced up as he processed this name, a series of conflicting expressions hurtling across his face.

'I thought you knew,' Kane said (eyebrows slightly raised), still chewing.

'How would I know?' Beede snapped, slapping down his book.

'Because you're *here*,' Kane said, 'and why else would you be? It's miles away from anywhere you'd ever normally go, and it's a shithole.'

'I come here often,' Beede countered. 'I *like* it. It's convenient for work.'

'That's just a silly lie,' Kane sighed, evincing zero tolerance for Beede's dissembling.

'Strange as this may seem,' Beede hissed, 'I'm actually in no particular hurry to get caught up in some sordid little situation between you and one of my senior *work* colleagues . . .'

'Well that's a shame,' Kane said, casually picking up his cigarette again, 'because that's exactly what's about to happen.'

Beede leaned down and grabbed a hold of his small, khaki work-bag – as though intending to make a dash for it – but then he didn't actually move. Something (in turn) held him.

Kane frowned. 'Beede, why the fuck are you *here*?' he asked again, now almost sympathetically.

'They make a good coffee,' Beede lied, dropping the bag again.

'Fuck *off*. The coffee is heinous,' Kane said. 'And just *look* at you,' he added, 'you're *crapping* yourself. You hate this place. The piped music is making you nauseous. Your knee is jogging up and down under the table so hard you're knocking all the bubbles out of my Pepsi.'

Beede's knee instantly stopped its jogging.

Kane took a quick swig of the imperilled beverage (it was still surprisingly fizzy), and as he placed the glass back down again, it suddenly dawned on him – the way all new things dawned on him: slowly, and with a tiny, mischievous jolt – how unbelievably guarded his father seemed –

Beede?
Hiding something?

His mind reeled back a way, then forwards again –

Hmmn

Beede. This rock. This monolith. This man-mountain. This closed book. This locked door. This shut-down thing.

For once he actually seemed . . . almost . . . well, almost *cagey*. Anxious. Wary. Kane stared harder. This was certainly a first. This was definitely a novelty. My *God*. Yes. Even in his *littlest* movements (now he came to think of it): knocking his disposable carton of creamer against the lip of his coffee cup (a tiny splash landing on the spotless nail of his thumb); kicking his bag; picking up his book; fumbling as he turned over the corner of a page, then *un*folding it and jumpily pretending to recommence with his reading.

Kane rolled his cigarette around speculatively between his fingers. Beede glanced up for a moment, met Kane's gaze, shifted his focus off sideways – in the general direction of the entrance (which was not actually visible from where they were seated) – and then looked straight down again.

Now *that* was odd. Kane frowned. Beede uncertain? Furtive? To actively *break* his gaze in that way?

What?!

Unheard of! Beede was the original *architect* of the unflinching stare. Beede's stare was so steady he could make an owl crave Optrex. Beede could happily unrapt a raptor. And he'd done some pretty nifty ground-work over the years in the Guilt Trip arena (*trip?* How about a gruelling two-month sabbatical in the parched, ancient Persian city of Firuzabad? And he'd do your packing. And he'd book your hotel. And it'd be miles from the airport. And there'd be no fucking air conditioning). Beede was the hair shirt in human form.

Kane took another swig of his Pepsi –

Okay –
But how huge is this?

He couldn't honestly tell if it was merely the small things, or if the big things were now also subtly implicated in what he was currently (and so joyously) perceiving as a potentially wholesale situation of emotional whitewash (Oh come *on*. Wasn't he in danger of blowing the whole thing out of proportion here? This was *Beede* for Christsakes. He was sixty-one years old. He worked shifts in the hospital laundry. He hated everybody. The word 'judgemental' couldn't do him justice. If Beede was judgemental then King Herod was 'a little skittish'.

Beede thought modern life was 'all waffle'. He'd never owned a car, but persisted in driving around on an ancient, filthy and shockingly unreliable Douglas motorcycle – c. 1942, with the requisite piss-pot helmet. He didn't own a tv. He found Radio 4 'chicken-livered'. He feared the microwave. He thought deodorant was the devil's sputum. He blamed David Beckham – personally – for breeding a whole generation of boys whose only meaningful relationship was with the mirror. He called it 'kid-narcissism' . . . although he still used hair oil himself, and copiously. Unperfumed, of course. He was rigorously allergic to sandalwood, seafood and lanolin; *Jeez!* An oriental prawn in a lambswool sweater would probably've done for him).

Okay. *Okay*. So Kane freely admitted (Kane did everything freely) that he took so little interest in Beede's life, in general, that he might actually find it quite difficult to delineate between the two (the big things, the small). He tipped his head to one side. I mean what *mattered* to Beede? Did he live large? Was he lost in the details?

Or (now hang on a second) perhaps – Kane promptly pulled himself off his self-imposed hook (no apparent damage to knitwear) – perhaps he *did* know. Perhaps he'd drunk it all in, subconsciously, the way any son must. Perhaps he knew everything already and merely had to do a spot of careful digging around inside his own keen – if irredeemably frivolous – psyche (polishing things off, systematising, card-indexing) to sort it all out.

But Oh God that'd be hard work! That'd take some real effort. And it'd be messy. And he was tired. And – quite frankly – Beede *bored* him. Beede was just so . . . so vehement. So intent. So focussed. *Too* focussed. *Horribly* focussed. In fact Beede was quite focussed enough for the both of them (and why not add a small gang of Olympic Tri-Athletes, an international chess champion, and that crazy nut who carved the Eiffel Tower out of a fucking *tooth*pick into the mix, for good measure?).

Beede was so uptight, so pent up, so unbelievably . . . uh . . . *priggish* (*re*-pressed/*sup*-pressed – you name it, he *was* it) that if he ever actually deigned to cut loose (*Beede? Cut loose? Are you serious*?!) then he would probably just *cut right out* (yawn. *Again*), like some huge but cranky petrol-driven lawnmower (a tremendously well-constructed but unwieldy old Allen, say). I mean all that deep inner turmoil . . . all that . . . that tightly buttoned, straight-backed, quietly creaking, Strindberg-style *tension*. Where the hell would it go? How on earth could it . . . ?

Eh?

Of course, by comparison – and by sheer coincidence – Kane's entire life mission –

Oh how lovely to hone in on me again

– was to be mirthful. To be fluffy. To endow mere trifles with an exquisitely inappropriate *gravitas*. Kane found depth an abomination. He lived in the shallows, and, like a shark (a sand shark; not a biter), he basked in them. He both eschewed boredom and yet considered himself the ultimate arbiter of it. Boredom terrified him. And because Beede, his father, was so exquisitely dull (celebrated a kind of immaculate dullness – he was the Virgin Mary of the Long Hour) Kane had gradually engineered himself into his father's anti.

If Beede had ever sought to underpin the community then Kane had always sought to undermine it. If Beede lived like a monk, then Kane revelled in smut and degeneracy. If Beede felt the burden of life's weight (and heaven knows, he felt it), then Kane consciously rejected worldly care.

A useful (and gratifying) side-product of this process was Kane's gradual apprehension that there was a special kind of *glory* in self-interest, a magnificence in self-absorption, a heroism in degeneracy, which other people (the general public – the *culture*) seemed to find not only laudable, but actively endearing.

Come on. Come *on*; nobody liked a stuffed shirt; nobody found puritanism sexy (except for Angelo who wanted to shag Isabella in *Measure for Measure*. But Shakespeare was a pervert; and they didn't bother teaching you *that* in O-level literature . . .); nobody – but *nobody* – wanted to stand next to the teetotaller at the party –

Hey! Where's the guy in the novelty hat with the six pack of beer?

   Kane half-smiled to himself as he took out his phone, opened it,
deftly ran through his texts, closed it, shoved it back into his pocket,
took a final drag on his cigarette and then stubbed it out.
   'So what's that you're reading?'
He picked up his lighter (a smart, silver and red-enamelled Ronson)
and struck it, lightly –

Nothing.

   After an almost interminable six-second hiatus, Beede closed his
book and placed it down – with a small sigh – on to his lap. 'Whatever
happened to that girl?' he asked mechanically (having immediately
apprehended the fatuous nature of Kane's literary enquiry).
Kane frowned –

Wow . . .
To answer a question with a question –
Masterly.

'Girl?' Kane stared back at him, blankly. 'Which girl? The wait-
ress?'
'Don't be ridiculous,' Beede snapped. 'The *little* girl. The skinny one.
I haven't seen her around in a while . . .'
'Skinny?'
Kane adopted a look of cheerful bewilderment.
   'The redhead,' Beede persisted (thoroughly immune to Kane's
humbug): '*Too* skinny. Red hair. *Bright* red hair . . .'
'Red hair?'
'Yes. Red hair. *Purple*-red . . .'
'Purple?'
'Yes . . .' (Beede yanked on his trusty, old pair of mental crampons
and kicked them, grimly, into the vertical rockface of his self-control).
'Yes. Purple.'
   Kane didn't seem to notice.
'Purple?' he repeated, taking some time out to savour the feel of this
word on his tongue –

Pur-ple
Purrrrr-pull

– then glancing up –

Ooops

– and relenting. 'You probably mean Kelly,' he vouchsafed, almost lasciviously. 'Little Kelly Broad. Lovely, filthy, *skinny*, little Kelly . . .'

'Kelly *Broad*. Of course,' Beede echoed curtly. 'So are the two of you still an item?'

An *item*? Kane smirked at this quaint formulation. 'Hell, no . . .' he took a long swig of his Pepsi, 'that's all . . .' he burped, '*excuse* me . . . totally fucked now.'

Beede waited, patiently, for any further elucidation. None was forthcoming.

'Well that's a pity,' he finally murmured.

'Why?' Kane wondered.

Beede shrugged, as if the answer was simply obvious.

'Why?' Kane asked again (employing exactly the same maddening vocal emphasis as before).

'Because she was a decent enough girl,' Beede observed stolidly, 'and I *liked* her.'

Kane snorted. Beede glanced up at him, wounded. He took a quick sip of his coffee (in the hope of masking any further emotional leakage), then – *urgh* – winced, involuntarily.

'Tasty?' Kane enquired, with an arch lift of his brow. Beede placed the cup back down, very gently, on to its saucer. Kane idly struck at his lighter again –

Nothing.

'So you think I had a problem with her?' Beede wondered, out loud, after a brief interval.

'Pardon?' Kane was already thoroughly bored by the subject.

'A problem? You mean with Kelly? *Uh* . . .' He gave this a moment's thought. 'Yes. *Yes*. I suppose I think you did.'

Beede looked shocked.

Kane chuckled. 'Oh come *on* . . .'

'What?'

'You *oozed* disapproval.'

'Did I?'

'Through every conceivable orifice.'

Beede's nostrils flared at this cruel defamation, but he drew a long, deep breath and swallowed down his ire.

'Okay. *Okay* . . .' he murmured tightly. 'So what do you think I "disapproved" of exactly?'

Kane threw up his hands. 'Where to begin?'

Beede folded his arms. Kane duly noted the folding. 'All right then,' he volunteered, 'you thought she was a tart.'

Beede blinked –

Tart?

'*You* know . . .' Kane's voice adopted the tender but world-weary tone of an adult describing something simple yet fundamental to a wayward toddler – like how to eat, how to *walk* ('So you put one foot . . . *that's* it, one foot, very slowly, in front of the other . . .') '. . . a tart; a harlot, a strumpet, a whore . . .'

Beede opened his mouth to respond, but Kane barrelled on, 'Although you shouldn't actually feel bad about it. I was fine with it. In fact – if anything – it was an *incentive* of sorts . . . I mean romantically.'

He paused for a second, musing. 'Isn't it odd how the disapproval of others can often contribute so profoundly to one's enjoyment of a thing?'

Beede opened his mouth to answer.

'Tarts especially,' Kane interrupted him.

'Well she certainly dressed quite provocatively . . .' Beede ruminated.

Kane waved this objection aside. '*Nah*. It was all just an act. Smoke and mirrors. A total fabrication. She was a sweetheart, an innocent. Her bad reputation was down to nothing more than a couple of stupid choices and some bad PR.'

'But you still broke up with her,' Beede needled.

Kane shrugged.

'Indicating that perhaps – at some level – it *did* actually bother you?'

'No,' Kane shook his head. 'It wasn't ever a question of virtue with

Kelly. It was simply an issue of trust.'

'Ah-*ha* . . .' Beede pounced on this idea, greedily. 'But isn't that the *same* issue?'

'Absolutely not.'

Kane smiled at his father, almost fondly, as if touched – even flattered – by the unexpectedly intrusive line of his questioning. 'She wasn't a tart. Not at all. But she *was* a thief, which is a quality I find marginally less endearing.'

Beede seemed taken aback by this piece of information.

'She stole? What did she steal?'

'*Huh?*'

Kane's attention was momentarily diverted by a sudden commotion outside in the car park.

'I said what did she steal?'

Kane struck his lighter again –

Nothing

'You really want to know?' he murmured.

'I just *asked*, didn't I?'

'Yes. Yes you did . . .' He sighed. 'She stole tranquillisers, mainly; Benzodiazepines . . .'

Kane struck his lighter for a final time and on this occasion a flame actually emerged and it was a full 5 inches high (he always set his lighters at maximum flare, even if his fringe paid the ultimate price for his profligacy).

'. . . Some Xanax. Some Valium. Some . . .'

He paused, abruptly, mid-enumeration –

'Holy *shit!*'

The flame cut out.

A man.

There was a man.

There was a man at the window, gazing in at them. And he was perched on a horse; an old, piebald mare (the horse wore no saddle, no reins, but he sat astride her – holding on to her mane – with absolute confidence). He was a strange man; had a long, lean, pale-looking face underpinned by a considerable jaw, grey with stubble; a mean mouth, sharp, dark eyes, thick, brown brows but no other hair to speak of. His head was cleanly shaven. He was handsome – vital, even – but with a distinctly delinquent air. He was wearing something strangely unfeasible in a bright yellow (a colour of such phenomenal intensity it'd cheerfully take the shine off a prize canary).

The window was horse-high, only; its torso banged against the glass, steaming it over – so the man leaned down low to peek in, as if peering into the tank of an aquarium (or a display cabinet in a museum). Kane couldn't tell – at first – what exactly it was that he was looking for, but he seemed absolutely enthralled by what he saw (seemed to take delight in things – like a child – quite readily). He was smiling (although not in an entirely child-like way), and when his eyes alighted upon Kane, the smile expanded, exponentially (small, neat, yellowed teeth, a touch of tongue). He reached out a hand and beckoned towards him –

Come

Kane dropped his lighter.
As the lighter hit the table-top Beede turned himself and followed the line of Kane's gaze. His own eyes widened.

The horseman kicked at the mare's flanks and pulled away. There was a thud of hooves on soil (God only knows what havoc he'd wreaked on the spring flower display in the bed below the window) and then a subsequent musket-clatter on the tarmac.

Kane shoved back his chair and stood up. 'Is the fucking carnival in town or what?' he asked (noticing the quick pump of his heart, the sharp flow of his breath). He'd barely finished speaking (was about half-way to the window to try and see more) when a woman walked into the room. She was holding on to the hand of a small boy. She appeared to be searching for someone.

This time it was Beede's turn to spring to his feet. The book on his lap fell to the floor. Kane spun around to the sound of its falling. '*Elen!*' Beede exclaimed, his face flushing slightly.

The woman did not acknowledge him at first. She merely paused, glanced from Beede to Kane, then back again, her expression barely altering (it remained bright and calm and untroubled. Almost serene). Kane saw that she had a large birthmark – a brown mole – in the curve of her nose, just to the right of her left eye, but it disappeared from view as a sheet of long, dark hair slipped out from behind her ear.

'Did Isidore bring you here?' Beede asked, trying (and almost succeeding) to sound less emotionally involved than before.

She looked a little surprised as she pushed back her hair. 'Of course not,' her lips pursed together in a brief pucker of concern, 'he's at work today.'

She had a soft voice. The accent wasn't Ashford but it was too vague for Kane to place it. As she spoke she released the boy's hand. The boy walked straight past Kane and over to the window, but instead of looking through it (he was a little short for this, anyhow), he turned, shoved his back against the wall, and pulled the curtain across the top half of his body (thereby casually obscuring what remained of Kane's view). Kane scowled (only the bottom half of the boy's torso was now visible), glancing from the curtain and back to Beede again. 'Did you *see* that creature out there?' he asked, his head still full of what'd happened before.

'This is my son, Kane,' Beede murmured to the woman, in a light, almost excessively straightforward way.

The woman nodded at Kane. She smiled slightly. She was very lean. Her clothes were long and hippyish, but dark and plain and clean.

'Elen is my chiropodist,' Beede explained.

'Hi,' Kane muttered, glancing distractedly towards the window again, focussing in on the boy, who – quiet as he remained – was rather difficult to ignore.

'Fleet,' the woman said – her voice mild but authoritative – 'please come away from there.'

'I owed Elen some money,' Beede continued (almost to thin air). He put his hand to his pocket, then thought better of it and leaned down to pick up his bag from the floor.

Kane noticed how he pronounced her name – not Ellen, but E-*len* – as if the 'l' had quite bewitched his tongue.

The boy ducked out from under the curtain (leaving it drawn), walked back over to his mother and stood at her side. He was small and wild-looking (four years old? five?); an imp; round-faced and wide-lipped, with pale skin, brown freckles and black hair. He stared at Kane, unblinking. Then he smiled. He had no front teeth.

'We were waiting in the bar area,' the woman said, glancing for a moment towards the window herself (as if sensing Kane's preoccupation with it). 'Fleet found a counter on the floor and put it into one of the machines. He won some money.'

The boy jiggled his hands around in his pockets and gurgled, delightedly.

'The barman said he was underage . . .'

'He is,' Beede interrupted.

Kane rolled his eyes, then displaced his irritation by taking out his phone and checking his texts again. The woman observed Kane's irritation, but showed no reaction to it.

'He gave me all of these,' Fleet interjected, pulling several packets of complimentary matches from his pockets, laughing and rotating on the spot, his face turned up to the ceiling, the matches clutched tightly to his chest. His mother put out her hand to steady him. 'He builds things with them,' she explained.

Outside the horse was still vaguely audible as it moved around in the car park. While Beede continued to search through his bag, Kane strolled over to the window, pulled the curtain back and peered out. The horse was visible, but way off to his left. It had come to a halt in the children's play area, where it stood, breathing heavily and defecating. The man was now struggling to climb off its back. But it was an entirely different man.

Kane blinked.

Entirely different. Tall. Nordic. Smartly dressed in some kind of uniform –

Imposter

He pushed his palms up against the glass and looked around for the canary-coated stranger, but nobody else was visible out there.

'How strange,' he said, turning just in time to see Beede's hand withdrawing from the woman's hand (he had passed her an envelope. She placed it into her bag, her eyes meeting Kane's, calmly).

'What is?' Beede asked.

'The man who peered in through the window a moment ago. The man on the horse. He's changed.'

'How do you mean?'

'He had a shaved head and a thin face. He was dressed in yellow.'

The boy suddenly stopped revolving. He grabbed on to his mother's skirts. 'Oh *dear*,' he whispered, then pushed his face deep into the fabric and kept it hidden there.

27

The child was definitely beginning to work on Kane's nerves.

Beede was staring at Kane, but his expression was unreadable (was it disbelief? Was it irritation? Anger? What *was* it?) The woman merely stared at the ground, frowning, as if carefully considering something.

'Did *you* see him?' Kane asked again.

'Uh . . . *no*. No. And I'm late – *work*. I'd better head off.' Beede spoke abruptly. He touched the woman's sleeve (she smiled), ruffled the boy's hair (the boy released his mother's skirt and gazed up at him), slung his bag over his shoulder, grabbed his helmet, his goggles, and rapidly strode off.

Kane watched him go, blankly. Then he blinked (something seemed to strike him) and he focussed –

What?!

Beede disappeared from view.

'Is anything the matter?' the woman asked, observing Kane's sudden air of confusion.

He turned to look at her. 'No.' He put his hand to his head.

'Yeah.' He removed his hand. '*No* . . . It's just that . . .' he paused, 'Beede . . . There's something . . . something *odd*.'

She nodded, as if she understood what he meant.

'What is it?' he asked.

She smiled (that *smile* again) but didn't answer.

'Do you know?'

He struggled to mask his irritation. She folded her arms across her chest and nodded again, now almost teasing him.

'Then what is it?'

'His walk,' she said, plainly.

Kane drew a sharp breath. 'His *limp*,' he exclaimed (as if this information had come to him entirely without prompting). 'He's lost his *limp*.'

'Yes.'

'But how . . . ? *When*?'

'A while ago now.'

'Really?'

She nodded. Kane scratched his jaw –

Two days' growth

28

He felt engulfed by a sudden wave of feeblemindedness –

Too tired
Too stoned
Too fucked . . .

He looked at her, hard, as if she might be the answer to his problem –

Chiropodist

'Did *you* get rid of it?' he asked.
She smiled, her eyes shining.
   Kane rubbed at his own eyes. He felt a little stupid. He steadied himself.
'Beede's had that verruca since I was a kid,' he said slowly. 'It was pretty bad.'
'I believe it was very painful,' she said, still smiling (as if the memory of Beede's pain was somehow delightful to her).
   He coldly observed the smile –

Is she mocking him?
Is she mocking me?

– then he gradually collected his thoughts together. 'Yes,' he said stiffly, 'I have one in almost exactly the same place, but it's never really . . .'
His words petered out.
She shrugged. 'People often inherit them. It's fairly common. Verrucas can be neurotic . . .'
   '*Neurotic*?'
Kane's voice sounded louder than he'd intended.
'Yes,' she was smiling again, 'when a patient fails to get rid of something by means of conventional medicine we tend to categorise it as a psychological problem rather than as a physical one.'
   Kane struggled to digest the implications of this information. His brain seized, initially, then it belched –
'But a verruca's just some type of . . . of *wart*,' he stuttered. 'You catch them in changing rooms . . .'

'Yes. But like any ailment it can be sustained by a kind of . . .' she paused, thoughtfully '. . . inner turmoil.'

The boy was now sitting on the floor and inspecting his matches. He shook each box, in turn, and listened intently to the sounds it made. 'I can tell how many's in there,' he informed nobody in particular, 'just from the rattlings.'

'We've met before.' Kane spoke, after a short silence.

'Yes,' she said.

(He already heartily disliked how she just *agreed* to things, in that blank – that untroubled – way. The easy acquiescence. The cool compliance. He connected it to some kind of background in nursing. He loathed nurses. He found their bedside manner – that distinctively assertive servility – false and asphyxiating.)

'You treated my mother,' he said, feeling his chest tighten.

She sat down on Beede's chair, facing him. 'I think I did. Years ago.'

'That's right. You came to the house. I remember now.'

They were both quiet for a moment.

'You'd just returned from Germany,' Kane continued, plainly rather astonished (and then equally irritated) by the extent of his own recall.

'Yes I had. I went there for a year, almost straight after I'd graduated.'

'I remember.'

He sniffed, trying to make it sound like nothing.

'You have an impressive memory,' she said, then put a polite hand up to her mouth, as if to suppress a yawn. This almost-yawn infuriated him. He didn't know why.

How old was she, anyway? Thirty-one? Thirty-three?

'No,' he said. 'It's just your mole. Your birthmark. It's extremely memorable.'

She didn't miss a beat.

'Of course,' she said.

'I'm sorry,' he struggled to repress a childish smile, 'that must've sounded rude.'

'No . . .' she shook her head, her voice still soft as ever, 'it didn't sound rude.'

Didn't *sound* rude.

Kane stared at her. She stared back at him. He took out his phone and inspected his messages.

'A psychiatrist,' she observed mildly, 'might call what you do with that phone "masking behaviour".'

He glanced up, astonished –

The cheek of it

– then quickly checked himself. 'I guess they might,' he said, returning casually to his messages and sending a quick response to one of them, 'but then you're just a foot doctor.'

She chuckled. She didn't seem at all offended. 'You have eyes just like your father's,' she murmured, gracefully adjusting the long hem of her skirt (as if hers was a life without technology, without *chatter*. A life entirely about thinking and pausing and feeling. A quiet life).

Kane's jaw stiffened. 'I don't think so,' he murmured thickly, 'they're a completely different colour.'

She shrugged and then sighed, like he was just a boy. She glanced down, briefly, at her son (as if, Kane felt, to make the connection 100 per cent sure), then said blandly, 'It was a difficult time for you.'

'Pardon?'

He put his phone away. The tone of his voice told her not to persist, but she ignored the warning.

'Difficult. With your mother. I remember thinking how incredibly brave you were. Heroic, almost.'

His cheeks reddened. 'Not at all.'

'Sometimes, after I'd seen her, I'd just sit in my car and shake. Just *shake*. I didn't know how you coped with it. I still don't. You were so young.'

She smiled softly at the memory, and as she smiled, he suddenly remembered. He remembered standing at the window and seeing her in her car, shaking: her arms thrown over the steering wheel, her head thrown on to her arms –

Oh God

His gut twisted.

He turned and gazed out into the car park. He was unbelievably angry. He felt found-out – unearthed – *raw*. But worst of all, he felt charmless. Charm was an essential part of his armoury. It was his defensive shield, and she had somehow connived to worm her way under it –

Damn her

He drew a deep breath.
 Outside he could suddenly see Beede –

Huh . . . ?

– walking through the play area towards the blond imposter and the horse. The imposter had now dismounted. He was touching his head. He seemed confused. Beede offered his hand to the horse. The horse sniffed his hand. It appeared very receptive to Beede's advances.
 'I wonder what happened to the other man,' Kane mused, then shuddered. Everything was feeling strange to him. *Inverted*. And he didn't like it.
 'Maybe there were two horses,' the boy said. He was now standing next to the table and fingering Kane's lighter. He looked up at Kane and held it out towards him. 'Red,' he smiled, 'that's *your* colour.'
The lighter was red.
 He showed his mother. 'See?'
She said nothing.
'See?' he repeated. 'He comes from fire.'
 'Don't be silly.' His mother took the lighter off him and held it out to Kane herself.
Kane walked over and took it from her. She had beautiful hands. He remembered her hands from before.
'I lived in the American desert,' he said to the boy, 'when I was younger. It was very hot. I once almost died in the heat out there. Look . . .'
He pushed back his sleeve and showed the boy a burn on his arm. The boy seemed only mildly interested.
 Kane was about to pull his sleeve down again when the woman (*Elen*, was it?) put out her hand and took a firm hold of his wrist. She pulled his arm towards her. She stared at the scar. Her face was so close to it he could feel her breath on his skin. Then she let go (just as suddenly) and focussed in on the boy once more.

'America,' Kane said, taking full possession of his arm again, drawing it into his chest, shoving the sleeve down, feeling like an angry child who'd just had his school uniform damaged in a minor playground *fracas*. As he spoke he noticed Beede's book on the floor. He bent down and picked it up. He shoved it into his jacket pocket.

'In a magic trick,' the boy repeated, plaintively, 'they would've had *two* horses.'

'How old are you?' Kane asked, glancing over towards the serving counter and noticing Anthony Shilling standing there.

'Five.'

'Then you're just old enough to keep it . . .' he said, showing Fleet his empty hand, forming a fist, tapping his knuckles and then opening the hand up again. The red lighter had magically reappeared in the centre of his palm. The boy gasped. Kane placed it down, carefully, on to the lacquered table, nodded a curt farewell to the chiropodist, and left it there.

TWO

'I'm Beede; Daniel Beede. I'm your friend. Do you remember me, Dory?'

Beede peered up, intently, into the tall, blond man's face, struggling – at first – to establish any kind of a connection with him. He spoke softly (like you'd speak to a child) and he used his name carefully, as if anticipating that it might provoke some kind of violent reaction. But it didn't.

'Of course.'

The tall, blond man blinked and then nodded. 'Yes. Yes, of *course* I remember . . .' He talked quietly and haltingly with a strong German accent. 'It's just that . . . *uh* . . .'

His eyes anxiously scanned the surrounding area (the road, the horse, the tarmac, the vehicles in the car park). 'It's just that I suddenly have the strangest . . .'

He winced, shook his head, then gazed down, briefly, at his own two hands, as if he didn't quite recognise them. '. . .*uh* . . . fu . . . fu . . . *fühlen?*'

He glanced up, quizzically.

'Feeling,' Beede translated.

The German stared at him, blankly.

'*Fee*ling,' Beede repeated.

The German frowned. 'No . . . not . . . it's this . . . this . . .' he patted his own chest, meaningfully, '*fuh*-ling. *Feee* . . . Yes. Yes. This *fee*ling. This horrible, almost . . .' he shuddered, 'almost overwhelming *feeling*. Like a kind of . . .' He swallowed. 'A dread. A deep dread.'

Beede nodded.

'. . . a terrible dread.' He moved his hands to his throat, '*Suffocāre*. Suffocating. A smothering feeling. A *terrible* feeling . . .'

'You're tired,' Beede murmured gently, 'and possibly a little confused, but it'll soon pass, trust me.'

'I do,' the German nodded, 'I do *traust* you.' He paused. '*Trost* you . . .'

34

He blinked. '*Troost.*'

'Trust,' Beede repeated.

'Of course . . .' the German continued. 'It's just . . .'

His darting eyes settled, momentarily, on the pony. 'I have an awful suspicion that this feeling – this . . . this . . . *uh* . . .'

'Fear,' Beede filled in, dryly.

'Yes . . . yes . . . *fff* . . .'

The German attempted to wrangle the familiar syllable on his tongue – '*Ffffah*. . .' – but the word simply would not come. After his third unsuccessful attempt (pulling back his lips, like a frightened chimpanzee, his nostrils flaring, his eyes bulging) he scowled, closed his mouth again, paused for a second, took stock, then suddenly, and without warning, threw back his head and roared, '*GE-FHAAAAR!*' at full volume.

The horse skipped nervously from foot to foot.

'*Urgh* . . .'

The German grimaced, wiped his chin with his cuff, then closed his eyes and drew a deep breath. On the exhale he repeated the word – '*Gefhaar*' – but much more softly this time. He smiled to himself and drew another breath. '*Fhaar*,' he sighed, then (with increasing rapidity), '*Fhaar-fhar-fhear-fear-fear* . . . *Yes!*'

His eyes flew open, then he scowled. 'But what am I saying here?'

'This fear,' Beede primed him.

'Yes. Of course. *Fear*. This *fear* . . .'

The German rapidly clicked back into gear again. 'I have a feeling – a . . . a *suspicion*, you might say – that this dread, this . . . this . . . this *fhar* may be linked in some way . . . *connected* in some way . . .' he jinked his head towards the pony, conspiratorially '. . . to *it*. To *that*. To . . .' he struggled to find the correct noun, 'to *khor-khor-khorsam* . . .'

He shook his head, scowling. '*Khorsam. Horsam. Hors.* Horse. Horsey. Horse. *Horses.*'

He glanced over at Beede, breathlessly, for confirmation. Beede nodded, encouragingly.

'But you see I'm not . . . I can't be entirely . . . uh . . . *certus*,' he scowled, then winced, then forged doggedly onward, '*certānus* . . .' He paused. '*Cer-tan*. I can't be certain, because it's still just an . . . an *inkling* . . .' he shuddered '. . . a slight shadow in the back of my mind. A hunch. Nothing more.'

While he spoke he distractedly adjusted the wedding band on his finger (twisted it, as if of old habit), then gradually grew aware of what he was doing and glanced down. 'What's this?'

His eyes widened. 'A ring? A *gold* ring? On my third finger?'

He glared at Beede, almost accusingly. 'Can that be right?'

Beede nodded. He seemed calm and unflustered; as if thoroughly accustomed to this kind of scenario.

'*Mein Gott!*' The German's handsome face grew stiff with incredulity. 'You're telling me I'm . . . I'm . . .'

'Married?' Beede offered. 'Yes. Yes, you are. Very happily.'

'*Seriously?*'

'Just wait a while,' Beede patted his arm, 'and everything will become clear. I promise.'

'You're right. You're *right* . . .' the German smiled at him, gratefully, 'I *know* that . . .'

But he didn't seem entirely convinced by it.

'So do you have any thoughts on where the horse may've came from?' Beede enquired, gently stroking the mare's flanks. She was exhausted. Her tongue was protruding slightly. There were flecks of foam on her neck and her ribcage. He was concerned that someone inside the restaurant might see them (a member of staff – the manager). They were in a children's play area, after all. The horse was plainly stolen. Did this qualify as trespass?

The German closed his eyes for a moment (as if struggling to remember), and then the tension suddenly lifted from his face and he nodded. 'I see a field in the middle of two roads, curving . . .' he murmured softly, his speech much less harsh, less halting than before, 'and beyond . . . beyond I see Romney. I see the marshes. '

He opened his eyes again. 'I was checking over a couple of vacant properties earlier,' he explained amiably, 'in South Willesborough . . .'

Then he started –

'*Eh?!*'

– and spun around, as though someone had just whispered something detestable into his ear.

'*WHO SAID THAT?!*' he cried.

'Who said what?'

Beede's voice was tolerant but slightly teachery.

'About . . . About South Willesborough . . . ?' He continued to look around him agitatedly. 'Was it *you*? Did *you* speak? Were *you* there earlier?'

'*Hmmn*. A field in the middle of two roads curving . . .' Beede mused (pointedly ignoring the German's questions), 'I think I know the place. And it's not too far. Perhaps a mile – a little more. We'll need to lead her back quickly. Someone might miss her. Do you have a belt?'

The German peered down at himself. 'Yes,' he said, and automatically started to unfasten the buckle.

'I'll take mine off, too,' Beede said, unfastening his own.

The German pulled his belt free, passed it over, then tentatively sniffed at the arm of his jacket. '*Urgh!*' he croaked. 'What on earth have I been doing? I smell *disgusting*, and look – *look* – I have horse hair simply *everywhere* . . .'

He began frantically patting and slapping at the fabric, but after a couple of seconds he froze – mid-slap – as something terrible dawned on him. 'Oh *Christ*,' he gasped. 'Oh *Jesus Christ* – the *car*. Where's the *car*? What on earth have I *done* with it?'

Beede had buckled the two belts together. He whispered soothingly into the mare's ear and then looped them around her neck. She was a sweet filly. She nodded a couple of times as he pulled the leather tighter.

On the second nod – and completely without warning – the German sprang back with a loud yell. The horse took fright and reared up. Beede clung on, resolutely.

'Hey, *hey* . . .' he hissed (managing – rather miraculously – to rein in both the horse *and* his temper), 'just calm down, Dory. She won't hurt anybody. She's worn out. Let's try and hold this situation together, shall we?'

'But I *hate* horses,' the German whimpered, hugging himself, tightly (the way a frightened girl might), and gazing up at the horse with a look of sheer, unadulterated terror. 'I absolutely . . . I . . . I *loathe* them . . .'

'That's fine,' Beede interrupted, '*I'll* lead the horse, see?'

Beede led the horse two steps forward. 'The horse is fine. Everything's fine. There's no need to panic. Everything's just *fine* here.'

But the German was still panicking. 'Oh *God*,' he wailed, 'if I've lost the car they'll sack me for sure. Then where will we be?'

'You won't have lost it,' Beede said determinedly.

'Why?' He grew instantly suspicious. 'How do you know? How can you be sure? Were you there?'

'No. *No*, I was *here*,' Beede pointed towards the French Connection, 'I was in the restaurant. I was having a coffee with my son. My son is called Kane. He's still inside, actually.'

As he pointed, Beede glanced over towards the window where Kane had stood previously. The window was empty. *'Coffee?'* The German peered over towards the window, scowling – *'Coffee?'* – but then something powerful suddenly seemed to strike him – a revelation – 'But of *course!'* he gasped. *'Kaffee* . . . kaff . . . *kaff* . . . Koffee. Coffee. I *remember* that. I *know* that. I *know* kaffee . . .'

He put a tentative – almost fearful – hand up to his own chin and gently explored it with the tips of his fingers. Then he smiled (it was a brilliant smile), then he gazed at Beede, almost in wonder.

'Beede,' he said, rolling the name around in his mouth like a boiled toffee. Then he clutched at his stomach (as if the memory had just jabbed him there), leaned sharply forward and took a quick, rasping gulp of air –

Oh God –
Oh God
Just to be . . . to be . . . to be . . .

He stared around him, quite amazed –

Where?

'Of course,' Beede smiled back, clearly relieved by this sudden show of progress (tastes and smells, he found, were often the key), 'of *course* you remember . . .'
He placed a reassuring hand on to the German's broad shoulder. 'Now – deep breath, *deep* breath – are you ready? Shall we get the hell out of here?'

Kelly Broad was sitting on a high wall, chewing ferociously on a piece of celery. She was passably pretty and alarmingly thin with artificially tinted burgundy hair –

Because I'm worth it

Her face was hard (but with an enviable bone-structure), her 'look' was urban – hooded top (hood worn up), combat mini-skirt and a pair of modern, slightly scuffed, silver trainers (the kind astronauts wore – devoutly – whenever they went jogging above the atmosphere). No socks (not even the ones you could buy which made it look like you weren't wearing any – the half-socks you got at JD Sports or Marks & Spencer).

Her legs were bare and white and goose-bumping prodigiously. But she didn't feel the cold. She had bad circulation, weak bones (fractured both her wrists when she was nine in a bouncy-castle misadventure. Earned herself a tidy £3,000 in compensation, and the whole family got to spend three weeks in Newquay; her gran lived there), a penchant for laxatives and an Eating Disorder –

Might as well bring that straight up, eh?

Un,
Deux,
Trois . . .

Bleeeaa-urghhh!

Although her eating habits (if you wanted to get pedantic about it – and Kelly did, because she was) were ridiculously orderly (the Weight Watchers' manual was her bible; she drew up a special weekly menu and stuck to it religiously, counted every calorie, took tiny mouthfuls, ate with tiny cutlery – just like Liz Hurley), so it wasn't actually a problem, as such; more of a . . . a *preference*, really. She simply preferred her food fat-free. It was a Life-Style decision (the kind of thing they were always banging on about in magazines and on the telly), and so all perfectly legitimate (especially when your own mother was too big to cram herself into an average-size car-seat – used the disability section on the bus – belly arrived home seven seconds before her arse – hadn't seen her toes since 1983 – *Feet?* They had their own fucking *passports* down there).

Kelly came from a bad family.
No. *No.* That was just too easy. They weren't bad as such (no, not *bad*) so much as . . . as *known* . . . as *familiar* . . . as . . . as –

Notorious
That was it

And only locally. Only in Ashford –

Well . . .

– and maybe in Canterbury. And Gillingham (where her older sister Linda supported The Gills – I mean *really* supported them – with a fist-guard, business cards, a retractable-blade). And in parts of Folkestone. And Woodchurch. And some of those smaller places which didn't really matter (except to the people living there).

In the local *vicinity*, basically. It wasn't *national* or anything (no special reports on *Crimewatch UK* – aside from a small, pointless item on *Network South East* – November 2001. And that didn't really count. It was probably just a quiet day – a craft fair had been rained off in Sheppey or something – and they had to fill up the time *somehow*, didn't they? Yeah. So the Broads copped it again – Uncle Harvey; Dad's oldest brother; the world's shonkiest builder –

Blah blah).

Notorious.
Like the Notorious B.I.G. The rapper. That fat American dude who got shot –

Bang
– dead. And then they made a documentary about him. And she'd watched it. And they'd said that he was actually a really nice guy (underneath. But fat. *Very* fat. That was partly what he was famous for. That's essentially what the BIG stood for). And his mamma loved him (which had to count for something). And when he died they made a tribute song for him. With Sting. And Puff Da – *Di* – Daddy.

Notorious.
Isn't that what Ashford people –

Gossips
Wankers

– liked to call the Broads? Wasn't that the word they preferred?
   Kelly sniffed.
Did it have to be a negative?
Notorious?

As in train robber?
As in sex offender?

   She pinched some pearlescent pink lipstick from the corners of her mouth.
I mean, wasn't Mother Theresa notorious? A notorious *saint*? (Remember that thing Kane told her – about Mother Theresa not being a saint at all. About how Catholics always wanted to keep the poor people poor by making them have lots of kiddies. 'Contraception murders love.' That's what he said she'd said –

Her mantra
Didn't sound very saintly, huh?

– but he was laughing as he'd said it. Maybe he was just taking the fucking mick. Like always. The fucker.)
   Hang on . . . who was that . . . that *Russian* geezer they'd called a prophet who actually had sex with just about everybody? And Boney M wrote a song called Ra-Ra-Rasputin all about his various pranks and everything?
   Wasn't he notorious (didn't they mention it somewhere in the lyric?)? And when they shot him dead, didn't he keep on getting up again? Like Freddie Kruger? Didn't he just keep on rising? Like Jesus or something?

Don't remember Mother Theresa pullin' any stunts like that –
An' if she did the papers would've been full of it, 'cuz Kane says The Pope owns the media –

Or is that the Mafia?

Uh . . .

Hold on a sec . . .

Did everybody notorious always end up getting wasted?
Couldn't you be something plain and simple like a notorious doctor (if you hadn't killed a patient? What about the bloke who created the first test-tube baby? Did he qualify?)? A notorious priest (if you hadn't messed with a choirboy)? Could you be a notorious . . . a notorious *sweetheart*? Yes?
No. It didn't sound right. A notorious *flirt,* maybe.
Kelly frowned and tucked in her skirt so the wind wouldn't lift it and show off her thighs. It was a little short –

Should'a thought of that

– and the fabric was rather flimsy (for something supposedly military – although she'd never yet seen anyone wearing a mini-skirt in a situation of mortal combat. Except for Lara Croft –

Tank Girl
That pretty cow in Alias *. . .*

– and she always did okay).
Kelly was sitting on a wall outside the Elwick Road Villas. It was a high wall facing a main road in Ashford's town centre. Her brother, Jason, had taught her how to climb it (before they'd put him away. Joyriding. His thirteenth formal offence –

Aw . . .
Unlucky for some, eh?).

Jason always knew the best route and the shortest cut (it was a fancy wall, built from some kind of rock –

Limestone?
Granite?

– there were bits where you could find a hand-hold and a foot-hold. Where you could pull yourself up).

Kelly took another bite of her celery. A car honked its horn at her. She didn't look towards it, merely raised her middle finger –

You twat

– and pulled her hood down lower.

Yeah. Notorious *slut* –

Stop thinkin' about it

Jason was her middle brother. Jason Broad. Twenty-one last Thursday. Inside for three years solid. Served eight months already. Father of four (two different mothers). At school Billy Sloane – *Sloaney* – had called him queer; Jase broke his arm in three different places (the canteen, the corridor, the playing fields) and no one – but *no one* – could ever seriously question his masculinity after that.

Had a heart of gold. He really did. Always took care of her (once shat on the bonnet of the car of a teacher she hated –

Jap car –
Hyundai –
Mr Whitechapel –
Fuckin' Northerner).

Jason was loyal –

Bottom line

– and you couldn't put a price on loyalty (as her dad always used to say –

Before he ran off to Oldham with the daughter of that pig who ran the chippie . . .
To get the police involved!
She was sixteen next birthday – and a slag – everybody knew it

The whole family had been barred from the shop, after –

Dad's legacy –
I mean we were hurtin' too, weren't we?
No decent chippie within a 2-mile radius . . .

– until Jason finally put the wind up them, and they moved to
Derby.

The new people were definitely much better – better batter, her
mum said; crispier. And they were cheaper –

Didn't have no teenage kids –

Not that it really mattered any more, now Dad was out of the
picture).

Nope. You couldn't put a price on loyalty. Kelly cleared her throat
(the celery was rather stringy) –

I'll say as much to Beede when the bugger finally gets here . . .

'Excuse me.'
Kelly frowned.
'*Excuse* me.'

She glanced up. A young woman was standing to her left, next to
the entrance gate. She looked vaguely familiar.

'What?'
'Are these your dogs?'

The woman indicated, haughtily, towards two large lurchers which
were collapsed on the pavement directly in front of her. Kelly gazed
at the two dogs, blankly.

'Nope,' she eventually volunteered, 'strictly speakin' they're my dad's.'

She smirked as she spoke (perhaps a little provocatively). The woman
didn't smile back. She was youngish –

ish

– and quite pretty. Black, with scruffy, nappy, mid-length hair (pushed
back from her face by an alice-band, no earrings, no make-up). Square
glasses. Arty frames. Dressed like a virgin –

Or Tracy fuckin' Chapman

Corduroy jacket, grey polo-neck . . .
Jeans by fuckin' Pepe or something

Kelly coolly surveyed her body –

Hmmn . . .
Junk in her trunk
But no spare tyre

The woman scowled. 'Well could you get them to move for me?'
'Why?' Kelly shot back. 'You too good to step over 'em?'

The woman placed her hands on to her hips (*Yup*. She was class – smart but bolshy – and Kelly could respect that). 'Of course not,' she snapped, 'I just don't want to *stand* on them.'

'They gets stood on all the time at home, mate,' Kelly dead panned, 'so don't you worry yourself, okay?'

She turned her head and gazed up the road. Counted to three. Over the sound of the traffic she could hear one of the dogs growling. Yeah. Right on cue. That was Bud.

'Excuse me.'

Kelly didn't turn back straight away.

'*Excuse* me.'

She turned and mugged surprise. 'Man, you still there?'

'One of your dogs just growled at me.'

'*No!*' Kelly gasped, throwing up her hands in mock-alarm (then plunging them straight back down again as she wobbled on the wall). 'Did he *really*?'

'Yeah. He did. And I'm in no mood for getting bitten, so would you ask them to sodding *move*, please?'

On 'move' Kelly threw her celery over her shoulder (finally engaging fully), pushed her hood back and pointed emphatically. 'You know what kind of an animal that is?'

The woman folded her arms, boredly. 'Of course I do.'

'Well tell me.'

'It's a lurcher.'

Kelly nodded. 'That's it. A Long Dog. A workin' dog. My dad used to go coursin' with 'em down on the Marshes . . .'

The woman looked disapproving (but only mildly). Kelly shrugged. 'Not any more, though. We got five of 'em at home altogether. My dad's up in Oldham. My poor mum has to look after 'em. Costs her a small fuckin' fortune, it does.'

The woman surveyed the animals, coldly. 'Well it's pretty hard to see what she's spending her money on.'

Kelly straightened her back –

Hoity!

– 'It's just old age as makes their ribs stand up like that,' she explained patiently. 'Soon as they eat anythin' they shit it right out again. Only thing different is it ain't in a can.'

As if on cue, one of the lurchers stood up, stretched stiffly, tottered (Kelly's rival snorted, under her breath), farted (she winced), put its nose to the pavement, located a scent, and staggered off in pursuit of it. The woman immediately took her chance; leaned boldly across the second animal and shoved the gate – the second dog didn't object – but the gate was locked.

'*Bollocks.*'

Kelly's eyebrows rose –

Get her

'So what the hell,' she asked smugly, 'd'you think I'm sittin' up here for?'

The woman didn't answer. She pressed the intercom.

Kelly sighed, piously. 'Intercom's broke. They're fixin' it. That's why the gates are locked.'

She pressed it again, anyway.

'If you wanna get in you'll need a key.'

Without warning, the woman kicked out her right foot and booted the wall with it. 'I'm meant to be *visiting* somebody,' she snarled. Then she winced as her toe registered the full impact of the attack.

'Feel better now?' Kelly asked, plainly delighted by this flagrant loss of composure.

The woman half-smiled to herself (embarrassed – but she was cute when she smiled). 'No. I don't, actually.'

The smile gradually expanded into an apologetic smirk.

'Ring 'em,' Kelly offered constructively.

'Can't. Haven't got my phone on me.'

Kelly removed her own phone from her pocket.

'What's the number?'

'Don't know off-hand.'

'Oh.'

Kelly put her phone away again.

The woman glanced up, remembering her manners. 'But thanks, anyway,' she murmured.

Kelly graciously tipped her head, then peered over towards the Villas. There were eight of them; grand; free-standing; Victorian. For the most part converted into flats – or 'apartments' as the twatty local Estate Agents liked to have it.

'You come to see that black geezer in apartment six?' she asked.

'Why?' the woman rejoined staunchly. 'Do people always visit residents the same colour as they are?'

Kelly pursed her lips. The woman removed the strap of a heavy-looking, leather satchel (the kind Kelly associated with teachers and social workers –

Yeah. That'd be right)

– from her shoulder and drew another step closer. 'You're one of the Broad girls, aren't you?' she said, her eyes slitting slightly as she gazed up at her.

Kelly slitted her own eyes right back. 'So what?'

'I was at school with your brother.'

Kelly didn't seem surprised by this information (like nits and the weather, the Broads got everywhere).

'Who?' she asked. 'Jase?'

'No. Paul.'

Kelly looked blank.

'Paul,' the woman reiterated slowly (which Kelly strongly resented), 'the devil worshipper.'

Kelly tossed her head. '*Satanist*,' she pronounced scornfully, 'and it was only a *joke*, anyways.'

The woman nodded. 'I knew that.'

Kelly jutted her chin out, just the same. She looked uncomfortable. The woman observed her disquiet.

'So how's he been doing lately?' she asked.

Kelly gave her a hard look, then, 'Fine,' she said.

'Is he still handing out shoes at the bowling?'

'Nope.'

'Oh. Moved on to better things, eh?'

Kelly tried – and failed – to detect any traces of irony in her voice. She glared at her, but said nothing.

'Well give him my best, if you see him,' the woman continued staunchly, almost (but not entirely) running out of conversational impetus. 'My name's Winifred. I was his partner in biology. We dissected a cow's eye together once – had a right laugh – before I transferred to Highworth in the fourth year.'

'*High*worth,' Kelly rejoined bitchily, 'well ain't *that* lovely?'

Silence

Kelly inspected her nails (bitten down to the quick) then neatly laced her fingers together. 'I don't see him that much,' she said primly, 'he moved to Readin'.'

'Reading?'

Far from being mollified by this information, Winifred's appetite for news seemed freshly enlivened by it. '*Really?*'

Kelly scowled. 'Yeah.'

'*Reading*, huh?' She mulled this over for a moment. 'Well *good* on him. Because let's face it,' she raised her brows, censoriously, 'no one was *ever* gonna to give him a proper break around here, eh?' She hesitated for a second (then promptly threw caution to the wind). 'Least of all your psychotic, bloody *sister* . . .'

Kelly shrugged (she just didn't want to go there). Winifred took another step closer.

'So can you actually scramble down the other side of that thing?'

'What thing?'

'The wall.'

'Oh . . .'

Kelly glanced boredly behind her. 'Dunno. Maybe.'

'I know it's a bit cheeky,' the woman wheedled (flashing that charming smile again), 'but would you mind taking someone a message for me?'

Kelly's eye-lids lowered, ominously. 'Man, do I look like your personal fuckin' courier or what?'

Winifred's smile did not falter. It continued blazing. She was shame-less, Kelly surmised –

All credit to her for that

– so she lifted up her legs and grumpily slung them over. 'Which block?'

'First Villa, flat three.'

'Right.'

She was already twisting around to scramble down when something suddenly dawned on her. She paused, mid-manoeuvre, gripping hard with her hands to stop herself from falling. 'But that's *Kane's* place,' she grunted, a hint of accusation in her voice.

'Yes.' Winifred made no apology for it.

Kelly pulled herself up again, kicking a leg back over (sitting astride the wall now, a hand pushed down on to her skirt to preserve her modesty). 'So what's your business with him?'

'With Kane?'

'Yeah,' Kelly growled.

'I don't have any. I'm here to see his dad.'

'Ah.' Kelly was plainly relieved. 'Well that's a shame, 'cos Beede ain't here, either. Neither of them are.'

'Are you *sure*?'

Kelly nodded. "Course I am. That's actually who *I'm* waitin' for.'

Winifred seemed mildly irritated by this news. 'But we arranged to meet at twelve,' she said petulantly, 'and it's ten past already. He's usually very reliable.'

'Yeah,' Kelly conceded, unhelpfully.

Winifred frowned and peered down at her watch. '*Damn.* I've got something I really, *really* needed to give to him,' she muttered.

Kelly rolled her eyes at this transparent little charade. 'So pass it over,' she volunteered boredly, 'and I'll stick it through his box.'

The woman gave Kelly an appraising look. 'Could I?'

'Well I'm not gonna *nick* it or anythin', if that's what you're thinkin',' Kelly snapped.

'I know that.'

Winifred opened her satchel and removed a large, brown envel-ope from inside it. She passed it up to Kelly. Kelly took it (the removal of a hand from her skirt causing a dramatic flash of her baby-pink g-string) and then placed it, neatly, on to her lap. A car horn sounded. The woman – Winnie – glanced over her shoulder. A boy was hanging out of a car window as it drove past, performing a wanking gesture. Kelly stared fixedly ahead of her.

Winifred took a few steps back, fastening her satchel again. 'I really do appreciate this,' she said, 'I'm in one hell of a . . .'

She flapped her hand.

Kelly nodded, sternly.

'Bye then,' Winnie smiled, 'and thanks.'

She turned and began to walk.

'*Hey*,' Kelly suddenly yelled.

Winifred spun around. 'What?'

'He never went to Readin',' Kelly blurted out, her cheeks reddening, holding the jiffy bag in front of her chest now – like a protective corset – and folding her arms over it.

Winnie looked confused. '*Who* didn't?'

'Paul. He died. Early last year.'

It took a while for this information to sink in. 'My God,' Winifred murmured softly, 'I had no . . .'

She paused again, her mind obviously racing. '*Shit*. I'm really *sorry* . . .'

She seemed stunned.

'Don't be.' Kelly was suddenly full of bravura (her hard eyes brimming with indignant tears). 'He overdosed. Solvents. *Cans*. He was addicted for years. That's why my sister always used to hit him. That's why he always had those awful fuckin' . . .'

she put her hand to her mouth, touched her chin, to illustrate, 'those spots, around here.'

Winnie shook her head. 'No. *No*, I didn't mean . . .' She paused, plainly in a state of some confusion. 'I meant . . .' she scowled, 'I meant that I was sorry because we *used* together,' she said finally, her own hand suddenly fluttering to her nose, her lips, 'we *started* using together, as kids.'

Kelly's face dropped.

Another car horn sounded. And before the woman – Winnie – could say another word, Kelly had stuck the envelope into her mouth, kicked her remaining leg back over the wall, and shoved herself off.

THREE

He just blocked it all out. It was as simple (or as complicated) as that. Denial – as the Americans were so fond of calling it – was Isidore's basic coping mechanism (his 'survival strategy'). That was how he dealt with it. And Beede (for all his cynicism) was sensible enough to just go along with the whole thing; the self-delusion, the subterfuge, the bunk, the bullshit.

He didn't want to push or to provoke or to challenge; because – bottom line – it was none of his damn business. And – more to the point – if he did (push, provoke, challenge etc), where would it actually lead?

Seriously?

What could be gained? Dory was (after all) just a man; a human being, battling – against horrendous odds – merely to function; to hold down a job; to raise a family; just to . . . to . . .

Oh God, here it comes –

. . . to *be*.

He was a simple man. A good man. He had integrity and dignity. He had pride –

A little too much, occasionally . . .

Dory was a person, not some psychological experiment. He was no benighted beagle or tragic lab rat; nobody's fool, nobody's victim – although Beede sometimes struggled to remind himself of this fact (he still harboured those Reformist tendencies in him – that persistent urge to just roll his sleeves up and dive in – no matter how diligently he might've tried to repress them).

51

It could certainly make things difficult (this 'denial'): the explanations, for one thing. Dory often 'displaced' his confusion on to the people surrounding him. Beede had read a book by R.D. Laing (*The Divided Self*) and several of Freud's case studies (Wolfman, in particular). He'd quickly picked up on all the jargon, and tended to use it – not because he liked it or trusted it – but because it was a convenient short cut, and short cuts – in working scenarios – were an issue of sheer pragmatism.

When it came to 'displacement', this particular situation was a perfect example. As they slowly picked their way back along the Bad Munstereifel Road (and it was a bloody treacherous hike, let alone with a horse in tow and your trousers sagging), at an approximate interval of every three to four minutes, Dory would turn and ask Beede (with complete guilelessness) why he had a horse with him, and what he thought he was doing with it (his territorial army background and his job in security made the whole thing even more dodgy; Dory – *this* Dory – had a ridiculously over-developed sense of propriety).

And whenever Beede said (as he was obliged to, because it was true), 'You took it, Dory,' or 'I found you with it – I was having coffee with my son . . .' etc – he could see Isidore's mind turning over, could see him putting two and two together (making five), could see him growing increasingly guarded and suspicious, as though Beede (for his own sick reasons – whatever they may be) was intent on surreptitiously inveigling him into some atrocious form of perjury.

Because in Isidore's mind (when he weighed it all up) the likelihood that he had stolen a horse himself (when he both feared and hated horses, and when he was intrinsically law-abiding) seemed somehow far less plausible than the likelihood that Beede had stolen it (or found it, or whatever) and that he had just 'blanked out' (as he sometimes called it) and then miraculously 'turned up'.

I mean wasn't that more plausible? Even from the outside?

Over time (their working relationship – their 'friendship' – had lasted about twenty-two months, in total) Beede had started to modify things. He knew that this was risky (perilous, even) but he simply could not stop himself. He'd long observed in Dory a kind of helpless paranoia (a desperate vulnerability) which somehow made the truth seem so immeasurably illogical (and stupid and *cruel*) that it was sometimes virtually impossible not to suddenly find yourself quickly inserting a small –

Tiny

– neat, white lie to try and make things more bearable. He knew that Elen sometimes did the same. It was difficult not to when you cared for a person. It was only natural (call it a maternal/paternal instinct) to feel a tugging need to assuage their distress in some way; to apply some kind of remedial blotter to the leaking ink of their misery.

So approximately ten minutes into the walk Beede had begun to modify the story (it was boredom, more than anything. Dory would keep on asking the same questions – again and again and *again* – until he felt satisfied by the answers; and if he wasn't satisfied he may well turn hostile. There might be –

God forbid

– an 'episode'.)

Consequently – according to Beede – the horse had simply 'escaped from a field'. Beede had 'just happened across it, wandering around in the road', so had gone off in pursuit of it, then Dory had arrived – 'in the nick of time' – and had helped him to subdue it.

In this new scenario Dory was quite the hero . . .

'Yes, I know you hate horses. Don't you see? That's what made the whole thing so . . . so *admirable*.'

The only problem with this approach was that Dory wouldn't automatically give up on all his former scraps –

Dammit

– and a few hours later there was always the risk that he might suddenly remember being in the play area (for example) and then get all agitated and jumpy, and the questions would start over. He was tenacious. He was suspicious.

Things were definitely –

Definitely

– getting worse on that score. Elen had said so herself (and Isidore had strongly indicated as much too, in some of his rare – but precious – moments of unselfconsciousness).

53

On the positive side (and there was always a positive side), he was actually 'going under' slightly less often than he had done previously; but when he did, he 'fell' much more quickly, was in deeper, and for significantly longer.

When he came to he was just a mess; he was in chaos. It was as if his brain had been placed inside a food processor (set on to its 'chopping' function); everything got hacked-up and jumbled together. And the end result? A horrible, indigestible mental coleslaw.

On this particular occasion Beede had taken the precaution of checking his watch at his very first sighting of Dory in the French Connection, and he'd calculated (another quick peek. *Yup*) that it'd taken twenty-five minutes for him to return to himself (*fully* return – so that he remembered his address, his wife, his child, his date of birth; all the basics, in other words).

Beede had been on hand for almost the entire process, and so far as he could gauge, things were definitely degenerating. Elen had told him that this'd happened twice before (a serious degeneration): once when they were first engaged, and once a short while after Fleet was born, when Dory had been forced to quit his job with Ashford's Fire Department (a severe blow from which he'd still barely recovered).

While Beede was certainly no expert, the attacks themselves seemed to have become far more . . . more perverse . . . more . . . uh . . . *tricksy* of late –

For want of a better word

More dangerous (even). They were stealthy. They seemed almost to creep up on him. They had no sense of propriety; were untimely, inexpedient and often socially embarrassing. They never (or very rarely) stood on any kind of ceremony. They were merciless. They were indecorous. They were *delinquent*.

Previously – and again, this was chiefly relying on the information which Elen had given him – they'd had a much more controllable evolution. They were constant but reliable. Were predictable. Were minimal. Had exhibited an internal *logic* of some kind.

Now there was something almost cruel, almost . . .

Vindictive?
Is that too emotional?

Now there were 'flashpoints'. And the paranoia was terrible. Really terrible. Much more severe than it had ever been (*ever*, Elen said). And the denial was absolute. But worse than all of this – worst of all – Dory had become – and this might not seem like much, superficially, but it was actually the most heart-breaking element of the whole thing – he'd become *humourless*.

He'd lost his ability to just laugh it all off. He was really – *really* – brought down by it. He was depressed. He kept saying (for example) that he was finding it 'hard to focus' (he'd been twice to get his eyes tested over the last six weeks. His eyesight was pronounced perfect, on both occasions).

He was barely sleeping. *Insomnia*. He'd always been a light sleeper (needed only four good hours, at most – like Margaret Thatcher), but there was no doubt – no doubt whatsoever – that sleep was a major factor in the whole scenario; a 'trigger'.

Nobody dared use the word 'narcolepsy', and certainly not in front of him (he was *German*. Self-reliance was his watchword – and clarity, and precision). There was a stigma – Dory felt – with this particular condition, because of its inevitable connection with childhood trauma; the underlying sense of an inability to *cope*. At some fundamental level Dory closely aligned coping with his masculinity (coping was something he needed to do, and do well, to be a successful male).

Isidore's finer feelings aside, however, narcolepsy was definitely one of the medical conditions which best fitted his particular combination of symptoms. It didn't fit completely (symptoms could be like that). Elen said it was as though Dory was missing a shoe, and narcolepsy was a slipper (ie they were related, but not entirely compatible). Beede found this description telling. He found it apt.

The other unsayable word was – but of course – schizophrenia. This word made everybody panic (even Elen). But it was not a fearful word for Beede. For Beede it was just a combination of letters which didn't even feature in his old *Pocket Oxford*. The closest they came to it there was 'schist'; a kind of crystalline rock, whose components were arranged in distinct layers. Beede liked that. He'd tried to tell Elen about it (the 'layers' ie the concept of something separate but unified), yet for some reason she seemed to gain no palpable sense of relief from the idea.

Of course Isidore had been medicated for his condition in the past – so far as it was possible (which wasn't very far at all), because every doctor he visited seemed to have a different opinion (and these medical practitioners were few and far between). Dory hated doctors – found them 'meddlesome' – flew into a blind panic at the idea of 'a diagnosis'. To be diagnosed was to be boxed up, to be compartmentalised, to be made separate, to be lost. For Dory a diagnosis represented 'the death of hope'. His optimism – and he *was* optimistic, by and large – thrived in unknowing.

There were some things (some symptoms – side-effects, you might say) which Dory simply wouldn't factor in during medical consultations (refused to, point-blank, Elen said), and this obviously made it very difficult for any kind of practitioner to complete their medical assessment of him. He could be extremely secretive (for such an extraordinarily 'open' person), as if protecting something precious – something vulnerable – inside of him.

And like nearly all people with serious long-term medical conditions, Dory associated medication – *being* medicated – with a lot of the bad stuff from his past (things from his childhood which he'd never openly discuss: his mother was over-protective, his father very controlling, the usual stuff). So he was heavily resistant to any kind of 'help' (medical, analytical), which obviously made things incredibly difficult . . .

'*Damn!*'

Beede suddenly (and unexpectedly) ground to a halt. He put a hand to his chest and drew a deep breath (he was surprisingly short of puff). As he exhaled, he quickly checked his watch. He cursed again. Dory – who was at least ten paces ahead (not even a vague sheen of sweat on him; he was fit as a cheetah) – heard the horse come to a stop. He turned, quick as a flash. 'Beede? Something wrong?'

Beede glanced up, almost guiltily. 'No. Nothing. Just a meeting . . .' he shrugged, 'I'm late. In fact I've already missed her. I completely forgot . . .'

'A meeting at work?'

'No . . .' Beede shook his head. 'Not at work.'

'At *home*?'

Dory looked flabbergasted (this was for comic effect, Beede presumed). 'Yes, Dory, at home.'

Beede crisply enunciated his response to try and railroad any potential ribbing. It wasn't a successful ploy.

'A *personal* arrangement?'

56

Still, Dory maintained his little act.

Beede found himself blushing. He had no idea why. He said nothing.

Dory's eyes flew even wider. '*What?* Beede – Mr *Daniel* Beede – actually *socialising*?!'

Beede's flushed but sombre face cracked into a smile (Ah yes. *This* was the real Dory. The real him. He could be tender yet mocking, could needle you in that special, gentle way of his which even the most ferocious curmudgeon would do well to take umbrage at).

'A *date*?' Dory rapidly expanded on his theme, his blue eyes twinkling. 'An *assignation*?'

'Yes. *No*,' Beede scowled. 'I didn't . . . It's just some . . .'

He started to walk again, then stumbled, slightly, on the narrow pavement '. . . some insignificant *person*,' he finished off, clumsily.

Dory seemed utterly delighted by Beede's coy evasiveness. 'Well perhaps you might ring her?'

He slipped his hand into his jacket pocket, then grimaced, and tried his other. Nothing.

'We need to cross before we reach the fly-over.' Beede quickly changed the subject, staring first down the road, then up it. He started off (firmly grasping his trousers) at a slow trot. Isidore glanced left himself, then followed.

They reached the other side (Beede now a little ahead) and walked rapidly onward. But after only a few moments, Beede abruptly stopped for a second time. Isidore found himself hard-up against the horse's rump. He took a quick step back. They were standing at the near-end of the fly-over. Cars and lorries were roaring past. Isidore frowned, glanced behind him, saw a small gap in the traffic and took his chance. He speedily overtook the horse.

Beede was staring down over the embankment to his left and frowning. He seemed deeply preoccupied. A large field lay ahead of them – a semi-circular meadow, full of bleached grass, young trees (huddled inside their protective, plastic sheaths) and a muddle of bushes. They were almost at the point where the road they were taking divided into three separate parts: one section charging boldly onwards, the other two curving sharply off and around to form the different sides (the valves, the ventricles) of a divided heart (or – in the pursuit of absolute anatomical accuracy – the two segregated cheeks of a pair of buttocks). Snuggled into the hinterland of that voluptuous curving were two good-sized plots. The one on their particular side currently contained a thin sprinkling of mixed livestock.

But Beede wasn't interested in the meadow (nor even in the animals). He was staring past it, towards the Brenzett roundabout which lay a short distance beyond.

Isidore silently followed the line of Beede's gaze.

'Oh *shit*,' he whispered.

It was his car – definitely his car. It was parked in the middle of the roundabout with the driver's door left wide open (a total hazard to all other traffic). A police car was pulling up behind it (no siren, but with its blue light rotating). Dory blinked (he didn't generally respond well to anything that flashed).

'Superb timing,' Beede said dryly. 'But don't worry ...' (he was extraordinarily composed) ... 'tell them the car was stolen while you were on the job, that you've just been phoned and informed that it's been dumped here. You can imply that the kids in question might've released the horse,' he glanced up at the filly, 'as part of the prank.'

Dory's eyes made sudden contact with Beede's – for a split second, perhaps even less.

'Quick thinking,' he murmured (instantly breaking his gaze), his clipped voice tinged with something corrosive –

Fastidiousness?
Suspicion?
Disgust?

'Naval training,' Beede demurred, with a casual shrug.

Dory half-smiled then jogged on, across the fly-over and a few yards beyond. Here he turned sharply, preparing to swing himself, lithely, over the crash barrier (this was a short cut), but before he did, he paused, glanced back towards Beede and shouted, 'You won't *tell* her, will you?'

Beede didn't respond at first.

'*Elen*,' Dory yelled. 'You won't *tell*?'

Beede shook his head, automatically. 'Of course not,' he shouted back. '*Hurry*.' He waved him on.

Dory sprang over the barrier, scissored his way between the saplings and then hurdled a second (wood and wire) fence, before clambering and lurching down the field's muddy embankment. At approximately the half-way point, his trousers started slipping; the fabric locked just above his knees, and he tumbled. It was a dramatic fall – a jester's fall – with all the additional frills and embellishments.

Beede closed his eyes (in an effort to repress a sharp bark of laughter –

Where did that urge come from?)

– then he turned his face away, waited patiently for a slight lull in the traffic, and moved implacably onward.

FOUR

An entry-phone engineer was taking what Kane could only (in all detachment and impartiality) call 'an obscene amount of interest' in Kelly's thigh area. She was collapsed on Kane's front step, both her legs stretched out stiffly in front of her, drinking from a flask of coffee and eating a Mars Bar (pulling back her lips as she bit down on it, almost in horror – like a donkey taking a Polo Mint from a suspicious-seeming stranger). He was crouched over her and gently massaging her upper knee as Kane drew closer.

Kane was not happy. His rage had two, distinct constituents. The first: simply that she was *there* (he was tired. He had dumped her. She was a pest). The second, that she was flirting. And this other man (his *rival*; a young man, looked Italian) had his filthy hands pretty much everywhere.

Kelly didn't notice Kane until he was almost upon them. When she did, she let out a small squawk and dropped the chocolate bar on to her lap (as though Kane was the caustic battle-axe in charge of her slimming club). The Italian glanced up (blankly, momentarily) then returned his full attention to her thigh (it was an appealing thigh. Even Kane knew that).

'How cosy . . .' Kane murmured, affably (brandishing his finely wrought shield of charm before him).
'Oh *Fuck*.' Kelly seemed mortified, almost frightened. 'This ain't . . . it's just . . . I fell off the *wall* and I . . .'

Kane was so unimpressed by the calibre of her excuse that he didn't even bother to let her finish it. 'Fell off the wall? How *awful* for you.' He smiled, falsely.

She grimaced. 'I was waitin' on Beede. I had a special package for him. The gate was locked . . .'
Kane seemed quite riveted by this story. 'The gate was locked, you say? *That* gate?' He pointed behind him, towards the open gate. 'How strange . . . And you were waiting for Beede? *The* Beede? *Daniel* Beede?'
'It fuckin' *was*,' she almost squealed, 'I *swear* . . .'

'Hmmn. A *special* package . . .' Kane mused.

Kelly looked down, then around her, in a sudden panic. 'Oh *shit*. Where *is* the fuckin' thing?'

Kane rolled his eyes. Kelly didn't even notice. She was still looking around for the brown envelope, visibly alarmed by its absence. 'I had a package. Some black girl gave it me. Cross my heart . . .'

Kane reached out his foot and gently poked the crouching Italian with it. 'Excuse me,' he said sweetly. 'May I interrupt you for a moment . . . ?'

The Italian turned, sharply (still crouching) and raised the flat of his hand. '*No*,' he said (in his threadbare English), 'get loss.'

He wasn't Italian. He had a heavy accent (mid-European, maybe an Arab, maybe Romanian). He was crazy-looking, like a sallow Frankie Dettori on some kind of growth hormone. Kane carefully reconsidered booting him for a second time. He was smallish, and thin, but the veins stood out on his fists like worm-casts.

Kelly struggled to get up.

'Oh *bollocks*,' she was muttering, 'I lost Beede's package. I'm in so much fuckin' *shit* . . .'

'What the hell are you doing?!' the Romanian bellowed (and in his indigenous tongue, so it was just a stream of crazy babble to the both of them), then, '*You*,' he continued, more haltingly (giving Kelly a firm glare), 'jus' *stay*! Okay?'

Kelly fell down again, shocked.

'*Wow*.' Kane took a small step back, as if the Romanian was a complex work of modernist art, best appreciated at a distance of several paces. 'This guy's a real *gem*, Kell. How on earth'd you hook up with him?'

'I already *told* you,' Kelly snapped, 'I was waitin' on *Beede* . . .'

'*Enough*.' Kane raised his hand in a gesture of weary compliance. 'I give in. Do what you like. I'm knackered. My head's totally mashed. Just shift out of my way, will you?'

He touched his fingers to his pounding temples.

The Romanian did not move. Kane tapped him on the shoulder. 'I said just *shift* . . .'

The Romanian sprang around. **'What are you?'** he demanded. **'Some kind of imbecile?'** Then, '*You! Go*!' he insisted, flapping Kane away as if he were some kind of vile bluebottle.

'Go *where*?' Kane tapped his index finger against his own chest. 'This is where I *live*, you moron. This is my *home*.'

Kelly attempted to struggle up again.

The Romanian turned – **'Idiot girl!'** – and firmly pushed her back down.

'*Ow*!' she expostulated, plaintively, as her bony arse made contact with the stone step.

At the sight of the Romanian manhandling Kelly, Kane completely lost it. He grabbed him by the shoulders – as if to spin him around again – but the Romanian was already moving smoothly of his own volition, and as he turned, his right fist turned with him. He punched Kane in the chest with it, then followed through with a hard left to his gut. They were powerful punches.

Kane doubled over with an embarrassing squeak. He saw the Romanian starting to lift his knee, then hesitating, as if re-considering delivering him a swift kick to the groin area (although it was still very obvious – even to him – that if the Romanian had seriously wanted to finish him off, he probably already would've. Those were amazing punches for a man of his stature – he was 5'5", at a push).

Kane remained down for a few seconds (catching his breath, consolidating, thinking this all over), before his watering eyes finally settled on the steaming coffee Thermos (Ye Gods! A *gift*!), and, quick as a flash, he'd grabbed it, straightened up, and thrown the contents into the Romanian's face.

The Romanian screamed. Kelly screamed (she was splattered, and the Romanian staggered sideways, accidentally knocking into her). Kane dropped the Thermos and heard the glass break inside of it (he took an active – almost adolescent – pleasure in the sound of its fracturing).

The Thermos had been open for some minutes and the coffee wasn't exactly boiling, but it was hot enough. The Romanian was scalded, yet seemed far more concerned by the damage to his clothing. He was hopping mad.

'This is my work shirt!' he yelled, pulling the still-steaming fabric away from his hairy chest, gesticulating wildly. **'You have ruined me!'**

Kane suddenly started laughing. It was a hoarse laugh (he was winded). He pointed, weakly, at the ruined shirt (it was hardly the most glamorous-looking garment he'd ever laid eyes upon). The

Romanian, meanwhile, had noticed his damaged Thermos. He snatched it up from the paving, almost howling.

'My *Thermos*!' he wailed (his pronunciation of the brand-name was – even to Kane's ears – rather endearing). **'What have you done?'**

At this point a second man arrived; another entry-phone engineer, potentially the Romanian's senior. He had Kelly's two lurchers with him.

'What's going on?' he asked the Romanian. The Romanian didn't answer. Instead he took the Thermos – his knuckles white with fury – and threw it, violently, against the nearest windowpane. The window – it was a large, double-glazed one – chipped but did not shatter.

Even so, the second entry-phone man was visibly alarmed by this display. 'Gaffar,' he gasped, 'are you off your fuckin' *head*?!'

Gaffar stood his ground, his arms at his sides, breathing heavily (like the Invisible Hulk, transforming), his fists clenching and unclenching ('the glass hasn't shattered, *dammit*' – his eyes were screaming – 'so now I might be obliged to *hospitalise* somebody').

'That's not even my window,' Kane said, still chuckling, still limply pointing, like everything was a joke to him.

The second engineer glanced down at Kelly. 'You all right there, love?'

Kelly nodded. Her eyes were closed now. She was resting her head against the door. Her face was very pale. One of the lurchers nuzzled her open hand. At its tender ministrations she emitted a gentle groan.

In the midst of all his hilarity, it finally dawned on Kane that she might not actually be bullshitting him about the fall. *Had* she fallen? He peered down at her, properly. He blinked (it was almost as though he hadn't seen her there before –

Kelly?).

His mirth evaporated. A shattered piece of shin-bone was poking out – like a discarded lolly stick – through the tight, smooth flesh just underneath her knee. The lower half of her leg was purpling and swollen to almost twice its normal proportions. Her trainer was off (lying on the ground nearby, next to her slightly mangled-looking Nokia). If her foot was a balloon, then it'd been pumped too full of air (looked like some kind of zeppelin sent up to advertise a discount shoe-store; or one of those themed lilos which kids loved to bob around upon, in the hotel pool, on holiday).

It was *gruesome*. As a boy Kane suddenly remembered shoving a piece of driftwood into the heart of a beached-up, blue-white jelly-fish (to see if it was alive, to see how it would react). That was her leg – what it reminded him of –

Christ –
What a cruel child I was

He glanced over at the Romanian. The Romanian was standing exactly as before (arms down, fists clenched, breathing, *breathing*). His cheeks were wet – were shiny – with remnants of the coffee. In the distance Kane picked out the insistent bray of an ambulance –

Hee-haw!
Hee-haw!

Oh *shit*.
If the Romanian had punched him again – right there, right then: square in the face – he would've considered it an act of the most extreme beneficence.

His full name was Gaffar Celik and he wasn't Romanian. He was a Kurd. He had just turned twenty-four. He was born in a poor town called Silopi, in Turkey, on the Iraqi border. His father had died – when Gaffar was only three – working as a Village Guard in a private army under the control of a Kurdish feudal lord. His mother had then taken them eastward (Gaffar, and his younger brother), first to Marlin (to stay with her widowed father), then on (when he passed) to be with her sister, in the beautiful mountainous village of Hasankeyf.

Hasankeyf was a kind of tabernacle to Kurdish culture (40 miles from Batman, straddling the Tigris River), and the sister was married to a man whose paternal line had found gainful employment for over twelve generations guiding tourists around the ancient sights there (the legendary caves, the remains of the old bridge, the magnificent obelisk, the beautiful, stone archway).

But few people visited them any more. The Turkish government had plans to flood the town as part of the Llisu Dam project, and so, gradually, one by one, the tour operators had wiped them from the cultural map (the south east had always been a difficult area). The decision – they insisted – was in no way political (to systematically flood all significant Kurdish landmarks? But what, they asked gently, was remotely contentious in that?).

Sometimes Gaffar felt like they were already submerged (there just wasn't actually any water, yet), that they had been abandoned, betrayed, cut off. But he was not bitter (had no *time* for bitterness). He merely felt a dreamy nostalgia (for a non-existent future), coupled with a tender, almost poignant, regret.

Occasionally – and with scant warning – things could turn nasty. Battalions of Turkish soldiers would suddenly descend upon them, *en masse*, and burn down people's homes (frighten them, move them on, accuse them of insurrection, of supporting the PKK and the Kurdish Revolution). Gaffar's family were just one among many (the working estimation stood at 70,000) to be methodically oppressed (and displaced) in this way. Eventually it all got too much and they fled north, to Diyarbakir: Town of the Black Walls, where – for a short while, at least – they felt a little more secure.

Gaffar's mother was a devout woman (especially since his father's passing. You might almost think – Gaffar sometimes thought – that she was 'making up' for something). She was a follower of the Alexi Sect (Alexi was Mohammed's brother-in-law; they were Shi'i, and persecuted – for radicalism – by the Sunni majority). Gaffar gave every appearance of conforming to this belief system. He had an actual, a *palpable* genius for pretending. Pretence was an essential part of his inheritance, of his *pathology*. He was proud of his duplicity (he didn't have much, but at least he had this; he *owned* it. It was *his*).

There was a secret, you see, about his father – something shameful and unspeakable – which, even when he was alive, they only talked about in whispers. And now that he was gone, it was either never mentioned or hotly denied. But it was still true, nonetheless.

His father had been a *Dawasin,* one of the Yezidis; the oldest and most singular of all the Kurdish tribes; a reclusive, secretive, clannish people who worshiped Malik Taus, the Peacock Angel. They believed that they were the last remaining direct descendants of Adam's line, that their race (and their race alone) was unbesmirched by the sins of Eve. They were *pure* (this was part of their patrimony), but they were not 'of the Book' (at least, not formally), and so, even amongst Kurds, they were both feared and despised.

Gaffar's father had been born in Sinjar, on the Syrian/Iraqi border (it was the Kurdish lot to be born on the edge of things, the perimeter; to be squeezed into the outer reaches; at worst to be persecuted, at best loathed and ignored). In 1975 the Dawasin in that area had been forcibly evicted from their land and placed into collectives.

Times were hard. He had drifted to Baghdad, searching for work. He'd left a wife and a daughter behind him, staying away – out of desperation (or so he claimed) – for many months in conjunction. In Yezidi culture absence was a crime of excommunicable proportions. And there was no coming back from it. So after a while, he didn't even try. His soul was lost from that point onward.

As if to underline this fact, categorically, he journeyed north, to Irbil, and became a denizen of the legendary Sheikhallah Bazaar, where he hired himself out as muscle in the trade of drugs, fake passports and illegal arms. He moved to Turkey on the back of his successes, changed his name (stole 'Celik' from a local mayor), converted to Islam and married Gaffar's mother.

He'd wanted (he claimed) to leave his former life behind. He even said he'd seen Jonah (Yunus) in a vision, where the whale was not a sea creature, but an enormous tent (a living thing, somehow, with ribs and teeth and organs), and it was crammed – full-to-bursting – with people he'd known in the past (his old friends, his enemies, his compatriots), and they were all slowly suffocating. But his own chest was full of air (like *he* was the whale, or the lungs, or something), and Jonah, on observing this fact, reached out his hand to him, and they walked clear – clear of the tent, of the bazaar – into a world beyond, into a promised land.

An epiphany.

Or this was the mythology. The truth was much simpler. Things didn't actually change all that much in Turkey (I mean the Kurds were persecuted everywhere, weren't they?). The fabric of his life remained virtually identical. He'd simply crossed over (or turned inside out, like a polythene bag). He was on the other side, now, but the leap he'd made wasn't gargantuan (like Jonah's whale), and it wasn't so much moral (or spiritual) as geographical.

He remained a soldier (but now paid by the state). The Guard were universally loathed. They were cruel and merciless. Some were just desperate, others, crass opportunists. Gaffar's father was ruthless, but not actively sadistic. He dispatched his duties efficiently. He took the occasional back-hander. He still thought like a traitor. And when he died (suddenly, on a landmine) his reputation was a distinguished one. He'd been fearless and brave and single-minded. He'd conformed. He'd fitted in. He was remembered by his compadres as an honourable man.

Gaffar sometimes wondered where his soul had gone (I mean which of the deities he'd served was the more forgiving, the more powerful?). It was a telling thought: but weren't all true nomads at their happiest in limbo?
Was God actually aware of that fact?

As he grew older it became increasingly apparent that Gaffar had fighting in his genes (in his *bones,* which he broke, then re-set, then broke again). It wasn't that he was angry (quite the opposite). His strength was rooted in his curious implacability.

From the tender age of twelve he fought for money. He was a gambler. He could win or take a beating – he didn't care which, particularly – so long as he was paid for it. He loved his family but he despised their life of grinding penury. He wasn't political (and in Diyarbakir it was difficult not to be) and he did not actively support the PKK (let's face it: when Ocalan was arrested, things actually got *better*: schools were opened, they could speak in their own tongue again . . . Ocalan was certainly a hero, but he was also a spitfire; didn't really care where his stray bullets landed, just so long as he satisfied his overall agenda.

He was single-minded – heroes often were – and matched the Turkish armed forces, blow for blow, in his ceaseless promulgation of violence and terror).

Politics were all well and good, Gaffar reasoned – ideals and such – but money was the language of progress. Money actually got you out of there; into the colourful world which flickered on the screens of the cable tvs in local cafes. Into freedom. Into Eden.

Gaffar was a bare-knuckle boxer, all over the region (developed quite a reputation, as he grew older, although eventually, inevitably, this began to work against him). The trick was in his stature. He was small, looked wiry. But underneath he was impregnable. His will was the iron rod in his spine which kept him standing (or told him the precise moment at which to fall). His will was indomitable. He was the God of his own insides.

But the whole world (alas) didn't start and end upon his skin's smooth surfaces. There was an outside (he could smell it, he could taste it. Sometimes it kicked or bit or bruised him). Outside all was chaos. And this chaotic outside – if it really wanted to – could suck you in.

There was no point resisting.

He got caught up (the hook went straight through his cheek) aged fourteen, fifteen, in the opposing currents of politics and corruption (dragged back and forth, aimlessly, between them). He hadn't tried, it'd simply happened; he'd attracted attention, had become almost a *talisman*.

He hung around in the backwash for a while (rejected by family, embraced by the local mafia, imprisoned for a year), then finally – out of sheer desperation – he struck a deal (it was the gambler in him). He risked everything (made promises to God, crossed his fingers, held his breath, you name it). And it *worked*.

Six long hours in customs and he was spat out, with due cere-mony, into the United Kingdom (thirty neat little bags of heroin killing time inside his colon).

King-dom?

They had a queen, they spoke English, they ate beefburgers and drank beer.

London. *North* London. Wood Green (no woods, not much greenery, but who cared? He was *here*. This was his big chance. His break for freedom . . .).

Hmmn

It'd looked better on the telly. And there was dubbing, too, in Turkey (or subtitles; *hell*, he wasn't fussy).
When people spoke it sounded utterly foreign. He couldn't react. He couldn't respond. He was rendered dumb. It terrified him.

Language (not just violence, or poverty) was now his determinator. The people he needed to get away from were the only people he could communicate with (everybody important spoke Kurdish here).

It was a different world – he could certainly vouch for that – but it was still run by the same rules (the sky the same colour, the ground just as hard, his belly just as hungry, the same battles for territory).
So he chugged on. Became a *Bombacilar* – a henchman for a gang in the Green Lanes area. Shelved his dreams of a boxing career. Supported Turkey in the football. Developed a taste for American lager.

Until everything crumbled – 22 January 2003. A vicious gang-fight on Green Lanes. A *massacre*. The accidental death of an innocent bystander. An armed swoop on a Haringey cafe. A police officer attacked with a kebab skewer. Illegal gambling. Nine arrests. Operation codename NARITA. Commanding officer Steve James and a friendly – a *very* friendly – interpreter. (*Oh that friendly interpreter! The dire threats she'd made! And the bewildering promises!*)

Her name was Marta. She was sixty-three years old, half-Cypriot and a widow, with a mixed degree in psychology and philosophy from Trent University –

Marta

She'd reached out her hand to him, and Gaffar had taken hold of it (it was a soft hand, smelled of hazelnut nougat and –

Mmmm

– Indian rose-water).
Marta, it soon transpired, was to be Gaffar's Jonah (although the

whale was not a tent this time, but the claustrophobic courtroom in which he'd calmly turned state's evidence).

Gaffar – like his father before him – had niftily slipped the border. And on the other side?

Ash-ford?
What a clumsy word

So this was where his journey ended. This was where he'd sunk his anchor. This was his port, his haven, his harbour. This was where he disembarked: a crummy job, an old shirt, his faithful Thermos (a leaving present from a favourite aunt). Two weeks rent paid up in advance . . .
This –

Ah yes

– was his Brand New Start.
But only so long as he did *Absolutely Nothing Wrong, Mate – D'ya hear?*

Someone had to take custody of the two dogs, so Kane (having first glanced around him for any other likely candidates – *bugger*. Not a one) reluctantly agreed to shoulder the responsibility.

Once the ambulance had pulled off, he ushered them both inside. The big one was a little snappy, but they trotted into the narrow corridor gamely enough, turning at the foot of the stairs (leading up into Kane's first-floor section of the flat) and gazing over at him, expectantly, as if awaiting further instructions.

Kane tried to move past them and the larger one growled –

Oh, really?

He tried again. This time it snarled, and the smaller one –

The little shit

– backed him up.

Right

Kane considered his options –

The pound?
Pest control?
The butcher?

Ten seconds later, there was a knock at the door. He answered, still musing. It was Gaffar. He was holding a large, brown envelope (which he'd discovered over by the wall) and a small, silver trainer. 'This *her*,' he said, proffering the trainer politely, like a down-at-heel Buttons in *Cinderella*.

'Pardon?'

Kane really was quite exhausted.

These two items belong to your skinny whore,' Gaffar reiterated.

'Oh . . . *yeah*,' Kane said, recognising Kelly's distinctive footwear, and then (much to his horror) the brown envelope she'd mentioned previously. '*Shit*. This must be for Beede. Thanks . . .'

He took the two objects, tucked them under his arm, and was about to close the door (a symphony of growling promptly resuming behind him) when his conscience briefly pricked him and he paused. 'So d'you get a roasting?' he asked abruptly. 'From your boss?'

'*Eh?*'

Kane mimed the throwing of the Thermos and then pointed to the chipped window.

'*Ahhh*,' Gaffar just shrugged, resignedly.

'The chop?'

Kane made a chopping gesture.

No response.

He thought for a moment. 'The *axe?*'

He made a dramatic slicing motion across his neck.

Gaffar's eyebrows rose for a second, then he nodded. **'Yeah, I'm** screwed, **but so what? I'm beyond caring**, *man*. **He thinks I'm a live-wire**, *huh*? **A troublemaker? Well he can stick his stupid opinions up his own arse. The bottom line is, I've had enough. I'm through. And that's my decision. I'm master of my own destiny**, see? **I don't care what he tells the damn authorities. He treats me like a slave**, yeah? **He pays like a . . . a cunt . . .** yeah? **I told him I could earn a better living out on the streets. I did that in Diyarbakir for an entire year. Lived like an animal, off my wits.'** Gaffar tapped the side of his head, meaningfully. **'He's a fool. An imbecile. I could devour his brains in one sitting and still feel ravenous.'** He paused for a moment, breathing heavily. **'You're right,'** he continued, vaingloriously, **'I should slaughter his entire family. Steal his money. Steal his car. Get the hell out of here . . .'**

As he spoke, Gaffar made a series of rather fetching little stabbing motions with an imaginary blade. On the final one, he symbolically disembowelled a toddler, then snatched some keys, which the toddler (rather mysteriously) appeared to be clutching.

Kane was scowling now, struggling to keep up with him. Gaffar observed his confusion (let it ride for a few seconds), and then, **'I'm just joking,'** he exploded, with a loud cackle, slapping Kane jovially on the shoulder, **'you big, fat, ugly** American *twat.'*

He continued to grin at Kane. Kane smiled brightly back. 'Correct me if I'm wrong,' he said, 'but I believe "American twat",' he drew a neat pair of speech marks in the air, 'is actually part of an *international* vocabulary – a *universal* language – which we all share.'

Gaffar mused this over for a second, apparently unmoved. *'Wow-wee,'* he finally murmured, dryly.

Kane sniggered (the man had *balls*, there was no getting round it). 'You're funny,' he said eventually, 'and you can take care of yourself. I respect that. Come on in. I'll dig you out a spare shirt. We can smoke some ganja. Some *weed*, huh? Then I *must* get some fucking zeds or I'll expire.'

'Okay.'

Kane pulled the door wider. Gaffar slipped smoothly past him to a muted *vibrato* of snarling.

'Just watch out for the . . .' Kane glanced over his shoulder, worriedly. *'Uh . . .'*

FIVE

Beede never locked the door which separated his and Kane's living areas. To do so would've shown a complete lack of faith in his son (and, by default, in his own parenting abilities). This decision 'not to lock' was primarily self-serving (Kane's feelings – or probable *lack* of them – barely entered into the equation). Beede's need to project himself as always open and accessible (a touching combination, say, of the old-fashioned Corner Shop – with their lofty code of personal service – and the modern, ruthless, all-nite Cash & Carry) was fundamental to his inalienable sense of the kind of father he wanted to be (or to *appear* to be, since in his mind these two notions were virtually interchangeable).

To boil it all down (which might take a while – there was plenty of old meat, hard lessons and human frailty in this particular broth), Beede was wildly cynical about the functions of paternity.

Was it Freud or Sophocles (Beede sometimes wondered) who first came up with the theory that all any little boy ever *really* wanted was to kill the father (strictly in the symbolic sense, of course)? Whoever ultimately took the credit for it (*Ah*, he could see them both now, queuing up at the Paradisical Counter of Philosophical Legitimacy: Sophocles slightly forward, a picture of genial equanimity; Freud, further back, but still scaring the living shit out of everybody), Beede definitely thought that they were on to something.

Although in Kane's particular case, his sheer indifference to his father (wasn't indifference a kind of murder, anyway? A death of care? Of *interest*?) was so strong, so marked, that to raise his hand against him – even figuratively – would've demanded just a tad too much energy. For Kane to actually get *angry* with Beede? Seriously? To take him on? To lose his *rag*?! You might as well ask a tropical fish to murder a robin (it simply wasn't feasible. It couldn't happen).

In bald truth, Beede's studious attempts to present himself as unfailingly approachable to his son were all just so much baloney. He actively avoided him – consciously, *un*consciously – at almost every available opportunity. But by being so unremittingly *there* for him (in the formal sense, at least) he cleverly *thwacked* the leaden ball of familial responsibility squarely back into Kane's court again (Kane was still young. He could take the burden. And it might actually be *good* for him to feel like something was wrong – or lacking – or missing – like he'd unintentionally fucked up in some way).

When it came to his door (its locking or otherwise), Beede honestly felt like he had nothing to hide. He almost believed himself transparent (like one of those minuscule but fascinating single-cell creatures which loves to hang around in pools of stagnant water), so certain was he of his own moral probity.

Of course everybody has *something* a little private about them (and Beede was no exception), but his firm apprehension was that once you started hiding things – once you got all sneaky and furtive – you automatically gave potential intruders the impetus to start hunting seriously. And that, he felt, would be a most unwelcome eventuality.

Visitors were rare, anyway. Kane was usually working (or partying) or crashed out. He didn't deal from home (oh come *on*). And nobody who knew Beede properly would ever consider turning up uninvited (he was a busy man. An 'impromptu' impulse was pretty much on a par – in his eyes – with spitting or extreme flatulence).

Even Kane kept his distance. Beede had the only kitchen in the property (open-plan – the wall had come down in 1971; his last ever concession to what he liked to call 'the modern malaise of interior renovation'), but Kane didn't cook, so that wasn't a problem (he had a kettle and a microwave gathering dust on his landing). Beede had a shower and a toilet (so spartan in aspect that they resembled something dreamed up by an over-zealous BBC props department for a gruelling drama about a Japanese prisoner of war camp) while Kane had a bath (which he absolutely *luxuriated* in), a toilet and a bidet. If they ever met or spoke, it was usually in the hallway, or at an appointed hour, at a preferred table, in a nearby cafe.

Imagine Beede's surprise, then, on returning home (after his protracted interlude with Isidore), to discover two recalcitrant curs snarling on the stairway, Kane – fast asleep – on his sofa (a saucer containing several cigarette stubs balanced precariously on the arm; Beede quickly removed it, with a *tut*), and a shirtless Kurd (with a blood-stained hanky tied clumsily around the fleshy area just below his elbow) sitting quietly upon an adjacent chair.

The washing machine was half-way through its cycle. The Kurd was peacefully occupied in playing some kind of dice game on Beede's reading table (all of his books now piled up, neatly, on the floor nearby). He was throwing two dice from a Tupperware beaker (the beaker into which Beede liked to drain off excess meat-fat from his roasting dish. It had a lid, usually, to keep the contents airtight. Beede had no idea where that lid had got to. The beaker had served him faithfully in this lone capacity since 1983. It must've been in a state of severe trauma).

'Good afternoon,' Beede said, quickly disposing of the tarnished saucer and then dumping his bag down on the kitchen counter.

The Kurd nodded briskly, picked up a pencil (Beede's pencil) and scribbled some figures on to a piece of paper (the back of Beede's water bill). Beede scowled. While he knew that it was unfair of him to blame the Kurd for Kane's apparent breach, he immediately took against him. 'I'm Daniel Beede,' he said curtly, 'and this is my home.'

'Gaffar Celik,' the Kurd muttered, barely even glancing up, '**and this is not my** home; **a fact I'm sure you'll soon be only too keen to acquaint me with,** eh?'

'**I speak a small Turkish,**' Beede answered, nonchalantly, taking off his jacket and hanging it up on the hook behind the door, '**from my time of the navy. You offend my pride with this words.**'

Gaffar winced, pantomimically, at his accent. '**Ever considered taking evening classes?**'

'Yes,' Beede back-handed, '**that is why we are conversation.** So what's *your* excuse, Mr Celik?'

'*Yip!*' Gaffar exclaimed, making as if to duck a punch, then rapidly drawing both fists to his chin (in readiness for some kind of counter-attack).

'Watch out,' Beede smiled, drawing up his own fists in a similar fashion, 'I was South-East Kent Boys Boxing Champion, 1956–1961.'

'*Wha?!* **You're a fighter, old man?**'

Gaffar was visibly moved by this information.

'Yes. I used to be. **In very far-back distance.** And less of the old, thank you very much.'

'I boxer,' Gaffar announced proudly, '**and trust me, I would've severely pulped your spotty, teenage arse back in '61.**'

'Oh, really?'

'Yes. **In my country I'm a celebrity** – *famous*, eh? – **for my amazing talents as a featherweight.**'

Beede appeared to take this bold personal declaration in his stride. 'Unfortunately the time-space continuum prevents us from categorically establishing the better man between us,' he murmured dryly, **'but I take you at you speak, eh?'**

'Let's roll for it, Greybeard,' Gaffar was smiling, **'I'll even give you a head start, as a mark of your seniority.'**

He removed a pound coin from his pocket and slammed it down, flamboyantly, on to the table.

Beede had no intention of playing dice. He hated all games (developed this deep antipathy during his long years in the navy). To Beede, game-playing was like aimlessly treading water in the fast-running Stream of Mortality; far better – he felt – to swim hard against the current, or to drown – spent and exhausted – in the attempt.

'Did that Tupperware pot have a lid when you found it?' he enquired. *'Huh?'*

'Lid,' Beede pointed and then performed a small mime.

'Ah,' Gaffar finally understood him and shook his head. 'Uh-uh.'

'Oh dear.'

'No problem,' Gaffar shrugged, **'we don't need one to play Par. Or Pachen, if you prefer.'**

'I suppose not . . .' Beede was mournful. He peered balefully over the back of the sofa at Kane (as if hoping to find the lid protruding from one of his pockets; perhaps jutting out neatly from between his buttocks) then glanced up again. 'So have you been here long, Gaffar?'

'Twenty-eight months.'

'No, I mean **in this rooms.'**

Gaffar inspected his watchless wrist. 'One hour.'

'I see.'

Gaffar vigorously rubbed his hand up and down on the goose-bumping flesh of his uninjured arm. **'Your friend's purple-haired whore broke her leg,'** he explained, amiably. **'She fell off the wall outside. I was helping her – I have a special genius for massage . . .'**

He pummelled the air, theatrically.

'Good *God* . . .' Beede was naturally alarmed by this news. 'She fell off the wall? Outside? Was it a bad break?'

Gaffar calmly ignored his questions. **'Then he – uh . . .** *Kane*,' he continued, nodding angrily towards the offending individual, **'suddenly turned up from out of nowhere and threw hot coffee all over me. Smashed my** Thermos. **Ruined my shirt. Got me the sack. And the** girl – whose leg was in a pretty bad way . . . uh . . .' he paused, ruminatively, 'Kelly. That her name . . . **she went off in an ambulance. Which was when,**' he continued, '**he kindly invited me inside and let the dogs maul me . . .**'

He pointed at the handkerchief on his arm.

'*Ah*. . . .' Beede suddenly caught on. He smirked. 'So would that be Pachen with *bluffs* you're playing there?'

Gaffar stared at him, blankly.

'No bluff,' he finally murmured, hurt.

While Beede wasn't entirely convinced by the accuracy of this stranger's report, he was impressed, nonetheless, by his good bearing and air of self-containment.

'I'm afraid Kane is my *son*,' he mused quietly, almost regretfully.

Gaffar's dark brows rose, but he didn't respond.

'I am his **father**, yes?' Beede persisted (like a rookie attending his first AA meeting; determined to confess everything).

The penny suddenly dropped.

'**What?**' Gaffar pointed accusingly towards the oblivious Kane. '**This big, fat, useless** *Yank* **is your seed?**'

Beede nodded. '**Cruel,** isn't it?'

Gaffar cackled, '**Well your arrival home was timely. I was just planning to fleece him.**'

'Then you would've fleeced *me*,' Beede declared, almost without rancour, 'because this is my flat. Kane lives upstairs.'

He pointed towards the ceiling.

As he spoke the washing machine clicked quietly on to its spin cycle.

Gaffar grinned, slammed down the Tupperware beaker (in brazen challenge), pulled a nearby stool closer and patted its seat, enticingly. '**Then let's settle this the traditional way, Old Champion,**' he wheedled. '*Come.* Come **and join me. Let's play**.'

Kane slept for three hours. When he finally awoke he found himself in his father's flat, curled up on the sofa (covered in a blanket: Beede's clean but ancient MacIntosh tartan, which had been so neatly and regularly darned over the years that the restoration work constituted more than a third of its total thread content).

The air was moist and scented (Gaffar had partaken of a shower – eschewing Beede's carbolic soap in favour of Ecover camomile and marigold washing-up liquid). There was some kind of tangy, tomato-based concoction bubbling away on the stove.

Kane blinked, dopily, as Gaffar emerged from the bathroom in an expensive – if slightly over-sized – Yves Saint Laurent suit.

He struggled to remember the exact course of events which had led him here –

Three Percodan
Seven joints
Half bottle Tequila . . .

His mouth was dry –

Dry

His stomach hurt. He shook his head. He cleared his throat. He inspected Gaffar more closely (his hands flailing around to locate his cigarette packet). Who *was* this man, again?

'Ah, you're awake. I just lifted £200 off your father,' the Kurd informed him, chirpily. *'Father,'* he quickly repeated. *'Beede*, eh?'

Kane sat up, alarmed. 'Is Beede here?'
The Kurd nodded. **'Now there's an intelligent individual. Very generous. Very hospitable . . .'** Gaffar expectorated, then swallowed, then blinked and swallowed again. **'But a miserable gambler . . .'** He shook his finger at Kane, warningly. **'Never, ever let the old man gamble with me again,** eh?'

'The bathroom?' Kane rapidly threw off the blanket, still panicked. 'Is he in the bathroom?'
'No,' Gaffar shook his head as he strolled into the kitchen. 'He – *uh* – **work.** He go. From . . .' he shrugged, 'half-hour.'

'*Jesus.*'

Kane closed his eyes for a moment, in relief. 'Thank *fuck.*'

Gaffar frowned, then abruptly stopped frowning as he peered into the bubbling pan on the stove.

'So did you explain about the dogs?'

Kane's eyes were open again.

'*Huh?*' Gaffar tested the edible medley (a large tin of Heinz baked beans with chipolatas). He winced –

Hot

– then sucked his teeth –

Too salty

How the English loved their salt.

'The dogs? The . . . uh . . . *Woof!* On the stair,' Kane valiantly continued, observing a cigarette-packet-shaped object in Gaffar's suit pocket. 'Did he see? Did you explain about Kelly?'

Gaffar half-smiled as he returned to the living area. 'Yes I do,' he said, with exactly the level of conviction most calculated to fill Kane with doubt. And then, '*Woof!*' he mimicked, satirically (with a huge grin), in a way that (Kane presumed) might be considered 'cute' in whichever godforsaken part of the planet he originally hailed from –

But not here

Kane rubbed his face with his hands (he was finding the Kurd rather exhausting). 'Would you get me some water?'

He mimed turning on a tap, holding a glass under.

Gaffar did as he was asked. He was accustomed to following orders. There was a kind of dignity in submission which the quiet ox inside of him took an almost active pleasure in.

'Thanks.'

As Kane drank he assessed Gaffar's suit.

'Nice suit . . .' He exhaled sharply as he spoke, then burped and wiped his mouth with his hand.

Gaffar nodded.

'Where's it from?'

'Beede.'

Kane blinked. 'No way.'

'Yes.'

'No,' Kane reiterated firmly. 'Beede would never own a suit like that. It looks foreign, for starters, and he religiously supports the British Wool Trade . . .'

Gaffar scowled. '*He* give to me. *Beede*. **In exchange for his losses**, yeah?'

'What is it?' Kane casually flipped open one of the front jacket flaps (feeling the seductive, semi-hollow crackle of his Marlboro packet through the lining). Gaffar immediately slapped it shut.

'Yves Saint Laurent,' he announced, haughtily.

'Not a chance, man,' Kane snorted. 'It's *gotta* be knock-off.'

Gaffar (rising like a pike to the bait) shrugged the jacket from his shoulders and showed Kane the label.

'*Wow*.' Kane perused the label at his leisure (it looked legitimate), while casually slipping his free hand into the pocket and removing his cigarettes. 'So there you go, huh?'

'So there you go,' Gaffar echoed, scowling, as Kane tapped out a smoke and flipped it into his mouth.

He pulled the jacket back on (wincing slightly as it snagged on his neatly re-bandaged arm). Kane relaxed down into the sofa again (*matches? Lighter?*), his expression one of tolerant bemusement. As he leaned he felt something crumple behind him. He shoved his hand under the blanket and withdrew a large, slightly dented brown envelope. He stared at it for a while, frowning.

Gaffar, meanwhile, had returned to the kitchen and was dishing himself up a large bowlful of beans. In the bread-bin he'd located a half-used wholemeal loaf from which he'd already torn a sizeable portion. He balanced the bread on top of the beans and carried the bowl over to Beede's desk, placing it down, carefully, on to the battered, leather veneer and taking off his jacket (hanging it over the back of the adjacent chair).

He sat down and began to eat, employing the bread as a makeshift scoop. Several mouthfuls in, he noticed a large World Atlas on a bookshelf close by, hauled it out, one-handed, opened it, and began casually paging through the maps.

Kane watched Gaffar for a while, patting away – like a zombie – at his pockets (impressed by the Kurd's apparent ability to make himself feel at home). The suit (Kane wryly observed) gave Gaffar the furtive air of a man struggling to pass himself off as Minister of Sport – or Information, or the Arts – in a tin-pot military dictatorship (somewhere much too hot) after his brother, Sergio (the ambitious, pissed-up lieutenant), had shot the bastard general and promptly stepped into his highly polished, size eleven lace-ups –

Ah yes –

The whole tragic socio-political edifice was currently hanging – like a badly mounted stuffed elk – on Gaffar's family resemblance, terror, and the faultless cut of his Yves Saint Laurent.

Sergio?
Man –
What am I on?!

   He finally located a box of matches (tucked down the side of the sofa), lit his cigarette and returned his full attention back to the brown envelope. He inspected the seal –

Not glued, just –

He kept his smoke dangling loosely from his lip as he popped out the flap. He peered inside – inhaled – and saw a thickish sheath of photocopied papers. He exhaled –

Hmmn

– and gently removed them.
   It was a very old book – forty pages long – badly reproduced and slightly blurry (although the frontispiece was in bolder type and so marginally more legible than the rest). It was written in Old English –

Well, old-ish . . .

Some (but not all) of the 's's were 'f's.

                    SCOGIN'S JESTS;
he read:

> *Full of witty Mirth and pleafant Shifts;*
> *done by him in FRANCE*
> *and other places.*
> *BEING*
> *A Prefervative against Melancholy.*

Then underneath that:

> *Gathered by Andrew Board, Doctor of Phyfick.*

This was followed by a whole ream of publishing guff.

Kane casually opened to the first page. He stiffened. On the blank, inner leaf, in pencil, somebody had written: –

So Beede –
There's a whole series of these things (one for each of the various monarchs' funny-men, although I didn't get a chance to look at any of the others). Apparently there was quite a vogue for them in the 1600s (and for several hundred years after that – I saw at least two editions of this one – the earlier called Scoggin's Jests *by an Andrew Board – 1626 – and this one, in which the spelling's more familiar, from 1796 – that's a 170-year gap!), indicating how popular these guys actually were (plus: note the celebrity publisher . . .)*

Kane returned to the front page again: –

Printed for W. Thackeray at the Angel in Duck Lane, near Weft-Smithfield, and J. Deason at the Angel in Gilt-Spur-Street.

He stared at this, blankly, for a while, removing his cigarette from his mouth (looking around for an ashtray, but not finding one, so tapping off the ash on to the knee of his jeans and patting it into the fabric), then turned back to the inside leaf and picked up where he'd left off: –

The information enclosed isn't considered especially reliable, though. This book was written years after John Scogin's death. Much of it will be based on either legend or hearsay (would've been considered 'tabloid', even at the time of its publication).

The actual story of his life (and a critique of Andrew Board, this book's compiler, who seems like a rather dodgy character – 'physician to Henry VIII', apparently) features in R.H. Hill's Tales of the Jesters, 1934 (and I wouldn't have a clue what his sources were), but – believe it or not – the text was registered unavailable (read as 'some miserable bastard stole it').

The librarian in the Antiquarian Books Section (who was actually quite chatty) sent me to go and see some journalist called Tom Benson who happened to be in the library on that day and in possession of an associated text called A Nest of Ninnies by Robert Armin (He's writing a book about comedy and is very interested in jesters', she said).

I tracked him down to the Music Section. He was a little hostile at first (you know how territorial these people can be), but after a brief conversation he admitted that he actually had his very own copy of Tales of the Jesters at home which he'd 'found' in a second-hand bookshop in Rye (this might've just been sheer bravura on his part – that whole 'journalists v academics' hornets' nest. Or maybe not).

The last section (in brackets) had been hurriedly crossed out.

Anyhow,

Kane continued reading:

I asked if I might borrow it some time (or even just make a copy of the relevant chapters) but he got a little prickly at this point and said he was still in the middle of using it, but that he would definitely call me when he was done (I gave him my number, although I won't be holding my breath). Then he told me some stuff over coffee (I bought the Madeira cake – it was a little dry) which you might find interesting. Will inform you in person.
The quality of the copy is poor (at best). This is because it was reproduced from a microfile. But I think you'll get the basic gist . . .
W.
PS If you need anything else – anything at all – you know you can always reach me on my mobile . . .

A number followed.

Kane cocked his head for a while – as if deep in thought – his eye returning, repeatedly, to the phrase 'I bought the Madeira cake – it was a little dry,' and then to the signature ('W').

Eventually – but somewhat hesitantly – he moved on to the text, proper. 'W' was right: the quality of the copy was very poor. And it was written in an ornate typescript (real migraine territory), which made the letters look like so many black ants dancing a woozy conga. After several minutes he succeeded in battling his way through The Prologue (his eye lingering, for a while, on a small rhyme at the bottom of the page): –

I Have heard fay that Scogin did come of an honeft ftock,
no kindred, and his friends did fet him to fchool at Oxford,
where he did continue until the time he was made Mafter
of Art,
where he made this jeft,

> *A Master of Art is not worth a fart,*
> *Except he be in Schools,*
> *A Batchelour of Law, is not worth a Straw,*
> *Except he be among fools.*

Kane's brows rose slightly. He closed the manuscript and reopened the envelope. He peered inside, then smiled and shoved in his hand, pulling out another (smaller) sheet of paper which he hadn't noticed there before. This was a receipt from The British Library, and detailed the costs of the photocopying. At the bottom of the receipt he observed – with a small start – the credit card details of one Winifred Shilling –

I knew it
The fucking Madeira cake –
Damn her

'Why?'
Kane jerked out of his reverie. Gaffar had twisted around on his chair and was now staring at him, quizzically.
'Sorry?'
Kane hurriedly shoved the manuscript and the receipt back into the envelope, licking the seal this time and pressing it shut.
'A look of thunder,' Gaffar exclaimed, helpfully providing both vocal (and visual) dramatisation of his words.

'*Oh* . . .' Kane's face rapidly showcased a disparate mish-mash of emotions (Picasso's cubist masterpiece *Woman Crying* seemed like traditional portraiture by comparison). He struggled to get a handle on the play of his features. 'It's . . . uh . . . *nothing*,' he almost ticked.

'Okay.' Gaffar nodded (registering Kane's inner turmoil, but taking it all with a pinch of salt: I mean, how hard could life *be* for this spoiled, flabby, Western pup?).

'I lost something,' Kane muttered, suddenly pulling himself to his feet (his hair falling across his face), 'that's all.'
He glanced around him (through the lank mop of his fringe), not entirely certain what he was searching for –

Beede?

  'Is lid?' Gaffar asked patiently, a small chipolata suspended delicately between his mouth and his bowl.
'Pardon?'
'Lid?' Gaffar indicated towards the Tupperware beaker on Beede's reading table.
'*Lid?*' Kane stared at the beaker, frowning.
'Ah, fuck it . . . *English*,' Gaffar murmured, turning back – resignedly – to his meal.

  Kane placed the brown envelope onto Beede's reading table (next to the contentious item of Tupperware), carefully balanced his cigarette there – its smouldering tip suspended over the carpet – and then kneeled down to inspect his pile of books. If there was one thing he could be certain of: Beede's books would speak (a-hem) *volumes* . . .

  On top of the pile (and it was a large pile) was what Kane – smilingly – took to be a real 'Beede classic': Derek Johnson's *Essex Curiosities*; Hardback. 1973. He picked it up and opened to the front flap –

Ah yes

'A representative collection of the old, curious and interesting objects that abound in Essex . . . for all those who cherish the heritage of the past and wish to preserve it for the future.'

Lovely

Kane put the book aside, with a grin.
Next up –

Ha!

Victor Papanek's *Design for the Real World*.

Brilliant!

Inside flap:

Ta-dah!

'A startling and constructive blueprint for human survival by a professional designer who accuses the Industrial design "establishment" of
mass negligence.'
(Oh God. The word 'establishment' stuck into those two, accusing
little inverted commas . . . How right! How po-faced! How deliciously
sanctimonious! How typically fucking *Beede*.) Kane sniggered, furtively,
then laid the volume down, almost fondly, turning – for a brief moment
– to take a quick puff on his cigarette –

Okay, okay . . .

He deftly returned his cigarette to its former position –

Soooo . . .

Third in the pile, a very new-looking paperback called –

What?!

The Yoga of Breath: A Step-by-step Guide to Pranayama by Richard
Rosen.

No

Kane picked up the book and stared at it, scowling (as if the
mere force of his disapproval – and incomprehension – might make

it disappear. But it didn't. It remained a steady weight in his hand; a neat 3*lb* tome of ridiculously incongruous NewAge hokum).

He slowly shook his head as he flipped it over and speed-read the sales pitch –

Blah blah . . . life energy . . .
Blah blah . . . self-transformation
Blah blah . . . breath and body awareness

Nuh-uh!

Beede? Reading a book about *yoga*? It made absolutely no sense (this strangely fashioned block simply wouldn't fit inside the box of traditional shapes Kane had painstakingly carved out for his father). He cast the book aside, hissing under his breath. It was a red herring. A *blip*. Some ditsy woman at work had loaned it to him – or that *damn* chiropodist with her stupid verrucas –

Hysterical?
Yeah
Ha bloody ha

The next book in the pile was larger and more traditional. Kane grabbed it –

Oh yes . . .

That was better: a thick, smart paperback (with illustrations) called *A History of Private Life: Revelations of the Medieval World*. He opened it, randomly, to a black and white reproduction of a small painting of a hairy youth (naked) from the fifteenth century, under which was written: 'The bear showed great affection for the child and suckled it for an entire year. Because of this feeding the child became as hairy as a wild beast and ate raw meat: *Valentin et Orson.*'

For some arcane reason Kane felt strangely comforted by this caption (something – however weird – translated from Latin. That was *him*, that was Beede: obscure, marginal, bookish, inaccessible . . .).

He sneered (feeling the comforting re-emergence of all his former prejudices), and turned back a few pages, his eye randomly settling

on a small sub-heading entitled, 'The Frantic Search for the Father'.
He started, slapped the book shut, and threw it down.

Paranoia

He closed his eyes (pushing back a sudden panic –

Push
Push)

– swallowed hard and tried to focus his mind again –

Tramadol
Yes

He imagined a small blister-pack in his pocket, rested an illusory
hand upon it, heard the neat click and the tiny rattle –

Ahhh

It worked just like magic.

Righty-ho . . .

Next up: three neat paperbacks, all by the same author: a
Dutchman called Johan Huizinga. These had been exceptionally well-
thumbed (even by Beede's standards – and he was nothing if not
thorough). The first was entitled *The Waning of the Middle Ages* (a
historical classic, it claimed on the back). Numerous pages had been
turned over at their corners (approaching a third of the total), and
there was still one of Beede's red pencils jammed rudely inside it
(Beede liked to underline relevant words and sentences as he read
– a strange quality in someone usually so circumspect – showing
very little respect, Kane always felt, for the integrity – and binding
– of a book).
He opened the text to its pencil marker and read (underlined
with great zeal): 'So violent and motley was life that it bore the
mixed smell of blood and roses.' 'Smell' had been circled and then
asterisked. Underneath that: 'After the close of the Middle Ages

the mortal sins of pride, anger and covetousness have never again shown the unabashed insolence with which they manifested them-selves in the life of preceding centuries.'

Next to this, in the margin, in block capitals, Beede had written: 'UNTIL NOW!'

Kane shut the book with a snort. His search became more impa-tient.

Another Huizinga book: *Men and Ideas: History, the Middle Ages, the Renaissance*, was tossed on to the floor, followed by – uh – *Homo Ludens: A Study of the Play-Element in Culture* –

Eh?!

– with its lovely cover (red and black, the kind of graphics favoured by the best casinos in 1950s Vegas). Sample quote: 'The human mind can only disengage itself from the magic circle of play by turning towards the ultimate.'

Wha?!

He sniffed. This was getting him nowhere, but that was okay, because it was pretty much where he wanted to be . . .

Right

A.R. Myers, *England in the Late Middle Ages;* Mary Clive, *This Sun of York: A Biography of Edward IV;* Joseph and Frances Gies, *Life in a Medieval Castle* –

Hmmn . . .

Was there some kind of *theme* emerging here? Kane frowned. It was a little strange, perhaps – this intense level of focus on such a partic-ular time-frame – but –

Aw heck!

– the history he could take. It was bone-dry, like Beede. The history made *sense* to him. It was old and silly and wonderfully unthreatening.

It didn't shock or unsettle or confound. It was dead. It was done. It was *after*.

Phew

   Next up –

Ay ay –

Shakespeare: The Complete Plays (markers in all of the *Henries* and *Richard III*), followed – hard-upon – by another ridiculously *hefty* volume: John Ayto's *Dictionary of Word Origins*. Kane lugged it aside, with a small grunt, boredly. Under that, Robert Burchfield's far more svelte and shapely *The English Language*. He flipped it over and ran his eye across a brief spiel on the back about how the mother tongue was so 'resilient' and so 'flexible' . . .
   'The English Language is like a fleet of juggernaut trucks,' he read, somewhat perplexedly, 'that goes on regardless.'

Really?!
Well, uh . . . Okay . . .

Under that –

C'mon, c'mon . . .

– a hardback: *Art of the Late Middle Ages* (purchased from Abebooks.com – the invoice shoved inside – from its original source of Multnomah County Library – at £29.50 – with shipping) –

Huh?!

Beede buying books on the *internet*?! Kane gently yuck-yucked –
Is this an end to the world as we know it?

   In this particular instance the front flap had been employed as a marker within the belly of the text. Kane opened the book to this place, casually. He inhaled sharply as his eyes alighted upon the stark, photographic reproduction of a sculpture entitled *Death Disguised as a Monk*. The sculpture consisted of an eerily animated skeleton – in wood, exquisitely carved – the bony skull and arms of which peeked out, ominously, from the sumptuous folds of a monk's cowl. Its expression was at once delirious – the gaping smile, the hollow eyes, the pointing finger – and . . . and *poignant*, somehow.

As he held the book several more pages flipped over, revealing a small, black and white illustration of a woodcut (1493) in which a group of skeletons performed a macabre jig over an open grave. Next to this image, in Beede's characteristic red pencil (that creepy, teacher-y, *bloody* pencil), he had written:

'DEATH –
He *said* it was a dance.'

Burning

Kane sniffed, then frowned, then shook his head –

Don't be ridiculous

He put the book down. He was at the bottom of the pile, now, with only one volume remaining:
The Encyclopedia of Witchcraft and Demonology by Russell Hope Robbins.

Kane picked it up. It was a heavy tome (old, hardback, the fine cover preserved in plastic). He looked for a book-mark and found one (of sorts), pulling it out as he turned to the spot. It was a business card for a company called Petaborough Restorations (no address, just a number). On the back of the card, in very shaky writing, Kane read: 'Peter's *exactly* what you need (Did an absolutely *superb* job on Longport for the Weald and Downland Museum). J.P.'

Kane gazed at this card for a minute, half-frowning, then casually pocketed it.

Good

He glanced down at the text. He found himself in the segment entitled 'Possession'. It consisted – in the main – of a series of lists. His eye settled, arbitrarily, upon one of them: a treatise (*Rouen*, 1644)

91

which detailed the eleven main indications of true possession. Next to each item on this list Beede had inserted a series of tiny, red marks. Item One: 'To *think* oneself possessed' carried a minute question mark. Item Two: 'To lead a wicked life' had a minuscule cross –

etc

Point Nine: 'To be tired of living [*s'ennuyer de vivre et se désespérer*]' had been strongly underlined –

Burning

Kane sneezed, hard, as he slapped the book shut (a sudden interest in the wonders of *Satanism*? Well this was definitely a turn up). He blinked, winced, inhaled . . .

No. *No*. Hang on – it *was* burning. For sure. He quickly glanced behind him –

Shit!

A cat! A fucking Siamese *cat*. Just standing there, its blue eyes boring into him, unblinking, its grey tail twisting up like a plume of smoke. He looked down and saw his Marlboro burning a hole in the rug. The cat lifted its head and then coughed (with just a touch of fastidiousness).

'*Fuck!*'

Kane lunged for the cigarette. The cat pranced away. Gaffar jumped up, with a hiss (Gaffar hated cats).

'You *bastard*!' Kane yelled, snatching up the still-red-embered stub and observing – much to his horror – the ugly, black hole in Beede's Moroccan rug.

'Shit, shit, *shit*.'

Beede loved his rug. Kane thought of it as Moroccan, but it celebrated – in words and pictures – some kind of crazy, phallic-shaped public monument in Afghanistan, surrounded by tiny planes (which looked like birds) with MINARET OF FIAM written on the periphery, semi-back-to-front. It was a ridiculous object. Kane remembered it – almost fondly – from his boyhood –

No –
Perhaps that's a false memory

Gaffar had already bounded over. He was staring down at the spot in dismay. He seemed to instinctively appreciate that this unsightly burn was a big deal for Kane (and Kane instinctively appreciated his awareness of this fact).

'Smoking could seriously damage your health,' Gaffar announced portentously, his accent almost cut-glass.

'You're not wrong there,' Kane murmured despairingly. 'Beede *loves* this stupid rug.'

'He go crazy?' Gaffar enquired.

'No,' Kane shook his head. 'Not crazy. It'll simply . . . *uh* . . . it'll *confirm* something . . .' He paused, then gave up. 'Yeah, absolutely fucking *psychotic,*' he muttered.

'Leave,' Gaffar said. 'I do. *Go!*'

He waved Kane away.

Kane glanced over at him, almost poignantly. 'You think you can *fix* this?'

Gaffar nodded. 'Turkish.' He pointed to himself, as if that was explanation enough.

'*Really?*'

Gaffar nodded. **'My mother, my grandmother, my great-grandmother,'** he lied, effortlessly, **'all sweated blood over the carpet looms of Diyarbakir.'**

'So you *know* about rugs? You think you can sort this out for me?'

Gaffar nodded again. '*Leave,*' he ordered, 'I am mend.'

Kane stood up just in time to observe the troublesome Siamese jumping lightly on to the kitchen counter. He glowered at it. 'I can't believe Beede's got himself a cat,' he murmured, taking a speculative step towards it, 'and a fucking *pedigree* at that. Beede hates domestic animals. Cats especially . . .'

He paused. 'At least . . .' He frowned, his voice petering out.

Gaffar hissed. The cat flattened its ears in response. Gaffar picked up Beede's Tupperware beaker and lobbed it at the cat. He scored a direct hit. He whooped. The cat kicked off the counter – its hackles up – and dashed, full pelt, into the sanctuary of Beede's bedroom.

Kane rapidly shot after it, across the living-room, through the kitchen, but then faltered – like a mime suddenly hitting an invisible wall –

Bang!

– just on the cusp of entry.

I mean Beede's *bed*room . . . ? His monkish cloister? His inner sanctum? His *lair*?

Beede's *bed*room? Was *nothing* sacred?

Kane drew a long, deep breath (steeling his resolve; throwing back his shoulders, sticking up his chin and *squinting*; like a heroic Sir Edmund Hillary trapped inside a *damnable* snowstorm), then entered, boldly, on the exhale.

SIX

She was lying on a trolley in the hospital corridor, propped up on her elbow and reading an old copy of *Marie Claire*. She'd already made firm friends with two of the porters, one of whom was still buzzing around in the background; perhaps imagining – even though she was obviously suffering from a serious fracture – that he might be on to a Good Thing here.

And what more could she expect (the porter's lascivious expression seemed to proclaim, as he slouched priapically against the Nurses' Station and hungrily appraised her)? She was a *Broad*, after all. They were a degenerate bunch. The now-legendary Jason Broad'd had his stomach pumped on the exact same Casualty Ward a mere eighteen months earlier, and had celebrated this momentous occasion with – wait for it – a can of Budweiser (downed it in one, the nutter)! Dr Morton almost had a coronary; was actually quoted as saying that 'Jason Broad should take out a restraining order *on himself*' (and if his current three-year prison sentence was anything to go by, then he'd pretty much followed the doctor's orders to the letter).

The whole family were delinquent (it was totally genetic): the dad, a child-fancier, the mother a basket case, the brothers all hoodlums, the sisters, sluts. The uncle was a trickster and the cousins, simpletons (although – so far as anyone knew – there was nothing concrete on the aunt).

Perhaps sensing herself the focal-point of somebody's attentions, Kelly suddenly glanced up –

Ah . . .
Patrick?
Is that his name?

She nodded and smiled politely. He smiled back –

Christ she wants me

– then turned and muttered something to the nurse on duty. The nurse sniggered, peering over. Kelly's mouth tightened. She looked down, her cheeks flushing.

The second (and rather more hands-on) porter had delivered Beede a message just as soon as he'd arrived at work: less a polite invitation to pop up and see Kelly, than a haughty – if carefully phrased – injunction (in the idiom of The Whips, this was definitely a Three Liner).

Even so, he didn't head up there immediately. He changed into his spotless white uniform, tinkered away at a faulty dryer, put on four wash-loads in quick succession, then took the service lift from his musty but well-ordered Basement Empire to the exotic, chaotic heights of Casualty (delivering a batch of clean towels to Paediatrics on the way).

As he strolled along the corridor, he observed (with some amusement) that Kelly had her nose buried in an article about a charitable Aids Trust in Southern Africa (whatever next? *Principia Philosophia*?).

'Better sort yourself out, first,' he volunteered dryly, 'before you apply, eh?'

She started, guiltily, at the unexpected sound of his voice, then her chin jerked up defiantly. 'Ha *ha*.' She slapped the magazine down, scowling.

'I believe you left your two dogs at the flat,' he continued (completely undaunted by his frosty reception). 'They're currently standing guard in the hallway. One of them mauled Kane's house guest.'

'*Screw* the blasted dogs,' she whispered crossly. 'Why ain't you returned my calls? Why've you been avoidin' me?'

Beede's brows rose slightly, but before he could open his mouth to answer she'd already charged on, 'An' *that* was your big mistake, see? I ain't no fool. You've been avoidin' me 'cos' you *feel* bad, an' you feel bad . . .' she poked a skinny index finger into his chest, 'because *you* stole those drugs from Kane and then sold *me* up the bloody Mersey. I've been thinkin' about it a lot – for *days*, in fact – and nothin' else adds up.'

Beede's expression did not change.

'So you fractured your leg?' he asked, at normal volume.

Kelly was briefly put off her stride by his refusal to engage with her. She *admired* Beede, after all. She didn't understand him –

Of course not

– but she respected him. She saw him as a being of an entirely different order –

Celestial/monkish

– a fraction cold, perhaps, but noble, defiant, honourable. One-dimensional –

Certainly

– a little *boring*, maybe. But entirely trustworthy. Above reproach – or so she'd thought – like the Good King in a fairy story.

'I fell off your stupid *wall*,' she grumbled.

'Why?'

'I was waitin' for ya. To have it out.'

'But why did you fall?' he persisted.

'I had a row.'

He didn't seem surprised by this. 'With whom?'

Kelly pushed her shoulders back, dramatically. 'That coloured bitch who killed Paul.'

'Ah,' Beede quickly put two and two together. 'That would be Winifred.'

She nodded (not a little deflated by his emotionless response).

'Anyway,' Beede spoke very gently (as if dealing with an Alzheimer's patient who'd been discovered trying to buy a cup of tea in the staff canteen with a tampon), 'he *isn't* dead, is he?'

'Stop tryin' to wriggle off the damn hook,' she growled.

'I wasn't ever *on* it, Kelly,' Beede said gravely (but there was an edge of steel in his voice). 'And Paul *isn't* dead. He's very much alive.'

'He's a fuckin' *vegetable*,' Kelly bleated. 'An' *she* did that. Said as much herself. It was *her* who got him started: took him under her wing when he was feelin' low, got him into dope an' sniff an' all that other shit. Then, once he was hooked, once he was well and truly *screwed*, kicked up her posh, little heels an' cheerfully buggered off.'

'If it makes you feel better to apportion blame . . .' Beede murmured, imperturbably.

'Private bloody *school*, a new bloody *life*. Fine for *her* . . .' Kelly continued, then she paused, as if only just registering his interjection. 'Yes.' She nodded. 'It bloody *does* . . .' (Beede smiled. He was familiar with Kelly's conversational stock-car racing – the dramatic zoom past, the sudden handbrake turn, the skid, the spin.)

'. . . though I ain't sure what you *mean* by that, exactly,' she finished off, scowling.

'If it makes you feel better to focus all your understandable *rancour* on somebody else – somebody who is, to all intents and purposes, quite extraneous to the situation – then that's perfectly understand-able . . .' Beede said benignly. 'In fact it's utterly human.'

Kelly was quiet for a while, then, 'You're head-fucking me,' she announced.

'Don't be ridiculous.'

'You *are*.'

'I merely stated a simple truth about your brother.'

'No,' she paused. '*No*. I'm wise to your tricks, see? On the surface you're pretendin' to be all sweet and kind and *charmin'* about it – like butter wouldn't melt – but underneath, what you're *really* sayin' – what you're really *thinkin'* – is that *I'm* somehow to blame for what's happened to him . . .'

'Not that you *are*,' Beede mildly demurred, 'but that perhaps – at some level – you *believe* you might be.'

Kelly gasped (her hand flew to her chest). 'You think I scragged my own *brother*?!'

'Now you're just being hysterical,' Beede snapped, barely managing to compose his features in time to nod, politely, at a passing Staff Matron.

'Fuck *off* I am!'

'Good. *Fine*. Whatever you say, Kelly.'

She stared up at him, in wonderment, the scales apparently fallen. 'Oh. My. God. You are *evil*.'

'I'd better get back,' Beede smiled, crisply (no point in a denial). 'It may've escaped your attention, but I'm actually meant to be employed by this hospital.'

'Yeah. That'd be right. *Off* you go, Grandad . . .' Kelly waved him away, airily. 'Back to work. Back to the *grindstone*, eh? Back to cleanin' your *dirty*, bloody laundry . . .'

Her voice oozed ill-will.

Beede didn't respond, initially, he just cocked his head and gazed at her, blankly, as if inexplicably baffled by the words she'd just uttered. Kelly shifted, uneasily, under his vigorous scrutiny.

Then – quite out of the blue – he smiled. He *beamed*. 'Have I got this all wrong . . . ?' he asked (suddenly the very essence of genial avuncularity). 'Or were you actually experimenting with a clever piece of *word*-play there?'

Before she could muster up an answer (she'd half-opened her mouth, in preparation, but had yet to rally her considerable intellectual forces – she was still in shock from the fall, after all), he'd patted her, encouragingly, on her bony shoulder.

'Because if you were, I'm *very* impressed, dear. Well done. *Bravo!*'

Kelly's eyes bulged at this near-perfect kiss-off.

'And by the way . . .' Beede continued, benevolently, 'if you were hoping for a visit from your *mother* any time soon . . .'

(Her mouth quickly snapped shut again. Oh *God*. The very *thought* almost calcified her entire bone-structure) – '. . . then you'll be delighted to know,' he purred soothingly, 'that she's here.'

The cat had found sanctuary in its basket. Only a piercing pair of china-blue eyes were now visible, peeking out at him, anxiously, from the creaking confines of its smart, wicker corral. Kane blew an idle raspberry at it, and the cat hunched down even lower, emitting a strangely haunting, dog-like yowl.

He glanced around him. It'd been a long while since he'd ventured inside Beede's bedroom, but during this considerable interim, a dramatic transformation – a *revolution* – had taken place.

Where previously Beede had been the master of decorative understatement (books, reading lamp, bed, eiderdown, matching Victorian dark-wood cupboard and chest of drawers) now the place was like some kind of Aladdin's cave: a veritable bring-and-buy sale of disparate objects, for the most part stacked up in crates (which now covered – floor to ceiling – three of the four walls).

The crates had been turned on to their sides, so that the items within were individually showcased; almost as if inhabiting their own miniature plywood theatres. Kane remembered staging theatrical endeavours of this kind himself, as a boy, in cardboard boxes; with badly painted back-drops, a batch of plastic animals and his Action Man – but –

Hey . . .

– surely Beede was taking things a little *far* here . . . ?

Even the cat's basket had been placed inside a crate. And each crate – Kane scowled as he bent down to inspect one – was tagged with a crisp, white label containing a date, a description of the item – eg:

> 13.08.2002
> Three coffee mugs c. 1997
> One bears the inscription: The world's best fisherman
> Cup three has slight chip on lip

– as well as a digital image of the item/s in question neatly affixed underneath.

Kane found himself staring at the photograph of the mugs for some minutes –

Has Beede completely lost his marbles?
Or is it me?
Is it the weed?
Has my fantasy/fact facility become utterly jumbled?

He was finally stirred from his reverie by a hoarse cough from the cat –

Hairball?

He moved over to inspect its crate (squatted down to read the label):

> 22.12.2002
> Blue-point Siamese
> 'Chairman Miaow', aka 'Manny'
> Three years old
> Neutered male

He stared at its photograph, then directly at the animal –

Hmmn.
A good likeness.

The cat returned his stare, unblinking.
   Kane's mind suddenly turned to the chiropodist –

Ella?
No
Ellen?

He thought about her hands and her long, plain, brown hair –

Uh . . .

   Then he focussed in on his foot. A small verruca, hidden underneath the arch (which he'd possessed – almost without noticing –
for seven years? Eight?) had actually been niggling him for several
weeks now (new trainers – he reasoned – with slightly higher insoles.
A different distribution of pressure, of body weight . . . That'd set it
off. Those tiny, jabbing sensations. Those sharp bouts of ferocious
itching –

Urgh).

   He flexed his toes and stood up. His phone vibrated inside his
pocket. He took it out and inspected it, stepping back. As he stepped,
he kicked into a tray of damp cat litter. The grey granules peppered
the surrounding carpet.
   '*Shit*,' he looked down, scowling, lifting his feet, gingerly.

Now what?

He shoved his phone away, squatted down and scooped a few of the
granules on to his hand, wincing, fastidiously, as he dropped them
back into the tray again. As they fell he noticed that the base of the
tray had been lined with –

Not newspaper, but . . .

– a letter . . . Handwritten. He tipped the tray up slightly to enable him to read it more easily. At the top of the page was the heading: Ryan Monkeith Road Crossing Initiative.

Ryan Monkeith? The name rang a bell, for some reason. He frowned for a moment, struggling to remember . . .

Ah . . . Yes!
But of course!
Ryan Monkeith – son of Laura – Laura with the dodgy tranquilliser habit – Blonde Laura – Scatty Laura . . .

It'd been all over the local news the previous year –

But Laura never . . .

– after he'd been killed crossing a road close to one of the new developments – a pedestrian blackspot . . .

The A292?
The Hythe Road?
The A251?

They were trying to build a bridge or install a crossing or something –

Weren't they?
In his honour?

– to be funded by his grandad or uncle or godfather. Some powerful local contractor . . .

Kane inspected the letter. It was the second page.
'. . . people like yourself,' it said, in a feminine hand, 'with your background in local politics, fundraising skills and the confidence of the local community . . .'

Kane snorted, dryly. The next section was smudged. But further down . . .

'. . . different sides of the fence, but after a tragedy of this magnitude we hope a certain amount of . . .' more smudging '. . . and that's why we feel your involvement would be especially . . .'

Blah blah

His eye was caught, briefly, by something at the bottom of the page –
'Isidore has been amazing – you'll be more than familiar with his energy and enthusiasm. He recommended you very highly . . .'

Gaffar popped his head around the door.
'Is fix,' he announced, smiling broadly.
'What? You fixed it already?' Kane slammed down the tray. 'You fixed the rug? *Seriously?*'

Gaffar threw out his arms in a shrug of pseudo-modest self-aggrandisement.

Kane followed him back through to the living-room. He located the precise spot where the burn had been (just next to the sidetable), squatted down and tried to find any sign of it. *Nothing.* Not a damn thing.

'*Jesus,*' he muttered, 'you've even . . . the burn went right through to the rough fibre underneath. How'd you get rid of that?'
'I just turned it around, you imbecile,' Gaffar explained, smiling, **'and hid the burn under the sofa.'**

Kane glanced up. 'So you're from Turkey? You really know about this stuff, huh?'
Gaffar nodded. 'Turk.'
Then he paused. 'Kurd,' he modified.
'Did you *train* in this kind of shit?'

'Are you kidding me?' Gaffar snorted, haughtily. **'Do I look like one of those rough-thumbed, short-sighted, carpet-weaving cunts?'**

Kane peered down again, feeling the spot with his hands.
He was in love with the job Gaffar had done.

'You're a genius, man,' he murmured, gazing up through his lank fringe again. 'What's your name? *Gaffar?* I owe you big-time, Gaffar. You are an unbelievable fucking *God-send.* You've saved my fucking *life* here.'

Gaffar tipped his head, bashfully (although he found himself a perfectly fitting receptacle for Kane's panegyric). 'Uh . . . an' *look* . . .' he clumsily stuttered, in his make-shift English, pushing his hand into his suit pocket and deftly withdrawing a small, neat disc of semi-transparent plastic '. . . Under sofa, *lid*, eh?'

Mrs Dina Broad had a wonderful facility for getting total strangers to do exactly as she wanted. It was something to do with her size, the tone of her voice (at once wheedling yet strident), her filthy tongue, and the considerable force of what a quality horse-breeder might call 'her character'.

Dina's manipulative genius was a happy coincidence, because she simply adored to be waited upon (to be bolstered and escorted, indulged and cosseted). In fact she absolutely demanded it. The cornerstone of her ideology was: *if you don't fuckin' ask, you don't fuckin' get* – a maxim which she used so often when her kids were young that – during a fit of high-spiritedness while working Saturdays in a print shop – her eldest son had designed her a t-shirt with this, her favourite slogan, emblazoned across the chest.

If Dina's life was a carousel (which it was anything but), then there was only enough room on the rotating podium (midst the high-painted roses, the mirror-tiles, the lovely organ) for a single pony; and Dina's was it (there was her name, in exquisite calligraphy, on a beautifully embossed tag around the neck . . . And just look at the mane: real *silk*. And see how straight the brow! How flared the nostril! How long the tail!).

Dina flew up and down (as her moods – and her blood-sugar levels – dictated), and the carousel just kept on spinning, with the music (Ah, the lilting music) never seeming to stop. It was Dina's show, entirely – paying customers could cheerfully go hang (Dina would supply the rope; would even – although it was a great deal of effort, and she *hated* effort – tie the noose herself. She was good like that).

The Dina Broad Show (like Celine Dion in Las Vegas) was a show that never ended (it just went on and on and *on*); but this low-budget extravaganza (in perfect Technicolor) by no means ran itself.

Nuh-uh.

There was the buffing and the oiling (to be regularly undertaken); the electrics (the wiring, the lighting, the amplification), not to mention the construction, the deconstruction, the reconstruction (this was a mobile – well, *semi*-mobile – proposition, after all), the ground-rent, the barkers, the cashiers, the crowd control . . . A whole *battery* – in other words – of tedious, time-consuming rigmarole.

Taken in total, The Dina Broad Experience had a technical staff numbering well over a dozen (the doctor, the social worker, the neighbour, the policeman), and Kelly Broad (poor, skinny, weak-boned Kelly) enjoyed the unique distinction of being at the very heart (or – depending on your take on things – deep in the colon) of this hard-working, poorly rewarded, long-suffering division.

Dina would not perform without her: *Fin.*

By a series of complex, Machiavellian ruses (there were two people in Casualty – aside from her own daughter – who were currently sharing a single crutch between them) Dina had somehow managed to commandeer a 'spare' wheelchair in the foyer, and a rather bemused-looking member of the general public (a willowy and slightly effete man in his sixties called Larry who was meant to be visiting his ninety-year-old aunt in an adjacent ward) was making a brave attempt at pushing her around in it.

'Aw *shit*, man!' Kelly gasped, grabbing a tight hold of Beede's arm. 'What the fuck's *she* doin' here?'

'She's your mother,' Beede explained patiently. 'She's visiting. It's part of her function.'

Kelly gave him a quizzical look. 'But she's never troubled herself visitin' me in hospital *before* . . .'

He stared down at her for a moment, almost with tenderness. It was difficult to decipher from the inflexible set of her gaunt features, but wasn't there a sudden, tiny gleam of childish delight (mixed in with an overwhelming air of bemusement) at the prospect of this most basic of demonstrations of maternal care?

His heart promptly went out to her.

'I should probably get on,' he muttered (not wishing to involve his emotional self any further).

'*Don't* go!'

She tightened her grip on his arm.

'I'm *working*, Kelly,' Beede explained, trying to disengage her claw-like fingers.

'But you don't know what she's *like* . . .' Kelly started off (almost pleading with him now), 'or how ticked-off she's gonna be with me . . .'

'It's not *real* anger,' Beede counselled, sagely, 'it's just *worry* . . .'

Kelly rapidly changed tack. 'Either you stay,' she threatened, 'or I'll tell Kane all about the drugs,' she reached for her broken phone with her free hand, 'I'll ring him. I'll *text* him. I *swear* . . .'

This was a foolish manoeuvre.

'Do exactly as you wish.' Beede coldly shook his arm free.

'If you go . . .' her eyes scanned the surrounding area, frantically, 'then I'll . . . I'll *leg* it.' She threw back her blanket and revealed her injury. He winced at the sight of it. She sat up and shifted her weight, as though fully preparing to hop off.

'Okay, *okay,*' he snapped, flipping the blanket back over again, 'I suppose I do need to have a quick chat with her about the dogs . . .'

Kelly's eyes flew wide. 'Are you *crazy*?'

'Pardon?'

'She'll *flip*. She'll go *spare*.'

'*What?*'

'Just . . .' Kelly put her hand over her mouth and spoke through a pretend-cough '. . . *trust me.*'

Dina (now perilously close), had already espied her daughter and was waving her walking stick at her (like a *Dr Who* Dalek, intending to exterminate).

'D'YOU HAVE *ANY FUCKIN' IDEA*,' she bellowed, from a distance of 12 or more feet, 'WHAT IT'S *TAKEN* TO *GET* ME HERE?!'

(Her prodigious rage came as a complete surprise to Larry, who'd been chatting with her, perfectly amiably, only moments before.)

Several people turned and stared. The less-busy porter glanced up, grimaced, and then quietly sidled off.

'You shouldn't've bothered, Mum,' Kelly murmured, all the stiffness disappearing from her backbone (rendering it floppy as a stick of soft liquorice). 'All's I did was break my stupid *leg* . . .' (she cuffed the leg, weakly, as if it was the limb's fault entirely), 'and I smashed my stupid *phone*, so I couldn't even . . .'

'*SCREW* YOUR STUPID LEG!' Dina yelled (indignant tears already brimming in her curiously mesmerising pipe-tobacco eyes). 'I'VE BROKE MY *FUCKIN' ARSE* GETTIN' HERE TODAY, KELL. SO WHAT *EXACTLY* D'YOU PLAN TO DO ABOUT *THAT*, EH?!'

The whole party was quiet for a moment, as if jointly considering the most feasible solution to this perplexing dilemma (I mean what *could* Kelly do?). No suggestions were forthcoming, although Beede (for one) appeared to be deriving a measure of laconic amusement from Dina's proximity. The woman was a legend, after all; she was Jabba the Hut with a womb, chronic asthma and a council flat. She was an old-fashioned bully – that much was clear – but her fury was swaddled by her considerable upholstery; her rage hijacked by blubber and then rapidly redirected into teary vulnerability.

Dina's laser-guided eyes (she could detect independent thinking at 200 paces) quickly alighted upon Beede's smirking visage. 'Pay a good price for that front-row ticket, *Mister*?' she enquired icily.

'Not nearly enough, I fear,' Beede answered smoothly.

Kelly stiffened. Dina sniffed the air, like a stag (he could almost hear her antlers rattling) and then turned to her daughter. 'That old stiff *botherin'* ya, darl?' she asked, thumbing towards him, rudely.

'This is Beede, Mum,' Kelly explained, endeavouring to facilitate a polite introduction. 'Kane's dad. I've told you all about him, remember?'

'Nope.'

Dina Broad shook her head, refusing, point-blank, to acknowledge this possibility.

'Yes I have. He *works* here . . .'

Beede stepped forward and offered Dina his outstretched palm. 'I'm Beede, Daniel Beede. Very pleased to meet you.'

Dina ignored his hand.

'He on Day Release from the fuckin' *morgue* or what?' she asked, with a sideways smirk.

'He don't work in the morgue, Mum,' Kelly spluttered.

'You sure?'

Dina gave Beede the once over. 'Been takin' the odd nip of *embalmin'* fluid, have we?' she enquired.

Beede smiled, weakly.

She leaned forward and peered down at his feet.

'What's up, Mum?'

Kelly leaned forward too, concerned.

'Eh?' Dina gazed up at her daughter, her eyes watering slightly with repressed hilarity. 'I'm just tryin'a read what that *tag* says on his toe, kid . . .'

'But he don't *work* in the morgue, Mum,' Kelly repeated, shrugging hopelessly, 'he works in the *laundry* . . .'

'Your mother seems a little confused,' Beede murmured (plainly eager to paddle awhile himself in Dina's metaphorical slip-stream). 'Is she operating two rinses short of her spin cycle, perhaps?'

Kelly's eyes bulged.

Dina's mirth evaporated.

'Oh yes? Oh *really*?' she exclaimed, straightening her back, her voice taking on a sharp, fluting quality. 'So you think it's a real *laugh*, do ya? A real, fuckin' *hoot*, eh? To rip the piss out of a poor woman who's stuck in a wheelchair?'

Beede mulled this over for a second, frowning. 'I'm not quite sure. Do you mean *literally* stuck?'

'It was the biggest one we could find,' Larry interjected (keen not to be found wanting in his capacity as Dina's temporary carer).

Everybody turned to stare at him, Dina with a look of especial ferocity.

He removed his hands from the chair and patted his damp palms on to the front of his jumper, 'I was only . . .' he muttered.

Dina spun back around to face Kelly again. 'Who *is* this man?' she enquired imperiously.

'I dunno. Who *are* you?' Kelly asked.

'Larry.' Larry said, 'I've come to visit my aunt.'

'Then FUCK RIGHT OFF AN' VISIT HER!' Dina yelled.

Larry took a quick step back, then paused. 'But I promised Matron that I'd return the . . .' he pointed, limply, to Dina's chair '. . . just as soon as we . . .'

Dina flew around and tried to swipe him with her stick.

Larry took yet another step back. 'There's no need for that . . .' he tried to caution her. She swiped again, this time making contact with his right knee.

'*Ow.*'

'Now GET LOST, *DICK*!'

The chair tipped, quite alarmingly, to one side.

'I think you might've developed a puncture,' Larry said (not intending to provoke, but succeeding, nonetheless).

Dina lobbed her stick at him. She missed her target. Larry scarpered.

'Okay,' Dina turned back around, snapped her fingers at Beede, and pointed. 'Go fetch.'

'Pardon?'

Beede's thermostat instantly clicked on to freeze (Kelly could almost hear his engine buzzing).

Dina immediately felt his chill (it was three-star), and pulled her coat tighter.

'Well what *else* does the old fart get paid for?' she grumbled, glancing over her shoulder (the stick had just been kicked out of the way by a very flustered expectant father). '*Oi!* D'you *MIND*?!'

'Beede's in charge of the *laundry*, Mum,' Kelly gently explained. 'He ain't a porter.'

'Okay,' Dina smiled, grimly. 'Well if *he* won't fetch my stick for me, *who* will?'

She gazed up at Kelly, moist-eyed (like an over-bred Pekinese begging pork rind at dinner). Kelly (who'd been virtually weaned on this particular look) started to get up.

'Just *stay* where you are,' Beede barked, immediately setting off to retrieve the stick himself. Dina whistled, appreciatively, as he bent over, then cackled, explosively, as he straightened up.

'I can't believe I smashed my damn *phone* . . .' Kelly tried valiantly to defuse the situation with a little light conversation, 'if I've lost all my numbers I'll go *feral*, I swear . . .'

'*Huh?*' Dina squinted up at her, boredly.

'They reckon it's a clean break . . .' Kelly yammered on, breathlessly.

'What is?' Dina interrupted.

'My *leg*.'

'Oh.' Dina sighed, expansively.

'And the doc who took the x-ray said I'd be done in a few hours. So if the shop's still open . . .'

'Which shop?'

'The *phone* shop.'

'Good idea,' Dina conceded. 'An' those brown shoes'll be ready at the cobbler's. You can grab 'em while you're at it. I got the slip here . . .'

She took her purse from the handbag on her lap and removed the slip from inside it.

Beede was now standing beside her, proffering her the stick.

'Keep ya *wig* on!' she cautioned him, handing the slip over to her daughter.

'I could grab us some take-away,' Kelly continued helpfully, 'for supper. What d'ya fancy, Mum? Thai? Pizza?'

Beede proffered Dina her stick again. She took it this time, with a sultry look.

'So you work here, then?' she asked (pointedly ignoring Kelly).

'I do.'

'Good. So you can push me over to Outpatients, *pronto*.'

Beede frowned, confused. 'But Kelly isn't even in surgery, yet . . .'

'*I* have an appointment, *stupid*,' Dina informed him imperiously, casually inspecting her watch. 'Blood test. Two-thirty . . .'

Beede glanced over at Kelly, his lips tightening (her face fell for moment, but then she rapidly rallied. The speed of the rallying – he felt – was almost the saddest part).

'But of *course* you do,' she murmured, scratching her head, '*Tuesday*. Two-thirty. I'd totally forgot . . .'

'One of these fine days,' Mrs Broad informed her, majestically, 'you might actually appreciate that not every little thing on this fuckin' planet revolves around *you*, Kell.'

She prodded Beede with her stick. '*Oi! You!* Uncle Fester! Let's *split*!'

Without further ado, Beede promptly stationed himself behind the chair and began to push. Five paces down the corridor – and still within ear-shot – he leaned gently forward and murmured, 'I must have a quick word with you about your *dogs* . . .'

Kelly gasped, ducked her head, stopped breathing, her thin body stiffening (as if preparing for some kind of monumental impact), but Beede kept right on pushing, and before she knew it, they were inside the service lift and the doors were firmly shut. How long had it taken? Twenty seconds? Less?

She took one deep breath, then another. Her hands gradually unclenched. She blinked. She glanced up and peered warily around her. Close by, a woman with second-degree burns on her knuckles was sitting – her head tilted slightly – and gawping.

'Show's over, love,' Kelly hissed.

Then she placed the slip for the cobbler's into the lining of her bra, plumped up her hair, threw back her skinny shoulders and pouted.

SEVEN

The Dog Warden (whom Beede had phoned from work with Dina's express permission – 'Just stare into my eyes – *deep* into my eyes. Good. Now does it *look* like I give a shit?') was actually so familiar with the Broads and their lurchers that he didn't even require an excuse, an explanation or a return address, he simply turned up – within the hour – clutching an unwieldy pole with a wire loop on the end of it to facilitate their subjugation.

Kane had seen this Draconian implement before – on one of the countless tv vet programmes – and was extremely keen to witness it in action. But as soon as the front door was opened, the dogs had leapt up and bolted (making a bee-line first for the warden, then his van), both their tails wagging, ten to the dozen.

'If this were Turkey,' Gaffar muttered, resentfully (as he and Kane stood listlessly on the front step together), **'I'd've blasted off the big one's** bollocks **for what he did to me earlier.'**

He took imaginary aim at the now fast-retreating van: '*BANG!*' (his competence with a firearm apparently uncompromised by his recent mauling), and then congratulated himself (in Kurdish) for the accuracy of his shot.

They trooped back inside again. 'D'ya hear what that uptight, little turd said to me out there?' Kane asked, indignantly, as he gave Beede's sitting-room a final once over.
'*Huh?*'
'The warden. He wanted to know if I'd given the dogs water – *water*, yeah? To drink? – and when I said that I hadn't – that I forgot – he completely went off on one. Said in high summer that'd constitute "a deliberate act of cruelty". Can you *believe* that crap?'
'*Fascist!*' Gaffar exclaimed.

Kane grabbed his jacket from the sofa and pulled it on. He idly adjusted the collar. 'Well they certainly won't be giving *him* his own cuddly, animal-welfare-based tv show . . .'
'Rolf Harris? *Fuck off!*' Gaffar snorted.

'*Bingo!*' Kane snapped his fingers. 'You like Rolf, huh?'

'I love,' Gaffar confirmed, emphatically.

'You *love* Rolf?' Kane smirked, suggestively.

'Oh yes,' Gaffar deadpanned, performing a painstaking mime in which he repeatedly violated Rolf Harris from the rear, 'I *love* Rolf.'

Kane gazed at him for a moment, in mute alarm.

'*I PISS YOU! HA!*' Gaffar burst out laughing.

Kane managed a weak smile as Gaffar jogged an exuberant lap around Beede's sofa, lifting up his knees and clapping his hands, Zulu-warrior-style.

As if prompted by the Kurd's sudden, thunderous show of good humour, Beede's phone began to ring. It was an old-fashioned, heavy-set, dial-tone phone c.1976, in bright, brick orange, and it lived – as befitted its lowly status – under his desk, behind a musty pile of old *Private Eye*s which he collected – or so he claimed – to donate to his dentist.

Kane ignored the phone completely. Gaffar completed his lap and ground to a halt, still grinning.

'So they featured this sweet, old girl on *Animal Hospital* once, yeah . . . ?'

Kane took out his cigarette packet (refusing – point-blank – to compromise his cool by responding directly to Gaffar's wanton display) and carefully removed a pre-rolled joint from inside of it. 'She had a Jack Russell. D'ya know that breed at all?'

Gaffar shook his head, slightly out of breath.

'A little, white dog – a terrier – a *digger*.'

Kane mimed 'dig'.

Gaffar nodded, his eyes drifting – every couple of seconds – towards the source of the ringing.

'Anyhow, there was something wrong with the animal – I don't remember *what*, exactly – so this old dear took it along to the surgery, and they filmed her for the programme, and Rolf asked her what its name was . . . *blah blah* . . . You're pretty familiar with the form, I guess?'

Gaffar nodded again. He was very well acquainted with *Animal Hospital* protocol.

'Yeah . . .' Kane carefully moistened the side of the joint, 'so this old

girl says, "He's called Bonus." And Rolf thinks the name's kind of cute
– *Bonus* . . . It means to get something for free . . . *Gratis.*'

'*Ah.*'

'So he asks her why the dog's called Bonus, and she says something
like, "I was walking home from work one day and I saw this little
dog running around. And it was obviously a stray. It was very dirty.
Very thin . . ."'

Kane mimed 'dirty', then 'thin'.

'Okay.'

'So she decided to take the dog home with her and to care for it. I
mean she saved its life, effectively. And she called it Bonus because
she got it for nothing. Like a gift from God.'

'Sure.'

'So then Rolf says, "Will you lift Bonus up on to the table so that
the vet can take a look at him?" And the old woman goes, "Would
you mind doing it *for* me?" And she's looking kind of anxious. So
Rolf says, "Why? What's the problem?" And the old woman says,
"Even though I took him home that day and looked after him and
loved him and have always cared for him the best way I possibly
could, he absolutely despises me. But only me. With everyone else,
he's fine . . ."'

'*Ah,*' Gaffar looked impressed.

'Yeah. The dog hated her. And it was all just pride, see? It resented
the fact that she had come to its aid in its time of need, when it was
truly *vulnerable*. It simply wouldn't forgive her for helping it, for saving
it, yeah? But it loved everybody else, was very gregarious, very friendly.
So Rolf could stroke it and pick it up and put it on the table, and the
vet could give it a painful injection, but if this kind, old dear so much
as went anywhere *near* it, it'd snarl and take a quick snap . . .'

'*What?!*'

'Because it was fucked up.'

The phone stopped ringing.

Gaffar shook his head, slowly.

'Yeah,' Kane shrugged, 'sometimes life can be a bitch like that.'

He finally located his matches, opened the box, took one out, struck
it and lit up his joint. Gaffar continued to stare at him, expectantly,
as if awaiting some kind of punch-line. But none was forthcoming.

About five seconds into this perplexing hiatus, Beede's phone began
ringing again. Kane glanced over at it, then back at the Kurd, then

down at the ash on the tip of his roll-up. 'So you're gonna be at kind of a loose end for a while now, huh . . . ?'

Gaffar grimaced.

'That's too bad.'

He inhaled on his joint. He suspended his breath.

'I've actually got a couple of jobs you can do for me,' he exhaled, with a slight cough, 'if you fancy . . .'

'Work?' Gaffar enquired, lifting his chin.

Kane nodded.

'For *you*?' his right brow rose, haughtily.

'Yup.'

Gaffar shrugged. 'Sure.'

They shook hands.

'Okay . . .'

Kane took another deep drag on the joint and then offered Gaffar the remainder. The Kurd took it. Kane gave him a long, searching look, then exhaled, sniffed and glanced back over towards the phone.

'So I'll need you to check up on Kelly . . . *uh* . . .' he grimaced, 'I'll be wanting to maintain a certain *distance* there, if you see what I mean . . .'

Gaffar looked blank.

'*Distance*.'

Kane measured out about a metre's span between his two hands. 'Me . . .' he lifted one hand '. . . and Kelly . . .' he lifted the other, 'never the twain shall meet.'

Still, Gaffar looked blank.

'So you could take her some food – salad, *fruit*, maybe. Some flowers. Make a quick delivery. Nothing too complicated . . .'

Beede's phone continued to ring.

'Can you drive?'

Gaffar's face suddenly lit up.

'Drive? Me? *Sure*.'

Kane moved over towards the door. 'Good. Then you can use the Merc. She's a dirty blonde. 220C. De-badged, of course. A strapping girl. *Exceptionally* reliable . . .'

He ushered Gaffar out into the hallway, yanking the door firmly shut behind them. But as soon as the lock clicked into its groove, he turned back, instinctively, and reached for the handle again. He didn't turn it, though – not at first – he just held on to it, loosely. He scowled. He struggled with himself. He proved unequal to the struggle.

'*Man* . . . You head on up, okay?'

He faltered, infuriated, on the threshold. 'Just let me quickly go answer that.'

'A bizarre coincidence . . .' Elen explained, picking up her mug, taking a small sip, and then quickly placing it down again (the tea was still very hot). 'She'd left a message for me at the practice. I was meant to be making a home visit this evening, but she was admitted last thing yesterday. She's having trouble with her pace-maker. I'd warned her about it the week before; her feet were unusually swollen during our last consultation . . .'

'Perhaps I know her,' Beede interrupted, pulling out a chair and sitting down himself. 'What's her name?'

'Mrs Bristow. *Evie* Bristow. Although everybody who knows her calls her Hat.'

'Really? Why?'

She shrugged, smiling.

Beede stirred his tea, removed the teaspoon and then couldn't find anywhere to put it, so pulled out a man-size tissue from a nearby box, folded it neatly in half, and placed the spoon on top (adjusting it, twice, to make certain it lay dead centre).

Elen watched this laborious process with an expression of wry amusement. He glanced up, absent-mindedly, caught her fond look, and started.

'The tea . . .' She indicated towards her mug, trying to defuse his alarm. 'It's delicious.'

'Good.'

Beede still seemed a little edgy.

Elen's smile gradually faded. 'Is everything all right, Danny?'

115

Beede frowned. His mother was the only other person who'd ever dared to use his Christian name in its abbreviated form (in her case, Dan). Yet Elen had always called him Danny, from the very first time they met, during a professional consultation (she'd seen his full name on the cheque he'd paid her with, and had used it, as a matter of course, ever since).

It still never failed to surprise him. He always felt a vague, nagging sense that she might actually be addressing another person, not *this* Daniel Beede, but some other, whom life – and its pitfalls – hadn't encouraged to prosper; a more approachable Daniel Beede; a more loveable one; more *cuddly*, even.

The only thing he knew for certain was that he actually bore no resemblance to this genial man (whom she appeared so determined to see in him), although a tiny part of him sometimes wondered whether he might not actually quite *like* to, occasionally (a brief excursion might be nice, into a world where fact was eclipsed by feeling), but whenever he started to experience these impulses – and it wasn't often – the hard, enamelled Beede within him swooped down from a great height and harried the gormless, hapless Danny; kicked him around a bit, then shoved him – without scruple – back into his box again.

He wouldn't have tolerated it from anybody else. But this was Elen –

Elen

– and everything she did was so effortless, so natural, so kind, so *unforced*, that to interfere (to block or confront or disrupt her), would've seemed like the worst kind of wrong-headedness.

'Yes. Yes. Yes, everything's fine,' Beede nodded, clearing his throat, 'absolutely fine.'

They were sitting at a desk in Beede's corner office. A handful of people were working in the laundry outside, and could be observed – going dutifully about their business – through a slightly wonky window in one of the two, make-piece, plasterboard walls (the other struggled valiantly to remain perpendicular while doing its level best to support the door).

The radio was blaring (Beede had a rota-system for choosing the channel – it was an inflammatory issue amongst the staff, whose ages varied – and today, much to his horror, it was tuned to 1Xtra). He leaned back in his chair and shoved the door shut.

It was a very small room – more of a cubby, really – and now, if possible, it seemed still smaller. He closed his eyes for a brief moment. If he remained motionless – and concentrated very hard – he could pick up Elen's distinctive scent of clove and peppermint (from the foot massage creams she used at work). It was a plain smell, and not particularly feminine, but he was almost ludicrously attached to it.

'So what happened, exactly?' she asked. She sounded tense. He opened his eyes, abruptly. He'd had no intention of worrying her.
'Nothing too apocalyptic,' he murmured, 'it was just a little . . . uh, *tricky*, that's all.'

He took a sip of his own tea and winced (it'd been brewed too long), then placed the mug down, gently, on to his desk again.

'He'd taken the horse from a field near the Brenzett roundabout . . .' he started off, casually.
She nodded.
'And I presume – although I can't be entirely certain – that he rode it to the restaurant along the dual carriageway . . .'
She grimaced.
'. . . which is . . . well, *you* know . . .'

'He absolutely *promised* me,' she interrupted, 'that he wouldn't do anything crazy like that again.'
As she spoke, Elen slipped both of her hands around her tea mug, as if to comfort herself with the warmth it exuded. She seemed profoundly regretful, and yet (at another level – and there was *always* another level with Elen) strangely detached.

'He was terribly confused when he came around,' Beede continued (not entirely ignoring her interjection, but feeling unable – through loyalty to Dory, principally – to trespass on to that particular discursive mine-field any further), 'and extremely suspicious . . .'

'He's petrified of horses,' Elen interrupted him, her voice still stoical. 'A pony stood on his foot once when he was just a toddler. If you know what to look for, you can see how the injury – the trauma – has taken its toll, subsequently, on his entire body-posture . . .'

'Yes,' Beede nodded, 'he did mention it. I mean the *fear*. He knew almost immediately that he disliked horses, that he was afraid of them. It was actually one of the very first things he seemed absolutely certain of.'

'Good.' Elen seemed bolstered by this.

'Although the horse *was* standing right next to us at the time . . .' Beede shrugged.

Elen continued to cradle her mug between her hands. Her hair fell across her face. She peered up at him, through it. 'So it wasn't just an accident?'

'What?' Beede scowled. 'That he was there? Where *we* were? No,' he shook his head, firmly, 'definitely not.'

'Oh.'

This obviously wasn't the answer Elen had been hoping for. 'But if you think about it . . .' she mused, 'I mean the actual *geography* of that area . . .'

'No.' Beede wouldn't concede the point, even to mollify her. 'If we were to calculate the odds – and I mean quite coldly, quite brutally – then I'd have to say that it was at least . . .' he ruminated, briefly, 'at least three-to-one *on* that he knew – strong odds, in other words.'

Elen frowned. Odds weren't really her forte.

'He *must've* known,' Beede pressed his point home, 'at some level.' She shook her head, slowly, as if still determined to resist his negative prognosis. 'But it wasn't very far . . .' she persisted, 'he was working in South Willesborough. I came to the restaurant on foot, but he may've seen your old Douglas in the car park. It's very distinctive, after all. It could've generated some kind of . . . of *spark*.'

Beede's ears suddenly pricked up. 'But how did you know that?' he demanded.

'What?'

'About South Willesborough?'

She seemed bemused by this question. 'Because he rang. He phoned me. Just before I left home.'

'Ah . . .' Beede nodded, then smiled (somewhat self-consciously). 'But of course. Of *course*. How silly of me.'

They were both quiet for a while. Beede fiddled idly with the teaspoon. It was a nice, sturdy piece of old-fashioned hospital issue with a reassuringly deep bowl and a broad, flattened tip. Age and over-use had given its original silver finish a slightly greenish hue.

'So did he let anything slip?' Elen asked.

Beede shook his head. 'Not a sausage.'

He glanced up as he spoke (she seemed mildly amused by his colloquial turn of phrase) and then, almost without thinking, he reached out his hand and tucked her hair, gently, behind her ear. The hair was so soft – so shiny – that it immediately slipped free again.

As soon as he'd touched her, Beede stiffened and then blushed (That was Danny! It was *him*!). Elen appeared completely unabashed. She casually pulled a hairband from around her wrist and tied back her hair into a ponytail with it.

'There,' she smiled, 'that's better.'

Her birthmark was now fully visible. It was about half an inch across – at its widest point – and just less than an inch long. It was in the approximate shape of Africa (although the southern tip was slightly flatter) and hung like a dark continent between her eyes, which, while also brown, were at least two shades lighter.

'He did mention that he'd been in South Willesborough immediately before,' Beede reverted – with an element of bluster – to his former train of thought, 'and we eventually found his car on the roundabout, close to the new exit. He'd left the door open. It was causing quite an obstruction. The police had just pulled up.'

'*God*. You should've phoned.'

Elen seemed about as close – in that instant – as she ever was to being fully engaged.

'I know, but he expressly asked me *not* to, and I just felt . . .'

He shrugged, grimacing.

'Compromised,' she nodded, understanding completely, 'of *course* you did.'

She reached out her hand and covered his hand with it.

He automatically pulled his hand away – she didn't appear to take this amiss – and then he smiled at her; a small, almost apologetic smile. She flattened her palm on to the desk and slowly pulled her arm back in towards her body again. Beede watched her lovely fingers (they *were* lovely) running smoothly over the coarse grain of the wood. He felt a sudden wave of excitement, then an equally sudden pang of recrimination. His eye settled, glumly, on the neat, gold band encircling her wedding finger.

'And it's all my fault,' she murmured, a finger and thumb from the offending hand now fiddling, nervously, with one of the buttons on her shirt, 'I *know* that . . .'

He was still watching the hand as it moved slightly higher and strummed the single-string-harp of her collar bone.

'I feel terrible about it,' she added, 'if that helps in any way.'

'Pardon?' He finally made eye contact with her. He hadn't heard a word.

'I said I'm *sorry*,' she reiterated (her cheeks flushing). 'This is all my fault. I should never have involved you . . .'

She paused, briefly – as if hoping for some kind of reassurance – but then rushed on, denying him the opportunity (had he taken it) to respond. 'Although if it's any kind of compensation, it's made such an amazing difference, simply sharing the burden with someone. It's been such a *relief* . . . And I'm just so . . . so embarrassingly . . . so *absurdly* grateful to you.'

She laughed on 'absurdly' – slightly hollowly – and then swallowed, involuntarily, on 'grateful' (so that it emerged in a half-gulp). Beede rapidly gathered his wits together (he'd been remiss before). 'Don't be *ridiculous*, Elen . . .'

He'd hoped to make this sound tender, but failed abysmally (his tender parts were as creaky, ill-used and rusty as the hinge of an ancient door).

'Yes.' She nodded. 'I mean . . .' she shook her head '. . . *No*. You're right. I should just . . .'

Her hand flew, briefly, to her mouth. She cleared her throat. Her hand dropped. She seemed quite composed again, but her lips were just a fraction too straight. He stared at her mouth, fascinated by this straightness. Then, before he knew it, she'd collapsed forward, buried her face in her hands and was sobbing. No sound. Just her shoulders – her fragile shoulders – jerking, rhythmically, up and down.

Beede was completely overwhelmed. He pushed back his chair (it screeched, maddeningly), glanced anxiously through the window, tensed his legs (as if about to stand up), but then stayed exactly where he was. Five seconds passed. Finally, he reached over for a tissue – it was a long reach – and then fell to his knees, proffering it to her. 'Please stop,' he murmured, 'crying won't help anyone.'

He processed these words internally and then promptly tore them into a thousand pieces –

You clumsy, heartless old fool!

He felt like an earthworm in the midday heat, trapped on an endless-seeming expanse of tarmac – crispening up, frightened. He longed for a moist, damp crack to crawl into; for the soil, the dank, the dark.

It took a mammoth effort, but he reached up his arm and cupped his large hand over the back of her small head (like a father might, with his son, or a priest, to a grieving widower). Elen responded to his touch. She drew a deep, shaky breath. She tried to control herself.

'Here's a tissue, you foolish thing,' he murmured.

She removed one hand from her face – it was soaking – and took the tissue from him, clenching it – like a child – for succour.

'I'm sorry,' she said, her voice just as calm and as soft as before. 'Everything's so . . . so *complicated*, that's all. And sometimes I don't really know . . .' she paused, 'how to . . .' she paused again, drew another deep breath, and then shuddered, in wordless conclusion. She looked exhausted. She dabbed at her face with the tissue.

Beede removed his hand. He twisted around and pulled his chair closer, then clambered to his feet and sat back down on it. They were knee to knee.

'You're still not sleeping.'

It was a statement of fact.

'No. I mean *yes*. I mean I'm absolutely *fine*. It's just the . . . the *roof*,' she back-pedalled, desperately, 'it's still leaking. And the builder, Harvey – Mr Broad – he keeps on stalling . . .'

'Harvey Broad?' Beede echoed, stiffening slightly. 'Harvey Broad is your builder?'

'And I've had a request from Fleet's teacher to come in and see her,' Elen continued (almost as if she hadn't actually heard him). 'I think there might be some kind of . . . of *problem* there.'

'But mainly it's Isidore,' Beede spoke with a quiet authority, 'he's much worse again, isn't he?'

She glanced up, dismayed. 'Isidore's *fine*. He's fine. He's . . .'

She groped around, desperately, for a better word.

'*Fine*,' Beede echoed, dryly. 'Yes. I get the picture. Even if he did just steal a horse and ride it, bareback, along a busy dual carriageway.'

Her former – somewhat shaky – resolve seemed visibly undermined by this callous summation. Her shoulders drooped, pathetically.

'So what now?' he asked, observing the droop with a bitter pang. She didn't answer him straight away. Instead, she unclenched the fist in which she'd held the tissue, observed it, balled up, in her palm, and then addressed her next few thoughts directly to it. 'Things were so much better when you were around,' she murmured, wistfully. 'He seemed so much more . . .' she paused, 'so much *easier* . . .'

Beede also stared down at the tissue – not a little jealously, at first

(I mean what had the damn *tissue* done to earn itself this gentle homily?).

'Easier in *himself*, somehow,' Elen continued (apparently undeterred by the tissue's taciturnity). 'But lately he's grown so . . .' she shivered, involuntarily, 'dark. *Dark*. Just . . .'

A long pause: 'just *furious*. Full of . . .'

A still longer pause '. . . *anger*. Bile. And then suddenly – out of nowhere – there'll be that awful, that cruel . . . the . . . the *laughter*,' she glanced up, fearfully, 'you know?'

Beede nodded. He did know.

'He's homing in on the boy,' she continued, warming to her theme now, 'more every day. And at night, if I rest – even for a moment – then he's up and he's gone. He just . . . just *flits* . . .'

Beede's expression did not alter. 'You need to use those new tablets I gave you.'

She shook her head, looking down, focussing all her energies – once again – on the tissue.

'Just for a *while*,' Beede wheedled. 'The other approach obviously isn't working.'

She shifted in her seat. 'I'd rather medicate myself,' she glanced up, anxiously, 'control myself. Don't you see? To do anything else would just feel . . .' she sighed '. . . *detestable*.' She paused, shrugged, smiled resignedly. 'And those other pills helped me enormously. They really did. I used them in conjunction with the ones from my doctor and was able to stay awake for several weeks, just taking quick naps, during the day, between clients . . .'

'That's crazy, Elen,' Beede interjected, harshly, 'and dangerous and short-sighted and irresponsible . . .'

'I honestly believed,' she interrupted, almost pleadingly, 'in fact I *still* believe, that if I could just keep a close watch on him, build up some kind of a regular . . . a *pattern*, then things might have a chance – however slight – of falling back into place again.'

She closed her eyes. She frowned. 'But everything's the wrong . . . the wrong *shape*, somehow.'

Beede was still furious. 'How on *earth* did you persuade me to get involved in all of this?' he asked (and it was a question as much to himself as to anybody). 'It's just . . . It's *madness*, don't you see? You're looking after a child, you're running a household, you're holding down a job . . .'

She dumbly nodded her acquiescence, a large tear forming in her eye and then sliding, plumply, down her cheek.

'You've lost so much *weight*,' Beede struggled, valiantly, to redirect his anger, 'you're so *thin*. I mean you look like you might just . . . just blow away.'

Elen shrugged (what did she care about that?). 'Dory's still exercising,' she murmured, trying – and almost succeeding – to maintain her fragile equilibrium. 'He's really, really *trying*. And it's so . . . so unbearably *sad*, somehow. He's doing the breathing – the yoga breathing – which is all very positive and empowering and everything . . .' she paused again, 'but there are just so many repercussions which he doesn't know about – which he *can't* know about – and I don't honestly feel like I can tell him – kill off that little bit of . . . of *hope*. But the more control he believes he has, the worse it becomes for everybody else. The less he goes under . . . I don't know . . . when he *does* go . . .' she bit her lip, 'it's just so much more *terrible*. I mean the *consequences*. . . . And if the police get involved again . . .'

She shrugged, helplessly.

'Dissolve a tablet into his tea,' Beede instructed her, 'or whatever he drinks before bed. That's the most difficult time, isn't it? The REM? When everything's in transition? He'll get to sleep much quicker. It'll be deeper. And that's *bound* to take the pressure off.'

'Oh *God*,' Elen clenched her hands together. 'If only it were that simple . . .'

'*Try*, at least,' Beede cajoled her. 'Think about Fleet. Your main priority has to be the boy. And yourself, obviously . . .' he paused, frowning, 'I've let you down recently. I can see that now . . .'

He scowled. 'We've been short-staffed here for a while. I've been taking too much on. And then there's this whole *Monkeith* situation. I seem to have become . . .' he shrugged '. . . horribly enmeshed in the whole thing . . .'

A look of fleeting interest crossed Elen's face. 'Well it's certainly a good cause,' she gently chivvied him, 'and so tragic. He was only eleven. Dory knows the godparents. He's been doing some leafleting for them.'

'I know,' Beede's voice sounded just a fraction sharper than before, 'it was actually Dory who recommended me to them.'

'Oh.'

Elen struggled to let the implications of this news sink in.

'But I can play around with my rota here at work . . .' Beede leaned over and grabbed a photocopied time-table from his desk, 'juggle things around a bit. I've certainly got some holiday owing. I can try my best over the next few weeks to keep up with him during the day again. And then you can have a rest. A proper rest. Believe me, things'll look ten times brighter after a couple of good nights' sleep.'

'But if he finds out . . .' Elen covered her mouth with her hand and stared at him, over her fingers, almost in panic. 'He's grown so suspicious. So paranoid. If he has *any* kind of inkling . . .'

'I know. I *know*.'

'And if he realises that we met up earlier . . .'

Beede stiffened. 'The trick is not to deny anything. If the worst comes to the worst, say you took Fleet out to do some shopping, that you stopped at the restaurant, that I was there with my son . . .'

'That's true,' she nodded, 'you were.'

She nodded again.

'The critical thing,' Beede continued doggedly, 'is that you need to get some rest – you both do; you *and* Dory – otherwise neither of you will be able to function properly.'

Elen patted her eyes with the tissue, then unfastened her hair to try and disguise their blotchiness.

'And as I said before,' Beede persisted, 'there's Fleet to consider . . .'

'It was such a surprise,' she said softly, changing the subject (exchanging one son for another), 'to see Kane there this morning.'

'I know,' Beede grimaced, 'apparently he goes there all the time. I had no idea.'

'I hadn't seen him in so long . . .' she smiled, vaguely. 'Not since . . . Well, since Heather . . .'

Beede tipped his head, momentarily at a loss, then his brows lifted. 'But of *course* – you would've met him as a boy . . .'

'He . . .'

Elen began to say something, then suddenly checked herself. 'He had a . . .' she gesticulated, vaguely, 'on his arm. He had a *burn*. He showed me.'

Beede frowned. 'On his arm?'

'Yes. He said he got it in the desert. In America.'

'I don't actually . . .' Beede slowly shook his head, then something struck him; a memory '. . . *Yes*. He does have a burn there. He got sunstroke as I recollect. It was very severe . . .'

He still wasn't quite following her.

Elen touched her own arm, ruminatively, in exactly the same place. Beede frowned, perplexed. 'Did he mention it for some reason?'

She opened her mouth to speak, but before she could answer, they were interrupted by a quick knock. A member of staff thrust an impatient hand into the office, proffering an invoice. Beede scrambled up and followed them outside. A terse conference took place, and then they headed off, Beede cursing, towards the storeroom.

When he returned to his cubby (five minutes later) Elen had gone. On his blotter she'd scribbled, 'Danny – Thanks. And SORRY. See you later. Godbless.

E.'

He ripped the page out, turned it over, sat down, picked up a pen in one hand and the phone receiver in his other. He pressed it between his cheek and his shoulder and he dialled the line for Casualty, then waited. As it rang he quickly wrote: Eva Barlow. He stared at it for a moment then scratched it out. Eliza Barlow (his next attempt). He crossed this out, too.

He frowned, gazing out into the middle distance, racking his brains to remember the proper name of the client Elen had mentioned with the malfunctioning pace-maker.

'*Liz?* Lizzie Brownlow?'

He grimaced.

'Damn.'

He slammed down the receiver.

'*Damn*.'

He leaned back in his chair, ruminatively.

'Cunning,' he eventually murmured, 'two names I would've remembered. But the nickname on top . . .'

He threw down the pen.

'That was clever.'

He picked up his mug of tea and took a quick sip of it –

Cold

He leaned over and took a hold of Elen's mug –

Virtually untouched

His eye casually alighted upon the tea-stained tissue where he'd rested the spoon, previously –

What?!

He peered around him, thoroughly puzzled –

But where . . . ?

EIGHT

It never rang; not *ever*. The last time Kane could actually remember (and the fact that he could still clearly recall this occasion – and in florid detail – said it all, really) was when his Great-Aunt Glenda (a true family gem) had died, aged ninety-six, in 1994.

To mark her passing, Beede's cousin, Trevor (who was horribly burned to death – a mere eight months later – in a tragic house blaze), had rung him up on that distinctive, brick-orange phone with a complex assortment of funeral arrangements:

1. All mourners to wear pink (she'd considered it a 'sacred' colour).

2. Lengthy, heartfelt readings to be performed (and then distributed in the guise of a commemorative pamphlet within a one-mile radius of her home in Esher, Surrey) from Kahlil Gibran's *The Prophet*, Joyce's *Dubliners* and *Problems of Reconstruction* by Annie Besant.

3. A proper, old-fashioned High Tea to be served, accompanied by home-made egg-custards, cinnamon buns (from Fitzbillies' traditional bakers in Cambridge), tumblers of apricot wine and her own *very* smoky blend of Lapsang Suchong.

4. Marigolds to form the centre of *all* her flower arrangements (she'd been a devoted gardener, but had suffered from chronic hayfever, and this cheerful, brightly coloured genus had been one of its main perpetrators. In consequence of this fact, she'd thought it might be 'a bit of a hoot' to make her final journey in a coffin absolutely *swathed* in the damn things: 'Bring along a jemmy,' she'd said, 'and if you hear a sneeze, then be sure and prise me out . . .').

She'd died – inevitably – in the depths of winter. Not a single humble British marigold to be had. The import costs had been astronomical and Beede had been furious (although his objections – he'd insisted – weren't so much monetary as environmental –
Yeah, right . . .)

Kane had just *loved* her for that.
And then –

But of course . . .

– there was his father's magnificently choleric expression as he stood, in church, determinedly booming forth one of Gibran's more flowery flights of fancy dressed in a crazily lurid, salmon-coloured shirt –

Absolute fucking class!

Even now, all these years later, Kane could distinctly recall over-hearing that landmark conversation through the cracks in his linoleum. He'd been upstairs stewing in the bath at the time – eight . . . nine Christmases ago. Ten, even.

And the phone had barely rung since (so far as he was aware – I mean he didn't stand *guard* over it or anything). It lived a very quiet existence (what could it comprehend, poor soul, of the advent of touch-tone, of texting and the internet?). It was almost superfluous (like Sleeping Beauty, in the midst of that great, big doze); to all intents and purposes, it was pretty much *dys*phonic.

Beede was resolutely ex-directory and nobody but distant (and now mainly dead) family had ever been privy to that particular number (even Beede's brother only ever contacted him via the hospital laundry).

But it had a fantastic bell. When it rang it produced an astonish-ingly pure, clear, old-fashioned sound; an elevated, almost ecstatic 'peal', a rousing, piercing, *energising* clamour.

Kane loathed phones. He really did. It was one of the few chinks in his easy-going armour. Yet it wasn't the technology itself that he objected to (Come *on* – he prostrated himself, hourly, at the altar of the disk and the drive and the chip), so much as the inbuilt element of surprise; the sense of a demand being made, then registered, then automatically responded to ('What am I?' he'd sometimes mutter. 'A dog to be whistled at?').

He used his own phone continuously (had to, for work), but he chiefly relied on its texting facility, and if – by chance – he was awaiting an urgent call, he'd set it on to vibrate (a vibration he could just about tolerate – it didn't shriek or keen or *insist*) and then shove it, care-lessly, into the front pocket of his denim jacket.

The brick-orange phone continued to sing.

Kane re-entered the flat, strolled over to Beede's desk, placed his hands on to his knees (bending from his hips, keeping his legs tensed

– like a linesman at a tennis match) and gazed down at the phone, scowling.

Still – *still* – it rang. He expostulated, sharply, then crouched down and curled his arm around the pile of magazines (accidentally snagging the top few with the turned-up cuff of his jacket and pulling them down on to the carpet –

Damn!)

He grabbed the receiver –

Wow . . .
Heavy

– then placed it, tentatively, to his ear. He didn't speak.
And at the other end of the line?

Silence.

'Hello?' Kane whispered, finally.
(Was this an entirely different world, this Beede-phone world? Was he speaking into some kind of supernatural vacuum, into a sphere utterly beyond everyday concepts of the here and the now?)
'Beede?'
Male. Young-ish. A pronounced German accent.
'No.' Kane stood up, smartly (the highly coiled, creamy-white wire connecting the receiver to the phone stretching itself, languorously).
'No. This is Kane, his son.'
'Kane?'
'Yes.'
Kane nodded.
'Beede's *son*?'
'Yes.'
'Is Beede there, by any chance?'
'Uh,' Kane glanced nervously around him, 'no. No, he isn't.'
'Oh.'

Long pause

'I suppose you could always try him at work,' Kane volunteered, helpfully.

'Yes. *Yes*. That's true. I could. In fact I *was*. But this number suddenly just . . . it just popped into my head. Out of the blue. It was really . . . really quite *odd*. So I grabbed the bull by the horns and I just . . . I *rang* it.'

'I see.'

'You know how that happens, sometimes?'

Eh?

Kane frowned and cocked his head.

'Although I'm not sure if he ever . . .' the German muttered, distractedly.

Pause

'. . . I'm not sure if he ever actually *gave* it to me. The number. I just plucked it from . . . How to describe it? I just plucked it from the air. From . . . from the *ether*.'

Longer pause

'Isn't that odd? Do *you* think that's odd?'

Kane cleared his throat, nervously, not really sure how to answer.

Silence

'Perhaps you could leave him a message?' he finally suggested (impressed by the quiet, somehow. It didn't drag. It was dynamic. It *crackled*. Was that a *German* thing? Did the Teutonic races have some special kind of strangle-hold on the high-quality conversational hiatus?).

'Beede's son . . .' The German mused, reflectively, as if calling something very peripheral to mind.

Kane said nothing.

'Beede's *son*, Kane . . .' he repeated, this time rather more emphatically.

Kane merely scowled.

130

'*Kane*. Yes. But of *course* . . .' (a connection was suddenly established), '*now* I remember: you shared a coffee together, didn't you,
earlier this morning?'

Was that a question, Kane wondered, or just a bald statement,
posing as one?

'Although – and I'm being brutally honest here,' the German confided,
'when I actually looked over towards the window – the window where
he pointed (and I can see it now, very clearly, in my mind's eye) you
were gone. The window was empty. So there was no way of really
. . . of really *knowing* . . .'

'We *did* meet,' Kane butted in, impatiently, 'quite by chance. Just
before lunch. At the French Connection.'

'That's *it*!' the German sounded gleeful. 'That's right! That's *exactly*
right! The *French* Connection! *Ha!*'

Kane took a small, nervous step back, a move which the phone
line gently resisted.

'What did you say your name was, again?' he asked, feeling a sudden,
sharp twinge of paranoia.

'So you're absolutely positive, then,' the German barrelled on, determinedly, 'and I mean *totally* certain that you met Beede there for
coffee this morning?'

'Why wouldn't I be?' Kane fired back, defensively.

'*God*, yes . . . I remember the fort . . .' the German muttered
(heading off, without warning, on a sudden tangent) '. . . the children's fort. The fort is significant, but I'm not entirely sure . . . *uh* . . .'

'Who *are* you?'

Kane was now officially freaked out.

'Isidore,' the man answered plainly (perhaps a little startled by Kane's
forceful tone). 'Didn't I say so before? I'm sorry. How incredibly rude.
Forgive me. I'm Isidore. *Dory*. Beede and I do the tours together.'

'Pardon?'

Kane didn't follow.

'The Ashford Tours. I'm the chauffeur. Beede's my guide.'

'*Ashford* Tours?'

Kane still wasn't quite up to speed.

'Yes . . . Although it's just a side-line, really. And your father's been
so caught up in his work at the laundry lately . . . Security's our main
function – keeping keys, guarding empty properties, a little light detective work . . .'

'Beede is your guide?'

Kane was struggling to catch on (I mean *Beede*? A *guide*? That old sourpuss? Welcoming people? Putting on a show? Being informative? Friendly? Obliging? Beede being *positive*? About modern *Ashford* of all places – the source of all his gloom? The heart of all his disappointments? Had the world finally gone absolutely bloody *barking*?).

'A great guide. A *brilliant* guide. Your father is quite a remarkable man,' the German observed, dryly (was it dryness, or something else?), 'but I'm sure you're already very well aware of that fact.'

'Oh yeah . . .' Kane mumbled, with a vague smirk, 'absolutely.'

His mind was momentarily drifting elsewhere. The children's fort. *Fort* –

Eh?

What was that?

He drew a sudden, sharp breath as he registered an unpleasant, pinching sensation in his forearm. He glanced down. He realised that he was now supporting the phone receiver against his shoulder and that his right hand was clutching – very tightly – on to his left arm (where the old sunburn scars were) –

Ow!

He blinked. He relaxed his grip –

What?!

The outer edges of his scar tissue had been reddened by the roughness of its manhandling. He scowled.

'But of *course*,' he suddenly found himself saying, 'it must've been you – on the horse.'

'Me?'

'Yes. You . . . Tall. Fair-haired. Wearing some kind of . . . of navy-blue uniform.'

The German seemed bewildered by this revelation. 'Me? On a horse? Riding? You actually saw me on *horse*back?'

'Yeah . . . Well, *no*. You were climbing off. You'd climbed off.'

'And you were there with Beede, you say? In the restaurant? Having coffee?'

Kane grimaced, impatiently. 'I think we already established that.'

He leaned forward and picked up the stray magazines from the carpet.

Silence

'And then?' the German asked, tentatively.

'What?'

As Kane carefully placed the magazines back on to the pile again he noticed a bank statement which'd been preserved, flat, between a couple of the editions.

'Then Beede left?' the German persisted. 'Is that how it happened?'

'Uh,' Kane considered this for a moment, eyeing the statement, casually, 'yeah. Quite soon after. Once the chiropodist arrived.'

'The *chiropodist*?'

The German's voice was hoarse with excitement. 'You mean *Elen*? The chiropodist? She was *there*?'

Elen
Of course

Kane glanced up, smiling.

'My *wife* was there?'

Kane's smile faltered.

'Good *God*.'

The German seemed overwhelmed by this idea.

'Although in actual fact,' Kane frowned as he remembered, 'the boy almost had me convinced that there were *two* horses . . .'

'Sorry? *What*? A *boy*?'

'Her son,' Kane paused, '*your* son. A sharp little character. He said that there were two. But if there were, then they were pretty much indistinguishable . . .' He paused again '. . . which I suppose they'd *need* to be, really, for the trick to work.'

'You're telling me that there were *two* horses?'

The German – rather slow on the uptake, Kane thought – swung from excited to panicky.

Kane stared down at the statement again, distractedly, then his brows suddenly shot up –

What?!
Holy fuck . . .

   'Was *Beede* on one of them?'
Kane continued to stare at the statement, as if mesmerised.
   '*Hello?* Are you *there*? I said was *Beede* on one of them?'
'No!' Kane snapped, exasperated. 'Beede was with *me*. I saw *one* horse. But the boy said that only by using two horses could you have managed the change-over so quickly. The swap. Like in a trick. A magic trick . . .'
   '*Swap?* Who swapped?'
The German sounded terrified.
'You and the other man. The . . .' Kane struggled to describe him, 'the strange . . . the creepy . . .'
'*Which* man?' The German rasped.
   Kane closed his eyes and tried to visualise –

Black
Yellow
Black

He shuddered, 'The *dark* man . . .'
   And then he found himself hissing – '. . . *Sssssss!*'
With no forewarning, his mouth was –

Good God!

It was *hissing* – 'Darkman*sssss.*'
   Kane quickly clamped his errant lips shut –

Where?

How?
What the . . . ?!

Isidore hung up.

PART TWO

FLEET

'There are many ways in which Fleet is much, *much* more advanced than all of the other children in his class,' Mrs Santa explained, encouragingly, 'his hand–eye coordination – for one thing – is really quite astonishing. And I mean *really* quite astonishing . . .'

She glanced over towards the play area in the corner of the classroom where Fleet was currently sitting and boredly constructing a small, neat structure –

A fort, was it?

– out of plastic bricks.

Elen detected a kind of anxiety in the glance. She felt a spontaneous knuckle of rage forming in her stomach (how *dare* she look at him like that? He was her *son*. She *loved* him), and then a balancing knuckle of sympathy (Oh *God*, he made her feel that way herself, sometimes).

These two contradictory knuckles were Elen's constant companions; and her gut was the boxing ring in which they staged their spats. 'Motherhood,' she told herself, bleakly: 'the pride, the humility.'

She tried to take a deep breath –

Breathe
Breathe from the stomach
(just like Dory said)
Kinking the back
Diaphragm flat, out, up . . .

They were sitting on two tiny chairs at a tiny table, like a couple of lady Gullivers amongst the Lilliputians. Elen couldn't actually remember entering the classroom, or how she'd actually got there. It was all just a blank, a fug. She stared over at the teacher, frowning.

'But then he might go and do something like . . . like *that* for example . . .'

137

The teacher indicated (perhaps slightly irritably) at the methodical way in which – before he finally positioned each and every individual brick – Fleet would run the nail of his thumb along the smooth plastic edge, then push the indented side, firmly, into his lower lip.

'He'll do that for whole hours at a time. And I mean whole *hours*, literally. That same, odd little ritual . . .'
This time her glance extended over towards the door.
Elen's own eyes followed, hard upon –

Oh my God
The Head Teacher –
Standing guard . . .

'He has a phenomenal memory . . .' Mrs Santa returned, some-what doggedly, to her positive sales pitch, 'although he's highly selective about the kinds of things that interest him. Very . . . *uh* . . . particular . . .'
Elen wasn't paying attention. She was still thinking about the Head Teacher and why he was out there –

Back-up?
Is something wrong?
Does she hate me?

She put a self-conscious hand to her cheek –

Is it the mark?

'But on the down-side . . .' Mrs Santa paused, stuck out her chin, gave a small, Jewish shrug –

Is she Jewish?

Elen stared at her. She was tiny, plump, wore her dark hair – pushed back today with a navy-blue alice-band – in a neat, sharp bob –

Is she?

'. . . his language skills are lagging way behind most of the other children's in his class. And his social skills are still very shaky – even after our previous initiative with the Bradleys' youngest . . .'

Elen blinked, snapping out of her reverie –

Oh my, yes –
The Bradley boy . . .
That ended badly

'He'll fall asleep at the drop of a hat – sitting at the table, or when I'm reading a story. Or he'll just curl up in a corner,' Mrs Santa twisted the engagement ring on her finger, smiling, almost fondly, 'like the dopey little dormouse in *Alice in Wonderland*.'

She cleared her throat and then waited for a response. None came.

'It's not that he's bored – at least I certainly hope it's not that . . .' she drew a quick breath, as if anticipating some kind of heartfelt affirmation of her teaching skills from Elen (she waited in vain), 'but he's definitely *tired*. And yet when he is awake, when he's on the ball . . .' she adjusted a gold link on the bracelet of her watch, 'he goes straight to the opposite extreme. He focuses too much . . .' she paused, speculatively. 'I'm sure you'll be aware of this yourself. He can try too hard. He can get too involved in certain projects – certain situations – and then get incredibly frustrated if things don't work out properly . . .'

'Is Fleet causing trouble in class?' Elen butted in, almost hopefully (there was something so reassuringly *normal* about the thought of a naughty, disruptive little boy).

Mrs Santa looked shocked. 'No. Absolutely not. In fact quite the opposite. If anything he's actually . . .' she winced, putting up a small hand to adjust the tiny, faux-Hermès-style silk scarf around her neck '. . . too well behaved. And too hard on himself. *Extremely* hard . . .'

Elen frowned. This was definitely not good.

'So you called me in today,' she spoke calmly and evenly (purposefully misinterpreting what the teacher was telling her –

This is a game, Elen –
Come on, girl,
Play)

– 'because he's *too* well-behaved?'

'Yes.' Mrs Santa nodded.

'And you really think that's a problem?'

Mrs Santa smiled. 'Problem seems rather a *harsh* way of putting it . . .'

'Right. *Fine.*'

Elen could feel herself growing defensive. She sensed a degree of soft-soaping. And, worse still, bobbing around, perniciously, beneath all those suds and lather: a hidden agenda. She glanced over towards the door again. The Head Teacher had ducked out of view, but she was certain he was still there.

'Some children find it difficult to concentrate,' Mrs Santa tip-toed onward, 'and some children are just . . .' she struggled to find the correct word, then gave up '. . . *too* concentrated. Fleet finds himself in this second category. He's very grown up for a boy of his age. In fact we've all noticed – myself, the classroom assistants, some of the mothers who like to help out sometimes – how much better he seems at interacting with adults than with other children of his own age . . .'

'Yes,' Elen was perfectly willing to take this on board –

Unreasonable?
Me?

'. . . Fleet's an only child,' she murmured, 'I suppose that must impact on him at some level . . .'

'We all think he's experiencing a certain amount of . . . of *stress*,' Mrs Santa rushed on (emboldened by Elen's apparent compliance), 'and that he's expressing it through particular . . .' she paused, as if searching for the least damning formulation '. . . behaviours. Tasks. Symptoms. *Habits.*'

'I see.'

Elen's voice was clear as a glass of spring water.

'He never seems quite able to switch *off* . . .'

Elen was quiet.

The teacher cleared her throat, nervously. 'We wondered whether there might be anything . . . anything *unusual* going on at home at the moment which could offer some kind of . . . of . . . ?'

She gazed over at Elen, appealingly.

'. . . Perhaps a recent family bereavement? The loss of a job . . . ?'

Elen said nothing. Mrs Santa filled the awkward silence by commencing a detailed inspection of the heel of her black court shoe.

'We have a hole in the roof,' Elen eventually volunteered, 'the roof's leaking.'

'Really?'

Mrs Santa seemed relieved by Elen's input, and yet somewhat nonplussed. Elen had a sudden sense of how it might feel to be a student who wasn't excelling in Mrs Santa's class (that atmosphere of 'tolerant' disappointment; of 'accepting' disquiet). She didn't like it. The angry knuckle tensed itself up inside her stomach again –

Cow

– then the second, gentler knuckle – the pacifier –

She's his teacher –
She just wants to help . . .

– predictably balanced it out.

'I know it mightn't sound like much,' Elen explained, patiently, 'but it's leaking directly above Fleet's bedroom. We've had to move all his . . . his *toys* down into the living-area. Everything's a little chaotic.'

'Ah.'

Mrs Santa tried to appear as if she'd been enlightened in some way by this explanation. She failed. She glanced down at her hands, then back over towards Fleet again. Fleet did a tiny, involuntary jump, for no apparent reason.

'Did you just see that?' she asked.

'What?'

'That little jump? That "tick". He does it fairly regularly.'

'Does he? Yes. Well that's . . .' Elen bit her lip '. . . that's something he . . . he *does*, occasionally.'

She smoothed down the fabric of her skirt and folded her hands across her lap. She knew she wasn't helping matters. She felt frustrated – impotent. There was so much she could contribute –

So much

– but she just . . .

Just . . .
No.
Can't.

Her eyes shifted over towards the classroom windows. It was a new building (everything was new here – for Isidore, something being 'new enough' was always a primary concern). She idly noticed how one of the smaller, higher windows had been left open. She gazed up at it, ruminatively. Her eyes moved to the square of putty surrounding the pane of glass. She could see – even from where she was sitting – that the putty had been interfered with. It was puckered; sliced; gouged out in some places.
She shuddered.

'We all want what's best for Fleet, after all . . .' Mrs Santa continued. 'Of course,' Elen was still distracted, still looking up at the window. 'So we wondered,' Mrs Santa grasped her moment, 'if it might not be an idea to book him in for a brief session with the child psychologist.'

'No.'
Elen immediately snapped back to attention. 'Absolutely not.'

Mrs Santa seemed shocked; less by the refusal itself, than by the casual manner in which it was delivered. 'But it's a perfectly *normal* procedure,' she emphasised, 'a significant percentage of our children end up seeing the psychologist at some time or other during their school career.'

Elen pushed her hair firmly behind her ears. 'What percentage would that *be*, exactly?'
Mrs Santa floundered, 'I don't know. Two . . . three . . .'
'That's not a significant percentage,' Elen was very calm, 'that's a *tiny* percentage.'

Fleet had completed his task in the play area. He yawned. He rubbed his eyes and then stood up. Elen reached out her hand towards him, almost as if appealing for his support.

'If you're concerned that there might be some kind of . . . of *stigma* . . .' Mrs Santa continued, staunchly.
'Yes I am worried,' Elen nodded, 'very worried. Because there would be.'
'The point is that we're extremely concerned about Fleet, and we simply feel . . .'

'The fact is,' Elen interrupted, 'that I'm not really the problem here. It's Dory, Fleet's father. He's German. He's very old-fashioned. He simply wouldn't tolerate the idea.'

'Fleet's father doesn't necessarily have to be involved,' Mrs Santa proclaimed boldly (glancing towards the child with a bright smile), 'it could simply be something that the school has instigated, something which just "spontaneously happens", so to speak.'

Elen seemed genuinely alarmed by this suggestion. Fleet was standing at her side, now. She slipped her arm around his waist and pulled him closer.

'I don't like the sound of that *at all*, Mrs Santa.'

Her gentle voice contained a strong warning.

Mrs Santa looked uncomfortable, as if a breach had been established and she – for one – was going to experience some difficulty in recovering from it. 'Well just think it over, at least. We're only trying to do our best for the boy,' she leaned forward and chucked Fleet, playfully, under his chin (he stiffened). 'We want him to be happy. We want him to excel.'

'Of course.'

There was a sudden, loud creaking sound directly above them. Elen glanced up. One of the classroom's suspended strip-lights had slowly begun to rock.

Mrs Santa glanced up, too.

'It's the breeze,' she said, 'it often does that.'

She clambered to her feet, walked over to the line of windows, picked up a specially adapted pole and pushed its metal tip through the high, open window's latch. She briskly pulled it shut.

The light continued to swing. Fleet stretched up his arm towards it, pointing his index finger. He paused for a second, then jumped again – a tiny, apparently involuntary jolt – before smiling and carefully touching that same index finger to his right shoulder (as if in some kind of convoluted boy scout salute).

Elen quickly stood up as Mrs Santa walked back over. She grabbed her bag to try and signal an end to their discussion.

'There, that's better,' Mrs Santa murmured. They all looked up towards the light again, their heads tipping, in unison, their chins lifting; like three, simple flower petals unfurling from the bud in a time-lapse-photography nature documentary.

At night he did his real work. You couldn't call it 'play', exactly. It was far too serious – too painstaking – for that. He'd been re-creating, in perfect miniature, the Cathedral of Sainte-Cecile (the world's largest ever brick-built structure) which was located (and this meant nothing to Fleet, he was six years old, and geography, to him, was just a clumsy four-syllable word) in the beautiful, French medieval town of Albi.

Fleet's tools: a trusty pair of children's paper-cutting scissors (the blades of which he'd secretly stropped on a stone until they were razor-sharp), some general-purpose adhesive (the white kind which came in a blue tub and smelled of marzipan), and matchsticks (in abundance; pristine – *never* spent – with the brightly tinted sulphured end cleanly lopped off).

He had a small black and white picture of the cathedral (a partial view – it was a monumental, many-faceted construction, 200 years in the making) which he'd discovered, by chance (at least, that's how he remembered it), aged four, in a French holiday brochure. He liked to keep it hidden (he didn't know why: instinct, perhaps) inside a folded strip of cardboard hoarded from a cereal packet, shoved under the dishcloths in the back of a kitchen drawer.

Sometimes he would creep into the kitchen at night with his torch, open the drawer and stare at the picture for hours, without blinking (or until his re-chargeable batteries faded). He would consume it, devour it. Then he would squirrel it away, and not feel the need to refer to it for days.

It was all a question of dimensions with Fleet, and of form: the scale of a thing, the logistics (what was feasible, what was not). Aesthetics didn't enter into it. Beauty was just something that worked. Beauty paid its way. It was infrastructure. It was superstructure. All the rest was simply floss.

He had no pictorial evidence of the cathedral's interior (which was legendarily beautiful, with an immense nave containing an Italian fresco of the Last Judgement, hundreds of sculptures, and one of the world's most impressive organs), but the inside of his matchstick monolith had been just as fastidiously re-created (was just as pristine – no bish-bosh job, this) as the exterior.

He'd made certain, educated leaps based on his tours of Ashford Church (the inside a crazy mish-mash of ancient period detail) and – but of course – two wonderful day trips he'd taken (aged three and a half and five) to the astonishing medieval village of Chilham, with its grand, stately home, thirteenth-century church and numerous timber-framed houses and cottages.

It was a big project –

Big

– and his parents weren't what you might call 'entirely behind it'. In fact they'd done everything they possibly could to try and disrupt him (financial and spatial restraints had been suddenly – and arbitrarily – imposed at various points, karate lessons were posited, extra reading classes, the bloody *cubs*).

Fleet was even suspicious – although this was sheer paranoia on his part – that the leaky roof scenario was yet another complex gambit they'd suddenly dreamed up to foil his progress (since his quality time alone with the cathedral had been profoundly undermined by it).

The truth was that Elen and Dory hadn't particularly minded the cathedral – at least, not at first. They'd found it charming; extraordinary, even (although – as was only to be expected – their tolerance of 'difference', or – worse still – of 'eccentricity', was entirely predicated by Isidore's own mental health scenario. The question of heredity was naturally an explosive one).

Fleet's burgeoning 'obsession' with structure (and they didn't even dare use this key word in private together) had been some time in the making, although Isidore held himself chiefly responsible for initiating this current phase (which they both thought especially severe), after he'd idly bought Fleet a small, Airfix aeroplane from a closing-down sale in a local toy shop.

His son had always been a frail, cerebral little creature – physically unadventurous – and his father (in whom nature found the perfect, working definition of 'robust') battled constantly to try and toughen

145

him up. He'd take him out for walks, or cycling, or to the park to mess around on the Adventure Playground. He tried to interest him in competitive sports.

Fleet absolutely dreaded these activity-based excursions, would be sullen, uncooperative, virtually monosyllabic. When his father threw a ball at him, he'd simply neglect to raise his hands, and if it hit him, he would buckle and fall, without a sound (like a tragic young soldier in a silent film, mown down, in his prime, on the front line).

Sometimes his mother joined them (acting as a buffer between her husband's enthusiasm and her son's recalcitrance) and he'd cling miserably to her skirts, begging her, in urgent whispers, to help him, to *save* him, to just take him *home* again.

Isidore felt like the whole world was alien to his son; that he was a stranger, dispositionally; that there was a quality within him which was fundamentally 'foreign' (this was something which he understood only too well himself – and why on earth wouldn't he? It was the keynote of his own existence; something, as a German, an outlander, that he battled constantly to overcome). Yet he found Fleet's total inability to fit in – the boy's effortless facility for bucking and chafing against even the most basic of social conventions – unbelievably infuriating.

Home life wasn't much better. When they'd moved to the new Cedar Wood development, Fleet had been inconsolable for weeks; kept feeling for the familiar walls of the old house whenever he walked in his sleep – as he sometimes would, when he was especially stressed – calling out, in sheer terror, when he couldn't locate them; or, worse still, they'd discover him, pushing, exhaustedly (tears streaking his cheeks, panting for breath) against a solid surface, as if fully expecting that it might desolidify in front of him . . . (or that *he* might, even).

During his waking hours he rigorously avoided the new kitchen appliances, quivered at the bathroom taps, baulked at the low-flush toilet and the dimmer switches. He even had to re-learn how to use his fork (exactly the same fork he'd used at their previous address); would hold it, loosely, in his hand, head tipped on one side, like a suspicious young thrush, inspecting the prongs with a mixture of fury and wonder.

It was all a matter of *context*, Isidore felt, and a question of adaptation. Neither of these concepts had any kind of hold on him. His dreamy, impish mind would simply wriggle free and he'd be set loose in the world again, unconstrained by anything.

It was an awful kind of liberty.

Model building – on the other hand – was something they could share in, something simple and quiet and relaxing; a perfect opportunity – or so Dory thought – for a little gentle father and son bonding. After the plane they'd made a tank (Isidore still taking the lead at this stage, Fleet mainly standing by, standing back, observing), then a sports car.

They'd graduated on to aquatic vehicles – a hovercraft, a submarine. Finally, a boat. A big one. Fleet chose the model himself (as a special fifth birthday treat). He plumped for a clipper (a 200 foot-er).

He built the bulk of the main structure, virtually single-handed, in just under three days (the age recommendation of the box specified twelve years and over) then got caught up in the rigging – tangled, knotted – spent hours on end perfecting the whole thing, even adding – much to Isidore's amazement – several home-made modifications where, apparently, 'the model wasn't proper.'

They'd visited the *Cutty Sark*, in Greenwich, as a family, when Fleet was just a toddler, and he'd completed a school project on deep sea diving (earning himself a much-coveted gold star), but these meagre, boat-related provenances were barely adequate – Dory felt – to justify the extent of his son's precocity.

There were – inevitably – a few gaps in Dory's memory at this stage (which didn't really matter – he told himself – since even the most superficially straightforward child's developmental progress was rarely – if ever – entirely linear) but the next thing he knew, Fleet was experimenting with the idea of making objects 'from scratch'. They'd messed around with clay (Fleet had screwed up his face; the clay was too gloopy, too glutinous, he was far too fastidious), then wood (Elen had stepped in and insisted – much to Fleet's irritation – that the boy was too small to handle sharp tools responsibly).

Then, finally, on an especially boring Sunday morning, Isidore had grabbed hold of a box of kitchen matches, rattled it, speculatively, tipped the matches out on to the table-top, unearthed a stray tube of glue in a nearby drawer, and quickly built a sentry box for one of Fleet's highly prized, enamelled Beefeaters.

That was it.

Fleet dived straight on in (not a whiff of uncertainty, no whining or faltering) and carefully began constructing a long, formal, looping creation (like an early piece of lace or crochet, or a dramatically enlarged chromosome – a cell, or a gene – cut open, stretched out, unwound). It was flat-topped, 2 inches wide, several feet long. It was beautiful.

'The Bridge', he called it.

His parents watched on in quiet bewilderment.

Elen immediately divined (it was a curious feeling, a *familiar* feeling) that something primal was connecting within him. She didn't know what or why. But she could see that he was spanning some kind of a divide (mentally, physically, symbolically), that this behaviour was unusual, that it was out of the ordinary.

Suddenly, without warning, 'The Bridge' was quietly placed aside and superseded (no fuss, no fanfare) by a menacing, fortress-style basilica. And with the arrival of this 'cathedral' it became patently obvious that parental participation was no longer an issue.

Isidore wasn't entirely certain (as a play-mate, or as a father) just how much of an influence he'd actually been on his son; whether Fleet's obsession reflected well (or badly) on him. He had a nagging – an *uncomfortable* – feeling about the whole affair. Had he led the boy, or had the boy – somehow, ineluctably – led *him*?

Fleet seemed happy (at least, to start off with), and that (they told themselves) was the important part. He seemed more confident, more at ease, was 'opening up' (asking for things, making lists, barking out instructions if anyone dared to try and join in).

As parents (as guardians, even, with a vested interest in his welfare) their enthusiasm had waned marginally when he'd expanded his architectural portfolio to include not only 'The Bridge' and 'The Cathedral', but a cluster of brand-new, subsidiary properties (a large, secondary building – down what was now 'The Hill' a-way – which he described as 'The Palace', then, shortly after, another structure, which he casually referred to as 'The Dungeon Tower'. He'd even commenced work on a water mill, whose connection to the other buildings seemed, at best, entirely marginal).

And everything (Elen quietly observed – although she didn't – for her own good reasons – confide in Isidore) was now suddenly on-going (happening all-at-once, burgeoning uncontrollably . . . like a . . . how to express it? Like the frantic, shifting interior of one of those toy kaleidoscopes, or a hall of mirrors, or a . . . a –

God help him

– some kind of a *disease*, maybe).

She tried to quell her increasing agitation by telling herself that Fleet'd seen development all around him (they were in a new-build property in a newly built area); the builder, the digger, the lorry, were all part of his locality; change was part of the milieu in which he lived and breathed and grew . . .

But it didn't work. It didn't mesh. It didn't entirely ring true.

Space was increasingly at a premium (the inside mirroring the outside in an funny kind of way). Everything – Elen observed, with an encroaching sense of terror –

Oh no . . .
I'm . . .
Can't . . .
Can't breathe

– was now thuddingly equal (Flat. *Reduced.* Like a beautiful, five-course meal, tossed into a large bowl and then devoured all in one go). Nothing took precedence. Nothing was ever rounded off (finished, *honed*). There was no sense of an end to it, of a neat conclusion. Of curtailment. Of *release*.

Elen knew all about the brochure in the kitchen drawer. She'd found it, looking for a tea-towel, and had made the connection. Its placement, she presumed, indicated something – she wasn't sure what – about Fleet's unconscious desire to involve her (she was, after all, the only person in the house to do the drying up; Isidore, in general, preferred to wash).

She'd kept it a secret. Isidore still firmly believed that 'The Cathedral' was just part of some magical 'dream landscape', that it was simply another perplexing facet of the boy's highly developed – if distinctly wayward – imagination (he *needed* to believe this, and Elen responded, automatically – as any considerate partner would – to whatever his needs were).

But she knew better. She'd been to the library and had looked up Sainte-Cecile in a Rough Guide travel book. She'd expanded her search on to the internet. There she'd seen a series of modern, photographic images of Albi, in all its glory (clinging to its hill, surrounded by water); then (with an increasing sense of claustrophobia) the Cathedral Basilica, the adjacent La Berbie Palace, the dramatic Dungeon Tower, the hooped colonnades of the St Salvy Cloister. Even the mill, sitting quietly downstream on the River Tarn.

And the bridge.

The *link* –

Oh God –
There it was

She traced its familiar, looping grandeur on the glaring screen with her index finger –

Yes
But of course –

Her wait was over. The worst had finally happened. This was the beginning.

This was the crossing.

They'd pushed the two boys together in class (what else to do?). They were both a little dippy. Steven Bradley had a Gameboy and a registered learning disability – *dyspraxia;* but very mild (words spilled out of his mouth in entirely the wrong order; he made regular trips to see the speech therapist in Canterbury). He could be clumsy –

Bless him

Came from a family of ten, so it was difficult, sometimes, for his parents (who were extremely well-meaning) to give him all the attention he so desperately required. He could be slow on the uptake, obdurate, even, but he was fundamentally a solid, sweet-natured boy.

Fleet on the other hand . . .

Hmmn

Fleet had . . .

What did Fleet have? Whatever it was, the parents wouldn't deal with it (were uncooperative, wouldn't face facts), which automatically rendered them a part of the problem. To care too much was a weakness all parents could quite reasonably be found guilty of, but to actively obstruct? To smother? To deny? Not only was it unhealthy, but in the voluminous wardrobe of parental misdemeanours, this was that fine-seeming, well-laundered garment hanging neatly alongside the foul and mouldering suit of abuse (contamination was always a real possibility when two items were hung so close).

Fleet wasn't a lost cause. Absolutely not. Because when all was finally said and done – with a modicum of support, a few one-to-one sessions, some firm guidance – they might actually be able to straighten the poor boy out (although he'd never be . . . not quite what you might call . . . well . . . *vertical*, exactly).

It was nothing insurmountable, in other words. But it *was* something (a blip, a phase – rather hard to put your finger on, really, without the benefit of professional input).

One thing was for certain: the boy was much smarter than he might initially appear. He was no Will o' the Wisp. No charming, harmless Puck. He was evasive, sly, elusive. And –

Why not let's just call a spade a spade, eh?

– you didn't have to hunt very far to find out who he might've learned *that* particular mode of behaviour from.

The mothers sat in Elen's brand-new kitchen (pale ash units, double-sink, waste disposal, grey marble counter) and enjoyed a pot of tea together. Fleet's father – the German, *terribly* handsome – Dory? Isidore? – had popped in to say 'Hi' (shook Mrs Bradley's hand, very formally, before heading upstairs for a quick nap. He'd been out on a job, he informed her – with an apologetic yawn – since eleven o'clock the night before).

Fleet (who didn't initially seem entirely delighted by their arrival) took Steven up to his bedroom and guided him, nervously (the boy was just an accident waiting to happen) around his model of Albi (which currently took up a significant proportion of the floor-space in there).

Steven (extremely polite, but essentially unmoved by the tour) listened, blankly, waited until it was all over (offering no comment), then perched himself on the edge of Fleet's bed, took out his computer and instituted his own kind of play (his head at an angle, his mouth falling slack, his fingers convulsing).

Okay

Fleet squatted down, picked up a boxful of matches and shook them, meditatively. He appraised his work. He mused. He calculated.

This arrangement suited them both perfectly (no pressures here, no expectations, no demands). Fleet worked away diligently on The Dragon Tower, leaving Steven entirely to his own devices.

Everything was proceeding in the best possible manner, and then . . .

Eh . . . ?

Fleet scowled. He suddenly found himself distracted by the computer's tiny voice. A tune. So simple. So repetitive. It hung in the air around him like a busy hover-fly. It buzzed. It troubled his ear. It *reminded* him of something. A *folk* memory. He cocked his head quizzically and focussed in on it, fully –

Zzzzzzzzzeeeee

Click –
Ah . . .

He closed his eyes, briefly.

Steven pressed *pause* and glanced up. 'What?'

Fleet looked straight back at him (his fingers slightly glue-ey). '*Huh?*'

Steven frowned, then looked down, released *pause*, and continued to play. He tried to concentrate, but something was interfering. He pressed *pause* for a second time.

'*Stop* that,' he demanded.

'What?'

Fleet didn't even turn around, he just continued to build, methodically.

Steven cocked his head to one side. Couldn't he *hear* it? The humming? Didn't it . . . ? Wasn't he . . . ?

It filled the air around them.

'*That*!' Steven exclaimed, pointing at nothing (his tongue twisting awkwardly).

Fleet slowly shrugged his shoulders and then continued on – doggedly – with what he was doing.

Steven sat in silence, frowning. He studied Fleet's breathing patterns from the back, to see if they might give him away.

'It's not *song* . . . not even *same*,' he eventually stammered.

'It *is* the same,' Fleet's voice was deadly calm, 'only it came from *before*.'

He continued to build.

'No,' Steven stammered. '*Not*.'

Fleet merely shrugged.

'*Not!*'

Steven looked down at his Gameboy. His hand was shaking slightly. He wanted to play – he *needed* to – but he was suddenly overwhelmed by an extraordinary sense of dislocation. He blinked, then he gasped. A gulf was opening up around him (was being scribbled – in thick, dark crayon – over the gleaming surface of his everyday world).

He sat on the edge of the bed, like a frightened nestling on the lip of a precipice, remaining perfectly still, hardly even breathing, until his mother had finished her tea and was standing at the bottom of the stairs, calling him –

'Steven? *Steven!*'

Then, and only then, could he blink back the darkness and run.

For the next two days, he didn't feel even the remotest inclination to turn his Gameboy on again.

The second time she literally had to drag him there. He kept telling her that he didn't like Fleet, that Fleet was mean, that he really didn't want to go and visit him any more. But the school had recommended it, and Mrs Bradley thought Elen was incredibly charming (quite the *loveliest* person. It took a little while to get to grips with her – *sure* – what with that severe, home-spun look; the dark, sober clothes, the long hair, the thinness, the birthmark – but once you did, there was something so . . . so *friendly*, so informal, so calm, so intelligent . . .).

And the house was so nice. And the area. Everything so new. Everything so . . . S*hhhhhh!* (Can't you *hear* that? The *silence*? No traffic, no dogs barking, no stereos blaring . . .)

Although on this occasion – it soon transpired – the marvellous quiet was to be interrupted (and quite notably), by a series of strange noises emanating from above.

Elen was cutting into a small, home-made fruitcake when the pandemonium first began. The mothers' eyes had met – in mutual alarm – across the table-top.

'Are they . . . are they *singing*?' Mrs Bradley asked (she couldn't actually remember ever having heard Steven sing before).

Elen gently pushed a slice of cake towards her.

'Yes. Yes, I think they must be . . .'

'But isn't your husband still working nights? Won't they disturb him?'

'No. That's . . . It's *fine*, honestly.'

Elen stood up – slightly flustered – and went over to close the door. Then a few minutes later, while she was refreshing the pot, she casually turned on the oven's extractor-hood.

All subsequent extraneous sounds were expunged by its *whirr*.

She'd gently questioned Fleet about his 'project' (this matchstick structure now took up the best part of their dining table – his bedroom having long since been evacuated because of the leak). She was especially interested in why it was that he hadn't completed the cathedral itself before moving on to some of the surrounding buildings.

'But what about *this* section?' she'd asked, standing on the cathedral's south side, where a large hole still gaped, unattractively, at the entrance.

'It's not finished,' Fleet had murmured.

'Then finish it,' she'd said.

He'd scowled up at her. 'It's not *finished*,' he repeated, as if speaking to an imbecile. 'They haven't *built* it yet.'

Steven had the most beautiful voice, and once he'd been set off, there was literally no stopping him (although he only ever really sang one song, and he sang it in what appeared to be a foreign tongue). When he did sing, though, his usually jumbled pronunciation sounded smooth and unhalting.

His speech therapist claimed that she'd seen this happen before (that it was relatively common, even). 'Remember Gareth Gates,' she'd said, 'with his terrible stutter, who finished up second on *Pop Idol*? Steven's like him . . .' she paused, speculatively '. . . although perhaps a little . . . *uh* . . .'

One of the volunteers in Steven's class was a member of Ashford Church's prestigious choir. With Mrs Santa's encouragement, she took Steven – and his mother – along to meet the choir master. Steven sang for him. In fact he sang – his shoulders back, his hands clasped, his tiny face all pinkly beatific – for upwards of half an hour.

The choir master had been both charmed and bemused.

'It's an early Madrigal,' he told them (over the continuing sounds of Steven's vocalising), 'in a kind of bastardised Latin. Or maybe Welsh or Cornish. Definitely not a tongue I'm especially familiar with . . .'

'D'you think he made it up?' his mother asked.

'I simply can't answer that.'

'D'you think you could make him sing something else?'

'I'm sure I could try.'

But when the choir master sat down at his piano and began to play, Steven put his hands over his ears, began rocking and screaming.

The instrument, the rhythm, the tempo, the pitch. They were all *wrong*. They were vile and cacophonous.

Modern.

He found it *disgusting*.

Elen couldn't help wondering why.

Why Albi?

At first she'd considered the actual *place* – its geography; its *historical* background – tales of religious strife were certainly legion; the basilica had been built by a cruel bishop –

Blah blah
Uh . . .

– Toulouse Lautrec had been born in the town, they'd built him a museum . . .

Hmmn

But after a while she decided to simplify things. She went back to basics. She began by considering the word itself, the name; its linguistic ramifications; the actual *semantics* (to do so, she'd found – in her extensive experience of problems of this kind – could often pay dividends).

Albi?
Al – bi?

Hang on . . .

If you inserted the 'I' (placed *yourself* in the picture), you got 'al-i-bi'.

Alibi

In Latin (she looked it up in a dictionary) that meant 'elsewhere'. I-am-elsewhere.
This funny little riddle just lodged in her head. And it stayed there.

Soon Steven was actually speaking – was chatting away, and with an amazing fluency – in this extraordinary new language of his, but only – Mrs Santa noted – when he was in (or around) Fleet's general vicinity. It was almost as if he felt Fleet might respond (but Fleet never did), as if he thought Fleet might actually understand.

And while Fleet wasn't ever aggressive (it wasn't in his nature to be), it was plain that he found the boy (and his language) both stupid and exasperating. He would turn his face to the wall, or simply walk away. He made his contempt quite obvious. Everybody noticed.

Eventually the home visits were gently discouraged.

Two weeks after Steven had entered the Special Care stream, he completely abandoned his strange, new tongue. He began to stammer and to falter again. He lost his curiously ecstatic air. He recommenced his relationship with the Gameboy (head cocked, mouth open, fingers jabbing), but he'd only ever play with the sound turned off. He was almost ludicrously punctilious on that point.

He took no interest in Fleet any more.

A while after that, when the dust had finally settled, Mrs Santa caught Fleet staring at Steven during break one morning.

'Is anything wrong, Fleet?' she'd asked.

Fleet's eye-line didn't alter. It remained fixed on Steven as he answered her.

'Steven should *stay* hiding behind the shapes,' he murmured, 'inside that funny little play-box of his.'

'Really?'

Mrs Santa tried her best to draw him out.

'Yes.'

'And why do you say that, Fleet?'

Fleet glanced up at her, a look of mild surprise in his impish eyes. 'Because that's where he's *safe*, Mrs Santa. All alone. In the quiet.'

'But of . . . of *course*.'

Mrs Santa delivered him one of her brightest smiles. She glanced nervously around her. Two girls were squabbling over a skipping rope –

Of course . . .

She rapidly marched towards them, determined to interfere.

ELEN

It wasn't all just corns and bunions –

Uh-uh

– No way.

Of course there was a *certain* amount of what a novice might term 'the run-of-the-mill stuff' (although for Elen, nothing was ever 'run-of-the-mill', because in her eyes every symptom – no matter how small or uncontentious – invariably belied a deeper cause, and uncovering something's origin, its genesis, was an essential part of the challenge of good chiropody; part of that special, 'transformative' magic – the buzz, the voodoo – which made all the hard daily slog – the cancelled appointments, the stroppy clients, the crazy hygiene – feel absolutely worthwhile).

Take bandaging, for example. Elen just loved it. As a small girl she remembered painstakingly binding the limbs and the torsos of all her dolls and her teddies with neat strips of fabric cut from old handkerchiefs (almost mummifying them, in several cases). It was just like weaving (was *artistic;* provided her with a similar kind of primitive thrill), but there was always that fascinating hidden variable in her line of work – a particular kind of condition, a certain shape of instep or toe, a preferred type of shoe – which made each and every application into something fresh and stimulating.

And it wasn't just the medical aspect. It was the mundane things, too. The chiropody minutiae: the pad, the splint, the plaster, the wedge, the gauze, the strapping, the brace, the stockingette –

Oh the smells –
And the whiteness –
Or – better still – the creamy-white –
The stretch, the non-stretch –
The earthy putty,

The sterilising tingle
The dizzy glue

Each item –

Oh, but look . . .
Aren't they all just . . . just beautiful?

– tidily arranged inside her briefcase (or laid out in that neat, spotless provisions drawer at her usual room in the practice). Every object *immaculately* packaged; each box and label so plain and clinical, so severe and uncompromising, so unapologetically –

Uh . . .

– generic

That was it!

– and *timeless*, too: the future/the past, all painstakingly rolled up into one hugely reliable sanitary bundle.

Elen liked the clean (*very* much – of course she did – she had to), but she absolutely *loved* the dirty: the malformation, the bump, the crust, the fungus. To Elen a foot was like a city, an infection was the bad within, and she was its ombudsman; making arrangements, sorting out problems, instituting rules, offering warnings.

On a good day she was a Superman or a Wonderwoman, doggedly fighting foot-crime and the causes of foot-crime (usually – when all was finally said and done – the ill-fitting shoe . . . Okay, so it was hardly The Riddler, or The Penguin, but in a serious head-to-head between a violent encounter with either one of these two comic-book baddies and an eight-hour, minimum-wage shift behind the bar of a 'happening' Ashford night-spot with a corn the size of a quail's egg throbbing away under the strappy section of your brand-new, knock-off Manolo Blahniks . . . *Well* . . . it'd be a pretty close call).

Elen firmly believed that she was making a difference.
She was nothing less than an evangelist for the foot. She was a passionate devotee. She worshipped at the altar of the arch and the heel.

Sometimes it wasn't easy. The foot was hardly the most glamorous of the appendages ('yer dogs', 'yer plates', 'yer hoofs'). No one really gave a damn about it (although – fair's fair – the acupuncturists had done a certain amount for the cause, and the reflexologists had sexed things up a little, but in Elen's view, the short-fall still fell . . . *well*, pretty damn short).

The foot had sloppy PR; it mouldered, uncomplainingly, down at the bottom (the fundus, the depths, the *nadir*) of the physiological hegemony. It had none of the pizzazz of the hand or the heart. The lips! The eyes (the eyes had it *all* their own way). Even the neck, the belly . . . the *arse*. Even the arse had a certain cachet.

But not the foot. The foot had none (the foot had Fergie, with her lover, sprawled on a deckchair, in the Côte du Tawdry).

The foot lived in purdah – in cold climes particularly. It was hidden away, crammed inside, *squeezed*.

Sometimes, as Elen dutifully chiselled into thickened wodges of hardened skin –

Ah, the bread-and-butter work . . .

– flakes of which would shoot like shrapnel on to her apron-front, hit her goggles, or fly past her ears, Sylvia Plath's poem 'Daddy' would suddenly pop into her head and take up a brief residency there. She'd learned it at school . . .

> *'You do not do, you do not do*
> *Anymore, black shoe*
> *In which I have lived like a foot*
> *For thirty years, poor and white,*
> *Barely daring to breath or Achoo.'*

Ah yes

She loved that poem.

If she'd actually ever thought about it – and she honestly hadn't – then she might have drawn a few, tired parallels between her own life and the life of the foot (that frustrating opposition of support and neglect). But then again, if she'd thought about it some more, she'd have realised that all struggles – foot-related or otherwise – could be encapsulated as some kind of battle between an object's natural function and its actual – often thwarted – circumstances.

Them's the breaks, huh?

Her own daddy (to extend the Plathian metaphor just one stage further), whom she'd admired devotedly (up until – and beyond – his premature death in 1989), had been a hard nut to crack; fair but irascible, sincere but undemonstrative, he'd worked his entire adult life in the Services. Elen had been a true Army Daughter (drilled, polished, guarded, wrapped up, packed off – sometimes left behind, sometimes shoved dutifully into a khaki knapsack).

There was never a happy medium with Dad: he was either perpetually absent or too resolutely there (like a badly focussed close-up –

Lobe –
Cheek –
Whoops!
Moustache –
Teeth –
Pore –

– in an amateur video), and each state (too little, too much) somehow rendered its opposite inexplicably traumatic.

He'd served four years in Germany, two, undercover, then was posted to Northern Ireland (where his iron nerve and skills in the realm of bomb disposal were deemed especially useful). He retired in '83 (well-decorated for bravery after the Falklands War).

Following two, brief years on Civvy Street (a wonderful reprieve for the family, but he'd found it hard to relax, felt drained and grey, seemed to sorely miss his old life of careless extremity) he'd joined the Metropolitan Police Marine Support Unit: the Underwater and Confined Space Search Team (even working – briefly – as a freelance safety consultant on the Channel Tunnel, although he'd resigned, in disgust, after their first fatality).

The circumstances of his own death had been profoundly unsatisfactory. He'd been one of countless casualties in the *Marchioness*

Pleasure Boat Disaster (a small Thames cruise ship, pole-axed, in the dark, by an unlit dredger).

'But what was he doing on the boat in the first place?' people constantly asked. Try as Elen might, she could never provide an adequate answer.

It'd all been so very sudden (so abrupt, so random, so incredibly *unfair*). He'd faced eternity so many times: head on, with such unfathom-able bravery; had gambled with life so fearlessly, only to be grabbed – *snatched* – from the rear; no chance to 'take stock' or 'make his peace'. Denied, at the last – and this was the cruellest part – that pious mantle of 'a noble sacrifice'.

Her mother (who'd long found the role of serviceman's wife an uneasy one) promptly remarried a dairy farmer and now lived a life of bucolic bliss in rural North Yorkshire.

Anxiety over the welfare of her father had glued Elen and her mother tight at certain points during her child- and teen-hood, but with his unexpected demise, the bond had slackened. And there'd been some ill-feeling over her mother's lack of involvement in the hard-fought campaign for a proper inquest ('You think if some random judge finds the cruise-ship company negligent it'll bring your father back to me?' she'd griped. And then, later – when things got really nasty – 'They don't decorate the wives, Elen. Sometimes, when a man risks everything so easily you have to stop and wonder what "every-thing" actually means to him . . .').

To cut things short: they were not so close now as they once had been.

Talking of fathers –

Yes
Good –
Moving swiftly on . . .

Franklin Charlesworth was the don. He was chiropody's Big Daddy. His absolute classic *Chiropody: Theory and Practice*, Elen had owned in hardback (in its 5th edition) just about as long as she could remember (it'd got to the point, in Germany, during school holidays – she was ten – when she'd read virtually every tome in the Base's library. So she'd borrowed this one. Pored over the pictures –

Oh my God!

What is that?!

– and had never troubled to take it back).

It was her Bible (that so-familiar frontispiece illustration of a septic bunion was her spiritual equivalent of Genesis – it was where everything first began). Charlesworth was definitely Moses (who else?). He delivered chiropody (or podiatry, as the Americans were so determined to call it) from the Dark Ages. He brought the tablets down from the mountain.

It was chiefly through his dedication, generosity, lateral thinking and hard endeavour that chiropody finally came to be recognised as a Medical Auxiliary (and won the Holy Grail: State Registration). It was the same text-book she'd used at college (her grades so superlative, they'd pushed her towards Surgery, but she'd resisted, for some reason).

Elen rarely dreamed, but when she did, Charlesworth provided her with the Foreword, the Contents, the Index, the Appendices. He represented so much for her (stuck a career-based *band-aid* over her emotional tribulations – such as they were), fulfilled all her wishes . . .

Uh . . .
Yes.
Skin diseases:
Count them off . . .

Primary Lesions:
The Macule,
The Papule,
The Tubercule,
The Vesicle,
The Pustule,
The Bulla,
The Wheal,
The Squames . . .

That's all eight.
Good.

Secondary Lesions:

Crusts,

164

Ulcers,
Scars,
Fissures.
Just the four . . .
Count them . . .
Uh . . .

Charlesworth was her guide, her inspiration and her mentor. He was her role model; the parent who was never absent. He was her constant, her anchor. He'd given so much, for so long; was so painstaking, so *fastidious* . . .

Sometimes she'd lie in bed at night and consider the many years he'd spent embroiled in the careful manufacture of corrective, protective and palliative foot appliances –

Oh those magnificent, one-off, hand-stitched surgical boots –
With the 'Charlesworth' splint, nestling softly inside . . .

Love could be rather like shoe-making, she'd quietly reason –

All in the finish –
And in the detailing . . .

For maximum comfort and minimum wear, your basic raw materials – be they plastic, synthetic, fabric or leather – had to be carefully – nay *scrupulously* – manipulated to fit. Over-the-counter, made-to-measure; it didn't really matter. There was definitely a craft in it.

218.

No, seriously . . .

That's Two *Hundred* (one, two, three, four, five –

Go on,
Count them)

– and Eighteen (one, eight) faults –

Yes, faults –
ie
Problems,
Botch-ups

– on your average New Build property.
218.

   She'd seen it on a television report. Some houses fared slightly better, they'd claimed, and some fared slightly worse. But 218 was the average –

Can that really be right?

   They'd also maintained – during this same incendiary broadcast –

Why oh why did I insist on staying up late?

Why didn't I just go to bed early, like Isidore said?

– that the sensible buyer should at no costs –

Under Strictly No Circumstances

– consider purchasing a New Build property situated either in, or around, a notable dip. This was because most New Builds were sited on meadowland – bogs – flood plains; on the outskirts of town; the left-over bits of land; bits that nobody had ever bothered with before –

But hang on . . .

– Which inevitably begs the question, 'Why?'

Exactly!
Hmmn . . .
Remote control –
Volume . . . uh . . .
Up

Were our ancestors all just thoroughly unadventurous? Were they obstinately – *neurotically*, even – attached to mounds and to hillocks? Was it merely a question of safety (of finding the best site to defend against the marauding invader)? Or was the population so tiny back then that they never felt the urge (there was simply no call) to build in these left-over places?

Finally (and here's the rub) did they perhaps *know* something about the kinds of environments best suited for human habitation? Had they worked out this equation themselves, over time, through a system of trial and error? Did they have more respect for the pitfalls of nature? Did they understand the land? And then did we –

Those damn politicians –
And those evil-bastard, money-grabbing contractors –
– just conveniently resolve *not* to understand? To forget all the lessons they'd learned, and to build on these marginalised sites anyway (while offering a swift –

arrogant

– but mechanical nod to that delightfully infallible modern double-act of 'progress' and 'technology'?

Infallible, that is, until they've got your damn money).

The bottom line (the programme stated) was that available sites were often empty for perfectly good reasons. If there wasn't landfill somewhere in the general vicinity (oozing a terrifying cocktail of poisonous gases out into the stratosphere), then there would definitely be water.

That horrible, interminable drip, drip, drip . . .

Elen and Isidore lived in a New Build. It was set in a slight dip (a little saucer), and she absolutely hated it. She'd always loathed New Builds (she'd never made any bones about this fact. At root – Isidore carped – she was a snob. 'So are you,' she'd say, 'but just of a different kind.').

Of course a tiny part of her quite liked the idea of something new, something *virgin,* but it was only a very small part, and it was dramatically overshadowed by the general thrust of her opinion –

Unfashionable, maybe . . .

– that something's intrinsic value was inversely proportional to its longevity –

The blackened frying-pan
The antique, diamond cuff-links
The family Bible

It'd been a sacrifice, but she'd made it in all good faith. She'd moved there for Isidore –

Clean slate,
New broom

– but it rapidly came between them. And the reasons? So far she'd tabulated 77 –

77 flaws

And while she knew that it was unhelpful, she simply couldn't stop herself. She kept an on-going list, in chalk, on a small blackboard in the kitchen –

Day sixty-four:
The garage door is sticking . . .

– and every entry (in tinier and tinier writing, towards the bottom) caused her husband immeasurable suffering. But she kept on tabulating.

73 had just been insignificant things (a chip in the woodwork, a cracked tile, the oven grill not wired-in properly). Four had been fundamental:

1. The dip (obviously). The autumn after they'd moved in, the entire front garden had flooded. And it didn't drain properly. And this had affected the front fascia. There was a great deal of mould. Black, dark green.

2. A crack in the kitchen. It wasn't horizontal (like all good cracks should be). It zig-zagged, like a child's drawing of lightning, and Isidore now thought –

Oh, great . . .

– that there might be a problem with one of the supporting walls.

3. The window-sills on the front of the house hadn't been fixed in properly (hadn't been made good). If you pulled at them, they either wobbled alarmingly or simply came away –

Actually came off

– in your hand.

4. The roof. It didn't work. If you stood in the attic, craned your neck and looked up, you could see shafts of light shining in. Dozens of them. And the problem was especially severe around the chimney where the damp had spread lower, had entered the plaster. In Fleet's room, the wall on the chimney-breast side felt as soft as icing sugar (you could push your fingers straight through the panelling) and the ceiling was starting to mould-up and to sag.

Power and Higson Ltd, the contractors –

All credit to them

– had been very sympathetic. They'd promptly sent around an independent surveyor, and he'd posited the precise sum they'd be willing to invest on 'making good'. But they were well behind schedule, and it was winter, and their workers were all fully occupied in maintaining the build elsewhere –

Oh. Dear.

    So they provided Isidore with a list of approved contacts for local firms who might – they believed – be able to do a good job. He left about thirty messages. He received only two responses. In both instances nobody was available to come over and even *assess* the job for the following two months.

    He grew desperate. He pulled out the Yellow Pages and thumbed his way through the relevant section –

Uh . . .

    A Priori Builders Ltd –

Okay . . . Uh . . . So that's . . .

He tapped in the digits, and waited . . .

Damn.
Engaged.

    His finger hovered – for the briefest of moments – over the redial button, but his eyes scanned onward . . .
AAABuilders and Plumbers PLC –

What?! You've got to be kidding!

    Aardvaak Builders inc. –

Huh?!

    Abacus . . .

Hmmn

Abacus Builders Ltd –

He called them. They answered. A meeting was set up for the following morning with Harvey, one of their key personnel.

Harvey arrived on time and made all the right noises (thought it was 'a good little house, mate, a solid little dwellin', just a few, small creases, and we'll iron them out, no problem').

He assured them – with all sincerity – that since they found themselves in 'a rather urgent predicament', a couple of his people would make a start on things by the following Tuesday ('The kid deserves his own room back, poor bugger. It's like a fucking *paddlin'* pool up here ... Look at his face! Just look at him! I think he might be in love with me. What's your name, kid-o? Fleet? Mum got knocked up in the Motorway Services, did she? *Eh?* Only kidding! Okay, Dad, we'll need to bang up some scaffoldin', straight off, and an absolute, bloody *ton* of tarpaulin . . .').

Harvey drove a bright red and gold, customised 4x4 Toyota Hi Lux with lifted suspension, imported, 39" Mickey Thompson tyres, an electric winch and PIAA lights, front and back. He took 'the boys' for 'a quick spin' in it. Elen stood and waited for them, out on the pavement. And she waited. And waited.

She checked her watch.

It was a full forty-three minutes until they finally returned home again. As Harvey re-entered the cul-de-sac – and performed a stately lap of honour – he sounded his siren.

It was a bastardised version of Madonna's 1986 anti-abortion classic, 'Papa Don't Preach', from the *True Blue* album.

'Do you remember Chicken Licken?' Elen whispered, tucking Fleet up for the third week in a row on the living-room sofa.

'*Uh*-uh.' Fleet slowly shook his head.

'He thought the sky was falling in.'

'Really?' Fleet looked fearful, as if he could quite easily imagine the sky caving in on him. 'Why did he think that?'

'Because he got hit on the head by a chestnut – or an acorn – and he thought it was the sky.'

Fleet pondered this for a while. 'Well that was very silly of him,' he finally announced, with a slight air of pomposity.

'*Exactly*.'

Elen gently adjusted his hair. His head seemed a little warm to the touch.

'It's only the ceiling,' she murmured, kissing him, softly, on the ear, 'it's not the sky or anything.'

The boy smiled and turned tiredly over, shoving his face into his pillow, hooking his feet together (as was his habit, each night, before slumber).

Elen stood up to leave.

'Well at least *he* likes the drip, drip, drip . . .' the boy sighed.

She froze, just for a split second, then she forced herself back into motion; pulling his duvet still tighter around him. 'When the builder comes,' she spoke brightly, normally, 'when *Harvey* comes, everything will be fine again, you'll see.'

The mark –

The blemish

– there was no getting around it.

When she was born they'd thought it might fade. But it did not fade.

The mark was the first thing she saw each morning, and the last thing she saw, each night, before bed. Five hundred years ago, they might've burned her for it. And she seriously thought – at some sick,

172

subterranean level – that they still *would,* if they possibly could (an unconscious suspicion remained. She saw it in people's eyes – the revulsion, the hostility, the nagging fascination).

The mark was undoubtedly a blotch on her good name. But it was *there*, dammit. So she'd had to work her way around it, she'd had to be strong, to look *beyond*.

She never gave even a hint that it bothered her; was casual, cheerful and straightforward, in general, but she was only a woman, and not devoid of vanity (people would come up to her, in the street, and tap her, gently, on the shoulder, kindly informing her that there was something . . .

Uh . . .

Oh!

Realising what it was – becoming embarrassed – apologising – then dashing off, humiliated. And those were the *nice* ones).

The mark was the first thing Isidore noticed when they'd crashed into each other at the ice rink in Folkestone. They were both seventeen.

She'd been visiting the coast for a weekend, to catch up with her father. Isidore had just completed a six-week School Exchange Programme in Tenterden. He was cutting loose in the summer, doing some casual work – mainly manual labour.

He wasn't actually wearing skates, but was walking, barefoot, on the ice. He was smiling, broadly, his boots hung around his neck by the laces. He looked a little crazy.

A representative of the rink's management team was already hot on his trail, and Elen – distracted by his feet (they were strong and tanned and straight) – missed a beat and tripped and span, spiralling straight into him.

The mark . . .

He'd thought it might be chocolate, or mud, or blood, as he'd helped her up. He even thought – for a split second – that *he* might've been the cause of it . . .

'Oh my God, are you all right?'

'You're German!' she'd murmured, taking his hand, glancing up at him, smiling. He saw at once that it was a mole of some kind. A beauty-spot.

He grinned his relief as she brushed the ice from her knees.

'Well whatever gave you that impression?'

She was exceptionally pretty. And the mark didn't really bother him.

He already had a well-documented genius for circumnavigation.

ABACUS BUILDERS LTD

Harvey Broad owned four mobile phones, three of which he kept neatly suspended, at his hip, in his 'builder's buddy' (a kind of construction worker's gun holster) which was fashioned out of an expensive-looking sandy-coloured leather ('This is a prototype, Guv. Have a guess at what kinda hide that is . . . *Pig?!* Pull the other one! That's Buffalo, mate. Straight up. Got her designed and crafted, to my own specifications, by a female in Norfolk who imports the skins, wholesale, from Yank-land and makes all kinds of shit out of 'em . . .').

Also dangling from this heavy-duty charm bracelet were a torch ('This here, my young friend, is the Surefire Millennium Magnum. Ain't she a pretty one? Wanna proper butcher's? Let me unhook her for ya. Nah, mate, nah. Don't touch. I'll run through all the functions just as soon as . . .

Right. So this baby is totally water and shock resistant. Blasts out 500 Lumens. See that? Take a guess at how much they rushed me for it? Take a wild guess . . . Five *pounds*? *Oi!* Does this kid know the value of money or *what*?! How does 392 *dollars* grab ya? I say dollars because this here torch is the first choice of the American Military; and trust me, those geezers don't mess around wiv' their hardware . . .')

A protective face mask ('New one every day, sure as eggs. Don't ever fuck around wiv' ya lungs. You probably couldn't tell by the look of me – I'm in fairly buff condition if I say so myself – but I only have three-quarters of the normal lung capacity for a man of my years. Got involved in a diving accident, in Malta, when I was still just a nipper. Bought me tanks off of some shonky army geezer. First time I used 'em the bastards imploded. I was 25-fuckin'-feet under water. Nearly finished me off, it did . . .')

A pair of wrap-around sunglasses, of the type generally favoured by slightly psychotic, recently widowed, Dodge-driving American octogenarians ('Believe it or not, my own dear wife Linda bought me these for thirty-odd quid off the Shoppin' Channel. QVC: *Quality, Value, Convenience*. They're totally, bloody indestructible. In the car I've got my Raybans – for smart – but these babies have what my oldest calls Unabomber Chic, and you just can't put a price-tag on that.')

A little hammer, a set of screw-drivers and some pliers. ('I like my tools how I like my women: small, well-crafted, lightly greased.')

A toy truck – a Monster Truck; a Dinky; 'Bigfoot 7', to be precise – neatly fashioned (by his own hand), into a key-ring for his customised Toyota.

Bigfoot 7 was originally (he told a bemused Elen) an F250 Ford Pick-up with a 540-cubic-inch engine which had been painstakingly fitted with four, huge wheels (by a man called Bob Chandler – 'a folk hero of the American car industry') to enable it to perform a series of stunts (chiefly – so far as she could gauge – to drive over a line of old cars and lay waste to them. She wasn't entirely sure why this was a good thing, and she didn't dare ask. It just *was*, apparently).

Harvey delighted in telling her how it took 'three men three hours to change a single, damn tyre. Imagine that? It's just completely bloody *fucked*!'). There were many Bigfoots ('I mean some of these babies can jump over 200 feet . . .'), but 7's claim to fame was that it had been used – to great effect – in the Hollywood classic *Turner and Hooch* ('You ever see that film? You never saw it? Are you *kiddin'* me?! I should lend you my copy. It's about a dog detective. Stars Tom Hanks. The boy'll fuckin' *love* it.').

Harvey was also the proud owner of three of the first four As in the building section of the local phone book: AAABuilders and Plumbers PLC – which he called 'Treble A' whenever he answered the relevant phone ('I always think it sounds a bit "Vegas", somehow, a bit plummy, a bit *flash*. Know what I mean?'), Aardvark Builders and Plumbers inc, the advert for which was slightly larger than most, and doubly distin-guished by a small etching ('I paid through the bollocks for that – excuse my French') of an anteater ('a straight-up mistake,' he told Elen, over his umpteenth cup of tea, on one of the rare occasions he actually visited their property, 'but if some Smart Alec gets all up on their high heels about it, I always says, "Well here's a nice idea, mate: why don't we just forget all about your plumbin' disaster and head off on a fact-findin' trip to the *f*-in' *zoo* instead?"').

Aardvark attracted chiefly a female clientele. Men, by and large, were impressed by Abacus Builders and Plumbers Ltd ('To this day, I still don't really understand what an Abacus is. No word of a lie, Helen. Apparently it looks something like a kid's toy.').

Three adverts out of the initial four (which – all things considered – was pretty impressive), but 'pole position' (as Harvey would have it) remained in the vice-like grip of Garry Spivey, genial (if iron-fisted) proprietor of A Priori Builders Ltd.

Spivey's apparently effortless alphabetical ascendancy rendered Harvey (his *deeply* competitive runner-up) almost incontinent with rage. In fact it was the very first subject he'd interrogate prospective clients on (through a highly unconvincing mask of subterfuge and bullshit . . . 'Just a couple of last things, Sir, to help out the suits in our Marketing Department . . .') before he'd even contemplate contracting to work for them.

Isidore (and Elen) were no exception –

Harvey (*cornering Dory while Elen went off to make some coffee*): So how'd you actually get to hear about Abacus?

Isidore: The phone book.

Harvey (*in tones of some surprise*): Not a *personal* recommendation, then?

Isidore: No.

Harvey (*rapidly removing a smart-looking electronic palm from his pocket and scribbling everything down on to it with a tiny, metal pen*): That's interestin', *very* interestin' . . .

Isidore: I just looked you up in the building section.

Harvey (*still scribbling*): Is that so?

Isidore: Yes.

Harvey: And Abacus was the first firm you tried?

(*The conversation is briefly interrupted at this point by a phone call in which Harvey is heard to tell his interlocutor: 'I don't know, mate, but it might be septicaemia. Yeah. Heel blister. Curse of the new trainer . . . Nah. 'Course I can't spell the fucker. I ain't a soddin' doctor.*

Tell him it's blood poisonin'. It's the same thing, yeah? Tell him to have a bloody heart, mate. This is Life or fuckin' Death, ya with me?')

Harvey (*slotting the phone away – Isidore noticed, idly, that it was the blue Nokia*): So you was tellin' me about how you initially came to contact us at Abacus . . .

Isidore: Yes. The phone book.

Harvey (*almost presuming*): And we was the first firm you liked the look of?

Isidore (*jocular*): Well I was hardly going to place all my trust in AAABuilders, now, was I?

(*No perceptible response from Harvey to this crushing piece of rhetoric*)

Harvey: So Abacus was the first?

Isidore: Yes . . . (*sudden pause*), actually, no. I believe yours was the second company I tried . . .

Harvey (*his ears pricking*): Oh yeah?

Isidore: Yes. But the first place I rang was engaged.

Harvey: I see. And you wouldn't happen to . . . ?

Isidore (*without hesitation*): A Priori.

Harvey (*in ominous tones*): Ah (*Harvey grimaces as he scribbles – all the more violently – on to his palm*).

Isidore (*craning his neck over towards the palm, slightly concerned*): Is that thing actually working?

Harvey (*still scribbling frantically*): What thing?

Isidore: The palm. I don't think you've turned it on.

Harvey has not turned the palm on.

Harvey (*irritably*): I keep the screen off to save the battery.

Isidore (*fascinated*): And it still functions that way?

Harvey (*very irritably*): Well I'd look like a bit of a fuckin' Charlie if it didn't, wouldn't I?

Isidore (*backing off, diplomatically*): Yes. Of course. Sorry.

Harvey (*slapping his palm shut, with a flourish*): Well, all's I can say is: the Gods must've been smilin' down on you that day.

Isidore (*bemused*): Pardon me?

Harvey: Mr Spivey and I are 'old acquaintances', shall we say . . .

Isidore (*still bemused*): Mr Spivey?

Harvey: Wouldn't trust him with a malfunctioning fuckin' toaster.

Isidore (*slowly catching on*): You mean the guy from A Priori? Is he bad news?

Harvey: Bad news?!
(*He snorts, derisively*)

Isidore (*alarmed*): What? A real rip-off merchant?

Harvey (*holds up his hands, as if in regretful denial*): Mate, I've probably said enough already. More than I should of (*taps nose*) . . . Professional conduct an' all that.

Isidore (*worriedly*): Of course. Of course . . . (*thoughtful pause*) Forgive me, Harvey, but haven't you and I actually met *before*?

Harvey (*surprised*): Come again?

Isidore: It might sound a little *crazy*, but I just suddenly had the strangest *feeling* that we'd . . . (*Dory frowns, confusedly*).

Harvey: Not that I'm aware of, mate.

Isidore: A long time ago, maybe . . .

Harvey shrugs.

Isidore: It might take a while to percolate, but it'll come back to me, eventually, I'm sure . . .

Isidore shakes his head, bemusedly, as Harvey deftly slips the palm into his jacket pocket.

He had astonishingly clean hands. Elen had quietly observed as much during their initial encounter ('You know how I do that, my love? Here's a little tip for ya: washing-up liquid an' sugar. Screw all the fancy stuff you can buy over the counter – that shite's just a rip off . . .').

And he was always immaculately turned-out; had a very distinctive 'look'; appearing to hold a particular strand of pseudo-American combat-style apparel in especially high regard (the kind which seemed like it might've been popular in the early 1990s with a certain type of butch but glossy San Franciscan homosexual).

His colour palate ranged through the bright whites, rich creams and pale olives (not, you might think, especially *practical* tones for a labourer); the sage-coloured, high-shine, front-zippered puffer jacket being his most essential garment (his closely shaven, well-tanned head sticking out through its neat, Chinese collar like the stalk of an apple, jutting, defiantly, from the sumptuous, swollen mound of its surrounding flesh).

Harvey spent over two hours a day at his local gym ('I used to Body Build competitively – back in the late seventies – before all the ladies got involved and turned it into a fucking circus').

He wore earrings in both ears; thick, gold hoops, of a size and style which teetered (Elen felt) on the brink of the effeminate. Of course (she told herself) only a real man (or a lunatic) could hope to get away with fashion *that* obvious.

Following Harvey's casual (yet *oh so regretful*) defamation of Garry Spivey, Isidore had proceeded to hire him on the spot (the sudden eye contact, the manly handshake, the quick nod). Elen (left determinedly on the sidelines, clutching a coffee pot) had been absolutely furious.

The evidence against him, she insisted, once he'd finally –

My God, doesn't the man have a home to go to?!

– taken his leave of them, was overwhelming: the clean hands, the fancy truck, the immediate start, two hours in the gym ('Two *hours*? Each *day*? Did you *hear* that?'), the suspicious-sounding heel-blister conversation (which Dory already deeply regretted repeating to her), and last, but by no means least, the somewhat pivotal issue of an estimate.

There wasn't one. Harvey cheerfully proposed that they, 'Bash it out as we go along . . .'

('Bottom line: if *you're* happy then *I'm* happy, sweetheart.' –

Sweetheart?!)

Isidore had gently pooh-poohed her objections.
'He's a *builder*, Elen,' he'd argued, 'not a candidate for Mayor.'
She'd thought this argument fatuous. It didn't pacify her.

'And what're the alternatives?' he'd doggedly continued. '*Seriously?* There *are* none. This is a boom town. We're desperate. Builders are at a premium . . .'

They were stuck between a rock and a hard place. They were screwed. Harvey wasn't their best bet, he was their *only* bet. She did, at least, have to concede him that.

Contrary to all her expectations, things'd started off well enough. Almost as if sensing Elen's misgivings (and determining, quietly, to respond to them), Harvey had arranged for the scaffolding to arrive, not merely on time –

Just on time, you say?!
Oh no!
That won't do at all!

– but a whole day early.

Isidore had been ecstatic ('This is absolutely fantastic, Elen, isn't it?'). But his ecstasy was short-lived.

While a third of it went straight up (during a brief frenzy of activity on that first afternoon), the following morning, at around eleven (with no explanation or prior warning), the scaffolders packed away their tools, jumped into their truck, and headed off.

Where, Isidore knew not (*where* didn't matter). What mattered was that they never came back.

They'd vamoosed. They'd turned-tail. They'd bolted. They'd *gone*.

The house (which'd looked fairly bleak *prior* to this new development – with its sagging sills, mouldy fascia and muddy garden) now peeked out, disconsolately, from beneath its perilous-seeming exo-skeleton like a sadly neglected poodle in an ill-fitting muzzle. The small garden (such as it was) had all-but disappeared under an unsightly pile of poles and planks.

Both Elen and Isidore became preoccupied by the idea that someone

might try and steal these paltry remnants (wasn't scaffolding valuable? And what was the insurance situation? Were they liable?). Isidore
left Harvey countless messages to this effect ('I mean I don't know if
the scaffolders are a part of your company, or whether you sub-let
out this side of the business, but I think it might be a little *risky* . . .').

Two days after leaving his fifth or sixth reminder, Isidore came home
to discover that a couple of small chains and padlocks had been
applied to the 'excess' scaffolding in order – he presumed – to render
it more secure. He was relieved (of course he was), but this wasn't
entirely the result he'd been hoping for.

A week after the advent of the padlocks (when their hearts seemed
in imminent danger of slipping down into their boots again) the boy
suddenly arrived: Lester; didn't look a day over fifteen.

Lester had a delinquent air about him (the base-ball cap, the unfocussed gaze, his skin a bright, purple-white – the approximate tone
of an undercooked chicken thigh bone). But his tracksuit bottoms
(Dory pointed out) were exceptionally dirty, and that had to be a good
sign (they were also three sizes too small. Perhaps he'd 'half-inched'
them, Elen mused, from another – even younger – boy in Harvey's
employ: an exceptionally hard worker who currently dangled, trouser-
less – poor lamb – from a half-swept chimney somewhere).

Lester (it soon became evident) 'lacked direction'. It was a full-time
job just to keep him working. And there was always some good reason
why he might suddenly feel the urge to slip away again: a missing tool,
a parole appointment, breakfast – eaten on the stroke of ten – lunch –
at twelve – and tea – at three – none of which did he ever opt to bring
along with him, but mooched off, mid-task, in a bid to track them down.

There were no fast-food emporiums in the local vicinity – 'This is
suburbia,' Elen patiently explained, 'and a very new area . . .' There
was only Tesco's at the – *ahem* – 'Community Centre', where Lester
was now a permanent fixture at the delicatessen counter. He'd developed a strong antipathy for 'the vicious old witch' working there, who
made him take a ticket – and wait to be called – even when it was
obvious that he was her only customer.

Very little seemed to stimulate the boy. He was so guarded – so sullen
and withdrawn – that Elen (as a mother) felt the kindly urge to 'draw
him out'. This was a mistake (she soon discovered), because there was
one topic – and one topic only – which Lester seemed to take an active
delight in: the multitudinous shortcomings of his unscrupulous employer.

'Don't matter how shit I am,' he grumbled, 'he don't even care. He never tells me nothin', and if he does, I never fuckin' listen. I mean would you? For three quid fifty a fuckin' hour?'

This unhappy information placed an already desperate Elen in an impossible situation: how on earth to confront Harvey over his financial (social *and* legal) transgressions without totally alienating him?

'I mean if this is Harvey functioning at his best,' she told a disconsolate Dory, 'then could you even *begin* to imagine how terrible a "go-slow" policy might be?'

Dory confided in Beede on the matter, and Beede (using his legendary 'business head') came up with the perfect compromise. The simple answer, he told him, was to side-step Harvey altogether. It was good advice and Dory took it, promptly promising Lester an extra £40 a week, tax-free, so long as he swore never to mention this delicate accommodation to his employer. Lester agreed – grudgingly.

Harvey had actually given Dory a 'special' number by which to make contact ('Priority line, mate. This is the line my wife and kids have . . .'). Sometimes, as he rang it and waited for the familiar recorded message to kick in (if his wife had this number, then she must've been well accustomed to falling back on her own resources), Isidore would idly muse as to which of the several phones suspended on Harvey's 'buddy' (if any) he was currently engaging with.

He didn't – at this stage – know that Harvey was running three separate businesses (that information came later, from Harvey himself, who saw no impropriety in it – would often, in fact, use it as an excuse: 'I'm runnin' *three* businesses here, mate, so maybe you could cut me a bit of fuckin' slack . . . ?!').

And he certainly didn't know (how could he?) that each business represented a different 'side' to Harvey (in much the same way that different outfits and accessories represented a different 'side' to Barbie).

Yet ignorant as he was, Isidore soon became convinced that there was some kind of *system* with the phones, that the phones were critical, that each one symbolised something different, yet fundamental –

But what?
And why?

'Don't you think you might be reading a little too *much* into all of this, Dory?' Elen had asked, gently, when he'd finally confided his phone fears in her. Maybe he *was* paranoid –

Maybe I am

– but he still felt like he could smell the unwelcome scent of I-Told-You-So oozing out from behind her sympathetic veneer –

So many secrets –
Where's the harm in just one more, eh?

   Isidore was now officially in New Build Hell.
He'd dreamed of a clean slate, a new dawn. But he'd been wrong to dream –

Bloody foolish
– naive, even.
   Sometimes he'd find himself staring at the carpets, the walls, and he'd see *history*. Right there. Starting up, unfolding, developing (*Bad* history, worse still . . .). And then, when he looked even closer, he'd distinguish yet another strand, another layer, underneath the 'new' facade. Embedded in the molecules. In the fabric of the building. In the . . . the *stuff*. Growing like a fungi. Spreading. *Encroaching*.
   When his mind took this kind of turn, he'd throw on some shorts, a vest, some trainers and he'd run –

Away
Just away

– anything up to 12 miles. At full pelt. Until his arms and legs grew numb.

Isidore could sometimes fall prey to attacks of paranoia, but in relation to Harvey his misgivings were justified (in fact they were absolutely spot on). Harvey *was* out to get him, and Elen knew it, but she had been skilfully manipulated by the builder into a compromising trade-off. She'd been side-lined. Her loyalties had been called upon, placed under duress, *compacted*, and then twisted.

Harvey had not – as yet – gone to work on their home, but he'd taken the time – and the effort – to go to work on *her*.

Three weeks after the scaffolding first went up (still no tarpaulin, and it'd rained every day since, bar one) Harvey had arrived on the doorstep mid-morning.

'You see before you,' he'd proclaimed dramatically (yanking off his puffer jacket and fastidiously shaking the rain from its delicate fabric: straight on to Elen's hallway carpet), 'a Man In Crisis.'

'*Ditto*,' Elen rejoined, holding up a brimming bucket (water was currently streaming down three of their upstairs walls. She'd emptied out a succession of bowls and pans on two previous occasions already that morning). Harvey stared at her, blankly. She bit her tongue.

'So what's the problem?' she'd asked, stepping aside to let him past –

Bright smile
BRIGHT smile

Harvey made his own way into the kitchen, pulled out a chair and sat down. As he answered her question he focussed, pointedly, on the kettle. Elen promptly walked over to it.

'Numero Uno: the Toyota's ignition is playin' me up . . .'

Elen grabbed the kettle and yanked off its lid. 'So how did you get here today, then?'

'The work van.'

'Ah.'

'I won't drive the Toyota in this kind of weather.'

'Right.'

Elen turned on the tap and filled the kettle.

'Ruins the paintwork.'

'I see.'

She turned the tap off again.

'Numero Two-o,' Harvey continued, 'my youngest girl is refusin' to come to Florida this year, and my wife's having a crack-up. Gerry is seventeen. Linda just don't wanna leave her . . .'

'So you're going away?' Elen spoke with some care as she pushed the kettle's plug into the socket. 'On holiday?'

'Yup. We always go mid-Feb. Winter sun an' all that . . .'

'Oh. Well that's very . . . *uh* . . .'

She couldn't think of the right word, initially ('soon' was her first thought). '. . . Inconsiderate,' she said, eventually.

Harvey glanced up, sharply.

'I mean of *her*.'

Harvey stopped scowling. 'Yeah. Well that's kids for ya.' He shrugged, resignedly. 'Only *then*, see, when I've *finally* convinced Linda that it's all good – that Gerry can stay with my sister for the three weeks . . .'

Three weeks?!

Elen's eyes widened.

'. . . She then decides that my sister's kid should come along instead. But Kelly – the silly cow – just went and broke her bloody leg. Plaster has to come off in the second week. So muggins here is expected to sort it all out, *and* pay for the privilege of gettin' it done private in the US.'

Elen did her best to look sympathetic as she grabbed a mug from the cupboard.

'I mean she's in *plaster*, Helen,' Harvey fretted. 'It's not like I've got nothin' *against* the kid, but it'll be boilin', fuckin' *hot* out there. She won't be able to get around without her crutches, go on any of the rides, take a dip . . .' he paused, squinting slightly over Elen's shoulder. 'That cupboard door's not set right . . .'

He sprang to his feet, whipping a screw-driver from his buddy. 'Shift over.'

In thirty seconds the door had been removed and then quickly realigned. He stood back, appraised his work, then winced, tutted, and got stuck into the next one along.

Elen watched, agog, as all sixteen doors were neatly and expertly re-hung.

When he'd completed this marathon (not, coincidentally, a job which featured in any shape or form on his lengthy 'to-do' list – or even on Elen's blackboard, for that matter) Harvey sat back down at the table, genially reappraised his work, took a rejuvenating swig of his tea, and swallowed, noisily.

'So it's cards on the table time,' he announced, experimenting by placing his weight first on one elbow, then the other. The table shifted. He frowned and peered underneath the table-top. 'Why's this thing wobblin'?'

He grabbed some pliers from his belt and tightened a bolt on one of the legs, then re-emerged, slightly puffed. He tapped the table again. It didn't wobble this time. He grunted his satisfaction.
'Thank you,' Elen murmured.

'The bottom line is this . . .' he said, acknowledging her gratitude with a curt nod, 'crazy as it may sound, I've taken quite a *shine* to you . . .' he picked up his tea and gulped down a second, large mouthful. 'You strike me as a good sort, somehow, even if your tea *is* bloody dreadful.'

Elen sprang to her feet. 'Has it gone cold? Would you like another?' Harvey didn't deign to respond, just continued to talk as she darted around the kitchen.

'An' that's why I'm going to tell you somethin' . . .'
He leaned forward, picked up a packet of biscuits (which Elen had yet to open – dark chocolate Bahlsens) and gave them a suspicious rattle. 'These kosher or what?'
'Uh . . .' Elen turned. 'Yes. I mean I don't know. They're German.'

Harvey threw the biscuits down again, grimacing. 'The plain truth is that I'm actually what you might call "a bit of a rebel" at heart. A "loose cannon", so to speak. Linda says I'm a "free spirit", which sounds a bit twatty, actually . . .'
He sniffed.

Elen opened the biscuit packet, slid four on to a plate and placed them down in front of him.
'Either way, the bottom line is this: I don't respond well to pressure. It's not that I can't, as such, but that I won't. It's a matter of principle, see? I simply ain't bothered. If someone keeps bangin' on at me to do somethin' – naggin' at me, pesterin' – then I just turn an' I walk – without a second thought – in the opposite direction. Because buildin' ain't simply a *job* for me, Helen, it's a passion, and I won't let anything or any*one* get in the way of that.'

Elen tried to respond appropriately to this curious declaration. 'Well

I suppose *most* people – when they're placed under a certain amount of . . . of *duress* . . .'

'Oh no.' Harvey was emphatic. 'I am not "most people", Helen, trust me. I am fucking *obstinate*. I make an art form out of it. I dig in my heels like a bloody *donkey*. Linda says they broke the soddin' *mould* when they made me . . .'

He stood up. 'I have four phones, see?'
Harvey indicated towards the three of his four phones which were currently visible, hanging on his buddy. Elen nodded.

'An' at the moment, your other half is on the blue phone. On the *Nokia*.'
Harvey tapped the Nokia with a warning thumb. Elen stared at the Nokia. Suddenly the Nokia had a somewhat ominous aspect. She gazed up at him, anxiously. 'So is that . . . is that *bad*, then?'
'No. Not *bad* exactly . . .' Harvey pulled an expression of infinite sadness. 'Just . . .'
He sighed.

'Right,' Elen pushed back her hair, impatiently. 'Oh dear . . .'
She glanced down and noticed that she hadn't yet removed the bag from his tea. She looked around for a teaspoon.

'Now the Siemens S55 . . .' Harvey continued, 'well, she's an absolute *corker* . . .'
'Really?'
Elen stopped searching. She simply removed the bag with her fingers –

Ouch!
Hot!

– and tossed it on to the counter-top.

'Oh yes. Absolutely. This little lady has 8080 pixels . . .'
Harvey took out his Siemens S55 and showed it to Elen, reverently. Elen stared at the phone, in silence. She noticed how – if she held her breath for a moment – she could hear the repetitive drip of the water as it hit the pans upstairs.

'An' this is my Sony,' Harvey took out his Sony, grinning, 'I *know* what you're thinking,' he chuckled, 'you're thinking, "Things have certainly come on a-way since then, Harve," and you'd be right. But that's me all over – a great, big softy . . .'

He was beaming at the phone. 'She's an old girl, but she's a goldie . . .'

Then he abruptly stopped smiling and slipped it away again.

'An' last, but by no means least . . .'

Harvey put a devoted hand to his heart (also, coincidentally, the location of his neatly buttoned shirt pocket) '. . . is the Motorola C350 . . .'

He removed it and inspected it, almost tearfully. 'But only my mistress and my lawyer have the digits for *this* baby . . .'

Elen gently placed Harvey's mug down on to the table. She grabbed the milk bottle, her serious brown eyes not shifting – even an inch – from his face.

'But then *you're* on the Nokia,' Harvey sighed, carefully slipping the Motorola away again, 'and I ain't saying – God forbid – that it isn't a *good* phone . . .'

Elen poured the milk. 'But it's not . . .' she interjected, helpfully, 'it's not the *best* phone?'

Harvey smiled and grabbed a hold of the mug's handle. '*Good girl*. I think we're finally gettin' somewhere . . .'

He sat down and toasted her with his tea, still smiling. Then his smile faltered for a second. 'Unfortunately, though, your *hubby* . . .' He rolled his eyes.

Elen frowned, panicked. 'Has . . . has Dory . . . ?'

'Upset me? *Nah*.'

Harvey shook his head, gazing down into his steaming mug with a look of profound anguish.

'Well that's . . .' She was confused. She bit her lip.

'Let's just say,' Harvey volunteered, 'that your husband was . . . *uh* . . . a little "inappropriate" with me when I first came around.'

Elen's neat nostrils flared slightly. This was three weeks ago. A whole *life*-time of dripping and misery and scaffolding. An agonising infinity of Fleet on the sofa-bed and Lester at the delicatessen counter. She pulled out a chair. Whatever else happened, this simply *had* to be made better.

'I mean I ain't gonna sit here at *his* table, drink *his* tea, speak with *his* lovely wife, eat *his* funny-lookin' German biscuits . . .' Harvey reached out for a biscuit '. . . an' rip into the man. But the fact is that he made it very clear – during our initial meeting – that I wasn't his first choice for the job. He effectively *told* me – to my *face*, Helen – that I was second best. And nobody – no *body* – who takes pride in what they do, enjoys hearin' that.'

'But are you sure?'

Elen was appalled.

'He made no bones about it, my love.'

She was silent for a moment.

'*Damn*,' she eventually murmured.

'I mean,' Harvey bit into the biscuit, 'I'm perfectly willing to believe that *I* might've contributed to the problem in some way – without actually realisin'. Because I'm a sensitive man, Helen, an *emotional* man. I feel things very deeply . . .'

He sighed (as if greatly moved by the thought of his own impetuosity). 'Perhaps I didn't get him *down* quite right, perhaps it's a *German* thing . . .'

Elen lunged for this straw. 'Dory *can* seem a little abrupt sometimes . . .'

Harvey acknowledged this declaration with a slight (almost indifferent) shrug of his shoulder.

'. . . a little . . . a little *abrasive*, even . . .'

She stalled, then drew a deep breath. '. . . But Abacus were definitely our first choice. Dory was dead-set on it. In fact he had to convice *me*. He thought you were an amazing find. He even said that. He said, "Harvey's an amazing find." He really did.'

'Bull*shit*.'

Harvey was implacable. 'Dory wanted Garry Spivey. He *wanted* A Priori.'

A Priori?

Elen blinked.

'No. *No*, I don't remember that at all . . .'

'First in the book, he said.'

Elen blinked again –

Which book?

Harvey's voice suddenly grew strident. 'I mean to actually *say* that, Helen – to *me* of all people. *First* in the bloody book!'

'A Priori?' Elen frowned, trying desperately to catch up. 'First? Are you sure?'

'Sure? Am I sure?' Harvey inadvertently spat out his mouthful of biscuit across the table-top. 'Of course I'm bloody sure! Of course I am! Garry Spivey is a cancer, Helen! He's a disgrace, a shit-heel, a bird-turd. I mean you don't know the half of it. You couldn't. The man is pure vermin. He has single-handedly dragged the East Kent building industry through the bloody sewers. He's a thorn in our side, Helen. A blight, a pest. He's a total fuckin' liability . . .'

During the second half of Harvey's impassioned declaration, Lester drifted past the open doorway. He was holding a small dog under his right arm – a dopey-looking spaniel. Elen had absolutely no idea where it had come from or what he was doing with it. Lester paused for a moment at the sound of Harvey's raised voice, half-smiling (seeming to effortlessly gauge the complex, emotional scene as it unfolded before him), then he shook his head, pityingly, and wandered off.

'The thing is, what your husband doesn't know,' Harvey was speaking again, and with great intensity (having taken a few quiet seconds to gather himself together), 'is that Garry Spivey and me go way back. We have what you might call "history". I had AAA in the yellow pages for twelve years. He was Alisdair Spivey and Sons. Worked with his dad – also, coincidentally, a tragic, fuckin' arse-wipe – an' everythin' was hunky-dory. But then, when his dad finally passes – lung cancer, may he rest in peace – he gets all up himself. He changes the company name. An' he bribes the twat who compiles the local Pages to give him first dibs. A Priori. Two words. Just out of spite. Sheer spite. And that's exactly the kind of grubby, petty, stupid little twat . . .'

Elen pulled out a chair and sat down.

'Maybe I'm being a little slow here,' she murmured, 'but AAA would come before A Priori, surely?'

Harvey sprang up (as if perched on the other end of a time-delayed see-saw). 'That's what I say. That's my whole point, Helen. Of course it bloody does!'

'So it's just . . .' Elen gradually worked it all out, 'it's just . . . just wrong, then?'

'It is wrong,' Harvey bellowed, 'it's bloody wrong!'

'Well . . .' Elen frowned, trying desperately to keep a lid on things, 'have you perhaps spoken to them about it?'

Harvey took a step back, blinking rapidly, as if in total astonishment at the naivety of this question. 'Have I . . . ? Have I *spoken*? Who the hell do you think I *am*?! I'm Harvey fuckin' *Broad*, woman! I have two bloody *restrainin' orders* out on me!'

'Oh . . .'

Elen tried not to appear even remotely alarmed by this information . . . 'I see.'

'I mean this is my *livelihood*, Helen. It's my life. My reputation. My *passion*.'

He gazed at her, panting slightly. Elen carefully knitted her hands together. 'So . . . so what *they're* saying, effectively, is that a single "a" comes before everything else?'

Harvey nodded. 'But the killer punch is the Latin. The *Latin's* the key. Latin always comes *first*, they say.'

'It does?'

Elen frowned.

Harvey sat down again. 'In the *Oxford English*, yes, okay, I can *accept* that. In the *old* version. Fair enough. But these are modern times, Helen. In the *Collins* I got at home they don't even *mention* any of that Latin stuff. In the *Collins*, AAA gets its own *listin'*: Amateur Athletics Association. It comes straight after AA: Alcoholics Anonymous. An' this ain't just no piece of old shite. This is the *Collins Modern Dictionary of the English Language*.'

Elen nodded. 'I do believe it's a very . . . a very *respectable* dictionary.'

Harvey suddenly leaned across the table, conspiratorially. 'I mean *you're* a doctor, aren't you?'

She flinched, somewhat taken aback by his unexpected change of tack. 'Well, uh . . . *no*, not . . .'

'But you're *familiar* with all that Latin shit?'

Elen paused. 'Well, *yes*. I know a little. But I'm just a podiatrist, Harvey. I'm a *foot* doctor. It isn't quite . . .'

'*Exactly!*' Harvey slapped his large, clean palm down hard on to the table-top. 'Podiatrist! That's Latin, right there!'

Elen tried to dissuade him. 'It's actually Ancient Greek. Podiatry is an American term. In Britain we tend to call ourselves chiropodists, but strictly speaking, *Cheir* means hand and *Pod* means . . .'

Harvey flapped a dismissive paw at her. 'Greeks, Latins, same fuckin' *difference*, mate. The point is this: it don't matter what kind of a doctor you are. You're a *doctor*. You're educated. You're *professional* . . .'

Elen flinched slightly.

'I mean don't get me wrong,' Harvey continued, 'we Broads have been in the buildin' trade for *years* – generations. We've been knockin' things up an' pullin' 'em down again for so long that it's *like* a profession to us. Point of fact, my great-great . . .' he flapped his hand impatiently, '*etcetera* grandad once wrote a very famous *book* about the most healthy way to build a house. This same man was a surgeon, too. A physician, and to *royalty*, no less. Also wrote what they call a "pamphlet" about astrology . . .'

'That's amazing,' Elen said.

'Yeah,' Harvey agreed.

'So we ain't *stupid* by any means. But when it comes to this whole A Priori issue I'm what you might call an "interested party". Nobody'll take me seriously. But *you* . . .'

Harvey appraised her, tenderly. 'You're just a member of the public. A professional female. An intellectual. So if you just happened to write them a letter . . . I dunno, sayin', for example, how you're educated and speak Ancient Greek, and when you went to the phone book you was *disappointed* . . . no, *no* . . . *shocked* to see A Priori in the wrong place . . .'

Elen allowed this all to sink in for a second. As it sank, Harvey continued to gaze at her, determinedly.

'Just a short letter,' he re-emphasised, 'stating how you're a doctor.' Elen carefully cleared her throat. 'So you really . . . you actually *want* me to do that?'

Harvey leaned back, sniffed, inspected his nails. 'Well it's up to you, obviously . . .'

He glanced down at his buddy, at his neat line of phones, then up again, pointedly.

Elen blinked. 'You actually want me to do that *now*?'

Harvey shrugged, as if he couldn't care less.

Elen slowly stood up and began looking around her – numbly – for a piece of paper. When she'd finally located a scrap, Harvey kindly loaned her his pen. It was a Parker.

ISIDORE

Isidore was not German. He was English. But being German seemed to work for him, so he stuck with it, he cultivated it. In fact he'd honed it to such a pitch now that he rarely even thought about it. It just fitted him, somehow, was comfortable, like a well-cut jacket (the maker's mark – the discreet tag – neatly located on the inside flap, but then gently scratched out –

A thumb-nail?
A flattened blade?

– until the embroidery had snagged and become unreadable).

Both of his parents had been teachers. His father, Laurie (second-generation London Irish – a lapsed Catholic, whose ancestors hailed from County Waterford, originally), was a huge, flame-haired, pale-skinned man – sandblasted in freckles – who specialised in the sciences. His mother, Clare (darker, much smaller; her grandparents, on her mother's side, exiled Jews, from Czechoslovakia), specialised in languages (Ancient Greek, Latin, French and German). They were enthusiastic travellers, and had toured extensively – throughout Europe, the Far East and Australia – during the early years of their marriage.

Laurie had suffered – man and boy – from both asthma and eczema, and had gradually evolved – through trial and error – into a keen proponent of alternative methods of healthcare. His favourite quote was by Father Sebastian Kneipp, founder of The Wellness Movement, who said, 'Those who do not find some time every day for health must sacrifice a lot of time one day for illness.'

He quoted it often, but always – like Pfarrer Kneipp himself – in a gently accented Bavarian-German (it was just too bad if the person he was quoting at was unfamiliar with this particular idiom).

Teaching could not hold them. In 1976, when Isidore was still quite young, they'd emigrated to Germany, intent upon establishing a Wellness School, or 'Kurhaus' – aimed principally at attracting English holiday-makers during the summer season; an evangelical establish-ment, brimming with health, good sense and cheerful discipline.

They spent two years in 'Kneipptown' (Bad Worishofen), learning the business of Wellness in all its configurations, then toured for a further six months, finally electing upon Bad Munstereifel – in the Northern Rhine Westphalia region – as the place to settle. It had much to recommend it: was a picturesque medieval spa-town (already steeped in the Wellness Tradition), full of neat, timber-framed houses, surrounded by an infinity of rolling, densely forested hills, clear streams and small mountains.

For 'Wellness', location was everything. The Kneipp Kur System was established upon The Five Pillars of Kneipp. These were Hydro (water therapy), Phyto (plant therapy), Kinesi (exercise), Dietetic (less meat, more cereal) and Regulative (early to bed, early to rise).

They bought – and renovated – an oldish (but not ancient) timber mill on the outskirts of town. It was big, but never – to Laurie's mind – big enough (which structure *could* be? His ambitions knew no bounds).

Only a small portion of the whole was to be their home. The rest, a labyrinth of tiny 'cells' (bed, sink, cupboard) and treatment rooms (pine-panelled, stone-floored, white-tiled).

The entire structure was circumscribed by an endless proliferation of copper piping, which fed into a seeming infinity of deep, ceramic baths, huge showers and wide basins (with gulping-hungry plugholes and giant, brass shower-heads, which hung from the ceilings – bent and top-heavy – like sinister, metal sunflowers).

And then, but of course: the Refectory (the busy clatter of cutlery at those endless lines of rough-hewn wooden tables, punctuated, every so often, by the odd, shrill squeal of the ecclesiastical-style benches as some foolish hot-head tried to stand up too suddenly), the awe-filled *hush* of the Consultation Room, the efficient, aromatic *clink* of the Dispensary (with its beautiful, white marble pestle and mortar, its tiny spoons and its delicate tweezers, its old-fashioned, brass scales – which were polished, every week, without fail, by a dutiful Isidore – and the shelves, and shelves, and *shelves* of fasci-nating, antique, green-tinted glass bottles, crammed with herbs and salts and tinctures and unguents).

All this space, and yet Isidore had no room of his own. Retreat – at home – was never really an option. His father was everywhere, inhabiting every corner. Isidore was only master of a small, cramped 'cubby', a slightly raised niche (or recess), moulded into the thick, old, stone wall of their living-room (by all accounts – his mother would opine proudly – an 'original feature'), where he'd carefully wedge himself – like a coin in a slot machine – to sleep each evening.

'Your playroom,' his father would tell him, chin up, gesticulating grandly, 'is the pine forest, the sweet meadow and the running stream. The whole *world* is your kingdom, Isidore. Was ever a child as blessed as you are?'

He knew that he was lucky.

Yet even in the midst of this apparent idyll – this lush, green Utopia – a shadow seemed to hang over the boy. Nothing too dramatic (at least, not to begin with); a slight veil – a *film*, almost – like an eye with a speck of grease in it, which blinks, then blinks again, and the grease spreads, and it thins, and the obfuscation is so slight, so minor, that it barely even impinges on the consciousness of the sufferer.

Its origins were – at least in part – linguistic. From the moment they'd arrived in Germany, Isidore was only ever permitted to communicate in German. Laurie's commitment to their new culture was absolute, and he needed his son's to be. If Dory dared to speak in English then he was not only ignored, but chastised (nothing too severe – a sharp word, a quick slap to the back of the knee – but these punishments seemed terrible to such a mild and timid boy).

As luck would have it, Dory picked up his new tongue rapidly; even growing (over time) to admire its merciless precision, its bite and cut, its fearless accuracy. But the transition hadn't been seamless (few transitions ever are). There'd been trauma suffered – at some level, however slight – and a tiny lesion had formed – a cut, a snag, a *tear* – between Dory's fragile sense of 'past' and his avowed – his *dedicated* – future.

This lesion didn't heal. It stubbornly persisted. And with time – and wear – it gradually abraded.

Words were at the heart of it; as if Dory's entire character was not only 'articulated' by Anglo-Saxon (in some obscure way – ie the rhythm of the diction, the complexity of the grammar, the elegance of the styling) so much as totally defined by it.

He'd sometimes complain of feeling 'a kind of niggling' deep inside of him – like a hunger, almost a *pining* – as if the old tongue still existed somewhere, still chattered away, uninhibitedly, like an underground stream, tirelessly searching for a fault at the surface – a crack, a furrow, a weakness – *anything* – to allow it to flood through and overwhelm him.

He was rightly fearful of this babbling (it groaned and chuckled, in stops and starts, like the cranky Kurhaus plumbing), and yet in some strange way, this subterranean conflict also served to buffer him. It was a secret – a flow; a Dionysian *current* – which couldn't be dammed, either by his own dogged conformity or his father's proselytising.

He had no proper name for it, but even if he had, he wouldn't've dared speak it. And there was actually no need (when all was finally said and done), because it spoke *itself*, constantly, creeping up on him – when he least expected it (while he was eating, sitting innocently in class, or out in the hills, walking) and blowing a sudden, icy blast of cold air on to the back of his neck; making him start and gasp, making the delicate hairs there stand stiff and erect.

Sometimes it would nudge him, furtively, whispering confidingly (grown-up things, secret things, things he couldn't – or didn't want to – understand). And sometimes it would just *pester* him, persistently – like a bad boy in class – elbowing him, nudging him, sideswiping and jostling him.

But it thrived – most of all – on ornate ambushes; lying low for hours – days, even – until he'd almost forgotten about it, then jabbing him, savagely, between the ribs, or shoving him, violently, from the back; sending him hurtling – hands out, eyes starting – *terrifying* him; making him roll up tight, into a ball, his arms over his head, his chin on his chest, his knees drawn in (like a spent fighter, receiving a kicking) until it finally emerged – powerful, victorious – from between his own lips, in the form of something which sounded suspiciously like . . .

But what?

A curse?

No . . .

A bellow?

No . . .

A cackle?

Well . . .

A laugh . . . ?

Uh . . .

Sometimes more of a . . . a *roar*, and sometimes just a titter. Sometimes a yuk-yuk-*yuk* or a hoarse guffaw or a tee-hee-*hee*, or a single, sharp *Ha!* (It was nothing if not variable).

Dory never really saw the joke, somehow.

In fact he'd swallow it back if he could – *bite* it back. The effort this took (the sheer force of will) made his eyes stream and his lips turn purple. It stropped his throat. It made him *burp*.

His deeply bemused father began prescribing chalk.

'Mein Gott. But how unbelievably *tedious* . . .' – the ten-year-old Isidore sometimes thought – 'to be the stranger everywhere . . .': at school, where the other boys still mocked his accent and the girls found him 'cute' (because he was small for his age) and treated him like a plaything. Then at home, where there were always visitors, cheerfully – confidently – appropriating the vista (in that *immediate* way, that *English* way), the children especially, who arrived, choc-full of vicious territorial bravura.

And as much as he might yearn to, he could not –

Just can't

– bring himself to speak with them ('Not in *German*. Like a stranger? *Never!* But not in English, either. What if *Father* should hear?'), and so they quickly grew tired of him. They called him 'dumb' and 'stupid'; 'weird', even. Sometimes they'd gang up on him (pelt him with pine cones in the forest, dunk him in the river), or – more often – they'd simply ignore him (like he was invisible, as if his 'difference', his 'foreignness', rendered him so).

But oh! How he admired their different clothes! The tunes they hummed! Their casual mobility! Their fantastic tv! Sometimes he'd hear them performing skits, or repeating catch-phrases to each other, and he'd stop, and listen, and just *drink* it all in. Devouring, not exactly the 'meaning' (it was incomprehensible – 'My parrot is sick . . .' meant nothing to him) but the rhythm. And that wonderful sense of blithe containedness at the heart of all humour (bizarre but self-perpetuating, like an Escher painting).

How complete they all were! How unified, how *whole*! How desperately – how violently, how *pathetically* – he envied them!

Rebellion was never really an option. Isidore loved his parents and he believed in their philosophies (why shouldn't he? They were all living, breathing proof of Kneipp's peerless efficacy).

At dawn he would rise with his father and they would walk together, barefoot, in the dew-heavy grass. Summer or winter, it didn't matter. It was a magical ritual, a 'fundamental'.

They would talk about everything. His father would discuss the process of photosynthesis or the life-cycle of the stag beetle, he would curse the folly of the British Trade Union Movement ('Thank God we are here, away from this indiscipline'), or question the motivation of Germany's Green Party. He believed in biology, but not in Ecology. Politics, he held righteously, was how you held yourself, what you ate and how you lived. It was a series of apparently mundane decisions. It was 'everyday', 'personal', radiated 'from within'. The other stuff? He'd snort, contemptuously: 'Isidore, my boy, just *showing off*.'

Clare (she quickly modified her name to Clara) would quote whole pages, verbatim, from Homer's *Odyssey* as she bustled, busily, around the Kurhaus kitchen. Isidore journeyed with her – sat quietly on a stool at the counter – weeping real tears for the unfortunate Odysseus (being hounded himself by vengeful Poseidon, appealing for help from the fleet-footed Athene, battling fearlessly with the Cyclops . . .

Take that, you . . .
Uh?
WAAAH!).

He believed in God. He believed in Cruel Destiny . . .

But where was *his* Ithaca? Where was the home from which he'd strayed, and for which he yearned – more than anything –

Anything

– to finally return?
Was it here? There? *Everywhere?*

It was definitely a puzzle.
And the answer to this riddle?
Closer, much closer, than he could ever have imagined . . .
Under his nose. In his mouth. On the *tip* of his tongue.

Three things:
1. The letter.
2. The skinny boy (Lester) and the disabled dog.
3. The paternity swab.

He'd been emptying a wastepaper basket into the dustbin when he came across an early draft.
It was written in Elen's neat hand –
Dear Mr Wrotham,

–it said –

I am writing, as a professional (*this was later crossed out*) as a doctor* and speaker of Latin* (**this had been clumsily inserted, in a different, scruffy, ill-formed script*) to draw your attention to the fact that there is a 'slight' (*replaced as*) 'serious' problem with the format of your current edition of the Ashford Region Phone Book . . .
That was it.

Underneath, in note form, and in that unfamiliar hand again

(presumably as a gentle reminder for the letter's second version, which must've been more successful than the first, because there was no sign of it in the bin – he'd checked) was written:

(1) A Priori – Garry Spivey (*the double 'r' in Garry had been force-fully underlined*).
(2) Say about the back-handers.
(3) Say your respectable.
(4) Mention AAABuilders Ltd but not that Im on a job 4 u.
(5) NB!!!****Quote the Collins Dictionary!!!

Eh?

Dory frowned and turned it over (as if an explanation might be neatly written on the back – ie: *Hello. This is Elen. It's the start of my menstrual cycle and I have gone temporarily insane.*
But no. Nothing).

He sat down and thought about the letter for a while. He simply couldn't make sense of it. Why would Elen be writing a letter to the phone book people? And about its *format* of all things?

It just . . .
She just . . .
She wouldn't.
No.

Then *who* . . . ? Who had prompted her to do so? And whose notes were those (on the bottom of the page)?

Harvey's?

Elen had made absolutely no mention to him –

None

– of a conversation with Harvey.

In fact Elen *hated* Harvey (insofar as Elen could possibly hate anybody) –

Didn't she?

I mean she *slandered* Harvey at every given opportunity . . .

Or have I got this all . . . ?
Am I . . . ?

Lester.

Lester!

Maybe it was for him? Maybe this was something for Lester's benefit? Maybe it was some kind of . . . of *reference* for the boy . . .

No.
It's a letter about the format of the phone book, that's what.
Oh God –
But it doesn't make any . . .

Dory suddenly crumpled the page up, in his hand. 'Damn her,' he murmured softly, his eyes filling with tears.
'*Damn* her.'

Sometimes he would see things – strange things; like a tiny, winged devil (for example), its claws caught up in the fabric of the bedroom curtains, or an exotic bird, cowering under an overturned teacup on the kitchen draining-board – and he would blink, and he would warn himself that he was asleep (that this was a brief, waking dream of some kind).
It happened fairly regularly. He was thoroughly accustomed to it. It was simply what he liked to call 'a trick of the mind'.
And so it was with the little dog. He'd been strolling out of the downstairs lavatory (still fairly preoccupied by some troubling issue at work) and he could've *sworn* that he'd seen a small dog trundling by

on a cart (heading out of the hallway and into the living-room, at a slow trot).

The dog was not *on* the cart so much as attached *to* it (by its back legs and hips, with two leather straps). The cart – a bright red colour, jaunty, almost gipsy-ish in design – was presumably some kind of replacement for its back limbs which – even from where he stood – seemed ill-formed and limp (possibly crushed – he idly mused – in a terrible accident).

He slowly shook his head. Then he grimaced. Then he turned, climbed upstairs, and forgot all about it.

Several days later he accidentally happened across Lester, in the kitchen, casually holding something under his arm –

Huh . . . ?

He drew closer. He blinked a few times, just to make sure. It was small. It was brown. It was definitely –

Definitely

– animate. And it bore –

No getting around it

– quite a *striking* resemblance to the creature he'd seen previously in his 'waking nightmare'.

Lester was making himself a cup of tea, one-handed. He seemed almost indecently familiar with the lay-out of the kitchen.

'Is that *your* dog, Lester?' Dory had asked, staring nervously at the forlorn, little creature and feeling a strange, tingling sense of *déjà vu*. Lester (balancing the dog on his hip, as though it were a baby or a rolled-up sleeping bag) glanced over at him in apparent astonishment.

'What's that?'

He appeared to be experiencing some difficulty in comprehending Dory's accent.

'The *dog*,' Dory pointed, 'is it yours?'

'*Mine*?'

Lester seemed genuinely shocked by the notion.

He quickly glanced down at the dog; firstly, as if to double-check that it actually *was* a dog, and secondly (once he'd established its fundamental dog-ness – Snout? *Check*. Paws? *Check*), whether it might reasonably be described as being *his*.

'No it ain't,' he eventually muttered (just the *slightest* hint of superciliousness in his voice – '*What?!* As if *I'd* own an animal like *that!*').

Dory had no particular fondness for canines. He'd never developed an affinity for them as a boy – his family hadn't ever owned one. His father had been almost hysterically fearful of animal hair (because of his allergies, although – ironically – he'd always been extremely passionate about horses; worse luck for Dory, whose horror of them bordered on the phobic).

The dog in question seemed very obliging. It wasn't a young animal. It had the dismal air of a creature which had seen better days: an animal which had journeyed – and possibly some distance – beyond its prime. When Dory inhaled, he caught just a suggestion of a whiff from it –

Mouldy wheat –
Wet sand –
Ammonia

He frowned and grimaced. His nostrils twitched.

Lester expertly slung the animal around his neck (the way some kinds of eccentrics liked to carry their cats) to free-up both hands to prepare his tea. It was a long dog (its extended spine better facilitating this unconventional kind of transport), although it certainly wasn't a dachshund (the only type of long dog Dory could actually name, off-hand).

'Then whose is it?' Dory persisted.

'*Huh*?' Lester's hearing seemed temporarily impaired. He was wearing a gangsta-style kerchief around his head (red, with tiny white stars – which might've been the source of his problem) and a pair of cream-coloured dungarees, which flapped a couple of dismal inches above his ankles, like two shabby sails against the skinny mast of his leg.

'Is it Harvey's dog?'

'*Harvey's* dog?'

Lester snorted as he picked up the kettle. 'Harvey don't *own* no dog, man. An' if he does, then *I'm* it. *I'm* Harvey's fuckin' dog.'

Lester tapped a self-righteous middle finger against his chest as he poured.

Dory chose to ignore this particular flight of fancy (Lester currently seemed to have a vested interest in presenting himself publicly as Harvey's tragic victim. His dupe. He'd increasingly started to dress – and speak – like one of the colourful panoply of characters in Alex Haley's *Roots*).

'Well if it isn't *yours,* and if it isn't *Harvey's* . . .'

'It ain't,' Lester reaffirmed.

'. . . then what exactly is it doing here?'

'It *lives* here,' Lester said, shooting Dory a sharp, slightly incredulous look.

'That's ridiculous,' Dory snapped.

Lester merely shrugged (as if long-accustomed to Dory's vagaries), grabbed the biscuit tin out of the cupboard, removed a gingernut and shoved it, whole, into his mouth.

'Well what are *you* doing with it?' Dory asked, infuriated.

Lester slowly chewed, then swallowed.

'I'm *carryin'* it,' he said, as if this truth was so readily apparent that Dory's question hardly warranted a response.

'But *why*?'

Lester's rolled his eyes. 'Because she's *paralysed*, Guv.'

'Good *God*.'

Dory's mind temporarily flashed back to the little, red cart. 'It can't walk?'

Lester's brows rose fractionally, as if to imply that, yes, this was generally what was to be understood in most English-speaking nations by the word.

'So how does it . . . ?'

Dory wordlessly mimed 'movement'.

'She drags herself around by her front legs,' Lester said, 'but it knackers her out. So sometimes she trots along on her little cart.'

'Cart,' Dory repeated.

'*Yes*,' Lester almost shouted, 'cart. *Cart*.'

Dory was temporarily lost for words.

The dog began panting.

'Stress,' Lester mused, gazing down at the dog and then over at Dory, sullenly.

The dog continued to pant. Dory was sure he could smell its ailing breath.

'You thirsty, Honey?' Lester gently murmured, carrying the animal over to a blue, ceramic water bowl (DOG inscribed – in bold letters – along its outside) and carefully placing her down next to it.

Dory had never seen this water bowl before. He had also never seen the food bowl (of a similar design) sitting by its side. The food bowl contained a modest handful of dried, brown pellets.

While he looked on, incredulously, Lester casually opened a cupboard (next to the sink), removed a bag of dog food and topped up the bowl.

'So let me get this straight,' Dory finally murmured, 'I have a disabled dog living in my home which I am both watering and feeding. It travels around on a small cart, and apparently it belongs to no one.'

Lester said nothing. The dog was staring up at him, poignantly. She was still panting. She had not drunk.

'I don't even know . . .'

Dory was staring at the dog now, quite overwhelmed by fastidiousness. 'I don't even *understand* how a creature like this might go about . . . I mean *how* does he . . .' Dory paused, delicately '. . . without . . . ?'

'*She*,' Lester interjected, cunningly side-stepping Dory's indelicate question about faecal hygiene with a bold statement of sexual orientation.

'Pardon?'

'Michelle.'

'*Michelle?*' Dory frowned.

Michelle?!

'It's on the *tag*, stupid.'

'It has a *tag*?' Dory stood to attention. 'Where? Around its neck?' He marched over to the dog, squatted down next to her and grabbed her collar. The dog did not shy away from him. She stared up at him – passive and unblinking – with her two indecently round, fudge-brown eyes –

King Charles . . .
Uh . . .

Dory carefully manipulated the collar until its silver tag was visible. On one side (scratched scruffily into the metal, apparently by hand) was the name MICHELLE. On the other side . . .

Dory blinked.
His own address –

But how?!

Lester crammed another biscuit into his mouth, carefully picked up his teacup, and then reached down and grabbed the dog.

'You're a real *caution*, mate . . .' he informed Dory, gamely, through his mouthful. Then he winked, as if in plain acknowledgement of some kind of subterranean covenant between them –

An 'understanding'?

Dory stared back at him, blankly . . .

What 'understanding'?

Did Lester honestly think he'd been taking the rise out of him? Or was it . . .

Uh . . .
The other way around?

Dory couldn't be certain –

DAMN THIS UNCERTAINTY!

On his way out, Lester idly tipped his head towards the kitchen table. 'An' she shits in a *box*,' he chuckled, coarsely, 'as if you didn't already *know* that . . .'
Dory – still squatting – glanced blankly ahead of him –

Yup

– sure enough: there, under the table, just along from the small, wicker basket with its comfortable, fleecy lining: a neat, plastic litter tray. And just along from *that*?

Oh dear God . . .
Surely not?!

A disturbingly large plastic carton of Wet Wipes.
For clearing up.

Over time, and with his father's guidance, he'd learned to control the worst of his behavioural excesses. But it'd taken a staggering amount of resolve, and a monumental effort of will. He'd had to be careful, heedful: *unstintingly* mindful. He could never relax. He could never 'let go'.

He'd had to watch himself, constantly – like a doctor, standing jealous guard over a favoured patient – to try and predict – with any kind of accuracy – how certain things (certain 'urges', certain 'impulses' – the 'tics', the 'jerks', the 'spasms') might ultimately 'play out'.

If he anticipated a problem (as he did, quite often), then he needed to do so well in advance ('Forewarned,' as his father was so fond of saying, 'is forearmed').

Cold water helped. Being entirely immersed. The release – the *shock*. And feverfew (the herb) –

Its taste!
So bitter!

Plenty of exercise (10-mile jogs, daily, as standard) and a very, *very* low protein diet.

And then, of course, there was The Witness.
Laurie had come across this concept in a German self-help book. 'The Witness' was the calm voice within, the authoritative voice, the dispassionate voice. It was not controlling. It did not demand or judge or dictate.

You found it when you closed your eyes (and emptied your mind, and looked around). It was strong and quiet and ever-watchful. The Witness stood proudly apart from the ego-driven side of the consciousness. It was the Civil Servant of the head. It did a little filing, made reports, took dictation. It was consistent and impassive and utterly reliable.

Laurie counselled his son to 'make a friend' of The Witness. To 'refer' to The Witness whenever things felt like they might be in danger of getting out of hand. He also taught him some rudimentary self-hypnosis techniques (involving touching certain body parts – the ear-lobe, the shoulder – and tapping them, repeatedly).

Each of these approaches – the exotic, the rudimentary – was more or less successful (there was no pot of gold at the end of Dory's rainbow; no get-out-of-jail-free card, no 'miracle cure'). Yet when taken *en masse*, they formed a workable 'control network', a kind of 'therapeutic mesh' (or safety net) which Dory (gentle Dory, *obliging* Dory) was more than happy to fall into.

That crazy river inside – that uncontrollable wave of words and hysteria – stopped flowing for a while. The tide withdrew. But it didn't disappear. It simply entered a different sphere – his dream-life – and controlled him from there.

On the day he turned sixteen (and with his father's help) Isidore designed and crafted a pair of strong, oak doors for his tiny cubby. Thick-cut, huge-hinged, padlocked. And every single night, from that time on, his parents lovingly contracted to bolt him in.

He blamed *Match of the Day*. An advert had randomly caught his attention (on one of the hoardings at the edge of the pitch –

Man Utd v West Ham).

– which said simply: DADCHECK.COM.

Dad-check?

Dad *Check*?

There were few things Isidore was absolutely certain of ('There's *nothing* certain in this world, my son,' his father always used to say – before his final stroke, the *really* bad one, after which he formally dispensed with casual conversation), but Elen's faithfulness was never in question. Her honour was unimpeachable. This was one of the few subjects on which Dory was *absolutely* unequivocal.

DADCHECK

But also he knew (with a feeling just as powerful, just as strong) that the boy was a stranger. The boy *did not belong*.

There was something . . .

And it wasn't that he didn't *love* him –

Oh God, no

He did. He loved him dearly –

There was just . . .

Put it this way: if the boy was a sum (a lovely little fraction; or a piece of calculus, say), then everything about him, superficially speaking, seemed *exactly* as it should be. He was all neatly spaced out, everything in the right place –

So to speak . . .

But the bottom line (and there was *always* a bottom line – in life, in arithmetic) was that he just *didn't add up*. The answer was wrong. Where there should've been a tick, there was a cross.
And it didn't matter how much he tried to ignore it –

That huge cross, in red ink –
That stupid, awful, ugly cross . . .

– it was still there. It was undeniable. It shouted – yelled, *screamed*
– out at him. .

Of course he didn't dare utter a word –

Not a word

– to Elen about it (a betrayal? At that level? How could she ever
forgive him?), but when the advert caught his eye (on tv – during
a *football* match – everything so perfectly *innocent*, so incredibly
calm and . . . and *ordinary* . . .) he quietly committed it to memory.

DADCHECK.COM

Dad/check . . .
He repeated the words to himself – over days, weeks, months – until
they were finally stripped of all their mystery. He rendered them
uncontentious –

Like cup,
Hat,
Cat,
Egg

He de-sensitised them . . .
Dad-check
Dad-check –

Heart-beat? Steady.
Breathing? Regular.
Sweat? Nope. None.

DADCHECK.
Dadcheck.

Dad –

Yawn

– Check . . .
   Then –

Bang!

– he accessed the site. He completed a small money order. He received
a neat package –

At work, of course . . .
The Release Form
The two swabs

– cornered the boy, one fine, winter morning, and made the whole
procedure into a nice, little game for him –

Fleet! Watch Daddy do this!
In my mouth . . .
See?
Shall I do it to you, too?
Shall we have a quick go?
Just for fun?
Open up!
One . . .
Two . . .

He posted it off.
   Several weeks later he received a letter. There'd been 'a problem'
with the swabs, an 'irregularity'. It was 'perfectly normal'. Would he
mind awfully repeating the procedure? For free?
   The boy was less cooperative the second time ('But why don't we
show Mummy? Or Lester? *Urgh! No*, Daddy! That tastes *really* funny!'),
but it was quickly done.
   More waiting.

Then someone from the laboratory rang his mobile.
'My name's Patricia Robbins,' she said, 'I'm an independent consultant
and I'm ringing about your Paternity Test . . .'
   'Do you have the results?' he'd asked, his heart speeding up.
'Yes,' she paused. 'Well, *no*. I mean, it's not quite as *simple* as that . . .'

'Not simple?' Isidore scowled. 'Am I the boy's father, or not?'

Patricia Robbins drew a deep breath. 'Is there any chance you might come in,' she asked, 'so we can talk this thing through, face to face?'

'No.'

Isidore was resolute.

'Okay. Well, the genetic blue-print . . .' she explained carefully, 'I mean I *presume* that you read all of the information enclosed with the . . . ?'

'Of course,' Isidore snapped.

'Then you'll be familiar with the idea that we draw our information from a series of coloured *rings* . . .'

'Yes. I remember.'

'Well the boy's genetic data . . .' she cleared her throat, anxiously, 'I'm afraid it isn't actually *in* colour.'

Silence

'I don't understand,' Isidore murmured, 'I mean . . . I just need to know . . .'

'Nor do I. I've never seen anything like it. The first swab was *confused*. In faded pastels. *Unclear*. We initially thought it was just a glitch, a problem with the procedure. But by the *second* swab . . . well, things had *really* degenerated. And it came out . . . *uh* . . .'

She paused.

'What?'

'It came out all . . .' She swallowed, nervously. 'It came out all . . . all *dark*.'

Isidore pulled the phone away from his ear. He closed his eyes. He called on The Witness. The Witness responded. It counselled him to keep his nerve, to bite his tongue, to proceed on, calmly, with the conversation.

He returned the phone to his ear again.

'Is the boy my son?' he asked, stolidly.

'Yes. I mean he . . . he *was* . . .' she stuttered. 'I mean I *think* he was – so far as I could tell . . . but *not* . . .' she cleared her throat, nervously, 'but he isn't . . . he isn't *now*.'

'What do you mean?' Dory's voice rose by an octave.

'I don't know,' she said, 'I don't *know* what I mean. It's just a blip.

You're just a blip. Science – if you think about it – *progress*, even, is defined by the very things it can't possibly take account of.'

Silence

'Perhaps it might be best to just take another test . . .' she suggested.
   'Is this a set-up?' Isidore's voice was hoarse and raw. 'Or some kind of horrible *joke*? Did *Elen* find out? Is that it?'
'We have counsellors,' she said, 'wonderful counsellors, who've been specially trained to deal with . . .'
'Am I the boy's *father*?' Dory yelled, tears running down his cheeks.
   'No.'
Patricia was unequivocal.
Isidore's jaw dropped.
   'But on a slightly more *positive* note,' she conceded, 'there's just a faint possibility that he might actually be *yours*. I mean from ten – maybe eleven or so – generations back.'
She paused. He heard some papers being shuffled.
'Although . . . *uh* . . . just to be on the *safe* side,' she averred cautiously, 'perhaps I might quickly retabulate that.'

PART THREE

ONE

'Oh *yeah*,' Kelly sneered, 'he can be the nicest bloke in the whole, damn *world* to start off with. Until you fall out with him, that is. Or until he falls out with *you*, more like. He'll be funny an' cuddly an' sweet – *nothin's* a hassle, *nothin's* too much trouble. And then, *just* when you're getting used to it, *just* when you're gettin' all snug an' cosy . . . *Snap!*'

She snapped her skinny fingers, to illustrate. 'He switches it all off. Quick as that. Turns cold as ice. Treats you worse than somethin' dirty he dragged in on his shoe. Wouldn't throw you a rope if you was *drownin'*, I swear to God . . .'

As she talked, her hands neatly and rapidly dissected her third consecutive clementine, clambering over the individual segments like a pair of frantic but purposeful albino spiders.

She suddenly glanced up.

'Oi! *Oi!* Dumbo! D'you understand a single, bloody *word* I'm sayin' here?'

Gaffar smiled, broadly. He thought she looked just beautiful. A princess, no less. Especially in the nightdress which he'd carefully chosen for her (and bought, with Kane's money) at the McArthurGlen Designer Outlet the day before –

Wednesday?

– Yes. Wednesday. When she'd suffered a severe reaction to the painkillers they'd prescribed her.

She glared at him, suspiciously, then carefully readjusted her décolleté. 'You don't have a fuckin' *clue*, do ya? I'm tellin' you about Kane, mate. *Kane.*'

'**Of course, yes.** *Kane.*'

Gaffar mock-spat on to the floor (believing this would please her. He was right. She was delighted). The patient in the next bed (*not* so delighted) expostulated sharply, then haughtily readjusted her bedspread.

'She thinks you're filth,' Kelly confided, with a dirty chuckle, 'foreign *muck*, yeah?'

'He *is* filth,' the woman interjected sharply, 'but then like *does* attract like, so they say.'

'*Oooh!* Get *her*,' Kelly squealed, palpably excited (this was obviously a fight she'd been itching for). 'I saw your hubby at visitin', love,' she trilled, 'and he ain't no fuckin' oil paintin', neither.'

'Didn't stop you from givin' him the glad-eye, though, did it?' the woman sniped.

'*Him?*' Kelly gasped. 'D'you think I need a trip to Specsavers or *what*?!'

'Baps hangin' out everywhere . . .'

Kelly shimmied her two shoulders, saucily. 'Well if you got it, why not flaunt it, *huh*?'

'An' if you *ain't* got it,' the woman hissed, 'then just do your best with the poor crumbs God gave ya.'

Kelly turned back towards Gaffar, with an air of great deliberation. 'Apparently,' she informed him gravely, 'her flaps got so loose after her fifteenth sprog that all her bits started fallin' out. The doctor was meant to shove 'em back up . . .'

Gaffar looked bemused.

'But he was far too *busy*,' Kelly continued loudly, 'so they got in the veterinary instead. He's that much more accustomed to gettin' his arm slimey . . .'

Kelly demonstrated the requisite technique (as Gaffar looked on), applying an imaginary coating of petroleum jelly (smearing it, thickly, right up to her armpit), then inserting her hand, screwing up her face, and groping around, wildly.

The woman turned away, disgusted.

Kelly still persisted.

'Good *Lord*!' she exclaimed (effortlessly adopting a top-drawer accent). 'So *that's* where Brian's been parking the Audi!'

Gaffar licked his lips, nervously, and shifted in his chair.

'How long till I get my *own* phone back?' Kelly asked, grabbing her replacement from the bedside table and inspecting it, irritably.

Gaffar shrugged.

'It's such *bastard* bad luck,' Kelly grumbled. 'I got all my important numbers on there . . .'

She threw the phone down again.

'Did you get all that stuff for my mum like I asked ya?'

Gaffar nodded. He pointed to a bag at his feet.

'An' the stuff for me?'

He pointed to a second, slightly smaller bag, next to it.

'Lemme take a quick butcher's . . .'

Kelly put out her hand, her eyes slitting, suspiciously. Gaffar lifted up the bag and placed it, gently, on to the bed. Kelly sorted her way through it, at her leisure, with a combination of nods and clucks ('Good . . . good . . . *Man!* I told you *Low Fat* yoghurts, didn't I? You stupid *goof* . . .').

She glanced up. 'Where's my salads?'

Gaffar looked blank.

'*Salads*, mate. Tomatoes. Cucumber. *Lettuce*. Where they at?'

Gaffar pointed, somewhat lamely, towards a bag of apples.

'*Apples*, you bugger. Full of bloody *sugar*. I need salads. Salads in a bag. Salads in a plastic fuckin' *container*. I don't bloomin' *care*. So long as they're salads. Sal-ads, yeah? So long as they're *green*, with no fuckin' *calories* in 'em . . .'

'Ah! Sal-ad!' Gaffar suddenly pretended to catch on. He shook his head. '*No* salad. They no salad in these shop.'

He waved his hand, dismissively.

'No *salad?!*' Kelly's jaw dropped (no *salad?!* I mean where'd he think this *was*? Fucking *Ethiopia*?). 'Pull the other one, mate, it's got *bells* on!'

Gaffar rubbed his chin. '*Tomorrow*. Tomorrow I bring you this salads . . .'

Kelly merely sucked on her tongue.

'You're too, damn skinny already,' Gaffar protested. **'What do you want** salad **for? You need some good protein. Chicken. Steak. Lamb. Not** salad. Salad's *shit*. **Just water with a dash of colour . . .'**

Kelly rolled her eyes, boredly, as Gaffar ranted.

'So you got the proper address for my mum an' everythin'?' she interrupted him. 'Please tell me you ain't gone an' forgotten *that* on top.'

Gaffar reached into his pocket and withdrew a couple of spent scratchcards.

'Don't let Kane see you usin' those,' she warned him, 'or he'll give you the world's *worst* fuckin' lecture. He *hates* the bloody lottery.'

Gaffar shoved the cards away again, felt around some more, and this time withdrew an address – in Kane's eccentric hand – on a scruffy piece of paper.

'Right. *Good*,' Kelly was satisfied, 'so Kane's lendin' you his car again, yeah?'

Gaffar shook his head. 'No car. Taxi.'

'He's payin' for your *cabs* now, is he?'

Gaffar nodded.

'*Wow* . . .'

She eyed him, jealously. 'He's never paid for *my* cabs . . .' she paused, ruminatively '. . . But then he *did* buy me a scooter for my eighteenth birthday . . .' She cocked her chin, smugly. 'Did he buy *you* a scooter yet?'

Gaffar simply smiled at her. She gave him a straight look. 'He got you dealin' for him already?'

Gaffar gazed at her, blankly.

'I fuckin' *know* he has. How'd you get a hold of all that smart clobber otherways?'

Gaffar shoved his hand into his pocket and took out his dice, a tiny blue pen (the kind you got free, in a bookmaker's) and a pad.

'Beede,' he said.

'Howzat?' Kelly scowled.

'Beede give suit. We play dice.'

'*What?*'

'You wanna play dice?'

Gaffar stood up, lifted the shopping bag back down on to the floor, then carefully adjusted Kelly's fold-out table.

'Mind my fuckin' *leg*!'

(The leg was partially suspended, above the bed.)

'Jesus *Christ*!'

Kelly pulled up her blanket, harrumphing.

Gaffar pointed at the grim, metal joists emerging from the plaster. '*Terminator!*' he pronounced.

She rolled her eyes.

He rested his hands on his hips. '*I vill be back!*' he intoned.

'Not if *I* have any say in the matter,' the woman in the next bed murmured (into the well-thumbed pages of a *Sunday Mirror* colour supplement).

'Well I *never*!' Kelly exclaimed, casually reinserting her well-greased arm again. 'So *that's* where Grandma stashed poor Rover!'

The woman hissed. Gaffar sat down. He picked up the pen and started drawing on the paper.

222

'What we playin'?' Kelly asked.

'*Pachen*. I show.'

He drew three horizontal lines and then intersected them with two vertical ones (leaving approximately a centimetre between each). When he'd finished the first one (the letter G inscribed neatly above), he commenced with the second (topping it off with the letter K).

'This you . . .' he said, pointing to the K graph, 'and this me.' He pointed at the G.

'So what kind of nonsense has Kane been up to?' Kelly asked nonchalantly (as if she didn't care a jot).

'Kane?' Gaffar glanced up at her.

'Yeah. What kind of shit's *he* been pullin' lately?'

Gaffar smiled and then shook his head.

'Why're you smilin' like that?'

Kelly pulled herself bolt upright.

'*Huh?*'

Gaffar pretended not to understand.

'Has he been slaggin' me off again?'

Gaffar cocked his head.

'Did he tell you I nicked those drugs off him? *Did* he? Because if he did it's a fuckin' *lie* . . .' she knuckled up her hands into furious fists. '*Man!* I can't *believe* he told you that . . .'

Gaffar shook his head. 'He . . . *uh* . . .'

'Because I *didn't*, all right? I've never done drugs. Apart from the odd bit of puff an' speed an' E, obviously. *Never*. An' he *knows* it, too. My brother was hooked on solvents. *Glue*. I've seen what terrible things that kind of shit can do to you . . .'

'Okay.'

'An' I'm still stuck in this damn *bed* – alongside that slack *bitch* – because of the stupid drugs they gave me in here. Look at my rash . . .'

She lifted up her blanket and showed him her belly. It was wall-to-wall hives.

'See?'

Gaffar winced, picked up the dice, and tried to start the game.

'I just can't *believe* he still thinks I stole off him. An' I can't believe he *told* you that, neither . . .'

Gaffar grimaced. 'I never . . .' he said, shaking his head '. . . we never talk.'

Kelly's pretty face closely scrutinised his. 'You *never* talk? Or you never talked about *me*?'

Gaffar pointed at Kelly and then shook his head.

'You *never* talked about me?'

'Uh-uh.'

Kelly was hurt. 'That's rich. We dated for eight solid *months*. What is his fuckin' problem?'

Gaffar shrugged. He shook the dice in his hand.

'So what *are* the two of you gassin' about all day, then?'

Gaffar's brows rose.

'I mean what's so *fuckin'* important, eh?'

Gaffar looked blank.

'Jesus *Christ*. I fell off his wall an' I broke my *leg* . . .'

'**Hey!**' Gaffar suddenly expostulated. '**Don't get so worked up about it! I'm here.** He send *Gaffar* . . . *huh?* . . . and for . . . for shop . . . **What more could a good whore possibly require**?'

He pointed at the bag.

'Yeah,' Kelly crossed her arms, sulkily, 'his little go-between . . .'

Gaffar merely sniffed.

'So what *do* you talk about, then?'

He rolled his eyes. '*Urgh*. No thing.'

'Bull*shit*!'

Gaffar sighed. 'We talk about . . . uh . . .' he struggled to think of anything, 'uh . . . *ah! Rug*.'

'What?'

'Rug. On floor.'

'*Rug?*'

'On floor. Beede floor. *Rug*. We talk.'

Kelly collapsed back into her pillows. 'Now you're just bein' a twat.'

'No. Is so true.'

'An' what else?'

'Uh . . . *Animal Rescue*.'

'Pardon?'

'He thinks I fuck Rolf.'

'*Rolf?*'

'He thinks I do fuck on Rolf.'

Kelly frowned.

Gaffar chuckled fondly as he remembered. 'Then we laugh.'

Kelly still frowned. 'Uh . . . *yeah*. Ha *ha*. Absolutely *hilarious*.'

She sucked on her lower lip. 'You boys are just *so* damn *sad*.'

Gaffar seemed untroubled by this assault. 'An' we watch Sky tv. We watch *uh* . . . Africa news. We watch . . . uh . . . Islam tv. Get piss. Get stoned.'

'Well that's just *great*. That's *dandy*. So I break my fuckin' leg. I get pins put in my *fuckin'* leg. I suffer a *major* allergic reaction to a drug which your *charmin'* pal has pretty much accused me – to my *face*, no less – of nickin' from him, and here you both are, spendin' all God's hours smokin' blow, drinkin' booze and watchin' Islamic bloody *tv* . . .'

'Yes.'

'I mean that ain't even a *proper channel*.'

'Is good tv. We watch Anthony Robbins. Guru. Infomercial. Many times. *Many* times. We watch . . . uh . . . Channel 4 race. We watch Text2Text. With **whore**. Tv **whore**. On phone.'

'You *freaks*,' Kelly gasped, 'you sad, fucking *freaks*.'

She crossed her arms.

Gaffar smiled.

'*Man*. That's just . . .' she gazed up at the light fitment, furiously, '. . . that's just *so* fuckin' typical. *Classic* Kane. *Classic* fuckin' Kane . . .'

Gaffar continued to smile, slightly hunched over, watching her furious ruminations, fondly.

'Don't *look* at me like that!' Kelly suddenly yelled.

He sat up straight. '*Wha?!*'

'Like some big, gormless *pup*!'

He shrugged, then pretended to adjust his face with his hand. His face was very rubbery. He pushed his nose across his cheek, like it was made out of Plasticene.

Kelly squealed, 'That's *disgustin'*! Stop it!'

Gaffar stopped.

'We play Tiger Woods PGA Tour 2001,' he informed her.

'Oh *God*, the fuckin' *golf*. Don't even *go* there . . .'

'Kane is play Justin Leonard. I is play Brad Faxon in big tournament for seven hour.'

'I hate that damn game,' Kelly hissed. 'I'm *haunted* by that fuckin' game. The sound of the bat hittin' the ball, the birds twitterin' in the damn *trees* . . .'

'Stick,' Gaffar corrected her.

'An' that stupid, fuckin' "*oooooaaawwwww*!" noise the crowd makes ever time you miss a shot . . .'

Gaffar nodded, sympathetically. 'I tell him we should play Super Mario, eh? Sims. *New* game . . .'

   'I bought him the 2002 edition of the golf for his birthday, and I swear to God he never even took off the cellophane wrapper. He's like, "No. I still enjoy 2001. There's still plenty of stuff for me to learn here."'

   'But he is good play for this game, huh?'

'Fuckin' *should* be, mate, he's wasted enough hours on it. An' I wouldn't mind, but he don't even *like* computer games. He only got the system in exchange for a bad debt an' the golf game was still inside. He claims he *despises* PlayStation . . .'

   'Kane *love* this game,' Gaffar reiterated.

'Did he give you the line about how it's an easy game to play but a difficult game to *master*?'

Gaffar stared at her, blankly.

'Just you wait. He'll tell you that. He *loves* to say that. That game is like a *religion* to Kane. I've never seen him more fuckin' contented than when he's playin' that stupid game.'

   'You hate this game, *huh*?' Gaffar observed.

'That Pebble fuckin' *Beach* course,' Kelly growled. 'Wiv' all the sounds of the waves in the background . . . ?'

Gaffar nodded, sagely. 'But this wave sound is better than his *music*, eh?'

   'His *music*?!' Kelly squealed. '*Man*, when I think about his taste in fuckin' *music* I just thank God we broke up.'

'Crazy music.'

'Desert fuckin' *rock*, mate.'

'Eh?'

'That's what it's called. Desert rock. Rock from the desert or somethin'. Did he play you The Meat Puppets yet?'

   '*Urgh!*' Gaffar threw up his hands.

'What a terrible, bloomin' *racket!*'

'Terrible!' Gaffar heartily agreed.

'Just a bunch of dirty, long-haired *dope*-heads wailin' an' screamin' over a howlin' guitar.'

   'I ask him for play Shania Twain,' Gaffar told her. 'I buy cd in Tesco.

Good cd. I show him this cd an' he is laugh in my face for half an hour . . .'

'Oh. My. *God*. I fuckin' *love* Shania!' Kelly interrupted him.

'Instead he is play this Stoneage Queens, eh? This Meat Puppet, this big *Dinosaur* . . .'

Gaffar winced at the memory.

'Shania is the best singer of all time,' Kelly declared, cuffing him on the arm.

'Shania is queen of the world,' Gaffar cuffed her straight back, 'Queen of this music world.'

'I can't believe you love Shania! I fuckin' *worship* Shania!'

'Shania is the most beautiful woman on this earth.'

'She's fuckin' *gorgeous*, mate. She is fuckin' *beautiful*. An' she's a good person, too, yeah? Beautiful on the inside *and* the out.'

They beamed at each other.

After two or three seconds Kelly actually realised what she was doing and quickly stopped herself.

She pointed at the paper, by way of a diversion. 'So how'd we play this stupid game of yours, then?'

Gaffar leaned forward, picked up the pen, and next to the various tiny boxes he began to write –

4x1, 4x2, 4x3, 4x4, 4x5, 4x6, 2x?, 3x?, 3x1/2x1, 1–5.

'Is *Pachen*. See?'

Kelly nodded.

Gaffar took the first throw to demonstrate. He got a five, a six, a one and three twos. He chuckled. He picked up the pen and ticked neatly in the box on his graph specifying 3x?. Then he threw again. Nothing. He passed the dice over.

Kelly shook them in her hand.

'Kane got sore foot,' Gaffar told her, in passing, just as she was about to throw.

She steadied herself. '*Huh?*'

'Foot. Hurt on foot. He phone, phone . . . Find foot doctor.'

'Kane has hurt his *foot*?'

'Yes. *Wart*.' Gaffar grimaced.

'Kane has a wart on his foot?'

'Yes. That is what happen. *That* is how we talk. Nothing at all with you and this drug.'

'*Fine* . . .'

Kelly promptly threw five sixes.

Gaffar's eyes widened as she picked up the pen and filled in her graph. She prepared for her second throw. 'So what are we playin' for?' she asked.

'*Huh?*'

'Cuz I ain't playin' for *nothin'*, that's for sure.'

Gaffar scratched his ear.

'Okay,' Kelly lowered her voice, 'here's the deal: if *I* win, you promise to tell me everything Beede's doin' . . .'

'*Beede?*' Gaffar looked perplexed.

She nodded. 'Beede. You *spy* on him for me. And I wanna know *everythin'*. I mean if that old boy *shits,* then I wanna know how much and where, yeah?'

Gaffar continued to scratch, ruminatively.

'And you can fetch me my bloody *salad*. I want my fuckin' *salad*, right?' She paused. 'But if *you* win . . .'

He stopped scratching and looked up at her, keenly.

Kelly thought hard for a while, frowning. Then her face suddenly cleared. '*Hand*-job!' she exclaimed, throwing down the dice for a second time, with an expression of high good humour.

Kane was haunted by his mother's pain. It was indelibly etched on him (chiselled into him, like he was a soft, sandstone carving). He longed – more than anything – to banish it from his mind (not wanting to *forget* exactly, or to . . . to *disrespect* – not at all – just to lessen the . . . to blank out . . . to edit . . .), but he could not.

Impossible.

As a boy her pain had been one of his earliest points of reference (am I hungry? Is it raining? Is Mummy in bad pain again?). It gave each day its substance (simply managing it, reducing it, ignoring it, enduring it). Her pain was at the heart of everything: it was the colour on their canvas, the scenery on their stage, the starring actor in their domestic drama.

He'd always known (and his mother – God bless her – had always warned him) that if he wasn't to be overwhelmed by it (stupified, *annihilated* – the way she ultimately had been) then he'd need – as a matter of basic survival – to create an emotional bypass of some kind.

He'd begun the early groundwork readily enough (while she was still around to guide him): worked out a route, completed some rough sketches, got a few useful quotes in. But it was a big job, a serious job, and when things had finally (and inevitably) proven too much for him (she was gone, life was shit, what the hell was the *point* in expending all this effort?), he'd taken what he took to be the second-best option: he glanced over his shoulder, stuck on his indicator, and pulled into a layby –

Brake,
Clutch,
Neutral . . .
Phew!

Not a cop-out –

Nope

– just a temporary measure.

It was a nice enough spot (a small expanse of grass, a shady tree, a picnic table), yet even as he sat there (eating a Cornetto), the hollow knell of her pain still continued to sound (like the low growl of a grizzly bear, hungrily ransacking a trashcan somewhere). It wasn't a deafening commotion. Not from here. It was really quite tolerable. And he was in no particular hurry to draw any closer (why *should* he be?). So he stayed. He encamped. He became a permanent transient.

He never spoke of it (the pain, the layby, the bear, the growling). Not to anyone. Didn't want to speak of it. Could not *stand* to.

Her agony – her unbearable forbearance – was just a part of him now. Embedded within him. Utterly secret. *Sacred*, even.

But then . . . then she'd gone and brought it all up again –

The chiropodist.
Elen –

– just idly, just *casually*, in general conversation.

   She'd pin-pointed something vulnerable on the map of him. She'd stuck a cruel tack in –

As a guide . . .
As a marker.

– then she'd fired a single arrow. It rose, it arced, it fell . . .

Ow!

She'd *pierced* him with it.

   And no matter how hard he tried – how much he fought and *wrangled* with the damn thing – he simply could not pull it out of him.

'You were so brave,' she'd said.

Brave?

   If only she *knew* (the nails he'd bitten. The tears he'd sobbed. The long nights – the terrible, endless, *sleepless* nights – full of pointless prayers to a heartless God). He shuddered at the memory.
   If that was brave, she could damn well *keep* it. A pack of wild horses wouldn't drag him back again.

Gaffar was waiting for Beede in the hallway, perched, uncomfortably, on the bottom stair.

Beede let himself in (not even bothering to switch the light on), slamming the door shut behind him, turning – in a kind of daze – and then glancing up, with a jolt. He hadn't expected to see someone sitting there.

'Gaffar,' he said, with a stiff smile, 'is that you? Are you still here?' Gaffar peered down at himself, speculatively, then glanced up again, smiling, grimly. 'Gaffar Celik – **like the proverbial bad smell, eh?**'

Beede bent down to pick up his post from the mat, then pulled off his helmet. He pushed his fingers through his hair.

Silence.

'Nice suit,' he said, finally, with a slight gesture of the hand, as if to break the ice between them.

'Sure,' Gaffar muttered, 'is *good* suit.' He shrugged.

'Perhaps . . . uh . . .' he shrugged again '. . . **a little on the roomy side**. But, *hey* . . .'

He winced, amiably.

'So you're staying upstairs with Kane?' Beede enquired.

'You ride motorbike?' Gaffar counter-questioned, pointing – with just a hint of incredulity – at Beede's battered and ancient piss-pot helmet.

'Uh, yes . . .' Beede peered down at the helmet, distractedly. 'An old bike. A Douglas.'

'*Hmmn*. Is so? I never *hear* of this bike . . .'

'That's probably because it's British.'

'Ah . . .' Gaffar snorted, dismissively, then folded up his large hands and slotted them, primly, between his thighs.

Beede walked over to his door and pushed it open. He stepped inside and then he paused.

He turned. 'So, Gaffar . . . Is there something . . . ?'

Gaffar glanced up, in apparent surprise. '*Nothing*. I just . . . *uh* . . . sit.'

'Right.' Beede nodded. '*Good*.'

He gently began to push the door to.

'*Nothing* . . .' Gaffar repeated (but with a touch more urgency this time), 'I mean is nothing for to trouble *you* . . .'

He hesitated. 'I mean is only *small* thing. **An insignificant little . . . uh . . .**' he pondered for a second '**. . . dilemma.**'

'I see . . .' Beede tossed his helmet, the post and his knapsack down on to the sofa. He seemed tired and preoccupied.

'Tough day?' Gaffar enquired.

'Is there ever any other kind?' Beede countered dryly, pulling off his leather gloves and observing – with some irritation – a slick of hair oil marking the hide.

'I was come to see you . . .' Gaffar cleared his throat, nervously, '*today*. In hospital . . . But then . . .'

He grimaced.

'Really?' Beede didn't seem especially delighted by the idea. 'The truth is that I barely have *time* for visitors, Gaffar – I'm always pretty busy down there . . .'

Then something suddenly dawned on him. 'Ah . . . I *see*. You wanted to come and apply for a job, perhaps? **Employment?** In the laundry?'

Gaffar's brows shot up, in horror. 'God, *no*,' he blurted out.

'Heaven preserve me!'

Beede looked piqued for a moment, then his irritation evaporated and he chuckled, wryly.

'Uh . . . *No!*' Gaffar back-pedalled, guiltily. 'Is because I *have* job, see? Job with *Kane*. *Good* job . . .' he paused. 'But this job *you* have, is *also* good job,' he continued, obsequiously, '*hard* job. Kane he say . . . uh . . .' Gaffar frowned. 'He say . . .' he paused, struggling to find the right words, **'it's almost like a . . . a dance . . .'**

He quickly stood up and gracefully threw out his arms, to illustrate. **'He says the hospital linen is full of shit and blood and vomit, but you grab it with your hands and you embrace it. You hold it to you, without pride but with . . . with acceptance. With love. Like a dancing partner. No sign of . . . of fastidiousness. He says it's really quite . . . quite . . .** beautiful – yes? Beautiful **to watch – although, of course, on another level . . .'**

Gaffar mimed himself retching, in total disgust.

'*Beautiful?*' Beede seemed taken aback. '*Kane* actually said that?'

Gaffar nodded.

'Good gracious.'

'Yes . . .' Gaffar tried his utmost to seal his advantage. 'Like . . . like beautiful *machine*. **Automata.'**

Beede's face dropped. 'Oh. *Yes*. Of course. I see what you mean . . .'

He suddenly looked tired again. He sat down, stiffly, on the sofa, pinched his sinuses between his fingers and remained – hunched over, his elbows pressing into his knees – for what seemed like an age. Gaffar hung around the doorway, uncertain whether or not to enter. After a certain duration he subtly drew Beede's attention to his continuing presence with a polite cough.

Beede opened his eyes and glanced over. 'I'm sorry, Gaffar,' he apologised, 'it's been a long old day and I'm not much in the way of company . . .'

Gaffar nodded, mutely, and took a small step back into the half-light.

Beede instantly took pity on him. 'But you said you had a problem of some kind . . . ?' he asked, straightening up, pushing back his shoulders, taking off his glasses (placing them, carefully, on to the arm of the sofa) and rubbing his face, vigorously, with both hands.

Gaffar scowled. '*Problem? No. No.*'

He shook his head, emphatically.

'I see . . . Well, I must've misheard you, then.'

Beede picked up his glasses and carefully reapplied them. He stared at Gaffar, enquiringly.

Gaffar took a step closer. 'Is just . . . **you could hardly call it a** *problem* . . . **More of a** . . .' he bit his lip, '**a puzzle . . . A hiccough. Yes. Hiccough. Something which . . . which recurs. Something which infuriates and disrupts, which persists. What's the** English **word for that?**'

'For what?'

Gaffar hiccoughed.

'A hiccough?'

'*Hey presto!*'

'Right . . .' Beede patiently awaited further elucidation, but none was forthcoming.

'Okay, a *hiccough*, eh?' he gamely struggled to improvise. 'So let's see . . . Is it an *immigration* issue, perhaps, or . . . or something connected to the local authorities?'

Gaffar flapped his hand, dismissively.

'Is it **policemans?**'

Gaffar snorted.

'Is it Kane?' Beede suddenly looked worried. 'Is he forcing you to do something that you feel uncomfortable with?'

At the mention of Kane's name, Gaffar placed his finger over his lips, hurried into the room and closed the door, gently, behind him.

'Is Kane upstairs?' Beede whispered. 'Don't you want him to hear us?'

'Kane is . . . *uh* . . . Kane is out,' Gaffar spoke at normal volume, 'in car.'

'Oh . . .' Beede paused. 'So is somebody *else* up there? The redhead? Kelly? Is it Kelly Broad? Is it something *she's* said?'

'No . . .' Gaffar shook his head. 'But is *with* her – this Kelly – I have . . .' he gesticulated.

'Hiccough,' Beede filled in, helpfully.

Gaffar strolled over, grabbed Beede's helmet, the post and his bag, placed them – carefully – on to the kitchen counter, then sat down next to him.

'What I need is . . . *uh* . . .' he scowled, exasperated, clenching his hands together, earnestly, 'I need friend . . . *Friend*?'

Beede stared at him, unblinking. For some reason his heart was sinking. He had a bad feeling.

'*Okay* . . .' he murmured.

'Yes. **In fact more of a . . . a** *confidant* . . .' Gaffar paused, specu-latively, '**actually, no. Not** *confidant*. **Just . . . just someone discreet, someone who doesn't need me to confide in them. Someone who takes things at face value. That kind of a person . . .**'

Beede said nothing.

Gaffar cleared his throat, carefully.

'Yes. So what I need . . . *uh* . . . I need for *you*, Beede, old man . . . *uh* . . .'

Gaffar swore under his breath.

'Just relax,' Beede counselled him, 'there's no rush. Take your time . . .'

'Is so. Yes. Is *good*,' Gaffar nodded, 'for because . . . uh . . . **What I need is a favour, okay? Do you get me? Just a small favour. But I don't want Kane to find out about it. I don't want anyone to know about it . . .**'

'A favour? From me?'

Gaffar nodded.

'Is it money?'

Gaffar blinked. *Money?!*

He glared at Beede, insulted. **'What kind of opportunist** *skank* **do you take me for?'**

234

'Oh. Right. Sorry. So *not* money . . .'

'No. Absolutely not. It's just a small demand on your time . . .'

'When?'

'In tomorrow morning . . .'

'Okay.'

Gaffar blinked (*Wow.* That was considerably easier than it might've been). '*Really* okay?'

Beede shrugged. 'Sure. As long as whatever you want me to do isn't illegal and doesn't take too long . . .'

'Not long,' Gaffar butted in, 'just few minute. Five minute. Is all.'

'Then that's fine. It's a deal.'

Beede reached out his hand and Gaffar took it. They shook.

'So what do you want me to *do*, exactly?' Beede couldn't resist asking.

Gaffar grimaced, he dropped Beede's hand. 'I need for you to go *shop*. I need for you to get for me, I, *Gaffar* . . .'

He pointed to his chest.

'Yes?'

'I need . . .' He drew a deep breath. '*Salad.*'

Beede stared at him, blankly. 'Pardon?'

'Salad,' Gaffar repeated (with an involuntary shudder).

'Salad?'

Gaffar nodded.

'Sorry . . . Did you just say "salad"?'

'Yes. Salad. *Salad.*'

'Salad? Like lettuce? Or tomatoes? *That* kind of salad?'

'Yes.'

'Right. And you need *me* to do that? You need salad but you have . . . you have no *money*, perhaps . . . ?'

'Oh no. I have money,' Gaffar insisted, 'I say before . . . I say I *have* money. Money is no problem. Kane give money – money for salad.'

As Gaffar spoke, Beede was staring down at the rug, with a frown. He was trying to think of the Turkish word for salad.

'Leaf!' he finally exclaimed.

'Not "leaf!"' Gaffar snapped. '*Salad*, you fool. **Salad. Salad.** Salad. **Salad.** *Salad.*'

'You want me to go *shopping* for you?'

'No,' Gaffar shook his head, 'I shop. *I* buy shop. But you – *you* – you shop salad.'

'So who's the salad for?'

Beede glanced down at the rug again. 'Kelly. Kane's **whore**.'

'And you want me to take the salad to her?'

'No. *I* take. So long . . .' Gaffar made a complex motion with his hands. '**So long as it's completely covered up. Packaged up. In a bundle. Wrapped up. And I don't have to look at it.**'

'How odd,' Beede murmured.

'What?' Gaffar straightened his back, defensively.

'My rug.'

'Rug?'

'Yes. My rug.' Beede pointed. 'I thought there was something wrong with it, and now I realise . . . There's nothing *wrong*, as such, but it's been . . . it's been turned around . . .'

Gaffar glanced down.

'Ah, yes,' he grinned, 'I do that.'

'What?' Beede seemed confused. '*You* turned my rug around?'

'Yes.'

'But why?'

'Kane.'

'*Kane?*'

'Yes. Kane **dropped his cigarette on it – or, to be completely accurate – that stinking cat knocked it off the little table with its pesky tail while he was searching through your books. Burned a small hole in it. Kane went nuts. So I told him I could fix it – told him my mother and my grandmother worked on the carpet looms of Diyarbakir . . . you know, blah blah . . .'** Gaffar scoffed, jovially '**. . . and – blow me – if he wasn't completely taken in by it! Swallowed it whole! So I sent him off to your bedroom – to seek vengeance on that filthy puss – then, quick as a flash, I'd moved out all the furniture, turned the carpet around, and placed it back . . .'**

Gaffar jumped up, to demonstrate. '**Oh my God! When he returned he fell to his knees, looking for the place where the burn had been . . .**' Gaffar fell to his knees, with a theatrical gasp. '**You should've seen it! It was hilarious! His face was a picture!**'

He glanced over at Beede. Beede did not appear to be overwhelmed by hilarity.

'Don't worry . . .' Gaffar tried to pacify him, **'it's only a tiny mark. You can barely even tell from this angle. And – let's face it – this carpet's hardly a priceless work of craftsmanship, is it? Just some cheap reproduction . . .'** Gaffar sniggered, **'I mean the Minaret of Jam? Afghanistan?!'**

'I appreciate your candour,' Beede smouldered.

'*Natch*,' Gaffar swiped a hand through the air.

'So Kane was going through my books, you say?' Beede murmured, tightly. 'Do you have any idea why?'

Gaffar shrugged.

'Because that just seems very . . .' Beede scowled, '*strange*. Strange behaviour. For Kane.'

'First he looked into the envelope,' Gaffar tried to remember the exact order of things, **'the brown envelope with the papers inside which Kelly – his whore – brought with her. He read them for a while and his face was like . . .'**

Gaffar pulled an expression of condensed fury.

'*This* envelope?'

Beede grabbed the aforementioned brown envelope from underneath an old newspaper.

'Uh . . . Yes.'

'But why would he look in *this* envelope?'

Beede pulled the papers out of it and inspected them, his eye settling, just briefly, on Winifred's handwritten note.

Gaffar shrugged again. 'I no idea. All I care for is *salad*.'

Beede gazed up at him, distractedly.

'Of course,' he eventually murmured, 'the salad.'

'In morning. We go Tesco Supermarket – Crooksfoot – *big* Tesco. Near hospital.'

'Right. *Yes* . . .' Beede struggled to re-focus. 'My shift starts at ten. So . . . uh . . . nine-thirty, say? Would you like a lift down there? On the bike?'

'*No!*' Gaffar widened his eyes, warningly. 'We meet in front. *Secret*, yes? By . . . uh . . .'

He made a pushing motion.

'The trolleys?'

'*Bingo.*'

'Okay. Out front, by the trolleys,' Beede confirmed, 'I'll be there.'

'God bless you.'

Gaffar took a small step back – bending his knee, dipping his head, graciously, his hands clasping together – as if offering his humble obeisance to the old man. But then he paused, mid-genuflection, peeking up through the deep pile of his luxuriant brows and indicating towards the rug, with a sly grin.

'So this was *damn* good joke, huh?'

TWO

He kept telling himself that it was the foot – the verruca – which was encouraging his thoughts to dwell on her. A small and previously dormant wart (hardly the world's most *alluring* thing) which was suddenly throbbing and smarting and *twingeing* him –

Twingeing . . .
Is that really a word?

   Although –

Uh . . .
Now just hang on there . . .

– was the foot *really* the spur? The root of it all? The instigator? I mean couldn't it just as easily be the other way around? ie his thoughts being absorbed by her –

The soft voice
The smooth fall of her hair . . .

– then frantically retreating –

The birthmark/patronising manner/pyromaniac son/his psychotic father

– and so turning, instead, by . . . by *proxy*, you might almost say, to the foot (which – because of some strange, fucked-up biological imperative –

Hysterical –
Didn't she actually say that?)

– had become the unwitting locus – the physical expression – of all his rancour.

Wasn't the wart just a collaborator? A patsy? Wasn't it simply giving him *carte blanche* to think about – to dwell upon – to *linger* . . .

On her?
Elen?
Or . . .
God –
Worse still (standing quietly behind her, almost eclipsed by her shadow):
Beede?

No.

No. It was the foot. It was the wart. It was the twingeing, the itching –

Now that truly is disgusting . . .

– and the occasional, entirely arbitrary dart of stabbing pain –

Ouch.
There it goes again . . .

It was definitely the foot. Because the more he dwelt on it, the more he realised that these irritating symptoms had been solidly in evidence since well before Monday's fateful meeting. Not quite so patently – so obviously – as they were now, not nearly so . . . so *belligerently* – but they *had* been there.

Although –

Yes . . .

– he didn't mind admitting (on the subject of mental unease etc) that he'd been somewhat alarmed (shaken up, even) by the letter from W. From Winnie. From Winifred. Because so far as he was aware (which wasn't very far – he couldn't honestly remember the last time he'd bothered asking Anthony – her father – about her general health/happiness/wellbeing) she'd moved permanently to Leeds (the university. Had some kind of fancy, post-graduate position in the History Department there).

He hadn't seen her for several years –

Four –
At the very least

And yet here was Beede, his father (dull old Beede, musty old Beede –

Mysterious old Beede?
Secretive old Beede?
Randy old Beede?! –

Urgh.

– Kane shuddered), conducting some kind of secret, but oddly *intimate* relationship with her (I mean all the stuff about the Madeira cake. Why would Beede give a damn about such trivia? Did Beede even *eat* cake? Did the fact of cake even offer up a tiny *blip* on Beede's psychological radar?

Because you wouldn't . . .

Cake?!

. . . you wouldn't even *mention* the cafeteria unless there was some kind of shared background in tea or food or . . .

Did Winifred even like cake?
He struggled to think. He tried to remember. Cake. Sharing cake. Enjoying cake together . . .

Nope.
Nothing.

Sharing tabs. Having sex. Smoking dope. Enjoying blow-backs. Yeah.
But *cake?*

Winifred Shilling – pill-fiend extraordinaire – sitting quietly with a fragrant pot of Earl Grey at her elbow in a suburban tearoom somewhere? Eh?!

Kane snorted, contemptuously.

Nah).

He glanced down –

Damn

The tip of his spliff had dropped off into his lap. And there was still a small –

Fuck!

– ember . . .
He cuffed it from his jeans and down on to the floor. He checked the fabric – no hole, but a tiny, brown . . .

Bugger

He took a final, deep drag –

Nope . . .
Dead

– then tried to push the damp dog-end into the ashtray, but the ashtray, it seemed, was already full to capacity. He frowned, then tutted, fussily. Some fool had shoved a *cigarette* packet in there –

Gaffar . . .

– he tried to remove it, manoeuvring it out so as not to spill ash everywhere. As the packet came free he saw – with a slight start – that it wasn't actually what he'd thought –

Not a packet . . .

He unfolded it, thinking it might be some kind of supermarket scratch-card. But no. A card – *yes*, certainly – but not a scratchcard. A *playing* card. A Jack. A Jack of Hearts. He gazed at it, blankly, as he shoved his dog-end into the ashtray. Then he blew on the card (to clean off the ash) and slipped it, with a small smile, into his pocket. As he pushed in his hand he felt *another* card. He frowned –

What . . . ?

Then he remembered. The card he'd taken from his father's book. The *business* card –

Yeah?

He pulled it out. But it wasn't the business card. It was *another* playing card. A *second* playing card. He stared at it, scowling.
The Joker.

The Joker?!

He delved back into his pockets again, searching for that *other* card – the business card.
Nothing.

Where'd it go?

And then he remembered the book. *Beede's* book . . .The one he . . .

Nope.

He inspected the Joker again. But it wasn't the Joker. It was the Jack. The Joker . . .
He turned the card over. He searched his pockets. The Joker was gone. He held the Jack and stared at it.
'Must've mis-read . . .' he murmured.

Ho-hum.

He shoved the card away, scowling, then peered up at her house –

Elen's house . . .

Because here he was –

Sure as eggs

– for all his well-rehearsed expressions of confusion/nonchalance/indif-
ference etc – lounging casually in his car (a mere three days since
their last encounter), planning on . . . expecting to . . . hoping to . . .

Uh . . .

He'd tried to track down her practice in the phone book, but hadn't
been able to find it there. She was married now and he didn't know
her surname, so he'd finally resorted –

Yes, yes . . .

– to a furtive inspection of his father's address book.
   He'd noted – with some interest – that she wasn't listed under 'c'
for chiropodist, or under 'e' for Elen, even, but under 'g'.

G?

He'd discovered other things, too. Further to the bank statement
(which he'd uncovered, accidentally, a couple of days previously) he'd
unearthed two old cheque books (*all* of the stubs –

Thanks, Pops!

– religiously filled out, if somewhat cryptically, in his own special short-
hand), some meticulous account books, several letters from the bank
manager (further to our meeting on . . . etc etc), and a demand from
a shonky loan company (dated 27 November) –

What the . . . ?!

That'd been the biggest shock.

Kane took out his cigarettes and sparked one up. He gazed over at the house again. He frowned. So was this the reason his father currently found himself over £38,000 in hock?

His mind dwelt, momentarily, on the envelope Beede had passed her in the restaurant –

How furtive he'd looked –

What was it? Love? Sex? Blackmail? (*Sex? Blackmail?!*

Seriously?! Knowing Beede, it was far more likely to be some kind of mealy-mouthed petition about the 'brutal coppicing' of a group of ancient Limes on the cycle track near the Stour Centre).

Whatever the reason, this certainly wasn't the kind of place he'd pictured her living in. Not Elen (*El-en* – he found himself tripping on the name – mid-syllable – just like his father had done).

Cedar Wood –

Cedar?
Wood?

– was a brand, spanking new development. Blank. Generic. Everything detached, or semi-detached. No personality. No atmosphere. No newsagents (for that matter), or chippies or pubs. No trees –

No woods – or cedars – that's for damn sure . . .

– just bushes. No birds . . .

He turned off the stereo, wound down the window and stuck his head out to make certain –

Nope

Just this awful, all-pervasive quiet. This *muffledness.*

He was shocked – quite frankly – by the feel of the place. He felt something within him revolt against it (the sense of quiet conformity. The dullness. The heart-sinking *blankness*). He was almost . . .

What?

Disappointed.

Oh come on . . .

As he sat and watched, a tall, thin, young man in scruffy work apparel suddenly appeared from around the side of the house. He was carrying a dog – a pathetic-looking spaniel – under one arm and holding what appeared to be an empty jam-jar in his free hand.

'*Bollocks . . .*' Kane murmured. He moved to duck down in his seat, but that same instant the young man glanced over.

'Aw *shit*,' Lester said, taking a quick step back.

Kane drew a deep breath, stuck his fag into the corner of his mouth, yanked the keys from the ignition, shoved open the door and clambered out.

'I ain't *got* it,' Lester began snivelling, 'an' you got no fuckin' *right* botherin' me at work, man.'

'You? *Work?!*' Kane scoffed.

'Leave me *alone*, man,' Lester seemed terrified.

Kane sighed, bored. This was just too bad. A fly in the ointment. But certain, well, *responsibilities* were inherent to the trade. He pulled his jacket slightly tighter around him, stiffening his body against the cold, then slammed the door shut (activating the alarm and the locks –

Click –
Beep-beep)

'*Don't hurt me, man*,' Lester all-but squealed.

'Got no choice, my friend,' Kane regretfully informed him, 'because if I don't, you'll paint me a pussy all over town, and *then* where the heck would business be at?'

Lester turned and bolted down the side of the house. Kane strolled casually after him, finally catching up with him in the small, paved rear garden where he was crouching – somewhat poignantly – behind a sheet on the washing line. Kane stooped under some socks. 'Put down the dog,' he instructed him.

'Uh-*uh*.'

Lester shot up against the brick of the back wall, shaking his head.

246

'Put down the fucking *dog*,' Kane reiterated, then he drew forward slightly, with a frown. 'What's in the jam-jar?'

'Nothin'.'

'Nothing?'

He moved in for an even closer look, blinking, for a second, through the smoke from his cigarette.

'Yeah.'

'You've got a jam-jar of nothing? Why?'

'I'm collectin' it.'

'You're collecting *nothing*?'

Lester nodded.

'Are you fucking *insane*?'

Kane snatched the jar from him and squinted in through the glass. Couldn't see anything. Saw nothing, in fact. Then he straightened up and punched Lester in the face.

Crack.

Lester's mouth flew open on impact. His skull smacked into the brickwork. The dog yelped as his grip inadvertently tightened around her. But his nose took the brunt of it.

'Okay, then,' Kane grinned, 'so here's to nothing . . .'

He toasted him with the jar and then handed it back.

Lester snatched the jar, his eyes smarting, the bone in the centre of his nose glowing whitely, as though it'd just been lightly dusted with phosphorescent powder. Then – on a count of three – warm, dark blood began to gush from his nostrils. Kane pulled a tea-towel from the washing line, yanked back Lester's head with a handful of his hair –

'Owwww!'

– and blotted his face with it.

'This all seems strangely familiar . . .' he mused, idly. 'Didn't I break your nose sometime before? Or was it your arm on that occasion?'

'Cracked my fuckin' *ribs*,' Lester hissed through the fabric.

'Ah . . .' Kane sighed, 'well there's surely some kind of *lesson* in this, my old friend . . .' he counselled, sagely.

'Hello? *Hello?'*

Uh-oh

Kane froze, mid-axiom.

A man's voice. Germanic.

'Lester?'

Kane turned. Then he took a quick step back –

Wha?!

His eyes widened. Directly behind him (about 2 feet away, at most), perched neatly on the washing line: a starling. A thin and greasy, yellow-beaked starling, cocking its head at him.

Kane stared at the bird. The bird stared back at Kane. Kane removed his cigarette from his mouth and flipped it down on to the paving. *'Shoo!'* he said.

As he spoke he heard the spaniel growling. A deep growl. A menacing growl. Then his eyes lifted – he didn't know why . . . instinct, perhaps – to an upstairs window at the back of the house. There he saw the boy (the strange boy. The imp) standing at the window and gazing out at him, impassively. Kane waved at the boy, but the boy didn't respond. Instead, he slowly – very deliberately – lifted up his hands and covered his face with them (but not in panic or alarm – so much as . . . almost as if in . . .

In warning?)

That same instant –

Oh balls

– he saw the mother, dressed in black, standing directly behind him. She looked . . . What *was* that look? Apprehension? *Fear?*

'Lester? Is that you?'

Again, the German . . .

Kane's eyes returned – fleetingly – to the bird. The bird shat down the sheet. Then it squawked. Then it flew at him.

'Shit!'

Kane dropped his chin and covered his face, instinctively. The bird hit him, with some force. He felt its beak slice into his knuckles.

He tried to swipe it away, but there was nothing.

'What are you doing?'

Lester was staring at him, warily, over the tea-towel.

'The bird . . .' Kane looked around him, his hands still up, still slightly panicked. 'Didn't you see it? The bird on the line? The starling. It shat down the . . .'

He pointed at the sheet. The sheet was clean.

'It *flew* at me. Didn't you *see* it?'

'Hello . . . ?'

The German had walked across the paved garden and was now standing on the other side of the sheet. He was talking down at their feet. 'Is everything all right back there?'

'Lester's banged his nose,' Kane observed brightly, drawing aside the sheet, like a theatrical stage-hand, to reveal a tragic Lester in all his newly bloodied glory.

'Good *God*. What happened?'

The German drew closer. Lester gesticulated, pointlessly.

'He's trying to stem the flow,' Kane said, still holding the sheet in his hand and failing to locate any bird dirt on it.

'It looks bad, Lester,' the German seemed shocked, 'it's swelling right up. Do you need a doctor?'

Lester shook his head, waved his arm and gurgled.

'Let me at least take Michelle from you . . .'

He reached out for the dog. The dog snarled.

'She don't like you,' Lester spluttered, through the towel.

The dog looked up at the German, her round eyes bulging, fearfully.

'I should drive you home,' the German murmured, withdrawing his arm again. 'You can't possibly do any work in that condition.'

He turned to Kane. 'Are you one of Harvey's people?'

Kane opened his mouth to respond, but before he could answer, Elen had come flying through the back door, down the steps and out on to the patio. She was clutching a pack of frozen peas. 'For the swelling,' she panted, 'here . . .' She removed the tea-towel. 'Hold back your head, Lester. Let me take a proper look . . .'

'Is it broken?' the German wondered.

'Was it the scaffolding?' Elen asked Kane, staring up at him, pointedly. 'A huge plank fell down this morning and almost decapitated the postman.'

'Well *something* certainly fell on him,' Kane murmured, noticing how much smaller she was than he'd remembered (five two? Three?), and how large her husband seemed by comparison. He was certainly handsome – in that blond way; that pure, square, *aryan* way. He was powerfully built. Muscular. Held himself gracefully, like an athlete.

Kane instinctively pushed back his shoulders and contracted the lazy muscles in his stomach.

Elen, meanwhile, was gently applying the bag to one side of Lester's nose. Lester bleated.

'Harvey left me a message about an hour ago,' the German was saying, 'promising to send someone this afternoon to have a look at it . . .'

'He's not one of Harvey's people, Dory . . .' Elen turned to her husband with a breezy smile, 'he's just a client. He's come about his foot. I'd completely forgotten. He has a . . .'

'Verruca,' Kane butted in (*just* a client? *Just?*). 'It's been driving me crazy, actually.'

'. . . an *appointment*,' Elen persisted, 'he has an appointment. He's not *with* Harvey.'

'Oh . . .' The German seemed disappointed. 'Well that's a pity . . .' He paused for a second, scowling. 'But didn't you use his *name* before . . . ?' he wondered (almost to himself). 'Didn't you say, "*Lester's* banged his nose . . ."?'

Kane nodded, unflustered. 'I've known Lester for years,' he said cheerfully, 'I dated his *cousin*, in fact . . .'

'His cousin?' Dory repeated. '*Lester's* cousin?'

'Yeah. Uh . . .' Kane glanced around him. 'I actually worked for a scaffolding gang in my teens. I'd happily take a quick look at it for you – perhaps tighten a few of the bolts up . . .'

Elen smiled. 'That's a very kind thought,' she said, 'but there's probably some kind of prohibitive clause in our Builder's Insurance . . .'

'Well, the offer's open . . .' Kane shrugged.

The German was still gazing at Kane, very intently. 'I have this strange feeling that we've met before . . .' he murmured.

Kane slowly shook his head.

'Are you sure? It's just . . .' He rubbed his chin, thoughtfully, '. . . there's something . . .'

As he was speaking, all the lights came on in the house behind them –

What?!
But how . . . ?

Kane suddenly became aware that it was growing darker –

Out here
By contrast . . .

– that it was almost . . . almost . . .

Dusk
Yes.

    'Would you mind holding the dog for a second?'
Elen briskly pushed a traumatised Michelle into Kane's arms. He looked
down. The spaniel's sharply domed, white head had been crowned
by three bright drops of blood. She was stiff to the touch, and bony,
like a factory-farmed hen.
He shuddered.
    'She's disabled,' Dory informed him (an edge of revulsion in his
voice). 'Her back legs . . .'
'*Oh*. I see . . .' Kane tried to arrange her more comfortably, but she
was shaking, uncontrollably.
'*I'll* take her.'
    Kane started, then turned. The small boy – Fleet – was standing
directly behind him, holding out his arms. 'She's frighted of strangers.'
'Fright*ened*,' his father corrected him.
    Kane passed the dog down to the boy, noticing, as he did so, that
his hands and his jumper felt curiously warm. Then suddenly cold.
Then wet.
'Oh *God*,' Dory murmured (missing nothing), 'I'm afraid she
must've . . .'
He winced, looking horrified. Kane gingerly prodded at his sweater.
It was sodden.
    'She's got a voluminous bladder for such a tiny scrap,' he mused.
'Fleet, put the dog down,' Dory shouted after his son, 'she's still doing
pee-pee . . .'
    Fleet was heading back into the house, at speed. He completely
ignored his father.

'*Fleet* . . .' Dory barked.

The boy disappeared into the kitchen.

Dory glanced over at Kane with a helpless shrug. 'She isn't actu-ally *our* dog,' he confided. 'She's an awful creature. I really have no idea how she ended up here . . .'

As he spoke, both Lester and Elen glanced over at him. Kane couldn't quite decipher their expressions (disbelief? Irritation? Incredulity?) but there was definitely a level of concord between them.

'Hold them more firmly,' Elen spoke softly, returning swiftly to her patient and readjusting the pack of peas, 'and keep your head back or you'll start to gush again . . .

'. . . You'd better remove your jumper,' she instructed Kane (without even looking at him). 'I'll pop it in the wash. It shouldn't take much more than half an hour.'

'No, it's fine – it's *fine*, really . . .' Kane began fobbing her off.

'But you must,' Dory interjected, plainly appalled. 'You can't possibly go anywhere like that. The *smell*, for one thing . . .'

He waved his hands around, fastidiously.

The smell?

Kane sniffed, deeply. He couldn't actually detect anything. 'It doesn't . . .' he began, and then suddenly he was quite overwhelmed – rabbit-punched – demolished – *abrogated* – by an unholy aroma –

Sweet Lord!

He staggered back a step.

The most . . . the most *terrible* stench. A smell so noxious, putrid and malodorous that it assaulted each of his senses, individually, then drew them all together and melded them – *soldered* them – into a kind of crazy disharmony. It wasn't just a scent now, so much as . . . as *sound*, as *colour*. He could *hear* it – it was . . .

Woah . . .

– it *hissed*, and the light cascaded off it – almost liquid, in a gush; glistening and pulsating. It was opalescent. It was *iri*descent. He felt ambushed by it, *saturated* in it.

252

'Oh God . . . oh *shit* . . .'

He clapped his hands over his nose, leaned forward and gagged, then took another clumsy step back into the sheet. But the feel of the fabric wasn't quite as it should be, it was like a . . . like a solid *wall* of thick, white smoke. He tried to push his hands through it and his hands were suddenly burning. His hands were on fire. He tripped –

Whooo-uuup!

– then he retched again. Violently. He began to cough, to choke. He felt the tender flesh straining in his throat.

'Take it off . . .'

The German was speaking. He'd moved over to assist him. He seemed very close – *too* close.

'Just pull it off . . .'

He yanked Kane's denim jacket from his shoulders, then grabbed at the sweater . . .

As his hands made contact with him Kane felt a sensation of such . . . a *ferocious* tickling. An *excruciating* tickling. He felt his skin goose-bumping and his nipples tightening.

'Please . . .' he gasped, flinching, his eyes watering, uncontrollably, 'I'm actually . . .' he panted, then he retched again. '*Fuck. No.* I'm perfectly . . .' he grabbed at the sweater himself, 'just let me . . .'

He tore the sweater off and threw it away from him, disgusted. It landed in the middle of the paving.

Jesus Christ.

He tried to catch his breath. He was panting and almost . . . almost *laughing*. He was high. Flying.

His entire body was still electrified. *Vibrating*. His heart was banging and hammering like an angry bailiff at the door of his chest.

And the smell? Different now. A sweet smell. A sharp smell. Blood? Filth? *Flowers?* Pumping through his temples, burning into his sinuses; acrid and savage, like singed plastic.

He sneezed, then winced, then blinked. Elen was standing next to him, holding the sweater in her hands. He gazed down at her, almost in wonder . . .

Roses.
No . . .
No.
Lilies?

Dory had moved several paces back.

'Perhaps you should drive Lester home, Isidore,' Elen spoke at normal volume, perfectly calmly, 'on the way to your evening shift?'
Dory peered down at his watch, '*Gracious* – the time . . . Yes. Of course. Good idea.'
He turned to Lester, put a hand on to his shoulder, and then slowly began guiding him through the washing.
'Keep your head tilted . . .' Elen reminded him.

'Will you be all right here?' Dory murmured as they passed.
'Of course. Keep that head *back*, Lester,' she reiterated, grabbing Kane's jacket from the crook of her husband's arm, passing it over to him and then motioning him, casually, towards the house.

'And do try not to bleed on the upholstery,' she persisted, smiling over at Kane as she spoke, almost sardonically. 'It's a company car, remember?'

THREE

The moment Gaffar left him, Beede promptly set about rearranging his old rug (and all of the surrounding furniture) with a fierce – almost *neurotic* – meticulousness. He turned the rug and angled it, precisely (using an old-fashioned, yellow-fabric, roll-up tape-measure), then slotted the sofa, the side-table and the small chair back into position by dint of those slight indentations in the carpet's weave which'd long been established by their former tenure. He stood over the burn for a while (breathing heavily), and inspected it, morosely.

It was a small mark, but ugly. He winced, placing a weary hand to his temples. They were thudding. Throbbing. He felt quite empty – hollow – like a neatly rinsed-out milk bottle. He could feel nothing – *hear* nothing – bar the sound of his own blood pumping –

Just . . .
So . . .
Exhaust . . .

He threw himself down on to the sofa and closed his eyes, with a heavy sigh. Then something odd suddenly struck him. His eyes flew open again.

'But what on earth did he mean . . . ?' he muttered. 'Just some cheap reproduction?'
He peered down at the rug, frowning. He felt . . .
He shook his head –

Don't be silly
Just tired
Too tired . . .

But he continued to sit there and to stare.
After several minutes he stood up. He scratched his chin. He dropped – carefully, somewhat creakily – on to his knees and he inspected the

255

rug more closely. He ran his fingers through its short, stiff fibres. Then he lowered himself on to his stomach (prostrating himself, as if for prayer) and took a long, deep sniff.

He closed his eyes and really concentrated. He sniffed again. Then he raised himself up, scowling.

'Smell's changed,' he murmured.

He scanned the room, slightly panicked, his anxious gaze finally settling on the large and precarious pile of books to which Kane had had recourse a mere three days earlier.

He reached out and grabbed the compact paperback of A.R. Myers' *England in the Late Middle Ages*. He held it in his hand for a minute and inspected the cover – not so much the illustration as the intimate, individual details of his own particular edition: the creases, the wear, the tiny marks in the patina.

He ran a gentle index finger up and down the spine which had been so well-flexed over time that the binding had cracked and whitened, rendering the title and the author's name virtually indecipherable.

He opened the book up. The first page was loose (he nodded slightly, remembering), and it was waterstained, too (again, a small nod).

He'd bought it second-hand. The price had been written, in pencil (£2), in the centre of that first, loose page, at the very top –

Good . . .

– and just to the right of the price was a stamp – a circular stamp – which read 'Davison School, Worthing'. There was another stamp – identical in colour (a faded blue-black) – slightly lower down, which read: 7 September 1971.

He flipped his way through the text, stopping, every so often, to inspect his own comments (scribbled messily but emphatically into the margins). As he paged, he visibly relaxed, appearing to find everything utterly familiar and in perfect order.

'It was an age of contradictions,' he read quietly, at one point, 'as vivid as the bright colours which it loved . . .'

He smiled, weakly, placed the book back on to the pile again, stood up, and walked through to the kitchen. He grabbed his post in one hand, and the kettle in his other (to confirm that it was full enough –

Yup)

– but then he froze, slapped down the letters, shoved his glasses up on to his head and gazed intently at the kettle's lid. Why did it seem so *different*, suddenly? He wobbled it, tentatively, between his finger and his thumb . . .

Hmmn

Was the *fit* less easy? He closely scrutinised each detail: the base, the filament –

Scandalously limed up –
What's wrong with me?
Should've sorted that out weeks back . . .

– the handle, the spout. Then he cursed, softly, under his breath. 'Enough, Beede, you old fool,' he murmured, '*enough.*'

   He pushed down his glasses, plugged in the kettle and strolled through to his bedroom where he was enthusiastically greeted by Manny, the cat. He squatted down and gave him a gentle pat. The cat's backbone arched in response, and his tail shot up. Beede smiled, then emitted a sharp, light, utterly instinctive *pswee-pswee* noise using his teeth and his tongue.

   The cat loved it, rubbing up against him – purring blissfully. Beede's eyes settled, flatly, on his bed –

Tired . . .

– on the counterpane, then dropped down lower, to the legs, then finally, to the carpet. He noticed – with a tiny fluttering in his chest – that the bed seemed to have been moved recently. Or nudged. Just by a couple of inches. He observed the indentation from its weight in the pile of the carpet.

   He stared at the bed again. It was heavy. Wooden. Darkly varnished. Victorian.

So what . . . ?
Or how . . . ?

He stood up and walked over to it. He ran his hand along the head-board. He looked for ridges, for scratches, for familiar imperfections. The cat followed him, tangling around his ankles, mewling.

He glanced down, as if relieved by the distraction. 'Hungry, are we?' He moved over to its 'food station' (ie its water bowl, its food bowl, its litter tray; all neatly arranged on a plastic mat – although the tray – as was the animal's habit – had been fastidiously nudged clear, and the granules from its several careful evacuations had been scattered over the carpet).

The food bowl was still half-full.

'So what is it, boy?' Beede asked. The cat gazed up at him, quizzi-cally, then its head snapped around as the kettle reached boiling point and turned off with a sharp *click*.

'Strong coffee,' Beede murmured, 'a *pint* of it. Care to join me?'

He headed back into the kitchen again, the cat at his heels. He opened the cupboard and removed a jar of Nescafé and a cup. He placed them both down on to the counter, grabbed a teaspoon from a drawer, unscrewed the coffee jar and dipped the spoon inside. His eyes settled – momentarily – on the first letter in his pile of post. He released the spoon. He reached out and picked it up. He inspected the address, irritably. He tore it open.

Inside was a copy of some minutes from a meeting of the Ryan Monkeith Road Crossing Initiative. He scowled as he glanced through them. His scowl deepened as he unfolded a handwritten note from a woman who signed herself Pat Higson/Monkeith which said:

> Beede,
>
> *Sorry you had to leave so early – hope you're feeling a little livelier by now. After you'd gone we took a vote on the contentious issue of Chairman (Tom didn't let me stand in the end. Think it was for the best, but Sarah Howarth did, and Jack Cowper(!!)). Isidore nominated you (in your absence) and I took the liberty of seconding him. The vote was all-but unanimous. So we dearly hope you'll do us the great honour of accepting this pivotal role in our small organisation!*
>
> *All details etc will be ironed out at our next meeting – Wed. 24th. 8pm. Our place again, I'm afraid (Hope the*

new Chair won't mind – I've heard he runs a tight ship!).
Yours . . .

As he read, Beede's jaw slowly stiffened. His eye returned to the line 'Isidore nominated you (in your absence) . . .'
'Damn him!' he gasped. 'But *why*?!'

He screwed up the letter and smashed it down, *hard*, on to the counter, then stood – stock still, eyes unfocussed, thinking deeply. The cat mimicked his reverie, his slim tail kinking, then sprang back, alarmed, as Beede exploded into life again: grabbing his helmet and his jacket, rummaging around inside his pockets for his keys and slamming his way, violently, out of the flat.

Once he'd gone, the cat jumped up, soundlessly, on to the counter and sat there, head cocked, listening intently to the Douglas's old engine (turning, cutting out, turning, cutting out, turning, catching, and then noisily accelerating).

As its clamour gradually faded he reached out a dainty paw and gave the contentious note a gentle tap with it, then watched – eyes narrowing, whiskers a-quiver – as it slid, seductively, across the counter-top.

'I'm sorry it's such a mess in here,' she murmured, bundling his sweater into the machine, yanking out the small detergent drawer, pouring in some washing liquid and adding a tiny drop of fabric conditioner, 'but our electricity cut out this morning – half-way through a washload . . .'

She gestured, wearily, towards all the chair-backs and the radiators which were currently festooned in towels, t-shirts and underwear –
Kane glanced around him –

Oh God, yes –
Her underwear . . .

Elen deftly programmed the machine and pressed the start button. As he stood there –

Stop staring at her bra, you twat

– his phone vibrated in his jacket pocket. It made him start –

Fuck –
Still feeling the after-effects of that crazy sensimillia . . .

'So,' Elen straightened up, smoothing down her skirt, 'shall I take a proper look?'
Her eye moved to his pocket where the phone quietly shuddered.
'Pardon?'
'The foot.'
'Oh. Yeah . . .' he frowned, glancing down, suddenly embarrassed by the notion of actual physical contact.
She observed his sudden reticence and smiled at him, teasingly. 'I thought you said you were in agony.'
'Yes. Well, *no* . . .' he back-pedalled, 'not *agony* exactly . . .'
As he spoke the dog trundled past him (her rear-end now attached – by a series of tiny, silver-buckled leather harnesses – to a jaunty red cart). Kane gazed on – somewhat startled – as she made her stately progress across the floor, her wooden wheels bumping and rattling against the reproduction slate tiling. She stationed herself, with a heavy sigh, directly in front of the washer-dryer.
Elen glanced down at the dog, fondly. 'The machine seems to mesmerise her. She'll stand there for hours, just watching the clothes turning.'

Wow

Kane put his hand to his head. He still felt slightly woozy.
'Are you sure you're all right?' she asked him. Her voice sounding distant, then very near. He blinked.
'Do you have any spirits?' he asked, sitting down, heavily, on a chair, 'whisky, maybe, or brandy?'
She leaned over and grabbed a hold of the vest which he'd in-advertently knocked down on to the floor. As she leaned her hair fell

against his shoulder. He inhaled it. The blackness of her clothing creaked. He felt a powerful urge to touch her.

'Do you think that's a good idea?' she asked.

'What?'

To touch?

'Perhaps a coffee would be better. Or some sweet tea? You look a little pale.'

Kane shrugged. 'Sure. Coffee – or tea, even . . .' he murmured, '. . . if you feel that's more appropriate.'

She gazed at him for a second – quite blankly – then she turned, opened the freezer and pulled out a bottle of frozen Stolichnaya. The bottle was so cold that it stuck to her fingers. She removed a tiny, highly decorated antique thumb glass from a cupboard, filled it and passed it over.

Kane took the glass and held it aloft, staring at it, in a kind of dreamy stupor.

'Is something wrong?' she asked, rolling the cap between her fingers.

'Are you familiar with the story of the Moscow Hotel?' he wondered.

'Pardon?'

He glanced up, distractedly. 'The label. On the bottle. It's a picture of the Moscow Hotel.'

She peered down at the bottle. She saw an uncontentious line drawing of a plain-looking building.

'Won't you join me?' he suddenly asked, with a slight smirk, saluting her with his shot.

'It's a little early,' she said.

He shrugged, knocked his drink back, swallowed, then shuddered.

'You were always such a *sober* little creature . . .' she murmured gently '. . . as I remember.'

Was it gentle?
Truly?
Or was it regretful?

'I wasn't little,' he snapped, 'I was fourteen – fifteen – a teenager.'

'Yes,' she tipped her head, thoughtfully, 'I suppose you were . . .'

'And as *I* remember,' he interjected, almost harshly (determined to

261

defend the honour of that once virulently hormonal adolescent monkey),
'I thought you were . . .' he frowned '. . . quite magnificent.'

Magnificent?!

She chuckled, wryly. 'You didn't get out much, *huh*?'
He grinned back at her.
'Although . . .' her expression grew serious, 'in retrospect . . .' she
looked at him, almost pityingly, 'you *can't've* got out much. Weren't
you your mother's principal carer?'
The smile died on his lips.
'So they needed to build this new hotel in Moscow,' he returned,
somewhat sullenly, to his former subject –

Why'd she insist on doing that?
On ruining things?

– 'and because the building was to be so close to the Kremlin, in the
centre of town – a landmark building – they commissioned two top
architects to come up with designs for it. When they'd completed
their plans, they sent them to Comrade Stalin so that he could tell
them which one he preferred . . .'
He offered her the glass back.
She didn't take it at once. She gazed at him, intently, then smiled,
took it, poured another large shot and downed it. '*Nasdravye,*' she
murmured.
He gave her a sour – almost withering – look. She promptly poured
and downed a second shot, then a third, before covering her mouth
with the back of her hand, leaning forward and coughing, hoarsely,
her hair swinging darkly across her cheeks, her eyes tearing up, like
some kind of wildly romantic girl consumptive –

No.
Stop that.

She cleared her throat. 'It's been a wretched day,' she croaked.
'So anyway . . .' he glanced down, unnerved, absolutely determined –

– not to engage with her emotionally '. . . the architect – or apparatchik, or whatever – takes the two designs to Stalin, to see which
one he likes better. And Stalin's not really paying attention. Perhaps
it's too early in the morning, or he's got a hangover, or he's still
thinking about that pretty young girl in the shiny-white underwear
who he watched in the gymnastics display the day before . . . '

She poured a fifth shot and offered it to him. He took it.
'. . . so instead of signing either one design or the other, he signs in
the middle of *both* and returns the plans with no further comment.'

He downed the shot –

Yup –
Good –
Better.

'Were they divorced by then?' she asked.
He glanced up, sharply.
'Who?'
'Beede and your mother.'

He was silent for a while; shocked.
'Yes,' he said, coldly, 'of course they were.'
'And then the two of you went off to live in America?'
He scowled. 'No. *Yes.* I'm not sure what you mean. They got divorced
when I was six or seven . . .'
'But she wasn't ill at that stage, was she?'

He could tell by the tone of her voice that his answer mattered to
her.
'No. Not exactly. I mean the *signs* were there . . .'
He refused (out of sheer spite) to let his father –

The canny bastard

– entirely off the hook. 'A certain discomfort. A *stiffness*. They
thought it might be arthritis. That's why we emigrated somewhere
warmer.'

'Somewhere hot,' she mused.
'Arizona. The edge of the desert. We lived in a mobile home – a

ramshackle kind of prefab – with rattlesnakes nesting beneath the floorboards and no air conditioning to speak of . . .'
'I thought rattlesnakes were notoriously shy.'
'They are.'

Silence

   'And when you came back?' she persisted.
'What?'
'Was she very ill?'
'Yes.'
'Terminal?'
He nodded.

Silence

'It's gradually coming back to me now . . .' Elen murmured. 'She had such beautiful feet. Powerful feet. Muscular.'
'She trained as a dancer when she was younger.'
Elen's eyes lit up.
'Of *course* – yes. I remember her mentioning that . . .'

Silence

'So they built *both* designs, then, in the end?'
   She leaned forward and took the glass from his hand. 'Because they were so afraid of Stalin that they didn't dare question his decision? Is that how the story goes? They integrated both designs into a single building?'
'Yes.'
Kane's voice sounded flat.
   'You know . . .' she frowned for a second, 'that story *does* sound familiar, now you come to mention it . . .'
She picked up the bottle and inspected it again. 'Although it doesn't look like anything special in the drawing . . .'
'They're knocking it down, anyway,' Kane glowered, 'so it doesn't really matter. They may've knocked it down already, in fact.'
   He took a sudden, mean kind of pleasure in the thought of the hotel's destruction.

'That's a great shame,' she said.

He shrugged. 'It was going to cost more to renovate it than to build something new.'

'But if you actually stop and think about it,' she ruminated, 'the hotel was important. A symbol of Russia's complicated past. A parable. I mean the fear, the power, the compromise, the confusion . . .'

'And the decision to knock it down,' he interrupted, 'is a symbol of Russia's future.'

She slowly shook her head. 'No. That doesn't necessarily follow . . .' she paused, 'and anyway, what kind of a future? One based on ignoring the mistakes of the past?'

'Sure. Why not?'

She looked surprised.

'But of *course* it follows,' he snapped (frustrated by her willingness to take him at face value). 'What you're not seeing is that it's all part of the *same* story. The same . . . uh . . . *trajectory*. You could almost say that the decision to knock it down is at the *heart* of the parable, that it actually tells us *more* about the Russia of today – the world of today – than the story of its construction told us about Russia back then.'

'How depressing.'

She smiled, wistfully.

'That's progress,' he shrugged.

'And so progress – in *your* view – is generally contingent on bull-dozing the painful stuff?'

He didn't answer.

She filled the glass and downed another shot.

He stared at her. She filled the glass again.

'Perhaps five's enough.'

'You're keeping count,' she muttered. 'How sweet.'

He glowered at her.

'Anyway . . .' she shook her head, glumly, 'I never get drunk. It's something about my constitution . . .' she put a graceful hand to her stomach and patted it. 'Solid as a rock.'

Kane grimaced. 'In my extensive experience,' he observed, dryly, 'it's always the worst kind of drunks who like to bend your ear with that kind of nonsense.'

She calmly downed her fifth shot then carried the empty glass over to the sink.

'When I was a student,' she shoved up her sleeves and turned on the tap, 'I once drank an entire bottle of surgical spirit . . .'

'If you *had* actually done that,' he said, bluntly, 'then you wouldn't be standing here now.'

'But I am.'

She peered over her shoulder at him.

Silence

'Yes. I suppose you are,' he grudgingly conceded.

'My father had recently drowned,' she continued, 'in an accident, on a commercial riverboat cruise, and I felt this almost . . . I don't know . . . this overwhelming *urge* to just blank everything out.'

She placed the glass down, gently, on to the draining-board. As she did so Kane noticed a clutch of terrible bruises: hand-prints, finger-prints, in a remarkable array of greens and purple-pinks, just above her wrists. She turned around, grabbed the vodka bottle and casually inspected the label again. 'Just like the Russians, I guess.'

'Weren't you ill?' he asked (struggling to remain focussed on the matter in hand).

'No,' she opened the freezer and placed the vodka back inside again, 'a dry mouth . . . a slight headache. I probably vomited most of it back up.'

She wiped her hands on her skirt and adjusted her sleeves.

The dog sneezed.

They both looked down at her.

Silence

And then – quite out of the blue –

'I thought you were magnificent too,' she said.

Kane froze. Had she actually just spoken? Out *loud*?

'And although she was beautiful – and she really *was*; I'm not just *saying* that . . . I mean she was so funny and so brave and what she *went* through was so horrible . . . But I never cried for her – outside, in my car, remember? Not once did I cry for her. The only person I ever cried for . . .' she paused, thoughtfully '. . . was you.'

She was staring at him – he could tell – but he didn't dare look

up. His eyes remained locked on the spaniel. He felt – he *couldn't*
. . . A maelstrom of emotion. Pain. Self-pity. Fury. Embarrassment.
  His phone began vibrating –

Saved by the bell

– but he made no move to answer it.
  And then suddenly –

Jesus

– there was this . . . this *shadow*. A dark shadow, in the kitchen. A
huge, dark shadow moving slowly towards him, gaining – with every
passing second – in both clarity and definition.
  Kane angled his head slightly and leaned back, to try and get some
kind of . . .

Good God –

An *old* man! Perfectly proportioned. Sharp-edged. Like a paper-cut.
Hunched over, scraggy, and vaguely, well, *comical* to look at . . . An
arthritic old man – hook-nosed, like Mr Punch or Don Quixote – sitting
astride a black, shadow donkey. The donkey was limping – lamely but
methodically – across the walls and the units and the tiling.
  And the old man's hand was holding up some kind of –

What was that?
A club?

– poorly fashioned *cudgel* . . .and he was brandishing it –

Uh . . .

– quite menacingly, high above his head.

  Fuck!

Kane quickly shoved back his chair, almost upsetting it, to prevent a
sudden succession of shadow blows from raining down upon him.

'*Fleet!*' Elen shouted. '*Enough!*'

Kane slowly righted himself, wincing. Straight ahead, in the doorway, stood the boy, his small hands held high and intricately knotted. Behind him? A precariously angled table lamp.

'Holy *shit*!' Kane gaped. 'Where the hell'd you learn how to do that?'

The boy opened his mouth to answer, but before he could, Elen had dashed towards him, grabbed his fingers and rapidly untangled them. 'You *know* you shouldn't . . .' she began, and then, '*Fleet!* What on *earth* . . .?'

She pushed the boy aside and strode into the room beyond, where the lamp was about to topple from its perch on a large pile of cushions. She caught it, switched it off, unplugged it, and placed it down, gently, on to the carpet.

Fleet watched her, impassively. 'Did I do bad, Mummy?' he asked. She scowled over at him. 'I'm afraid you did, Fleet. Yes. *Very* bad.' The boy's face crumpled. 'I didn't *mean* to,' he said.

Elen didn't relent. 'You *know* that you're not allowed to play with the light fitments or the electrical sockets . . .'

He shook his head. 'But I *didn't* know, Mummy. *Honestly*.'

She shoved her hair, brusquely, behind her ears. 'Well you know now. You mustn't *ever* do that again, do you hear me?'

Elen re-entered the kitchen and the boy trailed along behind her, still looking crestfallen.

'I don't understand you, Fleet,' she muttered, 'usually you *hate* touching electrical things . . .'

'Is Mummy upset?' he wondered.

'Yes. *No*. Just surprised . . . *shocked*. And she doesn't want you to do that again, all right?'

'It was only *fun*,' the boy muttered, grabbing on to her skirts and tugging at them.

'Fun for you,' she yanked the skirt from his grasp, 'but not for us. You frightened poor Kane. You gave him a shock.'

The boy gazed at Kane, unrepentantly.

'It *was* a great trick,' Kane conceded, with a shrug.

The boy half-smiled. Elen did not. 'You gave us *all* a bad shock,' she reiterated.

'Okay.'

The boy sniffed then yawned (already thoroughly bored of his mother's strictures). He grabbed a hold of her skirts again, '*Slœpan*, Mama,' he wheedled.

'*Schlafen*,' Elen promptly corrected him.

'What?'

The boy stared up at her, frowning.

'*Schlafen*,' Elen repeated.

'But that's what I just *said*, stupid!'

Elen's mouth tightened.

Kane idly watched on, observing the tip of the boy's head, the angle of his jaw. A pale face, a round yet oddly *girlish* face. Handsome, but with a touch of something . . .

Uh . . .

'If you're tired, Fleet, then you should go to bed.'

'No.'

He shook his head.

'But of *course* you must.'

'*Can't.*'

He stamped his foot.

'But it's nearly bed-time anyway . . .'

'*No.* Shut *up*!' he squealed.

Elen remained perfectly calm.

'I'll heat you a nice glass of milk . . .'

'*No!* I *won't!* I don't *want* to sleep,' the boy yelled, 'I want to stay awake, just like *you* do, and like *Daddy* does.'

Kane's gaze shifted back to Elen again, to see how she would react. She glanced up. He noticed – with some surprise – that her pupils were tiny – like pin-pricks.

The boy began grizzling.

Elen gently stroked his curls, then reached down and grabbed a hold of his hand. The boy suddenly unleashed a violent shriek. He sprang back, shoving the hand she'd tried to take under its opposite armpit, bending his knees, howling.

She gazed down at him, shocked. He howled again, even more dramatically. Kane stood up. 'I should go,' he murmured.

Elen was kneeling down, now, struggling to untangle the boy's arms. Finally, she managed it. 'You've got a cut,' she said, 'on your hand. Stop wriggling. Let me take a proper look . . .'

269

Kane peered over at the boy and saw it. The long scratch. The nasty tear.

He peered down at his own hand, then took a quick step back.

Elen glanced up at him.

'But what about your foot?' she asked, through the boy's pathetic keening. 'And your jumper?'

'It's fine . . .'

He continued to back away from her, suddenly struggling to . . . struggling for . . .

Can't . . .
Uh . . .
Trapped

'I can always . . .'

'Come and see me at the surgery,' she nodded, hugging the boy to her. 'Ask Beede for the number.'

'Thanks for the vodka,' he gasped –

Throat tightening up

– clutching (out of sheer habit) for the phone in his pocket, his keys, lunging clumsily for the door –

Must –
Get –
Need . . .
Uh . . .

– wrenching at the lock, then exploding – like a frantically resurfacing man-mole (its scrabbling claws unleashing a chaotic fountain of pebbles-roots-bugs-dirt . . .

Ahhhhh!)

– into the rich, deep pile of the navy night.

270

FOUR

'Forgive me. What awful timing. I should've thought to ring ahead . . .'

A startled-looking Daniel Beede addressed this awkward apology to an exquisitely set dining table and the four people surrounding it (while trying – and failing – to back his way out of the room into which he'd just that moment been unsuspectingly led).

'*Nonsense!*'

The tall, dark, vivacious woman who was entirely responsible for luring him there grabbed a firm hold of his arm and patted it, reassuringly. 'This is just perfect. In fact you couldn't have timed it better. We'd catered for six, then poor Cheryl's blind date got the jitters and stood her up at the last minute . . .'

Cheryl (an attactive, well-adjusted forty-nine-year-old woman) lifted an obliging hand to mark herself out from the other diners.

'Hi. That's me . . .' she smiled, winningly (apparently perfectly willing to embrace the myriad of comic possibilities engendered by having been recently snubbed by a man she'd never met) '. . . and no, for your information, he wasn't *actually* blind.'

The entire table tittered.

'Just *extremely* short-sighted, *eh*?!'

The man to her right nudged her, cruelly (again, the titters). As he nudged he accidentally pushed a side-plate into her wine glass.

Clink!

'*Tom*, you *oaf*! Watch the *crystal*!' Beede's companion hollered, good-naturedly. Beede winced.

'Doesn't care if I break it, mind . . .' the nudger complained to the fragrant but slightly worn-out blonde on his other side, 'just doesn't want to upset the *caterer*. A complete, bloody she-devil. Made Pat disinfect the refrigerator before she'd even *deign* to unpack the food from her van into it . . .'

'What's she got?' the second, rather more portly but equally expensively tailored man at the table enquired.

'Funny little hatch-back. A Citroën *Berlingo*. It's parked out the front.'

'Of course . . .' the second man snapped his fingers, in recognition, 'I think I saw it as we pulled up.'

The dazed-looking blonde – who wore a tight, white roll-neck and heavy make-up – gazed over at Pat, horrified. 'She made you clean out your fridge, Pat? I'm not being *funny*, but . . .'

Beede's affable companion shook her head. 'Tom's exaggerating, Laura. She just needed some extra room so I did a quick . . .'

'As God is my *witness*!' Tom interjected. 'I stagger home after a long day at the coalface, only to be sent straight back out – flea in my ear – to get some Dettox fridge spray and a bottle of *silver* polish. Arrive home for the second time, and blow me if she doesn't have me perched at the breakfast bar – like a disgraced schoolboy – polishing the cutlery!'

'Did a *lovely* job, Tom,' Cheryl sniggered, lifting up a dessert spoon, panting on to the back of the bowl and then buffing it, assiduously, with the sleeve of her top.

'Show them your fingers,' Pat instructed him.

Tom lifted up his hands. Every nail was blackened.

'How *awful*!'

Laura shook her head, horrified. 'I mean what's the point in getting a meal specially catered if you end up with hands looking like that?'

'He *offered*, Laura,' Pat struggled to pacify her. 'You should've *seen* it. All "yes Ms Sayle, no Ms Sayle" he was.'

'Is that her name, then?' Laura asked. 'Ms Sayle?'

'Well what kind of *sense* would the story make if it *wasn't*?' the car man sniped.

'Good *God*, Pat,' Cheryl spluttered (over the top of the others, half-way through a sip of wine), 'my idle, chauvinist brother actually *volunteering* to do some housework? Has the world finally gone *mad*?!'

'What do you *mean*?' Tom drew himself up, outraged. 'I'm a *completely* modern male. Ask the girls in the office. I make them a pot of fresh coffee, every morning, without fail . . .'

'You'd be quite astonished,' Pat *faux*-sniffed, 'how "modern" Tom can get around a clutch of attractive office girls.'

'*Attractive*?! *That* lot?!' Tom howled. 'Back me up, Charlie. Most of 'em are homely enough to stop the clock!'

'Stop the *what*?!' Cheryl snorted.

'The last time Tom brought me coffee in bed was when Max was three months old,' Pat sighed, all misty-eyed, 'on my twenty-fifth birthday . . .' she glanced around the assembled company, 'and how old is Max now?'

Tom began wailing.

'No! *Seriously!* How old is he?'

'Twenty-three?' Laura took a wild guess.

'Twenty-*four*!' Pat struggled to make herself heard over the general commotion. 'Getting *Tom* to lift a finger at home . . . ?' she threw up her free hand, despairingly. 'It'd be easier to get the Pope to fit a condom.'

'*Proper* coffee and everything,' Tom ignored his wife and continued to swank about his office achievements, 'in the *cafetiere* . . .'

'*Really?*' Laura looked suitably impressed. '*Proper* coffee? Charlie wouldn't know one end of a cafetiere from the other.'

'Don't be ridiculous,' Charlie snapped, 'of course I do.'

'No you *don't*.'

'It's a little plastic thing-y with a plunger . . .'

Charlie quickly mimed how to use the object in question.

Laura puckered up her lips, irritably.

'I'm *right* aren't I?'

'How *old* is she?' Cheryl asked Pat.

'Who?'

'The caterer.'

'Old enough to know better,' Tom grumbled.

'Young enough to teach an old dog new tricks,' Pat struck back.

'We'll get a good look at her when she brings out the starter,' Laura said, reaching for a stuffed, green olive from a nearby bowl, biting one end and inadvertently squirting the stuffing out through the other and straight down the front of her top.

'Oh *bugger*.'

She grabbed her napkin and began dabbing.

'Can't take you anywhere,' Tom moaned.

'I really should . . .' Beede used this brief, domestic interlude to try and start backing towards the door again.

'Don't be such a party pooper!' Pat clung tenaciously on to his arm.

'Pull out a pew,' Tom seconded her, 'there's plenty to go around.'

'I've already eaten . . .' Beede lied, a thin line of perspiration dotting his upper lip.

'That doesn't matter . . .' Pat insisted, 'it's just a *social* thing. We're one short and I'd be *so* grateful . . .'

'To be perfectly frank,' Beede brusquely informed her, 'I've got a fair bit of paperwork to be getting on with at home . . .'

'But it's our *Wedding* Anniversary,' Pat gazed at him, pleadingly.

'Sit down, old boy or I'll never hear the end of it,' Tom exhorted.

'If it's *me* you're worried about,' Cheryl delivered him a frank smile, 'then I absolutely promise to leave your virtue intact.'

'*Well* . . .' Tom muttered, 'until she's finished her second glass . . .'

'*Tom!* Stop provoking your sister!' Pat scolded him, yanking a reluctant Beede forward a step. 'Cheryl, this is Beede. Beede, this is Cheryl . . .'

Cheryl frowned. '*Bead*? As in necklace?'

'No. Beede as in . . .' Pat thought for a second. 'Yes. As in necklace, but without the "a" and with two extra "e"s.'

'So *not* as in necklace,' Tom rolled his eyes, long-sufferingly.

'And of course you know *Tom*,' Pat continued.

Beede smiled, curtly.

'*Everybody* knows Tom,' Laura exclaimed.

'And the woman with the embarrassing *stain* down her cleavage . . .' Charlie interrupted her.

'That's Laura, my sister-in-law . . .'

Pat paused as Laura waved a genial hello. 'And Charlie, my brother . . .' she cleared her throat, carefully, 'Laura and Charlie *Monkeith*.'

Beede stiffened as he reached out to shake Tom's hand. 'But of *course* . . .' he said, nodding sharply, like a tight-arsed but intensely respectful *commandant*, 'very pleased to meet you.'

'Beede just did us the great honour of accepting the post of Chairman on the Road Initiative Committee,' Pat continued, somewhat nervously, 'for Ryan.'

Silence

'I *must* actually . . .' Beede gently demurred.

'It's not embarrassing at *all*,' Laura brusquely interrupted him, peering down at her generously proportioned bust and rapidly dabbing again. '*Look*. It's almost come off.'

Charlie didn't look. Instead he pointed towards Beede's piss-pot. 'Come on a bike, eh?'

Beede gazed down at his helmet as if it were a curious tumes-cence which had just that second sprouted from the tips of his fingers.

'*Uh* . . .'

'I admire your fortitude, old boy,' Tom whistled, 'it's *stinking* weather for it.'

As Tom spoke Pat whisked away Beede's helmet and then placed her hands on to his shoulders to lift off his waterproofs. Beede started, involuntarily, as if her graceful hands were the clumsy mitts of an arresting officer.

'I'm *sorry*, Pat,' he insisted, 'but I'm afraid I *really* must . . .'

'Is it an old one?' Charlie asked.

Beede didn't answer. He was too busy fighting a losing battle to keep hold of his jacket.

'Didn't you hear it back-fire,' Tom asked, 'five minutes ago, pulling up?'

'Charlie here is a car and bike fanatic,' Pat informed Beede as she neatly folded his jacket over the crook of her arm, 'he owns that huge Jag' dealership on the edge of the Orbital Park, just across from the market . . .'

Beede nodded, despairingly, half an eye still fixed on the door. 'Yes. *Yes*. I'm familiar with the place,' he murmured.

Underneath his coat Beede was wearing his white hospital over-alls, the bottom half of which were partially obscured by a pair of voluminous, plastic, all-weather trousers.

The assembled company sat quietly for a moment and quietly assessed his unconventional garb. Beede looked down at himself, mortified.

'Remove your plastic trousers,' Pat instructed him, 'and then we can stick your all-weather gear in the laundry to dry off.'

'Drove a Ducatti for over twenty years,' Charlie fondly reminisced.

'Well you kept it in the *garage* for twenty years,' Laura corrected him, 'gathering a thick layer of dust.'

'That's simply not true,' Charlie snapped, 'I used to love taking it out on the road to follow the *Tour de France* . . .'

'You did that *once*,' Laura scoffed, 'the year we got engaged, then came staggering home – after three days, at most – with a dozen septic *blisters* all over your arse.'

'Beede drives an old Douglas, Charlie,' Tom quickly stepped in. 'Makes a racket like a constipated mule on a diet of beans, it does.'

'You'll probably need to remove your boots first,' Pat gently encouraged him.

'Uh . . .'

Beede glanced down. 'Yes . . .'

He noticed some suspicious-looking brown stains on the carpet behind him. 'Oh dear . . . I'm afraid I should've . . .'

A lean, fine-boned but imperious-seeming woman suddenly appeared in the doorway wearing a pristine serving apron and matching cap. She was holding a grand silver server piled high with tiny rolls. On espying Beede in the act of disrobing, she froze.

Pat glanced over, unabashedly. 'Is that the starter already, Emily? Because we've actually got one extra . . .'

'So we're back up to *six* again?' Emily enquired, icily.

'Yes we are.'

Pause

'I see.'

'Is that a problem?'

Longer pause

'No. But it'll put the entire first course back by *at least* half an hour.'

'That's absolutely *fine*, dear,' Pat beamed at her, 'just do the best you can.'

Beede miserably yanked off his boots and his all-weather trousers. He was now a vision of social inappropriateness in head-to-toe dazzling white.

Emily remained in the doorway, inspecting his attire, blinking rapidly.

'Are those the rolls?' Pat asked, grabbing Beede's boots and his waterproofs.

'Yes they are.'

'Well how about you slide those on to the sideboard and *I'll* do the honours while you take Beede's biking gear and hang it up in the laundry . . . ?'

Emily opened a disdainful mouth to answer as Pat bustled towards her, but Pat jinked in first. 'That's *wonderful*. You're an *angel*. She's an angel, *isn't* she, everybody?'

'. . . and if you could just open an extra bottle of *white* and stick it in the cooler . . . Bang the rolls on to the sideboard, dear . . . *that's* right. I'll deal with those later.'

Emily slid the rolls on to the sideboard and was then promptly swaddled with Beede's boots and muddy outerwear.

'Let's leave the helmet here, shall we?'

Pat displayed Beede's dented piss-pot on a highly varnished incidental table next to a beautiful vase brimming with fabulous pink and red imported peonies.

As Emily left the room she shot Beede a look of compressed rage. Pat had already grabbed the salver of rolls. She held them aloft, on the flat of an upturned palm, and sashayed around the table dispensing them with a pair of matching tongs.

'You'd never guess my lovely wife was once a cocktail waitress . . .' Tom sighed (with a look of quiet satisfaction), gently patting her rump as she passed him by.

'Yes you would,' Laura chided him, 'just look how beautifully she's carrying that tray . . .'

'That's exactly what he *meant*, Laura,' Charlie sniped.

'Pat and I first met when we were working as bunnies,' Laura informed Beede, 'in the seventies.'

'Is that so?' Beede said.

'Yes. Playboy bunnies,' she dimpled, 'with *wittle* white cotton-tails and *loooong* pink ears . . .'

Beede looked horrorstruck.

'I think Beede's probably already *perfectly* familiar with the concept of a Playboy bunny, Laura,' Charlie snarled.

'Beede,' Pat pointed to an empty place on Cheryl's left, 'you squeeze in there, next to Cheryl. That's right.'

Beede pulled out a chair and sat down. He removed a large, linen napkin from its silver ring and spread it out with methodical – almost exaggerated – care across his lap.

Cheryl watched on, intently.

'You have my intense sympathy,' she murmured, when he was finally done, 'bright whites can be such *bastards* to maintain, can't they?'

'So an old *Douglas*, eh?' Charlie returned staunchly to his former subject.

Beede glanced up, still struggling to process Cheryl's last comment.
'Pardon?'

'Dragonfly?'

'Uh . . . The bike? *Yes*.'

'As a point of interest, how long did that marque actually survive?'

'I believe they ended production in '56.'

Beede took a tiny, brown roll from his bounteous hostess.

'So what's the grunt?'

Beede's brows rose slightly. 'The engine's a 348cc horizontally opposed twin cylinder four-stroke.'

'Heavy, is she?'

'365lbs.'

'So top speed . . . I'm estimating seventy-odd?'

'Seventy-five, at a push.'

'How the hell d'you find parts?' Tom butted in.

'On the internet, mainly . . .' Beede tore his tiny roll in half. 'There's a handful of extremely useful dedicated sites.'

'So what do you *do*, Beede?' Laura suddenly interjected, plainly still mesmerised by the bright gleam of his uniform.

Beede placed the two halves of his roll down on to his side-plate. 'I run the Laundry Department at the Frances Fairfax.'

'The *laundry*? *Really*?' Laura looked astonished.

Beede nodded.

'*Wow* . . .' Laura continued to look amazed.

'Believe it or not,' Pat stepped in, leaning over his shoulder and filling one of his glasses with wine and the other with sparkling water, 'Beede here has actually been awarded the Freedom of the Borough for a lifetime of service to the community. It's an incredible honour.'

'The Freedom of the Borough?' Laura parroted.

'Yes,' Beede muttered, embarrassed, 'for what it's worth.'

'The Freedom of the Borough . . .' Laura repeated. 'What's that *mean*, exactly?'

'It means he can go anywhere he likes in the town without any kind of restriction,' Cheryl told her.

'Anywhere at *all*?'

'Oh *God* . . .'

Charlie shook his head, despairingly.

'Of course . . .' Cheryl smiled, 'his big speciality is turning up – at mealtimes – to demand a free feed.'

Beede shifted in his seat, uneasily. Laura frowned, as if not entirely convinced.

'There's an ancient custom,' Beede volunteered, spontaneously, 'among certain nomadic desert tribes which demands that whenever you meet a stranger on his travels you're duty-bound to feed and to water him: however much – or however little – food and water you actually have. It's a charming – even *altruistic* – tradition in many respects but entirely based on pragmatism, because – of course – if ever you find *yourself* in dire need then you can always depend on the kindness of others.'

Silence

'Apparently they were phenomenal speedway bikes . . .' Charlie observed.
'The Dragonfly? Yes.' Beede nodded. 'They were.'
'I have several lucrative contracts with the Saudis,' Tom piped up, 'and let me tell you, those people really *know* how to entertain.'
'So what did you actually *do*,' Laura asked, 'to get this Freedom?'
'Did you see the *look* that woman gave you?' Cheryl suddenly asked Pat, 'when you took the rolls off her?'
'What look?'
Pat seemed bemused.
'What *look*? You didn't notice the *look*?'
'*Was* there a look?' Tom asked.
'*I'll* say there was.'
'I have a friend who once managed the women's clothing department in the Marble Arch branch of Marks & Spencer's,' Laura told Beede, 'which is always *full* of Arabs. And she told me how one of her girls was crouched down – picking up some stock which'd fallen off its hanger – and as she was bent over this Arab came across and just and sat down on her.'

Silence

'How do you *mean*?' Charlie asked.
'He sat down on her back, like she was a chair or . . .' Laura frowned, 'or a *pouf*.'
'A pouf?' Cheryl repeated, blankly.

'Yes. Like a little chair without arms. A pouf. Or a footstool.'

'And an Arab *man* came and sat down on her *back*?' Tom repeated, as Emily re-entered the room holding a soup tureen.
'Yes.'

Silence

'Because apparently in Arabia it's quite commonplace behaviour. But my friend said she went up to him and she told him – very firmly – that we didn't treat our shop assistants in that way. Not here in England.'

Emily began ladling some soup into Tom's bowl, the corners of her lips tightened into a supercilious smile.

'In all my years of visiting the Middle East,' Tom mused, picking up his spoon, 'I've never witnessed the kind of behaviour you describe.'

Laura shrugged.

'If I may be so bold . . .' Beede said, 'that story has the slight ring of an urban myth to it.'

'A what?' Laura asked, as she jinked over to the side to receive her portion.

'An urban myth,' Beede repeated.

'He means a *lie*,' Charlie translated, somewhat unhelpfully.

Laura looked horrified. 'It's not a lie at all,' she insisted, 'my *friend* told me . . .'

Her eyes filled with tears.

Emily served Charlie. Charlie was grinning broadly, apparently utterly delighted by the trouble he'd instigated.

'That's *not* actually what it means at all . . .' Beede rapidly backtracked.

'*Isn't* it, though?' Cheryl asked.

'No. Urban myths are stories which possibly have some fundamental *basis* in truth but which become . . .' he paused, carefully, '*exaggerated*.'

'Kind of like a game of Chinese Whispers, Laura,' Pat explained, diplomatically.

'But a Chinese Whisper starts out one way and ends up *completely* the other,' Laura reasoned, 'and my friend actually *worked* in Marks & Spencer's. She was *there*.'

'In Marble Arch. Yes. We *know*,' Charlie interrupted.

Laura turned to him. 'Alice Wilson told me. *You* know Alice Wilson. She wouldn't just *lie*, would she?'

'Alice Wilson?' Charlie frowned. 'Oh *Christ*. You mean that awful cockney woman who runs the salon?'

Laura nodded.

Charlie rolled his eyes. '*Appalling* creature.'

Laura stared down into her bowl, her mouth tightening.

'I mean what were you *thinking*,' Charlie casually fished a prawn out of his soup and popped it into his mouth, 'idly repeating some stupid story she told you in the salon *here*, at Pat and Tom's anniversary dinner?'

Emily was now poised across Beede's shoulder with her ladle.

'I'm sorry . . .' Beede suddenly covered his bowl with his hand, 'but are there prawns in this soup?'

'It's a spicy Thai seafood broth,' Emily informed him, in clipped tones.

'It sounds delicious,' he smiled, grimly, 'but I'm afraid I'm extremely allergic to prawns.'

'Oh *dear*,' Pat said, 'I wish I'd known that.'

'It's fine,' Beede smiled, 'I'll just eat the roll. The roll's more than enough.'

He picked up his roll.

'Emily could always fish the prawns out . . .'

Pat tried to work her way around the problem.

'Uh . . . *No*. I don't think . . .'

'Could you do that, Emily?'

Pause

'I suppose I could *try*.'

'No, *honestly*, I'm allergic to prawns. If I eat even a tiny piece of prawn . . .'

'What happens?' Cheryl asked.

'I suffocate and die.'

'Oh.'

Emily moved back, stiffly, as if Beede's allergy might prove contagious in some way.

'Can you eat vegetable soup?' Pat wondered.

'I can eat pretty much anything so long as there aren't any prawns involved.'

'Well here's an idea then . . .' she smiled, 'Emily, I have some left-over vegetable soup from lunch in a Tupperware container in the refrigerator. Would you mind heating *that* up for Beede?'

'You want me to heat up some *old* vegetable soup?' Emily asked, aghast.

'Yes. You said the main course would be half an hour late, so hope-fully you should have . . .'

Pat inspected her watch.

Emily turned and left the room.

Pat glanced up, with a slight frown, surprised to see Emily gone. 'Well *that's* good then,' she said.

'Please,' Beede gestured expansively to the table, 'don't let your starters get cold on my account.'

'Are you *sure*?' Pat asked.

'Never more so.'

'Tom's already started,' Cheryl murmured, picking up her spoon.

They all commenced eating, except for Laura.

'I see no earthly reason why Alice would feel the need to *lie* . . .' she suddenly said.

'Please forgive my wife,' Charlie told the table, 'she's taking anti-depressants and they're making her a little . . .' he paused, specula-tively, reaching for the perfect word '. . . *irritating*.'

Laura's hand flew up to cover her mouth.

'So do you work on a *rota* system in the laundry?' Cheryl asked.

'Yes,' Beede answered.

'I was always under the impression that you worked alongside Isidore,' Tom interjected.

'*Isidore?*' Beede looked momentarily anxious. 'Yes. *Yes*. I *do*, occa-sionally,' he hastily conceded, 'on the local guided tours.'

'Isidore?' Charlie looked up from his soup. 'You mean the German who works for Jeff Ronsard over at Ronsard Security?'

Beede nodded.

'Lovely chap. Know him well. I provide their fleet. Jeff's an old pal of mine.'

'Aren't you *hungry*, Laura?' Pat enquired, tentatively.

Laura picked up her spoon and tried to eat a mouthful of soup, but her hand was shaking, almost uncontrollably.

'Would you like to come to the *bathroom*?' Pat asked, making as if to stand up.

'No,' Laura said, 'I'm fine.'

She paused. 'And I'm very sorry,' she added, 'if my behaviour's proved *irritating* to anybody this evening.'

'Don't be *silly*,' Tom chided her, fondly.

'You said it, old boy,' Charlie seconded him, perhaps a fraction less tenderly.

Laura threw down her spoon. 'That's *it*,' she hissed at her husband. 'You've been taking pot shots at me *all night* and I've had just about *enough*.'

'Let's go to the bathroom, Laura,' Pat stood up.

'I don't *need* to go to the bathroom,' Laura snapped, 'I'm not a *child*. Just *sit down*.'

Pat sat down, shocked.

'You're just tired,' Charlie told her, 'and a little *confused*.'

'I am *not* confused. I know *perfectly well* what's going on here.'

Emily re-entered the room, carrying a bowlful of soup. She whisked away Beede's empty setting and placed it down, reverently, before him.

'Nothing's going *on*, Laura,' Cheryl muttered.

'If you *must* know, Cheryl,' Laura snarled, 'hell'd freeze over before I'd look to *you* for support.'

Cheryl seemed taken aback.

'Is your soup warm enough?' Pat asked Beede. 'Because it didn't seem to take her very long . . .'

Laura also glanced over at Beede, as if perceiving *him*, at least, to be a dispassionate observer.

'Have *you* noticed him taking pot shots?' she asked.

'Uh . . .' Beede picked up his spoon. 'This looks *delicious*,' he said, dipping it into the soup and then consuming a large mouthful.

The soup was ice cold. He tried not to grimace as he swallowed.

'Is that good?' Pat asked.

'Wonderful,' he patted his lips with his napkin.

'Are you sure?'

'Absolutely.'

He took another spoonful.

'It's cold,' Cheryl said, peering down into his bowl, 'isn't it?'

'Not at all.'

'Am I not only *irritating* but *INAUDIBLE* now?' Laura yelled.

Beede leaned back, slightly alarmed, as Cheryl touched the side of his bowl.

'Ice cold,' she pronounced.

'Is it?' Pat asked.

'*Ice* bloody cold.'

'Are you sure?' Tom asked.

'*You* feel it.'

Cheryl picked up Beede's bowl and passed it over to her brother.

'Perhaps he has,' Beede quietly conceded '. . . been a little . . . a little *sharp* at points. But I don't think . . .'

Charlie glanced up from his soup, shocked.

'Sharp? Me? Absolutely not.'

'That *is* cold,' Tom pronounced, sticking his spoon in and trying some. 'Jesus *Christ*. It's disgusting.'

'*See?!*' Laura spat.

'But obviously I don't . . . That's just . . . that's . . .' Beede stuttered.

'You may be the new Chairman of the Road Crossing Initiative, Beede,' Charlie told him, perfectly cordially, 'but you are not – Thank God – the Chairman of my marriage.'

'No. Of course. And I wouldn't . . .'

Laura picked up her spoon and began eating, voraciously. Charlie glanced over at her. 'This soup is good, Laura,' he said, 'isn't it?'

'*Fuck. Right. Off*,' she sang.

'She shouldn't get away with that,' Cheryl told Pat. 'I mean how much are you *paying* her?'

'*I'm* paying her,' Tom said, 'and that soup is *ice* cold.'

Pat stood up. 'Should I call her in and tell her to heat it up?'

'Good heavens, no,' Beede tried to grab his bowl back, 'just finish your meals. I'm *enjoying* the soup. The soup's *fine* . . .'

'It's the *principle*, old boy,' Tom told him.

'But I just . . .I *don't* . . .'

'I mean how long does it take to slam a bowl of soup into the *microwave*?' Cheryl asked.

'*Emily?*'

Pat left the room, holding the offending bowl aloft.

'Imagine,' Tom said, fishing a prawn out of his own soup and devouring it, 'if we were in the Sahara Desert, Beede – a family of nomads – and Emily was our cook, and you arrived – at the last minute – and we were suddenly obliged to cater . . .'

The sound of raised voices emerged from the kitchen area.

'Oh dear,' Beede said.

Charlie finished his soup and threw down his spoon, with a clatter.

'Right,' he said, pushing back his chair, 'fag break.'

He glanced around the table. 'Fag break, anybody?'

'Good idea,' Tom stood up.

'Cheryl?'

'Gasping,' she said.

'Laura?'

'Is it still raining?' Laura asked.

'Jesus *Christ*, woman,' Charlie bellowed, 'where's your spirit of adventure?'

'Beede?'

Laura looked over at him. 'Smoke?'

'No, I . . .'

'Sixty-seconds,' Tom promised him, as they all trooped out.

Beede sat alone in the dining-room. He gazed, somewhat distractedly, at the partially eaten portions of soup, the cutlery, the settings, the rolls. He took a sip of his wine and then a sip of his water. He stretched out his legs and was surprised to feel his feet making contact with something soft and tactile –

A cushion?
A handbag?

He leaned over, flipped up the cloth and peered under the table. There he saw a cat – a Siamese cat. It gazed up at him, unblinking.

'Well *hello*,' he said, the top half of his torso disappearing from the cat's eye-line for a moment, then quickly reappearing, his hand pinching something, seductively, between its thumb and its forefinger, 'Fancy a bit of lovely, fresh seafood, do we?'

FIVE

It was almost dinnertime. As he picked a careful route along the ward (avoiding the hordes of stony-faced kitchen staff who were furiously shunting a series of heavily laden metal trolleys around) Gaffar was piqued to discover that Kelly already had a visitor –

Eh?!

A girl. A voluptuous girl; tall but very pale, with a mess of wiry, black hair. On drawing closer (approaching from the rear) he saw that her hair wasn't naturally dark. Her roots (more than an inch past showing) were actually a fine, copper brown.

She was visiting Kelly but they weren't conversing. The girl was staring off blankly into space while Kelly struggled to adjust the ring-tone on her new phone.

'Bloody *hell*, mate,' she murmured, glancing up, distractedly, at his tentative approach, 'ain't you got no home to go to?'

Before Gaffar could muster up a response she held out the phone, proudly. 'Hey! See what Geraldine brought me . . .'

Geraldine turned to appraise him.

'*Yah!*'

Gaffar leapt back, with a holler. Geraldine's mouth had been neatly sewn up with a piece of black string.

Kelly gave no appearance of having noticed his reaction – or if she had, then she'd plainly resolved to just let it pass. 'Gerry . . .' she graciously undertook the formal introductions, 'this here is *Gaffar*, Kane's little Turkish whore. Gaffar, meet my gorgeous cousin, Miss Geraldine Broad.'

'Not Turk, *Kurd*,' Gaffar modified Kelly's introduction slightly, offering Geraldine a friendly hand. Geraldine inspected his hand, then inspected her own hand, then lifted up her own hand, limply, then seemed to forget what she'd lifted it for.

Gaffar moved forward, grasped her hand, and shook it, warmly.

'Is she *problem* with this mouth?' he asked Kelly, as he shook.

'A problem? With her gob? *Nah*. The only real problem Gerry has is that she's thick as shit. *That's* why she sewed the damn thing up.'

Geraldine scowled at her.

'*Yaag!*' Gaffar looked appalled. 'Is she poss for *speak* like this?'

'Yeah. 'Course. It's only *cosmetic*. Fashion, yeah? If she's got somethin' important to say – which she never has, as it happens – then she can always pull the stitches out . . .'

'But it's nothing less than criminal!' 'Gaffar exclaimed. **'Whatever possessed such a beautiful girl to do something so hideous to her face?'**

Geraldine stared at him, blankly.

'Is crazy?' Gaffar asked Kelly.

'She's my fuckin' *cousin*,' Kelly scowled, 'she's a *Broad*. 'Course she's fuckin' crazy. We *all* are.'

Then she snorted.

Gaffar stared at Geraldine. Geraldine stared back at him, calmly. He thought she was quite beautiful with her skin as pale as steamed haddock and her eyes the colour of roasted aubergine. She wore a powerful perfume . . . Something heady and exotic. Something which smelled like jasmine. Like *chocolate*.

'I have never before *see* such a thing as this . . .'

He pointed to her mouth; the four tiny holes pierced above her lip-line, the four tiny holes pierced below, and the neat black thread connecting them in the cruellest of zig-zags.

Geraldine raised one, slightly quizzical eyebrow (as if to say, 'So where've you *been* all your life?').

'Turkey,' he promptly answered, 'Diyarbakir: **the Town of the Black Walls. A town with standards. If my sister ever came home looking like that I'd fucking kill her. Then I'd kill myself.**'

She shrugged, indifferent.

'Although I have no sister,' Gaffar added, as an afterthought, 'praise Allah.'

'She's a Goth,' Kelly informed him.

'Goff,' Gaffar repeated.

'Go*th*. G-o-t-h. Go*th*.'

'*Goth.*'

Geraldine shook her head, very firmly. Gaffar drew closer. 'Wha's this?' She shook her head, again.

Gaffar turned to Kelly. 'No. She say she no this . . . *uh* . . . "Goth".'

'Fuckin' *is*, mate.'

Geraldine shook her head and flared her nostrils slightly.

'Now you make her *piss*!' Gaffar exclaimed, delighted.

Kelly sat up straight. 'Well if you *ain't* a damn Goth,' she yelled, 'why'd you listen to Marilyn fuckin' *Manson*, wear antique fuckin' *lace* and sew your stupid *trap* shut? *Eh*?'

Geraldine shrugged.

'And check out her *boots* for Christsakes . . .' Kelly pointed, derisorily, 'only a fuckin' Goth'd wear boots like that.'

Gaffar looked down at her boots. They were heavy, black leather, knee-high boots with 6-inch, silver-plated, stack heels.

'Explain for Gaffar . . .'

Gaffar perched on the end of the bed, facing her. 'How you . . .' he pointed, 'how . . . **what're the actual logistics of this set-up?**'

He made a sewing gesture.

'What she does,' Kelly helpfully explained, 'is get a little bit of string – black, obviously, 'cos she's a total, fuckin' *Goth* – an' melts some wax on the end of it so she stiffens it up a bit. Then she threads it through the piercings and sews her mouth together. *Natch!* She used to have a fella who did the same thing, but they broke up.'

'Is so?'

Gaffar peered over his shoulder at Kelly. 'Man do this crazy thing, too?'

'Yeah. They think it's *art*, mate. Or some such. Stupid *twats*. But then they *split*, see? She wore him out. He said she just never shut up.'

Kelly made a jabbering motion with her hand. 'Much too *gobby* . . .'

Pause

Gaffar stared at Geraldine, quite transfixed.

'Jesus *Christ*,' Kelly snorted, 'I'm fuckin' *wasted* on you lot.'

'I never see this before,' Gaffar repeated, slowly shaking his head. 'Is incredible.'

Geraldine looked pleased. She almost grinned, but the stitching stopped her.

'See that?' Kelly exclaimed. 'She can't even *smile* properly. It's so fuckin' *tragic*.'

Gaffar nodded. He turned, confidingly. 'No blow job, eh?' he stage-whispered.

'Get *you*!' Kelly squealed.

Geraldine reached out a plump, white hand and softly cuffed his leg with it.

'*Ow!*' Gaffar yelled. 'Is *joke*!'

'Oh yeah?' Kelly interrupted. 'Like earlier? When I lost the bet? And you *seriously* thought . . .'

Gaffar looked indignant. 'Of *course* I thought – was *bet*!'

'Yeah, whatever. So'd you get the scooter yet?'

Gaffar reached his hands into his pocket and produced some keys. 'You've got it for a month, mate, *tops*.'

He nodded.

'And I ain't *ever* gamblin' with you again, see?'

He shrugged.

'So was my mum there when you picked it up?'

Gaffar winced. Geraldine's eyes widened, in horror. 'See this?' Gaffar said, pointing. 'Even your *cousin* is scare of you mother.'

'Everyone's shit-scared of her,' Kelly observed proudly. 'An' wait till you meet my *sister*, mate . . . Although she moved to Gillingham, so we don't see too much of her no more.'

'Big, *fat* . . .' Gaffar said, puffing himself up, '**like an ox. Like a small shed draped in a huge, lard corset.** I stay there *two* hour.'

'She make you hoover for her?'

Gaffar nodded.

'She make you wash up?'

Gaffar nodded.

'She make you massage her feet?'

Gaffar nodded. 'But this is . . . uh . . . soft feet. *Tiny* feet. Like . . .' he frowned.

'*Nah*. Them hooves is size sixes, mate. It's all just proportionate.'

'*Tiny,*' Gaffar repeated. 'Then I do . . . uh . . .'

He pointed to his shoulders.

'Your shoulders?'

'No. Is *her* . . .'

'*What?!* She made you massage her shoulders?'

He nodded.

'An' *did* ya?'

He shrugged.

'You *did*?!' Kelly shrieked.

He shrugged again.

'*Fuck me!* My old ma's got the *hots* for ya! D'ya *hear* that, Gerry?'

Geraldine nodded, gazing at Gaffar, slightly askance.

'I mean is that *fucked up* or *what*?!'

'I am *good* for massage,' Gaffar protested.

'Don't I fuckin' *know* it,' Kelly confirmed.

Silence

'So'd she get you to fetch her dinner?'

'*Yah*. Pizza. We share.'

'You shared a pizza?' Kelly scowled. 'Nuh-*uh*. My mum don't know the *meanin'* of the word.'

He nodded. 'Was *my* pizza. I bring.'

'*What?!* She ate *your* pizza?' Kelly cackled.

Gaffar nodded, mournfully. Kelly fell back on to her pillow. 'Man, what a *dick*. She walked all over ya.'

Gaffar grimaced. Geraldine stared at him, poignantly.

'This cousin is feel sorry for me,' he said, smiling at her. **'You have a lovely heart, and even lovelier breasts . . .'** He described her breasts in the air, appreciatively, with his hands. She looked a little shocked.

'So you fuck around with my scooter and I'll fuck around with *you*, mate,' Kelly informed him.

'I won't fuck,' Gaffar assured her.

'An' you can only keep it till my leg heals up.'

'Sure.'

Gaffar glanced over at the next bed. It was empty.

'Where she?' he asked, pointing.

'What? Her next door?'

He nodded.

'Dead.'

'*Wha?!*'

'Nah. Went home. *Cow*.'

She paused. 'Good riddance to bad rubbish. So what's up with Kane?'

Geraldine rolled her eyes.

'Yes. Is true,' Gaffar sighed, 'always this *Kane, Kane* . . .'

Geraldine rolled her eyes again.

'*HELLO!*' Kelly bellowed.

'Kane get foot . . .' Gaffar indicated towards his feet, 'at doctor. But when he come back is . . .'

Gaffar pulled a face.

'Upset?'

Gaffar nodded. 'Go to room. Bang door. **Masturbate.**'

Gaffar made a wanking gesture.

'*Pardon?!*'

'Yes. But is angry. No pleasure. *Anger*. This why I come here . . .'

'You're sayin' Kane came home from a foot doctor, then went straight into his room and *anger*-wanked?'

He nodded. **'Wank of rage.'**

He mimed wanking, fiercely.

Kelly looked stunned. 'That's *disgustin'*! You're takin' the fuckin' *rise* out of me!'

'Kane is *man*,' Gaffar told her haughtily. 'What is *girl* to understand?'

'Oh yeah?' Kelly sat bolt upright, indignant. 'You don't think *girls* do anger-wanks?'

'Never!'

''*Course* they fuckin' do!'

Gaffar snorted, contemptously.

'Geraldine. Don't *girls* do anger-wanks?'

Geraldine widened her aubergine eyes and slowly shook her head. Gaffar grinned.

'Fuckin' *hell*,' Kelly swore, 'why'd I even *bother*?' She paused. 'So who *is* this geezer?'

'For foot?'

'Yeah.'

'Is woman. He try find her. He no find her. For three days he say, "Is foot. Is sore foot." But Gaffar see . . .' Gaffar pointed to his eyes, 'is not *all* for foot. Is more . . .'

He raised his brows at her, suggestively. Kelly seemed shocked by this news.

'Whad'ya mean?'

'This also *Beede* doctor. Kane want this number but he will not speak Beede for asking. Is more *secret*. He say Beede have foot the same. Verruca. The *same*. And foot doctor say is foot *from* Beede. Crazy foot.'

He shrugged.

Kelly stared at him, mesmerised. 'I don't have a fuckin' *clue* what you're on about,' she murmured.

Geraldine sighed, deeply.

'She know,' Gaffar said, pointing to Geraldine.

'*Her?!*'

'Sure. **She's very intuitive. Very sensitive . . .**'

He smiled at her. She fluttered her long, false black lashes back at him.

'*Oi!*' Kelly interrupted. 'I'm here *too*, remember?!'

'Is same with letter,' Gaffar continued, 'you letter. First Kane see this letter an' . . .' he pulled an explosive expression, 'then I tell Beede, Ay! Kane read letter. Then Beede is . . . *Grrrrr!* Same. He say, "Is Kelly upstairs? Is Kelly in roof?"'

'In the roof? He thought I was in the *roof*?'

Gaffar shrugged. 'Beede is clever man. He see this *rug* is move. He is . . .'

'The fuckin' *rug* again?' Kelly exclaimed. 'What's the deal with Beede's fuckin' *rug*?!'

'I see in *dice*, yeah?'

'*What?*'

'If Gaffar play dice, he see . . .'

Gaffar pulled the dice out of his pocket and shook them, thoughtfully.

'Is like for . . .' he scowled, '**the way they hold them, the way they throw, the way they behave when they win or they lose. It speaks volumes. Those** Scientology **nuts need 2,000 questions. I only need three or four shakes of these little babies . . .** Is gift.'

'So what was actually in the letter?' Kelly asked.

'*You* know,' Gaffar shrugged, 'you give.'

'I *don't* know. Some black girl gave it me. I just passed it on. As a favour.'

'Is nothing,' Gaffar shrugged again.

'Well it must be *somethin'*. Otherwise everybody wouldn't be gettin' so worked up about it, *would* they?'

'Sure,' Gaffar conceded, 'is old . . . uh . . . **document. Some ancient** shit or other.'

'Well I wanna *see* it.'

'How?' Gaffar asked.

'I want you to *get* it for me. *Steal* it.'

'Sure.'

Gaffar shrugged.

'Thanks,' Kelly grinned at him, chuffed.

'Tomorrow.'

'Good. I'll be lookin' forward to that. You can bring it along with the salad. I can't even *look* at the shit they keep tryin'a force down my throat in here . . .'

She grimaced at a nearby nurse who was hurriedly removing a perfectly respectable-looking meal from one of the large, metal trolleys, then yelping as the heated plate singed her fingers.

Gaffar turned to Geraldine. 'You wanna ride? On scoot?'

Geraldine shrugged.

'In your *dreams*, mate,' Kelly sternly interrupted. 'You can't fit *her* on there too. It'll screw the suspension . . .'

'Sure, sure . . .' Gaffar waved his hand at her, dismissively.

'No fuckin' *way*.'

'Is food . . .' Gaffar pointed to an approaching nurse. 'We go.'

Geraldine slowly stood up, clutched a hold of her skirt (and the several layers of black netting peeking out from underneath it) then curtsied at Kelly, dramatically, like a dissolute rag doll determined to steal her moment in the chorus line of an especially bad Royal Ballet production of *The Nutcracker*.

'Up your arses,' Kelly muttered, to nobody in particular.

'Up *you* arses,' Gaffar echoed, charmingly, then he slipped his arm around Geraldine's soft waist and steered her away, quick-smart, turning – five steps on – and winking, mischievously, over his shoulder.

They looked ludicrous together, Kelly decided (glowering after them, furiously, as they paraded saucily down the ward). Gaffar was, after all, a conspicuous short-arse. Even by the most generous of calculations (and generosity wasn't featuring *high* on Kelly's current list of criteria), the Goth eclipsed him (in her heels) by at least half a metre.

As an adult, Kane felt almost entirely divorced from the child he once was. On the rare occasions he chanced to look back (and, by and large, he tried his damnedest not to) he saw a small boy with sandy hair, kneeling down, dutifully fastening his mother's shoe. Or blankly pushing her wheelchair. Or carefully washing her face with a pale, blue flannel. Or clumsily brushing her short, blonde curls (trying – and generally failing – to make the soft fringe stand proud).

He never looked back at this alien boy-Kane (this hollow child) with any sense of pride or tenderness –

Magnificent?
Was she out of her mind?!

– all he saw was a welter of mistakes, failures and botch-ups: a life brimming with bad news and worse news. A life of chapped hands, blisters and pressure sores. A life entirely composed out of small yet irksome physical details.

Perhaps the cruellest (and the most wretched) truth was that it'd never come easy. He'd loved her – certainly – but it'd always been a chore. He'd often felt ashamed of her. Angry with her. Sullen. Sometimes he didn't do up her buttons properly – on purpose, out of sheer spite – and she'd have to ask him to do it again. Sometimes he'd pretend he hadn't heard her calling. He'd make her wait: two minutes, three minutes, five, seven, ten. Sometimes he'd send her into coventry, or poke out his tongue behind her back, or break things, 'by accident'.

It *should've* come easier. But it didn't.
One time he'd poured hot soup on to her lap – her arm had unexpectedly gone into spasm and had smacked into the bowl as he held it (she'd always told him to rest it on the table, never in his hand, but wiping the drips from the bottom of the spoon, and then that careful, that –

Yawn

– interminable journey from the table to her mouth . . .).

The burns on her thighs had taken months to heal. He'd applied tube after tube of Calendula (the smell of it, even now, made his blood run cold). But she didn't punish or admonish him. She'd said she was fine ('I'm *fine* . . . Just tip some ice into a dishcloth. That's it. Quick,

quick. Try and keep it . . . that's right. That's good . . . That's . . .'). She refused – point-blank – to let him call out the doctor.

One time he just took off – he absconded – into the desert. He'd've been pushing eleven. It wasn't planned, exactly, but he packed a rucksack with four cans of Coke, five bars of chocolate and a large packet of pretzels. It was a great adventure. In those brief forty-eight hours he managed to acquire a winning combination of both minor sunstroke (hence the scars on his arm) *and* border-line hypothermia.

She'd waited, patiently, never thinking to raise the alarm, just trusting that there was something he needed to work out, and telling him, when he finally returned home (without tears or rancour, sitting calmly in a small pool of her own piss and shit) that if he could be depended upon to care for *her* – which he quite patently could (with this one, admittedly, somewhat *glaring* exception), then he should definitely be relied upon to care for himself. It was only *fair*, after all.

They'd returned to England – and to Ashford – shortly after. She missed the desert, dreadfully. Especially the skies. And the sunrise. It was his fault entirely, and he knew it, and he felt crushed by this knowledge. They'd moved into a drab sheltered flat on Hunter Avenue, opposite the playing fields.

Of course – for the most part – he'd always been there for her (just like she'd said). He'd been kind and he'd been tender. He'd loved her. Even now he could remember – with a smile – the sharp turn of her head, the elegant way she lifted her chin (that powerful – almost *palpable* – feeling she always gave him of natural grace under vicious attack), her ferocious sense of mischief, her passion for art, for music, the way she was always the first to laugh, to scoff, to swear (like a trooper) – at her pain, her illness and herself.

'The faster I flare up,' she'd always say, 'the quicker I cool down.'

And 'Brush off the shit,' was her other great favourite. 'Quick smart. Else it'll be liable to stick.'

'How'd you get my number?' she demanded.

'Your number?' Kane repeated, grimacing (*Fuck*. Now there'd be no avoiding it). 'I got it from my dad.'

He said this as if it were the most natural thing in the world.

'Your *dad*?'

'Yes. Yes . . .' he tried to sound bullish. 'Why? Is there a problem with that?'

'Uh . . . No. I suppose not . . .' Winifred paused, suspiciously. 'But your voice sounds different.'

'Don't be stupid.'

'I'm not being stupid. I'm perfectly serious. It sounds . . .' she paused, '*thick*. Kind of stressed.'

'I *am* stressed,' he said, trying his utmost to sound the opposite.

'And you're drunk,' she sighed, 'you've been drinking. Oh God, is it going to be one of *those* phone calls?'

'*Those* phone calls?' Kane echoed, with a dry laugh. '*Those* phone calls? Well that's kind of rich, isn't it, coming from you?'

'Yeah . . .' she sniggered (as if suddenly realising who it was that she was actually speaking to), 'that's true.'

He appreciated her ready candour (he'd always appreciated it).

'So what did I do?' she asked, in a tone of voice which implied it could've been any number of things.

'All I really need,' he said lightly, 'is to understand your sudden attraction to my father.'

'*Attraction?!* You *are* drunk,' she chuckled. 'Tequila.'

'No.'

'Vodka. You're terrible on pure spirits. They don't suit your body chemistry. It's important to understand what *works* for you, Kane. I always told you that, didn't I?'

'You did,' he said. 'When it comes to fucking-up *well*, you're the best possible teacher.'

'Thanks.'

He stared at the bottle of vodka on the table. He'd just bought it, at the off-licence. He stared at the picture of the Moscow Hotel.

'Was it the Broad girl who told you?' she asked. 'What's her name, again? Kelly?'

'No. I saw the package you sent. The letter.'

'Ah. The medieval thing. Wasn't that fascinating?'

'And I wondered . . .' he ignored her question, 'whether your sudden reacquaintance with my father might bear any relation to the fact that he currently finds himself over £38,000 in debt.'

A long pause

   'I'm *good*,' she murmured, perhaps a little shocked, 'but not *that* good.'
'Don't sell yourself short,' he said.
'Your father rang me up,' she said stiffly, 'because I'm a published author. It means I have ready access to the British Library . . .'
   'So why all the stuff about the Madeira cake?'
'*What* stuff?'
Kane adopted a girlish voice, '"The Madeira cake was a little *dry*" . . .'
'*Wow* . . .' she sounded almost awed, 'you really *did* read that letter . . .'
   Kane tried to brush it off. 'I'm worried about Beede,' he said, 'that's all.'
'*You?*' she snorted. 'Worried about *Beede*?!'
'Things change . . .' he reasoned.
'Nope. Some things are set in stone,' she said, 'and I'm pretty sure that's one of them.'
She paused. 'We're peas in a pod, you and I.'
   'And what *about* you?' Kane wondered, slightly on the defensive now (he didn't want to be a pea in a pod – certainly not a pea in a pod with *her*). 'Rushing off to Leeds. Writing a book. Developing a wild passion for a certain kind of plain *cake* . . .'
   'So are you dating the Broad girl?'
'Why?'
'Terrible family. But she seemed . . . well, *sweet*. Young. Too young. And too skinny. But I liked her.'
She sighed. 'It really was a shame about her brother . . .'
   Kane said nothing.
'I got him started, apparently . . .'
She tried to make light of it.
'You got everyone started. You got *me* started . . .'

Pause

   'So did you hear I got hitched?'

297

Kane's head jerked back.

'Congratulations,' he stuttered.

'He was a graduate student at ULU. Doing a PhD on Alexander Pope. You know, the poet . . .'

'Yes. I know who Alexander Pope is.'

'*The Rape of the Lock*.'

'I know who Alexander Pope is.'

'*What dire offence from amorous causes springs*,' she persisted.

'*What mighty contests rise from trivial things . . .*'

'I *know* who Alexander Pope is, Win,' he snapped.

Pause

'Anyway,' Winifred continued (plainly deeply gratified at having provoked the all-but unflappable Kane into a brief show of temper), 'he was from Haiti. Had the constitution of an *ox*. His family were all crazy. His father wrote *the* book about Jung. The one they use on all the college syllabuses. His mother was some kind of Voodoo High Priestess . . .'

'A *divine* union, then,' Kane sniped.

Winnie said nothing.

'Congratulations . . .' he pushed on.

'You already said that.'

'So I'm saying it again. And I'm meaning it.'

He did mean it. Yes. He did.

Silence

'You see my dad pretty much every week, right?'

'Pretty much.'

'And you never thought to ask?'

'About what?'

'Me.'

'No,' he was unapologetic, 'I mean why complicate things?'

'Of course,' she hissed, 'of *course*.'

Pause

'I forget now . . .' she eventually murmured, 'did I break up with you, or was it the other way around?'

'Both. You did all the breaking, but then you persisted in acting like I'd ruined your life.'

'Ah, yes. I remember now. I dumped you, but it was *completely* your fault . . .'

'What can I say?' Kane tried his best to shrug it off. 'I simply wasn't man enough.'

'That's true. You were weak.'

'Not weak, exactly,' he fought back, 'I just wanted to *enjoy* my vices – to kick back, hang loose. But you have this strange need, this *compulsion*, to turn everything into a test or a challenge or a question of fucking *honour*. It was exhausting. I was twenty-two. I just wanted to have fun.'

'Fun,' she echoed, dully, '*fun*.'

'You're one of life's big *adventurers*, Win . . .'

He wasn't sure if he was being entirely sincere.

'Yup. Got it in one,' she said.

'There you go,' he said, lamely.

'Christ, you were too, damn *cold*,' she said, harshly, 'and you're *still* cold, you bastard.'

'So you got educated, you got married, you developed a *passion* for Madeira cake . . .' he did his best to try and railroad her.

'I *always* asked Dad about you,' she said, sullenly, 'without fail. Every time we spoke.'

'Did you really?'

He was surprised by this.

'Yeah. Always.'

'And what did he tell you?'

'He said you'd put on a bit of weight. That you seemed bored, perhaps a little depressed . . .'

'*Depressed?*'

Kane was taken aback, but he did his best to mask it. '*Aw*, I never knew Tony *cared* so much,' he said.

Silence

'Anyhow, I got divorced.'

'I see.'

'There are some things . . . I dunno. Certain cultural *identifiers* . . . No, *signifiers* . . .'

'So that poor Haitian just couldn't cut the mustard?'

'Nope. He never "got" The Who. Didn't like *EastEnders*. And on the mustard tip, it was French every time, *definitely* not Colmans . . .'

'So the thing with Beede . . .' Kane butted in.

'And what I gleaned from my enquiries,' she continued, cutting and pasting her conversation, effortlessly, 'is that you've grown unashamedly *pedestrian* in your old age.'

'What?' Kane scowled –

Pedestrian?!

'Pedestrian,' she repeated.

'Just like my father, you mean?'

He battled to swallow down his fury.

'Good *God*, no,' Winifred exclaimed, 'not like Beede at all. The way I see it, we were completely wrong about Beede. Beede's great value. He's a maverick – a total hotspur. In fact I've become quite *enamoured* by Beede of late,' she half-joked. 'He's definitely an acquired taste.'

Kane rolled his eyes underneath his fringe.

'Stop rolling your eyes,' she said, 'underneath your fringe.'

He stiffened.

'You know,' she continued, her voice sweetening up, 'the more I actually stop and *think* about it . . .'

His eyes tightened. An alarm bell started to chime. He remembered her using that phrase in the past: 'The more I actually stop and *think* about it . . .'

Winifred stopping and actually *thinking* was never entirely a good thing. Winifred stopping and thinking often precipitated a sudden, wild leap into . . . into . . .

Where, exactly?

The wilderness?

The darkness?

The frying-pan?

The *shit*?

'Perhaps we should let this one go,' he said, warily. 'I *am* drunk. Vodka. You were right. And I'm feeling a little . . . *uh* . . .'

'But just when things were getting *interesting*,' she purred.

'I've gotta go,' he said, 'I need a pee. Someone's just . . . someone's banging on the door. Can you hear that?'

He held up the phone. There *was* banging.

'Okay,' she conceded.

'I loved the book, by the way.'

'Thanks.'

'It was great. Well done. You did good, Win.'

'I did *good*,' she echoed, mockingly, as he mumbled his hasty farewells.

SIX

They met on Kingsnorth Road, just along from the Post Office. It was shortly after ten. Beede was perched astride his Douglas, adjacent to the phone booth, his jaw set – and his arms firmly folded – against the cold east wind. He'd been waiting for approximately fifteen minutes.

Dory unwound the window of his Rover saloon as he drew up alongside him. 'You really should get a mobile,' he barked, 'that whole, "I'm in a phone-booth but I've only got twenty pence" routine could certainly grow a little thin . . .'

'How're your timings?' Beede asked (ignoring Dory's carping), hopping off his bike and leaning down towards him, his breath finely condensing. 'D'you want to head off somewhere?'

'I've only got ten minutes,' Dory said, glancing irritably towards the clock on his dash. 'Work's crazy right now.'

'That's plenty,' Beede shrugged, 'I only wanted to check up . . .' he faltered, 'I mean *catch* up . . .'

He turned, masking his slight embarrassment by pretending to make doubly sure that his bike was firmly positioned on its stand.

Dory didn't seem to register Beede's linguistic glitch. He merely nodded, abruptly, wound his window back up again, flipped on his indicator, pulled slowly forward and parked. Once the vehicle was stationary, Beede walked around to the passenger side, opened the door and clambered in.

'I'll switch the heating to max,' Dory muttered, leaning forward. 'You must be freezing.'

'It's certainly a little . . . *uh* . . .' Beede slammed the door shut and removed his gloves, '*nippy*.'

Dory adjusted the heating and then turned off his lights to preserve the battery. They sat quietly together for a few moments in the gentle gloom.

'I actually took the liberty,' Dory suddenly reached down into his side-pocket and lifted out a large, sealed carton, 'of getting you a coffee. A *latte*.'

'Thanks,' Beede carefully took it from him (his voice a little surprised, his fingers still leaden), 'that's much appreciated.'

Dory shrugged. 'I know how much you loathe these disposable things, but I was getting one for myself . . .'

'No,' Beede insisted, slowly easing off the carton's lid and then appreciatively inhaling the coffee's milky aroma, 'this is great. Just what the doctor ordered. My circulation's gone haywire. It's pretty damn cold out there.'

As he inhaled, the steam from the carton promptly condensed on to the lenses of his glasses.

'No sugar,' Dory said.

'Spot on.'

Dory reached down and withdrew a second cup. 'I'm still on my herbal tea regime,' he said, 'you know, trying to cut down on my caffeine intake . . .'

'I admire your self-control,' Beede peered at him, amiably, through the blur. 'In truth, I should probably be doing the same . . .'

He took a quick sip of his coffee. It was extraordinarily hot and extremely sweet. There were – at the very least – four sachets of sugar in it. On swallowing, his brows automatically arched and his glasses – correspondingly – shifted down his nose a way.

'Well that's . . .' he swallowed for a second time to try and flush some of the excess sweetness from his tongue, 'that's *definitely* hitting the spot.'

Dory nodded, apparently satisfied.

'So how'd it all pan out?' Beede wondered (maintaining a consistent – almost *unerring* – brightness of tone). 'With the police, I mean?'

Dory opened his mouth to answer, but before he could actually speak Beede entered a hurried plea on his own behalf. 'I've been ridiculously over-worked myself – flat-out in the laundry – or I would've rung sooner, obviously . . .'

'Obviously,' Dory echoed, peeling off the lid from his carton of tea. The car rapidly filled with the rich scent of chocolate.

'*Damn*.'

Dory stared into the cup. 'They've given me the wrong order. They've given me chocolate . . .'

Beede said nothing, just glanced at him, sideways (in his extensive experience of Dory – of *life*, in general – he'd discovered that what you might call 'true' mistakes were surprisingly few and far between).

'Is your coffee as it should be?' Dory asked.

'Absolutely,' he lied.

'*Damn!*' Dory repeated, staring into his cup. He took a sip and grimaced.

'It didn't pan out well . . .' he slung the lid on to the dashboard, reverting – with a scowl – to their former subject, 'unfortunately I'd left my phone in the car, remember?'

Beede shook his head, not quite following. His eyes wandered to Dory's lid on the dash, then beyond it, to the air vents at the base of the windscreen. A small, black writing pad – a jotter – had been temporarily placed there (or had accidentally slipped down into that position), and its pages were gently rustling in the warm breeze from the fan.

'My *phone*?' Dory repeated.

Still, Beede didn't catch on.

'Well the *story*, if you recollect,' Dory explained (his special emphasis on 'story' making his mixed feelings on the subject perfectly clear), 'was that a gang of kids had stolen my car, but I'd been *phoned* by someone to tell me where they'd dumped it . . .'

'Oh. Okay. But your phone . . .'

'Exactly. Still in the car. Sitting bang in the middle of the front *seat*, to be precise.'

Beede's shoulders tensed up. 'You think they noticed?'

'Well they're *policemen*, Beede,' Dory scoffed. 'It's just basic observation . . .'

'You could've had *two* phones,' Beede interjected. 'Some people do, apparently.'

Isidore stared at him, cryptically. 'In the same way that – just for the sake of *argument*, say – there could've been two horses?'

'Pardon?'

Beede was now totally all at sea.

'Forget it . . .' Dory shrugged. 'The bottom line was that they seemed to find the whole situation rather . . . uh . . . *perplexing*. No. *Improbable* . . . And then there were the *other* issues – the other *questions* – like whether I'd actually left my keys in the car – which I had – I mean, they were just dangling there, in the ignition . . .'

'That's not . . .' Beede cleared his throat, uneasily, 'that's not sounding like a *great* scenario, certainly.'

'I mean I work in security, and the police – as you already know – have this natural . . .'

He scowled, unable – temporarily – to latch on to the right word.

'Antipathy?' Beede cautiously filled in.

'Precisely.'

Beede slowly pushed his glasses back up his nose again.

'And as if *that* wasn't quite enough to contend with,' Dory continued (growing more querulous with every passing second), 'they then wanted to know *who* it was exactly that had phoned to inform me . . .'

'Well surely that's the easy part . . .' Beede shrugged, '*I* did. *Me*.'

'Pardon?'

Dory frowned at him.

'Wasn't that the whole point of the thing? Of the alibi? I phoned you. I recognised your car as I was passing. Then I went off to catch the horse and you eventually joined me . . .'

'Oh,' Dory said, dully, 'I see. Is that what we agreed?'

'Yes . . .' Beede paused, 'at least . . .'

'And is that what you told them?'

'Absolutely.'

'*Great*.'

Dory took a huge swig of his chocolate, and then swallowed, blinking furiously.

'So what was your story, then?' Beede wondered.

'I told them that a work colleague had rung. I didn't mention you. I wasn't specific.'

'Well I *am* a work colleague . . .' Beede frowned '. . . In fact – now I come to think of it – I believe they may've actually *asked* if we worked together at some point . . .'

'And you said . . . ?'

'I said "of course" – I mean we *do* . . .'

Dory nodded, frowning. 'Anyhow,' he took a third, slightly smaller, sip of his chocolate, 'they said if they needed to talk again then they'd get back in touch over the next couple of days . . .' he grimaced, 'but as yet I've heard nothing, so I'm just quietly hoping . . .'

'That it'll simply go away?'

'Exactly.'

'Touch wood.'

Beede lifted his fist and glanced around him. The dashboard was inlaid with a wood veneer. He rapped at it, smartly.

'That's plastic,' Dory muttered, curling his hands around his carton. He cleared his throat, then he cleared it again. 'God. I can really *feel* this chocolate taking a hold – you know? The caffeine – the *sugar*. I've grown so unaccustomed to it.'

'That's probably just stress,' Beede debunked.

'Probably,' Dory conceded, but then he deftly placed the lid back on to his cup and slipped it – with a small shudder – back into his side-pocket.

Silence

'I received a letter from Pat Monkeith today,' Beede tentatively introduced a new subject, 'informing me that I'd been nominated – and by *you* of all people – as Chairman for the new committee . . .'

Dory wasn't biting: 'I'm . . . I don't know . . .' he suddenly slumped down in his seat, shaking his handsome head, miserably, 'even after all these long years of trying to make good – of plastering over the cracks – of *white*washing and *bull*shitting – I still remain, quite simply, the world's most terrible . . . most . . . most *clumsy*, most *lack*-witted, most *ineffectual* liar . . .'

Beede snorted. Or – more to the point – he *found* himself snorting (a loud, cynical, *disbelieving* kind of snort). Then he blinked, shocked.

Dory stared at him, hurt. 'But I *am*.'

'Well hopefully . . .' Beede struggled to cover up his clumsy *faux-pas* '. . . hopefully some kind of major fraud or . . . or *murder* will've taken place over the last couple of days which'll completely snow them under and quietly enable you to just slip off their radar . . .'

He was joking. But not entirely.

'A gang rape,' Dory shrugged, 'or an indecent assault. That'd be *dandy*, huh?'

He delivered Beede a reproachful glare. Beede's eyes returned – inexorably – to the flapping journal.

Silence

'I'm sorry,' Dory muttered, finally, 'I don't mean to harp on about it . . . I'm just . . . it's just . . . I hate *living* like this, Beede. Lying. Taking risks. It's exhausting. I'm simply not . . . not *equipped* . . .'

'I know,' Beede patted Dory's arm, reassuringly, 'who on earth would be?'

'I find it physically draining.'

Beede nodded, vehemently.

'And I feel this overwhelming . . . this . . . this *huge* burden of guilt. This awful *weight* . . :' he pointed to the centre of his diaphragm '. . . right here. Crushing down on me . . .'

'That's just stupid,' Beede interjected tersely, 'and illogical.'

'Pardon?'

'It's pointless to feel guilty about something you have no control over.'

'Sure. *Sure.* I know what you're saying – I mean I understand your *logic*, perfectly . . .' Dory shook his head, 'but it's all just too *easy*, Beede. Don't you see? Because at some level I *am* responsible – I *must* be. And I simply can't allow myself to keep . . .'

'It's not a question of allowing . . .' Beede interrupted again.

'But it *is*!' Dory smacked down both hands, hard, on to the steering wheel (perhaps merely intending to express his frustration, or to add a little extra emphasis to his conversation, but somehow conniving to knock into the Rover's horn mechanism). The horn blasted, loudly.

Beede jumped back, alarmed. He almost spilled his coffee.

'Sorry,' Dory looked slightly rueful.

Silence

'Has something else happened, Isidore?' Beede murmured, on finally regaining his equilibrium. 'Something I don't know about? Something you haven't told me?'

Dory tipped back his head, with a soft grunt, and gazed up at the ceiling. He lifted his hand and gently massaged his throat, almost as if trying to ease the words out of it. When he eventually spoke his voice was uncharacteristically husky. 'Yes,' he said, 'it has.'

'Would it help to talk about it?'

Dory lowered his chin and stared straight ahead of him. He drew a deep breath. 'I took a paternity test,' he told the dashboard, coldly, 'for Fleet.'

'Sorry?'

Beede didn't know quite what he'd been expecting, but it certainly hadn't been that. 'You took . . . ?'

Dory nodded.

'But *why*?'

'I don't know. It was on a . . . a *whim*. It just . . . the idea just *came* to me. And I wish now – more than anything – that I hadn't. That I didn't. But I did.'

'Have you had the result?'

'Yes.' Dory nodded.

Beede stared at him, leaning forward slightly, tensed.

'And there's something else,' Dory continued, flatly, 'something almost *worse* . . .'

'Pardon?'

Beede still hadn't quite got his head around the paternity issue.

'It's Elen. She has these . . . these awful . . .' He winced.

'What?'

'Bruises,' he muttered.

'*Bruises*? Where?'

'Her arm. Just above her wrist. There.'

Dory indicated the approximate area on his own arm.

'I see.'

Beede was quiet for a while. 'Did she happen to mention how she got them?'

Dory nodded. 'She said she almost fell down some steps – at the McArthur Glen – but then someone put out a hand and grabbed her. Pulled her back. Quite roughly.'

'Maybe it's true . . .' Beede didn't sound confident, 'I mean maybe they did.'

Dory slowly shook his head. 'When I came home the other night and she was sleeping – she'd dozed off in front of the tv, waiting up for me – I quietly leaned over . . .'.

He slowly re-enacted the movement – the lean – and as he did so an icy chill surrounded Beede's heart.

'I quietly leaned over,' Dory repeated (still leaning, a strange and unsettling expression on his face – an almost *predatory* expression – but when he spoke, it was still with Dory's familiar accent, Dory's familiar voice), 'and I had a proper look. On closer inspection the fingerprints – the marks – corresponded – and I mean *exactly* – to the dimensions of my own hands.'

Dory held up his hands for inspection. They were uncontentious hands – innocent-seeming hands with long, slim fingers and neat, clean nails.

'Well that's . . . it could just be . . .' Beede stuttered.

'I tested it out, Beede – the fingers, the thumbs . . . And then – and I don't even know *why* I felt the urge to do this, I just did – when I pushed up her other sleeve . . .'

He swallowed, hard.

'*What?*'

'There were *more* marks. Marks inconsistent with the story as she'd told it. Almost as if . . .' he struggled to speak '. . . *you* know – as she'd been *held down* at some point . . . Pushed down. Against her will.'

Beede remained silent.

Dory straightened his spine, lengthened his neck, tucked in his chin and inhaled, deeply. He held his breath for several counts and then slowly released it.

'You're still doing the yoga?' Beede murmured.

'The Pranayama? Yes. It's pretty much the only thing keeping me sane right now.' He glanced over at him. 'I know I keep hammering on about it, but you really *should* buy the book . . .'

Beede shrugged.

Dory smiled. 'You think it's all rather too "New Age" to be taken seriously, eh?'

'Not at all.'

'But it's an *ancient* discipline . . .'

'New Age disciplines invariably *are*,' Beede said, disparagingly, 'but in the modern world they lack context – we just pick them up and then toss them back down again, we *consume* them. They have no moral claim on us. No moral *value*. And without that they're rendered meaningless, *fatuous*, even.'

'Here's the context,' Dory said, determined to persuade him, 'when I was a boy my father would constantly go on at me about something he referred to as "The Witness". The Witness – as my father expressed it – was this inner voice, this calm, authoritative voice . . .'

he paused, frowning. 'It's quite difficult to express – to . . . to *explain* – just off the top of my head . . . but in the early chapters of Richard Rosen's book he *also* refers to something which *he* calls "The Witness", and from what I can tell – and I find this oddly comforting, somehow, strangely *uplifting,* even – Rosen's Witness is pretty much *identical* – conceptually – to my father's.'

He gazed at Beede, intently, as if awaiting a response.

'So there's this *linguistic* connection,' Beede mused, 'to some arcane practice from your childhood . . . ?'

'No. *Yes*. I mean it transpires,' Dory continued (refusing to let Beede burst his bubble), 'that The Witness actually has its earliest origins in Pranayama. In the yoga of breath. Although in Sanscrit I believe the word they generally use is *Sakshin* . . .'

'I see,' Beede said, blankly rotating his coffee carton.

'It almost feels like a . . . I mean it sounds *silly* when I say it out loud, but it's almost like a kind of . . .'

He lifted his hands.

'*Sign?*' Beede filled in, dryly.

Dory shrugged, apologetically.

Beede gazed back at him, warily. 'So did you actually *ask* Elen . . .' he began.

'Rosen says that we can only get into *contact* with our Witness,' Dory plodded on, regardless, 'by divorcing ourselves from our everyday consciousness. By turning away from it. What generally happens is that over time, the . . . now how does he describe it? . . . the babbling *brook* of this consciousness – which basically consists of all our thoughts, our feelings, our passing desires, our physical and sexual impulses – slowly begins to overwhelm – or drown out – our inner or *real* sense of self, to the extent that we often find ourselves at a point where we actually believe that this everyday consciousness – or *citta* – *is* our real self. But the truth is that these momentary thoughts and impulses don't describe who we are *at all*. Quite the opposite. They actively *limit* it. And if we allow ourselves to identify too strongly with them then it results in what the yogis like to call *duhkha* – a kind of profound confusion, a feeling of deep misery . . .'

Dory leaned forward and lifted his journal from the air vent. As he lifted it, the pages flapped violently, like the wings of an injured bird. He immediately calmed the bird with a soft cooing sound and then drew it towards him, supporting it, gently, in both hands. He caressed its soft chest feathers with a tiny rotation of his thumbs, then spread out its wings – like a dark fan – with his other fingers.

Beede blinked.

Dory had opened the journal and was scanning one of his early entries. 'This is my journal,' he explained, 'Rosen insists that you keep one when you embark on the journey.'

'So how long is it now?' Beede asked.

'Pardon?'

'How long have you been . . .' Beede faltered on the word 'journeying', 'How long have you been *practising* now, in total?'

'Uh . . . Two months. And I'm not practising, as such, not completely. It takes about a year to learn all the basics.'

'And have you been feeling better for it?' Beede wondered.

'Yes.'

Dory was unequivocal.

'Really?' Beede seemed unconvinced. '*Significantly* better?'

'How do you mean?'

'During the eight or so weeks you've been practising, has everything . . . ?'

'Better?' Dory scowled. 'Yes . . . Well, *no* . . .'

'Correct me if I'm wrong,' Beede persisted (remembering what Elen had confessed to him, in the laundry, several days before), 'but I was under the impression that things had grown quite *difficult* over the past few months, that things might even have grown *worse* in some regards, less *controlled* . . .'

'Sorry?' Dory seemed confused. 'When did I tell you that?'

As he spoke he slapped the book shut. Beede watched his hands closely, sensing the bird squatting down, readying itself, *tensing* itself, as if intending to take flight. Dory was scowling. 'Over the past few months or so? I don't know . . . I thought . . .'

His eyes moved around the car, restlessly, then focussed in on the dashboard clock.

'*Christ*,' he said, 'it's late . . . I should've been . . .' He inspected his wrist-watch. 'I should've been well on my way to Charing by now . . .'

Beede stared at him, perplexedly, for a couple of seconds.

'Sorry . . .' Dory apologised, yanking down his seat-belt and fastening it.

'Don't apologise . . .' Beede grabbed his gloves and reached for the door handle, trying not to upset his carton of coffee.

'Ring me,' Dory said, 'and next time let's try and make it all a little less *ad-hoc* . . .'

'Now you come to mention it,' Beede told him, climbing out of the car, 'I've actually arranged some time off from work. I thought we might . . .'

'Great. *Fantastic*.'

Dory cut him short, leaning forward, pumping the clutch, reaching one hand for the gears and the other for the ignition. Beede continued to hold the door ajar as the engine roared into life.

'I *will* phone you,' he promised.

'You do that.'

Dory checked his mirror, then glanced over his shoulder. Beede slammed the door shut and took a step back.

Beede.
Beede.

He blinked. Dory had wound down the passenger window and was addressing him through it.

'Yes? Sorry?'

He inclined his head, slightly.

'I meant to tell you,' Dory shouted, over the din of the engine, 'I met your son.'

'Pardon?'

Beede leaned down still further.

'Kane. Your *son*. I saw him. I met him.'

'*Kane?*'

'Yes.'

'You saw . . . ?'

'Yes. He came to my house. This afternoon.'

Beede looked stunned. 'Kane came to your *house*? Are you sure?'

'He said he had an appointment. With Elen. Although she certainly hadn't *mentioned* it. He claimed it was for his foot. For a verruca. He didn't introduce himself, but I just . . . I *sensed* it was him. Call it . . .' he shrugged, 'call it *instinct*. In fact I recognised his *voice* of all things. His accent. You know . . . drawling, very distinctive, slightly American . . .'

Beede opened his mouth as if to speak, but he said nothing. His mind was racing.

'You look very different,' Dory said.

'How?' Beede put a hand to his face, panicked.

'Not *you*. You and *Kane*. Different from each other.'

'Oh. Yes . . .' Beede nodded, distractedly, 'I suppose we are very different.'

'Phone me.'

Dory smiled. He waved. He wound the passenger window back up. He pulled off, smoothly.

Beede stared after the car, his expression unreadable.

A white van sounded its horn. He started. He turned. The van's driver gesticulated, indignantly, as he slowly drew past him. Beede stared down at himself, vacantly. How long had he been standing there?

He noticed – with small grimace – that he was still holding the coffee carton. He flared his nostrils, shoved out his arm, tipped his hand, and poured the remaining liquid, angrily – almost *contemptously* – down on to the tarmac. Then he crushed the carton in his hands, paused, and then popped it – ever heedful of the environment – into his coat pocket.

'Lackwitted . . . ?' he muttered, heading for the kerb, scowling, '*lack*-witted? Where the hell'd he root up *that* particular configuration? Dim-witted, yes. *Dim*-witted I could almost accept – *almost*. But *lack*?'

It was a photograph; a picture of Kane, as a baby, sitting in a small, suburban garden, crammed into a plastic washing-up bowl (wearing a disarmingly sensorious – almost *Churchillian* – expression), totally naked but for a large, white hanky which had been knotted at each corner and plopped down, rather jauntily, on to his head.

Behind him sprawled a gorgeous, curly-haired blonde on a smart, plaid blanket, wearing a skimpy pair of purple, suede hot-pants, some flip-flops, a tie-dye vest and a huge-brimmed straw hat. She'd just made a daisy-chain and was hanging it – with a huge smile – around the baby's neck.

'So where the *fuck* d'you unearth the Goth?' Kane muttered, taking a swig of his beer and peering after her, suspiciously, as she sauntered off – in a girlish swirl of heels and black netting – towards the bathroom.

Gaffar didn't answer. He was sifting through a dusty, old shoebox full of photographs which Kane had removed (several hours earlier – he wasn't entirely sure *why*) from the top of his wardrobe.

'Leave those alone, will you?' Kane snapped. He was in a filthy mood. And nothing seemed able to lift it.

Gaffar quietly ignored him and continued sifting.

'Is something burning in the oven?' Kane asked, sniffing. The air was rich with the mingling scents of lamb and tomato and mint and cinnamon.

Gaffar shook his head. 'Is Kurdish meatball,' he said. 'Slow cook.'

'Did you ask Beede's permission to use his kitchen?'

Gaffar shrugged, insouciant (he hadn't).

'She's an incorrigible kleptomaniac,' Kane grumbled, peeling at the corner of his beer, label, 'did you know that?'

'Huh?'

'A thief. You literally can't take your eyes off her.'

'Thief?'

Gaffar looked up, briefly, then glanced down again. He was now staring at a photograph in which a younger Daniel Beede – with slightly longer hair, the same glasses but an *entirely* different – you might almost say *affable* – demeanour – graciously received some kind of special plaque at a large, social occasion from a gentleman wearing unthinkable quantities of gold jewellery and a three-tiered hat.

'Who this?' Gaffar asked, pointing to Ashford's then-Mayor.

'Not just a *normal* kind of thief – because that'd be fine, I mean she's a *Broad*, after all – but she'll literally steal *anything*. It's actually an illness. A compulsion.'

He leaned across the sofa and began feeling around inside the pockets of Geraldine's coat.

Gaffar continued to stare at the photograph, frowning. **'There's a** strange kind of . . . of luminosity. It's odd, but I've only ever observed this quality once before, in pictures of my own father, shortly after he left the Sheikhallah Bazaar, embraced Islam and journeyed to Silopi – the town of my birth . . .' He held the shot up for Kane's perusal: 'When exactly was this taken? Eh? *Kane?*'

Kane didn't bother looking up, so he turned the picture over and inspected the back (as he inspected, Kane removed a small, metal kidney tray from Geraldine's pocket of the type generally used in a hospital to deposit swabs or samples in). The photo wasn't dated. Gaffar sucked on his tongue, irritated. He was suddenly fascinated by this luminescent Beede.

'Well, well, *well* . . .' Kane chuckled, cupping his hands together and rattling four, small dice in them. Gaffar's eyes shot up, attracted by their familiar sound. He tapped, naively, at his jacket pocket, removed one, lonely die, gazed at it, appalled, then mutely held out his hand for the others. Kane passed them over and then delved back into the coat again . . .

Six used scratchcards.

'Are these yours?' Kane asked.

Gaffar shook his head.

'Good,' Kane grumbled, 'I *hate* those fucking things . . .'

He tried Geraldine's other pocket. 'A-*ha!*'

He withdrew Gaffar's set of house keys and cheerfully jangled them at him. 'The mystery is finally solved . . .'

'That evil vixen!' Gaffar exclaimed. 'She must've ransacked my pockets when we were riding on the scooter.'

'Yup.'

'Damn!' Gaffar looked disappointed. 'So that's the reason why her hands were crawling everywhere.'

Kane dug around some more. He gingerly removed the bottom half of an old pair of dentures.

'Are those hers?' Gaffar asked, shaking his head, horrified.

Next up, a book. A paperback. Kane stared at it for a moment. '*Jesus*. How'd she get a hold of this? It's Beede's. He dropped it, the other day, in the restaurant, and I picked it up . . .'

He inspected the front cover. There was something slightly unusual about it. Then he realised – no author's name. He turned to the back.

'*Cony-Catchers and Bawdy Baskets,*' he read out, somewhat haltingly, 'concerns the world of patriarchs, palliards and priggers of prancers, of autem morts and walking morts, of fraters, abraham men and rufflers – the elaborate, criminal anti-society of Elizabethan England . . .'

'Hang on . . .' he stared up at Gaffar, blankly.
'Huh?'
Gaffar wasn't paying attention. Kane slowly shook his head, frowning. 'For a moment back there – for a split second, as I read – I suddenly . . . it just . . . I dunno – it all made *perfect sense* . . .'

He opened the text, perplexedly, to where Beede had finally quit reading during their random meeting at the French Connection (the corner had been carefully turned at page 103). Here Kane's eye alighted on the sub-heading: 'Priggers of Prancers' and the following sentence: 'A prigger of prancers be horse stealers; for to prig signifieth in their language to steal, and a prancer is a horse . . .'

He re-read this sentence.
'A prigger of prancers be horse stealers; for to prig . . .'
'I already *knew* that,' he murmured.

'Beede knew of this rug,' Gaffar joined in, shuffling, distractedly, through some of the other photographs (in one there was an image of Beede, at ease, in full, white, Marine regalia. In another, a four-year-old Kane was snuggled up asleep in his pushchair with the woman from the previous picture crouched down behind him, grimacing theatrically as she held on to a rapidly melting ice cream. In a third, a ten-year-old Kane was gamely pushing the same woman around in a wheelchair. The woman was now totally transformed, but smiling).

'*What?!*'
Kane was gazing up at him, shocked. 'How could he tell? That burn had all-but *disappeared*. Jesus *wept*, the man's like some kind of pneumatic *hound* . . .'
Gaffar stared at him, blankly.
'Did *you* let it slip?'
'*Me?!*' Gaffar looked hurt.
'Was he furious?'
'No. Was *fine*. We *laugh*. He thought was big . . . uh . . . *joke*.'
'A joke?' Kane didn't look convinced.
'Sure. *Ha ha*.'

Kane glanced down at the book again, opening the text, randomly, and finding himself on page 57 in a chapter entitled: 'A Manifest Detection of Dice Play'. There, placed neatly between the folds of the pages, was a small, white card, a *business* card: Petaborough Restorations, he read. No address, just a number. He inspected the code. Was that Appledore? Tenterden?

'Petaborough Restorations,' he murmured, 'P.B.R.'

P.B.R.?

It rang a distant bell.

P.B.R.?

His mind turned back to a day or so before, when he'd been rummaging through Beede's old cheque stubs, struggling to decipher his impenetrable short-hand. P.B.R. He was pretty sure – no, *certain* – that he'd encountered these three letters, and repeatedly, somewhere.

He peered down at the book. A section of print had been heavily underlined towards the bottom of the page: 'At the gentleman's next returning to the house, the damsel dallied so long with the chain, sometimes putting it about her neck, and sometimes about his, that in the end she foisted the copper chain in the other's place, and thereby robbed him of better than forty pounds.'

?

Kane shut the book and inspected the cover. It consisted of a slightly yellowed detail from a sixteenth-century painting in which several gentlemen could be seen hunched over a table playing cards. The table was liberally sprinkled in gold coins. The only hand on display (to the viewer, at least) was one held to the fore of the detail where a heavily beringed gentleman clutched on to a Jack. He looked closer. The Jack of Hearts; and a blond, plump, slightly dissolute-seeming Jack, at that.

'Jack of Hearts,' Kane murmured.
He blinked.

Eh?!

He opened the book to page 103 again. 'A prigger of prancers,' he read. He shut his eyes for a moment. He saw a man, in yellow, astride a horse –

Holy fuck!

His eyes flew open.

The toilet flushed. He leaned sideways and tipped the kidney-shaped tray and the teeth back into Geraldine's coat pocket. He shoved the book down his side of the sofa.

'You're not gonna confront her?' Gaffar asked loudly, pointing indignantly.

'Christ no. It's a *sickness*,' Kane hushed him, 'it's not vindictive. It's pathetic. She can't control it.'

Geraldine re-emerged from the bathroom and sailed back into their orbit, quite the ship of state; magnificently serene, blissfully unaware.

'Shit. I'm suddenly really *hungry* . . .' Kane exclaimed, clutching on to his stomach, as if at once panicked and *delighted* by this sudden, very real, very powerful sense of appetite.

SEVEN

In Beede's dream he was hurling himself – at breakneck speed – up a steep, spiral staircase. The staircase was built of stone and it was dimly lit. As he climbed he felt panicked, angry – caught in the grip of some kind of emotional frenzy – but still astonishingly vigorous. So much stronger – *inside, out* – than normal. So much *lighter.* His limbs – legs, arms, chest – far more obliging, more supple, more resilient . . .

Huh?!

He ground to a sudden halt, his head snapping around –

What was that?!

He braced himself, gasping, against a cold, stone wall –

The stamp of a boot?
The clink of . . .
Eh?
A drawn sword?

He slitted his eyes, sweat trickling down the sharp furrows of his lean face –

Is it . . . ?
Are they . . . ?

Has he . . . ?

Then he found himself –

Ting!

– staring down – somewhat bemusedly – at his own two feet –

Feet?

He blinked.

Ting!

He stared down at them again –

My feet?

His feet – he blinked for a second time –

Ting!

– just to make *doubly* sure –

Yup –
There they both are . . .

– were tightly encased in a pair of tiny, leather shoes; ornate leather pumps, dramatically pointed. And the toes –

Ouch!

– were aching, were pushed together, were *cramped*.
   He roared. He found himself roaring; uninhibitedly, *potently*, without restraint, like an angry bull (or the anti-Geisha). He *bellowed* at his feet. He felt *enraged* by his feet (cooped, jailed, *corralled* by them) –

Stop, now

He struggled to control himself –

Stop now . . .

– but failed –

STOP!
QUIET!
ENOUGH!

He pulled himself straight, with a small, hoarse cough –

Yes.
Right.
Ahem . . .
Good.

– then promptly recommenced his climb. As he ascended, he felt buoyed by an overriding sense of *purpose;* by a steely, almost unassailable resolve.
    But the shoes –

Oh come on!

– the shoes were suddenly . . . They were *impossible.* They were unwieldy, impracticable, downright *unworkable.* The toes were ridiculously *long,* the stairs were unfeasibly *short* . . .
And the combination of the two . . . ?

Bedlam!

He began to jink himself sideways – like a crab – to preclude smashing the empty, pointed toe into the back of the stair, to allow the weight of each step to be taken by the heel rather than by only the tender, over-worked front pad . . .
    It was . . .

Uh . . .

He was . . .

Uh . . .

And just when . . .

Wow!

He glanced around him, quite amazed. He'd arrived at his destination, almost without realising. He threw out his arms with an exuberant *whoop* and rotated on the spot. He was standing (and twirling, and whooping –

Twirling?
Whooping?
Seriously?!)

– in the heart of an airy, cornflower-blue sky, suspended on a kind of a . . . a *roof*, a tower. And he was surrounded by . . .

What?

Tiles! A huge expanse of tiling. Beautiful tiling. *Ancient* tiling. He sneaked out a furtive hand and he *touched* the tiles. He *caressed* the tiles . . .

Ahhhh!

Then he found himself . . .

No!
Stop that!

– pulling the tiles loose, one by one –

Vandal!

– and holding them, stroking them, full of awe. He felt the weight of the tile, the strength of it, the undeniable *craftsmanship* . . .
And then suddenly –

Oh God –
Not again!

– that insidious – that *pernicious* – feeling of rage began bubbling up inside of him (starting in his stomach and burning all the way through him, like a dose of chronic indigestion) but this time it was coupled with –

Eh?

– a deep –

No . . .

– a *profound* sense of the *grossest* injustice. He felt aggrieved. He felt indignant. He felt bileful. He felt . . . he felt . . .

Different?

   Beede endeavoured to contain this colourful swirl of feelings within the needs, demands and limitations of his own character, his own *life*. It was a struggle (matching up the edges, trying to force this wayward spectrum of emotions to *cohere* with his own), and just as he was finally making some slight show of progress, he found himself –

But is this me, or is it someone else?

– sprinting to the edge of the parapet and gazing down –

Now hang on . . .

– and he was shouting –

Surely not . . . ?

– screaming –

Definitely not . . . !

– although he wasn't entirely sure *what* he yelled, or at *whom*, exactly . . .
   Far below –

Hello!

– he saw men –

Ants!
Black ants!

– in costumes, peering up at him; some laughing, some shouting right back, some gesticulating, coarsely.

Ahh . . .
So you think this is funny, do you?

– and before he knew what . . .

No!

– almost without . . .

No!

– he'd hurled down one tile and was lunging for another –

Wait!

– then another –

Stop!

– and another.
    Tiles smashed and shattered in the courtyard below him. Men scattered, running for cover . . . Until –

Huh?!

The crash of a door, the flurry of footsteps, the sharp nudge of steel between his shoulderblades.
    He gasped.
Was he afraid?

Am I?

    Was he?
No.
He *smirked.*
    He turned, lifting his arms, cackling victoriously; gloating, imperious, *exultant.*
Beede awoke –

Wah?!

    His eyes snapped open. He saw . . .

Wah?!

The cat.
The *cat*?!

    Yes. The cat.
The cat had crept into his room –

Ting!

– and on to his bed –

Ting!

– and was now sitting – bold as brass – square on his chest –

Ooof!

    Beede stared up at the cat. The cat peered down at Beede; quizzically, *perplexedly* – his ears pricked, his head jinked – a slight chime sounding, intermittently, from the bell on his collar.
    Beede didn't move. He remained where he was, hardly even breathing; blank, inert, supine . . .
    Then suddenly –

Ting!

– a chord was struck. He hauled himself upright –

Bell?
What Bell?!

– and the poor cat went flying.

'I feel regret . . .' Gaffar told the Goth, returning to the sofa (having carefully scrubbed out Beede's highly prized, Denby Pottery casserole dish in the left-over water from a bath he'd enjoyed earlier), throwing himself down, snatching the remote from her (she was watching re-runs of *The Osbournes* with such stony-faced concentration that it might as well've been a gut-wrenching two-hour special about ethnic violence in Rwanda) and turning it – almost out of habit – to the Islamic Channel just in time for the evening prayer '**. . . of course I do – I'm only human, after all. I left behind a mother, a brother, aunts, uncles,**' he counted them off on to his fingers, '**but I didn't do it consciously, not willingly. It was all just . . . just force of circumstance. My hands were tied,**' he held up his hands, pinned together at the wrists, to demonstrate, '**it was destiny. Destiny, yeah? I honestly believe that.**'

Kane emitted a gentle snore. They both glanced over at him. He was collapsed, post-dinner, spread-eagled on his favourite brown leather tv chair, his feet gently suspended on the inbuilt stool. Above him, an ancient, slightly torn poster of Haile Selassie was slowly unpeeling from the wall.

'You have family?' he asked, haltingly.

Geraldine nodded. Then she winced.

'Trust me,' Gaffar chastised her, 'if this bad family is *vamoose*, is go . . .'

He scowled. '**All those tiny ticks, those habits, those faults which always irritated you before, or embarrassed you in front of your friends, once you're gone – once they're gone – then those same bad things – those maddening characteristics – become a kind of emotional glue**

326

which sticks them to your heart, to your soul, which makes them live and breathe inside of you, become an indelible part of you, so that soon what you thought you wanted or needed or craved suddenly seems almost . . .' he shrugged, 'immaterial . . ."

The Goth stared at him, blankly, twiddling a stray strand of stiff, black hair around her little finger. He sighed and changed the channel, impatiently. 'I miss mother, *yes*? For her *cook*. Wonderful cook. When I is home she is say, "Gaffar eat, Gaffar eat" and is drive me *mad*. But now – *Ay!* Is . . . uh . . . **unforgivable cliché**, no? – now is I *think* of her and I go kitchen for to try make same *smell* or mother *taste*,' he shrugged, 'but is crap. Is *Gaffar* taste. Is change. Not so good.'

Geraldine took the remote from him, flipped off the tv, and then casually slipped it into her deep coat pocket. She stared at him, sympathetically.

'I think I see whole of *world* in this two black eyes,' Gaffar boldly romanced her, leaning across her lap and fishing it straight back out again. She lowered her lashes, modestly.

Kane snored, then shifted, with a disconcerted grunt. He was now lying on his side with his hands tucked between his legs. His breathing grew deeper.

'You are good for talk,' Gaffar said. 'Good for *listen*. Is easy for man to . . . **to unburden.**'

Geraldine took his hand and gently stroked the back of it.

Gaffar stared at the impressive array of silver rings on her fingers. One of them in particular was neatly inlaid with a piece of blue-black oyster shell which momentarily reminded him of the shimmer of a peacock feather.

He shuddered. He inspected it more closely.

'At sleep I dream of this . . .' he said, 'this bird. Big tail bird . . .'

He drew his hand away and described the fanning tail of a peacock.

'Peacock . . . ?'

Geraldine nodded.

'I keep on dream of this bird . . . **I'm on a long journey, alone, in the desert and I'm tormented by this terrible thirst** – need for drink, yes? – **I'm searching for an oasis – a well – in the faint hope of quenching it, and then suddenly I see this bird – this magnificent peacock – standing on the horizon. And it's strutting around, putting on a real show, raising and lowering and fanning its tail at me. I walk towards it, almost hypnotised, and as I draw closer I see that it's standing** by a well, a drinking well. I run to the well – delighted, obviously – to slake my thirst, but when I get there, there is no bucket or rope to lower down into it, so I lean over the wall of the well to peer inside – perhaps I might climb into it – I'm so desperate now – my thirst is so great . . . But hard as I try, I cannot see the bottom. So I grab a stone from the ground nearby and I throw it in. I wait, straining to hear the splash, but the pebble just keeps on falling. I hear it bouncing from the walls, reverberating, echoing, for many minutes and then finally nothing. So I turn – furious – to chastise the bird – this despicable bird – for leading me astray and . . . poof! It's disappeared. Vanished.'

Kane expelled a sudden gasp as he slept (almost as if in fascinated response to Gaffar's story). Gaffar peered up at the Goth – perhaps hoping for some kind of intelligent reaction – but she seemed completely preoccupied by the slumbering Kane. He turned to look at Kane, frowning. His eyes widened. Kane's head was thrown back, his mouth had fallen open, his breathing was sharp but deep and rhythmical. His eyes were blinking, rapidly. But his hands were the main thing. His hands – pressed between thighs – were twitching and jerking, involuntarily.

'Kane!' Gaffar called out, mortified, determined to awaken him. No reaction. He began to push himself up, intending to bound over and shake him, but before he could do so, Geraldine had grabbed his arm and had yanked him back down again. He opened his mouth to protest but she placed a firm finger upon his lips and smiled – just slightly – through her barbs of black string. Then she took his hand – with a salacious twitch of her finely sculpted brow – and pushed his fingers deep into her soft, warm lap, turning, simultaneously – very calmly and deliberately – to keep on watching.

It wasn't like any other building he'd ever seen; it was almost a cartoon – a *caricature* – of what a building might be. A truly terrifying construction (the proud work – he had little doubt – of some of the world's most warped and tyrannical imaginations).

The design itself was stark, impenetrable, *peerlessly* simple. The detailing was fastidious –

No . . .
Meticulous.

And the finish? Incomparable.

Kane felt a curious mix of emotions as he stood and he perused it: he was *awed* by its ambition –

Yes

– *sickened* by its barbarity –

Certainly

– *humbled* by its magnitude –

Absolutely

– and deeply –

No

– *profoundly* perplexed by the fact that this whole, titanic edifice – every damn *inch* of it – was built entirely (he reached out a questing hand) –

Uh . . .
Yup

– not from steel or aluminium or *glass* –

Nuh-uh

– but just basic, red *brick*. Hand-made, red brick –

More to the point

– *thousands* of them; *millions*, even –

Fuck . . .

Kane craned his neck –

Well that's one helluva pointing job . . .

Although –

How odd . . .

– as he touched it with his hand the brick suddenly seemed to blur and then transmogrify into . . .

Into what, exactly?

– wood. Tiny chips of . . . slivers of . . .

Uh . . .

(Like one of those old-fashioned, ridged and laminated cards he'd been so fond of as a child where the image is cleverly split into two, so that when you stare at it, straight on, you see one thing, but then, when you *angle* it, you see . . .

Uh . . .
No.)

Kane shook his head, withdrew his hand and stepped back so that wood returned – as if by magic – to its former constituency –

That's it –
Much better . . .

He was currently standing and gazing up at the East Entrance (he wasn't sure how or *why* he knew it was the East, he just did). The East Entrance was actually still under construction (a chaotic mish-mash of scaffolding and ladders; a huge, gaping *maw* in what was otherwise a flawless facade).

Right . . .
Good.

  Kane drew a long, slow, steady breath, steeled himself, glanced
furtively around him, yanked his hood down low to obscure his face –

Eh?
Hood?

– and stealthily entered the building.
  Once inside he observed (with a strange feeling of smugness) that
the basilica was constructed under fairly traditional lines –

Basilica?

– an oblong hall with a double colonnade and apse –

Apse?!

  Yet while the basic design of the interior was fairly uncontentious,
the *scale* of it was anything but.
It was gigantic –

Stupendous!

– and there was this –

Wow!

  – *ow!*

  – *ow!*

– this quite astonishing *echo* –

  – *ho!*

  – *ho!*

– so as soon as his boots hit the floor –

Granite?
Marble?

– he observed *another* pair of boots – the *same* pair, to all intents
and purposes – landing just a *milli-second* after; almost as if he were
two people, two explorers, two dreamy, mid-light voyagers . . .

Mid-light?
Hang on . . .

   It was evening –

But of course

– *definitely* evening. The giant hall was suddenly illuminated (or had
it always been?) by a thousand flickering candles. He sniffed. He could
smell cheap tallow. He could smell burning honey.
   And then –

What?
– without any kind of warning, the echo from his footsteps faltered
slightly – it adjusted itself; it missed a beat. He glanced anxiously
behind him – with a start. But there was only his shadow –

My shadow?
Really?!

   He gingerly lifted an arm. His shadow's arm lifted. It was a tiny arm.
He kicked out his leg. His shadow's leg lifted. It was a curiously *feminine*
leg. He pushed back his hood and tried to inspect his profile, but every
time he posed (to get the best possible slant on his features) the shadow
– like a twig in a game of Pooh-sticks – drifted gently out of view.
   He inspected his hands. His hands were very beautiful; a scholar's
hands. A gentleman's hands –

Still a gentleman's hands, eh?
After all this time?

– and there – very reassuringly – further up on the forearm; his burn.
He fondly recalled how he'd acquired it; setting fire to the barn –

Barn?!

His eyes quickly returned –

No.
That's just silly.
It wasn't . . .

– to those fine, scholarly hands. He smiled down at them, proudly,
spreading out his fingers and quietly perusing his uncallused palms,
his neat, clean nails . . .

A sudden *rustle* –

What?!

– from directly behind him –

Who?!

– caused him to spring sharply back, but way too late. She was
already hard upon him; a woman, lean; dark; distinguished; dressed,
from head to toe, in deepest mourning. He froze, certain he'd be
exposed –

Exposed for what?
To what?

– but she hurried straight on by him, as if she didn't even see him.
   He turned and observed her rapid progress down the aisle (her
skirts were long and black, the fabric seemed heavy – *shiny* – almost
as if wet, as if *water*logged. He stared at the floor, anticipating some
kind of damp trail, but there was nothing, only tiny tornadoes of dust
which danced and spiralled gaily in her wake).
   The woman – *The Mourner* (he didn't know why he felt the

strong urge to call her that) hastened on towards the altar, drew to an abrupt halt in front of it, crossed herself and fell into a deep curtsey. Her dark skirts rose around her like a singed blackcurrant soufflé.

As he watched her he felt something unexpected rise within him. A naughty urge? A *cackle*, perhaps? He held his breath, purely out of instinct, to *curtail* it, and as he held it he slowly began to – *Wa-hey!*

– to *levitate*.

He lifted straight up into the air; 2 feet, 4 feet, 10 feet, 20. He rose so high that he disturbed a wood pigeon from its roost. It clapped its wings, furiously, as it flew on by (and this single clap resounded around the ceiling, like a flurry of gunshot).

Then he panicked –

Oh shit . . .
How the hell will I come down again?

He exhaled, sharply – alarmed – and then he dropped –

Woah!

He suspended his breath again and held steady. He experimented with this system a few times –

Okay . . .

– then he tried to move forward, but it was difficult. He performed a kind of clumsy breast-stroke with his arms and made gradual headway.

Soon (in a blink) he was suspended directly above her –

The Mourner . . .
Who's she mourning for?

He exhaled gradually. It was a good feeling, a *warm* feeling. He slipped lower and lower, like the mercury in a cooling thermometer.

Twenty feet, 10 feet, 5 feet, he wobbled on 3. His shoes finally touched the ground, but so *lightly*. He stood on his toes, holding out his arms (like the poignant Christ carved in exquisite marble behind the altar).

He was mere *inches* from her. He breathed out – slowly and deeply – from his loin, from his belly, and then he inhaled the *scent* of her. He smelled . . .

Peppermint?
Clove?
Lavender?

He rose a delighted inch and then landed. He was aroused by her. She was standing now, and there was this irresistible *sliver* . . .

Uh . . .

– of white flesh on the back of her shoulder, peeking out like the slip of a moon from between the gloom of her dress and the pitch of her shawl. He fluttered out his hand and landed on it – like a moth, drawn to the light – with the soft pads of his scholarly fingers. She didn't move. She didn't react to the moth. She was muttering a prayer.

He rose and then fell again –

Ahhh . . .

This time, as he landed, he reached out both hands and slid them around her waist's tight hourglass. Her waist was so tiny he thought he might almost . . . *almost* fasten his hands around it. So he did. He clamped his hands around her, hearing – and thrilling to – the resisting creak of her corset; the aching groan of her stays . . .

His middle fingers touched each other. His scholar's thumbs touched each other . . .

Ahhh

He moved in still closer – so close now he was literally shoved up against her. He slid his hungry palms over the swell of her belly and then up, towards her breasts. His fingers pitter-pattered like rain on the gently rising dough of her chest.

Still, she did nothing. So he shoved his hands down –

Hard

– on to her breasts, from above, almost viciously, as if trying to push those neat, white buns back into the stern corset that supported them. Then he lifted them, sharply, and freed her nipples, rolling them between his fingers, with a satisfied grunt. Her nipples felt hard between his fingers as two cultured pearls.

He rose and then fell away.

Ahhh

He rose and then fell.

Because it was all in the breathing, see? Each breath sending a tiny pulse, a thrill, to his belly and his groin.
He breathed. He *breathed*. He squeezed her breasts. He pushed his face and lips into the tender white skin on the side of her neck.

And then suddenly, just when it seemed like he could do exactly as he liked, that he *would* do as he liked (that he might no longer be able to *stop* himself from doing so), she gasped and her head snapped around. Her eyes were wide. She seemed terrified. He saw her, in profile, and he *knew* her, but just as with his own shadow – when he tried to see her, to recognise her completely – the face lost focus and she was only . . .

Uh . . .

She struggled to turn and confront him, but he couldn't let that happen, he couldn't stop what he was doing –

Just can't . . .
Just need to . . .

– so he grabbed her arms, roughly, and pinned her to him, bruising her (he could feel the savage squeeze and crush of his grip against

the milky blancmange of her skin). He ground himself into her, into the blackness of her skirts, into the softness and the muffledness, like a ravenous man trying to land a fish from a fast-flowing river; and the fish is resisting – as all fishes naturally must – the fish is pulling the line taut – still tauter – but he counters, hungrily, he lugs, he wrestles, he strains, he *heaves*, and then, and then, and then . . . *smack!* –
Oh God!
Thank God!

– the fish jumps, it *springs*, spontaneously, unrestrainedly, out of the water.

EIGHT

'Did *you* put that bell on the cat?'

Kane had ventured downstairs, at dawn (okay, seven-thirty-*ish*); dazed, befuddled, and somewhat –

Uh . . .
Yuk

– *sticky*, to grab a bottle of milk from the front step, only to be unexpectedly *ambushed* by his father.

'Sorry?' Kane frowned, startled, slightly caught on the hop (he felt stained – *tattooed*, almost – by the sleep he'd just had. He felt it indelibly *inked* upon him. He felt . . .

Urgh

– he felt *filthy*).

'The cat?'

'Yes,' Beede nodded, 'I have a cat. A Siamese cat. I'm borrowing him. I mean I'm looking *after* him.'

Kane just stared at him, perplexed. 'What's that smell?' he said, finally.

'Smell?'

'Yes. Like . . . like smoke. *Wood*smoke.'

'Woodsmoke?'

'Yes.'

Beede sniffed, then shrugged. 'I'm not getting it.'

'Oh.'

Kane bit his lip, distractedly. Then he focussed in on Beede again. Beede seemed pale – strained – almost *stricken*. It wasn't a good look.

'I'm sorry,' Kane murmured (struggling to suppress a sympathetic pang), 'you were saying?'

'There's a bell on the cat. A *new* bell. Hanging on a collar around his neck. I was simply wondering . . .'

'No.' Kane shook his head.

'Are you sure?'

'Positive,' Kane insisted, yawning. 'Why the hell would I be putting a bell on a cat?'

'I don't know.'

'Talking of necks . . . Is something . . . *uh* . . .'

Kane indicated, tentatively, towards the offending area on his father. Beede moved a cagey hand to his shoulder.

'Have you pulled something? You look . . .'

Old

'*No*. It's fine . . .' Beede wrestled with himself. '*Yes*. I don't know. I think I may've sat up too abruptly in the night, and just . . . just *jinked* something . . .'

'*Ouch.*'

Beede shrugged, then winced.

'Perhaps it was Gaffar,' Kane volunteered.

'Pardon?'

'The bell.'

'The bell? You think?' Beede gazed up at him, keenly.

'Actually, no. Gaffar despises cats. Although . . .'

'What?'

'Maybe that's why. Maybe he put the bell on to try and keep some kind of *check* on it.'

'Is that possible?'

'No,' Kane snorted, 'it isn't.'

Beede scowled (Why was it always such a *dance* with Kane? Why was nothing ever . . . ?).

Kane sniffed at the air again. 'Woodsmoke,' he murmured, '*definitely*.'

He moved over towards the door. 'I'm just getting my milk,' he said. 'D'you want yours?'

'Yes,' Beede nodded, 'thanks.'

Kane went out, grabbed the milk, then came back in again, shivering. He handed Beede his bottle. Beede took it, then he winced.

'Have you taken anything?' Kane asked.

'Pardon?'

Beede pretended not to follow. Kane frowned. 'For your *back*. It's obviously . . .'

'It's probably just a cold,' Beede fobbed him off, 'in the muscle. In the shoulder.'

'Are you planning to go to work?'

'Of course,' Beede snapped. 'Why wouldn't I be?'

They stared at each other.

'I'll ask Gaffar about the bell,' Kane murmured, feeling around in his pocket with his spare hand for his cigarettes, unable to locate them. He turned towards the stairs. He gazed up at the stairs. He grimaced. Then he turned back around again.

'I have something for it,' he said. 'I mean I can *give* you something for it, something that'll help . . .'

'It's not a problem,' Beede said gruffly. 'If I'm desperate I can always take a couple of Anadin.'

'It's all perfectly kosher,' Kane persisted. 'I *know* about backs, remember? It's kind of my *speciality* because of . . . *uh* . . .'

Mum

Beede's eyes widened. 'Of course,' he butted in, keen not to venture a single step further down this particularly treacherous emotional bridleway, 'I appreciate the offer.'

Kane shrugged.

The unmentionable hung between them like a dank canal (overrun by weed and scattered with litter – the used condoms, the bent tricycle, the old pram).

'Well I'd better . . .'

Kane shrugged again, *hurt* (he'd tried to reach out, and he'd palpably failed, so that, he supposed, was that).

'Yes. *Thanks*.'

Beede inspected his milk bottle. Kane headed upstairs. He was at least five steps up when he could've sworn he heard something. A muttering. He paused. He peered over his shoulder. Beede had not moved. He was gazing down at the floor.

'Did you just say something, Beede?'

'Pardon?'

'Did you just *say* something?'

'No. *Yes*. I simply . . .' he glanced up, 'I just asked after your foot.'

Kane stared at him –

What?

'Your *foot*,' Beede reiterated, tightly. 'Is it feeling any better?'
   'My foot . . . ?' Kane glanced down at his foot, flushing. 'It's fine.'
'Apparently verrucas can be hereditary,' Beede informed him.
'Yes. *Yes*. Apparently so.'
(Had she told him that, too? *Elen?*)
   Beede was scowling again. He was passing the milk bottle from hand to hand.
'Is there something on your mind?' Kane asked (quite boldly, he felt, under the circumstances).
'I can always give you the number of another chiropodist,' Beede said, 'a *good* chiropodist, if seeing Elen doesn't quite pan out . . .'
   'Why? Don't you think Elen's a good chiropodist?'
'I didn't say that,' he snapped.
'But didn't she heal *your* foot?'
'Yes,' Beede conceded grouchily, 'in a manner of speaking.'
'Well either she healed your foot or she didn't heal it . . .'
'The foot's better – much better. But verrucas can be very persistent.'
'Neurotic,' Kane shot back, 'sustained by a kind of inner turmoil.'
   'Ah,' Beede smiled, grimly, 'so you had the little lecture, did you?'

Little lecture?

'Yes,' Kane said.
'*Good.*'
Beede's voice was bitter. His colour was high.
   'I actually remembered her,' Kane said, struggling to justify his position to his father (although he wasn't entirely sure *why*), 'from before . . . From Mum.'
'Ah.'
(Again, that deep canal, that unnavigable bridleway.)
   'And what's stranger still,' Kane continued, 'she actually remembered *me*.'

'I see . . .' Beede cleared his throat. 'Well I'm sure you're very *memorable*, Kane. It's just a complicated situation, that's all . . .'

341

'It's only a wart, Dad,' Kane scoffed.

Dad?

Beede flinched.

Dad?

'It's only a wart,' Kane repeated, blankly.

'So did she ask you for anything?' Beede wondered. 'When you saw her?'

'*Ask* me for anything?' Kane didn't follow. 'Like what?'

'I don't know . . . Drugs?'

'*Drugs?*'

'Yes. I just wondered if the conversation might've got around to . . .'

'*Drugs?!*'

'*Yes.*' Beede was defiant. 'Isn't that what people generally ask you for?'

Kane was appalled. 'What on earth are you talking about? She's a *foot* doctor. I have a verruca . . .'

'You went to her *house*, Kane.'

'*So?*'

'Do you make a habit of visiting the homes of *all* your healthcare professionals?'

'It wasn't . . .' Kane started.

'I mean do you make a habit of visiting your *dentist* at home?'

'I just turned up,' Kane was exasperated, 'on a whim. There was nothing sinister about it. My foot was hurting . . .'

'Oh *yes*,' Beede sneered. 'Your foot.'

Silence

'Did she tell you I went to see her?' Kane asked, suddenly anxious. 'Did she complain to you about it?'

'No.'

'So how . . . ?'

'Isidore. Her husband. He told me. He mentioned it in passing. He seemed . . .' Beede pondered for a moment.

'He seemed what?' Kane enquired.

'Bemused.'

'I see.' Kane shrugged (perhaps a touch disingenuously). 'Well I don't really know what *cause* he had to feel that way.'

'What *cause*? You just turned up at her *home* . . .' Beede threw out his hand, exasperatedly. 'Don't you think that's a little . . . ?'

'What?'

'Odd?'

'*Odd?*'

'Yes.'

'*No*. No I don't. She nursed my dying mother. We *knew* each other . . .'

'She didn't nurse her,' Beede snapped. 'She's a chiropodist. She massaged her feet – a couple of times, at best – ten long *years* ago . . .'

'I know exactly what she did,' Kane said, hoarsely, 'I know exactly what happened. I was *there*, remember?'

'All I'm telling you is that it's a complicated situation,' Beede struggled to keep a lid on things, 'her husband isn't 100 per cent well. She's under a great deal of pressure . . .'

'For *fuck's sake*, Beede, she's just taking a look at my *verruca*,' Kane remonstrated, still trying himself – at some level – to make light of it.

'Fine. But don't say I didn't warn you.'

Beede turned, abruptly.

'*Ditto*,' Kane hit back (somewhat childishly).

Beede paused. 'What do you mean?'

'Don't say I didn't warn *you*.'

'Warn *me*? About what?'

'About . . .' Kane scowled (I mean where exactly to *start*?), 'about Winifred.'

'*Winifred?*'

'Winifred Shilling. *Anthony's* Winifred.'

'What about her?'

'She's trouble.'

'Trouble?' Beede scoffed. '*Winifred?*'

'You'd better believe it.'

'At one time, yes, maybe . . .' Beede conceded, 'but not any more. Things've changed. She's grown up. She's moved on . . .'

'Moved on?' Kane butted in, incredulously. 'From *where*? From *here*? From *me*? Is that what you're suggesting? From *my* bad influence? Holy *Fuck* . . .'

'All I'm saying is that she's got her life back on track . . .'

'She's *poison*.'

'She loves her work, she published her book . . .'

Kane rolled his eyes.

Beede ignored him. 'She got married about eighteen months ago to some Haitian academic . . .'.

'And then they split. Because she's poison. Everything she touches turns to shit.'

'You exaggerate,' Beede scowled.

'I wish to God I did.'

'Then perhaps you're still too . . .' he mused, provocatively '. . . too *close* to the whole thing.'

'Too close? It's been almost four *years*.'

'Exactly. Four years. That's a long time.'

'Not nearly long *enough*,' Kane sniped, 'from where I'm standing.'

'Well I'll certainly heed your advice,' Beede allowed him, 'and I hope – by way of fair exchange – that you'll heed mine . . .' he paused. 'Although as far as Winnie's concerned,' he couldn't resist adding, 'you have absolutely nothing to worry about.'

Winnie?!

'I'm *not* worried,' Kane insisted haughtily, 'I just thought you should know.'

'Good. So now I do.'

'Good.'

They both turned. They both paused. They both took one meas- ured step forward, then another; like a pair of old adversaries engaging in a duel, but without weapons, or seconds, or anybody to call.

The surly, farting roar from the blackened exhaust of Beede's old Douglas had barely finished resounding off the walls in the hallway before Gaffar was padding nonchalantly downstairs (Beede's precious casserole dish cradled lovingly in his arms) and trying to gain access to the ground-floor flat.

He eased down the handle with his elbow and then nudged at the door with his shoulder, fully expecting it to just *give*, but it didn't, it *wouldn't* –

Eh?!

– so he placed the dish down gently against the skirting and tackled it for a second time using both hands.

Nope. Solid as a rock. He attacked it for a third time (*harder* – slamming into it with his hip, just to make sure) –

Nuh-uh

– but the door wasn't merely stuck, it was *locked*.

He drew a step back and stared at it, frowning. Then he shrugged, spun around and checked his appearance in the hallway mirror (he'd abandoned the suit and was wearing a smart, new outfit: black trousers from Burton, black shirt from Topman, black lambswool jumper and leather jacket from M&S, black boots from Clarks). He looked – to all intents and purposes – like a monochrome assassin.

But something was missing. He frowned. Then he reached out his hand and 'borrowed' Kane's favourite, hand-knitted, Dennis the Menace scarf from the heavily laden coat-rack (wound it around his neck – two, three, *four* times) checked his reflection again (wolf-whistled, approvingly), removed the keys to Kelly's moped from his trouser pocket, twirled them, jauntily, around his index finger, and briskly headed out.

'He's gone,' Kane said (glancing up from his well-thumbed copy of Philip K. Dick's *Beyond Lies the Wub*). 'There's only me here now, so why not save yourself the bother and drop the stupid act?'

He appraised her, somewhat critically, as he spoke. She was fully dressed but dishevelled, standing in her stockinged feet with her big toes bulging – like two wilful carp – out of their fishnet restraints. She had mascara caked down one cheek. Her lips were still sealed up.

She slit her eyes at him, leaned forward, removed the cigarette from between his fingers, jammed it, hungrily, into the side of her mouth and took a quick puff.

'There's tea and toast if you want it,' he said (eyeing her ample cleavage as she bent down, extra-low, to hand it back). 'God knows you must be starving after the night you've had.'

She snorted, dryly, strolled out on to the landing and returned – minutes later – armed with a laden plate and a steaming mug. She placed them both down on to the carpet, then dropped on to the sofa and began to unpick.

As her nimble fingers unlaced the string, she ran a speculative toe up and down Kane's shin.

'This day just keeps on getting better,' Kane mused, to no one in particular, 'first ambushed by my dad, then blandished on my own sofa by a Goth nymphomaniac.'

He returned to his paperback.

Geraldine snorted, enraged, and tried to knock the book from his hands with a well-aimed kick, but he was way too quick for her. He hurled the book on to the floor, grabbed her foot and began to tickle it. She unleashed a terrible squeak as she pulled the lace clear. 'What you tryin'a do?' she croaked (with all the fine vocal modulation of an eighty-year-old cockney fishwife), 'tear my fuckin' *face* up?'

Kane held on to the foot and squinted, dispassionately, down the line of her leg. 'Oh *dear*,' he murmured, his voice full of sympathy, 'how terribly *sad*. You appear to've mislaid your *pants*.'

She grinned at him, sliding down still lower and obligingly hitching her skirt up.

'Did you ever consider the benefits,' he wondered, casually inspecting her neatly shaven muff, 'of applying a few well-placed stitches down there?'

She yanked her foot from his grasp, pulled herself straight and adjusted her skirt.

'I'm guessing you didn't get around to telling Gaffar, yet,' Kane said, pulling his phone from his pocket and checking his texts.

'*Fuck off!*' she growled. 'We only just *met*. What kind of a *moll* do you take me for?'

He drew on his cigarette, gazing over at her, blankly.

'If you *must* know,' she admitted (slightly rattled by his stare), 'it weren't all that. He just wanked me off with his hand and then – because he did such a good job of it, as a special *favour*, yeah? – I let him cum in between my baps . . .'

She propped up her breasts and then shoved them together, to illustrate.

'Geraldine *Broad*,' Kane chuckled wryly, 'you incorrigible old *romantic* . . .'

'Give me some score,' she wheedled, 'and you can do the same if you like.'

'Don't be ridiculous,' he sighed.

She slid her hand on to his thigh. 'Okay,' she conceded, '*don't* give me no score . . .'

He stared down, frowning slightly, at her ring-laden fingers. 'So let me get this straight,' he murmured, 'you actually, honestly believe that it's possible to just side-step the truth – or *any* kind of basic, moral decision, come to that – by the simple but painful expedient of sewing your mouth up?'

She didn't react.

'. . . I mean you seriously think a few, tiny *stitches*'ll get you off the hook?'

She glowered at him.

'*Wow*,' he shook his head, pityingly, 'you're really messed up.'

'If you're *that* worried,' she sneered, snatching back her hand, 'then why didn't *you* say somethin'?'

'What? And spoil all your fun?'

She ignored him, bending down to pick up her mug. He pushed his cigarette into the corner of his mouth and returned to his texting.

'I shouldn't even be givin' you the time of day,' she grumbled, 'after the move you pulled on Lester.'

'He owed me money,' Kane shrugged.

'He owes *everyone* money.'

'D'you know anything about the job he's on?' Kane wondered.

She stared across at him, blankly. 'Job? Why would I?'

'He's over in Cedar Wood,' Kane tried to jog her memory, 'he's working for a German couple there.'

'Alls I know,' she informed him, 'is that if Lester's involved then it ain't lookin' good for 'em.'

'Although the woman – the wife – isn't actually German,' Kane corrected himself (his finger still jabbing at the phone), 'she's English. A chiropodist.'

Geraldine took a sip of her tea. 'They got a kid?' she asked.

'A son. Yes.'

'Well he *did* say somethin' about a kid. Dunno if it's on *that* job. But he loves this kid. He's crazy about him. If the kid says jump he's like, "Off which fuckin' building?" Sounds like the kid's a bit *simple* or somethin' . . .' she rolled her eyes, 'which means they gotta *whole* lot in common . . .'

Kane smiled, sympathetically.

Geraldine was encouraged. 'Says they got this big *castle* on their dinin'-room table. Made out of all these tiny bits of wood. *Matches*. The kid built it. The kid spends all his time buildin' it. Lester say's the kid's a real gem. Never stops goin' on about it. Says the kid's amazin'.'

'What kind of castle?' Kane asked.

'Like some kind of religious buildin'. Like St Paul's Cathedral, only foreign. An' he's built this kick-arse little city around it, Lester says. All tiny shops an' pubs an' shit.'

She took another sip of her tea, then clumsily adjusted her bra strap. 'He's been carryin' around this old pickle jar. I asked him what it was for the other day. He says it's for the kid. I'm like, "What's the kid want with an empty pickle jar?" He's like, "It ain't empty." I'm like, "What's it full of then, *air*?" He's like, "No you stupid, fuckin' whore, *fleas* . . ."'

Kane glanced up.

'Fleas?'

'Yeah. Fleas. He's collectin' fleas for the kid. I'm like, "Well I don't know why you're sniffin' around near *me*. I ain't got no fleas, you *twat*." Mum went fuckin' spacko when I told her. She's like, "I don't care what you do at work, Lester, but I won't have you bringin' that dirty crap back into *this* house . . ."'

She smirked, readjusting her strap again.

'Love your tits, by the way,' Kane muttered, in passing.

''Course you do,' she smiled, 'everybody does.'

He smiled too, still tapping. 'So how's Kelly bearing up?'

'Same as always. Broke her leg. Covered in spots. Hates your guts.'

'Good.'

She took a large bite of her toast, a mouthful of tea, reached out a greedy hand and plucked the fag from his mouth.

'Could you squeeze anything else in while you're at it?' he wondered.

'Why?'

She gazed at him, archly, as she took a puff. 'Whatcha got in mind?'

He glanced down at his watch. 'It's almost nine. Don't you have a job to go to?'

'Nope.'

'What about the salon?'

She blew a smoke ring then stuck her finger through it. 'They sacked me after they found out.'

He glanced up, frowning. 'Can they do that?'

'Whadd'ya mean, "can they?" They already *did*, thick-o.'

'But that's discrimination,' he explained. 'It isn't legal.'

'They said I could cut myself on the scissors or somethin' . . .'

'That's bullshit. It's not right. I can look into it for you if you like . . .'

'*Aw*,' she mocked him, 'my hero.'

'I'm serious.'

''Course you are . . .' She shrugged. 'I was sick of it anyways. That bitch of a manageress was always on my arse. I was glad to go, quite frankly.'

'Well don't say I didn't offer.'

'I won't, matey.'

She stubbed out his cigarette on the bottom of his trainer, placed the stub alongside the toast on her plate, then took another large bite.

'You've put on some weight,' he said.

'Yeah,' she spoke with her mouth full, 'it's all the drugs.'

'But it looks kinda hot.'

'I know it does.'

'So did you get around to telling your dad yet?'

'That's none of your damn business,' she snapped.

'Fair enough.' Kane shoved his phone away. 'Finish your breakfast,' he said, 'then empty your pockets and clear off. I've got stuff I need to do this morning.'

He bent down and retrieved his book.

'Not much to hang around *here* for, anyways,' she grumbled, grabbing her mug of tea, taking a deep draught of it, then belching so loudly – by way of vengeance – that Kane's lank fringe rocked.

A small but ruthlessly efficient band of chainsaw-wielding contractors were savagely laying waste to a tall line of trees on the edge of the forecourt. Beede was standing by the trolleys (next to the store entrance) and absolutely fuming as he watched their steady progress.

'I mean what's to be gained by that?' he couldn't stop himself from sniping at the kid who stacked the trolleys up.

The kid shrugged.

'They were serving a *purpose*: acting as a block to the motorway – countering the pollution, reducing the *racket* . . .'

The kid shrugged again.

'You'd be amazed at the level of bio-diversity which exists even in a superficially low-grade site like this,' Beede informed him, 'in the low bushes, the incidental scrub, the trees . . . I've actually seen several firecrests in that Scotch Pine over there.'

He paused. 'And a wren.'

'They're plannin' on expandin' the place,' the kid volunteered.

'Expanding?' Beede looked astonished. 'There's a brand-new store not half a mile away. How much more business can they possibly sustain here?'

'They're gonna extend the cafe, for starters. Move it upstairs, out the back . . .'

'Why?'

The kid shrugged.

'Move it *upstairs*?'

'Yeah.'

'Move it to the back and upstairs when the *vast* proportion of its customers are pensioners, or young mums with toddlers and prams?'

'They're puttin' in a lift.'

'A lift? But what on earth *for*?'

'So the mums can get their prams up.'

'That's absolutely typical of these people,' Beede grouched, 'to *create* a problem and then pointlessly throw money at it.'

He gazed over at the contractors, balefully. 'I mean where's the harm in just *leaving* things as they are?'

The kid shrugged. He looked at his watch.

Pause

'I'll *tell* you what their reasoning is,' Beede suddenly started up again. 'They move the cafe out to the back so that anyone who wants a drink or a snack has to traipse all the way through the store. And naturally, on their way there – human nature being what it is – they'll pick up a little something *extra*. It's just a scam – in other words – a cheap trick to encourage people to spend more of the money they don't have on more of the stuff they don't *need* . . .'

'I just work here, mate,' the kid said, starting to move off.

'Taking those trees down,' Beede persisted, 'will *significantly* impinge on your working environment. The air quality, for starters . . .'

'Who cares?' the kid sneered. 'It's just some crappy, old job anyway . . .'

'Rubbish,' Beede wouldn't let him have it, 'you're serving an essential function here – *uh* . . .' he inspected his name tag, '*Brian*, and don't you let anyone dare tell you otherwise.'

'I'm on my break now, mate,' Brian smirked, 'so they can tell me what the hell they *like* . . .'

'But I'm *serious*,' Beede maintained, 'your so-called "crappy" job is absolutely critical to the smooth running of this supermarket. You're a fundamental cog, a facilitator, a *lubricant* . . .'

The kid scowled.

'You're an essential component,' Beede persisted. 'If this store were a car you'd be something small but powerful: the *spark* plug, say. And you know as well as I do that without a spark plug this huge capitalist enterprise – this vast and impressive machine – simply couldn't start up.'

The kid continued scowling. He was still struggling to get past Beede's casual use of the word 'lubricant'.

'I mean look at it *this* way,' Beede continued, 'if an actress or a pop star or a footballer doesn't turn up for work one day, then what d'you imagine the consequences are?'

The kid shrugged.

'In real terms? There aren't any. The bottom line is that they *don't* facilitate. They simply entertain. If Capitalism was the ocean, all they'd be is the scum, riding on the crest of a wave.'

'*Rich* scum,' the kid muttered.

'That's a good point,' Beede allowed, 'and a fine pun. But the plain fact is that if *you* don't turn up for work then people can't shop. And if they can't shop, they can't *eat*.'

'If I don't turn up for work,' Brian observed dourly, 'then they get some other sucker in. Or they don't get someone in and the customers just have to shift their fat arses over to one of the *other* collection points to pick their trolley up.'

'But what if they're disabled?' Beede challenged him.

'Then they can get their shoppin' delivered on the internet.'

'And how many people are needed to facilitate *that*?'

Brian shrugged.

'Well let's count them off, shall we? There's the person at the computer – for starters – who *receives* the order, the person who goes out into the shop and *collects* the order, the person who *stores* it until delivery, the person whose job it is to *coordinate* the transport . . .'

'Excuse me,' a woman's voice suddenly piped up from behind him, 'but I can't find a trolley. One of the *little* trolleys. The ones with the metal thingy on the front which has a *clip* that you can pin your shopping list on . . .'

Beede glanced over his shoulder, irritably. He started. It was *Laura*. Laura Monkeith.

'*Beede?*' she looked equivalently stunned.

'Laura . . .' Beede stuttered. 'Good Lord.'

'Are you waiting for a trolley too?' she asked.

'Waiting . . . ?'

The kid took this as his cue to quietly slope off.

'. . . Uh *no* . . . we were just . . .'

Beede winced. He put his hand to his neck.

'They *never* have enough trolleys here,' she grumbled (the kid still within earshot), 'at least not the sort *I'm* always after . . .'

'Life invariably gets more complicated,' Beede promptly informed her, 'if your needs grow too particular.'

'I know,' she nodded, 'and they hire *Moguls*, too. It's store policy. I mean don't get me *wrong* . . .'

'I think you'll probably find,' Beede interrupted her, with a small smile, 'that the word you're searching for here is "Mongol". Although – strictly speaking – a Mongol is someone from Mongolia, which is a country in the remote, mountainous regions of the USSR . . .'

She gazed at him, blankly.

'The real *irony* is that you're not as far off-track as you might suppose,' he continued, 'because a Mogul – used in its original form – was actually a person of the Mongolian *race* – for example the Mongolian conquerors of India became known as "Moguls" because of their extraordinary wealth and power . . .'

Laura opened her mouth and then closed it again.

'I believe the word Mogul,' he doggedly persisted, 'is originally derived from the Persian, *Mughul* . . .'

'Can I just *say*,' she took a small step closer (rapidly putting their linguistic differences behind her), 'while I have this little opportunity, that I was sorry not to seem more *positive* when Pat mentioned your appointment to the Road Crossing Committee yesterday. The trouble is that Charlie isn't very *keen* on the whole thing, but Pat's got this bee in her bonnet . . .'

Now it was Beede's turn to stare at her, blankly.

'I mean it's not that he doesn't *like* the idea – he does – it's just the way he sees it, it doesn't really matter *how* many road crossings we build, or *where* they are, because they'll never bring Ryan back. And when Pat keeps harping on about it, it just makes him feel . . .'

'*Beede!*'

It was Gaffar (red-cheeked, slightly out of breath, wearing Kane's Dennis the Menace scarf). Beede turned, frowning, '*Uh* . . . Oh. *Gaffar* . . .' he blinked.

'Hello, Laura . . .' Gaffar grabbed Laura's hand and squeezed it, smiling, then he turned to Beede. **'What's up, old man? You look all cross, all red, all stiff . . .'**

Laura snatched her hand back. '*Gaffar*. What on earth are you doing here?'

'*Huh?*'

'Do you two know each other?' Beede asked, clutching at his shoulder. Laura turned to Beede, startled. 'No. Not at all.'

She glanced around her, slightly panicked. The kid was returning, pushing a long, silver worm of trolleys ahead of him.

'There's my trolley . . .'

She moved forward. 'That's *fantastic*. Well *done* . . . *uh* . . .' she squinted at his name tag, 'well done, *Brian*.'

She unlatched her trolley from the front.

'Oh . . .' She frowned, inspecting it, '. . . but there's no . . .' she pointed, '*you* know . . . the little metal thingy with the . . .' she paused for a moment, uneasily, weighing up her priorities '. . . Although . . . Forget it. It doesn't . . . I mean really *must* . . .'

She waved blithely at the assembled company and charged off.

Pause

'So that went *very* well, I think,' Beede deadpanned.

'She's trapped in this suffocating marriage,' Gaffar sighed, gazing poignantly after her. **'Separate bedrooms. Her son died last year. She blames herself for the whole thing because she was having an affair. Her husband's an insensitive pig who has no understanding of her needs. He's obsessed by this five-year-old** African macaw **which he got from an Exotic Bird Rescue Centre in** Canterbury. **He's taught it all the catchphrases from** Top Gear. **Sleeps with it. Takes it to work. Rings it – whenever he goes out – and leaves these idiotic messages on the answerphone . . .'**

'Laura *Monkeith*?' Beede asked.

'Always wants a bloody trolley with a *clip*-board,' Brian interjected. 'But I've seen her here loads and she never has no bloody *list* to pin on it.'

'*Yes* . . .' Beede frowned and checked his watch. It was late. *He* was late. '. . . Although I suppose your function in fetching the trolley for her,' he mused (almost to himself), 'is principally a *palliative* one.'

Brian stared at him, doubtfully.

'In other words,' Beede expanded, 'not only are you providing an essential service here, but you're also – at a more general level – caring for the very particular *emotional* needs of the community . . .'

As he was speaking, an especially large, high branch came crashing down on to the tarmac, followed by a loud, almost Bacchanalian roar from the small team of contractors.

'. . . Which is precisely *why*,' Beede concluded, with an angry flourish (not really even convincing himself with this tenuous piece of logic), 'if only for *your* sake, Brian, they should leave those *blasted* trees alone.'

NINE

Kane dialled the number. It rang for what seemed like an age, and then, just as he was finally abandoning all hope –
'Hello?'
A woman answered. An older woman, with a pleasantly mischievous voice. An engagingly *English* voice. A voice of the linnet and the sparrow. A voice of the bramble and the hedgerow.
   'Hi,' Kane responded, 'is this the right number for Peter?'
'Why?' she asked, curtly. 'Who wants to know?'
'I just need quick word with him,' Kane said. 'Is he around?'
   'Who are you?' she asked.
'A friend,' he said, 'well – a friend of a friend.'
'Stuff and nonsense,' she said, 'Peter doesn't *have* any friends.'
'Oh.'
Kane was taken aback.
   'He's utterly *friendless*,' she said, with evident delight.

Pause

'Well how *dreadful* for him,' Kane drawled, finally catching up.
'Isn't it, though?'
   'And how about you?' Kane wondered.
'How about me?'
'Aren't *you* his friend?'
'Good *God*, no.'
   'His wife?' Kane guessed.
'Peter? *Married?!* Don't be ridiculous.'
'His secretary, then?'
'Absolutely not,' she hotly denied in one breath, 'but in the *loosest* possible sense, *yes*,' she confirmed – somewhat quixotically – with the next.
   'His mistress?'
'We do share a bed . . .' she mused, 'and blankets and pillows, if *that*

counts for anything . . .' she paused, 'although the most *genuine* description of my overall role here would probably be . . .' she paused again, '. . . that of *maid*.'

'"A man needs a maid."'

Kane automatically quoted Neil Young.

'"Just someone to keep his house clean, fix his meals and go away,"' she quoted back.

'Marry me!' Kane exclaimed.

'So who exactly,' she staunchly ignored his flirting, '*is* this deluded friend of yours?'

Kane quickly grabbed a hold of the business card and flipped it over. 'J.P.,' he said.

'J.P.?'

'Yes. Peter worked with him on . . .' Kane inspected the card again '. . . on Longport, for the Weald and Downland . . .'

'Are you in a car right now?' she interrupted him. 'Are you driving?'

Kane was speeding up Silver Hill on his way home from visiting a client in the outer reaches of St Michaels.

'No. Not *driving* as such,' he lied, 'I'm just idling at a light, actually.'

'*Ssssh* for a second,' she hushed him.

He was quiet.

'You're driving a Mercedes, *C*220,' she said, 'and you're a liar. You're speeding up Silver Hill in completely the wrong gear.'

Kane double-blinked. He glanced into his rearview mirror and flipped down his indicator.

'Bear with me for one second,' he said, braking, changing gear and promptly pulling his car off the road.

'So how the *hell*'d you figure that out?' he demanded, brutally yanking his handbrake up.

'*Urgh*. Sticky handbrake,' she said. 'It's that particular model, I'm sure of it. I had one myself but I wrote it off – three-car pile-up, on my way home from a house sale in Cheam. It had the sticky handbrake and this tiny, maddening little *knock* when I drove uphill in fourth.'

Kane frowned. 'Were you hurt?'

'Excuse me?' she sounded briefly distracted. Her voice was a little further away from the receiver than before.

'When you wrote it off. Were you hurt?'

'Don't be an idiot,' she said, drawing closer again, 'it was a bloody *Merc*.'

'Good point,' he said.

'What colour's yours?'

'She's a blonde.'

'Mine too! Although mine was a mink. I called her The Mink . . .' She sighed, 'I do miss her dreadfully.'

'So what do you drive now?'

'A customised Lada.'

'What?'

'And a van. I have a small van . . .'

'A *Lada*?'

'Yes. A Lada. Why? Do you have a problem with that?'

'It's just an odd . . . an unusual . . . uh . . . *progresssion*. In terms of style.'

'Not at all. Where's your imagination? It's an absolute *gem*. I had it shipped over from Jamaica.'

'Jamaica? A *Lada*? Are you serious?'

'Of course I am,' she sounded vaguely insulted, 'they import them to use as taxis over there. They love them. Give a Lada a spray job, darken the windows, and *hey-presto:* you're transformed into some seedy, low-ranking apparatchik in a fabulous, Eastern Bloc spy drama.'

'Wonderful,' Kane said, flatly.

'It *is*,' she insisted.

'And you shipped it over from Jamaica?'

'Yes. Although they actually customise them in Hackney so it was a ridiculous way to go about things. But it felt right. It felt good. The car has a certain . . . *swagger* which you simply couldn't get any other way. A certain, indefinable *je ne sais quoi*. But enough of my Lada,' she said, 'when exactly did you speak to J.P. about Peter?'

'Yesterday,' Kane lied.

'Yesterday?'

She sounded surprised.

'So how'd you go about guessing I was on Silver Hill?' he tried to distract her.

'Pure conjecture.'

'Seriously?'

'No. Pure deduction, Watson. The engine was knocking – so I reasoned

357

that you were on a hill. Your phone reception is good, so I reasoned that you were nearby. I heard a fire engine siren sounding – in fact I can still hear it. I'm very familiar with the sirens from that particular station. We only live just around the corner . . .'

'You and Peter,' Kane said.

'We two,' she sighed.

A short silence followed in which Kane could've sworn he heard the distant pumping of a pair of old bellows.

'Is that a cigar?'

He took a wild guess.

'Yup. Just went out,' she said. 'Clever little *you*.'

Kane smirked.

'So how's J.P. bearing up?' she wondered.

He heard a match being struck.

'Pardon?'

She inhaled.

'J.P.'s health?'

'Uh . . . It's good. Pretty good. Fairly good. I mean . . .' Kane carefully hedged his bets, 'under the circumstances . . .'

'Yes . . .' as she spoke he could hear her pulling a tiny fleck of loose tobacco from her lip, 'although the "circumstances" – as you so aptly put it – aren't really what you might call *conducive* to good health, are they?'

'Uh . . . no,' Kane said.

'Quite the *opposite*, in fact.'

Kane cleared his throat. He sensed a problem. He grimaced. He took the bull by the horns.

'Am I missing something?' he asked.

'Yes.' She sounded perfectly cheerful. 'What you are missing is the small but necessary detail of J.P.'s tragic demise.'

'Oh.'

'J.P.'s dead. *Ka-put.* He died late last year.'

'God.'

'Bowel cancer,' she added, just for good measure.

'I see . . .' Kane bit his lip. 'Right. So now I guess – from where you're standing – I must be looking a little . . . *uh* . . . ?'

'Stupid? Yes.' She paused. 'And I'm *sitting*, actually. Or perching. On the edge of a counter.'

'Did you know J.P. well?'

'Well?'

Kane winced. 'I mean were you close?'

'Close? *Hmmn*. I don't know. Certainly not as close as you and he appear to be.'

'Okay,' he drew a deep breath. 'Just tell me straight . . .'

'J.P. was my brother.'

'*Shit*.' Kane was mortified. '*Seriously?*'

'Yes, *seriously*. It was all very serious. J.P. was very serious. His illness was very serious. His death was very serious. Death – in general – I find, can be like that . . .'

'I'm a dick,' Kane said.

'Truly,' she chuckled, 'I can't *wait* to tell Peter this story. Peter will think this all *terribly* droll.'

'Droll,' Kane parroted. 'That's one way of looking at it.'

As he spoke Kane heard what he presumed to be a small alarm of some kind sounding in the background.

'I'm all out of time,' she said, 'so let's cut to the chase, shall we? What's the real reason for your call?'

'I found Peter's number in an old book.'

'*What?*' she scoffed. 'Scribbled into the margins of some dusty tome?'

'No. On a *card* inside a book. A business card. And I was just interested . . .'

'Which book?' she scoffed. '*The Reader's Digest Compendium of Tall Stories*?'

'A history book,' Kane scowled, humiliated. 'I don't remember the title. A book about the criminal underclass of the sixteenth century . . .'

'Whose book?'

'My book.'

'*Whose* book?'

There was no escaping it.

'The book originally belonged to Daniel Beede.'

'No it didn't,' she demurred, 'the book originally belonged to me. It's that fabulous Penguin anthology edited by Gamini Salgado. I actually lent it to him.'

Silence

'Which I suppose would make *you* . . .' she cheerfully continued, 'his charming yet horribly degenerate son, Kane.'

'Yes. I suppose it would.'

'In truth I'd already guessed,' she confessed, 'I was just playing you along. I was on to you from the start. You have identical voices. Not the accent, obviously, because his is so beautiful and yours is quite appalling, but the timbre, the *tone*.'

'I'll have to take your word on that,' he said, hurt.

'Before I go,' she said, brusquely, 'because I really *must* . . . Have you considered selling your car?'

'Pardon?'

'The Blonde. Might you sell?'

He gave this a moment's consideration. 'Well it wasn't the *foremost* thought in my mind when I rang you . . .'

Then he paused and quickly reassessed, 'How much for?'

'Whatever you want. Whatever it takes. Just ask Beede – I'm old and rich and *incredibly* spoiled.'

'But what about the Lada?' he wondered. 'I thought the Lada had a certain . . . uh . . . *swagger* . . .'

'We'll do a deal,' she sounded delighted by the idea, 'we'll do a Part Exchange.'

'I'd need to *see* her first, obviously . . .'

'She's a he. I call him The Commissar.'

'I'll have to see *him*, then.'

'Fine. Come on over.'

Kane turned the key in his ignition. The Blonde coughed then started to hum.

'So how'd I reach you?' he asked.

'Reach me?' he could almost hear her smirking. 'But you already *reached* me, dear,' she said.

Gaffar was – much to Beede's intense exasperation – every inch 'the showman' on the fruit aisle (all he lacked was a spot-light, a costume and a drumroll): he serenaded the bananas; he juggled the apples; he plucked a black grape from a large bunch, balanced it on his chin, then flipped it up into his mouth and swallowed it, whole.

His jaunty mood was sustained – quite convincingly – as they journeyed through the vegetables: he was perky by the broccoli, tranquil by the onions, sanguine by the potatoes . . .

The first clue that anything was even *remotely* amiss manifested itself as they drew abreast of the avocados (a certain stiffness of gait, a sudden quietness). By the time they'd reached the tomatoes (a distance of 2 feet on, at best) his good mood had taken a serious nose-dive (nervous yawning, uncontrolled scratching, a thin line of sweat on his upper lip).

At the beetroots – **'God have mercy!'** – he seemed merely a shadow of his former, extrovert self: his complexion looked pallid, waxy, almost *ashen*; his lips were moist and quivering; his eyes started slightly from their sockets as they ransacked the shelves . . .

But the radishes, it seemed, were to be the final straw.

'No.'

He ground to a shuddering halt in front of them, gesticulating weakly.

'Is **enough**.'

He passed Beede the shopping list and the basket. Beede handed him back his knapsack and his helmet.

'Okay,' Beede sighed, 'let's just get this over with, shall we?'

And off he went.

He followed the list as best he could –

Cucumber, spring onions, celery . . .

– but there was some confusion around the issue of the *type* of mixed salad required, so he grabbed both – the bag and the sealed plastic bowl – and went off in search of confirmation.

Gaffar, meanwhile, was idling dreamily in the cheese aisle, quietly weighing up the distinct culinary virtues of Gorgonzola, Feta and minted Halloumi.

Beede strolled up behind him. 'So which is preferable?' he asked. 'The unenvironmental plastic tub or the horrendously overpriced shredded stuff in the bag?'

Gaffar turned, saw the tub held cruelly aloft, and promptly swooned.

He turned right at the public phone box and into Ox Lane (just as she'd instructed), then right again down Barnfield. 'There's a line of normal-looking houses,' she'd said, 'intersected by a small, dirt track. Take the track. And do watch out for the geese . . .'

'I'll drive carefully,' he assured her.

'No. I mean *you* watch out,' she explained. 'They're savages. Just sound your horn as you pull up, then sit tight. I can't come out myself – I'm right in the middle of something – so I'll send a dog to guide you. *Two* dogs. I'll send Koto and Pinch. Do exactly as they ask and you should be just fine . . .'

Should?!

She wasn't exaggerating. The geese (white-feathered, blue-eyed, mud-splattered, brightly beaked – beautiful geese, he supposed – if he'd been in a mind to consider a goose beautiful –

Am I in that mind?

– he gazed at them, quizzically –

Uh . . . No.)

– were strident, vicious and hysterical. There were about thirty of them, in total, and as soon as he applied his brakes they surrounded the car like a gang of little hooligans; battering at the paintwork, jabbing at the metal trim, honking cacophonously.

The general sense of affray was only exacerbated by the sudden arrival of five or six huge turkeys which patrolled the outer perimeter of the fuss, gobbling indignantly, like a posse of grey-suited prison guards, drawing back their necks, imperiously, shaking their wattles (like fat bunches of keys), and somehow producing a curiously hollow booming noise (*how?* With their throats? Their wings?), like the awful, reductive *bang* of a cell door closing at the far end of a distant corridor.

Kane unfastened his seat-belt and lit a cigarette. His hand – he realised – was shaking slightly. He tensed it up into an impatient fist and gazed around him, with a scowl.

It was certainly an unusual property –

A small farm?
A big smallholding?

He was parked in the cobbled courtyard which was full of old –

Junk

– farm machinery and surrounded by an ugly confusion of large sheds, barns and garages.

The courtyard itself was somewhat unkempt and exceedingly muddy. He adjusted his feet and peered down at his fine, white trainers –

Damn

The house –

Or cottage?

– (he glanced up again, wincing at the racket) seemed ancient (if not particularly charming); it was small, single-storey and entirely covered – ceilings, walls – in old, red tiles. It looked as if it'd once consisted of two storeys, but had hunkered down during an especially cruel storm, perhaps, or had taken a piece of bad news too much to heart, and had sunk, with an awful sigh, into the hollow refuge of its own foundations.

The windows were hung at awful angles. He shuddered. And the chimney? Utterly wonky. Like it'd been sloppily sketched on – as an afterthought – by a simpleton.

He checked his watch, then drew, impatiently, on his cigarette. He'd done just as he'd been instructed and had sounded his horn – *once, twice* – as he pulled up (how long ago now? Two minutes?

Three?) but there was still no sign of deliverance; no dog, certainly, although he could've sworn he saw a curtain twitch – in the cottage – and the hunched outline of a small figure within (possibly a child), carefully observing him.

He sounded the horn again (setting up a terrifying chain-reaction among his feathered compatriots, who blared back at him, discordantly), then reached into his pocket and withdrew a tiny, neatly sealed polythene bag containing five or six white tablets. He pulled open the seal, took one out and swallowed it. Then he slid his fingers back in, removed a second, and swallowed that, too. He closed his eyes for a moment and drew a deep breath.

In his mind's eye he suddenly had a clear vision –

No . . .

– an idea?

No . . .

– a perfect *memory* of geese – not *these* geese, but another breed, a different variety, a grey-brown variety with pink bills and pink feet –

All carefully dipped in tar, to preserve them, for the journey

There were hundreds of them – almost thousands – and they were being driven, in a messy line, a clucking, parping stream, along The London Road –

Hang on there:
Dipped in tar?!
Journey?!

He – Kane –

Right.
Yes.
That's me . . . .

– was sitting –

I'm high . . .
Up high

– he glanced down, in his mind's eye –

Good Lord!

– astride a pony, watching them pass with a sense of casual impatience. He was hungry. Part of him was idly wondering if he might steal one –

Steal a goose?

– but geese – he knew, from hard experience –

Really?!

– were far too noisy for casual abduction.
   He opened his eyes again.

Wow.

He inspected his scholarly hands –

?!

– which were anxiously fingering the polythene bag –

Just four left
Calm down
Calm down
Two was more than enough –

– then shoved it back, impatiently, into his pocket. He sucked on his cigarette. He thought about phoning again, or putting on some music . . .
   Then finally –

Finally

– (how long now? Five minutes? Seven?) a dog slunk into the courtyard from one of the larger barns. A sheepdog, but a terrible advert for the breed: skinny, sly-looking, filthy, with large bald patches along its flanks and an utterly naked grey-blue tail. It crawled along the cobbles, approaching the car at an angle, but never looking at it directly, and never confronting a goose (the geese – in truth – seemed all but oblivious to it). So submissive was the beast that it looked as if its nerve might just give, as if it might simply slink past . . .

And so it did. Straight past, into a shed opposite.
'Great.'
Kane folded his arms, irritated.

A minute or so later a second dog arrived; bigger than the first; fatter, but equally filthy. It seemed indifferent to the activities of the first dog. It sat, yawned, then leaned over and gnawed, neurotically, at its own hind leg –

Fleas.
Yes . . .

– Kane frowned –

I have a treatment for fleas –
A special powder . . .

– he chuckled –

What?!

He stopped chuckling. He shook his head. He blinked again, lifting his hand (like one of those ineffectual little cranes which clumsily snatches up small baubles in a glass box at the arcade) and suspending it, indecisively, above the horn . . .

Should I sound it?

But he held off.

The second dog (meanwhile) had stopped its gnawing and was gazing around the courtyard, casually. It sneezed. It surveyed the geese, nonchalantly. It slowly stood up –

Now what?

Kane frowned. He stubbed his cigarette out, keeping his eyes closely trained on it.

Then suddenly, without warning, the geese all turned, as one. Kane also turned. He saw the first dog – the sly dog – emerging from the opposite shed. And nothing had changed – so far as he could tell – it was still low to the ground, eyes askance but non-confrontational. Yet the geese had sensed something – a difference about it. Or maybe it was merely the combination of the two animals, in conjunction – a mathematical issue; a matter of basic goose geometry.

The second dog remained standing, its ears slightly pricked, its eyes glued on the first. The first dog carried on moving – slinking forward – very slowly. And gradually – almost miraculously – a path was forming. Waves of bright beak and white feather were parting – an escape route was being forged for him, a direct route from the driver's door to a large barn, opposite. Kane frowned, confused. He'd presumed (he wasn't really sure *why*) that he'd be escorted into the cottage.

Even so, he took his chance. He opened his door and slowly eased his way out. His exit was accompanied by a flurry of muted parping. Several geese rose up, flapping their wings at him. The second dog lifted its tail. That was all. The parping stopped. The wings were promptly folded.

Kane stood, indecisively, wondering whether to seek refuge in the barn or to throw caution to the wind and try and leg it over to the cottage. But his route was currently blocked. He took a tiny step forward (at an angle to the path) and became gradually aware of a monotonous humming . . .

No.
Not so much a hum, as . . .
Shit.
A growl

He glanced over towards the first dog. The first dog was crouched low and baring its teeth at him.

Fuck

He put his hand to his phone, and then caught himself doing it –

What are you gonna do, you prick?
Ring the Emergency Services?
Order a fucking pizza?

He dropped his hand and started walking to the barn. One step, two steps, three steps. Then the pills kicked in, or he changed his mind, or something –

Something?
A spirit of pure devilry?

– overwhelmed him and he turned and started running, sprinting, arms flaying – with a crazy *whoop* – towards the house.

What exactly happened next Kane couldn't entirely fathom. An explosion? An *implosion*? All he could really be sure of was that everything went to hell. That fragile sense of order, of equilibrium – collapsed. The geese went wild and attacked. The dogs – in turn – attacked the geese (as if this – at some level – was what they'd always secretly *yearned* to do). If there was a Pandora's Box for farmyards then Kane had just unwittingly lifted open its lid.

There was barking, braying, parping, howling, feathers flew . . . Kane felt a tearing at his legs. He put out his hand. Something inarticulate was yelled –

Is that me?
Or someone else?

A shot was fired –

A shot?

A goose was felled. Two geese –

With one shot?

– and the others scattered.

He glanced up, clutching his calf, cursing.

A woman stood before him, holding a shotgun. A tiny woman, sharp-faced, wearing a woolly hat, clogs –

Clogs?

– and a long, beige, butcher's-style apron.

She strode forward and gazed down at the geese. One was still moving. She slammed down a clog on to its throat and promptly dispatched it. Then she grabbed both birds (*huge* birds; one in either hand), hauled them up (by the neck) gave Kane a filthy look, turned and marched back over towards the cottage.

'Excuse me . . .' Kane said.

She glanced over her shoulder.

'Purrups jast di as yi *tald* nixt teem,' she said, gesticulating, irritably, goose in hand. '*Eejat!*'

Eh?

'So would you care to refresh my memory,' another – slightly more familiar, yet rather more imperious – voice suddenly rang out, 'about what it was *exactly* that I instructed you to do when you pulled up?'

He turned.

In the entrance to the barn stood a second woman, petite and lean, her bright-white hair pulled back into a glossy ponytail, a half-smoked cigar propped behind her ear. She had dancing, chartreuse-green eyes – boozy eyes – and a pair of the most astonishingly flirtatious charcoal brows: dark, hand-painted brows which decorated her fine-boned face like two fabulous pieces of Chinese calligraphy.

'You told me to sound my horn and wait for the dogs,' he said.

'Precisely.'

She wore overalls: scruffy, paint-splattered, in dark denim, matched with a pair of neat white gloves.

'So I sounded my horn and I waited,' he insisted.

'And the dogs came . . . ?'

'Yes,' he shuddered. The pills were kicking in (but hadn't they kicked in already?). 'Eventually.'

'And they cleared a route for you?'

  'Uh . . .'

He looked regretful.

'But you decided . . . ?'

  'I thought you'd be in the cottage.'

He pointed.

'But I'm in the barn, Kane.'

She pointed at herself. '*Hello*. This is *me* . . .' then smiled and indicated behind her, 'and this is the barn.'

  'I see.'

'Well I suppose it's going to be roast goose again,' she sighed, turning, 'poached goose, pan-fried goose, stewed goose . . .'

She disappeared from view. He didn't immediately follow her. He'd presumed (incorrectly, as it transpired) that she'd want to have a quick look at the car. And then there was this *smell* – a strangely evocative yet *familiar* smell – which'd wafted out with her –

Beeswax?

His eyes grew unfocussed as he sniffed the air.

  'What are you waiting for?'

'Huh?'

He started.

  She'd popped her head back around the door and was scowling at him, irritably. 'Not caused quite enough *carnage* for one day, eh? Secretly hankering after Round Two are we?'

'I hear you're planning on moving the cafeteria upstairs,' Gaffar could hear Beede saying, 'or out the back, or something . . .'

'Who told you that?'

A woman responded. She sounded nice. And normal. And uncomplicated.

'One of the young lads who shunts the trolleys around.'

'Yes . . . Well we're certainly planning some major *improvements* at the store.'

Gaffar opened his eyes.

'He's back,' Beede said.

Gaffar peered down into his lap. He was still in the cheese aisle, but propped up in a wheelchair. He was happy to discover that his crotch was still dry.

'Can you tell me your name?' the woman asked. She was crouching by his side.

'Who are you?' Gaffar asked.

'I'm Susan Pope . . .' she pointed to her name badge, 'assistant manager at the store.'

Gaffar proffered her his hand. 'Gaffar Celik,' he said. They shook.

'And how old are you, Gaffar?'

'Twenting-four.'

'And where were you born?'

'Eh?'

'Where were you first breath for this life?' Beede interpreted.

'Huh?'

'Born?' the woman repeated.

'*Ah* . . .' Gaffar finally caught on. 'Silopi. Turkey. Is shithole. Yes? **A border-town, full of vagrants and opportunists. Not a million miles away from this** shithole, actually.'

'And where do you live now, Gaffar?'

'Now?'

'Yes.'

'Here.'

Gaffar pointed down the cheese aisle.

'He lives on the cheese aisle,' Beede said, 'apparently.'

'I am love of cheese,' Gaffar confirmed.

Susan Pope nodded, slowly.

'He doesn't really live on the cheese aisle,' Beede explained, 'he shares the upstairs part of one of the villas on Elwick Road, with my son.'

Susan Pope frowned. 'I certainly hope you're not suggesting there's something *wrong* with the cheese aisle,' she said.

'Good God, no,' Beede responded, 'absolutely not. It's a marvellous aisle. In fact I'm struggling to understand how you could possibly improve it.'

'More cheese,' she said, 'bigger cheese.'

'Bigger cheese isn't automatically better cheese,' Beede counselled her, sagely.

'Oh yes it is,' she said.

'Where is this . . . uh . . . ?' Gaffar interrupted them, putting an anxious hand to his neck.

'The scarf? It's here. On the floor. With your jacket. I took them both off to check your vital signs,' Beede said. He reached down and retrieved them.

'Kane's mother knitted him this scarf,' he said, proffering it, tenderly. 'It'd be a shame to lose it.'

'Sure.'

Gaffar took the scarf and began rewinding it back around his neck.

'You should probably cancel the ambulance,' Beede told Susan Pope. 'He seems fine – quite back to his normal self.'

'Really?'

'Well as normal as he ever *gets*,' Beede averred.

'I am good,' Gaffar confirmed. **'I love passing out. When you come to it's like starting afresh. Everything feels clean and new.'**

'He loves passing out,' Beede interpreted, 'he's very accustomed to it. He's a boxer, by trade.'

'*Great* boxer,' Gaffar stressed. 'Champ.'

Susan Pope still didn't seem entirely convinced that he was all right.

'It was just the shock,' Beede said. 'He has this morbid fear of salad . . .'

'A morbid fear of *salad*?' Susan Pope echoed, taking out her phone. 'I have a ten-year-old at home who suffers from the exact-same complaint.'

'I'll wheel him to the canteen, if I may,' Beede said, 'and buy him a cup of sweet tea.'

'Good idea . . .'

Susan Pope stood up. She staggered slightly. 'My poor knees,' she sighed.

'Lovely knees,' Gaffar said, inspecting them.

'Oh dear,' she said, tutting, 'his eyesight's obviously still not quite up to scratch.'

'His eyesight's fine,' Beede insisted.

Her cheeks pinkened.

'I could always get a member of staff to ring through your shopping for you,' she twinkled, 'if that'll help.'

'That'd be great,' Beede said.

Gaffar started to push himself up.

'Sit *down*, Gaffar,' they chorused.

TEN

It wasn't so much a barn as a huge, converted storage space; a labyrinth of mysterious, dimly lit, air-conditioned rooms crammed with fascinating objects (mostly crated, or – in the case of some of the larger pieces – free-standing and fastidiously preserved in reams of brown paper and sheets of opaque plastic).

The rooms were connected by a warren of stark corridors with white walls and highly polished concrete floors, punctuated – at regular intervals – by heavy, metal, aircraft-carrier-style doors.

Kane felt like he'd inadvertently trespassed into the private back rooms of a museum, or a large art gallery, or an exclusive European auction house. Every detail – or lack of detail – oozed class; *refinement*; exuded that sense of effortless pared-downness which was – in Kane's not especially extensive experience – the exclusive prerogative of the extremely well-heeled.

'This place is deceptive,' he said, 'outside it seems ancient – kind of ramshackle – but inside it's fantastic . . .'

'You think so?' she shrugged. 'There was virtually nothing on this site when Peter first arrived, just the foundations of the old cottage. He built it all up pretty much from scratch – take a look . . .'

She pointed to a montage of photographs and architectural plans on a nearby wall. Kane walked over to inspect them. 'You weren't kidding,' he marvelled. 'It was literally just a field with some old rubble in one corner . . .'

'That's the site of the old cottage there . . .' she pointed. 'See? Those were the foundations. It was just a skeleton, a shell . . . If you look over here you can see a *very* rare photograph of how the farm once was . . .'

Kane gazed at a tiny, blurred picture of the original cottage and its surrounding outbuildings.

'Wow. It's pretty much identical.'

'Yup. It was a monumental project. A real challenge. Definitely a labour of love . . .'

'But why bother?' Kane wondered. 'Why not just build something new?'

'Where would've been the challenge in that?' she demanded.

Kane snorted, '*God*. It's no wonder he and Beede have so much in common. They're both men obsessed . . .'

He moved further along the wall to a slightly more recent image of a group of builders applying the last few tiles to the cottage's roof. One was lounging against the chimney, grinning widely, toasting the photographer with a bottle of champagne.

'Is that Peter?' he asked, pointing.

'No,' she smiled, reaching out a gloved hand and gently plucking a stray goose feather from the sleeve of his jacket. 'Let's head off, shall we? I won't put the lights on,' she continued, moving swiftly ahead of him, 'it's so wasteful if we're just passing through, don't you think?'

Kane drew away from the photograph and followed her, directed through the surrounding gloom by the sound of her voice and her jauntily bobbing ponytail.

'They're Russian Arsamas, in case you're interested,' she volunteered, waving the feather at him over her shoulder.

'Pardon?'

He was momentarily distracted by the sudden shudder of his phone. 'The geese. They're an especially ferocious breed, and terribly rare. Their bills are pink – you'll've noticed – not orange, like the descendants of the western greylag . . . '

She pulled open a heavy door, with a grunt. He reached out to help her.

'Fire door,' she puffed, allowing him to take the weight of it, then ducking through and walking on.

'They were raised as fighters,' she continued. 'They had this infamous Goose Pit in St Petersburg where they fought them as late as the turn of the last century. On the up-side they're very hardy – will withstand virtually anything the British climate can throw at them – but on the down: they're bad layers and the meat's abysmal. Gamey. Very tough.'

'So what's the point in keeping them?' Kane asked.

'What's the point?' she echoed, pausing and turning. He paused too, gazing down at her. She was small, exquisitely well-preserved and hard as a ball-bearing.

'What an *absurd* question,' she said, peering up at him, pityingly, still casually twirling the feather in her free hand. He could smell cigar smoke on her skin and in her hair.

He liked her. There was something . . .

What was it?
Mordant?
Ballsy?
Wicked?

'We used to worship geese,' she darted on. 'The *English*, I mean. Apparently when Caesar visited the island in 55 BC the primitive Celts kept huge flocks of them which were held sacred and never eaten. Geese've had this long and incredibly rich relationship with man. After the second ice age – when we evolved from nomadic hunters into farmers and cultivators – the goose was absolutely pivotal to the success of that transition; a kind of *civilising* force . . .'

They arrived at the base of a wide, oak staircase. Kane's phone shuddered, once again, inside his pocket.

'I had this *appallingly* handsome Russian lover in the sixties,' she confessed, taking the first step, 'a stone mason. Astonishingly talented but a revolting drunk. The Arsamas were his, originally – and a perfect symbol of the kind of relationship we had . . .'

She chuckled. '*You* know; fierce. Uncompromising. Passionate . . .'

She glanced over her shoulder at him, raising a single, sardonic, charcoal brow.

'The birds living here today are their descendants,' she continued, her breath quickening slightly with the exertion of the climb. 'I mean we always kept geese when I was a child – just your classic English whites and greys . . . My mother was raised in Essex and one of her favourite stories was of how she used to watch huge flocks of them being driven down from Norfolk to Smithfield Market. Over 8,000 birds at any one time. A journey of over 80 miles. She said they would dip the birds' feet in tar to help preserve them.'

Kane blinked.

'Pardon?'

'Tar,' she repeated, 'they dipped their feet in it.'

As she spoke she led Kane into a beautiful, high-ceilinged studio, awash with natural light.

He winced – struggling, at first, to adjust to the sudden brightness –

376

then gazed around him, awed. It was a massive room; like a glass-ceilinged chapel, a smart Docklands penthouse, and an Old Curiosity Shop, all rolled into one.

'What's that smell?' he asked.

'Wax and honey. I'm re-canvassing a painting.'

She pointed to a large, aluminium table in the corner of the room. 'It's a hot bench,' she explained.

Kane walked over and gazed down at it. There was a lead running from the table to a plug in the wall.

'And this table heats up?'

He tentatively touched it. It felt cool.

'The bench? Yes.'

His phone began shuddering. Peta tucked the feather into a large vase full of feathers which was standing on an old dresser nearby, then joined him at the aluminium bench, grabbed hold of a small pair of tweezers and carefully eased off a tiny fragment of the ancient canvas.

'There,' she said, holding it aloft.

He squinted through his fringe at it. 'Is that the actual painting, then?'

'The canvas *behind* the painting. Yes.'

'Come again?'

'These tiny pieces of fabric are the dead canvas. The canvas was disintegrating behind the paint – rotting away – and when that happens the paint begins to peel and fall. The work is lost. So we preserve the paint by suspending it in a mixture of warm honey and beeswax, then gradually pick off all the dead threads. It's an incredibly laborious, time-consuming process.'

Kane gazed down at the painting, quite fascinated.

'Is this what you do for a living?'

'As a living? God no. It's just a tiny part of what I do.'

He glanced around him, frowning. 'And does Peter work here too?'

'Peter?'

She seemed momentarily thrown off-kilter by this question. 'But of course. That goes without saying. Everything here belongs to Peter. It's Peter's bench, Peter's barn . . .'

'Peter must be loaded.'

'*Stinking*.' She shrugged. 'Although it's never been about the money with him. It's always been about the work. He insists that his prices are astronomical only because we live in a culture where an object's price and its inherent *value* are considered virtually one and the same thing.'

As she was speaking Kane's roving eye alighted on a large, wooden structure over to his left.
'Stocks,' he exclaimed, walking across to them. He reached out a hand to caress the ancient wood. It felt wonderful to the touch: rough, thicky-grained, almost primitive.
'It's a pillory,' she corrected him. 'Stocks are the ground-level version which they fastened around the ankles. The pillory constrains the arms and the head.'
'Is it still functional?'
'Absolutely.'
She strolled over to the pillory, reached up and opened one side of it.
'Try it,' she said, 'these holes are for your wrists, and this . . .'
'I know,' he said, 'it's for the neck.'
He carefully slotted himself in. She gently closed the top half around him.
'It's a tight fit,' he said, feeling a strain in his shoulders and a slight constriction in his throat. He started as he heard some kind of bolt being shot.
'People were considerably smaller then, remember,' she said, stepping back to appraise him. He tried to peer up at her through his fringe, but the wood fell too closely around his flesh for any kind of ease of movement.
She returned to the hot bench, bent over it again, and was soon deeply engrossed.
'Is it very old?' he asked, rocking his body back and forth. The structure was heavy. It barely shifted. His phone, meanwhile, shuddered silently in his pocket.
'Each individual element of the whole is totally legitimate,' she answered.
'How d'you mean?' he frowned. 'Is it a replica?'
'No. It's an original. Peter made it. He made two. This was the first, but he wasn't entirely happy with it.'
'Why'd he make it?' he asked.
'He made it for a museum of medieval life in Durham.'
'And what's wrong with it?'

'You tell me.'

'Pardon?'

He was concentrating on his phone. The vibration (she was right, he thought. I *am* addicted to it).

'You tell me,' she repeated.

'What's wrong? *Uh* . . . I wouldn't have a clue.'

He tried to inspect the structure, but it hurt to twist his head around.

'Your father couldn't guess either,' she observed, 'when I locked him in there.'

'Beede?'

Kane's competitive instincts were immediately activated. He struggled to examine the pillory again.

'Is it the metalwork?'

He didn't know why he thought so. He just did.

'Good theory.'

'The joinery. There's something . . .'

But what?

'. . . slightly *wrong*.'

'You're close . . .' She sounded impressed. 'They didn't do much mining in the late medieval period. Most of their metalwork was recycled – they'd simply smelt it down and re-use it. So there was a very specific kind of *finish* . . .'

'Hang on a second,' he interrupted her (having finally digested the full implications of what she'd just said). 'You don't mean to tell me you put *Beede* in the pillory?'

'But of course I did,' she smiled.

Kane blew a strand of hair from his eye. 'Seriously?'

'Ask him yourself if you don't believe me.'

She was still bending over the hot bench, working, methodically.

Kane pondered the idea of Beede in the pillory a while. He was both amused and perplexed by this unlikely concept: I mean *Beede* – the *indomitable* Beede – disempowered; held at bay; *constrained*?

'*Fuck* . . .' he swore (he couldn't help himself – the thought of it was simply so . . . so tantalising. So naughty. So *delicious*). 'Didn't he go nuts?'

'Beede?' She glanced up. 'Go nuts? Don't be ridiculous. He trained in the military. He was fine about it.'

'How'd you get him in here?'

'Pardon?'

'Did you use force?'

'*Force?*' she seemed astonished by this question. 'Against your father?'

'How else?'

'He climbed in himself. Voluntarily. The same way you just did.'

Pause

Kane cleared his throat. 'Was he in here long?'

'No. At least not by *ancient* standards . . .' she shrugged, 'four hours
. . . Maybe five.'

'Five *hours*?'

Kane was horrified.

'I didn't trust him,' she explained, her voice tinged with regret, 'not
at first. I'm naturally suspicious – in my line of work I have to be. And
he never actually *asked* to be released. He was too proud. And I never
actually *said* – I mean not in so many words – that I wouldn't release
him. I just left him in there, as a kind of experiment, really, to see
how things might pan out . . . '

'Your line of work . . . ?' Kane scowled, confused.

'And much to his credit,' she continued, 'he bore it all very bravely,
without complaint, which I thought at the time was wholly admirable.'

'Your line of work . . . ?' Kane repeated. Then suddenly everything
just fell into place. 'Good *God*,' he grinned, 'you're a *forger* . . .'

'In all honesty,' she confided, straightening her spine (with a slight
wince), 'that's not a word I've ever particularly *warmed* to.'

'Really?'

'No.'

She removed the cigar from behind her ear and rolled it, dreamily,
between her fingers. 'It just seems so . . . I don't know . . . so *coarse*;
so *limited* in its application, so *naive*, somehow . . .'

'And what about Peter?'

'Pardon?'

'Does he feel the same way you do?'

'Peter?'

She considered this question for a second and then nodded, emphatically. '*Exactly* the same, I'd say.'

'Ah . . .'

Kane beamed at her. She smiled straight back at him. They were flirting with each other.

'. . . It's all finally coming together,' he said.

'Is it really?'

She was searching the pockets of her overalls for a lighter.

'Yes it is. Would you like to hear my little theory?'

'Your little theory? Sure . . .' She found her lighter. 'Although . . .' she held it, poised in her hand, thoughtfully '. . . perhaps it'd be more fun if we waited for Peter? I'm sure he'd be just fascinated in what you have to say . . .'

'That's a fine idea in principle,' Kane conceded, 'but it *could* be rather a long wait . . .'

She shrugged.

'Or no wait at all,' he countered.

She appraised him, steadily.

'Just call it a gut instinct,' he smiled.

She appraised his gut, at her leisure. 'It's a charming gut,' she said finally, 'if just a fraction *soft*.'

'An infallible gut,' Kane insisted, tightening it up.

'So what's this infallible gut of yours telling you?'

'It's telling me,' he told her, 'that there *is* no Peter.'

She gazed at him, blankly.

'Peter's just another forgery.'

'*Urgh* . . .' she shuddered. 'That *awful* word again.'

'Sorry,' he apologised.

She popped the cigar between her lips, struck her lighter, leaned into the flame and puffed.

'In actual fact,' he continued, 'the *spelling's* a bit of a giveaway . . . Petaborough Reproductions. Peta, I believe, is the feminine form of the name . . .'

'I've often found that my most successful lies,' she finally stopped puffing, removed the cigar from her mouth and inspected the burning tip, '*you* know . . . those outrageous untruths, those *real* hum-dingers . . . generally benefit from the addition of the odd loose screw. If all the facts add up, if everything feels too neat and pat, if all the elements fall too readily into place, then you automatically arouse suspicion, because life simply isn't *like* that.'

Kane was frowning.

'Put it this way,' she continued, 'if the truth was a woman she'd be a whore. She'd be an extremely supple, highly sinuous, ridiculously wanton *slut*.'

'Let me get this straight . . .' Kane suddenly found himself panting slightly as he spoke (the former strain in his back was now a burning ache, his arms were cramping, his neck felt like a blade of grass endeavouring to support a bowling ball) '. . . Peta *Borough*? Does that make Borough your maiden name?'

She nodded, inhaling on the cigar, holding the smoke in her lungs, then exhaling, with a small cough.

'And you don't mind at all?' he wondered.

'*Mind?* Mind what?'

'Being named after one of Britain's most pedestrian towns.'

'Peterborough's a city,' she corrected him, pedantically.

'Never cared enough to find out,' he admitted.

'Well shame on you. It's a wonderful place. Its transport links are incomparable.'

'But why, I wonder,' he demanded, heading off on a complete tangent, 'did J.P. – your own *brother* – misspell your name on the business card Beede had?'

'And it has a fascinating history . . .' she maintained.

'Oh *fuck*,' he snorted, 'J.P. *isn't* your brother . . .'

She gazed up at the glass ceiling, piously. 'And then there's the cathedral,' she sighed. 'If ever you get the opportunity . . .'

'*Is* J.P. dead? Do you even *have* a brother?'

She just smirked. 'A lovely market. Several really wonderful restaurants . . .'

Kane was silent for a while. His phone vibrated. He tried to ignore it. A million tiny beads of sweat were forming on his forehead. She inspected the cigar again, fondly. 'Don't you think it *sweet*, though,' she enquired, 'the two of you – father and son, purportedly so very *different* – being immediately attracted to the exact-same object?'

'I was attracted to the table first,' he insisted.

'The hot bench,' she corrected him.

He paused, speculatively. 'Actually, no. That's not entirely true. I was attracted to *you* first.'

She snorted, jovially.

'You don't believe me?'

He peered up at her again, with an intense amount of effort.

'I think *you* believe you,' she smiled, 'and that's what really counts.'

'You think I'm full of shit?'

'Full to capacity.'

'And how about Beede?'

His head sank down again.

'Beede? Good *God*, no. The most straightforward man I ever met.'

'Oh come *on* . . .' he scoffed.

'His *life*, on the other hand,' she freely conceded, 'is extremely complicated.'

'Do you know Beede at *all*?' he wondered.

'I know him well enough.'

'Do you *like* him?'

'Like him? *Like* Beede?' she exclaimed. 'I'm utterly besotted.'

Kane's head jerked up –

Ow

He winced.

'You seem shocked,' she said.

'Not shocked, no . . .'

'Then what?'

'Perhaps just a touch disappointed,' he conceded.

'Why?' she demanded.

'Because you're gorgeous.'

'And?'

'And he's such a fool.'

'But such a *genuine* fool, don't you think?'

Silence

'So does Beede know?'

'Know what?'

'How you feel.'

She deliberated over this question for a second. 'Probably.'

'But you haven't actually told him?'

She glanced up, frowning. 'Why should I?'

'Why *shouldn't* you?'

'Because there wouldn't be any point. My feelings aren't reciprocated.'

'How can you be sure? Beede can be pretty hard to read . . .'

'Beede's easy to read.'

Kane was quiet for a while.

'I *was* attracted to you,' he murmured, almost sullen, now.

'So what do *you* do?' she cheerfully ignored him.

'For a living? Didn't Beede already fill you in?'

'Why would he?' she snorted. 'Beede never tells me anything . . .' She looked around for an ashtray but couldn't find one, so she walked over to Kane, pulled open his jacket pocket and tapped her ash into it. 'Not so much as a peep. In fact he was so evasive at first, so *secretive*, that I was actually obliged to go to ridiculous lengths to satisfy my curiosity.'

'But I thought you just said . . .'

Kane frowned, confused.

'I said that Beede was straightforward, not that he was willing to wear his heart on his sleeve.'

'So what did you do?' Kane wondered.

'How d'you mean?'

'To satisfy your curiosity?'

'I hired a detective.'

'You did *what*?'

Kane's head jerked up again.

'I hired a private detective. But he wasn't terribly good. And everything got ridiculously complicated. But – please God – let's not get dragged into all of *that* . . .'

She idly pushed his hair aside and stared into his face with her green eyes.

'So what did you find out?' he asked, struggling to meet her gaze.

She dropped his fringe, with a sigh, and returned to the hot bench. 'Nothing, really. Only as much as I've told you. That he was married, then divorced. That his ex-wife was ill. That he had a son who made his living from selling drugs . . .'

'I manage pain,' Kane interrupted her, haughtily, 'if you must know.'

She lounged against the bench, grinning. 'You consider it a *calling*?'

'Yes. I eliminate pain. I bring people relief when they can't find it elsewhere.'

Peta stopped smiling. 'Is this because of what happened to your mother?'

'No,' he snapped, 'it's because of what happened to me. *My* experience.'

'I see.'

'And my experience is that there's simply no need for it.'

'No need for what? *Pain?* You really believe that?'

'Of course. Why celebrate pain when you can celebrate pleasure?'

'Because of J.C., I suppose,' she answered, boredly.

'Who?'

'Jesus Christ. The crucifixion. We strive to be better people because we believe – or we're taught to believe, at least – that Christ suffered to deliver us from sin. And when *we* suffer – like Christ – we are brought closer to God, or if not God, then beauty. Without pain – the theory goes – we lose the ability to experience true ecstasy . . .'

'Sin? *Suffering?'*

Kane was having none of it.

'Too old-fashioned for you, eh?'

Kane gave this question some consideration. 'I mean it's not that I don't *like* antiques . . .'

'You like *me,*' she smiled, 'and I'm antique.'

'Exactly.'

'So what's *your* moral vocabulary consist of, then?' she wondered. 'I mean what are its parameters?'

'Is that a good cigar?' He ignored her question. He couldn't answer her question. And it seemed pointless, anyway.

'Why?'

'It smells good,' he grunted.

'It's very *pleasurable*, certainly,' she teased him. 'Would you like a puff?'

'I'd love one.'

Peta pulled off a glove and strolled over to him again. Kane tried to lift his head at her approach, but he could not.

'Poor boy,' she said, carefully sweeping his fringe from his eyes, then tightening her fingers around it and yanking his head up by his hair.

He grimaced. His face was glowing. His vision was bleary. He blinked, repeatedly. She made as if to proffer him the cigar, but kept it too far away from his lips for actual contact.

'Know about cigars, do we?' she teased him as his lips kissed thin air.

'A little,' he demurred, humiliated.

And then, before he'd even finished speaking, she suddenly pushed the cigar into his mouth. It hit his teeth. He tightened them around it. He bit into it. He took a deep puff. It tasted wonderful.

'Is that good?' she whispered softly, touching her nose to his ear.
'Fantastic,' he said, still holding on to it, still inhaling, his head spin-
ning (five hours? How the hell'd he *do* it?).
'Really?'

A droplet of sweat trickled down from his hairline. She stopped it
with her finger.
'Yes. *Really*,' he croaked. 'Is it Cuban?'
He was mortified to discover himself developing an erection.

'Nope,' she dried her finger, off-handedly, on the front of his t-
shirt, then snatched the cigar back and released his hair. His head
dropped, sharply. 'It's from the local *Spar*, you ignorant *goon*,' she
snorted, shoving it back into her mouth and turning away from him,
contemptuously, '£1.99, for a pack of four.'

She stalked – quietly, like a cat – across the oak floor and back
over to the hot bench where she grabbed a hold of her glove. She
gazed at him, ruminatively, as she pulled it back on. 'You do know
you're not locked in there?' she said.

Kane didn't respond. He remained exactly as he was.
'You're not locked in there,' she repeated. 'You do *know* that?'
Still nothing. No reaction.

She shrugged, removed the cigar from her mouth, and wandered
off in search of an ashtray. She found a blue and white striped saucer
propped up on the draining-board in the kitchen area. She extin-
guished the cigar on it and then tipped the stub into the rubbish bin.

'I only smoke the damn things,' she confided, 'to spur myself into
giving up.'
She sighed. 'Although it's disturbing how the mind – the *taste* – will
so readily adapt itself, if needs must, from something extremely good
to something so much worse . . .'

As she spoke Kane lifted his arms, tentatively. He felt the top half
of the pillory shift. He raised them again, this time more determinedly.
The pillory slowly creaked open, like a nutcracker.
And then, just as he thought he might've *actually* got away with it . . .
'Impressive hard-on, coincidentally,' she muttered.

ELEVEN

Gaffar took five sugars with his tea.

'Will you be taking any *tea* with your sugar?' Beede asked, looking on, appalled, as he tipped the sachets in, one after the other.

'I think this . . . uh . . . this pretty *manager* is hot for you,' Gaffar crooned, delightedly.

'Pardon?'

'Like father like son, eh?'

'How d'you mean?'

Beede seemed affronted.

'You like to play the angry, old bull, but there's definitely a touch of the randy, old goat in there somewhere . . .'

'So we definitely need to get to the bottom of this,' Beede interrupted him, carefully stirring his mug of oxtail soup.

'Huh?'

'This problem you seem to have with salad.'

'*Urgh* . . .' Gaffar waved his hand, dismissively.

'How long's it been going on?'

Gaffar took a small sip of his tea, then smiled, vacuously.

'And don't think for one moment that I'm falling for that ludicrous "simple Turk" act,' Beede snapped.

'Is no big deal,' Gaffar waved his hand again.

'You don't have any idea as to what's at the root of it?'

Gaffar shook his head.

'No clues at all?'

He shrugged.

'Well when did it all *start*? Do you remember?'

Gaffar frowned. 'Always,' he said, 'since boy. But not so . . .'

He grimaced.

'Not so severe? Not so bad? It's grown worse? Is that it?'

Gaffar nodded. **'Before it was simply . . . uh . . . a slight aversion . . .'**

'Before what?'

A woman with a pram hurried past them and inadvertently swept

Gaffar's collection of sugar wrappers on to the floor. He reached down to retrieve them.

'So what did your parents make of it?' Beede asked, once the Kurd had straightened back up again.

Gaffar stared at him, blankly.

'Your mother? Your father?'

As he uttered the word 'father', Beede observed Gaffar flinching slightly.

'Your father?' he persisted. **'Does he get leaf afraid sometimes same like what you do?'**

'Susa Pope . . .' Gaffar mused, gazing distractedly over Beede's shoulder. 'You get this lady number?'

'Pardon?'

'For phone?'

He mimed 'phone'.

'Susan *Pope*?'

'Sexy lady manager.'

Gaffar made a suggestive clicking sound with his tongue.

'Don't you *like* talking about your father, Gaffar?'

Beede went straight for the jugular.

Gaffar shrugged. 'My father he is long time . . . uh . . .' he pondered over the right word '. . . dead.'

'Oh. *Right*. I see. And your mother?'

'Tough as a pair of old boots,' he smiled fondly, **'God preserve her.'**

'So what age were you when he died?'

Gaffar shifted in his chair and peered under the table again, as if one of the wrappers might've secretly eluded him.

'Were you very young?'

'Sure. Young. He was hero,' Gaffar informed him haughtily. **'He died in the service of his country.'**

'Ah, *now* I get you . . .' Beede finally caught on. 'He was a soldier with the PKK?'

Gaffar looked horrified. **'A terrorist? Never! He was a proud Turkish citizen. He died on guard service in Silopi. He worked for the local Kurdish lord. He stepped on a landmine. I was three years old. My mother was pregnant with my brother. When I saw the body there were no legs left, no groin. They'd stuffed a spare pair of trousers with straw to protect our feelings. I saw it poking out at the ankles and at the waist . . .'** he shrugged. **'That's all I really remember.'**

'This was in Silopi?' Beede asked. 'Is that where your family hail from, originally?'

'No. I was *bor* Silopi. My mother family from Marlin. My father . . .' He shrugged, uneasily.

'Where?'

'Sinjar.'

'Sinjar? That sounds familiar . . . *Sinjar* . . .'

Beede considered it for a moment. 'Is Sinjar actually *in* Turkey?'

'Sure . . .' Gaffar nodded, unconvincingly.

Beede frowned. Gaffar took off his jacket. He hung it over the back of his chair. He seemed ill at ease.

'Nice jacket,' Beede said.

'New *leather*,' Gaffar grinned, half-turning and stroking the hide, patently relieved at the change of subject.

'Did Kane buy it for you?'

'Kane? No. Is Mrs Broad.'

'Pardon?'

'Kelly mother. Dina. Mrs Dina Broad.'

Beede looked confused. 'Dina? Dina *Broad*? *She* bought you a jacket?'

'Sure.'

Gaffar seemed completely unfazed by the idea.

'Dina Broad? But why on earth would she do that?'

'We go for shop. We two. She buy.'

He shrugged.

'She took you out *shopping*? Dina *Broad*?'

'Sure. Whas problem? We go. Taxi. Shop-shop. Is my idea. Shop for Dina. Shop for Gaffar.'

'And this is in exchange for . . . ?'

'Pard me?'

'For drugs, perchance?'

'*Drugs?!*'

Gaffar leaned back in his chair, surprised. 'For what is this?' he asked, almost indignant. 'For what is all this drugs-drugs? **You're a man obsessed!** You . . . Kelly Broad . . . **You're worse than each other!**'

'Then what else?' Beede demanded.

Gaffar scowled. 'What *else*? I walk dog. I do hoover. Massage. Even just little-bit chit-chat. Is good. Is enough.'

'You mean you're working as a kind of . . .' Beede frowned, 'gigolo cum . . .' he paused '. . . cum au pair?'

'I work for Kane,' Gaffar explained irritably. 'This Kane client. He want for client being *happy*. He send Gaffar. Gaffar is *bring* happy . . .'

Pause

'. . . Without all this *drugs* you so crazy about.'

'Did you hang a bell on the cat?' Beede suddenly asked.

'Pard?'

'The cat. The Siamese. Did you hang a bell on him?'

'Bell?'

'Ding! Ding! Bell. On a collar. Around his neck.'

'*Bell?*'

'Yes.'

Beede felt his shoulder tensing up again. He put a hand to it.

'No. No bell.'

'Oh.'

'What for I hang "bel"?' Gaffar scoffed.

'I have no idea.'

'Did *you* hang bell?'

'Of course not. If *I'd* hung bell . . . *the* bell – then I wouldn't be asking *you* about it, would I?'

'Okay.'

Gaffar scratched his head and then looked away, as if embarrassed on Beede's behalf –

Bell?!

Beede took a sip of his soup. A member of staff approached them clutching a carrier. 'I think this is everything,' she said. 'We took the precaution of wrapping up the greens in a double bag . . .'

'Great. That was very kind. Thank you.'

Beede took the carrier from her. She showed him the till receipt.

'Right. Of *course*,' he muttered. 'Do you have any cash, Gaffar?'

Beede peered over at the Kurd. Gaffar was engrossed in checking the texts on his new mobile phone.

'*Gaffar?*'

Gaffar glanced up. 'Cash? Sure.'

He delved into the pocket of his new, leather jacket, withdrew an indecently fat wad of mulberry-coloured notes, licked his thumb and peeled one off.

'Lid . . . Rug . . . Drugs . . . *Bell* . . .' he murmured, shaking his head as he passed it over. **'You need to get out more, old fella.'**

'So who's it by?'
As soon as he'd finished eating he'd been drawn back to the painting.
'That's the million dollar question. Medieval artists rarely – if ever – put a signature to their work. It's meant to be from the Cologne School . . .'

She was tidying away the remains of a basic lunch they'd just shared (water biscuits, blue Brie, cherry tomatoes and a jar of huge, home-made pickled onions, bobbing around like apples in a rich and luxuriant, dark malt vinegar).

'German?'
'Yes. Although obviously Germany – as we know it now – didn't actually exist back then . . .'
'Obviously,' Kane parroted.

'I'm hoping it's a Stephan Lochner,' she continued. 'He was a cut above most of his contemporaries – very heavily influenced by the Flemish painters of the time . . .'
'Which time?'
'1430, 1440. He died of the plague on Christmas Day, 1451.'
She went over to her desk and opened up a large scrapbook.

'Lochner is best known for his *Adoration of the Magi* which takes pride of place in the cathedral in Cologne . . .'
She turned the pages of the book until she reached a fine, colour reproduction of the painting in question, surrounded by a plethora of comments and observations written in a dark, blue ink.
'Come and look.'

Kane strolled over. It was a beautiful painting; a triptych. In the middle panel three wise men made offerings to the baby Christ.

'This is Saint Gereon,' she pointed to one of the side panels, 'and this is Saint Ursula . . .' she pointed to the other. 'They've augmented The Adoration with them because the two saints have a special relevance to Cologne. They were both martyred there.'

'Do you like it?' Kane wondered, detecting an element of fastidiousness in her tone.

'But of course,' she exclaimed, 'it's magnificent, don't you think? Finely observed, meticulously finished. A masterpiece of its time – of any time – although not, I'll admit, what you might call the world's most "emotionally involving" work of art.'

Kane didn't see fit to comment.

She turned the page over.

'What's that?'

He pointed.

'That's a reproduction of *The Paradise Garden* by the Master of Frankfurt. He's another contender, another candidate on my shortlist. He would've been one of Lochner's contemporaries . . .'

Kane drew in closer. It was an exquisite little piece. A fairytale-style walled garden containing eight quaint figures. The Madonna (although she looked more like a princess than a religious figure) sat in the centre of the composition reading a book. Around her a group of servants and a child (he presumed the baby Christ) entertained themselves with a series of innocent (if somewhat mundane-seeming) pastimes.

'Sweet, isn't it?' she said.

He shrugged.

'Although these works are never as straightforward as they look. In medieval art the messages are all *encoded* . . .'

He glanced up, suddenly intrigued. 'How d'you mean?'

'Well each figure, each colour, each bird and plant resonates at a symbolic level as well as at a physical one. An important symptom of what I like to call the "Medieval Disease" was that everything generally represented something else. People weren't encouraged to conceptualise, to question, to range freely. They were boxed in by Christian doctrine. They couldn't think in abstract forms. Everything was self-referential. It was an intensely restrictive system of thought . . .'

'Give me an example,' Kane demanded.

'The whole notion of "a garden", for starters. Medieval gardens would generally be divided into an inner and an outer area. This is an inner garden. You can see the walls which surround it. An inner garden is a highly formalised space, full of rules and elaborate structures. The outer garden represents "the untamed": the wild, the pagan, the uncontrolled, the fertile . . . The inner garden is based around the mead . . .'

'The mead? Isn't that a kind of drink?'

'No. Same word, different meaning. The mead you're thinking of is a beverage of fermented honey and water. This kind of mead is a lawn. In medieval times the lawn was planted with wildflowers because scent was incredibly important to them – here we see the violet, which is quite prominent. The violet represents humility – more specifically the humility of the virgin. She's referred to again in the roses in the borders. The red rose . . .'

She pointed to the rose. Kane nodded.

'That represents divine love. Initially Venus, and then, with the advent of Christianity, Mary. The purple or blue of the iris is traditionally a royal colour . . .'

'Royal Blue . . .' Kane interrupted.

'Exactly. And the Royal Blue represents the Holy Virgin as the Queen of Heaven. The columbine has petals which are shaped – to the medieval mind, at least – like a dove . . .' She sketched the approximate shape, in the air, with her hands. 'For that reason the columbine was taken to symbolise the Holy Ghost. Carnations – which were relative latecomers to Europe – represent the *in*carnation . . .'

'But what's the actual point in all of this?' Kane wondered, apparently nonplussed.

'The point? The point is to instil everyday objects with a devotional meaning. To underpin the commonplace with a profound sense of the holy. If God created the earth then the earth and everything in it must function simply as an extended homily to Him and His Work.'

'How *turgid*,' Kane drawled.

'No more turgid, I suppose,' she responded (half-smiling at his ready use of this unexpected word), 'than some of the apparently complex yet equally meaningless ramifications of modernity.'

He frowned at her. 'Such as?'

'*Uh* . . .' she gave this question a moment's consideration. 'Well how about your trainers, for starters?'

'My trainers?' Kane looked down at his feet, bemused. 'What's so complex about my trainers? They're just a basic pair of functional shoes . . .'

'Don't be ridiculous,' she scoffed. 'When you chose that particular make, that particular design, it was to send out a message. *Many* messages, in fact. But like the flowers in the border here that message is heavily encoded. Only a very specific kind of person will understand the exact nature of the message you're relaying. To me – for example – they're just a rather ungainly pair of white, rubber excrescences, but to someone who speaks the sophisticated dialect of Nike they represent a million different aspirational preferences. These artists . . .' she patted the scrapbook, fondly, 'speak the language of devotion. You speak the language of Capitalism. They're both equally meaningful on the one level, and both equally meaning*less* on another.'

'Oh come *on*,' Kane debunked her, 'I chose these shoes principally because they're comfy . . .'

'But you've been limping since you got here.'

'Have I?'

Kane stared down at his feet, mystified, then looked up again, with a frown. 'If you put your mind to it,' he muttered, 'it's possible to transform *any* basic transaction into a deep and meaningful psychodrama . . .'

She smiled.

'I mean for all you *really* know,' Kane continued (secretly pleased – and encouraged – by her response), 'the whole scenario might actually be *less* complicated than you think. Your artist might simply've *liked* red roses. Or've been especially good at painting them. I might've bought these shoes because I have unnaturally large feet and they were the only ones in the store that'd fit . . .'

'Not store,' she interrupted him, 'shop.'

He gazed at her, surprised.

'And you *don't*,' she said. 'You have perfectly normal-sized feet. And those shoes plainly *aren't* comfy. So why did you buy them, exactly?'

'If I wasn't wearing trainers, but brogues,' he evaded her, 'you'd probably decide I was sending out a message of *another* kind . . .'

'And you would be,' she maintained, calmly.

'What? A message that I *don't* like trainers, perhaps?'

'Exactly.'

'But d'you honestly think I'd be any less of a capitalist dupe for all of that? If I wore Doc Martens, for example, would I necessarily be more "free-thinking" or less constrained by social conditioning? Isn't that all just a part of the same bullshit conspiracy?'

'Doc Martens are manufactured in the UK,' she countered. 'They don't depend on the exploitation of third world labour . . .'

'It's entirely possible,' he speculated, 'that there may be serious Human Rights issues in the country – or countries – where they source their rubber . . .'

'Wouldn't life be so much *simpler*,' she deadpanned, 'if you could just manufacture your own shoes from scratch?'

Kane's phone suddenly began to vibrate. He pulled it from his pocket and inspected it, scowling.

'Although if you made your own shoes you'd be a shoe-maker,' she reasoned (half to herself), 'and in medieval times people involved in trades connected to the feet were generally ostracised.'

'Why?' He glanced up.

'Because people's beliefs were incredibly literal. They thought the devil had cloven hooves and that his followers did too. People who chose to work in trades relating to the feet were often suspected of an involvement with the occult.'

Kane's mind turned briefly to Elen: her neat hands, her modest dress, her birthmark.

'That's insane,' he said, impatiently stuffing his phone away again.

'I know. Life *was* insane,' she concurred. 'It was brutal, cruel, savage, and yet, by the same token . . .' she pointed to the image of the Madonna, 'breathtakingly beautiful.' She paused, and then quoted, ' "So violent and motley was life that it bore the mixed smell of blood and roses." '

He scowled at her.

'Johan Huizinga. *The Waning of the Middle Ages*. I first came across it in my late teens and it completely redefined my take on things. Huizinga's book celebrates a culture in decline – the *end* of a historical period – which was actually quite a radical undertaking at the time . . .'

'Which time?' Kane asked.

'The 1920s.'

'The end of the Great War . . .'

She nodded. 'Too often – in my experience, at least – history concentrates on the start of things, but why should a period's decline be any less significant?'

Kane shrugged.

'Huizinga outlines in the book,' she continued, 'why the Renaissance had to happen. How it set people free. How it liberated the mind by replacing the visual . . .' she pointed to the picture of the Madonna '. . . this complex medieval conglomeration of minute, self-referential *detail* – with the conceptual – with actual thought, unmanacled. It allowed people to think outside all of those stultifying ideological restrictions – those empty *forms* which were – to a large extent – deeply bound up in matters of social etiquette and faith. Central to Huizinga's argument is the idea that unity and truth were somehow completely lost – almost suffocated – inside this meaningless "aggregation of details".'

She paused. 'Not a million miles away – in many respects – from how we live life today.'

'You think modern life is *medieval*?'

Kane was patently going to take some convincing.

'Absolutely.'

'Give me one example,' Kane challenged her.

'Okay . . .' she gladly took up his gauntlet, 'if you ask any expert in the field what the single most notable social characteristic of medieval life was they'd probably say the bells. It might sound strange now, but bells pretty much defined the age. They tolled for every occasion – the start of curfew, the end of curfew, the arrival of a dignitary, the prospect of danger. Quiet was an anomaly. Life was all clamour. And now, after several hundred years of relative social calm and tranquillity, we've developed the mobile phone which also chimes – and must be *allowed* to chime – at every avaliable opportunity. But instead of bringing social unity, instead of connecting us more intimately to our social peers and neighbours, it actively divides us, it isolates us, it encourages an atmosphere of merciless self-involvement parading in the guise of spurious conviviality . . .'

'Fine,' Kane smiled, 'so you don't like the phone . . .'

She shifted her weight, leaned her hip against the desk, then calmly continued, 'In medieval life the higher echelons of society celebrated levels of cupidity – of excess; their huge *feasts*, their crazy *processions*, their ornate *costumes* – that were, by any historical standard, almost obscene. Here, today, deep inside the belly of the decadent West, we cheerfully do the same. We define our power and our status – just as they did – through meaningless and gratuitous acts of consumption. The phrase all you kids like to use, I believe, is *bling*.'

Kane smirked. He opened his mouth to say something . . .

'And how about their obsession with Courtly Love?' she demanded, jumping in first. 'The tournaments, the jousts, the chivalrous knights and all those bizarre and convoluted rituals of etiquette – those faux-historical games of *form*, which weren't actually historical at all; the cult of King Arthur, for example? All neatly echoed in our present-day passion for, say, *Star Wars*, or *The Matrix* . . . *The Lord of the Rings*. Harry bloody Potter. All invented mythologies. We inhabit these worlds as if they are real. We respond to them intellectually although they aren't *remotely* intelligent. We encourage our children to play computer games which seek to simulate life, to mirror it, because we're too afraid to let them step outside their own front doors. We allow them to fight violent, artificial wars on screen while we care-fully remove ourselves – and them – physically, from the consequences of actual conflict, with our long-range warheads and our missiles . . .'

'But how,' Kane quickly leapt in, 'can we be more violent *and* less, all at the same time . . . ?'

'It's the perfect medieval mind-set,' she exclaimed, 'don't you see? To experience something so intensely but as a strange kind of *denial*. I mean it's tragic,' she persisted, 'almost laughable, that our greatest invention – the computer – a device intended to set us free to live lives *unconstrained* by mindless detail – has actually ended up binding us more thoroughly to life's minutiae by filling the world with reams of useless – often unreliable – information; with this endless, this empty, this almost unstoppable *babble* . . .'

'Perhaps you underestimate normal people,' Kane said, quite appalled by her diatribe, 'both back then *and* now. Perhaps the largest percentage of us just slip under the radar, live life – quite happily – in that outer garden, that pagan garden, but history simply doesn't see fit to acknowledge our quiet and uncomplicated role in it.'

As he spoke she idly turned the pages of her scrapbook. 'Beede has this fascinating theory on language . . .' she said.

'Beede?'

'Yes.'

'What kind of theory?'

'It's complicated, but he thinks that the Renaissance took place – in Britain, at least – because of the evolution of English – that our language grew and developed towards the end of the Middle Ages and functioned as a necessary radicaliser, as a harbinger of the new. Because language won't be restricted. Because language is uncontainable. Like a fast-running river. It bubbles up and splashes and spills. English wasn't the obfuscating Latin of the Bible or the exclusive, courtliness of French. It had this unconstrained, grass-roots honesty and power. In effect, he thinks that our native language didn't just *describe* change, it actively *stimulated* it.'

Kane was staring down at the painting on the page she'd just turned to.

'Is that a Lochner?'

'Yes.'

'*Wow* . . .'

He drew closer to the image, both fascinated and revolted.

'It's *The Martyrdom of Saint Bartholomew*. Vile, isn't it?'

Kane nodded.

'What you need to remember,' she counselled, 'is that Lochner and his contemporaries lived lives of great extremity, of violent contrast. Huizinga says how the outlines of all things were much more clearly marked back then, and that's represented here, visually, in the very modern way in which the artist has outlined the silhouettes of Bartholomew's torturers . . .'

Kane inspected the silhouettes, frowning. Then he shuddered.

'It's hard to really understand the dark, for example, if you always have ready access to light, or the cold if you have constant access to heat, or real distance if you never actually *walk* anywhere . . .'

'Walk?' Kane scoffed. 'Did you ever try and do *anything* on foot in this town?'

'In *Ashford*?' she chuckled. 'Are you kidding? It's such an astonishing *muddle*, for one thing – such a *puzzle*. It's like history in paradigm. At its centre beats this tiny, perfect, medieval heart, but that heart is surrounded – obfuscated – by all these conflicting layers; a chaos of buildings and roads from every conceivable time-frame. It's pure, architectural mayhem. A completely non-homogeneous town, utterly half-cocked, deliriously ramshackle . . . And then, clumsily imposed on top – the icing on the cake – this whole crazy mish-mash of through-roads and round-roads and intersections and dead-ends –

398

Business Parks, Superstores, train stations, train tracks – which slice blithely through all the other stuff, apparently *aiding* it on the one hand, yet completely *disregarding* it on the other . . .' she paused, ruminatively. 'You're right: Ashford's a fantastic contradiction; a city which professes to celebrate journeying while being basically almost unnavigable on foot.'

Kane continued to stare at *The Martyrdom of Saint Bartholomew* while she spoke. He found the painting oddly mesmerising. In it he saw six men degrading a naked saint who lay on his belly (tied by two strands of rope, at his waist, to a table). The saint was fully conscious, and he didn't look especially saintly, or – his halo aside, obviously – particularly or indefinably different to his torturers. He could've been *any* of them.

And he wasn't just receiving the torture, passively, he was propping himself up, on to his elbow, and glancing over his shoulder (irate, almost) as one of his attackers – knife between his teeth – matter-of-factly prised back a huge, clean sheet of his skin.

Below the table, an old man casually and cheerfully sharpened the knives. Further along, a man dressed in white idly pushed a blade into the saint's thigh.

'What you see here is the spectacle of torture,' she said. 'Life back then was all about the spectacle: the noble majesty of princes, the pious grandeur of the Church, the extreme poverty of beggars, the righteous savagery of public executions. And the spectacle – in this instance – is rendered all the more awful by the casual demeanours of the men actually implementing it. In the Middle Ages they had no concept of leniency. They believed in the two extremes of cruel punishment or absolute mercy. Something was either right or wrong. There were no grey areas. No middle ground. A crime was an insult against society and God and it had to be punished – even celebrated – accordingly.'

'Well thank God for the grey areas, huh?' Kane murmured.

'You think modern life's all in neutrals?' she wondered.

'Isn't that what you've just been arguing?'

'I'd've thought you'd be hard pressed to find *anything* more black and white,' she smiled, 'than the British tabloid press. Or the deranged philosophies of Al Q'aeda, come to that . . .'

'How much is it worth?' Kane wondered, walking back over to the hot bench again (choosing not to engage with her any further on these points).

'Although – somewhat *ironically*,' she continued, undeterred, 'in medieval times it was principally the Islamic faith which strove to expand the world's intellectual boundaries – their Arabic translations of the early works of Aristotle, for example; and it was the advent of Caxton's Printing Press which helped to solidify and proliferate the English Renaissance through the ready provision of cheap, topical reading matter . . .'

Kane was bending over the bench and closely scrutinising the canvas. 'It seems so tiny,' he said, fascinated. 'I'd love to actually *see* it.'

'I paid 200,000,' she finally answered his earlier enquiry, 'which I thought was a snip.'

He glanced up, impressed. 'And how much will you sell it for?'

She shrugged. 'That's anyone's guess. It all depends on whether I can establish any kind of provenance . . .'

'You'll restore it yourself?'

'If I can. For the most part.'

'Will it take long?'

'Probably.'

'So who did you buy it from?'

She turned as he spoke, registering the sudden clatter of heavy footsteps on the staircase below them.

'An old German widow in Berlin. There's extensive water damage,' she murmured, strolling over to the door. 'The warehouse where it was stored was heavily bombed during the war . . .'

As she spoke a woman hurried into the studio. It was the woman from the courtyard; the tiny, incomprehensible woman with her scraped-back hair, her heavy clogs and her plastic apron. The apron was now streaked in what Kane presumed to be goose gore. She held her two hands out in front of her, fastidiously (as if she'd been caught on the hop and hadn't had the chance to scrub them clean). She was short of breath. She quickly patted a sheen of sweat from her forehead with the inside of her arm. A strand of hair had come loose from her tight bun.

'What's wrong, Ann?' Peta asked, gently tucking the errant strand behind her ear.

'Ya kiraysee jammun frund jast tooned ap, scratchud ta peases, raven lick a maddun,' Ann said, indicating behind her, with some urgency, 'a laft im inna kite-chen.'

Peta seemed surprised by this news. 'Was that wise?'

Ann shrugged. 'Well wat alse kad-ee du?'

'Okay. Fine. Well just try and keep him calm. Don't confront him, don't *scare* him. I'll come straight down.'

Ann nodded, turned and darted back off again.

Peta glanced over towards Kane. 'Something's come up,' she said, holding out her outstretched palm. 'I'm afraid I'm going to have to send you packing.'

'Where's she from?' Kane wondered, walking over and instinctively grasping her fingers (like a child looking for a mother's reassurance before crossing a busy intersection).

'Who? Ann?'

He nodded.

'The North East.'

'No. I mean originally. Romania? *Lithuania?*'

'The North East,' she repeated, 'near Sunderland.'

'Oh.'

Kane was perplexed. He stared down at his hand, in her hand. He blinked. For a moment he could hardly tell which of them was hers, which was his. The big hand? The small?

'You're right, though,' she conceded, 'it's an amazing accent . . .' she led him out firmly on to the stairwell and gently released him '. . . the best piece in my collection, actually; so raw, so spare, so rare, so *antique* . . .'

She gestured for him to lead the way, then followed – smiling faintly at his confusion – as they commenced their descent.

PART FOUR

DUNGENESS

'She'll have to stay in the car,' he told the boy, gruffly, 'her wheels will get stuck in the shingle.'

'But we can take the cart *off*, Papa,' Fleet wheedled, his face creasing up as if he might cry, 'and I can carry her.'

'She's too heavy,' his father insisted, 'she'll just get in the way . . .' He paused. 'I *told* you this would happen, didn't I? Perhaps now you'll understand why I counselled against bringing her. She's sick, see? *Disabled*. She's much better off at home. She's *happy* there . . .'

He peered down on to the back seat where Michelle currently sat on a large, black, plastic sheet. He was pleased to note that there'd been no unnecessary 'mishaps' so far.

Elen clambered out of the front passenger side, bent over and quickly swiped the creases from her skirt. She couldn't face another argument. It felt like they'd been arguing for the best part of the journey.

'Aren't you excited about seeing the lifeboat, Fleet?' she called over.

'Michelle wants to see the lifeboat, too,' the boy insisted.

'Michelle doesn't give a *damn* about the lifeboat,' Isidore snapped.

The boy's eyes filled with tears. He held both of his arms, stiffly, by his sides. His lower lip protruded and then started to wobble.

'*Please*,' Isidore's voice was hoarse, almost desperate, 'not another scene. I don't think I could stand it.'

'Mama?' The boy turned to face his mother. He held out his arms to her. Elen hurriedly made her way around the car. She squatted down in front of him, gently trying to force his arms to his sides again, but they remained stiff and unwieldy, like a rented deckchair which wouldn't fold properly.

'Did you take a peek at the Channel yet, Fleet?' she asked. 'See? Over there . . .' she pointed towards the flat, seemingly boundless grey splodge of water roaring hoarsely to the right of them. 'And the lighthouse? *Two* lighthouses. You're spoiled for choice here.'

'But why can't I bring Michelle?' Fleet persisted. '*Look* . . .' he pointed to an adjacent power line. 'Daddy brought *Phlégein* . . .'

Isidore stiffened at his son's casual use of this strange word –

Phlégein?
From the Ancient Greek?
To burn?

'Don't be *ridiculous*,' he barked.
He slammed the driver's door shut, quite furious.

'But you *did*,' Fleet squealed. 'Why can't I have Michelle if you have *Phlégein*?'

'D'you think it's going to rain?' Isidore asked Elen, stiffly. 'Should I unpack the waterproofs, just in case?'

'Yes. The sky's a little dark . . . Good idea,' Elen murmured.

Isidore marched around to the back of the car and yanked open the boot.

Elen turned to Fleet.

'Michelle has to stay in the car,' she chided him softly. 'It looks like rain. She'll get all wet and catch a horrible cold. You wouldn't like that now, would you?'

'I'll hold her under my jumper,' Fleet said.

'No,' Elen struggled to keep her temper in check, 'no you won't. She's going to stay in the car and that's that. She's happy in the car. She likes being in there. She's guarding the car. That's her job. *Look* . . .'

Elen indicated towards the window where Michelle's nose was currently pressed, her poignant eyes mercifully obscured by a small patch of condensation on the pane.

'Why doesn't *Phlégein* stay in the car?' Fleet whispered, conspiratorially. 'I don't *like* him, Mama. He's horrible. Why does Papa always let *Phlégein* come along? It's not *fair*.'

Elen drew a deep breath. 'We spoke about this before,' she said, 'remember? Mummy doesn't like it when you talk about *Phlégein*. It makes Daddy cross. Mummy doesn't want you to talk about it any more.'

'But why doesn't *Phlégein* stay behind too?' Fleet persisted.

Elen tried a different tack. 'Would you *like* it if *Phlégein* stayed in the car with Michelle?' she asked, her voice taking on a slightly ominous tone. 'Just the two of them? All alone?'

The boy's eyes widened.

'Let's not speak of this any more,' she said, hating herself.

Isidore slammed the boot shut.

'I can only find two mackintoshes,' he said. 'Yours and Fleet's.'

'Are you certain?' Elen stood up. 'I'm sure I packed yours with mine . . .'

'Positive,' Isidore insisted, throwing her mac over to her.

'Should I take a quick look?' she asked, catching it and shaking it out, just to make sure the two weren't caught up together.

'Fine,' Isidore snapped, 'if you think I'm incapable of hunting down a stray mac . . .'

'No,' Elen murmured. 'Of course. You're right . . . I'm just being . . . uh . . .'

She began to yank on the mac over her plain, black, knitted top.

'I don't like it here,' Fleet muttered, turning into the wind and hugging himself against the cold. 'It's ugly and messy and all . . . all *squashed*.'

Isidore unrolled Fleet's mac then reached out and grabbed hold of one of his arms.

'I can put it on *myself*!' Fleet screamed, snatching his arm back.

'Stop that! *Now!*'

Elen spoke sharply, pulling her hair free from the neck of her mac and trying to wrestle it into a ponytail.

They both glanced up at her, as if uncertain which of the two of them she was actually chastising.

'Fleet,' she added, as an afterthought, 'don't be such a baby or we won't go and see the boat after all.'

'I don't *care* about the boat,' the boy griped, 'I *never* cared about it.'

'You *like* boats,' Isidore growled.

'I don't *care*,' Fleet repeated.

Elen took the boy's coat from her husband and set about pulling it on. The boy sullenly complied to her brisk manhandling. Isidore scowled. He drew a deep breath and zipped his winter fleece right up to the throat. He locked the car and set the alarm –

Beep-beep

Fleet's entire body jarred at this unexpected sound. But then, almost immediately: 'Beep-beep,' he echoed, blankly.

'Well, *I* want to see the lifeboats,' Elen said, straightening up, 'and so does Daddy.'

The boy said nothing. He kicked out his foot and propelled a small pebble from the tarmac into the verge. The pebble made contact with the rattling brown skeleton of a dead plant.

'That's a Sea Holly,' Elen said, pointing, 'can you see the spiky seed-pods like tiny pineapples on top? And that's a Valerian . . .' she pointed further along. 'It used to grow wild in our old back garden – with the pretty cones of red flowers – remember? And that's a Sea Kale . . .' she pointed still further on. 'Or what's left of it. You can eat the leaves if you steam them. They taste like cabbage . . .' she paused. 'If we look hard we might find some interesting shells on the beach. Maybe even a fossil . . .'

'Do you have the train time-table with you, Elen?' Isidore interrupted her.

'The *train* time-table?'

'Yes. I handed it to you just as we were leaving.'

'Did you? Oh . . . Right . . .' Elen said, frowning.

'I gave it to you just as we were leaving the house. In the hallway. I was carrying the dog. I'd dug it out specially from the box of papers in the study . . .'

Elen slowly felt around inside the pockets of her mac.

'Well it's not going to be in the pockets of your mac,' Isidore snapped, 'you've only just this second put that on.'

'I don't *have* any other pockets, Dory,' Elen murmured.

'Where's your bag?'

'I left it at home. I didn't think I'd be needing it.'

'So you shoved it into your bag and then left your bag behind, is that it?'

She shrugged.

'Great.'

Isidore stalked off down the road, heading in the general direction of a large, solitary white shed positioned on a small ridge between the sea and the shingle.

Elen snatched a hold of Fleet's hand and trotted along behind him.

'I thought we were just visiting the lifeboat this time . . .' she shouted.

'I wasn't certain if the lifeboat station would be open, so I dug out the train time-table, just in case,' he yelled back. 'Fleet's never had the opportunity to ride on a miniature steam train before . . .'

'But it *is* open,' she gesticulated, helplessly, with her free hand, 'I mean it *looks* open, so we won't . . .'

'That's hardly the point.'

Isidore strode on.

'Ow!'

The boy suddenly ducked his head.

'*Now* what?' Elen glanced down, irritably.

'*Phlégein* hit me,' the boy grizzled, shoving the lower section of his face into the thick knit of his scarf, for protection.

'Look at me,' she instructed, still struggling to match her husband's pace. '*Where* did he hit you?'

'There . . .'

The boy indicated towards the side of his head, but still looked down – as if afraid to look up – his shoulders hunched.

'I can't see anything,' she puffed. 'Walk properly, Fleet. Don't be silly. Lift your head up.'

'He *did* hit me. I *felt* it . . .'

The boy tripped on a pot-hole and almost lost his balance. He kept a tight hold on his mother's hand, exaggerating the trip and forcing her to take the best part of his body-weight. She winced, biting her lip, then righted him, with a grunt.

'Well I can't see anything,' she panted. 'Show me properly . . .'

'No.'

Impasse

'Well if I can't see it,' Elen reasoned, her nostrils flaring, 'I can't kiss it better, can I?'

'I don't *care*. I don't *want* you to kiss it. I want to go *home*. I'm *tired*. I *hate* it here.'

'Fine.'

She stuck out her chin. She pushed back her shoulders. She continued walking. The boy kept his head down. She looked around her, defiantly. The sea hissed and crackled interminably, like a stylus stuck inside the final groove of an old LP.

The road they were walking (there was no pavement, just the wide expanse of pebble beach beyond) slithered through the plain landscape like a contorted mamba searching for a private nook in which to shed its skin. But there were no gulleys for it to crouch in. The sky, like the sea, was grey and unrelenting. The wind howled.

She inspected the sparse assortment of tiny cottages dotting the shingle around them. For the most part: ramshackle, wooden huts, old train carriages or ancient, flimsy-looking prefabs, often ornamented quaintly with the spoils of the sea – pieces of driftwood, skeins of seaweed, the rotting hulls of old rowing-boats, abstract hunks of what looked like rusty farm machinery, lop-sided flagpoles, broken anchors . . .

Each property was self-consciously open plan. There were no real fences – no boundaries – as if the fearless inhabitants were perfectly content to own both everything and nothing, concurrently.

She felt lonely – like one of those dilapidated huts: solitary, care-worn, *old*. She sniffed, mournfully. Her nose was running. She shoved her spare hand under her mac, angled it, carefully, then slipped it into a small pocket hidden inside the folds of her skirt. Here she felt the sharp edges of a neatly folded piece of paper. The time-table. Next to it? A tissue. But she didn't pull it out – not immediately. Her slim fingers dug down still deeper and touched something else. Something cold and metallic.

The *lighter*. Kane's lighter. She grabbed a hold of it, curled her fingers around it, drew a deep breath and *squeezed*; ducking her head, closing her eyes, almost smiling, as she etched its keen shape into the pliant flesh of her palm.

The lifeboat was out on call. The station was empty. Elen stood in the small shop, utterly panicked, desperate to find any visual evidence of this phantom vessel with which to distract her already dangerously recalcitrant son. She unearthed a pamphlet by the till: *The East/South East Stations and Museums Guide, 2002*. On the front was a photo of an orange, motorised dinghy bouncing through the surf manned by four volunteers in white crash-helmets.

'There we go . . . *That's* what it looks like,' she told him, pointing. Fleet didn't look. He was staring ahead of him, blankly, rubbing his index finger up and down on his lip.

The kindly woman behind the till instantly took pity on them. 'Is he *terribly* disappointed?' she asked, smiling down at the boy.

'Just a little,' Elen smiled back.

'Well there's a few nice photos of our actual launch – the *Pride and Spirit* – on the wall over there,' the woman said, 'just next to the door. And once you've shown him those why don't you pop outside and take a look at the launch tractor? If you're very good . . .' she spoke to Fleet directly, 'one of the men on standby might even start it up and take you for a quick ride. Would you like that?'

Fleet completely ignored the woman. He continued rubbing his finger on his lip.

'Wow,' Elen said, 'a *launch* tractor! Did you hear that, Fleet?'

Fleet gave no sign of having heard her.

'He's a little overwhelmed by it all,' she explained, with an apologetic shrug.

'Did you travel far to get here?' the woman asked.

'Only from Ashford.'

'Well that's not too bad, is it now?' The woman spoke to Fleet again: 'I'm sure Mummy will bring you back again very soon, and you'll be able to see the boat next time.'

'Of course he will.'

Elen squeezed Fleet's hand, encouragingly.

'Ow!' Fleet said, snatching his hand from his mother's grasp.

The woman smiled, distractedly. Another customer wandered into the shop.

'We mustn't get in the way,' Elen said, stepping back from the counter, 'I can see it's all systems go today . . .'

The woman nodded. 'There's a trimaran in trouble on the other side of Rye Harbour,' she explained, checking her watch with a slight air of anxiety, 'the crew've been out for around half an hour . . .'

Elen hadn't actually given a second's thought since her flustered arrival at the boathouse to the crew and the probable reasons for their absence. In fact she'd given little thought to anything beyond mollifying her husband and pacifying her son. As the woman spoke her cheeks reddened. She felt mortified, ashamed, *embarrassed* for having allowed her own pathetic, little, domestic drama to play itself out in a theatre generally reserved (and deservedly) for tableaux of a far more heroic stamp.

'You all do such an amazing job,' she gushed.

The woman ignored this. 'Why don't I go and have a quick chat with one of the men and see what we can arrange?' she said.

'That's terribly kind of you. Fleet will be thrilled . . .'

As she spoke, Elen placed a warning hand on Fleet's shoulder. Just in case.

The woman smiled at the new customer. 'I won't be a minute,' she said. 'We've just got to try and muster up something *extra*-special to turn the day around for this little chap . . .'

The new customer chuckled, sympathetically. The woman headed off.

Elen turned to the new customer, embarrassed. 'He loves boats,' she said. The customer gazed down at Fleet, benignly.

'What's your favourite kind of boat?' he asked.

Fleet didn't answer.

'He built a model of an old clipper once,' Elen said. 'From a kit. Made a really good job of it, didn't you, Fleet?'

'Gracious me!' the man exclaimed. 'That's quite impressive, isn't it?'

Fleet grimaced. He gazed up at his mother.

'I want to go home now,' he said.

Elen shot the customer an agonised look. The customer smiled.

Elen took Fleet over to the wall near the door. Here – just as promised – were a series of smart, colour photographs of the station's Mersey Class launch, both on and off the water.

'These are some pictures of the wonderful lifeboat which is normally stationed here,' she told Fleet (determining to make up for her previous inadequacies); 'and the *very* brave people who sail on it.'

Fleet gazed up at the photographs, blankly. Then, 'But there *isn't* any boat here,' he said.

'*This* is the boat,' Elen explained. 'It's called the *Pride and Spirit*. It's out at sea right now rescuing some people who've got into trouble on a trimaran.'

Silence

'A trimaran is a boat with three hulls,' the other customer explained, helpfully.

412

'Aren't those lovely, bright colours?'

Elen pointed to the boat's blue and orange finish. As she reached up her sleeve slipped back revealing the row of fading bruises circling her wrist. She quickly dropped her arm.

'I don't know,' Fleet said, yawning nervously, 'I want to go home. Where's Papa?'

'Daddy?'

Elen glanced around her.

Through the open door of the shop she saw Dory deep in conversation with one of the standby volunteers. The volunteer was handing Dory a leaflet. Dory was writing down his phone number on to a piece of paper and passing it back.

Dory looked tall and handsome and extremely dashing. Quite the part, in fact.

'Oh God, what on earth's Daddy doing now?' she murmured, her throat contracting.

Fleet turned to look.

'John likes the water,' he confided (with a slight smile), 'almost as much as he likes fire.'

'Hush now,' Elen whispered as the woman from behind the till came bustling back into the shop.

'That's all fine,' she said, beaming. 'Toby says he'll happily show your boy around the tractor if you just head on out there in the next five minutes or so . . .'

'That's fantastic,' Elen enthused. 'Say thank you to the kind lady, Fleet.'

Fleet gazed up at the woman. 'John burned down the barn,' he said.

'Really?' The woman seemed briefly thrown off her stride by this unexpected piece of information. 'Which barn?' she wondered.

'The barn in Oxford.'

'Ah. I *see* . . .' she suddenly caught on. 'And was there much damage done?'

'Oh yes,' Fleet nodded, enthusiastically, 'because he locked all the beggars inside. He wanted to burn them alive, but mostly they just got suffocated in the smoke.'

The woman blinked.

'Oh dear,' she finally responded. 'Well that wasn't very *nice* of John, was it?'

413

Fleet shrugged. 'Served them right,' he opined, manfully.

'Gracious me,' she exclaimed, 'but what about all their poor families? What about their mummies and their daddies? Wouldn't *they* have been upset?'

'No,' Fleet seemed unmoved by her argument. 'It was good,' he insisted, 'because that's when John *knew*.'

'Knew what, exactly?'

'That he needed to abandon the sheltered world of *academe*,' Fleet pronounced, almost as if by rote, 'and pursue his fortunes in the real world.'

The woman looked over at Elen, quite amazed. 'They won't half come out with things at that age, eh?' she laughed.

'He's terrible,' Elen tried to smile back, 'I just can't take him anywhere.'

'I don't *want* to go anywhere,' Fleet muttered, suddenly reverting back to his sullen self, 'I want to go *home*.'

'Right . . . *Good!*' Elen almost sang, pointing towards the exit like an actor, glibly improvising stage directions in an amateur panto. 'Let's go and see this fabulous *tractor* thingummy, shall we?'

'We might've had a slim chance of catching the damn thing,' Dory spluttered, 'if you'd've just broken into a slow *trot*.'

'A slow *trot*?' Elen's breathing was still jerky and irregular from the intense bout of exertion she'd just undergone. 'We *sprinted* the last hundred metres, Dory. I literally had to drag Fleet along behind me. Didn't you hear him screaming?'

'I turned around at one point,' Dory scoffed, 'and you were collecting flowers from the roadside . . .'

'*Flowers?!*' She seemed stunned. 'Are you serious? It's the middle of winter. How could I possibly be collecting flowers? He dropped his *glove*, for heaven's sake. We went back to grab it.'

'Oh. Right.'

He had the good grace to look slightly shame-faced.

'We should've come in the car,' she upbraided him (still deeply insulted by the 'flowers' comment). 'It was just too far on foot.'

'It's not even half a *mile*, Elen . . .'

Dory continued to fight his corner.

'Fleet's only five years *old*, Dory.'

'Five *years*?!' Dory exclaimed. 'I could walk for entire *days* when I was five years old. I once walked seventeen *kilometres* when I was about five. Barefoot. By the time I arrived home the soles of my feet were completely black with dirt and dried blood. It took literally *weeks* before the stain wore off.'

'Well that's hardly the kind of conduct I'd *advocate* for a young child,' Elen rebuked him, quite horrified.

'Whyever not?' Dory casually waved her reservations aside. 'I absolutely thrived on it, as I recall.'

She looked away, with a grimace.

'What's your problem?' he asked.

'I don't have one,' she answered, 'I just wish we'd driven, that's all.'

'I do believe,' he murmured silkily, 'that you've already made that point.'

As he spoke Elen noticed – from the corner of her eye – a man and a woman about two tables along shooting them furtive, slightly disapproving glances. Dory also noticed. He leaned back in his seat, cleared his throat, then calmly inspected the brand-new time-table which he'd just picked up from the ticket office for the Romney, Hythe and Dymchurch Railway ('Thirteen and a half miles of mainland railway in miniature . . .').

Elen unfastened her hair and shook it out. Fleet, meanwhile, was crouching under the table, quietly humming a sweet – almost inaudible – little tune while strumming away, dreamily, on his upper lip.

They were waiting for their lunch at The Light Railway Cafe. The cafe's fish and chips (according to the station guide) were apparently much vaunted in the local area.

Dory placed down the new time-table. He peered over at the nosy couple. They were silently consuming their meal, but still maintaining a steady interest.

'Fleet,' he murmured (concerned that his son's unconventional behaviour might be the real source of their fascination), 'please come out now.'

Fleet didn't budge.

'At least it hasn't started raining yet,' Elen sighed, staring out of the window towards the huge nuclear power plant which – from this particular angle – completely dominated the sky-line.

'So there won't be another train for the best part of an hour . . .' Dory inspected the new time-table again, pretending not to be concerned by his son's total lack of compliance.

'To be perfectly honest,' Elen confided, pouring Fleet's apple Fanta from the can into a glass, 'I don't think a long train ride is really what today needs.'

'How d'you mean?'

Dory looked surprised.

'Well Fleet doesn't *like* trains, does he? They upset him. Remember Victoria?'

'Victoria?' Dory scowled. Then the penny dropped. *Victoria*. God . . . *Yes*.

'I wouldn't even mind,' Elen continued (obviously minding very much), 'but it took about twenty minutes to persuade him into the *car*, and I only managed that by agreeing to bring the dog.'

Dory didn't comment. He picked up the time-table again.

'We're meant to be trying to *relax*, aren't we?' Elen persisted (but with an edge of timidity in her voice). 'As a family, I mean?'

'Relax? On a day out?' Dory seemed quite astonished by the sugges-tion. 'Surely if you want to relax you simply stay at home and do nothing? This is a *trip*, Elen. On a trip you're active – vigorous. You experiment. You *explore*. You try and expand your child's horizons . . .'

'That's all very *laudable*,' Elen conceded, 'but I think it might be a mistake to try and run before we can walk . . .'

'Fleet?' Dory leaned back in his chair (ignoring her last comment). 'Mummy's just poured you your Fanta. You'd better come out and drink it.'

Silence

'Fleet,' he repeated, 'come out now, please, and have your Fanta.'

Silence

'Fleet . . .'

416

'Dory . . .' she interrupted him, quietly.

'Fleet . . .'

'Dory!' she almost shouted. He stared across at her, startled.

'I'm sure he'll come out when he's good and ready,' she murmured.

'But he *can't* just sit under the table, Elen,' Dory struggled to keep his voice at an angry whisper. 'Next you'll be advocating giving him his *meal* down there.'

'Let's just . . .'

She smiled and gently cradled her coffee cup in her hands . . . ('Let it go', or 'Try and behave like two civilised adults', or even, 'Enjoy the moment', this gesture seemed to say).

Dory grimaced. He straightened up. His nostrils flared. Elen tipped her head forward to cover her face with her hair.

'You're still upset with me, aren't you,' he suddenly rounded on her, 'for giving that lifeboatman our telephone number?'

'What?' She seemed taken aback. '*Upset?* No. *No*. You've got it all *wrong* . . .'

'Have I?'

'*Yes* . . . It's just . . . I just . . .' she drew a deep breath, then glanced over towards the couple two tables along, 'I simply wasn't expecting . . .'

'But where's the *harm* in just having a chat?' Dory butted in.

'Fleet,' she suddenly rocked back in her seat and gently cuffed the boy away from her, 'stop messing around with my skirt.'

Dory gazed at her, blankly, as she admonished the boy. Then he blinked. Then he gazed at her again, almost in awe, as if he hadn't actually *seen* her – not for hours, not for *days* . . .

Elen . . .

With her birthmark. Her graceful demeanour. Her soft, brown hair. Sitting opposite him.

Right there.

'Did you apologise to the man with the tractor?' she asked, glancing up, distractedly, and then freezing for a moment – almost with surprise – as she gauged his strange expression.

'Tractor?' Dory repeated, blankly.

'Toby. The man with the tractor . . . Fleet. *No!*'

She cuffed the boy away again.

'Toby?'

'The volunteer.'

'Oh *yes* . . . but of course,' Dory rapidly caught up, 'of *course* I apologised.'

'It was all just so . . .' Elen shuddered, traumatised.

'I said he'd been ill,' Dory whispered, 'I said his grandpa had just died.'

Elen stared at him, blankly. Dory took a sip of his coffee. He paused. 'I mean what *else* could I say? It was horrendous. A simple "sorry" without any proper explanation . . .' he shrugged '. . . It just wouldn't have felt quite enough . . .'

'*Yes* . . .' Elen frowned, biting her lip. 'But . . .'

'But *what*? But *nothing*. It was utterly humiliating. You should never have . . .'

'I couldn't *help* it,' Elen exclaimed. 'The woman in the shop . . .' Her jaw stiffened.

'Anyway . . .' she struggled to rein in her fury, 'he was *fine* when you took him for a spin with Harvey the other week.'

'Was he?'

Dory stared at her, cryptically.

'*Wasn't* he, though?'

'If having a terrible tantrum qualifies as "fine", then yes, absolutely . . .'

Elen's jaw dropped. 'A *tantrum*? But why didn't you . . . ?'

He shrugged. 'I didn't want to upset you.'

She was stunned.

'I wanted to save you the unnecessary *distress*,' he maintained.

'But surely there are *some* things . . .' she argued.

'Why?' he demanded. 'Do you always make a habit of telling *me* everything?'

'*Yes*. Of *course* I do . . . I mean . . .' She frowned.

'Everything? Every *little* thing?'

As he spoke a waiter approached the table, his arms heavily laden with their food.

'Okay, two adult portions . . .' he slipped the steaming plates down carefully in front of them, 'and . . .'

He glanced around him, looking for a child.

'Sorry. *Yes* . . .' Elen reached out for the plate. 'He's playing under the table . . .'

418

As she reached her jumper slipped back revealing the familiar pattern of bruises on her wrist.

Dory flinched. The waiter handed her the plate, appearing not to have noticed.

'Enjoy your meal,' he said. Then, 'You too,' he added, directing his words at their feet.

Silence

The waiter headed off. Elen placed Fleet's portion next to his Fanta. 'Your dinner's here, Fleet,' she said softly, 'do come out and eat.'

Fleet promptly emerged from under the table and sat down on his chair.

'Good boy,' she said, and patted his shoulder.

Dory picked up his knife and fork, plainly infuriated by the child's eagerness to oblige his mother.

'Anyway,' he said gruffly, referring back to their former conversation, 'I handled it. It was fine.'

'I still would've appreciated being told,' she said, spreading a paper napkin on to her lap then reaching over to grab Fleet's, unfolding it and tucking it into the neck of his jumper.

'Will you make Mummy very happy by using this fork?' she asked, picking up the fork and showing it to him, gingerly.

Fleet stared at the fork. He nodded. He took a hold of the fork.

'Good boy,' she said, returning to her own meal.

Dory peered over at his son. His hold on the fork was, at best, erratic. He stared at him, frowning. Then – 'Fleet, I think you're eating with the wrong hand,' he said.

Fleet continued to prod at his food – clumsily – from a peculiar angle.

'Why don't you use your *other* hand?' he asked. 'Because I'm sure it'd be much . . .'

'My other hand is full up,' Fleet informed him.

'Full up? Of *what*?'

Fleet lifted his other hand. The other hand contained a tissue, a train time-table and a red lighter. He placed them all down, gently, on to the table-top.

'But where on earth did you get *this*?' Dory asked, reaching out for the lighter.

'Mama's pocket,' Fleet said simply, swapping his fork into his other hand and commencing to eat his meal with it.

Dory stared at the lighter, blankly, then his gaze shifted, pointedly, to the old train time-table.

Elen's brown eyes, meanwhile, remained calmly focussed on her plate.

There were two lighthouses – the old and the new. The old – no longer in use, painted black, open to the public – stood adjacent to the railway (with its Light Railway Cafe) and several hundred yards east of the nuclear power plant.

The new lighthouse – taller, leaner, smartly emblazoned with black and white stripes – stood further down the coast, like an upended hornet, its vicious sting supplanted by a powerful lamp, which blinked – calmly and benevolently – into the Straits of Dover.

Since the long, pebble-strewn spit on which they found themselves was so exceptionally flat and uncluttered (little more, in effect, than the brazenly exposed flesh of the immodest sea-bed) it was possible to see the two lighthouses from virtually every vantage point. With this in mind, Dory had concocted an entertaining plan to take a photograph of his son in which – by a quirk of perspective – he could make it appear as if the child were a tiny Goliath, supporting the new lighthouse in his outstretched hand.

But the boy wasn't being cooperative.

'Just hold up your arm and flatten out your palm . . .' Dory explained (for what felt like the hundredth time), adjusting Fleet's unwieldy limb to the perfect angle, 'then stay still – *very* still – okay?'

He took several steps back. He lined up the shot. He was just taking the picture – his finger pressing down on the shutter – when Fleet –

Click

– dropped his hand.

420

'Damn.'

Dory waited a couple of seconds for the digital image to reconfigure. Had he managed to snatch the shot before . . . ?

Uh . . .

The picture sprang into focus on the tiny screen –

Nope

'Fleet?'

'What, Papa?'

'That didn't work. You moved. It won't work if you move. So you need to lift your hand up again and keep it *still* this time, okay? Just like I showed you before . . .'

'I don't want to,' Fleet grizzled, 'it *hurts*.'

'What do you mean, it *hurts*? How can it possibly hurt?'

'It *does*,' Fleet insisted.

'He's too young,' Elen said, 'to really grasp the concept . . .'

'Well let *me* do it first,' Dory snapped, passing her the camera, 'so he can get a general idea of what I'm trying to achieve from looking at the image on the back . . .'

Dory went to stand in line with the new lighthouse. He glanced over his shoulder. He posed. Elen tried her best to recreate the trick.

'Could you just . . . ?'

She waved him forward.

'Forward?'

'Yes. And then drop . . .'

'What?'

'Just drop . . . That's it . . .'

She struggled to get the whole image into focus.

'Drop *what*?'

'You just did it. Your hand . . .'

'Where? Here?' He dropped his hand still further. 'Like this?'

'No. You just . . .'

She took another step back, 'Yes. Good. Perhaps lift it a little higher now . . . And if you could just *twist* your . . .'

'It should actually be possible,' he sniped, 'if you're going about this *intelligently*, to sort all these details out from *your* end.'

'But you're so much *taller* than Fleet, and it's . . .'

Dory dropped his arm and strode towards her.

'This is stupid. You go and pose and *I'll* take the picture . . .'

'But I don't . . .'

Elen hated being photographed.

'We can *wipe* it,' he insisted, coolly gauging her displeasure. 'It'll be *fine*. I just want Fleet to get the gist of what I'm trying to do here . . .'

Elen went to stand in front of the lighthouse. She held out her hand. Dory carefully shifted around and angled the camera. 'Big smile.' Elen smiled, weakly.

He took the shot. He waited for the shot to reconfigure. He stared at the screen. The picture appeared . . .

Shit

He blanched at the dark circle of bruises on her outstretched wrist. He quickly pressed 'delete', muttering something under his breath about the battery running low, then turned the camea off.

It took half an hour of concerted effort to cajole the boy to the top. Dory led the way. Elen supported from the rear. Fleet was squeezed in between them – the jam in their sandwich.

The real problems started on the second floor when the wind suddenly rose and the skies opened up. Sheets of rain slammed fiercely into the walls and against the small, deep-set windows which allowed neat squares of natural light to flood on to the stone stairwells.

Fleet became convinced that the lighthouse was unstable, that the lighthouse was *rocking*, that it might conceivably *fall* – then blow away; fly down the beach and into the sea, like a hollowed-out lobster shell. Elen tried to distract him with the choice selection of ancient artefacts on display – 'See how different this old lighthouse used to look, Fleet? Before they painted it?' – but Fleet wasn't willing to be distracted.

'I don't like it, Mama,' he bleated. 'It's going to fall over. I'm *dreadful* frighted. I want to go down.'

'But when you get to the top,' she told him, 'you'll be able to see for miles and miles. All the little boats out to sea. All the little houses . . .' she paused, deviously. 'In fact you may even be able to see *Michelle*, sitting in the car . . .'

His eyes suddenly lit up.

'And will Michelle be able to see *me*, Mama?'

'Very possibly, yes. If she's looking the right way . . .'

'*Really?*'

His face broke into a smile.

'Absolutely. And I'll tell you what *else* we'll do . . .'

'*What?!* What *else*?' he interrupted her, jumping up and down.

'We'll *wave* at her. Very hard – like this . . .'

Elen waved, maniacally. Fleet squealed his delight.

'And will Papa wave, too?' he gasped.

'Of *course* he will. You'll wave at Michelle, too, won't you, Dory?'

Elen turned to face her husband with an expression of mute appeal. '*Dory?*'

Her eyes scanned the room. Dory had disappeared. She paused, frowning, then tipped her head and listened carefully. Above the snarl of the wind and the rain she heard the clatter of footsteps rapidly resounding – like distant cannon fire – on a higher level.

'And will we *say* anything to her?' Fleet wondered.

'Pardon?'

Elen focussed in on the boy again, distractedly.

'Will we *say* anything to Michelle, Mama?'

'To Michelle?' Elen struggled to maintain the light tone in her voice. 'Yes. Of *course* we will. We'll say, "Hello, Michelle! Look! We're up here! Hello, Michelle!" and then we'll all wave our hands again, like *this* . . .'

She waved. Fleet copied her, using both hands, laughing uproariously.

'So shall we go now?' he gasped, eager to set off again.

'Yes, let's.'

Elen turned grimly towards the stairwell. Fleet skipped on ahead of her – to the foot of the stairs – and then commenced a mad scramble up.

'Not too *fast*, Fleet,' she tried desperately to wrangle him, 'and do take care. And always make sure to hold on to the *rail* . . .'
'*Yes*, Mama!' he hollered back, then: '*Hello, Michelle! Hello, darling Michelle!*' he trilled.

The last flight wasn't curving, but straight, and not stone, but steel; little more than a reinforced ladder.

As they started to climb, the sound of the rain striking the large, glass dome directly above them reached a noisy crescendo. But then half-way up, it just stopped. The wind dropped. The storm – it seemed – had blown itself out.

'Take your *time*, Fleet, keep it steady . . .' Elen panted after him, struggling not to snag her feet in the fabric of her skirt.

The boy – like a tiny, hyperactive monkey – scrambled effortlessly to the top. He whooped. He ran around the huge glass lamp, screaming. Elen carefully eased her way up behind him.

'*Fleet!*' she gasped. 'Calm down! Stop running! The floor's a little damp. Just try and be *careful* . . .'
She glanced around her, anxious for any evidence of her husband, but there was none. Just to her left, however, was a hatch – a tiny door, which had been left slightly ajar (a small pool of water had formed just inside of it, on the floor). The hatch led out on to a thin, steel and wire balcony which – from what she could see – traversed the entire circumference of the dome.

'Can we go out and see Michelle now, Mama?' Fleet asked, pointing eagerly to the hatch (he'd already realised that he was too short to see through the windows properly).
'I suppose we can,' she said, dubiously, 'but only if we move very slowly, very carefully. Mummy will go out first and then you can follow . . .'
She eased her way through the hatch, then turned and guided the boy.

'Where's Papa?' the boy asked, gazing around him, apparently unfazed by the fact of being suspended – quite precariously – hundreds of feet up.

'Uh . . .'

She tried to steady her breathing. 'Hold on to my hand now. I think he must be a little further . . .'

She led him, slowly, to the right, her back pressed up hard against the masonry. Then –

'*WAAAGH!*' the boy suddenly lunged forward, with a roar.

Elen's heart nearly jumped from her throat. '*Fleet!*' she shrieked, grabbing on to his hand still harder. 'Don't *do* that!'

'But *look*, Mama!' the boy squealed. 'It's *Phlégein!* Down there!'

He pointed, exultantly. 'See, Mama, *see*? Just flying round and around! He can't *find* us up here!'

The boy flung himself – for a second time – at the thin, metal rail. '*Wooo-hooo!*' he bellowed, then he ducked.

'Fleet. *Fleet* . . .' Elen struggled to attract the boy's attention. 'If you don't calm down we're going straight back inside again. D'you hear?'

'What's Papa doing?' Fleet asked, unpeturbedly, from his squatting position.

'Pardon?'

'*Papa* . . .' he repeated, pointing.

Elen turned. Further to their left, down on the floor, huddled into a poignant ball: Dory. He was soaking wet. He was sobbing uncontrollably. He was shivering.

'Right,' Elen whispered faintly, 'let's head inside. *Quickly* . . .'

She pushed the boy back towards the hatch.

'But what about Papa?'

'He'll be fine. I'll deal with him in a moment, once you're all safe inside . . .'

Two seconds elapsed.

'But what about *Michelle*?!' Fleet suddenly wailed.

'You'll see her in a minute, I promise.'

Elen yanked open the hatch and pushed down the boy's head to try and manoeuvre him through it. He resisted.

'But I can't *see* Michelle from inside, *can* I?!'

'Yes you can. I'll lift you up. Trust me. It'll be fine.'

She pushed him still harder and bundled him through.

'Now I want you to stand there, very quietly, very calmly, so I can

go and fetch Daddy,' she instructed him, sternly, from the other side.
'But I want to see *Michelle*, Mama!'

'And there's something *else*,' she struggled to distract him, 'something *very* important, that I need you to do for me . . .'

She spoke with quiet authority.

'What?' He gazed at her, sullenly.

'I need you to count to one hundred, but *very* slowly. Okay?'

The boy didn't respond.

'And when you've counted to one hundred – but *very* slowly, yes? – we'll all wave at Michelle, then we'll climb down the stairs again, then we'll go straight into a newsagent's and buy *fifty* boxes of matches.'

'*Really?*' Fleet's eyes lit up. He was profoundly impressed by the generous nature of this exchange. '*Fifty* boxes, Mama? Are you *sure*?'

She nodded, sagely. '*Fifty* boxes, Fleet. But only – let me stress this very clearly so you don't misunderstand me – *only* if you count, very, *very* slowly. Like this:

one .... two .... three ....'

'When should I start?' he asked eagerly.

'Only once you close your eyes, *then* you can start, but very, *very* slowly, remember? If you count too fast you won't get all the boxes. The slower you count, the more boxes you'll get.'

She began to withdraw.

'Will I stand up while I count, Mama?' Fleet wondered, determined to get every aspect of the transaction correct in order to maximise his prize.

'Yes,' she paused, 'you must stand very straight and tall. No messing around, no running about. Just close your eyes and concentrate *very hard* on what you need to do.'

The boy nodded. He closed his eyes. He drew a deep breath . . .

'One .... two ....'

The bird had found him. It was perched on the rail, shaking the rain from its greasy, black wings and chattering hysterically.

'Fly!' she hissed, taking a swipe at it. It fell off the rail with a euphoric squawk and somersaulted through the air.

'Dory?' she spoke, tentatively –

No response

'*Dory?*'

She reached out and softly touched his shoulder. He opened his eyes and peered at her, suspiciously, from under the crook of his arm.

'Elen?'

'Are you all right down there?'

He blinked.

'Yes,' he said (almost peevishly), 'I'm just upset about the *view*.'

'The view?'

He nodded. She glanced around her, dazedly, at the crazy, icy, grey and gold panorama spread out below.

'Is something *wrong* with the view?'

'Don't be *silly* . . .' he scolded her, 'of *course* there is.'

'Okay,' she drew a deep breath, 'so what's wrong with it, exactly?'

'The port, *obviously*,' he scoffed.

'The port?'

'Yes. The port. The old harbour. I can't see the old harbour. They've gone and put this . . . this *horrible* . . .' he waved his hand, with a shudder, towards the power station, 'this *thing*. This box. This *idea*.'

'The power station?'

'Is *that* what you like to call it?'

She nodded.

'I see.'

He sniffed, fastidiously.

'So they've put the power station in front of your . . . ?'

'Yes. The blah-bleugh station. The *bleugh* . . .' he interrupted, cruelly, almost vomiting the phrase back at her.

She gazed over towards the power station. 'Which port do you mean?' she wondered. 'Rye?'

'Rye?' he scoffed. '*Rye?!*'

'*Not* Rye?'

'Old *Winchelsea!*' he exclaimed.

'Winchelsea?' she frowned. 'But isn't Winchelsea a town? Isn't it perched inland? On a hill?'

'Not the New Town, the *Old* . . .'

He slowly began to uncurl.

'I'm all *wet*,' he said, irritably, patting at his clothes, 'what happened to my mac?'

'We forgot your mac at home.'

'Although . . .' he paused, thoughtfully, 'I *like* the wet, don't I?'

He peered up at her with a slow smile.

'*He* likes the wet,' she corrected him, sharply, 'not you.'

'The wet,' he repeated, 'the . . .' he sneezed, '*weit* . . . the *weit*, the *våat* . . . no . . .' he shook his head, confused, '*vaad* . . . *vaad?* No . . . *no, votur* . . . yes? . . . *vater?* . . . water?'

'Perhaps we should go inside,' she suggested.

'Inside?' he frowned. 'Why?'

'Because Fleet's in there, and I don't want to leave him alone for too long.'

'Fleet?' he rolled the name around on his tongue. '*Fleet* . . .'

'Fleet. Your son. Don't you remember?'

He frowned, then he paused, then he smiled. 'Oh God, yes . . . Fleet. Your boy.'

'*Our* boy.'

He gave her a strange look.

'Why are you looking at me like that?' she asked.

He glanced down at himself, evasively. 'Did I fall?' he wondered.

'Perhaps,' she responded. 'Would you like to get up?'

'Yes.'

She offered him her hand. Dory slowly clambered to his feet.

'I'm bigger,' he said, 'than I remember.'

He gazed down at his fingers. 'And my hands . . .'

'Hold on to the rail and I'll help you back,' she said.

'What a terrible storm,' he sighed, accepting her help, shuffling his feet along, very slowly. 'Where's Fleet?'

'He's inside.'

'Pardon?'

His eyes flew wide.

'He's inside, Dory. He's fine. He's counting.'

'You left him *inside*? In the *tower*? All *alone*?'

'He's fine,' she emphasised. 'We'll be with him very soon . . .'

428

'Oh . . . Okay . . .' He readily accepted her explanation. 'Good.'

His gaze returned, idly, to the power station.

'Why does it sing?' he asked.

'*Uh* . . .' she frowned.

'We'll need to move it,' he continued, matter-of-factly, 'to try and see what's left behind.'

'Here's the hatch . . .' she encouraged him towards it, 'and that's Fleet inside, counting . . .'

Fleet had reached the grand total of twenty-three. He was counting *very* slowly.

Dory allowed himself to be manoeuvred through the hatch.

'I am very big, now,' he informed the child, cheerfully, crawling through on his hands and knees. 'In fact I'm *huge* . . . Look!'

Fleet opened his eyes and appraised his father.

'Hello, John,' he said, softly, 'will you be visiting us for very long?'

JURY'S GAP

They were heading for the port. Elen was driving. Fleet was in the back (fifty boxes of matches piled up all around him). Dory – drier now, and warmer, ensconced in a replacement jumper – was holding court in the front passenger seat (Michelle balled up snugly on his lap), regaling Fleet with blood-thirsty vignettes from savage Old Winchelsea's long and highly chequered history.

There were brutal yarns aplenty: tales of smuggling, of piracy (a problem endemic to the port: 'Those unprincipled scum'd plunder a *robin* if its chest was bright . . .'), of filth, contagion and vicious armed attack.

The 'bastard French' (Elen winced at his language) had virtually razed the place in 1360 with an invading force of 3,000 men. They'd slaughtered so many townsfolk that the graveyard couldn't hold them and their bodies were unceremoniously piled – like human ballast (Dory described the scene, with an almost palpable relish) – five or more deep, into local embankments.

He also detailed (helpfully mapping out the local geography, in the air, with his finger) how a concerted (but ultimately disastrous) policy of land reclamation in the Romney Marsh region – principally instituted by the greedy Church – had unleashed untold environmental (and economic) damage further down the coast by encouraging many of their fine, natural water courses to silt up.

'There was a terrible storm,' he remembered (Fleet listening, all agog), 'a *legendary* storm. It raged so fierce that the tide didn't ebb. It flowed twice – like a final, cruel judgement from a vengeful God. The flooding and loss of life in the old town was catastrophic. And when the tide finally withdrew, all that remained of that once great port were its shattered foundations, hidden, acres deep, in slime and mud . . .

'But canny King Edward,' he continued, 'remained unbowed. He knew the value of the place, strategically. So he quickly devised a plan to transport Winchelsea – lock, stock and barrel – up on to a nearby hill, to rebuild her afresh – and that's exactly what he did, and that's exactly where she stands today; daintily pulling up her skirts from the thirsty River Brede as it licks and laps about her pretty ankles . . .'

Suddenly (and completely without warning), just as they entered the tiny, nondescript villiage of Jury's Gap (a raggle-taggle line of cottages fringing the road, which dutifully adhered – in turn – to the tall sea wall), Dory broke off from his story-telling and lunged wildly for the steering wheel: '*Stop*, Elen! *Quick!*' he yelled.

Elen panicked. She swerved. She applied the brake. They skidded. A car behind them honked its horn.

'Dory, *no!*' she exclaimed, guiding the car off the road. 'You *can't* just . . .'

She stopped the vehicle, with a slight jerk, applied the handbrake, then turned, in shock (her eyes wide, her hands shaking).

'*Look*,' Dory exclaimed, completely ignoring her agitation and pointing, with an exultant grin, towards a nearby cottage.

'Look *where*, Papa?' Fleet asked, gathering his matchboxes up off the floor.

'For *Sale!*' Dory whooped, clapping his hands together.

'*What?!*' Elen scowled, incredulous.

'For *Sale*,' Dory reiterated, cuffing her, flirtatiously, on the shoulder. 'Don't you *remember*?'

Before she could answer he'd bundled the dog up under his arm, had sprung from the car, and was heading towards a small, ill-maintained, plasterboard bungalow. It was up for sale. There was a sign out the front.

'What's Papa doing, Mama?' Fleet asked.

'I don't know,' Elen murmured. 'He seems to be going to look at that house.'

Dory strolled through the gate (it was off its hinges) and down the path. A moment later and he was knocking boldly on the front door.

'He's knocking on the door, Mama,' Fleet said, now perched up on his knees, his arms curled around her headrest.

'Yes, Fleet. I can *see* that . . .'

After a short pause the door was opened by a young girl (perhaps sixteen or seventeen years of age); a slightly plump, eccentric-looking creature sporting a voluminous, grey mohair jumper (full of holes, pulled down almost to her knees), a pair of over-long, baggy jeans (which were extravagantly split and frayed at her heels) and scruffy, blonde dreadlocks, yanked back from her face into a shapeless, olive-green crocheted hat (with the charming addition of a clutch of small, plastic daisies poking intermittently through the knit). Dory spoke to her.

'What's Papa saying?' Fleet wondered.

'I don't know.'

The girl – initially suspicious – was soon smiling and nodding. She reached out her hand and patted Michelle's head.

'She's patting Michelle,' the boy said.

Dory turned and pointed towards the car. The girl glanced over. She nodded again. Dory waved his arm at them. He beckoned them to join him.

'Oh *God*, no,' Elen groaned, covering her mouth with her hand.

'He wants us to go, Mama,' Fleet said. 'Shall we go? Shall we go now?'

Dory gesticulated again, this time more keenly.

'Okay,' Elen said, turning around, 'we should go. But I need you to be a good boy for me, Fleet. I need you to be very calm and grown up. Do you understand?'

She gave him a meaningful look.

'Of course, Mama,' Fleet said.

They climbed out of the car. She took him by the hand. They made their way, swiftly, over towards the property. By the time they'd reached the front step Dory was already half-way down the hallway.

'I don't know,' he was saying, 'it's the same but *different*, if you see what I mean . . .'

He turned. 'Elen, Fleet . . . this is Gaynor. She's very kindly agreed to give us a quick tour around Aunt Mary's old home.'

Gaynor nodded her welcome to them both. 'I only wish my Dad was in,' she said, 'he's the real expert on the area. Works behind the bar on The Ranges. He's lived here all his life – grew up on Broomhill Farm . . .'

Dory's face broke into a delighted grin. 'We always bought our eggs there,' he said.

'Really? *God*. My dad never stops banging on about how it was always his job to clean out the chicken shed. The smell was just terrible, he says. He *hated* those birds . . .'

'Perhaps we knew each other?' Dory speculated. 'What's his name? Is he my age? A little older?'

'His proper name's David Thomas, but everyone calls him Chubby – Chubby Thomas. He was born in 1954. I'm the youngest of eight,' she smiled, 'what my mum likes to call "an afterthought".'

'Chubby . . .' Dory considered the name as they followed her through to the kitchen. 'It rings a vague bell, actually. But he was possibly a little old to've been a regular playmate . . .'

He glanced around him. 'Gracious me,' he exclaimed, 'the old *range* . . .'

He walked over to a large, black Aga and ran a fond hand along the rail.

She nodded. 'It's always been there. We've never actually managed to get it working but it was too heavy to shift. Dad's ripped out pretty much everything else over the years . . .'

'I can *see* that . . .' Dory shrugged, benignly. 'But it still has the same . . .'

'Atmosphere?' she filled in. He nodded.

'Is the cottage very old?' Elen interrupted.

'Not ancient, no. But a good age for around here . . .'

'And there's still direct river access out the back?' Dory enquired.

'The Gut? Sure . . .'

She opened the back door. A gust of cold, sea air blasted inside.

'My aunt used to call it a "drowning river" . . .' Dory stepped forward and poked his head out. 'She'd never let me swim in it. I remember I built a raft one year but she wouldn't let me float it out there . . .'

'It's very reeded up,' the girl conceded, pulling the door shut.

'So you're selling?' Elen asked, brightly.

'Yes. My parents have split and my mum needs her half to set herself up. Dad's really pissed off about it, though. He loves the old place and property's so expensive round here . . .'

'Will he be able to afford to stay in the area?'

She nodded. 'He's moving to a tiny shack on the other side of the Gut which he inherited from my grandad. You can see it from the back window if you crane your neck . . .'

Elen walked over to the window to take a look but the reeds were too high to see anything beyond.

'I mean it's just a *shed*, really. Nothing to write home about. But he's hoping to get planning permission and to do a bit of work on it . . .'

'What about you?' Elen asked, turning.

'Me?'

'Where will you go?'

'I'll move into Camber, probably.'

'At the end of the day,' Dory observed, portentously, 'we're all just custodians, *eh*?'

The girl smiled at him, vaguely. 'So was your aunt German, too?' she wondered.

'No. Not German. My father was Irish. She was his oldest brother's wife. Widowed in the war. Her name was Mary Erwitt. A lovely woman. Big-boned. Red-haired. Wonderful cook. Kept herself to herself, really, so far as I can remember. God-fearing. A devout Catholic . . .'

'That's *amazing* . . .,' Gaynor interrupted, excitedly, 'because when we first moved here the place hadn't been decorated for what seemed like *years*; the wallpaper was really ancient, and all of the paintwork . . . And in almost every room – even the toilet – there was a small nail banged into the plaster with the bleached-out shape of a crucifix around it. So we knew someone really religious had lived here once. Mum's Catholic too, but lapsed. Those funny, little crosses used to completely freak her out. She was always on at Dad to repaint the place, but he took ages to get around to it. We had all kinds of weird junk hung up on the nails to try and cover the marks – just for her peace of mind, really – old calendars, bits of material, teddies, *sombreros* . . .'

'Is your daddy *very* fat?' Fleet suddenly butted in.

'*Fleet!*' Elen chastised him.

The girl burst out laughing. 'No. Not when he was a boy, but he's certainly fairly hefty now . . .' she winked. 'Enjoys the odd swift pint if you know what I mean . . .'

She described a huge, imaginary belly, with her arms. Fleet stared at her, anxiously.

'They called him Chubby because of his *cheeks*,' she explained. 'He had chubby, red cheeks as a child. They used to pinch them to make them redder. Like this . . .'

She leaned forward and pinched Fleet's cheeks. Elen smiled. Fleet stood stock still, visibly enraged.

'Would you like to take a quick look at the living-room?' she asked Dory, straightening up.

'Ouch,' Fleet murmured, under his breath, as they followed her through, 'that *hurt*.'

They entered the tiny living-room. There was barely enough space in there for the four of them, the tv and the sofa.

'This must've been quite a squeeze for the ten of you,' Elen said, looking around her, aghast.

'Crazy,' the girl grinned, 'but crazy-*good*.'

Almost one entire wall was mounted with fishing trophies.

'Your father likes to fish, I see . . .' Dory murmured, leaning in closer.

'Most of those are mine, actually,' she confessed.

'You're a *fisherwoman*?' he marvelled, gazing at her, somewhat incredulously. 'Who'd 've thought it?'

'*Dory!*' Elen quickly upbraided him, but Gaynor didn't appear to take offence.

'Don't worry,' she smiled, 'everyone's always surprised when they first find out.'

'You must be very good at it,' Elen murmured, shooting Dory a dark look.

'So did you live here long?' Gaynor wondered as Dory walked over to the old fireplace and ran his hand – in a familiar manner – down the side of the thick, stone-clad chimney.

'Long? *Here?* No. I'd say about a year. But I visited often in the summer. My parents moved around a lot. She was my favourite aunt . . .'

'It's a cosy house,' the girl shrugged, 'I've always liked it . . .' She paused. 'But there's loads of work still needs doing – some dry rot in the attic . . . problems with the roof. Whoever ends up buying it'll probably just knock it down and build something new. That's generally how things tend to go around here . . .'

'Ah-*ha*!' Dory finally found what he'd been hunting for.

'What?'

She moved forward, intrigued.

'A letter, a tiny initial I once carved into the stone . . .'

He pointed. She drew in close. There, carved into the stone, a scruffy letter 'D'.

'How strange . . .' she murmured, frowning, 'I always thought . . .'

'Good heavens,' Elen exclaimed, glancing down at her watch. 'It's almost two, Dory. We must go. We're late already . . .'

'You always thought what?' Dory asked.

'I have a brother, Dylan. I always thought *he* . . .'

Pause

'In fact I'm *sure* . . .' the girl persisted.
'No. Not *that* one,' Dory corrected her, completely unfazed, 'further back . . . see?'

She leaned in still closer. There she saw a second letter; smaller, older, beautifully etched.
'My full name,' he smiled, 'is Isidore.'
'Wow,' she seemed visibly shaken, 'I can honestly say that I've *never* laid eyes on that before . . . '
'But it's not an *i*, Papa,' Fleet said, pulling in close himself and peering up, 'it's a *j*.'
The girl inspected the letter again, frowning. As she did so, Dory turned to Elen and raised one strong, blond brow, very slowly and deliberately. Elen didn't react. Dory returned his attention to the boy.
'That's just the Germanic style, Fleet,' he calmly assured him.

'*Dory* . . .' Elen persisted, grabbing Fleet's hand and guiding him away, 'the *time* . . . remember?'
'Of course you're right,' he sighed, 'we should go. But it's been lovely reacquainting myself with the old place, Gaynor. And showing the *boy* around, obviously . . .'

He tousled Fleet's hair as they all trooped down the hall to the front door. Here, they said their quick farewells and Dory mooched off, dreamily, down the pathway, placing his spare hand, wistfully, on to the broken mechanism of the rusty gate as he passed through. But Elen didn't follow him – not straight away.

She turned back, briefly.
'It was incredibly sweet of you,' she said softly, 'to take the time to show us all around. And I know it's meant the *world* to Dory . . .' she paused, cautiously, 'but please, *please* promise me,' she continued, 'that in the future you'll try and be extra wary when strangers call . . .'

'Of course,' the girl nodded, slightly taken aback by Elen's sober tone. As she nodded a small, plastic daisy fell from her hat. Fleet bent down and grabbed it.

'I'd hate you to think that you've done anything wrong here,' Elen persisted, 'and I don't mean to alarm you, but if *I* were your

mother . . .' she shrugged, 'or your *dad* for that matter . . .'
Words failed her. She shuddered. Her eyes filled with tears. Then she
darted out her hand and squeezed the girl's arm.

'Of *course*,' the girl repeated, staring down at Elen's fingers, confusedly, 'I completely understand . . .'
'Good.'
Elen smiled, then turned and headed swiftly down the path, sweeping
a recalcitrant Fleet firmly along behind her.

'Bye-*bye*, Gaynor,' he sang, over his shoulder, before neatly pivoting
around as they passed through the broken gate, grinning, victoriously,
and cheekily waving the little, plastic daisy at her.

WINCHELSEA

He just couldn't quite *locate* himself.

'I just can't quite . . .' he kept muttering, shaking his head, looking around . . . 'I just can't quite *orientate* . . .'

The tiny, picturesque town of Winchelsea (so small it was almost a play town – an ornamental town) appeared to be completely empty – although its houses were all newly painted and their gardens were uniformly pristine.

It was a beautiful place, but deserted.

'It must've been evacuated,' Dory boldly surmised.

After several minutes of driving around, they eventually spotted a frail, somewhat beleaguered inhabitant forging a gradual path up the lonely High Street. Dory rolled down the car window as they drew alongside her.

'Did something bad happen?' he asked.

'Bad?' she echoed, carefully readjusting her walking frame. She seemed a little hard of hearing.

'Yes. Something bad? An armed attack? Or a *contagion* of some kind?'

'Sorry?'

'Is everybody *dead*?'

She looked shocked.

He pointed, increasingly panicked, towards Fleet on the back seat. 'Because I have the boy, see? I need to be especially careful. I have the *boy* with me this time . . .'

Elen deemed this a good moment to gently accelerate. The car slowly pulled off with Dory still declaiming, loudly, from inside of it. The old woman stood and stared after them, bewildered.

Elen's dearest wish at that point was to drive straight home, but Dory wouldn't hear of it. 'I simply need to . . . to *locate* . . .' he kept repeating, almost poignantly, 'to set this all *straight*, somehow . . .' he tapped at his head, 'in here. I need the two different things – the two ideas – to just . . . to *unify*.'

So she parked on a street adjacent to The Lookout (by the Old Strand Gate) where there was a famously stunning view over the marshes below (the Royal Military Canal, the long road into Rye, the remains of Camber Castle, Winchelsea Beach, Dungeness – the power station and the lighthouse, both twinkling, vaguely, in the Channel – even France, on a good day), and led him by the hand (although he insisted on leaving the boy behind: 'as a precaution') to take in the vista.

The wind was biting and it was threatening to rain again. Dory gazed down, in silence, for several minutes, yet no matter how hard he tried (and he *was* trying – the powerful wave of his reason crashing, indomitably, against the sheer cliff of his instinct), he seemed incapable of feeling any kind of rapport with the landscape.

'But where's the great forest, Elen?' he finally murmured.

'I don't know . . . Fallen?' Elen suggested tentatively. 'Or cut down?'

'And the river? The Brede?'

'Shrunken, perhaps, or . . . or *diverted*.'

He gazed at her, astonished. 'But what about the pilgrims?' he asked. 'How will they manage? How will they set *sail*?'

'They won't,' Elen said, softly. 'There *are* no pilgrims, Dory.'

'No *pilgrims*?!'

He shot her a scathing look then turned on his heel and began striding, rapidly, downhill.

'Dory?'

'There will *always* be pilgrims, Elen,' he bellowed over his shoulder.

'Dory!'

'No. *No* . . .' he gesticulated impatiently, 'I *must* find the water.'

He strode on, defiantly.

'Dory!'

He didn't respond.

She stood, clutching the car keys, uncertain whether or not to try and follow him on foot. But Fleet was alone, and she didn't like to leave him unattended for too long. So she ran back to the car, unlocked it and wrenched open the door, only to be greeted by the unwelcome spectacle of a doleful-looking Michelle, hunched over on the driver's seat, adrift in a large pool of her own feisty urine.

'Look, Mama!' Fleet chortled delightedly from the rear. 'Michelle's driving!'

'*Fleet!*' Elen exclaimed, dismayed. 'I thought I *told* you not to move her from the plastic cover. Now she's gone and done her business everywhere . . .'

She gingerly lifted the dog and surveyed the damage.

'Oh *God* . . .' she shook her head, horrified. 'This is a *company* car, Fleet. What on earth will Daddy say when he sees the mess she's made . . . ?'

'Nothing,' Fleet observed, phlegmatically, 'because he isn't here.'

Elen leaned over, removed a handful of tissues from the glove compartment and did her best to wipe the dog clean. Once she'd finished, she dumped her, unceremoniously, into the back.

'Mind my *matches*, Mama!' Fleet squealed.

What?!

She saw that he had matches spread out all around him.

'What are you *thinking*, Fleet?' she reprimanded him. 'You *know* you're not meant to play with those until the sulphured ends've been chopped off. It's too dangerous. They aren't *toys*. Now put them away.'

He stared at her, insolently.

'I said *put them away*!'

She began frantically dabbing at the saturated seat fabric.

'I need the toilet, too, Mama,' Fleet informed her, making no perceptible effort to tidy his mess up.

'Well you'll have to wait,' she snapped. 'We're in a hurry.'

She continued dabbing.

Fleet gazed out of the window, glumly.

'Put the matches away, Fleet,' Elen warned him, 'or I'm confiscating the lot – for *good*.'

She carefully laid out a wad of dry tissues over the worst affected areas then took off her mac and arranged it over the top. She sat down, slammed the door shut and attempted to fasten her seat-belt. But she was clumsy. Her hands were cold and unwieldy. Her fingers slipped. She cursed under her breath.

'Where's John?' Fleet suddenly piped up.

'Daddy's gone for a walk . . .'

'Yes, I *know* Daddy's gone,' Fleet persisted. 'But where's *John*, Mama?'

Before she knew quite what she was doing, Elen had spun around and had grabbed the boy's shoulder. '*Never* call him that again,' she gasped, shaking him. 'It's Daddy. It's Papa. It's Dory. It's *Isidore*. *Never* use that other name again. *Never!* D'you *hear* me?'

The boy stared up at her, coldly. She stared back at him, appalled. 'Just tidy that mess up,' she whispered, removing her hand, with a shudder. '*Please*.'

The boy didn't move.

She turned back around and lunged for her seat-belt, yanking it, violently, across her chest and then pushing it, viciously, into the requisite slot.

'*Click*,' Fleet said, as the two disparate parts made sudden contact.

The boy spotted him first. They'd just visited the public toilets on Winchelsea Beach (which stood adjacent to the playing fields in a site known locally as The Old Harbour) and had clambered up the steep sea wall to take a cursory peek at the Channel.

The tide was far out and the beach lay before them: a series of sharply graduating shingle banks, concluding in a smooth, delicately rippled expanse of golden sand. This sand was interspersed – at steady intervals – by deep swathes of sticky mud which'd been colonised by wading birds: oystercatchers, mainly (parading around, elegantly, in their suave black and white), a handful of hyperactive plover (dashing in and out with the waves like little wind-up toys), and a lone, peerlessly methodical dunlin (slipping its long beak into the goo like a conscientious nurse checking a patient's temperature with an antique thermometer).

The beach – while wind-swept and desolate – felt oddly inhabited (*peopled*, even) by the serried ranks of tall, wooden groynes which'd been neatly – almost miraculously – deposited into the sand, like a scruffy line of tin tacks half-tapped into plasterboard ('They're to stop the beach from washing away,' Elen explained, much to Fleet's burgeoning dismay. 'But where will it wash *to*, Mama?' he asked, querulously).

Each individual groyne had been moulded by the sea into its own highly idiosyncratic form. There were giant spoons, warning fingers (pointing, arthritically, into the lowering sky), and huge needles (their glimmering eyes sometimes threaded by discarded clumps of multi-coloured fishing twine, frayed scrags of synthetic turquoise rope, or long, coarse tangles of pungent, browning kelp).

Dory was way off in the distance, small as an ant, up to his knees in sludge and slime.

'Papa!' Fleet yelled.

Elen put out a hand to quieten him. '*Hush* now,' she murmured.

'But why?'

'Because the wind's too strong. He won't hear you.'

She paused, squinting intently into the weak afternoon light.

'Can you tell which . . . *uh* . . .' she cleared her throat '. . . which *coat* Papa's wearing, Fleet?'

'Coat?' Fleet barely blinked. 'The *yellow* coat, Mama.'

She winced, then nodded, then folded her arms across her chest. 'I wonder what he's searching for?' she murmured, almost to herself.

'Papa's looking for the *trees*,' Fleet told her.

'Trees?'

'Yes. He's remembering the great forest. He's looking for the trees.'

'He's at the wrong end, then,' a deep voice suddenly interrupted them.

Elen turned, surprised. A man stood behind them, a tall, lean man in late-middle-age; a slightly dishevelled but nevertheless distinguished-looking man, garbed – almost head to foot – in ancient oilskins and an improbably long pair of black, rubberised wading boots. He held a spade and an old bucket in his hand.

'Pardon?'

'The forest's further along,' he explained, pointing with the spade. 'Down that way, over towards Pett Level.'

'A forest,' Elen frowned, 'on the beach?'

He nodded. 'The petrified forest. *Dimsdale* forest. It's only ever visible at low tide.'

'What's in your bucket?' Fleet asked, trying to peer inside, but Elen restrained him.

'Worms, son.'

'*Yuk.*'

Fleet grimaced. Then he threw back his shoulders and stuck out his chin. 'I knows Gaynor,' he swanked.

442

'Who?'

The man looked confused.

'Gaynor. She does fishing. And she gets lots of medals for it. I *saw* them.'

'Gaynor Thomas?' the man asked.

'I got this,' Fleet said, ignoring his question but removing the little daisy from inside his coat pocket, 'from her funny hat. *Look*.'

He displayed the daisy on the palm of his hand.

'I know Gaynor well, as it happens,' the man said, bending down to inspect it. 'She's something of a local legend. We've fished together often. She's a very talented young lady.'

'My papa lived in her house,' Fleet informed him, pointing over towards Dory who continued to stagger around – somewhat aimlessly – in the mud.

'Did he indeed?'

'Yes.'

'Well that's very interesting. Does your . . .' he hesitated before using the word, 'your *papa* like fishing too?'

'No. And *her* papa is very red and very *fat*.'

Fleet blew out his cheeks and paraded around, 'fatly'.

The man's stern face broke into a smile.

'Don't be so *rude*, Fleet,' Elen murmured, grabbing his hand, eager to steer him away.

'Can I look at your *mathek*, please?' Fleet asked, refusing to be steered.

'My what?'

The man frowned, confused.

'Your *mathek*,' Fleet repeated.

'My . . . ?'

'Maggots,' Elen interrupted, 'you mean *maggots*, don't you?'

Fleet grimaced, irritably.

'They aren't maggots,' the man patiently explained, 'they're worms.'

'*Beita*,' Fleet gasped, peering, excitedly, into the bucket, then rapidly withdrawing, with a terrified squeak.

'What's that again?'

Fleet fiercely gnashed his teeth at him.

'Ah . . . You mean *bait*.'

Fleet gnashed again.

'Or *bite*, eh?'

Fleet nodded.

'We'd better go and find Daddy,' Elen said, half-turning towards the distant Dory.

The man turned too, and as he turned one of his rubber boots discharged a small, flatulent sound.

Fleet snorted, ribaldly. The man glanced over his shoulder, in surprise.

'Guess what?' Fleet said.

The man half-turned back. 'What?' he answered, gamely.

'John was hiding in the queen's chamber when the queen bent over and made air . . .'

Fleet bent over himself – to illustrate – and produced a loud, farting noise with his mouth.

'*Fleet!*' Elen chastised him, horrified.

'And when she'd done it,' Fleet continued, unrepentant, 'she said . . .' he adopted a high, fluting voice, '"The same is worth to me twenty pound!"'

The man's brows rose.

'So John bent over – in the corner, where he'd been hiding all the while and *spying* on her – and *he* made air, only much, much *louder* . . .'

Fleet promptly produced a second, even more resounding raspberry

'. . . And then John says . . .' he paused, judiciously, '"If yours is worth twenty then *mine* is worth *forty*!"'

He cackled, uproariously, at his own punch-line.

The man seemed uncertain how best to respond.

Fleet stopped cackling. 'It was very *loud*, see?' he explained, 'so it was worth more pounds.'

'Yes,' the man half-glanced towards Elen, his eyes twinkling, 'I think I follow the logic of it.'

'John was always making fun of the queen,' Fleet continued, 'because nobody else dared. They all hated her at court.'

'Did they indeed?' the man said.

Fleet nodded. 'She grew up with soldiers . . .' he winced, fastidiously, 'she was *vulgar*.'

'*Vulgar?*' the man echoed, plainly surprised by the boy's sophisticated vocabulary.

Fleet nodded. '*Vulgus,*' he modified.

'Do you actually understand what that word means?' the man enquired, intrigued, 'or are you simply repeating something you've heard?'

'Something I heard,' Fleet freely admitted. '*John* told me.' He shrugged. 'I've never even *seen* the queen . . .'

'So what do you think John means when he says that the queen is vulgar?' the man asked.

Fleet thought hard for a moment. 'It means she's *stupid*,' he declared, 'and she doesn't have any . . .' he paused, frowning, '*finus* . . . no . . . *finesse*,' he corrected himself.

The man glanced over towards Elen. 'How old is this child?' he demanded.

'Five,' Elen murmured. 'He'll be six in July.'

'*Five?*' he seemed startled. 'But his language skills are nothing short of astonishing . . .'

'Yes . . . well he's . . . he's not *normally* quite this talkative,' Elen observed (plainly somewhat confused herself by this rare display of loquaciousness).

'Look at Papa!' Fleet suddenly yelled.

They both turned. Dory had fallen to his knees in the bank of mud (it was now slowly enveloping his thighs) and was patting at it, naively (almost like a baby), as though experimenting with its texture.

'My youngest daughter,' the man explained (obviously struggling not to be distracted by this curious spectacle), 'was also a gifted child, so I know exactly what the pressures are – I mean as a parent – the particular kinds of *challenges* it generally gives rise to . . .'

'*Gifted?*' Elen echoed, dumbfounded.

'Have they picked up on it at school yet?' the man wondered.

'At school?' Elen slowly shook her head. 'Uh . . . no. *God*, no. If anything they probably feel he's a little *under* the average . . .'

'*Under* the average?' The man seemed amazed. 'They must be deaf and blind . . .'

Elen said nothing.

'I mean he's only five years old and he's using synonyms. He's experimenting with the Latin root. Surely that's exceptional by *any* standard?'

Elen's cheeks reddened with a combination of pride and anxiety.

'John told his wife that the queen was deaf,' Fleet began chatting away again, 'so when the queen summonsed her to court to talk about all the bad things John had done – to try and get her to make him stop – his wife shouted at the queen so that the queen might hear her. Then the queen shouted back because John had told the *exact* same thing to the queen about his wife . . .'

He giggled. 'Instead of making things better, they was just *shouting* at each other. And the more they was shouting the more crosser they got . . .'

The man listened intently to the boy's chatter, his head cocked.

'He got paid back in the end, though,' Fleet ran on, with apparent satisfaction, 'because the queen told the king about it.'

'And what did the king do?' the man wondered.

'Nothing. But he warned John, in private. He said, "Stop teasing the queen!"'

'And did he?'

Fleet looked astonished. '*Stop?!* Of course not. The next day he pulled down his trousers in the queen's private chambers . . .'

'His *trousers*?' the man repeated, alarmed.

'Yes. It was *horse*play . . .' Fleet trotted gaily around on the shingle, whinnying. 'He was pretending to be a *horse*, see?' he chortled.

'Goodness me. And how did the queen respond?'

'She was furious. She went straight to Edward and she forced him to choose . . .'

'Between her and John?'

'No. Between John and Jane Shore.'

'Jane Shore?' The man scowled. 'How does *she* enter the story?'

Fleet rolled his eyes, despairingly: 'Edward was in *love* with her, of course.'

'In love?'

'She was his *maîtresse*.'

'His *maîtresse*?'

'Yes.'

The man mulled this over for a moment and then the penny suddenly dropped. '*Ah*,' he said, 'his *mistress*. I *see* . . . So who did he choose?' he asked.

'He chose his *hure* . . .'

'*Fleet!*' Elen chastised him. 'Enough!'

But Fleet ignored her. 'He told John to leave the court, and said if he *ever* came back he would set the hounds on him . . .'

He snapped at the air again: '*Beita!*'

'So did John ever dare come back?' the man wondered.

'Oh yes,' Fleet smiled, as if delighted by the question, 'John *always* comes back. That's the whole *point*.'

446

'And did the king set the dogs on him?'

'Yes.' Fleet nodded. 'But John was too clever for him. Because when he came back he brought a fast hare, hidden in a sack. He waited for Edward to release the dogs, and then, when they was right in front of him, he set the hare free . . .'

Fleet re-enacted the scene.

'*Weeeeeee!*'

The man chuckled.

'. . . and it ran and ran . . .' Fleet clapped his hands, laughing, watching the hare, cheering it on, 'and the dogs followed the hare and not John, see?'

'My. That was very clever of John,' the man indulged him.

'Yes. And John thought the king would think so, too. But he didn't . . .'

'Enough now, Fleet,' Elen interrupted. She smiled over at the man, apologetically.

'So what did the king do?' the man asked, ignoring her intervention and squatting down, stiffly (in his ungainly boots), so that his head was now at a level with Fleet's.

'It was very hard for Edward,' Fleet explained, 'because John always made him laugh. John wasn't like the other fools. He was *educated*. He was a scholar. He went to Oxford, you know. John was a Master of *Farts*.'

The man blinked.

'John had lib . . . *liber* . . .' Fleet scowled, trying to wrangle the word.

'*Liber*,' the man interrupted, glancing up at Elen, 'is Latin for "free". It's at the root of the modern English words liberty and libertine . . .'

Elen smiled, then nodded, almost too brightly.

'I'm actually quite a keen, amateur linguist,' he added, by way of explanation.

Fleet didn't seem to register this interruption. He just ploughed on, regardless: 'The queen wanted to throw John in the tower,' he said, 'but the king still loved John, so he came up with a clever idea . . .'

'Did he indeed?'

'Yes. He called John to him and told him to return the hare.'

The man frowned, confused. 'How d'you mean, exactly?'

'The fast hare. The king said he wanted it. John said, "I can get you another hare, but not that one. It's a fast hare and it's gone . . ."' Fleet paused, speculatively. 'Although not in those words, because they spokes in all different ways back then . . .' he grimaced. 'But the king wouldn't change his mind. He said, "I don't care if it's gone, John. I want it and you shall bring it to me."'

'Well he's the *king*,' the man shrugged. 'He can do as he likes, I suppose . . .'

'Exactly,' Fleet nodded. 'But John says, "Where will I look?"'

'Good point . . .'

'And the king says . . .' Fleet paused as if he was about to say something highly ingenious, 'the king says, "Thou must look him as well where he is *not*, as where he is."'

The man bent in still closer to the boy, frowning. 'Say that again?'

'Thou must look him as well where he is *not*, as where he is.'

'I see. *Okay*. And is that what John did?'

'Yes. He *had* to. Because that was what the king wanted.'

'And did he ever find the hare?'

'The same fast hare?!' Fleet exclaimed. 'Don't be *stupid*! He was never *meant* to find it.'

'*Fleet* . . .' Elen interrupted.

'The king *knew* he would never find it. That's why he asked.'

'My. So is that how the story ends?'

'No,' Fleet shook his head, regretfully.

'It *isn't*? Dear oh dear . . .' the man glanced up at Elen, with a smile, but Elen wasn't smiling.

'John was very angry about being sent away,' Fleet explained, 'but he pretended it was all a joke – same as he *always* does – and just as soon as he got a chance he escaped his guards and he climbed up on to the roof of the palace. There was tiles all around him, so he grabbed one and he threw it down into the courtyard . . .'

Fleet mimed John hurling down a tile: 'Then another one, and *another* . . .'

Fleet threw down more tiles, with ever-increasing violence.

'Everybody was running away and hiding. They was *scared*. They thought he was gone mad.'

'Gracious!' the man was plainly riveted. 'So what did the king do next?'

'He sent his soldiers for him and they dragged him down from the roof. The king was very, very cross. He asked John *why* he was throwing down all the tiles from his roof, but John just laughed and said, "I am looking for the fast hare." And the king said, "Why would you think a fast hare might be hiding in my roof?" And John said, "I'm looking for him where he is not."'

Pause

'It was meant to be funny,' Fleet said, with a shrug.
   'Who told you this story?' the man asked, fascinated.
'John told me.'
'Really? Is John your friend?'
   Fleet gave this a moment's thought, then, 'No,' he said.
'He's not your friend?'
'No. He's not my friend because he hurt my mama.'
   As he spoke Fleet pushed up the sleeve of his mother's jacket, revealing the fading ring of bruises around her wrist.
Elen yanked the sleeve back down again, quick as a flash.
   The man straightened up, pretending not to have noticed.
'You have an astonishing child,' he commended her.
Elen nodded, a strand of her dark hair falling across her face.
'My youngest daughter,' he continued, 'was extremely precocious at his age.'
   'Your youngest?' Elen held Fleet firmly in front of her (one hand on each shoulder). 'How many children do you have altogether?'
'Three. Although . . .'
'I see . . .'
Elen shoved her hair brusquely behind one ear.
   'Does the boy excel in any other areas?' he asked.
'Excel?' Elen frowned. 'No. Well . . . *yes* . . . I suppose he's pretty good at building things,' she conceded. 'He's built an entire town out of matchsticks. A cathedral, a water mill, a *bridge* . . .'
   The man's face lit up. 'How *extraordinary*. My daughter trained to be a civil engineer. She *loved* to build things . . .'
'The gifted one?' Elen enquired politely.
'Yes. My beautiful Eva,' he pronounced her name with an almost unbearable poignancy, 'her two great passions were building and the beach. She *lived* out here as a child. In fact they once filmed a feature on *Blue Peter* about the extraordinary sand structures she constructed . . .'
   'How old is she now?' Elen interrupted, glancing, distractedly, over her shoulder.

'Eva would've turned twenty-seven this year.'

'Ah . . .' Elen turned back. Then she blinked, uneasily, as she gradually registered what'd just been said.

'Your daughter's *dead*?' she asked, almost incredulously.

'Yes,' he answered simply.

'God. I'm so *sorry* . . .'

'She went missing about five years ago,' he explained, 'Although . . . well, they never managed to retrieve the body . . .'

He gazed down at Fleet. 'She was working in Darfur, in the Sudan,' he expanded. 'She was taken hostage by a local militia. They held her for three weeks and then nothing else was heard of her. The police believe she was decapitated.'

Elen looked stricken. She didn't know what to say.

'How terrible,' she finally muttered.

'Yes.' He cleared his throat. He looked down for a moment. He regained his composure. He looked back up. 'I'm Charles, by the way . . .' he said, 'Charles Bartlett.'

He held out his hand to her. Elen hesitated for a second, then she took his hand and shook it.

'I'm Elen,' she said, 'and this is Fleet.'

'Fleet?' he stared down at the boy, benignly. 'What a *fine*-sounding name for such an agile young fellow . . .'

Fleet gazed up at him, blankly.

'You *are* fleet,' he amplified.

Fleet nodded. He *was* Fleet.

'I don't know if you're interested,' Mr Bartlett continued, 'but I've compiled a wonderful treasure-trove of material about gifted kids over the years. It's my area of special interest. I was once a teacher, by trade. In fact I was lucky enough to help establish the National Academy for Gifted and Talented Youth. It's a government-funded initiative. Are you at all familiar with their work?'

'No.' Elen shook her head. He looked a little disappointed.

'They sound very interesting, though,' she quickly added.

'They are,' he smiled, mollified. 'In fact they run some amazing residential summer programmes, although he's way too young for those right now, but I do have some incredibly useful books back at home – some pamphlets, contact addresses . . .'

'That's certainly a very tempting offer . . .' Elen started, 'but . . .'

'You'd be doing *me* the favour,' he insisted. 'I'd love to see them put

to good use and space is in fairly short supply at home right now –
my older son's just separated from his wife . . .'

Elen opened her mouth to speak, then closed it again.

'I mean I live literally 20 yards away,' he continued, 'just the other
side of the wall. The little place directly behind the toilets: Kennel
Cottage. That's the chimney . . .' he pointed to a small, smoking
chimney only a stone's throw from where they stood.

Elen turned (once again) to peer over towards Dory. Dory – as if
timing this manoeuvre purely for effect – suddenly toppled, face-first,
into the mud.

'Look at Papa!' Fleet whooped.

'Good God. Is he . . . *uh* . . . ?'

Mr Bartlett nervously readjusted his spade (as if he might be called
upon – at any moment – to dig Dory out).

Dory slowly pulled himself up straight, and then fell, dramatically,
back –

Splat!

'Yes . . . *No*. He's . . .' Elen struggled to find an adequate explanation, 'he's just being . . .' she frowned, 'uh . . . *silly*,' she concluded,
as Dory commenced a strange, clumsy back-stroke in the mud.

'It must be freezing,' he said.

'Yes,' she answered stiffly, 'it must.'

As the three of them stood and watched, Dory slowly clambered
on to his feet again. He was now entirely coated in mud. He began
wading towards them, arms akimbo, like some kind of B-Movie
Monster.

'Did you drive here?' the man asked.

'Yes. We live in Ashford, we're just . . .' Elen shoved her hair behind
her ear, 'just passing through, really . . .'

'Well why don't I dash back home and quickly pile what I can find
into a plastic bag for you?'

'Really? That would be . . . I mean . . .'

'Absolutely. It'll take five minutes, tops.'

Charles Bartlett smiled, grabbed his bucket, and strode off.

Dory, meanwhile, was cheerfully interacting with the long line of
groynes. He engaged one in conversation (chatting away with it, very

amiably, for a minute or so) then moved further along and politely asked another to dance. It spurned his advances (and quite forcefully, by all appearances). Instead of gracefully retreating, however, he drew in still closer and repeated his request. He received a resounding slap for his troubles, and reeled dramatically back, clutching his cheek, cursing. He immediately approached a third (utterly undaunted by the previous rebuttal) and whispered something salacious into its ear. This groyne seemed more compliant than the former. It murmured something saucy in return. He guffawed. Then he put out his arms and they began to dance. Or at least . . .

Uh . . .

Elen frowned.
Was it dancing?
She quickly grabbed Fleet by the hand.
'Let's get you back into the car,' she told him.
'But what about Papa?' he whined.
'Papa's coming.'
She headed off, determinedly.
'But what's Papa *doing*?' Fleet asked, glancing over his shoulder.
'Papa's dancing, Fleet. He's just dancing.'
She frog-marched him along the top of the wall and then straight down the flight of steps on the other side.
'Michelle's in the car, remember?' she told him, guiding him down, speedily. 'She'll be missing you by now, won't she?'
'Yes,' Fleet said (as if quite certain of this fact), then he paused and peered around him, scowling. 'Where did the nice man go to, Mama?'
'He went back to his house,' Elen muttered, keen to keep the boy moving. 'He's gone to fetch us a few books.'
'Really? Where's his house?'
'Over there . . . Behind the toilets . . .'
Elen pointed towards the large, square toilet block and then gently pulled him on. Fleet grudgingly complied.
'Is he a dog, Mama?' he suddenly asked.
'Pardon?'
They were striding along the tarmac, heading towards the car.
'I said is he a *dog*, Mama?'
'A dog?' she looked flustered. 'Why?'

'Because he lives in a kennel.'

'No . . .'

She began searching for her keys. 'He doesn't . . . that's just . . .'

'Then why does he live in a kennel, Mama?'

'It's not a kennel, Fleet. It's just *called* a kennel.'

'Can Michelle come too?' Fleet persisted.

'Come where?'

'To his kennel.'

Elen located her keys.

'He doesn't *live* in a kennel, Fleet. He lives in a cottage.'

She deactivated the alarm on the car.

'But can Michelle come, anyway? Just in case?'

'In case of what?'

'In case it really *is* a kennel?'

'No.'

'Why not?'

She unlocked the car. She opened the back door. 'I need you to climb inside now, please.'

'But what about the *kennel*, Mama?'

'There *isn't* a kennel, Fleet . . .' She helped him inside. 'Say a big hello to Michelle.'

'Hello, Michelle!'

He reached out his arms to embrace the dog.

'Right,' she told him, 'I'm just going to fetch Daddy.'

She slammed the door shut.

'Stay put, okay?' She waggled her finger at him, sternly, through the window.

It was the smallest, quaintest, daintiest house imaginable – more like the bijou cabin of a jaunty, Congolese paddle-steamer (scythed from its original base and then dumped, unceremoniously, on to the beach-front) than a formal place of residence.

As she rapped on the knocker (a small, brass fox which glanced cheekily over its shoulder – the hinged appendage being fashioned from its lustrous, brush tail), she noticed a dark slick of mud on her cuff.

He answered promptly and welcomed her inside. He was wearing a pair of old jeans and a slightly creased, green jumper over a pale blue shirt with a thin, red, woollen tie knotted loosely at his throat. He seemed very different now from how he'd appeared on the beach: smart and yet dishevelled. Intellectual. *Bohemian*, almost. His hair was longer than she'd imagined – brown, flecked with grey, curling up at his collar. And he smelled – she couldn't help noticing – of sandalwood and sea-spray. No. *No* . . . Sandalwood and glue. A *nice* smell.

'I'm sorry I took so long,' she said, squeezing past him into the tiny hallway, 'I just had to . . .'

She gazed around her, in awe.

The cottage was minute and filled – literally to its rafters – with papers and with books. She found herself stepping over a large pile of old files just in order to gain access.

'Don't worry,' he insisted, keen to mitigate her anxiety, 'it's taken me a while to find everything I was searching for. I'm afraid the place is a little . . . *uh* . . .'

As he spoke he observed the back of her long skirt draping itself over the pile of files and the fabric pulling tighter as she slowly moved forward.

'Hold on a second there, let me just . . .'

He bent down and lifted the hem.

She turned, surprised.

'*Oh . . .*'

'Sorry. Your . . .'

'*Whoops!*' She lost her balance. He let go of her skirt and grabbed her arm. She crashed into the wall, upsetting a pile of books. He crashed in after her, upsetting another. The files also toppled and reams of articles, exam papers and letters slithered out over the tiles.

Behind them, the door slammed shut and then blasted back open, gusting a small tornado of correspondence down the hallway.

'Chaos!' he exclaimed, laughing, his arms now propped either side of her.

'Oh *God*, what have I . . . ?'

She tried to bend over to retrieve the papers. He took a quick step back to allow her room to manoeuvre, but as he stepped his heel slid on a shiny, plastic, folder binding and his legs shot out from under him. He hit the opposite wall and then crashed to the floor, a third pile of books cascading around him.

'Ow.'

He was still laughing (clutching at his spine), but more ruefully, this time.

Elen crouched down to assist him. She took his hand. He had beautiful hands: long, lean fingers with neat square-cut nails; fine but active hands – cut and calloused in places (one fist in particular bearing at least two plasters).

'Are you all right?' she asked, plainly concerned, preparing to pull him up. 'That was quite a fall . . .'

The door slammed shut and then blew open again. They both glanced towards it, instinctively. Their eyes widened.

Standing there, almost filling the entire door frame (having offered scant warning of his approach – no steady crunch of footsteps on the shingle path, no casual knock, no tentative call) towered a filthy, steaming bogman, a huge, marshy spectre, a prehistoric *remnant* of some kind.

'Dory!' Elen exclaimed, dropping Charles's hand and clambering to her feet. 'Aren't you keeping an eye on Fleet?'

Dory didn't respond. He just smiled. Only his eyeballs and his teeth remained uncongealed by slime.

'Uh . . . Charles,' she stammered, 'this is my husband, Dory – Fleet's father . . .'

'How do you do?' Charles quickly pulled himself upright. 'You have a wonderful son . . .' he proffered Dory his hand. 'He does you enormous credit.'

Dory ignored Charles's hand, jinked deftly around him, pushed roughly past Elen, kicked his way through the piles of books and papers, strode purposefully down the hallway, turned left and disappeared from sight.

'I'm sorry,' Elen said, gazing after him, mortified. 'I'm afraid he's . . . he's . . .' she struggled to locate the requisite word . . . 'he's . . . well, he's *German*,' she finished off, flatly.

'Oh . . . *Yes*. Of course.' Charles nodded and carefully closed the door, double-checking that it was properly latched this time.

Elen half-turned and noticed – to her horror – a large patch of mud on the wall where Dory had shoved past her. Charles also noticed. His brows rose slightly.

'If you could get me a J-cloth,' she began, 'maybe *dampen* it a little . . .'

'Don't worry,' he smiled, bending down to try and straighten up the files (several of which now bore large, muddy prints on them).

'But if I can wipe it down quickly . . .'

'I'll wait until it's dry,' he said firmly, 'and just brush it off.'

She knelt down to assist him, chastened.

'I'm actually meant to be redecorating,' he added, 'throwing some stuff out, hanging some shelves . . .'

His hand touched hers as they reached for the same scrap.

'Will Fleet be okay?' he asked, quickly removing his hand. 'Waiting alone in the car?'

'He has the dog with him,' she answered, 'the spaniel. Michelle. But I shouldn't be too long . . .'

'You're right,' he straightened up (with a slight grimace), 'I can sort this out later.'

Elen also stood. She patted down her skirt. She shoved her hair behind her ear.

'I've put a small *box* together . . .' Charles Bartlett politely indicated the way (this act rendered all the more stark in its chivalry by the boorish behaviour of the mud-drenched Dory). Elen walked ahead of him, picking her way, carefully, down the corridor.

The box in question (and it wasn't especially small) stood open on a battered, walnut-veneered desk in a corner of the tiny living-room. She glanced around her: more books (literally thousands of them), two lovely, brown, antique leather smoking chairs (nestled in the lap of one – like a cat – a small, black, somewhat incongruous-seeming laptop), an ancient record player perched on top of an old Bird's Custard Powder crate (a messy worm-cast of LPs writhing along behind it), but no evidence of Dory to speak of. Although – she frowned – there was a door . . . Partially ajar, in the opposite wall, with what looked like – but *was* it? – a small, muddy smear above the handle.

Charles Bartlett came over to stand beside her.

'Of all the books I've ever recommended,' he told her, reaching inside the box, 'I've always found that parents find this one by Sally Yahnke Walker especially useful . . .'

He held it out to her. It was called *Stand Up For Your Gifted Child: A Survival Guide for Parents of Gifted Kids*.

'It's published by Prufrock Press,' he continued, pointing to the spine, 'they tend to specialise in this area, so it's definitely worth heading to their website every once in a while to see what new stuff they have on offer . . .'

Elen took the book and quickly flicked through it.

'Giftedness can be a mixed blessing,' he continued, 'because if a child is bright but their talents aren't properly nurtured – if they aren't challenged or *stretched* – then those early gifts can so easily go to waste. Clever kids tend to get bored easily – as you'll probably have noticed – and because children are – by their very nature – fundamentally conformist, instead of drawing attention to their predicament and demanding something better they'll prefer to just coast, or – worse still – they'll become disruptive. I've a theory that some of the baddest apples in society are those gifted kids who've somehow slipped under the radar, intelligent kids who've ended up redirecting their positive energies – through simple frustration – into negative acts.'

'Is it American?' Elen asked, closing the book and turning it over. He nodded. 'They're leagues ahead of us in this particular field, and much more accepting – as a culture – of excellence than we are. While we've always had a strong tradition of tolerance in this country, we tend to confuse excellence with superiority. We think intelligence is elitist, is snobbish, even. Bright kids make us uneasy. Although . . .' he pulled a handful of printed sheets from the box, 'it's not all bad news. We've made some good progress over recent years. There's the National Association for Gifted Children – which I mentioned earlier, and the World Class Tests . . . Have you heard of them, perhaps?'

Elen shook her head.

'Well I've enclosed a few of their dummy papers here . . .' he passed her the sheets. 'You'll find everything you could possibly need to know about their organisation on www.worldclassarena.org . . .'

He pointed to the internet address at the top of a page. 'It costs a certain amount to sign up to the programme, but it's definitely a good investment. By submitting Fleet for the tests within his age range you'll really be able to challenge him – put him on his mettle – see how he holds up against the national average . . .'

Elen looked horrified.

He chuckled, sympathetically. 'Don't look so worried. There's no obligation. It's just one of a whole host of possible courses of action . . .'

He returned the book and the papers to the box. 'It's often just nice to have a few different options . . .'

'I'm afraid it might take me a little while to get my head around this whole thing,' she murmured. As she spoke, a loud noise – something akin to a snore or a snort – emerged from the adjacent room. Charles Bartlett turned, surprised.

'What's this?' Elen quickly shoved her hand into the box and removed a second book.

'Uh . . .' he turned back. '*Oh* . . . Yes . . .' He looked vaguely embarrassed. 'I just thought you might . . .'

'Isn't that your name?' she pointed. The book – entitled *The Lily of Darfur* and subtitled: *The Liquid Life of Eva Bartlett* – was written by a Dr Charles Bartlett.

'You're a doctor?'

She glanced up at him.

'Gracious, no,' he snorted, 'not a proper doctor – a *useful* doctor. Just a doctor of modern languages.'

'And this book is about your daughter?'

He nodded.

Elen inspected the beautifully reproduced black and white cover photograph of a young woman sitting squarely – confidently – astride a huge, bald-kneed, baleful-eyed camel. She was a strong, lean, fierce-looking creature, scowling down (somewhat exasperatedly) at the photographer, dressed entirely in white robes (her dark hair obscured by an Arabic-style headscarf). She was holding the camel's reins in one hand and what looked like a map of some kind – or an architect's plan, perhaps – in the other, with an old rifle supported casually across her lap.

'The Lily of Darfur?'

He nodded. 'That's what they called her. About five months after she disappeared we received a large, brown envelope containing over 400 letters, most of them written in unschooled Arabic. Many from children. And that one, special phrase – that poetic tribute – was used in virtually all of them . . .'

Elen turned the book over and inspected the photo on the back. This second image was of Eva (aged about seven), standing on a beach in her swimwear, her dark hair curling around her pinched, little face, scowling (once again), her arms folded, defiantly, across her chest and a small plastic spade propped under one elbow. Behind her, the sea was slowly devouring a huge, ornate sandcastle, a magnificent structure which reminded Elen (in spirit, at least) of some of the early works of that wonderfully eccentric and devout Spanish architect –

'*Gaudí*,' Charles murmured (as if reading her thoughts). 'For about six months all she'd do was talk about Gaudí, think about Gaudí, emulate Gaudí's work . . .'

'Did you always know Eva was special?' she wondered.

'Every parent thinks their own kid is special,' he shrugged, 'but yes, I suppose we did. Eva had an old soul. From her first days on earth she had this . . .' he shook his head, 'this strangely *exhausted* quality about her. And this unquenchable thirst. This *hunger*. It could be quite terrifying just being around her. She was such a creature of extremes. So vulnerable – lost – *haunted* even, yet so joyful, so inquisitive, so *eager* . . .'

As he spoke Elen's eye ran down the assorted eulogies on the back cover: Winner of the Prairie Rose Standard, Joint Winner of the International Origins Award, Shortlisted for the Mary Trask Prize for Non-fiction, and then, 'Rich, dark, funny, heartbreaking; a book which grapples with the fundamental issues of how it feels – and what it *means* – to be human.' *Sunday Times*.

'Essential reading for both parents *and* non-parents. A truly modern parable.' *Daily Express*.

'Not hectoring, not preachy, but funny, cruel, horribly unrelenting and *real*. Superb.' *Time Out*.

'Unputdownable. Savage but redemptive. Tender but dispassionate. An unalloyed tear-jerker.' *Marie Claire*.

'A book which really makes you hate yourself for having poked fun at the "clever kid" in class. Heart-breaking.' *Sunday Mirror*.

'[The Lily of Darfur] should be sent out, free, to every college, every nursery and every school in this country. It's required reading.' Marie Knoakes, *Health Issues*, Radio 4.

'This book not only changed my mind, it transformed my world.' John Myers MBE.

Then, at the very bottom, a highlighted strip which read: Soon to be made into a Motion Picture.

'What amazing reviews,' Elen exclaimed.

'Publisher's guff,' he shrugged, 'I'm convinced they make half of that stuff up . . .'

'Do they?' she looked shocked.

He took the book from her and placed it firmly back into the box. 'But is there a film?' she persisted.

He nodded. 'It came out late last year.'

'Was it any good?'

'Good?' he frowned, plainly conflicted. 'Uh . . . Let's just say the jury's still out on that . . .'

'Really?'

She continued to stare up at him, expectantly.

'It was called *The Very Special Child*,' he finally elucidated. 'I was played by John Cusack. My wife was the girl who played Phoebe in *Friends*. I met her at the premiere, in fact . . .' he laughed, wryly. 'She was extremely charming . . .'

'And who played Eva?'

'A young actress called Maya Coales. Have you heard of her?'

Elen shook her head.

'No. Nor had I. But she was tremendous. She'd been a regular in kids' tv drama for years, apparently, but this was her first major role. She was passionate about the part. Incredibly conscientious. She actually came to live with us for a few weeks before she began filming . . .'

'That must have been strange,' Elen murmured.

'Not only strange but extremely challenging . . .'

'How, exactly?'

'Well . . .' he gave his answer a few, brief moments' consideration '. . . because I suppose I'd taken a kind of *refuge* in the book – almost without realising it – in the act of writing it, crafting it, *honing* it. It was like this perfect, totally self-contained little bubble . . .' he frowned, 'but then suddenly this young woman turns up, and she's asking so many questions. Questions I hadn't been able to ask before, questions I hadn't *wanted* to ask. Questions I'd *avoided* to some extent . . .'

He cleared his throat and grimaced.

'Don't be so hard on yourself,' Elen murmured.

'I'm not . . .' he scowled, confused, 'or if I am, then it's because I *need* to be. It's important not to forget, not to . . . I don't know . . .' he scratched at his ear and mused for a moment. 'The awful truth is that in some sick and twisted way writing the book has allowed me to become the inadvertent *beneficiary* of Eva's tragedy – all the literary plaudits, the glamorous film premieres, the financial rewards . . . They don't sit comfortably with me, and nor *should* they. Because no matter how you look at it, we made mistakes with Eva – I mean as parents – *serious* mistakes. Eva was a special case. We needed to . . .' he shook his head. 'There were things we could've done. Things we *should've* done . . .'

'But Eva's *gone*,' Elen said softly. 'Isn't that punishment enough?'

He smiled at her, vaguely. 'Writing the book was one thing,' he confided, 'but to sit there – in the cinema – and suddenly see everything flashing past in this awful, brash technicolour. To see Eva's life so . . . I don't know . . . *reduced*. To see everything drawn in such stark, simple strokes . . .' he shook his head. 'Her life was the opposite of that. It was chaotic and fragile and contradictory . . . just . . . well, a *mess*, really . . .' he shrugged. 'If there's one thing I've learned from all of this it's that life – *real* life – can't ever be drawn that neatly and cleanly. Eva's life was a jumble of bad lines, smudges, half-erased ideas . . .'

'A mess of sweat and blood and snot . . .'

'*Exactly*.' He nodded, emphatically. 'One of the worst things about the film was how they dealt with her death. Eva was kidnapped by the SLA – the Sudan Liberation Army, but in the film they confused them with another anti-government militia called the JAEM – who have strong Islamic connections. They implied that the troubles in the Sudan were based on an Arab/African conflict, although the truth couldn't actually be more different . . . It's an economic, a political – an *environmental* – catastrophe, not a cultural one. And that was something which Eva herself felt very strongly about . . .'

'When my father drowned,' Elen suddenly interrupted him, 'I did everything I could to lay blame – to seek retribution. It was exhausting and horrible and – I don't know . . . counter-productive, even, but it kept him alive. It made him *breathe* again. And at the time I really needed that. It's what got me through . . .' she shrugged. 'I suppose what I'm trying to say – in my own clumsy, roundabout way – is that Eva gave her life for what she believed in. Hers was such an enormous sacrifice. And perhaps you just need to keep reminding yourself of that fact. Step back and really allow her choices to *mean* something, respect them, allow Eva and what she was to transcend all this other stuff – all the pointless regrets and the misunderstandings. Because if you can't . . .' she shrugged, helplessly, 'then you're diluting what's *true* about her . . .'

She frowned. 'If you feel confused or depressed about things, just try and focus in on the pure *idea* of Eva, on the gestures she made, the defiance she showed, on the *moment*, the *fire* . . . Remember that everything else is just a distraction. An aside. A footnote . . .'

He stared at her as she spoke, frowning slightly. He focussed in on her eyes, at first, then his gaze moved to her mouth.

'That's beautiful,' he murmured softly, once she'd finished.

She turned and glanced around the room, embarrassed.

'Have you lived here long?' she wondered.

'Uh . . .' It took him a moment to snap out of his reverie. 'Yes. *No*. I mean I don't really live here. It was a holiday home when the kids were young, and now it's my retreat. My study. It's where I come to work, mainly . . .'

'It's lovely. Very . . .' she smiled, '*cosy*.'

'An awful mess, you mean?' he said, teasingly.

'No. Very cosy. Very *snug* . . .' she grinned.

Silence

'I suppose I should be thinking about getting back . . .'

She reached out and grabbed a hold of the box.

'She didn't die,' he said, suddenly.

'Pardon?'

'I couldn't . . .' he frowned '. . . this is *ridiculous*.' He put a hand to his forehead. He seemed intensely confused.

'Eva didn't die,' he repeated. 'It wasn't . . . I mean I don't even know why I'm *telling* you this. I just can't keep on . . .' he almost burst out laughing. 'It's just . . . It's become . . . The truth is that she faked her own death.'

'*What?*'

Elen's grip tightened on the box.

'She fell in love with a Sudanese warlord. Not even a warlord, actually – a least there'd be a kind of *glory* to that – just some local small-time thug. She converted to Islam. She simply wanted to disappear, she said. So they concocted this scheme. She wanted to be dead to *us*. Her family. Her past. Her former dreams. So she killed herself. She killed the Eva she was. But she *isn't* dead. She's alive. I went to the Sudan. I *found* her there . . .'

'But what about the book?' Elen asked, appalled. 'And the *film*?'

'The book had already been published. The film was in post-production. I went on a kind of pilgrimage because of some of the things that young actress – Maya – had brought up . . . And then, when I found out – I mean how ironic, when you think about it . . . this story was so much more extraordinary, so much more harsh and cruel than *anything* those movie people could've conceived of . . . And when I found out . . . well, I just couldn't *bear* . . .'

He covered his face with his hands.

'Good God,' Elen said, staring at him, in horror.

'Yes.'

They remained silent for a while.

'I was a failure,' he said. 'As a father, as a teacher . . . even as a chronicler of my own daughter's demise. And my punishment is to be internationally celebrated for the very thing I was a failure at.'

'What about your wife?'

He shook his head. 'I didn't tell her. I haven't told her.'

Elen looked astonished.

'I just couldn't bear to. I tried to but she wouldn't . . . she *couldn't* . . .'

'How long since . . . ?'

'Three months.'

'And what will you . . . ?'

'I don't know. I just don't know. '

'But when you *met* her again, didn't she . . . ?'

'*Nothing*. No emotion. She was wearing the veil. She spoke to me in Arabic, through an interpreter. She never even made eye contact.'

'But are you *sure* that she . . . ?'

'Nobody forced her. Nobody *could* force Eva. Everything she'd done was of her own free will. She said that for the first time in her life she felt truly herself. Truly complete. Truly happy. She said the old Eva was dead and that the person who stood before me was just a ghost . . .'

Elen's grip slipped on the box.

'Are you all right there?' He quickly moved towards her.

'Thank you. No. It's fine . . .'

She glanced around her, anxiously.

'Eva made me swear to keep her secret,' he continued. 'She begged me. She told me to consider it as my one, last duty to her as her father.'

He paused, observing Elen's unease. 'But *enough* . . . You must get back to your son,' he said.

Elen opened her mouth to speak, but nothing came out. She seemed overwhelmed.

'Just try not to think too badly of me,' he murmured, 'if you possibly can . . .'

Her eyes widened. 'Think *badly* of you?' she expostulated, 'How could I? How could I possibly? I'm *honoured* . . .'

She smiled at him, then she frowned. 'I'm just . . . This isn't really . . . I just need to . . .' she looked around her. 'Would you mind . . . ?'

She tipped her head, nervously, towards the adjacent room.

'Yes. I mean no. Not at all. Of *course*. Go through.'

She walked to the door and peered gingerly around it. There was a tiny room beyond; a monkish cell, no more than seven feet square. It consisted of a small bed, a sink and a window covered by a pale, grey blind. Curled up in the bed lay Dory, sound asleep, wrapped up in some blankets and a hand-sewn, patchwork eiderdown.

'Oh God . . .' she glanced over her shoulder, 'he's climbed into your bed. And there's *mud* . . .'

She gestured, limply.

Charles Bartlett came to join her. He gazed down at Dory.

'Is he asleep?'

'Yes. *No*. I'm not sure. He suffers from a rare form of narcolepsy. Sometimes his behaviour . . .'

'It's fine. You don't have to explain . . .' he took the box from her. 'I'll carry this out to the car. Don't worry about the mess. Take as long as you need . . .'

He quickly withdrew.

Elen shoved her hair behind her ears, drew a deep breath, closed both eyes for a second – as if calling up some special reserve of patience or forbearance – and then leaned in towards the bed.

'Dory?' she whispered.

He didn't respond at first.

'*Dory?*'

She gently touched his mud-coated cheek.

Dory's eyes suddenly flew open, he knocked away her hand and sat up, abruptly.

'What's that?' he asked, touching his head, panicked. 'A spider? A rat? Is it the *bird*? That *infernal* bird?'

'Relax, Dory,' Elen spoke quietly and calmly. 'You've been asleep, that's all. You've been asleep in bed.'

Dory held his arms out in front of him, horrified. 'But my *skin's* flaking off . . .'

'It's not your skin,' she explained, gently drawing back the eiderdown, 'it's just mud.'

'My skin's flaking off,' he repeated.

'It's not flaking off, Dory. It's fine. *You're* fine . . .'

'I feel strange.'

He looked around him, scowling. 'Are we at sail? Are we in France?'

'No. We're not at sail. We're in England.'

'Who are you? Are you French? Are we in France?'

'We're in England, Dory. I'm Elen, remember? It'll all come back to you soon enough.'

'What is this?' he asked, putting his hand to his lips. **'What is this in my mouth? What are these strange shapes?'**

'Just words,' she answered.

'Words? **Are we speaking English?'**

'No. We're speaking French.'

'But why are we speaking French? Who speaks French? Do I speak French?'

'A little, yes. And German, too. But we can speak English, if you prefer.'

He gazed around the room, frowning.

'This isn't my room,' he announced.

'No. It isn't your room. You've just been resting here . . .'

'This *definitely* isn't my room.'

'No.'

'This definitely isn't the house in Cheapside.'

'No . . .' she frowned. 'This isn't your room. But the car's parked outside. And Fleet's in the car. Remember Fleet? He's waiting in the car with Michelle.'

Dory suddenly threw his legs out of bed and placed his feet, firmly, on to the wooden floor. 'Then let's go,' he said. But he didn't move.

'Take your time . . .' she cautioned him, grabbing the eiderdown and trying to fold it. 'Don't do anything until you're quite ready . . .'

'Ready for what?'

'Don't move until you feel strong enough . . .'

He stared down at his hands. '*Mudde*,' he mused, idly.

Then he scowled. '*Modde*,' he modified.

'Mud,' Elen casually corrected him, almost without thinking. Then she winced, realising her mistake.

Dory drew a sharp breath. 'I'm *sorry* . . .' he threw back his shoulders and gazed up at her, haughtily, 'but who are *you*?'

She gently placed the folded eiderdown on to the end of the bed. 'I'm Elen,' she said softly, 'I'm your wife.'

'My wife? My *wife*?!' he seemed to find this thought entirely preposterous.

Elen nodded.

'And my wife is . . . my wife has . . .'

He pointed towards her nose, almost shrinking back, in horror, '. . . a *mäl*?'

'A mole. Yes, I do,' she responded calmly. 'A birthmark.'

He considered this notion for a while. '*Mal* . . . Mole . . . *Moll* . . .' he slowly permutated, '*Moll* . . . *Molest* . . . *Molestus* . . .' He suddenly clapped his hands together, delighted. 'Surely there must be some kind of *joke* in this?'

Elen just stared at him, blankly.

'Very well,' he sighed, piqued by her refusal to play along (as if *familiar*, in some way, with this strange dynamic between them), 'then let's go . . .' He stood up, sulkily. He grabbed a blanket from the bed and wrapped it around his upper body, forming a deep cowl around his head.

'Let's *go*, woman,' he repeated, more urgently this time, his voice oddly muffled by the dense swathes of fabric.

BECKLEY, NO, *NO* . . . BIXLEY WOODS

The smallest slip of the tongue was all it took to set everything back in train again.

She'd taken a wrong turn at Rye – went left at the bridge instead of right – and had headed uphill towards the lush greenery of Peasmarsh instead of down and around and through the flat marshes of Brookland.

She pulled over, once she realised, and unfolded the map, determined to navigate a new route home through Beckley and then Tenterden.

Dory (who'd been silent until this point) turned to stare at Fleet, who was curled up with Michelle, fast asleep, on the back seat. 'But who on earth *was* that man?' he asked, tiny flecks of dried mud peeling from around his mouth as he spoke.

'Pardon?'

Elen glanced up from the map, surprised to hear his voice.

'That man. Who was he?'

'Which man?'

'The man in the house. The man in the tie.'

'Oh *him* . . . His name was Charles. Charles Bartlett. He's a writer, apparently . . .'

'I see.'

Dory nodded.

'We met on the beach,' Elen explained. 'We were standing on the shingle . . .'

'The three of us?'

'No. Just Fleet and I. The tide was out. You were down near the sea, in the mud, searching for the forest . . .'

'Sorry?' Dory raised a hand to silence her, his expression incredulous. 'I was searching for *what*?'

'A forest.'

'A *forest*?'

'Yes.'

'On the *beach*?'

'Yes.'

  'But why in God's name would I have been doing that?'

'I don't know,' Elen shrugged, 'in fact I'm not even sure if you *were* – it was Fleet's idea. He seemed convinced. He said you were looking for the forest and I said, "How could there possibly be a forest on the beach?" Then suddenly . . .'

  She caught his expression and abruptly stopped speaking.

'Don't falter *now*,' Dory muttered dryly, 'not when it was all starting to sound so *convincing* . . .'

'It's not a matter of convincing you,' Elen said, 'it's just the truth.'

'And the truth,' he continued, boredly (as if he'd fallen prey to this particular brand of questionable logic a thousand times before), 'is sometimes rather less coherent, less *believable* than it might be, eh?'

  'But it *wasn't* odd as it turned out,' Elen did her best to ignore him, 'it wasn't odd at all. Because there *was* a forest. Charles was walking past and he overheard our conversation and he told Fleet that there *was* a forest, a petrified forest, but only at low tide, and slightly further along . . .'

  'A petrified forest?'

'Yes. In fact I think it's quite famous. You probably read about it in the guide book at some point . . .'

'And I was searching for this forest?'

'Yes. At least . . .' She frowned. 'Well – to be fair – you didn't actually *say* . . .'

'And did I find it?'

'No. I don't know. I didn't ask . . .'

  'And this man, this . . . this *Charles* character,' Dory interrupted her, 'he was just strolling past at the time?'

'Yes. He'd been digging for worms. He was dressed in oilskins. He had a bucket and a spade.'

  'Dressed in oilskins? A *writer*, you say? Digging for worms?'

'Yes.'

'How wonderfully . . .' Dory shrugged, wordlessly, smiling broadly, as though thoroughly delighted by the extravagance of her explanation.

  'What?'

She sounded defensive.

'Colourful. How wonderfully *colourful* that all sounds.'

'It didn't *seem* colourful,' she said, almost sullenly, 'it just seemed . . .'

'What?'

'I don't know. Embarrassing. *Invasive*. I just wished he would go.'

'But he didn't, did he?'

'No. He didn't. It was complicated. He was chatting away to Fleet, and then he mentioned that he had a daughter, and I said, "How old is she?" – just to be polite – and he said, "She's dead, actually. She was kidnapped in the Sudan and then decapitated." At which point . . .'

'Let me just get this straight . . .' Dory murmured. 'He had a daughter . . .'

'Eva.'

'He had a daughter called Eva who was kidnapped in the Sudan, and once he'd shared this information with you, you calmly resolved to lock up our five-year-old child in the car and go *home* with him?'

'I didn't leave Fleet alone. I wouldn't do that. I left *you* looking after him.'

Elen tried her best not to sound resentful, but didn't quite manage it.

'Bear with me for a second . . .' Dory scowled, 'because I'm experiencing some difficulty in pulling this all together, *spatially* . . . Wasn't I on the beach at the time, searching for a forest?'

Elen pursed her lips. 'I'm not sure what you're trying to imply,' she said sharply, '– or *why* you're trying to imply it – but his interest was in Fleet. He had this long conversation with *Fleet* . . .'

'So you said.'

'Fleet reminded him of his daughter – his dead daughter.'

'Why?'

'I don't *know* why. Because she liked to build things. She was very precocious. She was a gifted child.'

'So he had this long conversation with Fleet about what? About building?'

'Yes. *No*. He had this long chat with Fleet about . . .' she frowned, '. . . about history.'

'History? About *history*? How extraordinary. I don't believe I've *ever* had a long chat with Fleet on that subject.'

Dory almost sounded forlorn.

'*Exactly*. It was odd. I won't pretend it wasn't odd. It was definitely out of character. Fleet just suddenly grew very . . . very animated. I was as surprised by it as you are . . .'

'Fleet had met this man before, perhaps?' Dory reasoned.

'Never.'

Elen was unequivocal.

Dory leaned back in his seat and thought for a while.

'I know it sounds a little . . .' Elen began.

'Yes it does,' he agreed.

Elen stared down at the map again.

'Why do you have the map out?' he asked, as if he'd only just noticed.

She glanced up at him, confused.

'The map,' he reiterated. 'Are we lost?'

'Not lost, no . . . I just . . . I took a wrong turn in Rye. I was heading for the marshes but now I'm . . .' she pointed, 'I'm here, half-way to Beckley . . .'

'Bixley,' he corrected her, drawing in closer, his eyes instinctively drawn towards the greened-in sections.

'I thought we could drive home through Beckley and then Tenterden . . .'

'*Cock* Wood,' he suddenly pointed to a small area on the map (a mere inch to the right of their current location), 'is *that* where we're headed?'

Elen gave him a strange look. 'No,' she said, 'we're heading home.'

'And here . . .' he grinned (moving his finger a couple of inches along), '*Sluts* Wood . . .' he sniggered, coarsely, and then, '*Hookers* Wood! Who would've *thought* it, eh?'

'Don't be silly, Dory,' she said, her voice almost inaudibly low.

'Birch Wood, Gilly Wood,' Dory rapidly reeled off the place names, prodding the map with his finger, jabbing at it, savagely, almost ripping through the paper, 'Kicker Wood, Twist Wood, Spouts Wood, Stocks Wood, Lord's Wood, Pond Wood, Gray's Wood, Glover's Wood . . .'

'*Stop* that, you'll tear it,' Elen exclaimed, knocking his hand away.

'Where *are* we?' he asked, almost menacingly.

'We're near Beckley. I told you . . .'

She tried to flatten out the map where he'd dented it with his finger.

'Bixley,' he corrected her.

'*Beckley* . . .'

She pointed to the town of Beckley.

'No,' he said, refusing to look, 'that's just a lie. I'm not a fool. I *know* what you're up to, Elen . . .'

'It's not a lie, Dory.'

'It's not a lie, Dory,' he mimicked her.

'What's *wrong* with you?'

'He just happened to be walking past?'

'Who?' she almost wailed.

'*Who?!*'

He suddenly began reciting something, off pat, in an incredibly precise and cruel parody of her voice: 'Next time you feel depressed or confused,' he cooed, 'just try and focus in on the pure *idea* of Eva, on the *gestures* she made, the *defiance* she showed, on the *moment*, the *fire* . . . Remember that everything else is just a *distraction*. An *aside*. A *footnote* . . .'

He paused, then, 'Oh Elen!' he continued, in equally asinine (but now intensely male) accents. 'That's *beeeautiful!*'

Elen's jaw dropped.

'You were listening?' she asked, stunned. 'You were *spying* on me all the while?'

Dory glanced out of the window. 'Where *are* we?' he asked, as if he hadn't actually heard her.

'But that's . . .' she frowned, confused, 'that's not *fair*, Dory.'

'Not *fair*?' he snorted.

Elen said nothing.

'Where *are* we?' he persisted.

'I *told* you, we're just outside Beck– . . .' she faltered. 'We're just past Peasmarsh, on our way to Rolvenden.'

He stared at her, blankly. 'Who am I?' he asked.

'What do you mean?'

'Who *am* I?' he repeated.

'You're *Dory*,' she exclaimed, reaching out to try and touch his arm, to offer him some kind of comfort. 'You're *Isidore* . . .'

'Really?'

He jerked his arm away from her.

'Yes.'

'*Really?*'

'Yes.'

'Are you absolutely *certain*? Absolutely *sure*?'

He continued to stare at her, fixedly, a half-smile playing around his lips.

'What do you want from me, Dory?'

Her eyes filled with tears. 'Just tell me what you want me to say and I'll *say* it . . . '

'This feels all wrong,' he suddenly announced, '*I* feel all wrong . . . Everything's all . . . all *awry* . . .'

He reached for the door handle.

'*Stay* in the car,' Elen implored. 'It'll be fine. Just give it a few minutes and it'll all become clear. I *promise* . . .'

'Bixley,' he repeated, obdurately, stabbing at the map with his muddy finger. She peered down at her lap, frowning. He was pointing to a large, wooded area: Bixley Wood. The small town of Beckley lay just above it, and Beckley Wood, somewhat confusingly, lay directly below.

'Bixley,' she said, finally apprehending the small kink in their linguistic wallpaper, 'Bixley. Of *course*, yes . . .'

She glanced up, keenly. But it was too late. *She* was too late. Dory had sprung from the car and had begun to run, the muddy blanket flying out like a cape behind him.

PART FIVE

ONE

'You're pullin' my fuckin' *leg*, mate!' Kelly exclaimed, leaning forward and giving Gaffar a playful slap.

'No,' Gaffar insisted, wincing theatrically. 'If I pull *leg* you hit Gaffar even *more* hard . . .'

'*Aw*. An' a piece of shit *comedian* to boot,' she grinned.

He shrugged.

'Pass it over, then.'

She held out her hand, expectantly.

He delved into his jacket pocket and pulled out the envelope.

'So it was in his bag all along?'

'Sure. He was go for buy cup tea . . . and . . . *urgh* . . . mug stinking English beef soup. Leave this bag for the chair. So I take quick . . . *uh* . . . look. Is in bag. So I . . .'

Gaffar made a furtive snatching motion. Then he shrugged.

'But the door to his flat was *locked*, eh?'

'Yes.'

'Well that's a little bit *odd*, for starters, don'cha reckon?'

'Why?' Gaffar shrugged again. 'For me is make good sense. You lock door if you fear for *thief*.'

He pointed to himself.

She stared at him, quizzically, plainly nonplussed by this sudden show of conscience. 'Get over it, mate,' she scoffed, 'he's the one who thieved from his own son's stash an' then let *me* take the fall for it, remember?'

'No.' Gaffar shook his head. 'Is other reason. I *know* this Beede. This Beede is good.'

'Looks is Deceivin',' she murmured.

'Eh?'

'It's a reggae song. *Looks is deceivin', man*,' she sang, '*Don't underrate no man* . . .'

Gaffar cringed at the sound of her voice.

'Fuck *off*, you minge!'

She slapped him again, this time with the envelope.

'Enough!' Gaffar pushed the packet away, irritably.

Kelly was naturally compelled (by his show of irritation) to whack him for a third time. Gaffar clambered to his feet, bolshily.

'Keep your *wig* on, Guv!'

He continued to stand. He avoided her keen gaze. He scratched at his armpit.

'Somethin' fishy's goin' on here,' she murmured, suspiciously. 'You can't even look me in the *eye*, this mornin'. What gives?'

'Eh?'

'Was it *Gerry*? Is that it? Did you cop off with the little strumpet?'

'Eh?'

'*Gerry*, you nonce!'

He stared at her, blankly.

'You *did*,' she squealed, clapping her hands, maniacally, 'I swear to *God* you did . . .'

She was almost disappointed.

'What? You think I fuck?' Gaffar looked horrified. 'With this Goff?'

'*Goth*, you idiot . . .'

She appraised him, steadily, her cheeks flushing. 'Can't you keep it in your pocket, or what?'

He looked indignant.

'She's got the pox. Did you *know* that?'

'Pox?'

'The pox. Disease. Hep A. Like Pammie Anderson does.'

'Pammie?'

'*Baywatch*. Like Pammie.'

Kelly described a huge pair of breasts in the air with her hands.

'Did she tell you about this?' Gaffar demanded, outraged.

'Tell me what?'

Gaffar continued to look affronted.

'Tell me about the pox? Of *course* she did. She's my cuz, you fool. She tells me everythin'.'

Gaffar looked horrified.

'She tell you about this *breasts*?'

'Whose breasts? Pammie's breasts? What about 'em?'

'But where's the point,' Gaffar demanded, hotly, **'in sewing your mouth up, if you're still going to blab all over town about it?'**

'You did the deed at Kane's, then?' she asked, crossing her skinny arms across her chest.

'No.'

Gaffar resolved to deny everything.

'At *her* place? With her *dad* sniffin' about?'

She winced, fastidiously.

'No.'

'On my *scooter*?!'

'No.'

'*Man!* That's *filthy*! You better disinfect the damn *seat*, I swear to God . . .'

'*No.*'

'I want it *bleached*.'

She scowled up at him. He scowled back at her.

'Ah-*ha*!' he suddenly exclaimed, throwing up his hands. '**I bet she** texted **you! The little** Jezebel! **How else could you've found out so quickly?**'

'Did you get me my *salad*?' Kelly demanded, changing the subject, plainly disgusted.

Gaffar nodded. He pointed, sullenly, towards the bag.

'Can I have a *look* at it or what?'

'*Here?*'

'Whadd'ya mean, "here"? Of course "here" . . . Pass it over.'

'No.'

Gaffar shook his head.

Kelly's jaw dropped.

'Whadd'ya mean "no"?'

She lunged for the bag. Gaffar kicked it away from her.

'You're *bruisin'* it. You're *ruinin'* it. Pass it *here*, you ignorant *twat!*'

'No.'

'I *HATE* you,' she bawled.

'Same,' Gaffar declared.

Then he leaned in and he kissed her.

It was after six when she rang, and dark outside. He was still at work, poring over his office computer where half an hour earlier (in the midst of sorting out a VAT wrangle) he'd casually *Googled* the word Sinjar and one thing had rapidly led to another.

He picked up the receiver.

'Hello? Laundry,' he'd murmured.

'*Danny*. Thank God you're there,' she gasped.

His heart flipped.

'Elen?'

He quickly leaned over and shoved his office door shut.

'*Elen?*' he repeated, his neck jarred by the long stretch.

'Yes,' she answered, her breathing erratic. 'It's me. I'm here. Sorry . . .'

He thought he could pick out the sound of Fleet – wailing dramatically – in the background.

'Where are you?'

'I'm in Flackley Ash. At the hotel. They've let me use the office phone . . .'

'Is something wrong?'

'It's Dory,' she murmured (covering her mouth with her hand as she spoke). 'He's gone.'

'*Gone?* Where?'

'He just . . .'

Pause

In the background Beede could hear her conversing quietly with someone . . .

'*No. He's fine. An orange juice would be lovely. And some crisps. Beef and Tomato? That would be . . . Say thank you to the kind man, Fleet . . .*'

'Elen?'

'Hello?'

'Are you all right?'

'Yes. I'm good. Fleet's just a little bit . . .'

Pause

'*That's it, darling. You go and fetch . . .*'

Another pause

'*Michelle will be fine. She's asleep in the car. All cosy in the car. You eat those crisps. Just don't tip up the . . .*'

'Danny?'

Beede blinked.

'Hello?'

'Sorry. Fleet's a little tired. I'm afraid he's making rather . . .'

'Dory's gone?' Beede repeated.

'It's been a terrible day . . . I mean really almost . . .'

She covered her mouth with her hand again (he presumed to stop the boy from overhearing) '. . . *unbelievably* bad.'

'And you're in Flackley Ash? Just outside Beckley?'

'He ran off. We've been searching for hours but it's dark now. And he's covered in mud. He'll be freezing. It's awful out there. Wet and icy. I found some of his clothes caught up in the brambles – a vest, a sock, one of his shoes . . . He had this . . . this *blanket* . . .'

'Should I come?'

'I can't call the police.'

'Absolutely not. I'll come.'

'You'll need a torch. A strong torch. And wear something warm – a scarf, a hat. I'm not quite . . .'

Beede inspected his watch. 'Okay. I'll need to dash home. I'll fill a flask. Get some provisions. I'll be forty minutes. Will you be all right until then? Can you stay in the hotel?'

'I don't know. Fleet's a little fractious. I might wait in the car. I'll be in the car park . . .'

'Have a brandy. Have something to eat. There must be a takeaway in the area. Have you eaten?'

'Yes. I mean *no*. That's a good idea.'

'Just hold tight and I'll be there.'

'I will. Thank you. And I'm really *sorry*, Danny,' her voice shook, 'I didn't know who else to . . .'

'I'll be there,' he repeated, a warm glow rising in his stomach. 'Everything will be fine. All right? Just stay strong. Just hold on.'

Three seconds . . . four . . . *five*. That was all it took. He was struggling
to manoeuvre The Blonde in the busy courtyard – was slowly reversing –

Mind that old plough . . .

– then pulling forward again . . .

Uh . . .
Whoops!
Small hole in the cobbles . . .

    It was dark. Everything was a little close, a little *cramped* . . .
The Blonde's headlights were on full, and as he laboured at the wheel
(his eyes slightly unfocussed, his hands clenching then unclenching,
turning, *turning* . . .) they glanced off the tiled facade of the tiny
cottage, bouncing against one of the windows, and shining, momentarily, deep into the small room beyond –

Kitchen?
Or dining-room, was it?

– (he saw a roaring fire in the hearth, a table, chairs, an *Aga* . . .).

    As his headlights penetrated the room (scything mercilessly through
the nets) they briefly illuminated the strangest, the most *baroque* of
tableaux . . .

Like in a . . .
Like in one of those . . .
What's he called again?
La . . . Lu . . . ?

480

He blinked.

Lochner?

Three people. No –

No . . .

He felt a sudden, not entirely pleasant jolt of recognition . . .

Four.
Four people . . .

Peta –

Naturally –
Nothing surprising there . . .

– standing in an open doorway (having just entered the room, presumably) looking vaguely startled, vaguely . . .

Uh . . .

– alarmed. And then there was the serving woman –

Ann?
Anna?

– the Northumbrian. She was just to her right, close to the table. She had her hands on her hips. She was shaking her head and speaking. He could see her lips moving.

Then sitting down in front of her – directly in front of her – was Dory. *Isidore.*
Kane recognised the huge German immediately, although . . .

But why?
How?

– he was filthy and all-but naked (his modesty only preserved by a dirty-looking blanket). He was shivering (violently, uncontrollably). His arms and his shoulders – the skin there – seemed all –

Ripped?
Scratched?
Mauled?!

Kane shuddered.
   But the most perplexing part of the whole –

Uh . . .

– scenario was definitely the blindfold. He'd been blindfolded. His eyes and ears had been bound up with what looked like a . . .

Dishcloth?
Tea-towel?

   And the fourth?

What?

The fourth person?

No.

It's . . .
Perhaps it's just the dark –
Or a deep shadow . . .
Or the flicker of the fire . . .

Kane blinked. Almost as if . . .

?

He blinked again.

Yes.

The shadow hung over Isidore. The shadow . . . it . . . the shadow wasn't doing what Isidore did. The shadow –

Dark

– was doing its *own* thing. The shadow was pestering him, it was molesting him. The shadow was *spiteful*. It was tweaking at the blindfold. And every time it tweaked, Isidore would jump, gasp, slap his hands to his eyes, check that the fabric was still in place, that the folds were still holding . . .

Ann finished speaking. Peta seemed to answer her. She was shaking her head. And then . . . and suddenly . . . the shadow was gone, or if not *gone*, exactly – then . . . then it'd *diminished* . . . the light had altered, maybe, or the *slant* he was at, the *angle* . . .

The shadow was now . . . it was much smaller, *daintier* . . . it was . . .

What, though?

– A moth? A bat? A bird?

But how . . . ?

– or was it just a spark from the fire? An errant piece of kindling? A tiny, gaseous flare from a damp piece of coal?

Kane *saw* the bird, and yet he did not *see* it. The bird floated, like a speck, like a piece of smut (a tiny midge, perhaps), which'd been trapped (crucified) in the surface moisture of his eye –

Ow!

He tried to blink it out. But it wouldn't go. It hurt. It niggled him. He stopped blinking. The bird (or the *idea* of the bird – or the speck, or the bat or the shadow) was angry about something – Kane could feel the creature's rage, rasping in his throat, like a dry kind of burning –

Like before . . .
Remember?
The rasp –
The cut –

Acrid.
Like . . . urgh!
Like melting plastic . . .

And before Kane could stop it –

Can I stop it?
Do I even want to?

. – the bird was hurling itself at Dory's blindfold and tearing at it, wildly.
Kane gasped, feeling – in that second – as if *he* were the bird, as if *he* were the rage, the fire, the attack –
and Isidore – in turn (he was *sure* of it) felt him –

He feels me

Isidore threw himself forward, with a yell, his arms flying up, his legs kicking out, somehow managing –

You fool!

– to smash his head, blindly, unwittingly, into the corner of the table.

Crack!

Isidore froze. He swooned. He fell.
Peta threw out her hands. Ann ran towards him.
Kane's own arms kept on moving –

Must leave
Must keep steering

– and the car kept on turning. Until . . .

Chicken shed –
Old garage door –
Rusting pile of antique bicycles –
Dirt track –
Nothing.

'Albi,' he found himself muttering, nonsensically, as he drove back on to Barnfield, Ox Lane, Silver Hill . . . Then, *'No.'* He shook his head, violently. He was still shaking.
Al-*i*-bi.

The Latin
Remember?

I. Am. Not. Here . . .

His unconscious mind began tapping out a series of incomprehensible morse-code messages to him.

Eh?

He struggled to decipher them –

I. Am. Elsewhere . . .
It said.

'How strange,' he murmured, just resolving to go with it, to flow with it (like Winnie had always taught him) –

Relax, now
Don't panic . . .

How *strange*, though . . .
Almost as if his thoughts were a war drum (or a tom-tom or a bongo) being deftly played by a mysterious hand on the other side of a very distant, very stark and yet beautiful snow-capped mountain.

'So Beede' – she read, scowling, 'There's a whole series of these things (one for each of the various monarchs' funny-men, although I didn't get a chance to look at any of the others). Apparently there was quite a vogue for them in the 1600s (and for several hundred years after that – I saw at least two editions of this one – the earlier called Scoggin's Jests by an Andrew Boord – 1626 – and this one, in which the spelling's more familiar from 1796 – that's a 170-year gap!), indicating how popular these guys actually were (plus: note the celebrity publisher . . .)'

Kelly returned to the front page again:

'Printed for W. Thackeray at the Angel in Duck Lane, near Weft-Smithfield, and J. Deason at the Angel in Gilt-Spur-Street.'

She grimaced.

Eh?

'The information enclosed isn't considered especially reliable, though . . .' she quickly read on. 'This book was written years after John Scogin's death. Much of it will be based on either legend or hearsay (would've been considered "tabloid", even at the time of its publication).
    'The actual story of his life (and a critique of Andrew Broad, this book's compiler . . .'
Kelly's eye flipped back . . .
    'The actual story of his life (and a critique of Andrew Board, this book's compiler . . .'
Her eye flipped back . . .
    '. . . and a critique of Andrew Board, this book's compiler . . .'
She quickly turned to the front page of the document:
'Gathered by Andrew Board, Doctor of Phyfick.'

Phyfick?

She re-read it: 'Gathered by Andrew Board . . .' then slowly shook her head and returned to the letter. 'The actual story of his life (and a critique of Andrew Broad, this book's compiler . . .' she grimaced '. . . who seems like a rather dodgy character . . .'
She grimaced again '". . . physician to Henry VIII", apparently . . .)'

Her eyes widened '. . . *features in R.H. Hill's* Tales of the Jesters, *1934 (and I wouldn't have a clue what his sources were), but – believe it or not – the text was registered unavailable (read as "some miserable bastard stole it.").'*

Kelly threw down the photocopied sheets on to her bedspread. She picked up her phone and began texting a message.
GFFR MADE A PASS, THE FCKER! it said, *I ND 2 C U! PRONTO! K. XX*
Then she went back and deleted the *XX*.
Then she went back and deleted the *I ND 2 C U! PRONTO! K.*
Then she went back and deleted *THE FCKER!*
She re-read the message: *GFFR MADE A PASS* and grunted her satisfaction. She sent the message.
She grabbed the photocopied sheets again.
'*The librarian in the Antiquarian Books Section,*' she read, one brow slightly raised now, '*(who was actually quite chatty) sent me to go and see some journalist called Tom Benson who happened to be in the library on that day and in possession of an associated text called* A Nest of Ninnies *by Robert Armin (He's writing a book about comedy and "is very interested in jesters", she said).*
'*I tracked him down to the Music Section. He was a little hostile at first (you know how territorial these people can be), but after a brief conversation he admitted that he actually had his very own copy of* Tales of the Jesters *at home which he'd "found" in a second-hand bookshop in Rye (this might've just been sheer bravura on his part – that whole "journalists v academics" hornets' nest. Or maybe not).*'

The last section (in brackets), Kelly observed, had been hurriedly crossed out.

'*Anyhow,*'

She continued reading:

'*I asked if I might borrow it some time (or even just make a copy of the relevant chapters) but he got a little prickly at this point and said he was still in the middle of using it, but that he would definitely call me when he was done (I gave him my number, although I won't be*

holding my breath). Then he told me some stuff over coffee (I bought the Madeira cake – it was a little dry) which you might find interesting. Will inform you in person.
'The quality of the copy is poor (at best). This is because it was reproduced from a microfile. But I think you'll get the basic gist . . .
W.

'*W?* W for *Whore*,' Kelly muttered, thickly.
She glanced up –

Kane

There he stood, large as life, at the foot of her bed.
'Fuck-a-duck,' she said, tossing down the booklet, 'that was quick.'
'How's the leg?' he asked.
'D'you get my text?'
'So the rash didn't actually reach your face?' he said.
She pulled down the neckline of her nightie to reveal her thick swathe of fading hives.
'Ow,' he murmured.
'I'm *allergic*,' she said. '*See?*'
She glared up at him, vengefully. He seemed unaffected by her look. He appeared pale, distracted.
'Are you all right?' she asked, releasing the fabric.
'Fine,' he said. But he didn't look fine. He looked odd. Dishevelled. And he . . .

Urgh

– she sniffed the air, bemusedly.
'You stink . . .' she muttered, 'like a bomfire or something.'
'*Bon*fire,' he corrected her, with a smile.
'That's what I just said.'
'No. You said bo*m*fire.'
'Exactly.'
'Bom-fire. B-o-m. It's bo*n*fire.'
His neck and his shoulder suddenly convulsed as he spoke. He put a hand to his head.
'Are you all right?' she repeated.

'I was looking for my dad,' he said, peering around him, vaguely, as if Beede might be anywhere. 'He wasn't at home and he's gone from the laundry . . .'

'Why?'

'Pardon?'

'Why are you lookin' for him?'

'Why . . . ?'

His eyes alighted on the photocopied sheets. 'What's that you're reading?'

'What's what?'

She quickly flipped back her counterpane to try and obscure them.

'That,' he pointed, undeterred. 'How'd you get a hold of it?'

'Uh . . .'

'Did Beede give it you?'

'Beede?'

'Yeah.'

He put his hand to his head again.

'D'you wanna sit down for a minute?'

She pointed to a chair. He went and sat down on it. As he moved she noticed that he was limping slightly.

'Did you hurt your foot?'

'My foot? No. It's just my trainers . . .'

'Oh. So you got my text, then?'

'Your text?' he murmured. 'Sure. Sure I did.'

'And?' she persisted.

'And what?'

'Ain't ya pissed?'

'Pissed? Why?'

'Why?! Because that stunted Turkish *prick* made a *pass*,' she paused. *'And* he trashed my fuckin' salad . . .'

'Right . . .'

Kane grimaced, then he nodded, then he reached a distracted hand to his phone as it vibrated in his pocket. Kelly gazed at him with a look of burgeoning incredulity. It took several seconds for him to even register her disquiet.

'What kind of a pass?' he finally asked.

'That must be some high-calibre fuckin' *zong* you're on,' she observed, tightly.

He ignored her. 'What kind of a pass?' he repeated.

'*Duh!*' she threw up her arms. 'He *snogged* me.'
'Ah . . .'

Kane's eyes wandered aimlessly around the ward.
'On the *mouth*.'
She pointed to her mouth (it was a sweet, little mouth).
'*Here* . . .'

'I see . . .'
He idly noticed how a nearby window had been propped permanently open with the aid of a balled-up surgical glove. He shivered, involuntarily.

'Is that all you've got to say?' she asked, hurt.
His eyes slowly returned to her. 'How d'you mean?'
'Is that the best you can *muster*?'

Muster?!

His brows rose a fraction. 'So you think I could do better?' he smiled, finally engaging with her.
'Yeah, actually.'
'How?'
'Ditch him.'

'What?' He abruptly stopped smiling.

'Sack him.'
'*Seriously?!*'
'One hundred per cent.'

'Just for a kiss . . . ?' Kane slowly shook his head. '. . . *Nah.*'
'Why not?' she demanded. 'You ditched me in a flash, an' we dated eight, solid *months*, so why not ditch him?'
'Because.'
'*Because?!*'
'Because it's *different*, Kelly.'
He sounded bored, like this was tired, old territory.

'*Different?* You don't know him from fuckin' *Adam*, mate. He could be anyone. He's takin' the damn *piss* . . .'
He rolled his eyes.
'And it ain't only me as thinks so, neither,' she continued hotly, 'he's been givin' my poor old mum the runaround . . .'

'Your *poor old mum*?!' he grinned.

'*Yeah*. Playin' with her feet. Walkin' the dogs. She even took him out *shoppin'* . . .'

Kane chuckled, delightedly.

'He's been schmoozing my *mum*, Kane,' Kelly exclaimed, riled by his hilarity.

'So where's the harm in that?'

'Where's the *harm*? It's *sick*, for one thing. An' she ain't got the *money* to support no Toy Boy, for another . . .'

'*Sick*? Sick of your poor old mum to have a bit of fun?'

'*Fun*? He's been leadin' the poor cow *on*.'

Kane suddenly stopped grinning. 'Maybe he actually fancies her,' he said, in all apparent seriousness.

'Fuck *off*!'

'*Jeez*,' Kane slowly shook his head, 'the arrogance of the young . . .'

His eyes returned, almost inexorably, to the propped-up window. 'Well he can't fancy her *that* much,' she sniffed, 'if he went an' porked Gerry behind her back.'

'He didn't shag her,' Kane said.

'The ignorant *fuck*,' she scowled.

'He didn't shag her,' Kane repeated.

'All he needs now,' she ignored him, 'is to make the moves on my sister an' he'll have the full bloomin' *complement* . . .'

'God, no,' Kane muttered, 'surely even Gaffar couldn't stoop *that* low?'

Kelly stared at him, open-mouthed.

'And what about your aunt? Doesn't she count?'

Kelly flared out her nostrils and sucked on her tongue.

'Anyway,' Kane maintained, 'he didn't shag Gerry. He just came between her tits.'

'*What?*'

'She told me. She said he came between her tits. They didn't shag.'

'Oh. My. *God*.'

'Her tits *are* amazing,' Kane added, almost as an afterthought.

Silence

'I honestly don't believe you just said that.'

Kelly's back was straight as a ramrod.

'Said what? That her tits are great? Whyever not? Her tits *are* great. It's an objective *fact*.'

'That ain't the point, Kane.'

'That's *exactly* the point . . .'

'No.'

She seemed cut to the quick.

'Of *course* it's the point,' he maintained (pretending not to notice), then, 'Those bastards fired her from her job at the salon, did she tell you?'

'He's a thief,' she interrupted him, coldly.

'Who is?'

'Gaffar.'

'*Gaffar* again? Are you *obsessed* with the poor man? What did he steal?'

She pointed to the photocopied sheets.

Kane looked bemused. 'But why?'

'Why what?'

'Why would Gaffar steal those?'

She shrugged, scratching at her nose. 'I dunno . . .'

'Maybe because you *asked* him to?' Kane speculated.

She glared at him, wordlessly.

'Jesus *H*, Kell.'

He slowly shook his head.

'You thought I stole those drugs an' you sacked *me*,' she whined, rapidly back-pedalling, 'but I *never* stole them . . .'

'Fine.'

Kane shrugged.

'Whaddya mean, "fine"?'

'I believe you. I believe you didn't steal them. I apologise for accusing you. I was wrong.'

'It was *Beede* what stole them,' she blurted out, unable to contain herself.

He stared at her, blankly.

'Beede,' she repeated, almost guiltily.

'He *told* you that, did he?'

'No.' She shook her head, plainly surprised by the casualness of his reaction. 'I worked it out.'

'How?'

'I dunno. He stole them to pay back the bitch who killed Paul. Your *ex*. Seems like those two've been gettin' pretty *cosy* . . .'

'That's bullshit,' Kane scoffed, 'and, strictly speaking, Paul isn't actually *dead*, is he?'

Her jaw dropped. 'That's exactly what your stupid *dad* said . . .'

'Well he isn't, is he? He's just . . .'

'What *is* it with the two of you lately?'

She gazed at him, perturbed.

Kane stood up. 'I gotta go,' he murmured, 'I need a smoke . . .' He felt around in his pockets for his cigarettes. 'And I'm sorry about all that other shit,' he said, pulling out his phone and inspecting it '. . . the drugs, your leg . . .'

'All that other shit?' she echoed, blankly.

He shoved the phone away again. 'I'll have a quiet word with Gaffar. I'll tell him to back off . . .'

He spoke with great sincerity, almost tenderly. She continued to stare at him, passively, as if dazed.

'And I'm really sorry about your mum . . .'

He pulled out his fags.

'My mum?'

She frowned, slowly emerging from her stupor.

'I told Gaffar to be nice,' he tapped a cigarette out and stuck it into his mouth. 'It was just part of the service.'

'Back up a minute . . .' she scowled, 'I ain't followin' . . .'

'I told him to do it. I *paid* him.'

She allowed this news to sink in for a second.

'An' *muggins*, here?' she demanded, pointing to herself, indignantly.

'Pardon?'

He was searching for his lighter.

'Did you tell him to butter *me* up?'

'In your case,' he smiled, removing the cigarette and propping it behind his ear (as a tutting nurse marched by), 'he didn't take much asking . . .'

'*Wow* . . .' She slowly shook her head, her few paltry illusions finally shattering, 'I honestly can't believe what a *tit* I've been. What an unbelievable fuckin' *tit* . . .'

He found his lighter. An old blue *bic*.

'. . . What a total, brainless, fuckin' *ditz* . . .'

He glanced up.

'You was just *bored*!' she exclaimed, almost as if delighted by this cruel insight. '*That's* the honest truth of it. There *was* no mystery. You just wanted rid an' I was too clueless to see it . . .'

'It wasn't like that,' he maintained.

'Bollocks it wasn't.'

'Look . . .'

'Fuck off,' she interrupted, flapping him away with her bony hand.

'Please don't get all narky, Kell . . .'

'Narky?' The veins stood out on her neck. '*Narky?!* You think *this* is narky?'

'Okay,' he shrugged, 'whatever. You can think what you like . . .'

'I will,' she said, still flapping.

He pointed to the photocopied sheets. 'Should I return those to Beede for you?'

'Nah. Don't trouble yourself,' she snapped.

He stared at her, perplexed.

'I'm *am* sorry,' he muttered, shrugging. 'You're a funny girl, a *sweet* girl . . .'

'Fuck *off*, already,' she hissed, turning her sharp face away and slamming her head, violently, into her pillow, then lifting it, cussing, and repeating the process, twice.

TWO

Beede shone the torch into the rear of the car, briefly illuminating the hunched-up form of a small, sleeping child, covered in a messy pile of clothes and coats and blankets. The dog sat nearby, stiff and alert, her huge, round eyes reflecting the light of the torch eerily back at him.

'I'd've kept the heater on,' Elen said, shivering, 'but I was worried the battery might go flat.'

She looked terrible, bedraggled.

'You must be freezing,' he exclaimed, reaching out his hand to touch the damp fabric of her sleeve, 'and you're soaked through . . .'

'It rained steadily,' she said, 'while we were searching . . .'

'Drive him home,' he told her gently, 'and have a warm bath, a hot drink. That'll soon sort you out.'

She nodded, but she didn't seem to be listening. Her eyes were scanning the dark horizon.

'Drive him home,' he repeated. '*Seriously*. There's nothing more you can do here.'

'We were talking about the woods,' she said, 'and then there was this stupid . . . this *misunderstanding*. He mentioned Bixley several times. It seemed important. He had this strange kind of . . . I don't know . . .' her voice gradually petered out.

She unfolded the map and pointed. 'I found his shoe and his jumper here . . .' She pointed again '. . . This is where he left the car.'

'That's about 3, 4 miles,' Beede calculated. 'So he was travelling at speed . . .'

'I just headed straight for the wooded areas,' she shrugged, helplessly, 'more out of instinct than anything . . .'

She passed him the map as if she couldn't bear touching it any more, as if she was disgusted by it, by the places that it had unwittingly led her. Her hands were shaking.

'Thanks.'

He took it, folded it and thrust it into his coat pocket.

'No,' she said. '*No*. Thank *you*. I don't know what I'd've done if you hadn't come.'

She stared down at the damp tarmac, utterly drained and forlorn, swaying slightly in the blustering wind.

'Come here,' he suddenly found himself murmuring, holding out his arms (or if it wasn't him – and how *could* it be? – then it was the gentle one, it was *Danny* who called to her). She moved slowly towards him as if propelled not so much by whim as by a terrible inability to actually resist anything. He drew her, protectively, to his chest. She fell against him, a dead weight at first and then she suddenly reached out her arms and clasped her hands tightly around him, pushing her face into his neck with a tiny expulsion of breath. Her nose was icy against his skin. He flattened out his palms and gently patted her back. She felt so tiny to him, so thin, like some kind of fragile mouse or bird, and her hair was so soft, smelled so sweet, like marzipan and fresh linen.

He touched his cheek to the side of her head. His lip almost brushed her ear.

She was shivering. She was icy.

'You're so cold,' Danny whispered, 'slip your arms under my coat.'

She nodded and unfastened her hands. He yanked open his coat and enveloped her in it, pulling the front flaps either side of her and securing them with his arms. She nestled against him, her own arms pulled up close in front of her at first and then gradually – as she felt his warmth – her hands flattened against his chest and then worked their way around his ribs, around his sides, around his back, until they made contact with each other, then one hand fell, slid slowly down, until it reached the waist of his trousers. On the left-hand side – where his shirt had come untucked – her icy fingers touched his skin.

He shuddered, closed his eyes and breathed her in.

She snuggled up still closer. He thought she might be crying.

'There,' he whispered softly, 'hush.'

'I felt so lonely,' she said, 'so *cold* inside, and the day went on forever. And everything I *did* . . . everything I *said* was just . . .'

Her body shook.

He lifted his hand and cupped it around the back of her nape, pushing his fingers into the delicately boned base of her skull, then gently angled her head under his chin, her cheek into his collarbone.

'Save me,' she implored him, pushing her smooth forehead against the gap in his shirt, but Beede didn't hear her (Thank God he didn't hear her – what could Beede do, after all?), only Danny heard and Danny said, 'I'll look after you. I'll take care of you. Don't worry any more. You're perfectly safe here.'

'I feel safe,' she said, breathing into him, and he could feel her lips parting and the warmth of her breath on his skin.

Kane was standing in the steamy bathroom (the door propped open to improve the ventilation), carefully greasing back his wayward blond mane with the aid of a small quantity of coconut hair oil. He'd recently bathed and shaved, had applied a modest amount of cologne, was wearing a clean, grey t-shirt, a soft, white, Adidas hoodie and a new pair of dark-blue, engineered Levis. He looked pristine.

'So,' Gaffar said, wandering in and pulling off his leather jacket. 'You speak for Kelly, eh?'

'I had a call from Hinxhill at five,' Kane said, perusing the blur of Gaffar in the fogged-up mirror. 'Did you finally make it over there?'

'Sure.'

'And Kempe's Corner?'

'Sure.'

'How was the weather?'

'*Urgh*. Bad. Is *rain*, eh?'

'And the scooter?'

'Slow for start . . .'

Gaffar impersonated the engine with a series of dry, hacking coughs. 'Piece of shit. *Italia* . . .'

He turned and indicated fastidiously towards the splashes of mud on the back of his trousers.

'How was Martha?' Kane wondered.

'Crazy,' Gaffar said. 'She make me read from book, but . . .' he shrugged.

'The poetry?' Kane smiled, fondly. 'The tiny little yellow hardback? Emily Dickinson?'

Gaffar looked blank.

'Or was it Blake this time?'

Gaffar shook his head. 'I dunno. Was all crazy.'

'Martha *loves* Emily Dickinson.'

'Crazy woman.'

'And Bert?'

'Nothing. No words.'

'Really . . . ?'

Kane turned to face him, concerned. 'He didn't actually speak?'

'Nothing. Jus, "Why *you* here? Where is this *Kane*?"'

'Did he seem depressed at all?'

'Sure he was depress.'

'Was he clean?'

'*Clean?*' Gaffar frowned. 'Sure he was clean.'

'Well that's generally a good sign. Whenever Bert gets seriously miserable his hygiene's always the first thing to go. I'll need you to keep an eye on that for me, okay?'

Gaffar nodded. Kane returned to his hair again. 'Bert was pretty much a tramp when we first met – had this huge, long beard, filthy nails, lived in absolute squalor. Never washed. Was physically overwhelmed – he told me once – *emotionally* overwhelmed by the touch of water. Being caught out in a rainstorm would leave him virtually disabled – I mean for *weeks*. Beaten. *Pummelled*. He's just wired all wrong. You'd be surprised how many people are, how difficult their lives can be . . .'

Gaffar nodded again, his eyes ranging, boredly, around the room. 'The medication he'd been prescribed was a disaster,' Kane continued, '*totally* inappropriate to the range of symptoms he had. His doctor simply couldn't give a shit. Didn't have a clue. He's one of those old-school, stiff-upper-lip types who thinks a warm bath and a good meal are enough to cure 95 per cent of all human ills. My involvement with him goes *way* back. He actually cared for my mother before she died – kept her *criminally* undermedicated right up until the end. He's an intergalactic *twat* . . .'

Gaffar slowly began unwinding Kane's scarf from around his neck. He plainly wasn't focussing.

'I wondered where that thing'd gotten to,' Kane observed.

Gaffar grunted, unapologetically.

'So did he let you bring in his firewood?'

'Huh?' Gaffar stopped unwinding.

'Bert. Did you bring in his firewood?'

'Sure. *Sure*. And I do wash up, like you say. I turn on radio, for bit music, and then . . .'

Gaffar threw up his hands, grimacing.

'*Fuck*. You messed with his *radio*?!' Kane spun around, horrified. 'Bert has ears like a friggin' *bat*, I *told* you that. He's very sensitive. *Incredibly* sensitive . . .'

'I have chicken,' Gaffar said, thumbing over his shoulder, 'is roast, whole.'

'Yeah?' Kane's horror was immediately assuaged by the prospect of food. 'Is it still hot?'

He sniffed at the air, hungrily.

'Sure. You wan eat? You go out?'

'Go out? In *this* weather? No way.'

'Oh. Okay . . .'

Gaffar gave Kane's smart outfit a meaningful once over then shrugged and wandered off.

Kane held his hands under the warm tap until the grease melted from his fingertips, then he strolled into the living-room, threw himself down on to the sofa and lifted his bare feet – with a slight wince – on to the coffee table. On the tv was a dramatic re-enactment of a true-life adventure in which two men were trapped high on a mountain in a raging blizzard. They'd tied themselves together, for safety, but one man had just slipped off a sheer precipice and was now dangling, unsteadily, in the pitch dark, hundreds of feet below the other.

The camera – having investigated the unenviable circumstances of the fallen man in pornographic detail – suddenly switched back to studying the plight of the man who hadn't fallen. He was struggling to sustain the weight of his partner. He couldn't pull or grip on to the rope properly. He was exhausted. His fingers were severely frost-bitten. He was in serious danger of slipping down himself.

'Cut the the rope, man!' Kane exclaimed, leaning forward and gently massaging one of his feet. 'It's his own stupid fault. He's just gonna drag you down there with him . . .'

As he spoke he peered at his foot. He frowned. His feet looked different, somehow. The toes appeared compressed, almost squashed, as if they'd been squeezed – over time – into a bizarre, triangular mould. The big toe slanted dramatically inwards, and there was notice-able callusing on several of the smaller toes.

He inspected his other foot. It looked similarly mis-shapen. He wiggled his toes. They felt stiff, almost arthritic –

Hmmn

He leaned back again, grimacing, remembering his mother. He remembered her feet – her dancer's feet: distorted, bulbous, over-arched and ugly – he remembered massaging them for her some-times, as a boy, as a special treat.

While considering his mother's feet he noticed a slight, fluttery feeling in his stomach (which he promptly dismissed as an excess of appetite –

When did I last eat?).

He wriggled his toes again (then *again*, almost obsessively), in a determined bid to try and loosen them up a bit.

Gaffar, meanwhile, was in the hallway, whistling jauntily, dishing up the chicken. He served it with a cold ratatouille, some hummus and several toasted pockets of pitta bread.

He brought two plates through and passed one to Kane with the useful addition of a small piece of kitchen roll to be employed as a serviette.

'You're a God,' Kane said, taking it from him and swinging his feet back down on to the floor again.

Gaffar sat next to him, then glanced over and espied (with a disap-proving *cluck*) Kane's newly greased head pressed up against the upholstery. He nudged Kane to make him lean forward, then placed a spare piece of kitchen roll over the headrest to try and preserve the fabric from the impact of his hair oil.

'*Aw*, thanks, honey,' Kane said.

'So . . .' Gaffar stretched out his legs as he grappled with a chicken wing, 'you speak for Kelly?'

'Yeah . . .' Kane nodded, leaning back again, balancing his plate on his stomach, tearing off a small piece of bread and scooping up some ratatouille, '*Yeah*. She told me all about how you trashed her salad.'

'*Wah?!*' Gaffar gaped.

'She said you trashed her salad and then you snogged her. She was absolutely, fuckin' *livid* about the whole thing . . .'

Kane chewed on his mouthful, dispassionately.

'For *why* she say this?' Gaffar asked, infuriated.

'Did you happen to see Beede lately?' Kane wondered, swallowing.

'Beede?'

'Yeah. He's not at home and he wasn't at the laundry . . .'

'I been work, eh? *Hard* work,' Gaffar gesticulated irritably, 'how I'm suppose see him *there*?'

He snorted, infuriated.

'Do they eat much hummus in Turkey?' Kane wondered, peering at it, inquisitively.

'Sure.'

'Really? I always had it pegged as a Greek speciality.'

Gaffar shrugged. 'Is Greek, Arab, *Turk* . . .'

The mountaineer who hadn't fallen suddenly began hacking with a knife at the rope which suspended his partner in a desperate bid to save his own life.

'They crucified him for this,' Kane said. 'Did you ever read about it?'

'Huh?'

Gaffar squinted at the screen.

'He cut him off. It's a total breach of climbing etiquette. But he'd've died otherwise, for sure. The real irony is that even though they both actually *survived* as a direct consequence of what he did, he was treated like some kind of criminal – a *pariah* – in mountaineering circles for years afterwards . . .'

Kane scooped up some hummus on a second chunk of pitta. 'There are many imponderables in this life of ours, Gaffar,' he murmured, 'but one irreducible fact is that people who climb mountains are invariably cunts.'

'*Sheeesh*,' Gaffar exclaimed, gazing at the screen. '**What a treacherous rat! Is he seriously gonna cut that?**'

'Kelly told me to sack you,' Kane said, gently popping the bread into his mouth.

'Pard?'

Gaffar turned from the tv, with a slight start, at the exact moment that the knife finally sliced through the rope.

'Yeah . . .' Kane chewed and then swallowed as the suspended mountaineer dropped, like a stone, into an apparently bottomless icy fissure. 'She wanted me to fire you. *Seriously*. She claimed you were romancing her *mother*.'

'*Huh?*'

'Dina Broad.'

Kane smirked. He performed an obscene gesture with his hands.

Gaffar looked astonished. 'Dina Broad?' He paused. 'Dina *Broad*?!'

'Yeah. And she was furious about Gerry, too. She said all you needed to do now was fuck her sister, then you'd've tried it on with her entire family . . .'

Kane chuckled as he tore off another piece of bread, his eyes returning, irresistibly, to the drama on the screen. 'Which I actually thought was kinda *funny* . . .'

'*Sister?*' Gaffar was still struggling to catch up.

'Yeah. She has a sister. A fucking psychopath. Lives in Gillingham. You ever been there?'

Gaffar shook his head. Kane suddenly winced and then quickly adjusted the position of his right foot.

'Don't bother. She's a Nazi. Built like a brick shithouse . . .'

'All this Broad girls is big *mouth*, huh?' Gaffar threw down his chicken wing, piqued.

'You better believe it.'

Gaffar glowered at the tv. The falling mountaineer had been fortunate enough to land on a small, jutting shelf, about 20 metres into the icy fissure. He lay there, unconscious, for a while.

'It's always been kinda hard to gauge these things with Kell,' Kane mused, 'she's a *Broad*, after all – but I got the weird impression this afternoon that she was protesting a little too much, you know? Like somewhere deep inside of her – and I mean *way* deep inside – she might've been feeling just a teensy-bit conflicted, a teensy bit *jealous*, if you see what I mean . . .'

'*Huh?*'

Gaffar's head snapped around. 'Jealous? For *why*?'

Kane shrugged. 'That's the million dollar question, my friend.'

Gaffar stared at him, quizzically.

'Her mother's a total piss-taker – that goes without saying – but Kelly's hardly a pushover. It might seem that way at first – to the casual observer – but the dynamic between them is so much more complex . . . It's hardly a coincidence, for example, that Kelly's so skinny and Dina's so fat. There's a measure of co-dependency there. Kelly doesn't just starve herself but she actively *facilitates* Dina's weight problem. It's like she derives some strange kind of pleasure from feeding her mother, from fattening her up, from doing everything she can to effectively *disable* her. It's a complicated relationship. For Kelly, looking after Dina – being indispensable to Dina – makes her feel important. It's an essential part of how she places value on herself . . .'

Gaffar frowned.

'. . . Then suddenly here *you* come along with your massages, your Mediterranean good looks, your shopping trips . . .'

Kane smiled, inscrutably, as he pulled a stray piece of skin off a thick slice of chicken breast and then shoved it into his mouth.

'But Kelly is for *asking* me to look after this mother!' Gaffar exclaimed, indignantly.

'Yeah . . .' Kane chewed and swallowed. 'Who can possibly understand the vagaries of the female mind, eh?'

Gaffar turned back to the tv, dissatisfied.

'See that?' Kane said. 'He's fractured his leg. The rope's been cut so he can't climb back up. He knows that if he stays put he's gonna die, so his only possible chance of survival is to gradually lower himself down – into the darkness – still further . . .'

They continued eating.

'Did you happen to notice,' Kane suddenly quizzed him, 'how Beede's locked the door into his flat?'

'Beede?'

'Yeah. He locked his door.'

'Sure.' Gaffar nodded.

'You noticed that?'

'Sure. In morning. I take . . . uh . . . *dish*? For cook? But door is lock.'

'The really strange thing about it,' Kane's eyes remained focussed on the screen, 'is that Beede *never* locks his door. I don't think I've ever *seen* that door locked. I didn't even know that there *was* a lock on it.'

'Maybe he fear thief?' Gaffar speculated.

'Kelly did mention how she'd asked you to steal some papers for her,' Kane volunteered.

'Sure.'

Gaffar didn't trouble himself in denying it. 'But this lock is *before* I steal paper.'

'Before?' Kane frowned. 'So how'd you go about it?'

'Uh . . . I steal from Tesco,' Gaffar murmured, as if this key piece of information was of no real interest, 'from Beede bag.'

'Tesco's?'

Kane looked at him askance.

'Ya.'

'You saw Beede at Tesco's?'

'Sure.'

'Really?'

'Sure.'

'But . . .' Kane frowned, confused '. . . but Beede hates Tesco's. He never goes to Tesco's. He disapproves of Tesco's.'

As Kane spoke he reached down again, wincing, towards his foot.

'Okay,' Gaffar opined, unhelpfully.

'Well it's a fact,' Kane insisted, 'Beede hates Tesco's. He loathes the impact of big supermarkets on the High Street. He always shops locally. It's not just an idle preference, it's ideological.'

Gaffar shrugged.

Silence

'So what was he doing exactly when you saw him at Tesco's?' Kane wondered.

'Uh . . .'

Gaffar picked at his teeth a while, thoughtfully.

'Was he shopping?'

'Sure.'

'Did you happen to see what he was shopping for?'

'I see him *uh* . . .' Gaffar frowned, 'is in *front* supermarket, yeah? With lady. He is *talk* with this lady.'

'A woman? What did she look like?' Kane's chin suddenly jerked up. 'Did she have brown hair? Did she have long, brown hair?'

'No. No *brown* hair. Is *blonde*. *You* know . . . is this lady . . . *uh* . . . Mon-*key* . . .'

'What?'

'Mon-*key.*'

'A *monkey* lady?'

As he spoke, Kane's shoulder convulsed, dramatically.

'*Fuck.*'

He grabbed at it, then grabbed at his plate, to stop it from falling.

Gaffar stared at him, perplexed. 'No *monkey*, Mon-*key.* Laura Mon-*key.*'

'Oh *shit* . . . I get ya,' Kane exclaimed, 'Mon*keith*. Laura Mon*keith* . . .'

Gaffar snapped his fingers.

'So he was talking to *Laura*?'

'Sure.'

'Outside *Tesco's*?'

'Sure.'

'*Wow.*'

Kane dwelt on this for a moment, still rubbing at his shoulder. 'So lemme get this straight: they're in the middle of this private conversation, yeah? This *intimate* conversation – close to the trolleys, out front, when you – Gaffar – just suddenly, quite randomly, roll up and surprise them?'

'Sure.'

'How very odd . . .'

Gaffar shrugged, indifferent.

'But you were discreet?' Kane asked. 'With Laura, I mean?'

'Sure,' Gaffar nodded, blithely. 'I go. I say hello.'

Gaffar re-enacted a jovial wave.

Kane winced (this wasn't the response he'd been angling for). 'And what did Laura do? Did she acknowledge you? Did she seem pissed off at all?'

'*Piss?!*' Gaffar grinned. 'She is *shit her pant*! This Laura she is saying, "I never see this Gaffar! I don't know of this Gaffar!" Then she is run away.'

Gaffar impersonated a panicked Laura running off.

'She was embarrassed?'

'Exact.'

'Okay . . .' Kane nodded, thoughtfully. 'So just as an idle point of interest, Gaffar, do you happen to recall that long discussion we had – a couple of days ago – about client confidentiality?'

Gaffar gazed at him, blankly.

'Client confidentiality,' Kane reiterated. 'That chat we had. About how I tend to think it best – as a rule – *never* to acknowledge any of our clients in public . . . I mean except with their express say-so, obviously?'

'*Ah* . . . Yes. Sure.' Gaffar nodded.

'You *remember* that?'

'Sure,' Gaffar repeated, amiably.

'Right . . . *Good*.'

Kane stared at the tv a while, frowning.

'So once Laura had run off,' he soon doggedly recommenced his former line of enquiry, 'you casually stole the document from Beede's bag?'

'No. *No* . . .' Gaffar seemed to find this notion quite ridiculous. 'First we have tea.'

'Tea with Beede?'

'Sure. We talk.'

Kane's brows rose slightly.

'You *talked*? What did you talk about?'

'Uh . . . chit-chat: shop, tree, pretty manager, *bell* . . .'

'Bell?'

Kane's ears pricked up.

'Sure. Bell on cat.'

'Oh *God*, yes . . .' Kane chuckled. 'That friggin' *bell* . . .'

Gaffar continued to eat his meal.

'So what did you say?' Kane wondered.

'Eh?'

Gaffar glanced up, mid-mouthful.

'About the cat. Did you *admit* to hanging the bell on it?'

Gaffar gazed at him for a few seconds, wordlessly, as if quite astonished.

'What's wrong?'

Kane took another bite of pitta.

'Wrong? . . .' Gaffar slowly swallowed his mouthful. 'You thing *I* hung bell?' He pointed to his chest. 'Gaffar? You thing *Gaffar* hung bell?'

'Uh . . .' Kane frowned (seeming to have nothing vested in this issue, either way), 'I dunno . . .'

'Okay . . .' Gaffar gently placed his plate down on to the coffee table. 'So . . . *Okay* . . . **Let me finally get this thing straightened out, once and for all,** eh?'

He spoke slowly and deliberately. 'I. *Me.* Gaffar. Not. Hang. Bell. Cat.' He drew a deep breath. 'Understan? Gaffar . . .' he pointed to his chest, 'is *not* hang bell cat.'

'Right.' Kane nodded. 'Fine. Whatever.'

Gaffar gripped firmly on to his knees with both hands. '. . . **Because it's starting to weigh me down a little – the whole** cat **thing, the whole** bell **thing . . . First your father insinuates it, and then you do. Yeah? And I'm not entirely sure if the confusion that's developing between us here is based on some fundamental linguistic or cultural difference, or if I'm actually just living in a complete** fucking *nuthouse* **– but the fundamental facts of the matter – as I see them – are that I've been keeping myself** pretty *busy*, yeah? **Cooking meals, cleaning the flat, dressing my wound, carrying firewood, picking up dog shit, giving massages to bad-tempered, bloated, 25-stone harpies, visiting the hospital, buying** *salad*, **making out with a silent, huge-breasted, voyeuristic** Goff **as you blithely masturbate in your leather tv recliner . . .'**

'*Goth*,' Kane corrected him.

'**. . . stealing papers from people's bags,**' Gaffar continued, undaunted, '**riding a badly engineered Italian** *scooter* **all over this godforsaken town while your stinking** English **weather** pisses **endlessly down . . .** Pretty damn *busy*, yeah?'

'Absolutely,' Kane said, nodding.

'**On that basis, I'm sure you can imagine,**' Gaffar continued, '**that it comes as something of a surprise to me – perhaps even a shock, at some level – that you and your father seem so determined to believe that I,** Gaffar, **in the midst of all this frenzied – if fundamentally pointless – activity, somehow have the time – or the inclination – to hang a stupid** bell **on an ugly** fucking *cat*.'

He stared at Kane, somewhat short of breath, his dark eyes bulging. '*Okay?*'

'Sure,' Kane shrugged.

'*Okay?*'

Silence

Gaffar picked up his plate and recommenced with his meal.

'Feeling better?' Kane enquired amiably, after a brief duration.

'Fuckin' *lid*,' Gaffar muttered, 'fuckin' *rug*, fuckin' *drug*, fuckin' *salad*, fuckin *cat* . . .'

He screwed up his napkin and threw it down at the coffee table, in disgust.

They both watched tv a while.

'So you didn't, then?' Kane suddenly enquired.

'Pard?' Gaffar turned and stared at Kane, blankly.

'You didn't?'

Gaffar continued to stare.

'Hang the bell, I mean. You *didn't* hang the bell on the cat?'

Gaffar remained utterly motionless.

'*Ding! Ding!*'

Kane mimed the ringing of a tiny bell.

'*Miaow!*'

He impersonated a cat.

Silence

Gaffar slowly closed his eyes. He remained dangerously quiet for three – five – seven seconds and then –

'*Ha!*' he suddenly bellowed, his eyes flying open again, darting forward and slapping Kane (perhaps a fraction too firmly), on his thigh. 'You's *funny* guy, *eh*?'

Kane shrugged, modestly.

'No,' Gaffar insisted loudly (as if addressing a crowded public meeting), 'is *true*. You's *very*, very funny guy.'

Kane smiled.

'*Funny*, huh? In Turkey we has this *word* for funny guy like you,' he paused, dramatically, '**tiny cock!** Eh? **Baby cock! A man with a dick so small, so infinitesimal, it's the approximate size of a newborn child's. Tiny cock . . . mini cock. Peanut cock . . .**'

'Aw, *shucks*, man,' Kane interrupted him. '*Enough* already – you're *embarrassing* me here . . .'

On the tv, the fallen climber screamed out in agony as he began clumsily binding up his badly fractured leg. Kane patted his full stomach as he watched this painful process, then he burped, slid his empty plate on to the coffee table, leaned forward and peered down at his feet. He wiggled his toes and then gingerly stood up.

'You know what?' he murmured, feeling around inside his pockets for his car keys, his phone, his cigarettes. 'I actually gotta head outa here. Some stuff I forgot about. Stuff I need to take care of . . .'

He strolled into his bedroom to find his shoes and his jacket, was gone for several minutes and then returned, carrying an old pair of scuffed, brown Bludstones.

'You should keep on watching this,' he told Gaffar, indicating with the boots towards the tv, 'the next bit's fantastic. He cracks up. His mind starts to wander and the whole film turns into some crazy kind of *acid* trip . . .'

Gaffar stared at Kane, intently, as he spoke, an inexplicable smile playing around the corners of his lips.

'In fact there's a fine lump of hash in the old Gold Blend jar if you wanna make a night of it . . .' Kane continued, slightly unnerved by Gaffar's look. He pulled on his boots, with a grimace, then furtively rubbed at his nose (surreptitiously, while he was still bending over) in case something vile was hanging from it.

Gaffar's darkly ironic gaze continued to follow him as he prepared to exit.

'Great dinner,' Kane yelled over his shoulder, as a parting shot. '*Fantastic* dinner. Cheers for that.'

Gaffar's eyes narrowed slightly as Kane disappeared from view, then he turned and busily recommenced his meal, wondering – with an idle shrug – how long the small square of kitchen roll which was currently affixed to the back of his head might reasonably be expected to stay in situ.

THREE

She was hardly *overburdened* with stuff to occupy herself, and Gaffar (the horny, little runt) had gone to all the trouble of –

A-hem

– *borrowing* it for her, so she lounged back in her bed, propped up on her pillows, and she read it, at her leisure, from cover to cover.

It took ages (the lettering was all squiggly and the actal copy-quality was shite), but she read every damn *page* of it – every damn *word* (even the ones – and there were plenty of them – which she didn't have the first clue what they meant – like 'parbraked' or 'whiting' or 'apothecary' or 'tapster' –

?!).

And it was quite funny (actually) and stupid and *dirty* . . . all about con-tricks and wise-cracks and sex and bums and farts (especially farts); not the kind of stuff she could imagine *historical* people thinking about (or talking about or *doing*) – or *Beede* reading (or thinking about, or doing) either, for that matter.

There was this one story (for example) where Scogin (or Master John, or Master Scogin, or *John* Scogin – the geezer whose adventures the book was describing) played a prank on his college pals so he wasn't obliged to go hungry during Lent . . .

Lent?

Kelly called over a passing nurse and asked her if she knew what Lent was, and the nurse explained how she wasn't entirely sure but she thought it might be the few weeks between when Jesus died on the cross and when he rose again –

'Oh *yeah* . . . Like in *Carrie*? At the end of the film? When that evil fucker who threw pig's blood at her is layin' roses on her grave an' then – *Pow!* – this hand breaks out thru the soil an' grabs for his throat?'

'Well . . . Yes. *Kind* of . . . Jesus pushed back this huge boulder which was blocking up the entrance to his tomb . . .'

'So he was *mad*-strong, huh? Like a Power Ranger?'

'Yes . . . Well . . . he obviously had supernatural gifts of a *sort* . . .'

'An' he was all covered in *bandages*, weren't he? Like a mummy? I *remember* that from R.E. at school . . .'

'Yes. *Yes*. Bandages or . . . or maybe *robes* . . .'

'Wow. *Awesome*. An' *then* what?'

'Uh . . . I'm not entirely sure. He *spoke* to a few people, I imagine, to prove that he'd risen again . . .'

'Sprang out on 'em? Really shat 'em up? Big, meaty *nail* wounds still on his hands?'

'Uh . . . Well maybe not *quite* so . . .'

'Wow. An' then they *still* went on an' voted him God? Even after all his shady behaviour?'

'Uh. Yes. *Yes*. I suppose they did.'

Pause

'*Aw*. Check out your *face*! I'm jus' rippin' the *piss*, love.'

Anyhow, from what she could gauge, Lent was the time *in between* these two distinct phases (about six weeks or so, the nurse estimated) although the haughty old geezer in the bed opposite – who was *much* too good to mix with the other patients on the ward and spent all his days hidden behind drawn white curtains (Reverend Jacobs, they called him – because, Kelly supposed, he was totally Cream *Crackers* . . .

Geddit?)

– interrupted the nurse at this point (through his drapes, no less) and told her (in no uncertain terms, either) that she didn't know diddly-squat . . . 'Lent – you silly *goose* – starts on Ash Wednesday and commemorates the time when Jesus retreated into the desert and battled with his conscience for forty days and forty nights . . .'

Eh?!

'An' who the hell asked *you*, you interferin' old Gobshite?'

More properly, Lent was a time when religious people, people who went to church ('Yeah, yeah, *Catholics* and stuff') liked to cut back on sweets and booze . . .

'What? You mean like goin' on a special *diet* for Christ?'

'Exactly . . .' the nurse nodded, glancing anxiously towards the drawn, white curtains.

'Why?'

'Well to prove their *faith*, I suppose . . .'

'*Beezer!*'

'And to show they have some understanding of Christ's suffering, by suffering a little themselves . . .'

'*Brilliant!*'

'And then, when it's all over – at Easter – they can eat as much as they like.'

'*Yeah?* Chocolate eggs an' shit?'

'Yes.'

'An' Jesus is *cool* with that?'

'Yes. *Yes*. I believe he is.'

Anyway, Scogin wasn't meant to eat too much (or get pissed) during Lent (this was in olden-times, so everything was inevitably much more: *you* know . . . *yawn*) and he didn't have any spare money (any *wonga* – no *dosh*) to creep out of college and spend secretly at Nando's (or down the boozer, or wherever), so he came up with a cunning plan to get free entry into the college pantry (where all the food was stored – *Duh*!).

He did this by pretending that his 'Chamber Fellow' (the nonce who shared his room, poor bugger) was ill. It was the time of The Black Plague, and because none of the other scholars wanted to catch what the poor Fellow had, they gave Scogin the keys to the kitchen so that he could prepare him his food while nobody else was about (to avoid cross-contamination an' shit). Once Scogin had the keys, though, he just took what he liked (Lent be blowed, eh? He feasts like a king!).

After a few weeks, however, people started to get suspicious ('Oi! Where the hell's that lovely leg o' lamb?!') and they demanded to see the sick Fellow's 'water' (his piss – they wanna test it), but instead of providing them with a sample, Scogin held a burning candle to the poor Fellow's nose (an' his *lips*, so they blister up) and the sight of his apparent 'contagion' was so terrifying to behold that the Masters stopped harassing the conniving pair and allowed them to keep those precious keys for a few weeks longer.

Scogin and his Chamber Fellow consequently lived the Life of Reilly throughout all of Lent, eating what they liked, drinking and carousing, until Maundy Thursday when they enjoyed a huge, final blow-out at the college's expense –

Eh?

'Oi. *You*. Behind ya curtains. Old Smarty-pants. What's Maundy Thursday when it's at home?'
'Maundy Thursday' – his disembodied voice wafted through, 'is the last Thursday before Easter Friday. And I'm *delighted* to discover that you like my pants so much.'
'Ha *ha*. I don't like your pants. I *hate* your pants . . .'

Pause

'. . . So what's the *point* of it?'
'Well, traditionally it's a day on which the monarch likes to hand out cash gifts to paupers, but in terms of purely *religious* observance, it's generally celebrated,' he continued, somewhat dogmatically, 'with the old-fashioned custom of *feet* washing.'
'Fuck off, you nutter!'
'Look in the Bible and see for yourself – John XIII. XIV . . .'

A neat, hardback, King James Bible – its pages held together by an elastic band – came scytheing through the curtains towards her, landing – with a *thwack* – against her cast.

'*Ow!* Watch out! You tryin' to take Bible Bashin' to a whole new level or *what*?!'
Kelly grabbed the Bible and checked the reference (it took some time to find it): John XIII. XIV:

'If I then, your Lord and Master, have washed your feet, ye also ought to wash one another's feet.'

Que?!

Scogin and his Chamber Fellow (to get back to the *nub* of the matter) actually imbibe so royally on Maundy Thursday that the Chamber Fellow eventually passes into a dead faint (drunk as a skunk), at which point Scogin cheerfully strips him naked, rolls him up in a sheet and runs around the college telling everyone he's dead.

The remaining Masters all duly line up to inspect the body, sober preparations are made for a burial, and everything's proceeding very smoothly, when (*Aaaaarrrrrgh!*) the drunken Fellow suddenly awakens, takes fright, jumps to his feet and begins running around in a total panic. The Masters start yelling and screaming (thinking he's some kind of ghostly apparition), which makes him panic all the more and run still faster, until (inevitably) his scant coverings promptly fall off (yet more screams from the Masters). It's at this point (as he's sprinting about, in the raw, his goolies flapping) that Scogin takes the opportunity to commence yelling: 'A miracle! A miracle!', as if testifying to an act of Otherworldly Intervention (It's *Easter*, now, dammit! He's gonna be dining out on this sacrilegious little farce for *weeks*!).

!?
Hmmn . . .
Well maybe it weren't actually so funny as all that . . .

When the nurse arrived to serve her dinner (an hour or so later) Kelly calmly refused it. 'I'm dietin' for Jesus,' she announced piously (she just *liked* the idea, somehow). 'Oh . . . An' would you mind returnin' this holy *cosh* to Greta Garbo over there?'

The nurse did as she was bidden, returning the Bible ('Thank you, nurse,' he purred, 'that's *extremely* kind of you'), but then, when she attempted to serve the Reverend his meal: 'You know what? I think *I* might diet for Jesus, too . . .'

Pause

'. . . Although a nice, tall glass of iced tomato juice certainly wouldn't go amiss . . .'

Pause

'. . . a little squeeze of lemon, if it isn't too much trouble . . .'

514

Kelly glanced over towards the curtains, with a scowl.

'. . . with just the tiniest *dab* of Worcester Sauce,' he murmured, 'to render it more palatable.'

And then, once the nurse had gone: 'You don't mind if I keep you company?' his disembodied voice enquired, cordially.

'I don't mind *what* you do,' Kelly snapped.

'Holy *cosh* . . . ,' he mused. 'That was actually quite funny. Well done *you*.'

Kelly rolled her eyes.

'So you like giving things up, then, Kelly?' the Reverend asked.

'I'd like it if *you* gave up,' Kelly opined, returning to her reading.

'Could I ask you a special favour?' the Reverend wondered.

Kelly glanced over at the curtains for a second time.

'Nope.'

'It's just that now we're on this *fast* together . . .'

'Whaddya mean? *Fast?* I ain't on no fast.'

'Now that you're dieting for *Jesus* . . .'

'Who *cares* why I'm dietin'?!' she expostulated. 'It ain't none of your damn *business*.'

'But it *is* my business,' he maintained calmly, 'Jesus is my business, which makes *you* my business.'

Kelly threw down the photocopied sheets with a frustrated hiss.

'Why're you in here, anyways?' she asked, crossing her arms. '*Brain* tumour?'

'I'm here because God willed it,' he informed her.

'*Fuck* off!'

'He struck me down three times . . .'

'What? With his *fist*?'

'. . . and each time,' he ignored her, 'I was blessed with a singular vision.'

Silence

'An' what do the doctors make of *that*?' she asked.

'Of *what*?'

'Of God's willin' it an' stuff?'

'The doctors don't give a hoot about God's will. They think it was probably a minor stroke.'

'But God told you *different*, huh?' she sneered.

'Yup.' Reverend Jacobs seemed very sure on this point.

Kelly snorted, derisively, and grabbed a hold of her papers. She tried to find her place, but couldn't.

'If God made you sick,' she reasoned, slitting her eyes, 'then why don't he make you well again?'

'Ours is not to reason why,' the Reverend quoted.

'How old are ya?' she asked, scowling.

'I'm forty-two.'

(*Hmmn*. A mite *younger* than she'd calculated.)

'Old enough to know better . . .' she mused.

'Absolutely *not*,' he informed her, curtly. 'And I pray I never *shall* be, either.'

She stared at the curtains, quizzically. 'Why'd they keep your curtains shut?'

'It's the *glare*,' he sniffed, 'it makes me dizzy. The environmental *stress*. I'm actually wearing dark glasses behind here.'

Kelly pondered this for a moment.

'What kind?' she asked.

'Calvin Kleins,' he answered promptly, 'but a nice pair.'

She frowned.

'Are you a *real* Reverend, or is it your street name or your *tag* or what?'

'I suppose you could call me a kind of missionary. I work mainly in Canada. I've been on a sabbatical in England for seven months . . .'

'I broke my leg in three places,' Kelly promptly interrupted him, 'fallin' off a wall, an' I'm allergic to prescription painkillers . . .'

She paused, "spose you prob'ly think God had a hand in that, *too*, huh?'

'I try *not* to think, in general,' the Reverend sighed. 'I find those intellectual Christians such a *bane*, don't you? I'm what they call a "Charismatic". I'm sensitive. My relationship with God is predicated not on thought but on *love*.'

?!

Kelly slowly shook her head and returned to her papers. After a minute or so, however, she suddenly looked up, with a nervous start, swore, turned sharply and peered behind her, scowling, as if a mischievous hand had just snapped at her bra strap.

He didn't know Bixley Woods well. He'd visited them once, at best, ten (possibly even fifteen) years ago. It'd been spring – he recalled – and the Bluebells had been in full splendour; the forest floor a dense and seemingly infinite tapestry of gently shimmering cobalt-blue.

He'd been especially moved (he remembered) by the plight of the Wood Anemones, which – like the plainer, smarter sister in a Brontë novel – had been gradually shoved (by their more popular sibling) into the wood's inhospitable outer margins, where they clung on, tenaciously, seeming to positively thrive in the poor soil and dappled shade there. They were such fragile plants, so plain and sweet and tender . . . He smiled, fondly. But that was spring – his smile rapidly dissipated – and this was winter.

Once he'd left Elen –

Elen –
No . . .

Stop.

– he'd driven – his breath still irregular – along the A268, took a left at Two Hoven's Farm and pulled on to Bixley Lane. It was ludicrously dark here and so unimaginably wet that he felt like he was ploughing though a vicious jar of black Quink.

He changed down a gear as he headed past the old saw mill and a couple of small cottages, then put his lights on bright as he drew beyond. The woods crowded ever closer, glowering down at him, encroaching.

He didn't want to stop, but he took an old Landrover in a small layby –

Abandoned?
Dumped

– as a signpost (a pointer) and parked up close to it, in the hope of shading his bike (in its lee) from the worst of the weather.

He was quite wet already (tiny rivulets of water trickling down his back). His scarf was damp. He wore a woolly hat (which he'd hurriedly yanked from his rucksack after removing his helmet) and his thick, leather biking gloves. He had a compass – hung on a black cord around his neck – which he quickly inspected. He tried to pull out the map, but it was tipping down and the wind howled, so he thought better of it.

He was wearing solid boots (biking boots) but this didn't equip him for the voluminous puddles and the sticky expanses of mud on the initial track. It was a wide track. A good track, really, all things considered. He had a torch. Without a torch any kind of progress would've been totally unfeasible.

He trudged into the darkness, calling out, woodenly, at ten-second intervals.

'Dory?'

He felt strange – *surreal* – as if this wasn't actually a real search, just a pretend search, a search in a film, perhaps, which had already been carefully scripted to fail.

'*Dory?*' he called. 'Isidore?'

Two minutes in and he was drenched. He felt hopeless.

'*Dory?*'

After five minutes, he entered the pine forest. The weather wasn't nearly so extreme here and the ground was softer underfoot. The soles of his boots were cushioned by rotting ferns, old moss and pine needles which stuck to the mud he'd already accumulated until soon his feet were like two, huge, weighted blocks.

He stopped for a moment, out of breath, closed his eyes and tried to inhale the forest. He sniffed (as if desperate to reactivate his storm-battered senses, his curiously fragile sense of self), but the only thing to enter his nostrils was water. Water from the perpetual drip on the tip of his nose. He coughed.

He moved doggedly onward. Soon the wide track fractured into a dozen much smaller paths. He inspected the compass, shivering, then took a bold step forward and almost fell. A tendril of Bramble had hooked on to the sleeve of his coat. He pulled it off, cursing, but as he pulled he noticed something – a piece of cloth. He reached out for it, unhooked it and drew it closer to his face. He grimaced –

Boxer shorts . . .

He wrung them out and shoved them (grimacing, fastidiously) into his pocket.

'*Dory?*'

He felt overwrought. He felt too *old* to be heroic. Too *old* to be brave and dependable. Too *old*.

He tried to look around him, to focus, but his glasses were streaming. 'Dory? Are you there?'

Then, quite out of the blue – with almost no warning – his hackles rose. It was entirely unconscious – unwitting – *automatic*.

'*Dory?*' he pivoted on his heel. 'Is that you?'

He lifted his torch from ground-level, into the rain-soaked black, then gasped, stepping back, almost tripping.

Behind him – 7 feet away, at best – stood a stag. A giant stag. 'Holy Mary,' he said.

The stag gazed at him, blankly. It seemed dazed. It was an old one. Its horns were broken. Its pelt was thick in certain places (the shoulders, the rump), but intensely threadbare in others.

'Holy Mary,' he repeated, panicked, feeling the beat of his heart, almost *entering* his own heartbeat (through a funnel, a dark funnel, through his . . . his *head*? Where? His *ear*?) and then suddenly – an entirely *different* sensation (and yet the *same*, somehow) – he felt the beat of the stag's heart, he felt himself crushed up against it, against this bold and extraordinary *counter*-beat – he felt the stag's ears pricking up, turning towards him, he felt himself sucked in – the two beats merging and becoming one, pumping in tandem – charging on, *careering* on, in a riotous, shuddering gallop, twice as strong, twice as powerful – the same beat, the same breath, the same . . .

He took a second, blind step back, then a third, his boot hitting a tree trunk. He tried to push himself up against the tree, to become the tree (as he'd become the stag) but his rucksack blocked his body.

The stag glanced over its shoulder, away from him, distractedly. He felt the individual bones rippling in its neck.

He could still feel its heart, but softer now. The flare of its nostril . . . 'Heart,' he thought, then, 'hart. *Hart* . . .'

He scowled –

No.

'*Dory!*' he yelled, swinging the torch around.
'*Dory?!*'
He returned the blaze of the torch to the deer, but the deer was disappearing into the darkness, sinking into the darkness, being engulfed by the squall . . . Its beat gradually grew softer.

'*Dory!*' he yelled again, and as he yelled something hit him, square on the head.
He froze for a second, blinking, terrified, then he laughed – a cone, a *pine* cone! He took a small step forward, still laughing, searching for the cone with his torch, and as he searched – still chuckling, oddly engrossed, *childishly* engrossed in the search – a large, heavy branch came crashing down on to his back.

'I had three visions,' he told her, a little later on that evening (as she swallowed her pre-lights-out medication).
'Yeah,' she murmured, boredly. 'You already *said* . . .'

'In the first,' he continued (refusing to be put off), 'a man is standing next to a house. Everything seems fine. And then the house simply collapses. *Totally* collapses. But it's like in that old Buster Keaton gag – that black and white short – where the house falls around him but the man remains standing, apparently unhurt, in the middle of all this mess and chaos . . .'

'Hmmn. *Fascinatin',*' she said, picking up her phone and sending a quick text.

Nite MumXX

'In the second vision I saw a sheep leading its lambs to slaughter. Or if it wasn't a sheep it was a duck, or . . . or some *generic* creature . . . Animals aren't really my *bag* . . . But the *kind* of animal it was doesn't really matter — it was a *symbolic* image, a *metaphor* . . .'

''Course it was.'

'And in the third I saw a boy awaken from a long, deep sleep. He sits up. He looks around. He speaks. He says two words, very clearly . . .'

'Oh yeah? An' what's he *say*, Rev?' she asked, idly.

'I'm not sure. I don't remember.'

'Great.'

Kelly checked her texts. There was one from Gerry, one from her aunt, one from her dad, one from Jason, one from Gaffar and one from her mum.

Eh?!

She scowled, mystified.

'And now I'm dieting for Jesus,' he said, with apparent satisfaction.

'Well bully for you, mate.'

She rapidly scrolled down the messages and pressed ENTER.

FOUR

He was huge, or at least he appeared to be. A veritable titan. He was in his late thirties, early forties, heavily built with a pallid complexion (but flashes of high colour on his nose, chin and cheeks), wore a large, thick moustache (with tinges of red in it), a deer-stalker hat and an impressive collection of all-weather gear, topped off by a smart, camouflage jacket decorated with – Beede squinted – what looked like a bizarre photographic *montage* of twigs and leaves.

He was shining a torch directly into Beede's face as he lay – prone and winded – on the forest floor. Beede didn't realise (at this point) that it was actually *his* torch.

'Well that wasn't very clever of you,' the giant observed mockingly, 'was it now?'

He was drunk, Beede surmised. His breath reeked of alcohol –

Rum?
Brandy?

Beede slowly pulled himself up into a sitting position and blinked, owlishly, into the light. He flexed his shoulder, then his neck, then his leg. He felt a little stiff and creaky, but there was –

Thank God

– nothing sprained or broken, so far as he could tell.

He frowned, then put a tentative hand to his face –

Damn . . .

He'd somehow managed to dislodge his glasses in the fall. He pulled off his gloves, stuffed them into his pocket, then felt around, clumsily, on the ground surrounding him. As he reached out, blindly, a

522

cold, wet snout suddenly made contact with his bare skin. A warm tongue licked his knuckles. He snatched his hand away, alarmed.

'*Enough*, Gringo,' the man snapped. Beede squinted into the darkness. Just to his left he made out the rough outline of a small and extremely overweight, pure-white Jack Russell.

The man drew a step closer and peered rudely into Beede's face. 'You're getting a bit long in the tooth for this kind of lark, aren't you?' he asked.

'Pardon?'

Beede adjusted his hat which was currently hanging – somewhat rakishly – over one brow.

'A bit long in the tooth, a bit *old* . . .'

'I seem to have lost my glasses in the fall . . .'

Beede continued to pat at the floor around him.

The stranger shone the torch helpfully on to the ground, then took a step back.

'Careful not to stand on them,' Beede cautioned him.

'Nothing happens in these woods,' the man informed him, slurring his words a little, 'without me or Gringo here knowing about it.'

'Is that so?'

Beede glanced up, distractedly.

'She's been hard on your trail for the past twenty minutes,' he stared down at the dog, fondly, 'all in a bait, she was, so I left her to it. She tracked you down a real treat, she did.'

'Can you see anything?' Beede asked (neglecting to mention that he hadn't actually been in the woods that long). 'I really can't function without them . . .'

'No,' he said, barely even bothering to look.

'Are you *sure*? They must be around here somewhere.'

'I heard a voice calling out earlier,' the man said. 'Was it you?'

'Probably . . .' Beede was crawling around on his hands and knees now. 'I'm searching for someone. A friend of mine . . .'

'A *friend*?' he sneered.

'Yes.' Beede glanced up. 'Perhaps you'll've seen him? Tall, blond, German . . . He might've appeared . . .' he paused '. . . distressed.'

'A *male* friend?'

'He's German,' Beede continued, 'but he speaks excellent English . . .'

Beede stopped his search for a moment as something odd suddenly dawned on him –

The branch –
The fallen branch . . .

'Where's the branch gone?' he asked, rocking back on to his heels.
'What?'
'The branch. The branch that fell on me.'
The man stared at him for a second, blankly, and then, 'Oh. Yes. The branch. I moved that off,' he said, 'I threw it over there somewhere . . .'
He gesticulated, vaguely, towards the distant undergrowth.
Beede frowned. He felt a brief moment's disquiet.
'Isn't that *my* torch?' he asked.
'No.'

Pause

'Yes.'
'Could I have it back, then?'
Beede held out his hand. The man passed it over, sullenly.
'That's a good torch,' he said, 'very powerful.'
'It's an old torch,' Beede said, 'I've had it for twenty-odd years.'
'An oldie but a goldie,' the man quipped, leering down at him.
'So you live locally?' Beede asked.
'Me?'
He pointed to himself, stupidly.
'Yes.'
'Roundabout.'
'In Beckley?'
'Roundabout Beckley.'
'It's a filthy night to be hanging around in the woods,' Beede mused.
'We patrol these woods,' the man said (placing his hands on to his hips, as if rehearsing some kind of formal speech), 'summer, autumn, winter, spring – come rain or hail or shine.'
Beede nodded, his eye casually alighting on what he took to be –

No.
Surely not . . .

– some kind of ornately decorated, American-Indian-style –

Holster?
No.
Scabbard?

– *sheath* hanging around the man's waist. A sheath for a sword. Or a large hunting knife, perhaps.

'So you spend a lot of time here?'
He stated the obvious.
'I do.'
'Are you a warden of some kind? A gamekeeper?'

'You could call me a warden,' the man nodded. 'You could call me,' he paused, self-importantly, 'the *Guardian* of the Woods.'
'The King of the Woods, eh?' Beede murmured.
'What?'
'In ancient English myth there was this perplexing figure called The King of the Woods. He guarded a large Oak in the centre of the forest. He never slept . . .'

'I wouldn't know anything about *that*,' the man demurred, taking an unsteady step back.
Beede aimed the torch down at the forest floor again and bent over to recommence his search. He felt a sharp spasm of pain in his left shoulder as he moved it –

Ouch

'Did you see the deer?' he asked, suddenly remembering the deer, almost with a jolt.
'I've seen deer,' the man said, 'I've seen *plenty* of deer. But not tonight.'
'There was a huge deer,' Beede said, 'a stag. An old stag. Standing about 7 or so feet away. A magnificent creature.'

'I lost my bird,' the man said (defensively, almost competitively). 'I wasn't just hanging around.'
'Pardon?'
Beede glanced up again.

'My kite. My red kite. I keep birds of prey.'
'And you lost it?'
'Yes.'
'A red *kite*?'

'Yes. I flew him this afternoon – in the clearing just to the south of here – and while he was flying this other bird started to bother him, to *harass* him – which they will do, sometimes. It was a dark bird, a small bird, probably just a starling. But fierce. *Crazy.* Really caught him on the hop – put him on his mettle – until suddenly he got it into his *stupid* head . . .'

He tutted, 'He was an *ounce* over. Just an ounce. But that was all it took.'

'An ounce?'

'Yes. He was too heavy to fly . . .'

'If you fly them when they aren't hungry,' Beede said (plainly very familiar with this concept), 'then there's no incentive for them to return. They're remarkably pragmatic creatures, aren't they?'

'It's all about weight with birds of prey,' the man continued (as if Beede hadn't actually spoken). 'If they aren't hungry then they won't come back. He was an ounce over his flying weight, but I flew him anyway. I suppose I got too cocky, too *bold* . . .'

As he spoke he drew a large flask from his jacket pocket, unscrewed the lid and took a long swig of its contents. He shook his head, bitterly. 'I thought there was a *bond* between us – a strong bond – but I was wrong. He deceived me. I was a *fool* – a soft-touch. I shouldn't've trusted him.'

He proffered Beede the flask. It smelled of rum and coffee.

'Thanks,' Beede said warily, 'but I'm fine.'

'Suit yourself.'

The man scowled at him and then took a second, even longer swig.

'Will he survive out here?' Beede wondered. 'In this bitter weather?'

'No.'

Silence

'He'll die.'

The man shoved the flask away again as Beede continued his search. 'I don't know how I'll get home without my glasses,' Beede murmured, growing increasingly pessimistic about his chances of finding them. 'I couldn't possibly *drive* . . .'

'Where to?' the man asked.

'Pardon?'

'Where's home?'

526

'I live in Ashford.'

'*Oh.*'

The man grimaced, as if coming from Ashford was somehow unconscionable.

'I'm *Beede*, by the way,' Beede straightened up and held out his
hand, 'Daniel Beede.'

The man stepped forward (he *was* huge: 6'4", 6'6" . . .) and grabbed
hold of Beede's outstretched fingers. Then he squeezed them (Beede
winced), and *squeezed* them. He held on to them for four – perhaps
even five – seconds longer than Beede might've thought appropriate.
He had huge hands. Spotlessly clean. Dry. Surprisingly warm.

'You have very cold fingers,' the man slurred, '*very* cold.'

Beede managed to disengage himself from the man's tight grip and
then continued his search. Gringo joined in. She sniffed around in the
pine-needles with an audible enthusiasm. Then she began to dig. Soil
and needles flew everywhere.

'Careful, girl,' Beede cautioned her, flinching, not sure if her contri-
bution was entirely helpful. But the dog ignored him. The man stood
by and watched, making no effort to restrain the dog or to help in
the search himself.

After several minutes, Beede stood up again. 'I just can't seem to
find them,' he said, worriedly.

'What will you do?' the man wondered.

'I don't know,' Beede shrugged (perhaps a fraction irritably).

'Well at least the rain's stopped,' the man volunteered.

Beede peered up into the sky. The rain had stopped and the wind
had calmed, but the cold was even fiercer than it had been previously. His hands were almost frozen. He shuddered, then shoved his
hand into his coat pocket and withdrew –

Eh?

– a piece of unfamiliar fabric. Damp. He blinked as he unfolded it –

Oh, yes . . .

The pair of boxer shorts. He shone the torch at them for a moment,
then he scrunched them up and shoved them away again, pushed his
hand into his other pocket and withdrew his gloves. He pulled them

527

back on, then slowly ran the torch over the forest floor one final time.

'It's like they've just vanished,' he said, mystified.

'Are those your shorts?' the man asked. His voice had a new, slightly menacing tone to it.

'Pardon?'

'In your pocket. The shorts. Are they *yours*?'

'Uh . . .'

Beede put a tentative hand to the pocket.

'No,' he said, 'I found them in the Brambles. A few minutes ago. I thought they might actually belong . . .'

He paused, judiciously. The man stared at him, in silence.

'I should probably start to try and work my way back,' Beede said, turning and aiming the torch in the approximate direction of the larger track.

'These woods are packed full of mischief,' the man murmured, 'like you wouldn't hardly believe.'

Beede opted not to comment. He grabbed hold of his compass.

'Due north east,' he said cheerily, inspecting it closely in the torchlight. He pointed the torch ahead of him again. Everything was just a blur.

'The things I've seen,' the man said, his voice suddenly an unsettling mixture of rage and longing, 'behind the trees and in the bushes. Things I can't get out of my mind . . .' he slammed his hand, hard, into the side of his own head. 'Just can't seem to get *rid* . . .'

'Right,' Beede said abruptly. 'Well good luck with the kite. I do hope you find it.'

He took a rapid step forward.

'Hey . . .'

The man called out. Beede half-turned.

'Your glasses!' He pointed towards his feet. 'Down there. *Look!*'

Beede directed the torch to the the place he'd indicated. As he angled it he could've sworn he saw something glinting in the man's hand. A blade, perhaps. A long blade. His heart began racing. 'I can't run,' he thought. 'If I run then I'm done for.'

'I am the Guardian of the Woods,' the man's voice boomed, portentously.

'I don't see the glasses,' Beede said (at normal volume).

'I am the Guardian of the Woods,' he boomed again.

'I spent ten years in the Merchant Navy,' Beede announced. He

528

spoke with confidence. He threw back his shoulders. He tried to look like a proposition.

'You know what they say about sailors,' the man sneered.

'I *don't*, actually,' Beede said, sharply.

'Anyway,' the man continued, 'you're looking in the wrong place. I meant over there . . .'

He pointed to his left, and as he pointed he staggered slightly.

'I already searched over there,' Beede said, firmly.

'Perhaps you should look again,' the man said, thickly.

'No,' Beede stood his ground, 'the glasses are gone. I don't want to waste any more time on this.'

He turned.

'*Here* they are!' the man exclaimed.

Beede glanced over his shoulder. The man was holding out his huge hand. Inside his hand were what looked like a pair of glasses. Beede paused. He turned the torch on to the man's hand. Yes. They were definitely *his* glasses. They stared at one another. The man's other hand (his right hand) was hidden behind his back.

?

Beede suddenly heard a curious grunting sound and redirected the torch downwards. There he saw the dog – Gringo – rocking back on to her haunches and panting.

'Is your dog all right?' Beede asked.

'I am the Eyes of the Wood,' the man intoned, sonorously, drawing his hand from behind his back. The hand held a knife; a long, sharp hunting knife.

'Good for you,' Beede said, 'but I'm actually more concerned about your dog right now . . .'

'I am the *Ears* of the Wood,' he chanted, almost trance-like.

'She seems in some discomfort,' Beede persisted.

'I am the *Heart* of the . . .'

He shot the dog a quick, sideways glance. The dog was panting quite loudly.

'Stop that, Gringo,' he said harshly. Then, 'She's *fine*,' he insisted.

'No. No she isn't. There's blood,' Beede murmured, 'there's definitely blood . . .'

'Don't be a *fool*.'

'It's pretty bad,' Beede said, drawing in closer. 'I'm virtually blind without my glasses and even *I* . . .'

'*Where?*' he butted in.

'Her hindquarters. At the back. It looks like a . . . a *haemorrhage* of some kind.'

The man crouched down. 'Shine the torch on her,' he instructed. 'More closely. Up closer.'

Beede shone the torch. There was blood everywhere, but it appeared black in the torchlight. The man reached out his hand and lightly touched this dark stain, perhaps believing that it was just a shadow.

'Oh *shit!*' he exclaimed, feeling the warmth of it, seeing it leak on to his fingers. 'What the hell's *happening* here?'

'Pass me my glasses,' Beede instructed him, 'so I can take a proper look.'

The man hesitated.

'I *know* about dogs,' Beede lied.

The man handed him his glasses. Beede put them on. He squatted down. 'She's whelping,' he said, matter-of-factly.

'What?'

'She's whelping. She's pregnant. She's giving birth.'

The man looked astonished, then appalled, then enraged, 'Don't be disgusting,' he growled. 'She's ten years old. She's *neutered.*'

'Look at the size of her nipples,' Beede insisted, 'they're all distended . . .' His eyes widened. 'Good *Lord*. I believe I can almost see a *head* – the crown of a head . . .'

The man sprang back, in horror, almost losing his balance. He held out his knife, as if to defend himself with it.

'That's a lie!' he yelled.

'It's no such thing,' Beede said calmly. 'Whether you like it or not, she's giving birth.'

'She's neutered,' the man repeated, 'she's a virgin. She's a good girl. She's ten years old.'

Beede stretched out a hand to try and aid the poor creature.

'Don't *touch* her!' he roared, brandishing the blade.

'Calm down!' Beede snapped. 'You're upsetting her. She's stressed enough as it is. And she's *old*. She's probably as mystified by all of this as you are.'

Gringo had fallen on to her side and she was panting, heavily.

'Who did this to her?' the man yelled, brandishing the knife again (as if Beede might've been responsible). 'Which dirty, interfering *bastard* did this to my girl?'

'That head looks rather large,'Beede observed. 'It's as much as she can do to squeeze it out . . .' He grimaced. 'She might need some help . . .'

Gringo's breathing became more strained.

'*Enough!*' the man gasped, overwhelmed. '*Stop* this, Gringo! Get up. *Up*. *Up!*'

The dog tried to struggle to her feet and then collapsed back down.

'You're being ridiculous,' Beede snapped, 'and you're confusing her.' The man continued to hold out the knife, but his confidence was starting to waver.

'Put that knife away,' Beede instructed him. 'I need you to hold the torch.'

The man stared at him, terrified. 'What will you do?' he asked.

'Nothing. Not a damn thing until you calm down and put away your blade.'

He took off his rucksack and began unbuckling the main flap. The man slowly slid his knife into its holster.

'Is she going to die?' he asked.

'Not if we keep our heads about us,' Beede said, passing him the torch and then removing a clean shirt and a clean vest from inside. 'We need to keep her warm . . .' He wrapped the shirt around the dog, 'and we need to stop her from going into shock . . .'

'*Gringo! WHY?!*' the man bellowed, starting to sob uncontrollably.

'Hold the torch *properly*,' Beede barked. 'Control yourself. I need to see what I'm *doing* here.'

'I don't want her to die,' the man whined, 'don't let her die. Please don't let her die.'

'Okay, Gringo,' Beede whispered, pulling off his gloves, stroking the dog's head, trying to reassure her. 'You're doing fine. Good girl. You're doing fine.'

Gringo pushed.

'That's it, girl, a couple more of those and we'll have it sorted.'

'*Pull* it!' the man yelled hysterically. '*Grab* it! Get it *out* of her!'

'*Quiet!*' Beede snarled. 'If I pull too soon I could cause a rupture . . .' The man squeaked.

Beede touched the pup's head. 'Come on, lad, you're almost out, you're nearly there . . .'

'It's HUGE,' the man squealed.

'It's big,' Beede confirmed, 'but she's doing a grand job. Good girl, Gringo, one more push. That's it. One more push . . .'

Gringo pushed again. The pup was almost half-way out now. Beede slowly tried to ease its progress. Gringo pushed again. The pup plopped neatly into Beede's hand followed by a quick mess of afterbirth. The man dropped the torch, in shock.

'For God's sake,' Beede admonished him, 'pull yourself together. We need some *light* here . . .'

'Sorry.'

He picked up the torch and pointed it at Beede again.

'Not in my *eyes* . . .'

He redirected its blaze.

The puppy was still neatly contained inside its shiny, amniotic membrane.

'What's wrong with it?' the man asked, horrified. 'It just looks like snot.'

Beede carefully held the pup up close to the bitch's face. She sniffed at it, fascinated, then inspected the umbilical cord, opened her mouth and bit it cleanly in half.

'Well done,' Beede congratulated her. 'Now you just need to tear the membrane . . .'

Instead of inspecting the pup, however, the bitch seemed far more interested in the afterbirth. She licked at it for a few moments and then took a furtive bite.

'Leave that alone! Don't be filthy!' the man admonished her.

'She'll want to eat it,' Beede muttered, still preoccupied by the tiny pup, 'it's only natural. *Instinctive*. She knows it'll be full of vital nutrients . . .'

As he spoke he gently tore away the membrane then cleared any spare mucus from the pup's face with his thumb. When this was done, he rubbed it, gently, with the vest. The pup opened its mouth and mewed.

'Good,' Beede said, 'that's the first one sorted. By rights I should let it suckle, but the conditions here are hardly conducive. I think you should probably just store this little fellow inside your shirt.'

The man stared at him, horrified.

'It'll die otherwise. It's freezing cold out here. Take it. Put it inside your shirt, but make sure you don't smother it . . .'

The man didn't move.

'*Take* it!' Beede hissed.

The man reached out his hand. He took the pup. He stared at it, in wonder.

'Inside your shirt,' Beede repeated, returning to the mother. 'Okay, Gringo, how're we doing here?'

He rested a gentle hand on the dog's womb. She'd given up on the afterbirth and was panting again. He wrapped the shirt closer around her.

'Is there someone else inside there, girl? Have you got your breath back? Are you going to try and push again, eh?'

Gringo tried to push.

'That's it. That's the way . . .'.

Gringo pushed again. Then again. Another head began to crown. 'That was quick,' Beede said, glancing up, 'usually the wait is longer. But the pup doesn't look nearly so large this time . . .'

The man had now tucked the puppy inside his shirt. 'Well done, Gringo,' he said, moving forward slightly, his voice wavering with emotion. 'That's my girl.'

The dog pushed.

'She's responding positively to the sound of your voice,' Beede encouraged him. 'Keep on talking.'

'Well done, Gringo,' he repeated. 'Clever Gringo.'

The dog pushed again.

'Don't *die*, Gringo . . .' His voice cracked. Tears began rolling down his cheeks again.

'Try and hold it together, will you?' Beede said brusquely. He softly stroked the dog's head. 'Okay, girl,' he murmured. 'We're gonna need one more big push. That's it. One more. One more *big* push . . .'

Gringo pushed.

The second puppy plopped out into Beede's hand, followed by its own sudden squelch of afterbirth. Once again Beede held the pup up close to the bitch's face, but on this occasion she refused to pay it any heed.

'We're going to have to cut this ourselves,' Beede said; 'hand me your knife.'

'What?'

'Your knife. Pass it over.'

The man put his hand to his waist and fingered the handle, but he didn't look happy.

'*Quick,*' Beede snapped.

'But you *can't* use my knife,' he protested, 'it's brand-new. It's a top-of-the-range Japanese *Warrior's* knife.'

'I don't give a *damn* what kind of knife it is,' Beede informed him, holding out his hand, refusing to be gainsaid.

The man slowly pulled out the knife. It was insanely sharp and at least 50 centimetres long. Beede lay out the pup on the vest, took a hold of the knife, held it an inch or so from the pup's torso and cleanly sliced through the cord.

'There.'

He passed the knife back and picked up the pup. The man almost gagged as he inspected the blade, then he grabbed the vest and polished the blade with it.

Beede tore away the anmiotic membrane and then closely inspected the second pup. It felt cold in his hand. 'This fella doesn't feel too smart,' he said. 'The bigger one was probably resting on top of it inside the womb . . .'

He cleared mucus from the tiny puppy's airways.

'*Vest*,' he instructed brusquely. The man passed it over. Beede rubbed the body with the vest –

Nothing

He rubbed again and blew warm air into the puppy's face. 'Come on, little one,' he murmured.

Gringo, meanwhile, had turned around and was sniffing at the second afterbirth. Beede blew into the tiny pup's face again, then he tossed it, gently – like a bean-bag – from hand to hand. He massaged its little ribs. Then he held it upside down.

'It moved its arm,' the man said.

'Did it?'

Beede wasn't so confident. He cocooned the tiny pup in his hand. It still felt cold and lifeless. He blew on it, then he rubbed it, vigorously, with the vest again –

Nothing

He decided to try mouth-to-mouth. He inserted his little finger between the puppy's tiny jaws.

534

'What are you doing?'

'Mouth-to-mouth.'

'Is that safe?'

'Safe? Who for?'

He painstakingly pushed down the puppy's tiny tongue, then affixed his lips closely around the creature's muzzle and exhaled. The puppy's ribs rose. Beede sucked the air out. The puppy's ribs fell. He exhaled again. Then he inhaled. Exhaled. Inhaled. At the close of the seventh cycle, he stopped. He inspected the pup. The puppy remained completely flaccid. It was inanimate. It was dead.

He closed his eyes for a moment, defeated, and then –

Pow!

– he suddenly sensed the stag – that grand, old stag; not as an actual entity, but as . . . as a *beat*. He *felt* the stag – its raw, untrammelled energy. He felt its pulse, in the ground, like a fast-approaching train. He felt the beat thundering towards him. And then –

Bang!

– it hit him. He rocked back. He felt it reverberating inside his eardrum, inside his head – his forehead – butting into him, like a hooligan – then travelling down, through his veins, his airways, into his throat, a *suffocating* pulse. He almost gagged, almost choked. Then on . . . into his shoulder –

Argh!

(He bit on his lip to stop himself from screaming)

– then down, still further, jerking and shuddering, into his arm, into his wrist . . .

Until –

Huh?

– it cut out. It was *gone*.

Beede kept his eyes closed, barely even breathing. He focussed in on his hand. He *sensed* his hand; the cup of his hand, the sanctum . . .

Eh?

– the *goblet* –

Eh?!

– the *Communion*, and there, in the centre of it, the tiny puppy suddenly jolted, then it coughed.

Beede opened his eyes.

'It's alive,' he said, his voice devoid of emotion.

The puppy coughed again. Beede gently massaged its ribs for a minute and then handed it over. The man took the second pup and placed it, gently, inside his shirt.

Gringo was still gnawing at the second afterbirth.

'You'll need to get everybody home,' Beede said, 'into the warm. Where's your car?'

'I have a Landrover . . .'

The man pointed. He seemed quiet now, almost deflated. His eyes looked strangely hollow.

Beede shoved away the vest, pulled on his gloves and threw his rucksack over his shoulders. 'I'll carry Gringo,' he said, wincing. 'You lead the way . . .'

He carefully wrapped Gringo in the shirt again, then picked her up. She was heavy. She kicked out her legs, in protest.

'Right. Good. Let's go,' Beede said, tightening his grip on her and starting to walk, sucking on his lip as he slowly moved forward, feeling the unexpectedly warm, metallic tang of blood on his tongue.

FIVE

'*Dead?!*' Kane repeated, sounding perfectly astonished, 'When? *How?*'

'I don't know. He just . . .'

Kelly began sobbing, violently, as he accelerated rapidly away from a set of traffic lights.

'Did you speak to your mother?'

''*Course* I did, *Dumbo.*'

'Is she okay?

''*Course* she's okay.'

'And your dad?'

'He switched his phone off. He sent a text. He don't wanna talk. He ain't good wiv' stuff like this.'

Kane opened his mouth to speak.

'An' don't you *dare* say,' she quickly interrupted him, 'that it's all for the best.'

'Okay,' Kane said gently, 'I won't.'

He paused.

'But it is.'

'We gotta fetch the body,' she wailed. 'We gotta sort out the fuckin' *funeral.*'

'Good point.'

Kane pulled on to a roundabout and then turned right.

'Mum ain't up to it, Jase is in the clink, Linda don't give a fuck, an' I'm stuck in *this* shithole . . .'

'Don't worry,' Kane murmured, 'I'll help you sort it out. I'll get on to it first thing. That's a promise.'

'But who's gonna sit with the body?' she bellowed.

'Sit with the body?'

Sit with the body?!

'Sit with it while it's still *warm,*' she blubbered.

'Sit with the body, Kell? Are you *sure*? D'you think that's entirely necessary?'

'Of *course* it is! Of *course* it's necessary,' she began to hiccough, hysterically (in the background Kane could hear somebody talking to her – a nurse, *two* nurses, both trying their level best to calm her down).

'It's lights out,' she mewed, 'an' I'm keepin' up the *WHOLE FUCKIN' WARD!*'

'Just hold on a second . . .'

Kane glanced into his rearview mirror, turned on his indicator and gently pulled off the road.

'I *CAN'T* hold on, fuck-wit!'

He braked, drew to a halt, stuck on his hazard lights . . .

'Are you still there, Kell?'

All he could hear now was a high, shrill squall.

'*Kelly?*'

'His body's stuck in some *morgue*, an' he's all a-fuckin' *lone!*'

'He'll be in a chapel of rest,' Kane lied. 'They'll have a priest sitting with him.'

'He *came* to me!' she bawled. 'He came an' snapped my *bra* strap, Kane!'

'*Pardon?*'

'I swear to God. They said he died at eight. At eight someone snapped my bra strap. I *felt* it. He always did that when we was kids. He snapped my bra strap. He *came* to me, Kane.'

'You wore a bra when you were a kid?' Kane said, struggling to get this all straight in his head.

'When I was twelve, *thirteen*, stupid! My first bra. He used to love takin' the piss.'

'Right.'

'An' stop raisin' your fuckin' *brows* like that!'

'I wasn't raising my brows, Kell . . .' Kane lowered his brows. 'You're obviously very upset . . .'

'I need someone to *sit* wiv' him, Kane.'

'I already said – they'll probably have a priest . . .'

'They *won't* have no priest. They don't give a *shit!*'

'Or if not a priest, then one of the nurses who looked after him on the ward . . .'

'*BALLS!*'

(More hushing.)

'They keep tryin'a shove a load of *tablets* down my neck . . .'

   'Ask for a *Sinequan* . . .'

'FUCK OFF, KANE!!!'

'I'm just . . .'

   He tried to think on his feet.' . . . I suppose I could get *Gaffar* . . .' he murmured. 'Uh . . . Did you speak to Gaffar yet?'

'*What?!* Why the fuck would I wanna speak to *him*?!' she yelled.

   Kane smiled. 'So you *did* speak to him?'

Pause

'Yeah.'

'Was he helpful?'

'What does *he* know?! He's just a little, Turkish *DICK*.'

'A *Kurd*. A Kurdish dick.'

'*WHATEVER!*'

(More hushing.)

   'Look. I'm in my car. I'm on the Romney Marsh Road. I'm right in the middle of something. D'you have the number of the hospital on you?'

   Kelly blew her nose, noisily, then she cleared her throat. 'I got it on my phone.'

'Right. Find it – quick as you can – send it to me, and I'll sort something out.'

'I just don't want him to be on his *own*, Kane . . .'

'That's fine. That's fair enough. I'll sort something out. I'll go myself or I'll get Gaffar . . .'

   'Whoever goes, I want them to light candles and say a little prayer. I want it like Paul Burrell did for Diana, yeah?'

'Who?'

'Paul Burrell. The butler. He went an' he sat with her. An' he lit *candles*. I want candles . . .'

   'Okay.'

'You promise?'

'Yes. It'll be fine. I'll ring Gaffar now. I'll order a cab. He'll be there in a couple of hours . . .'

   'Thanks . . .'

She sniffed, poignantly. 'An' I *mean* that.'

'It's nothing. It's the very *least* I can do.'

Half-way through saying it, Kane realised that he *meant* it –

Huh?

'I'm sorry,' he added (quickly glancing over his shoulder – as if the truth was a cruel assassin which was slowly and methodically tracking him down).

'Yeah, yeah,' she sighed.

They both rang off.

He dialled Gaffar's number. Gaffar answered immediately.

'Yah?'

The line was terrible.

'Gaffar?' Kane shouted. 'It's Kane.'

'So?'

'Can you hear me?'

Kane winced as a large cargo of static came slamming into his ear.

'Man . . .'

He opened his car door and clambered out –

Holy Fuck –
It's freezing out here

'Gaffar?' he grimaced against the cold.

'Kane?'

His voice sounded clearer.

'You spoke to Kelly?'

'Sure.'

'Her brother died.'

'Sure. I speak Dina. Then I ring.'

'How was she?'

'Dina?'

'Yeah.'

'Is okay.'

'Well I need you to do me a huge favour, man.'

'Huh?'

'I need you to go up to Reading. Reading, yeah? Where the brother

is? At the hospital? Call yourself a minicab. Call Simo. Ask for Simo. He'll cut you a deal. The journey'll take about an hour and a half. Be sure and get a quote up front, though . . .'
'Sure.'
'I need you to sit with the body tonight.'

Pause

'Sure.'
'Will you do that for me?'

Even longer pause

'Sure.'
   'Okay. Call the cab now. Wrap up warm. It's fuckin' *freezing* outside. Take plenty of cash. I'll text you the address just as soon as I have it. You're gonna have to bullshit the people at the morgue that you're related. A step-brother or something. Paul Broad, his name was. Okay?'

'Sure.'
   'You wanna write that down?
'Sure.'
(No sound of any attempt being made to write it down.)
   'Or I can text that through if you prefer . . .'

Silence

'And Kelly wants candles. Try and get candles.'
'Sure.'
'Thanks, man. You're a brick.'
   Kane hung up.
He stood in the darkness for a second, shivering slightly, staring at his phone, and then –

Thwack!

A large, frozen object plummeted down from the heavens and crashed into the roof of his car.

'He has some kind of a feud under way with the local vet . . .' Beede explained as Peta knelt over the bitch and gave her back-end a cursory inspection. 'He doesn't have the first idea how to cope. This whole situation has taken him totally by surprise. He's a wreck – began shaking like a *leaf* when I threatened to leave . . .'

'How mortifying,' Peta drawled.

'He's just a little . . . *well* . . .' Beede frowned and glanced nervously over his shoulder.

They were standing in a filthy, brightly lit double garage on the outskirts of Beckley.

'And he *lives* in this place you say?'

Peta's keen – somewhat mercenary – gaze slowly took in the single camp-bed, the Calor Gas heater, the ill-concealed, heavily stained chamber pot, the bizarre array of antique army boots, the ancient wardrobe with the badly hung door and broken mirror, the collection of magazines about oriental weaponry, the bales of hay, and the strange combination of furniture, old junk and animal cages lining the walls.

'His mother owns the house, but they barely speak. He has a key. He comes and goes as he likes. Apparently the bitch belongs to her. She's insanely protective of the animal. He said she'll go crazy if she finds out what's happened. And in the *wood* of all places.'

'Well at least it's warm in here,' Peta muttered, straightening up and shoving her hands into her coat pockets.

'Is the box a good size?' Beede enquired.

She inspected the box. 'It's perfect. And there's plenty of newspaper, which is ideal.'

'She's stopped bleeding now,' Beede observed. 'Do they usually lose that much blood when they whelp?'

'Not that I'm aware of. Perhaps one of the pups was in breech . . .'

She peered over at him as she spoke, with a frown. 'You've bitten your lip. Did you realise?'

'Uh . . . Yes.'

He touched his lip, self-consciously.

'Does it hurt?'

'No.'

'And your shoulder?'

Beede's mouth twitched. 'That's nothing. It's fine . . .'

He seemed embarrassed by her attention.

'But you're holding it differently – stiffly . . .' she maintained, ignoring his pique. 'Isn't it bothering you?'

'No. Not at all.'

She walked over and calmly placed her hands on to his shoulder. He flinched at her touch but she persisted. 'Where's the source of the discomfort? Is it the side of the neck?'

'It's honestly not . . .'

She pulled back the collar of his coat and loosened his scarf, then slipped her hand into the gap and applied a light pressure with her fingertips.

'There?'

He grimaced. She'd hit the spot.

'Is that *terribly* tender?'

'No . . .' he used the sudden, keening wail of a car-alarm outside as an excuse to move away and readjust his scarf. 'Is that your car?'

'My van isn't alarmed.'

She remained exactly where she was, her hands still held aloft, staring at him, slightly hurt.

He cleared his throat. 'I really didn't expect you to come. I just rang because I wanted a quick word with Ann. I know she's had a fair amount of experience in this area . . .'

Peta raised an imperious brow.

'Not that you *haven't* . . .' he rapidly backtracked.

She crossed her arms and gazed around the room again. 'You never cease to amaze me,' she said. 'I mean the *situations* you connive to get yourself into . . .'

He scowled.

'There's actually some good stuff in here,' she murmured, 'against all the odds. *Interesting* stuff . . .'

She walked over to inspect a large, ornately framed, deeply homo-erotic print of a fifteenth-century Italian painting of Saint Sebastian, his lean, naked torso completely riddled with arrows. Close to that was a headless shop mannequin with two, small, individual dartboards clumsily etched on to each breast. A dart was still hanging from the left nipple (the right-hand one having been completely obliterated by overuse).

'I could sell this for a fortune,' she smiled. 'There's a greasy little misogynist I know who owns half of Aldgate – works in the city . . . He'd just *die* . . .'

Next to the dummy was a badly stuffed fox.

'*Urgh*. D'you suppose he did this himself?' she asked. Beede merely shrugged. Next to the fox was a brightly coloured 1950s roll-up, fabric St John's Ambulance demonstration chart of the lower abdomen.

'He's one of those *wood* people, isn't he?' she sighed, trailing a bored finger around the kidney. 'One of those strange, sexually repressed, borderline-deviant males who likes to make a habit of hanging around in the woods at night . . .'

'Perhaps you should *collect* him,' Beede opined, acerbically. 'Do you *own* any sexual deviants yet?'

Her mouth tightened at its corners. 'A few,' she said, shooting him a dark look.

Beede crouched down and affixed a mewling puppy to a spare teat.

'I spoke to Kane this afternoon,' she said casually, walking over to one of several cages and peering inside.

'Pardon?'

Beede glanced up.

'Kane,' she repeated. 'Your son.'

'*Kane?*'

Beede's eyes flew wide behind his glasses.

'Yes. It was *very* odd. He just rang me up, out of the blue. Said he'd found my business card in an old book . . .'

'What did he want?' Beede demanded.

'I don't know . . .' she shrugged, pretending not to notice the urgent tone of his voice. 'To talk, I guess. Just to chat . . .'

'About *what* exactly?'

'About you, mainly.'

'About *me*?'

'Yes.'

'But why on *earth* . . . ?'

She turned and gave him a scathing look. 'Because the poor child doesn't really have the first idea who you *are*, Beede.'

Beede's jaw stiffened. He seemed stunned by her impertinence.

'Did you get rid of him?' he asked, roughly.

She shook her head, surprised. 'Of course not. I invited him over. In fact I made him an offer on his car.'

Beede's jaw tightened – if possible – still further.

'He was sweet,' she continued blithely, moving into a far corner and picking up an old, rather dusty policeman's truncheon. 'Quite charming. We shared lunch.'

'*Charming*,' Beede spat, standing and turning to face the garage doors (as if uncertain of being able to remain civil in front of her), '*that'd* be right.'

She placed down the truncheon and turned around herself. 'So did we finally establish what it was exactly that *you* were doing in the woods tonight?' she wondered airily.

Beede kept his back to her. He glanced over at the side-entrance as if hoping that the garage's owner might return. But he didn't.

'I was searching for someone,' he said, finally.

'Who?'

'A friend.'

'A good friend?'

'Yes,' he said, defensively. 'A fairly good friend.'

'And this friend was seeking refuge in the woods?'

There was a trace of mockery in her voice.

'Yes. I had reason to believe that he was.'

'Does this friend make a *habit* of seeking refuge there?'

'No,' he snapped. 'Not that I'm aware of . . .'

'So why . . . ?'

'His *partner* asked me,' Beede interrupted. 'His wife. He hasn't been well. He was distressed. They had an argument and he climbed out of the car. He ran off.'

'I see . . .' she nodded. 'Well the conditions are hardly *propitious* for an overnight excursion . . .'

'Exactly.'

She smiled, wickedly. 'Must've been some hum-dinger of a row, though . . .'

'Yes. No. I mean I wouldn't really know . . .'

'What was it about?'

'I don't know,' he repeated, turning around.

She strolled to another part of the room and began picking through the rubbish again. 'And the wife?' she murmured, almost inaudibly, holding up a small, chipped, alabaster bust of Queen Victoria.

Beede put a nervous hand to his mouth. He investigated the cut on his lip with his index finger.

'She's obviously very worried,' he said, dropping the hand, 'so she asked for my help.'

'D'you think he's still there?'

'Where?'

'In the woods.'

He shrugged. 'I wouldn't have a clue, Peta.'

She glanced up when he used her name.

'Then it's a fruitless quest,' she said, holding eye contact with him for a second.

'Very possibly,' he conceded.

She turned. 'And on one of the coldest nights of the year . . .'

He nodded. He couldn't deny it.

'Well all I can say is that this wife must be a *very* persuasive character,' she mused, inspecting Victoria in profile, now.

He scowled.

'Did you think of contacting the police?'

'*No* . . .'

Beede frowned. 'I mean, he's been in trouble with the police before,' he elaborated. 'He didn't . . . He wouldn't . . .'

'And the wife?' Peta persisted. 'What's *she* like?'

'Nice,' Beede insisted. '*Normal*. A chiropodist. They have a child – a son . . .'

'Will you go back?' Peta interrupted.

'Pardon?'

'To the woods? Will you return once you've finished up here?'

'Uh . . .' Beede scratched his head. 'Yes. I mean I suppose I must . . .'

'Then I'll come with you,' she said. 'I have Pinch in the van. He's an absolute gem. If *anyone* can help track down your man . . .'

'No.'

'But I *insist* . . .'

The garage's owner suddenly came slamming back inside. He was heavily laden.

'No iodine,' he panted, dumping his various provisions down on to a nearby table, 'but I've got Dettol . . .'

'That's a disinfectant,' Peta clucked, marching over, 'not an antibacterial agent.'

'Or there's TCP . . .'

'That's more like it.'

She grabbed the bottle and inspected it. It seemed rather old. She unscrewed the lid. There was rust inside the cap. She grimaced.

'And I've defrosted some liver in the microwave . . .' he continued.

'Will she eat it raw?' Beede wondered.

'And milk?' Peta enquired, before the man could answer, 'and cotton wool?'

'Full cream,' he said, removing a carton from a carrier bag, followed by a small swab of cotton wool.

'Good. Well done.'

Peta took the TCP and the cotton wool and went over to sterilise the tips of the pups' cords with it. She grabbed them, one at a time, and dabbed gently at their bellies.

'I'm sterilising the cords,' she explained. 'And for future reference, if the mother refuses to bite the cord herself, then it's best to either tear it or to cut at it but using a rough, sawing motion. This second cut . . .' she held up the smaller pup, 'is rather too close to the body. It's preferable to leave about 2 inches in order to prevent the risk of an umbilical hernia . . .'

'Will he be all right, d'you think?' the man asked, concerned.

She shrugged. 'It looks fine – I mean, so far as I can *tell*. All being well, the cords should fall off in a few days' time . . .'

The man began to pour some milk into a bowl.

'If she's lost blood then you should provide her with plenty of iron: meat, milk, even a vitamin supplement. Cod liver oil, perhaps. You can buy capsules at your local pet shop. And don't exercise her too much,' she expanded, 'just take her out for a quick trot on the lead, allow her to empty her bladder, then bring her straight back inside.'

The man nodded.

'No more of those mysterious, nightly excursions,' she persisted.

He scowled.

'I see you have an interest in Japanese Art Swords . . .'

'What?'

The man stared at her, still scowling.

'Samurai swords?'

'Oh. Uh . . . Yes.'

He put a tentative hand to his hip.

'I actually have a couple of wonderful, early Tokugawa period Katana,' she said nonchalantly, 'a matching pair – short and long from around 1630 – the Ogatana *and* the Kogatana . . .'

The man blinked. 'Are you serious?'

'Of course I'm serious,' she snapped. 'In fact I also have a *used* Waki-sashi, and a very, *very* rare, early Muromachi period sword which is *incredibly* beautiful and well over 3 foot . . .'

'A *used* Waki-sashi?'

The man turned to Beede. 'That's the special sword a Samurai uses to commit suicide.'

'I know,' Beede said.

'They slice open their stomachs with it,' the man added.

'I know,' Beede said.

'I have the most marvellous Edo period Japanese Samurai Helmet, too,' Peta continued, 'pre-1700. A 62 plate Suji Kabuto by Nobuiye, a master of the Myochin School.'

'The Waki-sashi,' the man persisted. 'About how much would that . . . ?'

'I acquired it as part of an exchange,' Peta said brusquely. 'It's a small but precious piece of Japanese cultural history. The value is an irrelevance, really . . .'

'Oh.'

The man frowned, bemused.

'You don't *own* an object like that,' she clarified.

The man nodded, plainly baffled.

'I'm impressed by some of your little nick-nacks,' she cast out a benevolent hand, 'I see you have a Victorian burr walnut credenza up against the back wall. It has a replacement marble top, and the fabric has rotted away behind the fretwork, but I like it. If you're *very* good I might be persuaded to give you forty quid for the thing . . .'

'Seventy-five,' the man shot back.

'Sixty,' she conceded. 'And trust me, I'm on a hiding to nothing here. Credenzas are all-but impossible to integrate into the modern home . . .'

'I got it at the dump,' he said.

'A scavenger, eh?' she mused, picking up a filthy, old jug from the table and inspecting the marks on the bottom of it. 'That's exactly how I started out, although I can rarely find the time any more. I restore antiques. It's labour intensive. I'm what they call money-rich but time-poor . . .'

'D'you like the look of that?' the man asked.

'It's Royal Doulton. A late nineteenth-century ewer. An Emily Stormer, I believe. But there's a small crack in the rim . . .'

'Ten quid,' he said.

'Five.'

'Done.'

'I'll round it up to eighty if you tell me you still have the brass bucket which fits inside that Regency mahogany planter with the openwork slats . . .'

She pointed.

'I never had any brass bucket, no.'

He shook his head, forlornly.

'That's a shame. Then I'll take it off your hands for a tenner.'

His face brightened.

Peta reached into her coat pocket, withdrew an old, leather wallet, unclipped it and removed a bundle of notes. She counted out £75.

Beede glanced over at the man. The man was rubbing his hands together, smiling, delightedly.

'A *used* Waki-sashi,' he murmured.

'These chaps should be weaned in around five weeks' time,' Peta said, slipping the wallet away again, slapping the notes down on to the table, propping the Doulton ewer under her elbow and indicating towards the pups, 'you can start them off on solids in about three, but only if they gain a sufficient amount of weight. Try them on baby cereal and warm milk. If the bitch's condition declines then she *must* go to a vet. I have a good man in Tenterden. I'll give you his number. Tell him Peta sent you . . .'

Peta recited the vet's number. The man grabbed a nearby pad and wrote it down, very carefully.

'Beede,' Peta turned to Beede, 'would you be so kind as to give our friend here a hand loading up my van with the credenza?' she paused, her bright, green eyes twinkling. 'And do try and be *extra* careful with the mirror, dear, *won't* you . . . ?'

She stared at him, blankly, as if she'd just opened her door to a complete and utter stranger –

A double-glazing salesman . . .
A Prophet of Jehovah . . .

'Sorry. I know it's a little *late* . . .' he said, his cheeks reddening slightly at the coolness of his reception.

'Of course,' she murmured. 'Of *course*. You've come for your jumper. It's folded up in the washing basket . . .' She glanced over her shoulder. 'I'll quickly run and grab it. Fleet's in the bath. I shouldn't really . . .' She was deathly pale. Her hair was in disarray. Her eyes were red-rimmed.

Just tell her, you fool . . .

He steeled his nerve and then opened his mouth to speak, but before a single syllable could leave his lips, her worn face broke into an unexpected smile. She reached out her hand.
'You've actually got . . .'
She grabbed something from the back of his head, then held it up close to her face to inspect it. 'What *is* this?'

He stared at the white napkin, flummoxed, and then, 'Oh *shit*,' he said, mortified, 'how'd *that* end up there?'
'Like a little halo,' she said, her face softening. Then she stepped back and pulled the door wider.
He grabbed his opportunity and quickly slipped past her.

'Isn't it freezing?' she asked, closing the door with a shiver and then turning to apprehend him. She paused. 'Are you all right?'
'I just had a call . . .' Kane said, his hand returning, neurotically, to the back of his head.

'From Beede?' she interrupted, showing as much animation in that moment (he felt) as she ever really might.

'*No*,' he said (irritated), 'from my ex-girlfriend. Her brother just died. He was in a coma . . .'

'How sad,' she murmured (struggling to hide her disappointment). 'How old was he?'

'I don't know. Twenty-one, twenty-two . . . But that wasn't the weird part . . .' he continued. 'I was standing by the side of the road, having just finished the call, minding my own business, staring at my phone, and then suddenly this . . . this *thing* came plummeting out of the sky – like a *stone* – and crashed into the roof of my car.'

'What kind of a thing?'

'A bird.'

'Really? What kind of a bird?'

She glanced, distractedly, towards the stairs as she spoke.

'I don't know exactly. A sparrowhawk, maybe. It was reddish in colour.'

'A kestrel?'

She turned and started walking.

'No. Different. Bigger.'

'Then maybe a kite? A red kite?'

'Well I guess it doesn't really *matter* now,' Kane trailed along behind her, 'because it was dead.'

'It must've died mid-air,' she reasoned, starting to climb the stairs, 'on the wing, mid-flight.'

'But that's the strange thing,' Kane said. 'It was completely frozen.'

'Oh.' She frowned. 'So maybe it froze to death. It certainly feels cold enough out there tonight . . .'

She was half-way up the stairs now. The stairway, Kane noticed, smelled quite strongly of damp.

'And it had no eyes,' he interrupted her, 'the eyes had been torn out.'

She stopped in her tracks. He almost slammed into the back of her. He reached out his hands to steady himself. One hand touched her waist. He quickly withdrew the hand, as if burned.

'Sorry,' he muttered.

She half-turned. 'What did you do with it?' she asked.

'I guess I should've just tossed it into the undergrowth,' he said, shrugging, 'the damn thing dented my *roof* . . .'

'But you kept it? You brought it with you?'

He nodded.

The boy began screaming for his mother from the bathroom.

'Go and fetch it,' she said, 'I'd like to see it.'

He stayed where he was, confused.

'Fetch it,' she repeated.

'Now?'

'Yes. Go and get it. I want to see it.'

'Muuuummmmy!'

Kane paused for a moment, surprised, and then he turned and jogged back down the stairs, out through the front door and along the short garden path to his car. He quickly disabled the alarm, retrieved the bird from the front passenger side, winced as he held it, grabbed an old Sainsbury's carrier bag from the floor at the back and wrapped it around the bird, then carefully carried it inside.

But by the time he'd returned, she'd disappeared. He waited for a minute or so in the hallway, unsure whether to go up and find her. He could hear her conversing with the child in the bathroom.

'Hold up your arms,' she was saying, 'quickly now. You don't want to get all cold again, do you?'

Pause

'What's that on your arms?'

'Where?'

'Those rashes. They look like flea bites. Gracious me . . . there are *dozens* of them . . .'

'I'm hungry, Mummy,' the boy said.

'But I don't understand all these *bite* marks, Fleet. Daddy powdered the dog a few days ago, didn't he . . . ?'

'I'm *hungry*, Mummy!'

'I can make you some warm milk . . . But we'll need to put some calamine lotion . . .'

'I want an egg in it.'

'In your milk?'

'Yes.'

'Okay. After we've put on the lotion I'll make you milk with honey and a dash of nutmeg, how would that be?'

'And an egg.'

'Okay. With an egg. And how about if for a *special* treat I tuck you up in *my* bed. Would you like that?'

No audible response

'Good. Then let's go and get you settled.'

As he listened to her talk (his eyes unfocussed, the frozen bird held to his chest, a dopy smile teasing the corners of his mouth) Kane observed a slight movement at the far end of the hallway. He focussed in on it –

?

It was the dog. The spaniel –

Angela?
Sarah?
Michelle?

'Hello, girl,' he murmured.

The dog wasn't hitched to its cart. It was dragging itself along – somewhat laboriously – by its front legs, the two back legs hanging flaccid (almost *boneless*, like rubber chicken wings) from the base of its spine. Its progress was agonisingly slow. Kane watched it, quite fascinated (by the various techniques it employed, the different muscles it used, the physical adjustments it made . . .) as it inched its way gradually forward.

'It *is* a kite . . .'

Kane almost jumped out of his skin. Elen was standing beside him again.

'Sorry,' she smiled, 'did I alarm you?'

'No. It's fine. I was just . . .'

He held out the bird to her but she didn't take it from him, just moved around him, carefully inspecting it from various angles.

'Totally frozen,' she murmured. 'You were right.'

'It's absolutely *solid*,' Kane said, his eyes alighting on her chin, her nose, her lips. 'My hand's gone numb just holding it . . .'

'And the eyes . . .'

She stared at the bloody sockets, grimacing, then reached out a tentative hand and gingerly touched her finger to the top of its head. As her finger stroked the bird's domed crown its beak suddenly snapped open, almost as if she'd pressed some kind of hidden mechanism.

Kane dropped the kite, with a yell.

'*Jesus*,' he gasped. 'How'd you *do* that?'

Elen just stood there, frowning.

'What d'you think it means?' she wondered, slowly pushing her hair behind one ear.

'*Means?*'

'A kite. A *red* kite. I wonder what it represents . . .'

'*Represents?* You think it's an omen? A sign?'

He gazed down at the bird, anxiously.

'Don't you?'

She picked up the kite, inspected it again, then gently placed it inside the carrier bag.

'A sign?' Kane mused. 'What kind of a sign?'

'I don't know.'

Kane suddenly thought of Peta.

'I love your hair like that . . .' Elen interrupted his brief reverie.

Kane's eyes refocussed and he smiled down at her.

'. . . That's just how Beede wears his,' she continued.

Kane's smile faltered.

'So what will you do with it?' she wondered, apparently oblivious.

'Pardon?'

'The bird. What will you do?'

He shrugged. 'I don't know. Bury it, I suppose . . .'

She nodded. 'That's a good idea. I might have room in the back garden,' she said, 'or there's a cemetery directly opposite where I work . . .'

She hung the bag on an empty coat hook. The hook promptly fell out of the wall.

'Two hundred and nineteen,' she announced, picking the bag up again and hanging it on the next hook along, then heading off down the hallway, grabbing a hold of the dog as she strolled past and propping it, easily, under her arm.

Kane followed her through to the kitchen where she placed the dog into her basket, washed her hands, dried them on a dishcloth and then indicated that Kane should do the same. As he obliged her she gazed over at him, frowning. 'You're still limping,' she said. 'Is it the verruca? Are you in pain?'

'No,' he lied.

'You should come and see me at the surgery. It's on Queen's Road, just left of the Mace Estate. It's only a short spit from your flat.'

As she spoke she removed a carton of milk from the fridge, poured a large quantity into a pan and began heating it up. Half-way through, she carefully turned away and sneezed, violently.

'God. I think I may've caught a chill. I got soaked earlier. My clothes are still all damp . . .'

She held up a dark sleeve for him to feel.

He ignored the sleeve and reached out to gently brush the fabric covering her right collarbone with the back of his hand instead. The tips of his fingers tickled her jaw.

She dropped her arm and took an unsteady step away from him, then turned back to face the counter, quickly separated three egg yolks, plopped them into the warming milk and whisked the mixture, adding a generous pinch of nutmeg.

Kane walked over to the kitchen table. On top of it was a large box. On top of the box was a book. He picked it up. '*The Lily of Darfur*,' he read. He stared at the picture of the woman on the cover. 'Wow. She certainly looks like a force to be reckoned with . . .' he mused, his eye resting on the gun.

'Yes. Apparently she was . . .' Elen added a tablespoonful of honey to the milky mixture. She peered over her shoulder at him. 'I met her father today, out walking on the beach. It's his book. He wrote it.'

'Dr Charles Bartlett,' Kane read out loud, and then (in suitably stentorian tones), 'Rich, dark, funny, heartbreaking; a book which grapples with the fundamental issues of how it feels – and what it *means* – to be human.'

He sat down at the table and opened the book to the first printed page, a short preface . . .

'*If there's only one thing that my long – and for the most part wonderful – acquaintance with Eva Jane Bartlett has taught me,*' he read, '*it's that more often than not, the act of love is all about letting go . . .*'

Kane snorted, sarcastically. 'So where'd he mine *that* little gem from?' he wondered. 'The book of Hallmark?'

'It's true, though, isn't it?'

Elen continued whisking.

'Yeah? Well that's clichés for you . . .' Kane grimaced.

'But as a *parent*, especially . . .' she frowned.

'I wouldn't know about that,' Kane brushed her off.

'Well just look at you and Beede,' she persisted, turning from the stove, 'he's always encouraged you to follow your own muse hasn't he?'

'Trust me,' Kane muttered. 'When it comes to Beede and I you don't have the first idea what you're talking about.'

'You're right,' she shrugged, 'I can only judge Beede by the standards of friendship, but as friends go . . .'

'As friends go,' Kane interrupted, dryly, 'I'm sure he's been *very* friendly.'

Elen froze. Kane casually returned his attention to the book. After thirty seconds or so he glanced up. 'I think the milk might be about to . . .'

An angry hissing sound interrupted him. She turned – with a start – and quickly removed the milk from the hotplate, cursing as she dumped the whisk into the sink.

'Would you like some of this?' she asked, refusing to look at him.

'Sure,' he said. 'Why not?'

She removed three mugs from a cupboard and set them out.

'Perhaps this is just another Hallmark cliché,' she murmured softly as she poured, 'but until you have kids of your own . . .'

'When I do,' he said tersely, 'then I'll be sure to send you a card.'

She finished pouring the first cup, picked it up, and turned to face him, holding it out. 'So tell me,' she said.

'Pardon?' He glanced up from the book, saw the proffered mug, reached over and took it from her.

'Tell me what it was that Beede did,' she insisted, 'that was so unbelievably bad . . .'

'You know what?' Kane laid down the book and cradled the mug in his hands. 'It really is the strangest thing, but every time we talk I somehow get the feeling like the conversation we have is the *same* conversation . . .'

'You mean a conversation you don't like?'

She looked hurt again. Baleful.

'No . . . not . . .' he frowned '. . . I mean the *same* conversation. As if I'd never been away. As if the conversation had never actually stopped . . .'

'I don't think I understand what you mean by that,' she said, dully.

'You look exhausted,' Kane murmured, staring up at her, pityingly.

'Did you feel like he *neglected* you?' she persisted. 'Is that it?'

'No. Beede never did anything wrong,' Kane suddenly felt tired himself, 'not explicitly. If he had, then maybe I could've forgiven him. But Beede *never* does anything wrong. Everything he does is right. Everything he does is for the best possible reasons, with the best possible motivation . . .'

'So you hate him because he's good?'

'I don't hate him.'

She stared at him, unblinking.

'Okay . . .' Kane folded his arms. 'So you *really* want to know?'

She nodded.

'Fine.'

He drew a deep breath and opened his mouth to speak.

'Actually . . .' she suddenly glanced up towards the ceiling, tipping her head slightly, listening. 'Just . . . Just *hold* that thought for me,' she instructed him.

SIX

The Reverend slowly regained consciousness, yawned, scratched his nose, gradually eased open his eyes and lazily focussed them in on . . .

Eh?!

– a skinny, burgundy-haired girl with a badly broken leg, who was perched on the side of his bed and staring down at him, intently, like some kind of ravenous owl.

'What on earth are you *doing*?' he whispered, shocked.

'You never said you was black,' Kelly berated him, at normal volume.

The Reverend considered this for a moment. 'I didn't think I'd *need* to,' he said.

'*Why?*'

'*Shhhhh*. Because I didn't think it was *relevant*, quite frankly.'

'Well it ain't.'

'Well if it ain't – *isn't* . . .' he corrected himself, 'then why did you feel the need to *raise* the issue?'

'Well if it ain't an issue,' she deftly back-handed, 'then why'd you feel the need to *avoid* it?'

The Reverend tried to adjust himself – to pull himself up into a sitting position – but his freedom of movement was restricted by Kelly's weight on the counterpane.

'For heaven's *sake*, girl,' he expostulated, irritably, 'what *time* is it?'

'Quarter-past-I-don't-give-a-shit,' Kelly said, promptly.

'How long have you been sitting there?'

'Hours.'

'*Hours?* Doing *what*, exactly?'

'Thinkin',' she sighed, 'just thinkin'.'

'But why think on my bed,' he demanded, 'when you have a perfectly good bed of your own?'

'Why?' She gazed down at him, bemused (like the reason was as obvious as the nose on her face). '*Why?!* Because I wanna *know*, of course.'

'*Know?* Know what?'

'I wanna know about *Paul*, stupid!'

'Who?'

'In your dream. The kid who woke up. I wanna know what he said. I wanna know if he said the same thing my brother did . . .'

'It wasn't a dream,' the Reverend interrupted her (somewhat preciously), 'it was a *vision*.'

'Yeah, yeah. So what did he *say*?'

The Reverend continued to scowl at her. She was actually rather an attractive young scrap.

'D'you not think there might be some kind of impropriety?' he asked. 'I mean in your being here, on my bed, at night, after lights out?'

'Are you a poof?' Kelly delicately enquired.

'Absolutely not.'

'Then yes,' Kelly confirmed, 'it's definitely a bit dodgy.'

'I'm a Reverend,' the Reverend upbraided her, 'I don't *do* "dodgy".'

'So what *do* you do?' Kelly asked, raising a suggestive brow. 'Just for the *record*, I mean . . .'

'That's none of your damn *business*!' the Reverend hissed.

Kelly appraised him, frowning. 'Do they even *have* black people in Canada?' she wondered.

'They have black people everywhere,' the Reverend snapped.

'My brother died,' Kelly informed him.

'I know.'

'How?'

She slit her eyes at him, suspiciously.

'Because you yelled the whole ward down for half an hour.'

'Oh. Yeah . . .'

'And I feel very sorry for you,' he said, 'if that helps at all.'

'Thanks . . .'

She continued to stare at him.

'. . . I *think*.'

'So will there be anything else?' he asked.

'Yup.' Kelly nodded. 'Either you tell me what he said or I'll tickle your feet till you piss the bed.'

She began Incy-Wincy-Spidering with her fingers down the counterpane –

Pause

'Oh for *heaven's* sake,' the Reverend expostulated. 'It wasn't *your* brother. Visions aren't *specific*. They're symbolic. God isn't literal, he speaks in *metaphors* . . .'

She straightened up. 'Why?'

'Because that's how he's always done it.'

'So what did he *say*?' she still persisted.

'Who? *God*?'

'*NO!* My *BROTHER!*'

'*Shhh!*' he winced, cowering. 'I don't *know*. I honestly can't remember . . .'

'Okay. Fine . . .' Kelly recommenced her slow finger-crawl.

Silence

'Oh *bollocks*,' the Reverend cursed, quickly drawing his feet up.

Kelly stared at him, surprised.

The Reverend sniffed, then gently cleared his throat.

'*Well?*' Kelly persisted.

'Well *what?*'

'Well what did he *say*?'

'Oh bollocks,' the Reverend repeated. '*That's* what he said.'

Kelly's eyes widened, in amazement. 'Oh *bollocks*?'

'Yes.'

'In a *vision*?'

'Yes.'

'A vision from *God*?'

'Yes. And that's *precisely* why . . .' he looked slightly embarrassed, 'I didn't want to make an *issue* out of it . . .'

'Oh *bollocks*? Are you *sure*?'

'Completely.'

The Reverend nodded.

'Oh *bollocks*?'

'Say it enough times,' he snapped, 'and you'll wear it out.'

Before he'd finished speaking, however, Kelly had abruptly leaned forward and cuffed him, delightedly, about the head.

'*Ow!*'

'Spot *on*!' she gasped. 'He *swore – real* loud – that's what the nurse said . . . *Man!*' Her eyes were now as bright and round as two new beach balls. 'Would you ever *believe* it?!'

The Reverend shrugged.

'High five,' Kelly volunteered, offering him her flattened palm.

'My arms are stuck,' the Reverend demurred, 'under the counterpane.'

'So fine,' Kelly beamed, chucking his pious cheek, instead, 'you win. It's a deal. Where do I sign up?'

'Sign up?'

The Reverend frowned.

'Yeah. You *convinced* me. You worked your magic. So how'd I join?'

'Join? Join *what*?'

'*You*, mate. The Church an' shit . . .'

'You want to join the *Church*?'

'Yup.'

Kelly nodded.

'To follow *God*?'

'Yup.'

Kelly nodded again.

'To dedicate your life to Jesus Christ?'

'Yeah. An' if you want *my* opinion,' she expanded airily, 'then fuck Ashford, mate, we wanna go to *Africa*, do some *important* work – help out all those little orphan kiddies with AIDS . . .'

'*Africa?!*'

'Yeah. I got this article . . .' she reached down into the front of her nightdress and scrabbled around for a while. 'Hold on a sec . . . It's fallen under my . . . *Here* we go . . .'

She pulled out the relevant, neatly folded-up page from *Marie Claire* and threw it at him. It hit him on the chin then bounced back down on to the counterpane.

He freed his arms, grabbed it and unfolded it.

'I don't understand,' he said, after several moments' quiet. 'This is an article about the benefits of solar energy.'

'Huh?'

Kelly snatched it from him and perused it herself. The article was actually a detailed exposé on the environmental devastation generated in third world countries by their unnecessary dependence on bottled gas. Kelly flipped the page over. 'It's on the other side, you *twat.*'

The Reverend took the page back and gazed at it, terrified.

'But you don't even know what my *denomination* is,' he finally blustered, glancing up. 'You don't even know what kind of Church I'm a member of.'

'Well *he* knows . . .' she shrugged, pointing skyward, 'an' *he* obviously reckons it's solid.'

'But that's . . .'

'I mean *think* about it, Rev: God pushed me off a wall to get me here, yeah? You said so yourself. Then he gave me my *allergy* to prove to Kane how I was innocent. Then he sent *Paul* over at eight, on the dot, to snap at my bra strap. Those was *my* signs. An' he gave *you* a special vision all about the whole thing – which was *yours*, see? So I don't rightly *care* what kind of a Church it is, yeah?' She threw up her hands. 'That's just *blah*, that's just *details* . . .'

'But what if I don't want you to follow me?' the Reverend quavered.

'*Boo shucks.* That ain't your choice . . .' she shrugged. 'An' it ain't *my* choice neither. It's God's choice, yeah? Whether *we* happen to like it or not.'

She sprang down off the bed. 'Now you get yourself some shut-eye,' she sternly instructed him. 'Okay? 'Cos we got a *whole* lotta shit to sort out come sun-up . . .'

She leaned over and snatched the Bible from his bedside table.

'What are you planning to do with that?' he asked, warily, as she shoved it under her elbow, steadied herself, and slowly began to hop.

She paused. 'Whaddy'a *think* I'm gonna do?' she demanded.

He shook his head.

'I'm gonna *read* it, Dumbo!'

She took another hop, wobbled slightly, regained her balance, and then (*just* as he was starting to get his confidence back, *just* as he was commencing to lean back and relax), she spun around and made as if to fast-bowl it at him – over her shoulder, at speed, like a seasoned pro (although she didn't actually let go). He ducked (just the same), with a yell, and it was at *this* point (the sneering porter told the credulous lab assistant, over coffee, the following morning) that she lost her footing, grabbed for the Reverend's drapes (to stop herself from falling), and brought the whole edifice – the curtain, the rail, the joists, the plaster, large chunks of the actual *ceiling* – crashing down around them.

'He was raised in Silopi – which is a Turkish border town – but his father grew up in *Sinjar* . . .'

'Iraq,' Peta murmured.

'Exactly.'

It was just after twelve and they were sitting together, companionably, in Peta's beat-up old van (the heating blasting out on full capacity) pouring themselves beakers of strong, milky coffee from their own individual, tartan flasks.

'Our flasks are all-but identical,' Peta observed, wrapping her cold hands around her beaker and taking a tentative sip.

'Yes,' Beede glanced over, anxiously, 'how odd.'

'Why?' she demanded.

'I inherited this flask from my mother,' he promptly evaded her.

'Me too.'

'Really?' he deadpanned, 'You *knew* my mother?'

She groaned as he withdrew a KitKat from the rear pocket of his rucksack.

'But the Kurds are fundamentally a nomadic tribe . . .' Peta quickly returned to their former subject, 'so there's nothing especially strange about . . .'

'I know,' Beede interrupted her. 'He did seem very ill at ease, though – very *uncomfortable* – when I raised the subject of his father . . .'

'His father was a Village Guard, you say, in a feudal Kurdish army?' Beede nodded.

'Well they're a notoriously despised breed – even amongst their own . . .'

'Yes. But that aspect of it didn't seem to bother him. He said his father was a hero, that he was killed in service after stepping on a landmine. He was just a small boy at the time and yet he clearly remembered his father's comrades bringing the body home. They'd stuffed a spare pair of trousers full of straw – to save the family's feelings – but they hadn't done a terribly good job of it. Gaffar said there was straw poking out from his ankles and his waist . . .'

'That's a grisly story,' Peta conceded, 'but why might it generate this tremendous fear of salad? A fear of *straw*, yes, or a horror of amputation, perhaps . . .'

'He's a fascinating young man,' Beede expanded, 'a boxer. Has the most astonishing presence, amazing posture . . .'

'But is it only salad he's afraid of?' Peta demanded. 'Not *all* vegetables?'

'Just salad. Specifically lettuce. I think he'd probably be perfectly fine around a tomato – say – even a cucumber, at a push, but grew increasingly anxious in the supermarket because of the necessary physical proximity of these items with the one thing he was *really* phobic about . . .'

'I knew a girl who was petrified of buttons once,' Peta volunteered.

'That's apparently quite a common phobia,' Beede nodded.

'It was the thought of a button "coming loose" which terrified her . . .'

'Really?'

'She couldn't even say the word, or write it down or type it . . .'

'So how did she ever manage to raise the issue?'

'She didn't. It was just something I observed. Even as a child I had a powerful interest in detail . . .' she shrugged.

'Did she ever recover from it?' Beede wondered, unwrapping his KitKat and breaking it in half.

'Yes. She went into therapy eventually. We met at a school reunion about ten years ago and I interrogated her about it. She claimed that it was a complex phobia – the complex ones are much harder to resolve – because she wasn't so much afraid of the buttons themselves as of what they represented. For ages the therapist thought it was a sexual fear . . . a fear of disrobing . . .'

'No surprises there, then,' Beede observed, cynically.

'But after a while they discovered – following some bouts of deep hypnosis – that she'd swallowed a button as a baby. It'd become briefly lodged in her throat . . .'

'Hmmn . . .' Beede gave this scenario some consideration. 'So you think it's possible that Gaffar might've had an experience along similar lines?'

564

'Well it's not inconceivable.'

Beede frowned. 'I have another theory,' he said, 'but it's quite a strange one . . .'

He offered her half of his KitKat. She thanked him and took it.

'In a spare moment earlier this afternoon I actually did a web-search on Sinjar and got some rather bizarre results . . .'

She bit into the chocolate and then frowned as she chewed. 'This is soft,' she said, grabbing the packet and inspecting it. 'The sell-by date is February 1997.'

Beede ignored her. 'Obviously there was all the run-of-the-mill stuff – political, *geographical* . . . But hidden in amongst it . . .'

'1997,' she repeated, snatching the remainder of the bar away from him. 'I doubt even Pinch would risk something of that vintage . . .'

Pinch sat bolt upright in the back of the van, on hearing his name uttered.

'In fact . . .'

Peta offered the chocolate to Pinch. Pinch sniffed at it, gently took it from her, and then devoured it, with relish.

'Chocolate is bad for dogs,' Beede idly observed as Peta rolled down her window and spat out what little still remained in her mouth.

'*Balls* . . .' she cursed, 'I just dribbled it down the side of the door.'

She wound the window back up again. Beede took a few, quiet sips of his coffee.

'So, hidden in amongst all the geographical stuff?' she prompted him.

'Yes,' he unscrewed his Thermos and carefully topped up his beaker, 'there was a ream of information about this ancient Kurdish tribe, this outlandish *sect*, known as the Dawasin . . .'

'The what?' Peta frowned.

'The Dawasin, sometimes also known as the Yazidi, I believe – or *Yez*idi, the spelling varies on individual sites . . .'

'I've heard of them,' Peta butted in, 'an ancient Kurdish sect. There's a large community in Germany of all places . . .'

'Apparently so, there's several hundred thousand of them – in total – but one of their main populations was in Sinjar, until Saddam Hussein took it into his head to steal their traditional lands and cram them into collectives in the mid-1970s . . .'

'Are they Moslem?'

'No. At least other Moslems don't consider them so. That's another big part of the problem . . .'

'So what do they believe?'

'I'm not sure. It's all kept very hush-hush. But from what I can tell their faith contains elements of Christianity, Judaism *and* Islam. They hold the Bible and the Qur'an sacred, but they have their own holy book written by their own special prophet, Shaykh Adi. It's called The Book of Emergence – I can't remember the Kurdish title off-hand . . .'

She smiled. 'I think we can forgive you that . . .'

'They worship a fallen angel,' Beede continued, 'called Malik Taus. He's also known as The Peacock Angel. They believe that evil is as much a part of divinity as good . . .'

'How very modern of them . . .' Peta quipped.

'Yes. Although Malik Taus isn't the devil, strictly speaking, because he repented his fall – for 7,000 years – during which time he wept seven large jars of tears which he used to put out the fires of hell . . .'

'Gracious.'

'And God isn't an active presence, either. He created the world but then he withdrew. Shaykh Adi and Malik Taus control the world's destiny now.'

He paused. 'They're fanatical purists. You can't join or convert. You have to be born into the tribe.'

'Why?'

'Because they believe – and this is the really crazy part – that they're the last remaining direct descendants of Adam's line which hasn't been besmirched by the sins of Eve . . .'

'What?! *How?*'

'I'm not sure,' he shrugged, 'but because they're so pure – I mean racially – they're insanely clannish and secretive. They never discuss or practise their religion openly, never marry outside of the sect, and if you leave the community for over a year then you risk excommunication, which means that your soul is effectively lost forever.'

'Okay . . .' Peta pulled a smallish, Tupperware container from her bag, prised open the lid and produced two home-baked rock cakes from inside. She passed one over to Beede. '. . . So how exactly does this relate to your friend?'

'Well there was one fact which sprang out at me . . .'

He took a quick bite of the rock cake.

'These are wonderful.'

566

'Yes. They're one of Ann's specialities . . .'

   Peta took a bite herself.

Beede quickly chewed and swallowed. 'The Yezidis actually believe that lettuce is evil.'

   'No!' Peta almost choked on her mouthful. 'That *must* be apocryphal!'

'It's always possible – I mean I gleaned this information on the *net*, after all. But from what I could tell, a hatred of lettuce, of salad, is a deep-seated part of Yezidi culture. Malik Taus hid inside a lettuce patch at one point and so lettuces are associated with evil and all Yezidis are extremely cautious around them . . .'

   'So you honestly think . . . ?'

Beede shrugged. 'It just struck me as rather strange, that's all.'

   'But does – uh – *Gaffar*? Is that his name?'

Beede nodded.

'Does Gaffar practise any religion that you know of?'

   'He's a Moslem, a Sunni Moslem. But not an especially dutiful one. I get the impression that his mother is fairly traditional, quite devout. It's possible that he might suspect something about his father's past – I mean if I'm on even remotely the right track here, then I'm guessing that his father may've been raised among the Dawasin and then left the tribe at some point, travelled over to Turkey, converted, got married, started a new life there . . .'

   'But this is all speculation . . . ?'

'Yes. Entirely.'

   'Will you ask him about it?'

'Perhaps. I'm not sure. I'm in two minds on the matter – it might not really be my place . . .'

'Your *place*?' Peta parroted. 'How come?'

He just shrugged.

'I mean isn't the phobia sufficiently disabling to justify your involvement, whatever the consequences?'

'It's certainly quite bad. Quite extreme . . . But if he *doesn't* know – by some strange fluke – well, the wider ramifications could be absolutely *fascinating* . . .' Beede turned to look at her, his eyes glimmering. 'Because what it would potentially mean is that this isolated young man had somehow sustained a kind of unconscious memory of this extraordinary and singular culture from his genetic past. A kind of mystical or spiritual *imprint* . . .'

Peta frowned. 'He might've had clues. There might've been – what do they like to call it? – *uh* . . . A certain amount of *leakage* from the family in general . . .'

'Of course.'

'And something else to factor in,' Peta continued, 'is that this is a culture he can never fully regain, that he can never actually *experience* or have ready access to. If his father was excommunicated . . .'

'That's also true,' Beede nodded. 'It does seem very paradoxical, very *cruel* in a way – to discover something so monumental about yourself which lives on, just out of reach, and can never be recovered.'

'And especially hard to bear,' Peta expanded, 'when everything about our modern culture seeks to engage, to democratise, to *convert* . . .'

'The Dawasin are certainly a bizarre anachronism,' Beede agreed.

He smiled. 'Gaffar's such an amazing creature, though. Such a paradigm . . .'

'How so?'

'Well, because he's been stripped of literally everything – his past, his home, his *history*, even – and yet there he stands, utterly unbowed, just readying himself, quite calmly, for life's next big assault . . .'

'*You're* quite extraordinary,' Peta murmured, shaking her head.

'Me?' He turned to look at her, surprised.

'You'll happily spend a night tramping around the woods,' she informed him, tartly, 'in freezing mid-winter, on a doomed quest to find a lost friend. You'll search the web trying to unlock the secrets of a random Kurd's psyche, but when it comes to your own flesh and blood, your own *son* . . .'

'That's hardly *fair*,' Beede snapped.

'Why not?'

Beede glowered down at his rock cake. He felt a strong urge to throw it at her, to clamber out of the van and disappear, but it had started to rain – huge, round drops which smashed down in a thousand, mean little rabbit-punches on to the windscreen.

'Why *not*, Beede?' she repeated.

SEVEN

She didn't return for over forty minutes. After two he took out his phone to check his messages. He sent a quick text to a client and a quick text to Gaffar. He put his phone away again. He carefully inspected his hands. He frowned. He chewed off the jagged tip of a broken thumb-nail. He inspected his hands for a second time. He stopped frowning. He took out his phone. He re-checked his texts. He read a perplexing message from Kelly which simply said, *I 4give U –*

Eh?

He debated ringing her, decided against it and texted her instead (*uh . . . Thanx, I think . . .*).
   He looked at his watch –

Late

– then gazed around the kitchen. His eye alighted on his mug of sweetened milk. He took a small sip of it and grimaced. It tasted strange. Rich. Thick. And there was a dense skin on the top. He ran a tentative finger along his upper lip then stood up, walked over to the sink, poured the eggy-milk down the plughole and washed out his cup.
   Once he'd completed this task he noticed the dirty pan – how the milk had burned into a glutinous, brown mess on the base of it. He grabbed hold of it, found a scouring pad, some detergent, and scrubbed away, assiduously, until all the burned milk was gone –

Good

He placed the pan on to the draining-board, rinsed out the whisk, then set about cleaning the top of the hob – where the milk had boiled over – shining it up to a perfect finish with a small piece of kitchen towel.

He leaned against the oven, with a sigh, and gazed around the room. He took out his phone. He held it in his hand, scowling, swore under his breath, and shoved it away again. He inspected his watch. He went and sat back down, then stood up, as if intending to go, but didn't move. He cocked his head and listened –

Silence

He frowned. He inspected his watch. He glanced around him. He picked up the book by the doctor about his antsy-looking daughter. He sat down. He flipped through it . . .

Then the letters started to arrive. Slowly at first, then more and more frequently. All of them in Arabic. The Foreign Office had translated them, as best they could . . .
'She was a lovely girl,' said one, 'with a huge soul, a generous spirit . . .'
'When she smiled,' said another, 'the world always felt like a better place.'

Kane snorted and tossed the book – contemptuously – back into the box. He pulled up his hood (like a sullen teenager), then crossed his arms and gazed around him.

Hung over the back of a nearby chair were three, tiny child's socks, none of which matched. And on the table just in front of them? Something he hadn't noticed before –

A scarf?
A shawl?

He reached out and grabbed a hold of it (it *was* a scarf. A long, grey scarf. Soft. Knitted) then closed his eyes and pressed it to his face. It smelled of cloves . . .

Yes . . .

– and of chestnuts, and of winter – of old charcoal smoking in a brazier. It was still damp. He frowned. Something was tickling his cheek. He opened his eyes and looked down –

Mud.
Flecks of mud . . .

He carefully picked them out of the grey fabric, one by one, then rolled the scarf up, into a tight ball, to see how small he could make it –

Pocket size?
No –
Too big.

He grimaced and pressed it to his face again. He buried his nose into it, burrowed into it and stayed there for several minutes. It was then that he saw –

Huh?!

– the *goose* wings. Clear as day. In his mind's eye . . .

Eh?

– and he was busily engaged in fastening them together –

Are those my hands . . . ?

– with some twine –

Twine?

?!

– then slinging them over his shoulders, with a guffaw, and tying them into place –

Just like Icarus

– before starting to climb.

Climb?

The sound of running water distracted him from his reverie. He opened his eyes and glanced up at the ceiling. There was a crack. A long crack, which extended virtually the entire . . .

What's she doing up there?

He frowned –

Showering?

He stared down at the scarf again, bemused. He hesitated for a moment and then pushed his face into it for a second time.

Soil

He saw soil. And it was French soil (he was certain of it). And he was scooping up this soil with his hands and he was slowly, carefully, piling it inside his shoes. His boots. His tiny, hand-made, exquisitely stitched, ludicrously pointed boots . . .

Then there was a rumbling –

Eh?!

He definitely heard a rumbling –

Almost a . . .

He opened his eyes. He saw the dog. She was standing (as best she could) on the kitchen tiles in front of him and she was growling. She was baring her teeth at him.

'Hey . . .'

He leaned down towards her to try and calm her. She continued to growl. Not at *him*, he soon realised . . .

'Is it the scarf?' he asked, proffering it to her. She backed off, still growling.

Kane threw down the scarf and stood up. His chair squeaked against the tiles. He felt strange, almost intoxicated. He thought about having a smoke to calm his nerves. He gazed down at the dog. The dog seemed perfectly fine again. She was dragging herself over towards her water bowl.

Okay . . .

He took a quick turn around the table to burn off some energy. After two or three steps, though, he stopped. He stared at his feet, at his Blundstones . . .

Ow!

He was sure there was something . . .
   He squatted down, untied a lace on one boot and pulled it off. He stared inside the boot –

Nothing

He tipped the boot upside down –

Nothing

He frowned. He inspected his sock –

Nothing

He slowly and suspiciously put the boot back on. He stood up. He stamped his foot. It felt fine.

Hmmn.

He began walking around the table again. On his way around he noticed a large, dark-blue, *faux*-military-style jacket hung up on a peg on the back door. He stared at it, scowling, then he walked over and quickly slipped his hand into one of the jacket pockets. He withdrew a small, brown pill bottle without a label on it and a neatly rolled-up length of bandage. He shook the bottle. He unscrewed the lid, frowning, and peered inside of it. The bottle was half-full of large, unwieldy-looking white pills. He tipped one out on to the palm of his hand and stared at it, still frowning, then he gently touched the tip of his tongue to it –

Eh?

He touched his tongue to it again –

Chalk –
Just chalk.

He tipped the tablet back into the bottle (his head cocked, nonplussed), replaced the lid and returned the bottle and the bandages to the pocket. He reached into the second pocket. This pocket was full of plastic . . .

Rubbish

He withdrew a small piece of packaging and was just set to push it straight back inside again when he paused and took a second look . . .

What?!

It was the packaging for a cat collar – but a *special* cat collar: a collar for a cat, with a *bell* on it. And shoved in alongside that? A Polaroid. A crumpled-up Polaroid. He carefully straightened it out. It was a photograph of a cat. A cat wearing a collar. A cat wearing a collar *without* a bell attached. And not just *any* cat, either –

Oh no . . .

It was *Beede's* cat. Beede's *Siamese* cat –

Manny?
Is that his . . . ?

A door suddenly slammed shut in another part of the house. Kane quickly returned the photo and the packaging to the coat pocket and turned around, panicked, grabbing his cigarettes from his jacket –

I was just gonna pop outside for a quick . . .

Elen looked dazed – dreamy, *distracted*, even – as she drifted back into the kitchen. She'd changed her clothes and her hair was now wet – newly washed – falling in thick, dark tangles across her shoulders. She was wearing a dressing gown (a plain, brown dressing gown) which was loosely fastened with a belt. And under that? Nothing but a short, thin, pale grey slip.

As she entered the room she was dabbing at her face (her eyes, at least) with the sleeve of the dressing gown –

Crying?
Was she . . . ?

And because her arm was lifted the dressing-gown belt had come loose. Kane could see the lean lines of her body beneath it, the slope and lift of her small breasts, the jut of her hip-bone, the neat angularity of her knees . . .

She didn't immediately acknowledge him. She simply walked over to the table, picked up the grey scarf and buried her face in it. Her shoulders shook a little. Kane almost moved towards her then, but still, something stopped him.

Elen drew a deep breath, threw down the scarf (almost in disgust), turned and walked over to the sink. She stared into it for a while, blankly. She sniffed, forlornly and clumsily scratched at the back of her calf with the toes of her other foot. Kane stared, his lips parting, at the pale, soft flesh behind her knees.

Then he dropped his cigarettes. They landed on the tiles with a clatter.

'John?'

She spun around, terrified, almost losing her balance, grabbing on to the cabinets behind her, her eyes wide, her nostrils flaring. She stared at him, wildly, almost blind – it seemed – with fear. Then she began blinking, very rapidly, as if not entirely sure . . .

'Kane?'

At first she seemed astonished by his presence, and then (almost in the same instant) just as astonished that she'd somehow connived to forget that he was there.

'Oh *God*. I just . . . I didn't . . .'

She grabbed at her dressing gown and pulled it tightly around her.

Kane bent down to retrieve his cigarettes in a brave attempt to mask his dismay.

'You were gone for so long . . .' he murmured, straightening up again, 'I was just going to . . .'

'How *stupid* of me . . .'.

She looked around her, confused.

'What was I *thinking*?'

She slapped the side of her head, with frustration, slightly harder – perhaps – than she should have.

'Don't worry about it.'

He didn't like to see her slap herself.

'No. It's just . . . I went upstairs to check on Fleet,' she paused, frowning, 'didn't I? And then . . . Then I must've dozed off. I was sitting on the bed . . .'

She scratched at her head and felt her wet hair . . . 'Yes. Then I went to have a shower. I washed my . . . I was just feeling so . . .' she shuddered. 'Isn't it cold? Is the heating on? It feels so cold.'

She quickly walked over to a heater and felt it with her hand. Her hand was shaking, he noticed. It had almost a blueish pallor.

'I should go,' Kane said, feeling mortified. 'In fact I *must* go . . . I've got . . .'

He turned and tried the back door. It was locked. He looked for a key. He saw one. He twisted it and tried the door again. It remained tightly shut. He glanced up. There was a bolt, at the top. He unfastened it and pulled the door wide. He stepped outside.

'You did the washing up . . .' he heard her, still babbling, still anxious. 'That was so . . .'

He began striding across the patio tiles towards the side-gate.

'Kane?'

He glanced over his shoulder.

She was standing on the back step, her arms wrapped around her. She looked tiny. Her feet were bare.

'Kane?'

She stepped down on to the patio tiles.

'Go back inside,' he said irritably. 'You'll freeze.'

'Please don't leave.'

'Go back inside,' he repeated firmly.

'No.'

She was shivering. Her teeth started chattering. But she didn't move.

'Don't be stupid,' he said, almost angry now. 'Go back inside.'

'Don't leave,' she said, 'I'm very sorry . . . I wasn't . . .' Her voice was almost inaudible. He closed his eyes for a moment. He clenched his hands into fists. He was infuriated by her.

'You're tired,' he said.

'I just want to speak to you,' she said. 'I just need to tell you something.'

'Tell me what?' He turned. She didn't answer. She just continued to stand, as before.

'Tell me what?' he repeated.

She held out her hand, plaintively.

'I should go,' he said, but then he took a tentative step towards her.

'Just one second,' she promised.

'Fine.'

He walked straight up to her. He stood in front of her, almost too close. He stared down at her, intimidatingly. But she wasn't intimidated. Instead she reached up, with both hands, and gently grabbed the white hood on either side of his face, then slowly, very deliberately, she stood up on to her tip-toes and pulled his head down towards her. Soon both of their faces were obscured by the hood's dense fabric. Their noses were almost touching, and their lips.

'What do you want?' he murmured, mystified.

'What do you want?' she echoed, then she wobbled slightly. He reached out his hands and found her waist, her ribs. He fastened his hands around her and supported her. She opened her mouth slightly, as if to speak, but she didn't speak. She just lightly exhaled on to his upper lip. He opened his mouth, too. Their lower lips touched. Her breath was warm and smelled of milk. He felt the cold tip of her nose almost brushing his cheek. Neither of them moved.

'Mummy?'

As quickly as it had begun, it was done with. She was there, then she was gone – back into the house again to deal with her son.

Kane felt shaky. He pushed back his hood. He put out an unsteady hand to support himself against a piece of scaffolding. The scaffolding creaked and shifted. He quickly let go again. He glanced up, shoving his hand into his pockets and taking out his cigarettes. He tapped one from the packet and propped it between his lips. He located a box of matches, opened it, removed a match and struck it. He lit his cigarette, shook the match out and tossed it down, grimacing, on to the concrete.

'Well it's none of your damn *business*, for starters,' he growled.

'I didn't say it was,' Peta shrugged, 'I just said it was perplexing, that's all . . .'

She paused. 'Which it is.'

'Kane and I are very different,' Beede insisted.

'No. That's not true. From what I can tell you're actually very similar . . .'

'Similar? You think so?' he sneered. 'Well maybe *that's* at the root of it, eh?'

'Perhaps.'

She refused to be intimidated.

Silence

'Very *similar*,' Beede scoffed.

'You both take things so much to heart . . .' Peta murmured.

'*Kane?!*' He blinked at her, astonished. 'How can you possibly think that? You've met him once. Trust me, Kane takes nothing to heart. He lives in the moment. If he doesn't like a situation then he walks away from it or he devours a pill to blank it out . . .'

Peta looked shocked. 'That's harsh, Beede . . .'

'He's a thief,' Beede maintained calmly, 'a dealer.'

'He eliminates pain,' Peta neatly recontextualised. 'He brings people relief.'

Beede snorted, contemptuously.

Peta ignored this. 'Weren't you ever close?' she asked.

Beede shrugged. 'There was never really *room* . . . Heather was always so . . .'

He shook his head, irritated.

'What?'

'I don't know . . . *Needy*. Overpowering.'

'Even before she was ill?'

He nodded. 'Kane was her refuge – her retreat. He was just this tiny, open, credulous little receptacle into which she poured all her dreams, all her frustrations – her disappointments. She was just one of those characters . . . Very funny, very charming, openly manipulative – sometimes almost . . . I don't know . . . almost *hilariously* so. And beautiful – intensely beautiful. People just loved to be around her, to do things for her. Kane was no exception . . .'

'But didn't the relationship concern you?' Peta asked.

'Pardon?'

'Well it doesn't sound entirely . . .'

'Healthy? Functional? No. It wasn't. And naturally I spoke to her about it. I warned her. But she didn't care. It was just her nature. Her *way* . . .'

Beede idly picked a currant out of his rock cake and gently pressed it between his forefinger and his thumb. 'Heather stifled the boy. She always did. And for my part, I was always determined that if there was one thing I could do for him – as a man, a father – it would be to leave him to his own devices. Not to criticise. Not to control. Not to manipulate or to judge. And that – to the best of my ability – is what I did.'

'Was it difficult?'

'It nearly killed me . . .' he smiled, grimly. 'But that which doesn't kill us . . .'

He paused. 'And in hindsight it was probably a mistake. The damage – the trauma – was way too deep. Kane quickly confused freedom with *licence* . . .'

'What about the divorce?' she asked (determined to understand every detail of the scenario). 'How did that work?'

Beede popped the currant into his mouth. 'She squeezed me out,' he shrugged, 'or I squeezed myself out. It just ended. We were relieved. There were no ill feelings on either side.'

'None?'

'No,' he glanced over at her, blankly, 'there were always other projects, other demands on my energy . . .'

'But then she fell ill?'

'Yes. *Yes*. Although it wasn't quite as dramatic as . . . I mean it was all very slow, very gradual . . .'

He frowned.

'Why the frown?'

'Because . . . I don't know . . . Because it all *sounds* very dramatic, very tragic, even, and to a large extent it was, but the illness wasn't entirely ... It wasn't ...' he continued frowning, 'I mean doctors often like to imply that particular kinds of people – particular kinds of characters – have a sort of ... of *predisposition* towards certain types of ailments ...'

'Like a choleric person developing an ulcer, say?'

He nodded. 'In Heather's case the illness seemed like a cruel but strangely coherent articulation of the person she already was. I mean she wasn't a shirker – God forbid. Absolutely not – she was a *dancer* for Christ's sake ... They're machines, they're completely driven, totally indestructible right up to – and sometimes *beyond* – the point of collapse. But Heather made a career out of projecting herself as vulnerable, as embattled, as winsome and fragile, while underneath – below all those layers of connivance, below all that tinsel and netting and ribbons – was this astonishing feistiness and vitality, which is what people responded to, and which – God knows – *I* responded to at some level. It was what I loved about her, and what Kane loved too, I don't doubt ...'

'So she moved to America?' Peta interrupted.

'Yes. Early on. They thought the warm, dry weather ...'

'And you didn't mind her dragging your son along?'

'*Mind?*' Beede looked surprised. 'Of course not. It just seemed ...' He shrugged again. 'Inevitable, I suppose.'

'You'd detached yourself,' she sighed, 'even at that stage.'

He grimaced. 'Perhaps.'

He took another bite of his cake. Peta returned hers, virtually untouched, to its Tupperware container.

'Were you pleased when they came back?'

'Oh yes.'

He nodded. 'I was relieved. For her sake as much as Kane's. They moved into the bungalow on Hunter Avenue ...'

'And how was Kane by that stage?'

'Kane?'

'Was he different? Had he changed?'

'Uh ... I don't know. He was always a good boy. He had a wayward side. He certainly doted on his mother ...'

'And you?'

'Me?'

Again, the surprise.

'Yes, how did Kane feel about you?'

Beede slowly shook his head, as if it hadn't actually occurred to him to consider this before. 'I couldn't honestly say . . . I tried to be there for him, I suppose. But I had this sense that he'd moved on, that he didn't really *relish* my involvement, that he'd . . .'

'What? Grown up? Grown beyond you? Become an adult?'

'No. *Yes.*' Beede nodded. 'I suppose he *had* to some extent. He was so amazingly attentive. So diligent when it came to Heather. He'd become her partner – her *dancing* partner – if you see what I mean. Her rock. Her support. He always knew the best thing to do, what tablet to take, what number to call . . .'

He suddenly scowled. 'Until, of course . . . *Well* . . .'

He shook his head. He put down his cake. He glanced over towards her, with a shrug '. . . until he *didn't*, obviously.'

He clasped his hands together and stared out through the rain-splattered windscreen.

'What happened?' she couldn't resist prompting him.

He sighed. He lifted his glasses and rubbed his eyes. But didn't seem to object to being prompted.

'They were living downstairs at that point. I'd divided the flat into two parts. I was upstairs. The pain had been especially bad, I remember, especially gruelling. But there was actually a reason for that – it later transpired – because she'd been stockpiling her painkillers, her sleeping pills. She'd been planning for months to commit suicide.'

'Did Kane know?'

'Oh yes. *God* yes. He was intimately involved. Her motor skills were so diminished by the end. She found it difficult to swallow. And then there was always a danger that she might regurgitate what she'd taken once the process was actually under way. She didn't want to risk that. Kane was an integral part . . .'

He fell silent.

'How old was he?'

'Fifteen. It was all so cold, so *calculated*. His sixteenth birthday was just two days away.'

'Did he want his mother to die?'

Beede turned towards her, scowling. 'Of course not. He loved her. He *doted* on her. But he would've done absolutely anything she'd asked him to do.'

'So then what?'

'I don't know, exactly. They had a special day together. They celebrated his birthday early. There was a *cake*, I remember . . . and presents . . .'
He bit his lip. 'And once that was done, once that was over . . .'
He closed his eyes and pinched the bridge of his nose. Then he opened them again and drew a deep breath.
'She'd taken the requisite amount,' he calmly continued, 'whatever that was . . . She'd actually passed out. From what I could glean afterwards she'd been "dead" – in Kane's mind, at least, without any detectable pulse, he said – for twenty minutes or so . . .'
He smiled. 'But the human animal is a resilient beast . . .'

'She wasn't dead?'

'No. She suddenly started to twitch, to gasp, to move about. An awful kind of seizure . . .'

'Kane must've been terrified.'

'He panicked. He went to pieces. As luck would have it, though, I'd just come home from work . . .'

'So you walked in on the whole thing?'

'No. *No* . . . I was working unsociable hours at the time. I'd just crawl home in the afternoons and slip straight into bed. I rarely saw the two of them. We were all so bound up in our own lives, our own routines . . . Anyhow, the next thing I knew Kane was shaking me awake. He was hysterical. He said his mother had tried to kill herself. He said he needed help.'

'*He?*'

'Yes . . .' he glanced up, 'not *she*. Not *she* needed help. He needed help. I thought about that a lot, after . . .'
He shrugged. 'Anyway, I ran downstairs, I saw her. It was . . .' he winced '. . . a terrible sight.'

'And Kane?'

'Hysterical. You've got to help me, he kept saying, so I tried to sit her up, I tried to make her . . .'

'Is that what he wanted, though? To revive her?'

'No. I don't know. Yes. I mean he loved her. He was traumatised . . . He certainly didn't try and stop me at that stage, although I do remember that he became quite distressed when I rang for an ambulance . . .'

He slowly shook his head. 'In all honesty I don't think he knew himself. That was the problem. It wasn't the kind of decision he should've been called upon to make . . .'

'But weren't you tempted to just leave her? To let her die? That was what she'd wanted, after all . . .'

'No.' Beede's answer was immediate. 'Absolutely not. It didn't dawn on me. And apart from anything else I could've been considered an accessory, which would've been a disaster for Kane. The boy had to be my priority. I couldn't jeopardise his future care . . .'

'But you never actually asked him?'

'Asked him what?'

'What he thought you should do.'

'There wasn't time . . .'

'But you said he was her partner, her *rock*, surely . . .'

'He came and woke me up. He was floundering. He'd lost control. He requested my help . . . And another thing,' he continued staunchly, 'if I'd left her to die, Kane may well have been haunted by his involvement – tormented by it, even – later on . . .'

'Are you sure of that?'

'Of course I am. How could he *not* be? He was a *child* . . .'

'He was the adult. You said so yourself.'

'*I* was the adult. *Heather* was the adult.'

'So you revived her?'

He nodded. 'I did my best. And the ambulance was mercifully prompt.'

Silence

'So how long before she . . . ?'

'Before she died? Months. Almost a year. She was profoundly brain-damaged. But still she *knew* somehow . . . There was this powerful, this *palpable* sense of . . . of rage, of disappointment.'

'God.'

'Yes. It was awful.'

'And Kane?'

'Totally devastated. Furious. Mortified. He blamed me, obviously. And at some level I suppose he blamed himself for not having had the strength to sit it out.'

'Didn't you ever try and talk to him about it?'

'I tried. Of *course* I tried. But the situation was on-going. It was fluid. There was never a perfect opportunity. And it was complicated. It was too difficult – for both of us. There was no . . . no *groundwork* . . . no . . . no *rapport* . . .'

Beede suddenly paused, agonised, as if an awful truth had just dawned on him. 'I suppose there never really *has* been . . .'

Silence

'. . . Ever.'

Silence

'God. I was an abysmal dad,' he said.

Once the boy had finally been persuaded to head upstairs to bed again, they sat together, stiffly, at either end of the sofa, a small pile of folded bed-linen placed between them like a buffer.

Elen had taken the opportunity to yank on a pair of loose, black sweat-pants and a huge, navy-blue jumper – (five sizes too large for her), which Kane presumed (with a slight sinking feeling) belonged to her absent partner.

'When someone dies,' she said, staring straight ahead of her, kneading anxiously with her agile fingers at the jumper's hem, 'it's like they suddenly become a *part* of you. I mean at first there's the grief, this huge *void*, this terrible sense of loss, but then one day you wake up and you find yourself eating the same cereal they ate – salted porridge, in the case of my dad, which I'd always really *loathed* before . . .' she paused, 'then buying the same kind of clothes – a certain type of *vest*, for example, which I started getting for Isidore, made out of this special Irish yarn, which really makes him *itch*, he says,' she smiled, dreamily, 'but which my dad had always worn . . .'

At the mention of Isidore's name, Kane glanced towards her, with a frown.

'And he loved Monkey Puzzles,' she continued. 'The trees?'

She glanced back at him, very briefly.

Kane nodded.

'He'd always point and yell, "Monkey Puzzle!" whenever we drove past one – it was like some great, big joke which I never really caught the punch-line of . . . But I even found myself doing *that* . . .' she shook her head, smiling, 'and Fleet's just as bemused by it now as *I* once was . . .'

'My mother used to sing this stupid song about Aspidistras,' Kane reminisced. 'She had the most awful voice . . .'

'Then one day I looked into the mirror,' she interrupted him, 'and I saw *his* face staring back at me. I'd never considered the resemblance before. I mean I don't think there even *was* one . . . But suddenly our foreheads, our *jaws* . . .'

She ran a gentle finger along the sharp line of her jaw.

'Even tiny things – phrases he used, hand gestures, *smells* . . .'

'They definitely settle on you once they're gone,' he said, 'like a strange kind of *powder* . . .' His mind turned, momentarily, to the bottle of pills in Isidore's pocket. 'Like a fine layer of chalk.'

'But it takes ages, doesn't it? The same way it takes a while for the dust to settle after you've replastered a wall or a ceiling . . . ?'

'Months,' he nodded, 'years, even . . .'

They were quiet for a while.

'So what did she want for you?' Elen suddenly wondered.

'Want?'

'Your mother. What were her dreams for you?'

Kane frowned. Then he smiled.

'She always thought I'd be a carpenter,' he said.

'Really?'

'Yup. I used to whittle away at things, as a boy. I was actually quite good.'

'A carpenter?' Elen considered this for a moment. 'I can't really imagine that.'

'I used to make woodcuts. Old-fashioned, oblong woodcuts . . .' He approximated the shape and size in the air with his hands (and as he did so he had a sudden, sharp memory of his father's cheerful indifference to his painstaking endeavours). 'I did these amazing *Star Wars* ones, full of all this incredible detail . . .'

He shook his head, fondly.

'What happened to them?'

'I don't know. I guess they must be at the back of a wardrobe some-where . . .'

'So why did you stop?'

He shrugged. 'I just lost interest, I guess.'

He never encouraged me.
I was never really good enough.

'A talented carpenter can always find work,' Elen volunteered.

'I carved her a cross,' he mused, 'but it was never finished. *God*. I've not thought about that in years . . .'

'Is she buried locally?'

'No. There was a family grave just outside Aylesbury, in Buck-inghamshire . . .'

'Wood's so mutable,' she sighed.

'Everything's mutable,' he responded blithely, 'that's why it's impor-tant to savour the moment.'

'Oh *God*,' she suddenly exclaimed, covering her mouth with her hand.

'What?'

He jerked forward in his seat, concerned.

'I've just had a *thought* . . .' she turned to face him, her eyes full of wonder.

'*What?*' he repeated.

She grinned at him. 'You must finish it.'

'Pardon?'

'The cross. You must finish it. Complete it. Take it to her . . .'

He frowned. He wasn't especially impressed by the idea.

'I mean finish what you started . . .' she ran on excitedly.

'Find *closure*, eh?' he said, scratching four, tiny, deeply ironic speech marks in the air.

She looked hurt. Then, 'Yes,' she said. 'Why not?'

He reached for his cigarettes.

'May I smoke?' he asked, taking them out.

'No,' she slowly shook her head.

'Why not?' he demanded petulantly. 'Doesn't your husband like it?'

'The smell,' she explained, 'will get on to Fleet's bedclothes.'

She put out her hand and patted the small pile of linen. As she reached out he saw the mean line of bruises on her forearm.

'Of course.'

He quickly put his cigarettes away again, frowning.

'And no, Dory *doesn't* actually like it,' she expanded (somewhat unnecessarily, he felt).

As she spoke the dog – Michelle – appeared in the open doorway. Kane stared at her, moodily.

'What happened to her legs?' he wondered.

'Her legs? Michelle's legs?'

He nodded.

'I don't really know. I think she was probably born that way. The legs are malformed. They never grew.'

'Have you had her for long?'

'God, no. Only a month or so. She just . . . *uh* . . . she just kind of turned up.'

'What?' Kane scoffed, thinking of Beede and the cat. 'Just landed on your doorstep with the special little cart attached?'

'Isidore – my husband,' Elen explained, frowning, 'sometimes he does things – *initiates* things – and then forgets . . .'

'Did he build the little cart?' Kane asked, smirking (still niggled, at some level, by the smoking ban).

'No.' Elen shook her head. 'At least . . .' she frowned, 'I'm not entirely sure . . . Although it's beautifully made, *exquisitely* made, like a tiny work of art . . .'

'Did he bruise your arms?' Kane wondered (as if this question was of exactly the same order – the same *calibre* – as all the others he'd just asked).

'Pardon?'

'Dory. Your husband. Did he bruise your arms?'

Elen turned to apprehend him, shocked.

Kane calmly met her gaze. 'You said that sometimes he initiates things and then he forgets, I just presumed . . .'

'No,' she drew back from him, visibly appalled. '*God*. How awful. What an awful thing to . . .'

She pulled down her sleeves, offended.

'I'm sorry,' Kane apologised, 'I must've got the wrong idea. It was just something Beede said . . .' He shook his head. 'It was nothing.'

'It was an accident,' she persisted.

'Good. Fine. You don't need to explain.'

'I slipped on a patch of black ice while out visiting a client, and someone – this man – they just . . .'

She paused. 'Beede? Did *Beede* say something?'

'No. Nothing important.'

'What did he say?'

Kane looked uneasy. 'He just warned me to keep my distance, that's all.'

'Keep your distance?' she seemed surprised. 'Keep away from *me*, you mean?'

'Yes.'

'Did he say anything else?'

'Yes. He said the situation at home was complicated, that your husband wasn't well . . .'

'And that was all? That was all he said?'

Kane thought about the drugs.

'Yes. That was all.'

'So he warned you off? Beede warned you off?'

She looked forlorn.

'He was right to,' she added. 'It *is* complicated.'

She glanced down at her arms. 'But Dory didn't do this.'

'I'm relieved to hear it,' Kane said, glancing over his shoulder. 'So where is he tonight?'

He tried to sound nonchalant.

'Dory?'

Her chin jerked up. 'He's at work. He's just at work.'

'I see.'

She suddenly drew her legs up, folded them tight into her body, pulled the baggy jumper over the top of them, yanked it down to her ankles, manoeuvred her arms from the sleeves (withdrew them inside), wrapped them around her legs and balanced her chin on her knees. She stared straight ahead of her like a grave, blue Sphinx. 'I must put the dog to bed,' she murmured, 'otherwise she'll just drag herself around, peeing all over the place . . .'

'Can I give you a hug?' Kane asked.

'What?'

She turned, hostile. He didn't dare repeat it.

'I'm just so *tired*,' she sighed, 'and it's made me a little fractious, I'm afraid. I'm not quite myself.'

'Then you should sleep.'

He prepared himself – mentally – to go.

She closed her eyes. 'I can't. I can't sleep. I just keep on waking up.' She opened her eyes again. 'I wish I could sleep.'

'I can give you something,' he said, gauging her reaction, coldly. She quickly shook her head. 'No. I need to stay alert in case Fleet . . .'

'*I* can keep an eye on the boy,' he insisted. 'And I give you something to make you relax,' he expanded, 'which'll definitely help . . .' 'If I relax I'll just shatter,' she smiled, slightly self-consciously (as if perfectly aware of how dramatic this sounded), 'like some beat-up, old windscreen.'

'Damned if you do . . .' he told her, watching on possessively as she gently tipped her head against the arm of the sofa, her long, dark lashes slowly fluttering to a close. After a while her breathing deepened.

He leaned over towards her, then, instinctively reaching out his hand to brush the damp tangle of hair from her forehead, her cheek, her throat, but not actually making contact – not *daring* to make contact – just holding his fingers aloft, mere inches from her skin, like a scrupulous pianist too enthralled by the thought of a tune to presume to play a note.

EIGHT

'You *forgive* me?'

'Yeah . . .' Kelly slapped her Bible shut and grinned into her mobile's mouthpiece, almost beatifically, 'yeah, I *do*, as it so happens . . .'

She was sitting – legs akimbo – in a badly broken wheelchair, on a busy hospital corridor, alongside a lightly slumbering Reverend, patiently awaiting their latest x-ray results.

'But *why*?' Winifred demanded, her words slightly slurred. 'I mean for *what*?'

'Because I've found God an' I wanted to make my peace,' Kelly informed her, cheerfully. 'I sent the same text to everyone in my address book . . . *Uh*,' she frowned, concerned, 'an' if you don't mind my sayin', you sound just a tad *pissed*, love.'

'So let me get this straight: you suddenly got this overwhelming *urge* at . . . uh . . .'

Pause

'. . . five past eleven – pretty much on the dot – to forgive everyone you ever *met*?'

'Yup,' Kelly nodded. 'That's about the sum of it.'

'But *why*?'

'I already said,' Kelly shrugged, unperturbed, 'because it was the *Godly* thing to do . . .'

'The *Godly* thing?' Winnie snorted.

'Yeah. *You* know, clean slate an' all that . . .' she paused, thoughtfully, 'or maybe you *don't*, come to think of it . . .'

'So which God are we talking about here?' Winnie enquired (as if Gods were just something you might select at the cheese counter).

'*Which* God?' Kelly was incredulous. 'Don't be stupid! *The* God. The God who *found* me. *My* God.'

'*Urgh* . . .' Winnie hiccoughed. 'I'm suddenly feeling ever so slightly *sick* . . .'

'An' because of Paul,' Kelly calmly continued, 'I'm forgivin' you for *Paul*. Paul died. He's dead.'

Pause

'Yes,' Winnie spoke extra slowly, as if engaging with an imbecile, 'I know that. You already told me that, remember?'

'No I didn't, as it happens,' Kelly maintained, swapping her phone to the other ear (and inadvertently nudging the Reverend awake as she did so). 'Well I *did*, but I didn't, because he weren't actually dead at that point.'

'Pardon?'

'I fibbed.'

'You did what?'

'I fibbed. I porky-pied.'

'You *lied*?' Winnie struggled to digest the full implications of this news. 'But that's just . . . I don't understand. Why on earth might a person *do* that?'

'*Oi!*' Kelly harrumphed. 'Climb down off your high horse. It was *you* as got him snortin' *glue*, remember?'

The Reverend delivered her a warning glare. She delivered him one straight back.

'Well strictly speaking . . .' Winnie slurred, 'I mean to be completely fair, we kind of got started *together* . . .'

'*Balls!*' Kelly exclaimed. The Reverend nudged her, sharply. She drew a deep breath and stared up at the ceiling. 'But who cares – *whatever*. It's *over* with, yeah? A done-deal – *kaput*. I forgive you. So let's just leave it at that, shall we?'

'How'd he pass?' Winnie demanded, patently still suspicious, 'and *when*, exactly?'

'Late this afternoon. He was in a coma. He sat up, he said, "Bollocks", an' then he died. Just like that.'

As she spoke Kelly's raised eyes moistened.

'He said *what*?' Winnie chortled.

'Bollocks.'

Kelly wasn't chortling.

'He sat up and said bollocks? He was in a coma? Then he sat up and he . . . ?'

'Yeah,' Kelly growled.

'Are you serious?'

'Never more so.'

'Honestly?'

Kelly drew a deep breath. She clamped her lips together (this forgiveness business plainly wasn't all it was cracked up to be).

'Yeah, *honestly*,' she finally ground out.

'So how long was he in this coma for?'

Winnie's tone was now marginally – but only *very* marginally – more sober.

'Two years.'

'Two *years*?!'

'Christ,' Kelly expostulated. 'You growin' *spuds* or what?'

The Reverend clucked. Kelly shot him a black look.

Silence

'So you've forgiven me, huh?'

'Yup.'

Kelly rested a gentle hand on her Bible.

'But what if I don't *want* your forgiveness?' Winnie wondered.

'Come again?'

'What if I don't want it? What if I'm not *interested* . . .'

Kelly rapidly lifted her hand.

'Then you can fuck right off,' she spat, 'because you're forgiven, and there ain't bugger-all you can do about it.'

The Reverend slapped her arm.

'Ow!'

'Well I'll need to forgive you too, then,' Winnie graciously insisted.

'Huh?'

'For lying to me in the first place.'

Kelly gave this some thought. 'Fair enough,' she conceded, 'though as grudges go, it's hardly in the same *ball*-park . . .'

'Well that's a matter of opinion.'

'No it ain't. It's a fact.'

'Yes it is.'

'No it ain't.'

'So where'd you get my number?'

'Huh?'

Kelly was briefly thrown off her stride.

'Was it Kane? Did he give it you?'

'*That* skank? No. I got it from the envelope.'

  'The envelope? Which envelope?'

'The one I delivered for ya. As a *favour*. An' while we're at it . . .' Kelly continued, 'that old story . . .'

'Which one?'

'The one in the envelope.'

'You mean the stuff from the British Library?'

'Yeah.'

  'What about it?'

'The man who wrote it, the doctor . . .'

'What about him?'

'Nothin' . . .' Kelly cleared her throat, guardedly, 'I was just *interested*, is all.'

Pause

'Why?'

'*Huh?*'

'Why? *Why* were you interested?'

'Why the hell *shouldn't* I be?' she snapped.

  'Uh . . .' Winnie gave this question some consideration. 'No reason, I suppose. He was a fascinating character . . .'

'Yeah?'

'Yeah.' She paused, speculatively. 'So you obviously took a quick peep inside the envelope . . . ?'

'Yup.'

'Well that was wrong – a total breach of etiquette, of *faith* . . .' Kelly scowled.

'But I forgive you.'

  Kelly continued scowling. 'I'll tell *you* somethin' for nothin', Miss Clever-Bum,' she volunteered.

'What?'

'For all your fancy education, you ain't much of a *speller.*'

'Rubbish,' Winnie shot back, 'I'm an excellent speller.'

'No you ain't. You couldn't even get his *name* right.'

  'Whose name?'

'The doctor's name.'

'Of course I did.'

'No you didn't.'

   'Well there's probably a perfectly good reason for that.'

'Oh yeah?'

'Yeah. And if you'll just hold your horses for one second then I'll . . .'

Long pause

'Hello?'

'Keep your knickers on. I'm just fetching my notes. I'm finding the page. Here we go. Board. Andrew Board – b-o-a-r-d, or Boord – double "o" – or Boarde – b-o-a-r-d-e – according to where it is that you happen to look. I actually had *two* copies of the original text, and one was much earlier . . .'

'So?'

   'Well they spelled words in a variety of ways back then.'

'Who did?'

'Everyone.'

'Huh?'

   'The language was in flux.'

'Come again?'

'English,' Winnie sighed, exasperated, 'the *language*, it wasn't always set in stone. It grew, it *developed*. Nowadays it's considered such a funda- mental part of the national character, the culture, something we're all so sure about, so proud of, but back then it was just a baby – a fledg- ling. It was still finding its feet, still being painstakingly sewn together. And all the rules which we now take so much for granted . . .'

   'Hang on a sec . . .' Kelly was confused. 'So if there weren't no *English*, then what did we speak?'

'Pardon?'

'If there weren't no English then what did we speak, I mean *before* we could speak?'

'We spoke French. Or Roman. Or Norse. Or Latin. Or a series of local dialects, I suppose . . .'

   'French?' Kelly was horrified. 'Us English spoke *French*?'

'Yup. We still do. Where d'you think *pleasure* comes from, or *naive* or *liqueur*?'

   'But then . . .' Kelly was growing increasingly confused, 'but then how did they all *chat*? I mean amongst themselves? *Before*?'

'I imagine they just muddled along as best they could. That's one of the main reasons why the doctor's story's so interesting. He actually wrote one of the first truly English texts . . .'

'He did?'

'Yup . . .'

A brief scrabbling amongst papers . . .

'The doctor – believe it or not – was also a monk.'

'A *monk*?' Kelly reached out and grabbed the Reverend's arm. The Reverend quickly snatched it back.

'Yes. A monk of the London Charterhouse. A Carthusian monk, which is the strictest possible order.'

'How strict?' Kelly demanded.

'Well he was a vegetarian, wore a hair shirt, lived a life of abject poverty . . . strict as you like, really. And he joined early. He joined when he was still underage . . .'

'How old?'

'I don't know. A kid, most probably. A teenager. But it was a tricky time to be affiliated to the Church . . .'

'Why?'

'Because Henry wanted a divorce, so he separated with Rome.'

'An' then what?'

'Well the monks were basically screwed. He stole all their lands and money. He made them choose between their faith and their monarch – swear an oath of conformity. Many of them refused and were persecuted – imprisoned, placed under house arrest, deported. Boorde, too, more than likely – he was a bishop at one stage, I believe . . . *Uh* . . . Bishop of Chichester – 1521 . . .' she paused, distracted. 'What's that strange noise?' she demanded.

'It's only me,' Kelly squeaked, 'I'm just excited.'

'Excited? Why?'

'Because . . .' Kelly simply couldn't hold it in any longer, 'because he was my fuckin' *grandad*,' she exploded.

'*Sorry?*'

'The *doctor*. He was my *grandad*. My great-great- . . .'

'Dr Andrew *Board*?'

'My pops was always goin' on about how we had this great-great-great- . . .'

'. . . etc . . .'

'. . . who was a *doctor*. A doctor to the *king*. Dr Andrew Broad. An' he said how he wrote this book all about how you build a proper house . . .'

'Board, Broad . . .' Winnie tried this on for size. 'Good Lord. How *odd* . . .'

'An' I always used to think it was just more of his old *bullshit*, yeah? I mean why would a doctor write a book about . . . ?'

'That's a good point,' Winnie interrupted, 'a valid point. But the plain fact is . . .' (she suddenly sounded rather excited herself) '. . . that he *did* . . .'

'Fuck *off*!'

'He wrote . . . I mean these are just rough *notes* . . . but I've written, *The boke for to lerne a man to be wyse in bylding of his house for the helthe of his soul*. Uh . . . I'm not sure if that's an independent text or if it's just part of *The First Boke of the Introduction of Knowledge*, which he also wrote . . .'

'Bloody hell.'

Kelly turned to the Reverend.

'This is too weird,' she said.

'Broad/Board/Boord,' Winnie murmured. 'Who would've thought it?'

'It's fuckin' *monster*,' Kelly shook her head, astonished, 'it's *huge*.'

'His *The Dyetary of Health* was actually one of the earliest medical works to be written in English,' Winnie returned to her notes again, 'which gives it great philosophical significance. Apparently the *OED* traces the first uses of several general words to that particular book . . .'

'The *OED*?'

'Yup. The *Oxford English Dictionary*.'

'*Shit* . . .' Kelly gasped, 'my Uncle Harve's gonna pop his fuckin' *clogs* . . .'

'Although – on the down-side – there's some question over the authorship of the work that I photocopied . . .'

'Which work?'

'*Scogin's Jests*.'

'But you said in that letter you wrote,' Kelly rushed on, 'about how it was all a bit dodgy. About how *he* was a bit dodgy . . .'

'Did I? Oh. Well as I already mentioned, there were certain . . . uh

'. . . confusions . . . about the authorship of the Scogin book,' Winnie said carefully. 'I mean there's obviously still loads more to find out . . .'

'Really? You'd *do* that?' Kelly very nearly bounced out of her chair. 'Uh . . . well, *yeah* . . . I suppose I could always head back down to the library. Or you could always try the internet. I already looked for Scogin – so did Beede – and he didn't have a single entry, but *Boorde* on the other hand . . .'

'*When?*'

'Sorry?'

'When will you go back?'

Winnie frowned. 'To the library? I dunno. I mean how much more do you really . . . ?'

'*EVERYTHING!*' Kelly bellowed, her voice shaking with emotion. 'This might sound stupid, yeah, to someone like you, someone all educated who wrote a fancy book, but I always thought we Broads was just . . .' she paused, judiciously, 'just *shit* . . .'

'Well you were obviously wrong.'

Winnie smiled as she spoke.

'I know. It's another *sign*,' Kelly was buzzing now, 'and it ain't just about *me* this time, neither. It's about *all* of us. Because God loves you too, yeah? You're a *part* of this thing, no matter what. Just like the Rev here . . .'

Kelly squeezed the Reverend's shoulder. The Reverend winced, pained.

'Hang on a second . . .' Winnie paused, confused. 'A part of what?'

'The puzzle. The *picture*. Like the Reverend said, God *made* me fall off the wall that day . . .'

'The wall?'

'When I fell off the wall an' bust my leg . . .'

'You did *what?*'

'An' then I met Gaffar. An' I was allergic to painkillers. An' Gaffar stole the envelope. An' I read the papers, an' I met the Reverend. An' the Reverend had this *vision* that Paul would say "Bollocks". Then he did. An' now we're goin' to Africa. And my grandad was a *monk*. He dieted for Christ too. An' it's all because I fell off that wall. Because of *you* . . .'

'You're just babbling now,' the Reverend soberly interjected. He leaned in closer to Kelly's phone. 'She's just babbling,' he informed Winifred.

'Who's that?' Winnie demanded.

'It's the Rev. Ignore him. He's only in a bad mood 'cos I brought down the roof . . .'

'You did what?'

Winnie sounded bewildered.

'Like I told that stupid nurse, it was a total, fuckin' *accident* . . .'

'Kelly . . .' The Reverend nudged her.

'So will you go?' Kelly demanded, ignoring him. 'Will you look?'

'To the library?'

'Yeah.'

'Well I'm sure I'll probably be heading into town at *some* point . . .'

'*BRILLIANT!*'

Kelly paused, inhaled, at which juncture the Reverend snatched the phone from her. 'It was just a *metaphor*,' he said, 'God speaks in metaphors, as I tried my best to explain to her. And forget Africa. She's getting way ahead of herself on that count . . .' he paused. 'And there was *no* impropriety. Doesn't matter what they say. My curtains were only closed because I have a certain *sensitivity* . . .' he inhaled, sharply, 'in fact the doctor's just heading over, so if it's all right with you, I'll draw a neat, little *veil* around this peculiar interlude and bid you a very . . . uh . . .'

He took the phone from his ear and stared at it for a moment, trying to figure out how to end the call, then something else occurred to him and he returned it to his ear. 'Are you still there?'

'Yeah,' Winnie answered, suddenly quite exhausted.

'Just to set the record completely straight,' the Reverend continued, 'I'm actually a *High* Anglican. It was a *High* Anglican vision. Nothing remotely radical, or weird, or New Age or – God forbid . . .' (he quickly crossed himself), 'Evangelical . . .'

He removed the phone from his ear again, finally located the right button, and cut Winnie off with it.

'I really don't mean to be a liturgical *bore*,' he informed Kelly, passing her the phone, 'but we need to discuss the concept of The Fall – as a matter of some urgency . . .'

'Jus' gimme a *kiss*, you big ape,' Kelly exclaimed, throwing out her arms, beaming. And then, as she proceeded to envelop the Reverend in a robust hug: 'D'ya hear that, Doc?' she demanded, over the Reverend's twitching shoulder. 'We Broads got *class*, yeah? We got *breedin'*. We got *pedigree!*' she cackled. 'Just like the fuckin' *dog*-meat! Like *chum*! Like all those natty little mutts at *Crufts*. We're *up* there, mate. We *arrived*! We pulled it *off*! Ding-*dong*!' she hollered, her gleeful voice echoing down the corridor. 'Ding-bloomin'-*dong*!'

He gently covered her with a blanket, walked over to the light switch (it had a dimmer mechanism on it), glanced around the room for a final time and turned it off. He strolled into the kitchen to ensure the back door was locked. It wasn't. So he turned the key and shot the bolt.

On his way out he noticed a small pool of liquid on the tiles. He grimaced, crouching down to inspect it –

Dog piss

– then quickly grabbed some paper towel and cleaned it up. Once this was done –

Yuk

– he went to try and locate the dog.
'Michelle?'
He peered along the hallway –

Nope.
So where . . . ?

He observed a door, slightly ajar, just off to his left – a room he hadn't been into before . . .
'Michelle?'
He paused, his head slightly cocked, listening intently. Was that a sound? A *whimper*? He pushed the door wider and felt blindly along the wall for the light. He found the switch. He pressed it. The light came on. He winced. It was a bright light – just a bare bulb (the

shade having been removed at some point). He looked around for the dog. He spotted her. She was cowering under the table. He pushed the door wider, took a tentative step towards her and then –

Good God

He froze.

It was actually a dining-room – by no means a huge room – mostly taken up by a table and six chairs (several of which had been placed against the walls – to better improve access to the table, he supposed). And on top of the table? Crowning it? Over-running it? *Eclipsing* it?

Holy Moly!

A crazy, chaotic, matchstick town: a cathedral . . . a palace . . . a bridge . . . a *water* mill . . .

Wow

Kane slowly moved forward, so hesitantly at first that it was almost as if he thought the matchsticks might all collapse (that they might not actually be glued). Then he stood and he stared, quite agog.

After a minute or so he gradually began prowling around the table, intently apprehending each individual model from every angle, finally drawing to a halt (right back where he'd started) on the southern side of the large cathedral.

This was surely the pinnacle – the *pièce de résistance*? A wildly ambitious, terrifyingly meticulous, insanely ornate and yet perfectly magnificent structure (as yet unfinished). It was also . . . *well* . . . oddly . . . *uh* . . . (he scratched his head, bemused) . . . strangely . . . *uh* . . . –

Familiar, somehow . . .

He blinked. He drew in still closer, concentrating so intently on the finer details that he was barely even breathing now. He nervously reached out a tentative finger . . .

'Don't!'

A voice spoke.

He turned, withdrawing his hand, surprised. It was the boy –

Huh?

He glanced down at himself. He suddenly realised that he had fallen to his knees. He was kneeling.

'I *know* this place,' he exclaimed, 'I had this incredible *dream* . . .'

'John saw it while he was in France,' the boy automatically responded, rather like a tour guide. 'He thought it was beautiful. He often thinks about it.'

'No . . . you don't understand,' Kane repeated, barely even registering what the boy was saying, 'I had a *dream*, but it was *exactly* . . .'

'I know,' the boy brushed him aside, contemptuously. 'We *all* dream about it.'

Kane frowned, confused, as the child drew abreast of him.

He was still on his knees.

'How d'you mean?'

'Did the bird do that?' the boy wondered, inspecting Kane's knuckles dispassionately.

'Do what?'

Kane half-turned.

'*That*,' the boy pointed, 'on your hands.'

'*Huh?*'

Kane inspected his palms.

'No, *silly*, on the *back* . . .'

The boy turned his hands over –

Ouch!

Kane winced at his touch. The skin on his fingers felt swollen; stretched, incredibly sensitive. He gazed down at them, horrified, expecting second-degree burns, at least, but there was nothing visibly wrong with them. He blinked –

Nothing.

Perfectly fine.

Perfectly smooth.

'There's nothing wrong with my hands,' he said, clearly spooked.

'Oh.'

The boy shrugged.

Kane paused, frowning. 'So you actually *saw* the bird?'

'Did you meet the pretty lady?' The boy ignored his question, smiling mischievously. 'The pretty lady, over there,' he indicated towards the far side of the cathedral, 'by the altar?'

Kane's cheeks flushed as he remembered his dream.

'John loves to hide,' the boy confided, peering inside the cathedral now, through its half-finished southern entrance, 'to creep up, *very* slowly and then . . . *WAH*!' he turned, springing forward, with a yell.

Kane almost tipped over, backwards, in surprise. The boy cackled, delighted. 'He's always doing it to Mummy,' he chuckled. 'It's *funny* . . .' He chuckled again, but then after a few seconds his smile faded into a frown. 'I wonder where he's taken Daddy this time,' he murmured.

'John?' Kane echoed, struggling to regain his former composure. 'Is he one of the contractors?'

'Who?'

The boy began scratching at his arms, irritably.

'One of the builders?' Kane reiterated (remembering how Elen called out this same name a short while earlier, in the kitchen). 'Is he one of the people working on the house?'

'*No*, stupid . . .' The boy shook his head, smiling, and then, '*Yes*,' he rapidly changed tack, nodding his head, a sly look flitting across his face. He continued to scratch.

Kane glanced down at his hands again – still slightly paranoid – but once again his skin felt smooth to the touch. It felt fine.

'So did your daddy build this?' he asked, turning towards the cathedral.

'*Him?*' The boy snorted, contemptuously, his scratching growing ever more intense. '*He* couldn't build this.'

'Don't do that,' Kane instructed him, reaching out to restrain him, 'you'll draw blood if you're not careful.'

The boy knocked his hand away, still scratching, defiantly.

'Show me your arms.'

Kane grabbed a hold of one of the boy's wrists and pulled up the sleeve of his pyjama top. The right arm was covered in a mess of tiny, bleeding bites. He grabbed the left arm, pushed back the sleeve and paused. On the soft flesh of the left forearm (punctuated by yet more bites) was a birthmark. A pale, pinkish birthmark. He stared at it for a moment, surprised.

'Are these *bites* of some kind?' he demanded, after a short pause. 'Flea bites,' the boy nodded. He indicated towards a glass jar on the table. Kane glanced over at the jar. He remembered seeing the jar before: it was the same jar Lester had been carrying – the jar of nothing.

'It's empty,' he said, but even as he said it he remembered his conversation with Geraldine, the conversation about . . .
'No it isn't!' the boy grinned, delighted. 'It's all full of *fleas*. We've been *training* them to live in the cathedral. We glued cotton to them. Invisible cotton . . .'

'*Invisible?*'
'Yes. Lester brought it. It's *special* cotton . . . Look . . .'
The boy opened a small drawer in the side of the table and withdrew a normal-seeming spool of black thread.

'Now you see it,' he said, beginning to unwind a dark strand from the spool. 'And now you *don't*!'
Kane looked down at the cotton. The boy was right. As soon as a strand was unwound it all-but disappeared.

'How *odd* . . .' He drew in closer, intrigued. The boy handed him the spool. Kane took a strand of the thread between his fingers and tensed it against the reel. 'I've never seen this stuff before. It's almost like a very fine kind of *fishing* twine.'

'Lester says his mummy uses it.'
Kane inspected the end of the spool: 'Coats 100% Nylon Invisible Thread,' he read, '200m. Matches All Colours.'

'Give it back now,' Fleet demanded. Kane passed it over. The boy returned it, punctiliously, to its place in the drawer. While he did so Kane picked up the empty jar. He peered inside. Sure enough, on closer inspection he was able to see dozens of tiny black dots with a series of fine, floating strands attached.

'So how do they breathe?' he asked. 'I mean with the lid screwed on?'
'I don't know,' the boy shrugged.
'Perhaps there's just enough air trapped inside . . .' Kane mused.
'We must feed them,' the boy said, taking the jar from him.

'Feed them?' Kane echoed.
The boy rolled up his pyjama sleeve. Kane was horrified. 'You've been feeding them on your *arm*?'

The boy nodded, unperturbed. 'Daddy put powder on Lester's dog,' he explained, indicating towards the spaniel. 'We was using her to feed the fleas, but now we *can't* . . .'

'Lester's dog?' Kane echoed.

The boy glanced over at him, in alarm, as if he'd been unintentionally caught out. Then his face closed up.

'So Michelle is *Lester's* dog?' Kane reiterated.

The boy shrugged.

'Does your mother know?' Kane wondered.

'*Know?*' the boy surveyed him, haughtily. 'Know *what*?'

'About the fleas. And about who Michelle actually belongs to?'

'Don't be *stupid*!' the boy exclaimed.

Then he paused for a moment, another sly look crossing his face. 'John needed some money, so he made a special *powder* for killing fleas,' he announced, 'but it wasn't *really* a special powder – it was just chalk. And on Sunday he sold it for a penny to all the wives at church. Then after a few weeks the wives came to find him. They was cross. They said, "Your powder doesn't work. The fleas are worse than they *ever* was." But John says, "Of course the powder works." The wives say, "No. It doesn't. We want our money back." So John says, "Well how did you *apply* the powder?" And the wives say, "We shook it from the jar – on all our clothes an' our sheets an' our blankets – that it might kill the fleas." Then John begins to smile as if they are *very* foolish. So they say, "*Why* are you smiling?" and he says, "But of *course* it won't work if you shake it from the jar! You must feed it to the fleas on a little spoon, one by one, and then, when they have eaten their fill they will lie down and die – but *only* if you feed them one by one."'

Fleet put his hand to his mouth and sniggered. 'The wives was very cross with John, but there was nothing they could say.'

Kane watched the boy, closely, as he told the story.

'That's a very funny story,' he said, once the tale was finished, 'John must be extremely clever to fool all those women like that.'

'He is,' the boy nodded.

'Does your *daddy* like that story?' he continued, in exactly the same light tone. 'Does *he* think John's funny, too?'

The boy looked surprised by this question, then confused.

'No,' he answered, looking down. 'I don't know.'

'And your mummy?'

The boy glanced over his shoulder, nervously. 'Mummy doesn't like me to talk about it,' he said.

'Oh,' Kane nodded. 'So Mummy isn't too *keen* on John, then?'

The boy took a step back. He shook his head, conflicted. 'She *does* like him,' he said. He lifted his hand to his mouth and began stroking his finger along his upper lip '. . . but sometimes . . .'

The stroking grew more frantic.

'Right . . .' Kane glanced around him, wanting to mollify the boy. 'So how will we go about feeding these fleas?' he asked.

The boy continued to stroke his upper lip. He glanced up at Kane, but he didn't speak.

'I suppose we could always use *my* arm,' Kane volunteered, taking off his jacket and rolling up his sweatshirt sleeve.

The boy dropped his hand. '*Really?*'

'Sure. Why not?'

Kane showed him a tantalisingly bare expanse of flesh on his arm.

The boy strode to the table and grabbed the jar. He expertly twisted all the protruding strands of twine around his index finger, then slowly unscrewed the lid. He lifted the fleas into the air, like they were a group of invisible girls attatched to the invisible ribbons of an invisible maypole.

'Give me your arm,' he instructed.

Kane held out his arm. The boy tried to settle the fleas upon it. Kane winced as they landed, jumped and then re-landed.

'It might take a while,' the boy said.

'That's just fine,' Kane smiled, turning his face away, repelled, as they started to suckle.

NINE

Beede drove straight in to work – after a long, cold night of fruitless searching – feeling numb, physically drained and demoralised. The first thing he discovered, on arrival, apart from an irate member of staff camping outside his office who – for no reason they could fathom – was suddenly being charged Emergency Rate tax (Beede promptly made up the difference in his wages, without scruple, from petty cash) was a note from Kelly. It was scribbled on to the back of a Get Well Soon card (*Dear Jeremy, Get well soon, Son! Lots of love, Dad*) which featured (Beede frowned at it, horrified) a badly taken photograph of a woman's breast with an amateurish-looking mouse's face (and whiskers) drawn on to the soft, pale flesh around the nipple (a very large, *pink* nipple, which was apparently meant to signify the mouse's snout) in some kind of – he looked closer –

Good Gracious . . .

– felt-tip or make-up pencil. It was obscene. It was ugly. It was awful.
   He clutched at his shoulder, grimacing, then opened a desk drawer and searched for some Aspirin. He couldn't find any. He slammed the drawer shut (irritated) then jarred his shoulder again in the act of doing so –

Ouch!

   He turned the card over, with a scowl. On the rear of it Kelly had written –

Oi! Join the 21st century, Grandad! Get yorself a mobile!

And then, directly underneath, in capital letters:

I FORGIVE YOU, MATE!

XXKelly

Then under that:
PS. I think we <u>both</u> know what for – but Im so over it now you would not even believe!!
Then under that:
PPS – I found GOD!!!! Or he found <u>me</u>, more-like! (Swank Swank!)
Then under that:
PPPS. Paul died (yestrdy. aft.), but don't wrry. Im really OK about it.

Then under that: .... *PPS. Going to Africa to become a Saint!*
[followed by a little drawing of Africa – which looked nothing like Africa – with a small halo above it] *WAH!!!!!!!!*

Beede sighed, gently pinched the bridge of his nose, threw the note into the wastepaper basket and picked up his phone. He dialled Elen's number. It rang several times before it was finally answered.
    'Hello?'
Beede almost did a double-take.
'Dory?'
'Yes?'
'Good *God* . . .'
    'Hello? Beede? Is that you?'
'Yes. Yes it's me. So when did . . . ?' He quickly stopped himself. 'I mean how *are* you?'
'Fine. I've only just got in, actually. I was out working. Out all night working . . . [*hand placed over the receiver*] . . . *No*, Fleet. Put it down. That's for your toast. You *know* you don't just eat it off the spoon . . . [*pause*] Hello?'
    'Dory? Hi. Is this a bad time? It's early . . .' Beede glanced at his watch. 'I wasn't really thinking straight . . .'
'Uh . . .' Dory paused. 'I'm afraid Fleet's still finishing off his break-fast. Elen's already left to see a client. I'm in charge of the school run and he's being rather . . . [*hand over receiver again*] . . . Absolutely *not*. You do *not* feed the dog from the table. Go and wash your hands. That's *completely* unacceptable . . . [*Pause*] Beede?'
'Hello?'

'Can we meet up later, perhaps? You could come over here if you like. Are you at work?'

'Yes. I mean . . .' Beede was scowling, confused. 'So you've acquired a dog?'

'Pardon?'

'You have a *dog*?'

'A dog? Uh . . .' Dory grunted, tetchily. 'Yes. I'm afraid we do. A spaniel. A wretched little thing, actually. Her back legs are all . . . *Fleet!* [*loud wailing in the background*] . . . I *warned* you about that, didn't I? It's your own, stupid fault. Now take off your socks and go and wash your feet. I said *take off* . . . Don't spread it all over the floor! [*Pause*] Beede?'

'Yes?'

'I'm sorry. The dog's made a mess on the tiles and Fleet's just walked straight through it. I'm going to have to . . .'

Beede was gazing out (hollow-eyed) through his small window into the laundry as Dory spoke, idly scraping his thumb over the day's growth on his cheek –

Desperately need a . . .

– then suddenly –

Huh?

– he stiffened to attention –

Elen!

He saw Elen standing there. He saw Elen in the laundry. He saw Elen, conversing with a member of staff and then turning, with a smile, and walking towards him.

'Beede? Hello? About ten, then? Ten-thirty?'

'Yes,' he almost barked, feeling his heart starting to race, his skin redden. 'Absolutely. That's ideal. I'll see you then.'

He slammed down the receiver and stood up, adjusting his shirt collar, brushing a self-conscious hand through his hair. Elen knocked.

'Come in.'

The door opened.

'Danny!' she gasped. 'What a relief! Thank God you're here. I just had a hunch . . .' she'd grabbed a hold of his arm and squeezed it, gratefully, struggling to catch her breath. 'Did you get all my messages?'

'Messages?' He glanced over towards his answering machine. The red light was flashing.

'No matter,' she ran on. 'He's home. Stumbled in about an hour ago, dressed in this filthy, old tracksuit. Flip-flops. No explanation. This awful *bruise* on his forehead . . .'

'I know. I just rang . . .' Beede admitted, shutting the door behind her, and using this manoeuvre as a means to dislodge her grip on his arm.

'He answered?'

She seemed alarmed by this prospect. They were still standing in close proximity. She was wearing a soft, loose, black, roll-neck jumper and slim-fitting black jeans tucked into a pair of plain, knee-high leather boots. Her hair hung over her shoulders in two loose plaits.

He indicated, stiffly, towards the spare chair. 'Yes. But it was fine. He was busy with Fleet . . .'

He wished she would just move away. He was overwhelmed by her proximity. He closed his eyes, momentarily.

'Are you all right?'

He opened his eyes again. She was staring up at him, frowning.

'Fine. Just a little tired. I seem to have pulled a muscle in my . . .'

She put out a quick hand and felt his forehead. 'You're warm. Much too warm. And you've got a tiny, little blood blister on your lip. Did you stay out all night?'

'Uh . . .'

He tried to take a step away from her but simply backed into his chair. He sat down, heavily.

'I'm fine,' he said.

'You're not actually intending to *work* today?'

She glanced over at the rota on the pin-board above his desk, but she couldn't make any sense of it.

'No,' Beede shook his head, 'I left in rather a rush last night so I just popped in to . . .'

'Let me drive you home.'

'No. I'm fine. I've got the bike.'

'Don't be ridiculous. You're obviously in pain. Your cheeks are all flushed.'

'It's nothing,' he tried to brush her concern aside, 'just a little stiffness in the mouse . . .'

He frowned.

Mouse?

His mind turned to Kelly's card.

Forgiven

'I mean mussell,' he said, 'muscle,' he quickly corrected himself. But that was all it took, because suddenly, butting its way, determinedly, into the gap (the chink – nudging itself in between those tiny hurdles of meaning) came the stag; that huge, powerful, old stag with its sturdy gait, its broken horns, its unflinching look.

Then (hard upon) he felt a corresponding tremor running through his arm, as if a mouse were under his skin, inside his vessels, scurrying through him, hunting for something.

'No.'

He opened his eyes –

Were my eyes closed?
Did I just speak?

She was kneeling down in front of him. 'No,' she repeated firmly, 'I'm definitely coming home with you. If you insist on taking the bike then I'll follow. I'll cook you some breakfast. It's the very least I can do.'

Beede started to object again, but he wasn't really concentrating. He was thinking about the mouse. The scurrying mouse.

'Just *humour* me, Danny,' she pleaded, grabbing his hand.

He could smell her hair as she leaned towards him. Her hair smelled of roses. He smiled. Then he winced. His nostrils quivered. *Blood* and roses, he thought.

'A present? For *me*?'

Gaffar proffered her the bag, with a grin.

She took it and opened it. Inside were a pair of white, knee-high, fun-fur boots. Yeti boots.

'Is for to match,' Gaffar explained, 'on foot.'

'*Aw!* To wear wiv' the old plaster-cast? To balance me out, like?' Kelly kicked off her slipper, delighted. 'What a *sweetheart*. Bang it on, will ya?'

Gaffar carefully slipped the boot on to her foot.

'*Wow.*'

She held out her leg and inspected it, grinning. 'That's dapper,' she chuckled, tousling his hair. 'Thanks, kid.'

'You is *dress*, huh?' Gaffar observed, straightening up again, indicating towards her clothes.

'Yeah. I'm just waitin' to get signed out. The doctor's due in an hour . . .' she frowned. 'So where'd you get that bruise?' she wondered. 'It's a fuckin' *corker*.'

'Bruce?'

Gaffar looked mystified.

'That *bruise*, Dumbo. On your forehead.'

'*Ah.*'

Gaffar put a hand to his forehead.

'You was in Readin', yeah?'

'Reading? Sure.'

'You sit wiv' my brother then, or what?'

'Uh . . .'

Gaffar frowned.

'Wassup?'

'I get this *tex*,' Gaffar promptly changed the subject, 'to say you is *forgive* Gaffar, eh?'

'*Forgive* you?' Kelly echoed. 'Sure . . .' Then she frowned, suspicious. 'What *for*, exactly?'

Gaffar closed his eyes and tensed up his shoulders, as if steadying himself for some kind of violent attack. 'Okay . . . *Okay*. So this stupid hospital is *close*,' he confessed.

'*Closed?*'

He opened one eye. 'Sure. This morgue . . .'

'The morgue was *closed*?'

He nodded.

'Fine.'

Kelly shrugged. 'I mean I know you're full of *shit* – I ain't a *fool* or nothin' – but fine.'

Gaffar was taken aback by her reaction. He was almost disappointed.

'*Fine?*'

Kelly nodded. 'You was on a hidin' to nothin' there, mate – a wild-goose chase – 'cuz Paul was *here* all along, see?'

'Goose?'

'No. *Paul*. My *brother*, yeah? He was here. God brought him here. He snapped on my bra strap. It took me a little while to realise, yeah? Paul was wiv' God. An' God was right here . . .' she swallowed, blinking, suddenly full of emotion, 'on *this* ward.'

?!

'Did they mess with your medication again?' Gaffar murmured, staring at her, quizzically.

'Thanks for the boots,' she repeated, 'they're lush. And now I need you to help me up. There's somethin' I gotta do.'

'Huh?'

'I need a piss. An' then I wanna go an' find the Rev. They moved the Rev . . .'

She pointed to the ceiling, by way of explanation. Gaffar inspected the ceiling. There seemed to be a large hole in it.

'For *piss*?' he reiterated.

'Yeah. I need a piss. You can come an' hold the doors open. The nurses are all busy. Help me up.'

She held out her hands. He assisted her, gently, to her feet, then passed her her crutches.

'An' you can grab that while you're at it,' she suggested, pointing to the large, brown envelope containing Beede's photocopied document which was poking out of her half-packed sports bag. Gaffar snatched up the envelope, bent it in two and shoved it into his back pocket.

'So what *did* you do all night?' she asked him.

'Pard?'

'Went to some shonky gamblin' den, eh? Got bladdered? Played dice? Crowned it all wiv' a big punch-up?'

Gaffar scowled, patently unnerved by the accuracy of this synopsis.

'You speak for Simo?' he asked, quickly glancing over his shoulder, paranoid.

'Simo?'

'Drive? From mini-cab?'

'So how much did ya bag?' Kelly demanded.

'Eh?'

'Wonga, mate. Greens. Boodle. Mazuma. Because I definitely want half of it.'

'Half?'

'No kiddin',' she persisted. 'Either you give me what's due or I ring up your pal Kane an' tell him how you sold us all down the fuckin' *swanny* last night, kicked up ya size nines an' went gamblin' instead.'

'Half?' Gaffar reiterated.

Kelly deftly slipped her hand inside his coat pocket and withdrew his wallet. She opened it up.

'Fuck me. You're *well*-pelfed!'

She removed a portion of the notes, then handed him the wallet back. Gaffar snatched it from her, glowering.

'*Oi!* Don't get all *narked*,' she chastised him. 'This is for a good cause, yeah? This is for *God's* work, ya *get* me? I'm on his pay-roll, now.'

She crossed herself (the wrong way around) then stuffed the notes into her skirt.

'Right. Let's head off. I'm fuckin' *bustin'* for a slash.'

She indicated the way. Then she stopped.

'*Balls*. I forgot my Bible. It's on the bed. Just grab me my Bible, will ya?'

'Bible?'

Gaffar leaned down and grabbed the Bible. He held it in his hand and inspected it, frowning.

'You need this Bible for to go *piss*?'

'Yeah,' she confirmed. 'When I was into East 17, yeah? The band, yeah? I wouldn't even fuckin' *fart* – 'scuse my French – without my picture of Brian in my pocket. I had it all reinforced wiv' sticky-back plastic – to protect it, yeah? So I could wipe the lippy off his gob whenever I smooched it,' she shrugged, resigned. 'That's just how I am, I guess.'

He proffered her the Bible. She took it from him, kissed it, then passed it back. He gazed at her, incredulous.

'I'm gung-ho, Gaff,' she chuckled, hopping along, unsteadily, in her fluffy, new boot, 'I'm a *nutter*, a ditz, a turd, a ding-bat . . .' she shrugged. 'But that's *corking*, mate, it's peachy – it's "all wool an' a yard wide" as my old nan used to say – because here's the *important* bit . . .' she turned to face him, her eyes shining with pride, and enunciated very slowly – very *cleanly* – to ensure he understood '. . . that's *exactly* how God loves me, *see*?'

'But you're being ridiculous . . .' Kane was down on his hands and knees (his phone gripped, unsteadily, between his shoulder and his ear), digging through an assortment of junk in the back of an old wardrobe '. . . I mean he didn't actually *say* anything, did he? He didn't actually *mention* that we knew each other . . . ?'

Pause

'I know, but Beede's not *like* that. I already told you, he has his own shit to deal with – trust me . . .'

Pause

'Well if you'll just *calm down* for a minute . . .'

Pause

(Scowling) '*Where*, exactly?'

Pause

'*Why* not?'

Pause

'The *parrot*?' Kane burst out laughing. 'Now you're *really* being para-noid.'

Pause

'I'm *not* laughing, I'm just . . .'

Pause

'Fine. Yeah . . . Although I'm definitely not increasing the amount, because you're actually doing really . . .'

Pause

'*Listen.* You're doing really *well*. There's no need to jeopardise all the hard work we've put in just because . . .'

Pause

'Okay. Well it's your funeral . . .' Kane rolled his eyes, straightened up, withdrew a smallish, oblong object wrapped up in newspaper from the wardrobe, crouched back on to his haunches and inspected his watch. 'I know the area. I'll look for your car. But just *calm down*, all right? And give it about half an hour . . .'

Pause

(More eye rolling) 'I know. *Yup.* Bye.'

He threw down his phone and began unwrapping the parcel. As he pulled off the paper it became clear that the single object was in fact *two* objects which had been carefully stored away together. Kane smiled as he flipped them over to take a proper look. He stared at them both, intently. His smile slowly faded.

'*Man.* But these are just *shit*,' he murmured.
He held one up even closer to his face to inspect the finer detail –
'*Jeez.* This is *dreadful* . . .'
He held it at arm's length again. 'I mean I can barely even tell . . .'

His musings were interrupted by the sound of the front door slam-ming –

Eh?

He tossed the woodcuts back into the wardrobe, grabbed his phone, shoved it into his pocket, checked for his car keys and sprang to his feet.

'*Gaffar?*' he yelled, striding through the flat and out on to the landing (only pausing to grab a pop-tart from the toaster and stuff it, whole, into his mouth). 'I'm *onto* you, you sneaky *fucker* . . .'

He bounced down the top three stairs, then ground to a sudden halt. There, just in front of him, stood Elen and Beede. Gazing up at him. Together.
Beede had his hand resting lightly –

Paternally?

– on Elen's shoulder. She had her hair in two sweet plaits. She was wearing slim-fitting black boots.

Kane nearly choked on his pop-tart.
'Sorry,' he put up his hand to his mouth, 'I thought you were someone else . . .'

'Kelly's brother died,' Beede observed stiffly, trying the handle on his door, then realising – with a small start – that it was locked. 'Did you know?'
'Uh, yeah,' Kane murmured, noticing a tiny, little blood blister on his father's lip. 'She rang me last night. It was all very sudden. Very quick . . .'

His eye shifted to Elen. She was standing at Beede's side, completely at her ease, gently smiling up at him. She indicated, with her finger, to the side of her mouth. Kane frowned, then, '*Oh* . . .' He rubbed at his cheek.

Jam

'Well that's *something*, I suppose,' Beede conceded as he retrieved the key from his coat pocket.
'And a little more . . . *uh* . . .' Elen pointed to her chin.

'I actually need to have a quick word with you about Gaffar,' Beede muttered. 'Later, perhaps?'
'Is something wrong?' Kane enquired, still dabbing and swallowing.
'Absolutely not,' Beede frowned, as if shocked by the suggestion (by

Kane's patent lack of *faith* in his Kurdish pal). 'It's a kind of . . . *well* . . . a kind of *cultural* issue.'

'*Cultural?*' Kane frowned.

Beede unlocked the door and pushed it open. He politely waved Elen inside and then promptly followed her, closing it – firmly – behind him.

'Thanks. *Great*. Nice to see you, too,' Kane muttered, remaining where he was for a while, scowling – deeply irked – like a schoolboy dismissed by a peremptory headmaster. Then he quietly descended the remaining stairs, inspected his teeth in the hallway mirror –

Urgh

– rubbed at them, vigorously, with his index finger and grabbed his ancient, grey, crombie from the coat-rack. He slowly put it on, listening out – quite nonchalantly, he felt – for any audible snatches of conversation from inside Beede's flat.

'. . . this weird, old . . . uh . . . *habit* I guess you'd call it,' Elen was speaking, and her voice was much louder – much clearer – than Kane might've anticipated, 'I mean this was *way* back when we very first met – before things got quite so . . .' her voice quavered a little (did it? Or was she just bending down as she spoke – or *sitting*? Perhaps sitting down on the sofa?) '. . . so horribly *complicated* . . .'

'Damn,' Beede swore (making a rattling sound), 'I'm all out of Anadin.'

(Kane visualised Beede's First Aid tin – bright blue, rusty-hinged – which was generally stored on a top shelf in the kitchen).

'I'll run out and get you some . . .'

Elen's voice grew still louder.

Kane sprang away from the door, panicked.

'No. It really doesn't *fmwah-fmwah*. I'm actually *fmwah-fmwah-fwah-fmwah*.'

Kane grimaced and drew closer to the door again. It sounded like Beede was filling a pan – or a kettle, perhaps – with water.

'I thought we both agreed that you'd try and put your feet up,' Elen gently chastised him, her voice growing fainter.

'Don't be silly,' Beede insisted, 'it's much *fwah-wah-fmwah-fmwah-fwah*.'

'Well at least let me *fmwah-wah fwah-wah wah fmwah*,' she demanded.

'How *maddening*,' Beede suddenly exclaimed, 'the washer's playing up inside the cold tap . . .'

(Strange squeaking noise as the tap is manipulated.)

'. . . It must've perished, I suppose . . .'

(Sound of cupboard door being opened and shut.)

'Sorry,' he apologised, 'you were telling me about *Dory* – this strange habit of his.'

'Oh . . .' Elen sounded momentarily distracted. '*Yes* . . . Well he'd just *fmwah-wah-wah fwah fmwah fmwah-wah fwah* . . .' she returned – somewhat haltingly – to her anecdote, 'I mean without *fmwah wah fwah fwah,* and when the person answered he'd tell them that [*her voice grew much clearer again*] he'd lived there, as a boy, and that I was his girlfriend, and that he'd told me all about it, and would they mind terribly if we just took a quick look around . . .'

'You never mentioned this before,' Beede's voice suddenly sounded incredibly close – so much so that Kane leapt back towards the mirror again (where he frantically pretended to readjust his fringe).

'I honestly hadn't thought about it in years . . .' Elen sounded guilty, 'I mean he only ever did it a few times . . .'

'How many times?'

(Beede again, still close, sounding rather tense.)

'I don't know – five, maybe six . . .'

'And what part did *you* play, exactly, in this curious, little deception?'

Huh?

Kane frowned at what he took to be Beede's unnecessarily cutting tone.

'Did you simply go along with it?'

'Yes.' Elen responded simply, unequivocally. Kane smiled. He touched the back of his hand against his cheek, then glanced up and saw himself in the hallway mirror – the dreamy eyes, the goofy look – and dropped his hand, appalled.

'At first I honestly *believed* him,' she continued. 'It sounds stupid now, I know, but I was completely taken in. I thought he *had* lived in those places. The first couple of times at least . . .'

'And he never set you straight? You never interrogated him afterwards?'

'No. Not that I can clearly recollect. We spoke mainly in German back then. My vocabulary was somewhat limited. And the relationship was new. It was far less . . . well, *vocal* . . .' her voice petered out.

'But that still doesn't make any sense, Elen,' Beede all-but snapped. 'It's illogical. How could he possibly have lived in those places when he was born and raised abroad?'

'But he wasn't,' Elen said calmly.

Pause

'Pardon?'

'He was born here, in England. His parents were Londoners. They emigrated to Germany when Isidore was a boy.'

'Oh.'

(Beede sounded shocked.)

'And in my own defence,' she continued, 'I suppose I was just a little more naive back then. Dory was always so plausible. And the whole thing was so bizarre, so out of character, so *unlike* him. You know yourself how straight he is, how repressed, how *law-*abiding . . .'

'Yes.'

(Although Beede didn't sound entirely convinced.)

'And I guess,' Elen persisted, 'that I probably found it quite *funny* in a way. *Exciting*, even. We were young. Things weren't nearly so . . .' she cleared her throat '. . . so fraught between us back then.'

Her voice faded somewhat towards the second half of this speech. Kane leaned in closer to the door. It sounded like she was standing in the kitchen now.

'The point is that *wah fwah-wah fmwah-wah fmwah* . . .'

Kane scowled, exasperated.

'. . . I mean not in *years*, but then yesterday, out of the blue, he suddenly forced me to pull over the car, leapt out, and went to *wah fwah wah-fmwah wah-wah-fwah*. This tiny, little *fwah-wah-wah* . . .'

'An *old* house, you say?'

Beede's voice sounded more distant again, too.

'Oldish. But not *that* old.'

'Who answered?'

'This young girl – this very *fmwah-fwah-wah wah fwah*.'

Kane placed his ear directly against the crack in the door.

'So what did you do?'

'I didn't really know *what* to do. I just grabbed *wah-fmwah wah fwah fmwah fmwah-wah*. I mean it's not that I didn't *trust* him . . .'

'Did she show you around?'

'Yes.'

'And did he seem quite . . .' Beede paused, judiciously '. . . quite *himself*?'

Elen paused, too.

'Yes. I mean . . . *yes*. A little manic, perhaps.'

'So what happened?'

'Well he suddenly came out with all this amazing *detail* about how the place had been when his old aunt had lived there. It was incredible. How he'd built this *wah fmwah fmwah-fwah-wah* . . .'

Kane rolled his eyes.

'. . . Even all this crazy stuff about his aunt being a very strict Catholic, and how she'd had crucifixes hung up everywhere, at which point the girl – Gaynor – who certainly appeared to be taking the whole thing with quite a pinch of salt – although maybe that was just *me*, I mean *my* paranoia – suddenly told this story about how when they'd first bought the place there'd been all these marks on the wallpaper – shadows – from where crucifixes had obviously been hung before . . .'

'Perhaps he'd noticed one of those shadows as you were walking around?'

(Sound of refrigerator opening.)

'No. They'd redecorated. This was *years* ago . . .'

(Clanking sound.)

'Does this *fmwah* smell all right to you?' she enquired. 'It's the day after its sell-by date . . .'

(More clanking.)

'There should be a new one. Hang on . . .'

(Still more clanking.)

Pause

(Sound of teaspoon rattling around inside a mug.)

'What you need to bear in mind,' Beede pontificated, 'is that even twenty or so years ago a standard Catholic home would've had *fmwah-wah fmwah-wah* on *fmwah-wah* all over the house . . .'

'Of course. But it was just . . .'

   'Is that pale enough?'

'Yes.'

(More stirring. Sound of objects being placed on to a tin tray. Clanking sound. Noise of refrigerator closing.)

   'I don't mean to put a damper on things,' Beede's voice grew much louder, 'but you'd be astonished how easy it is for someone with a very basic knowledge of human psychology – or in possession of certain behavioural techniques – to infer things from an environment, and simply – by the power of suggestion, by picking up subtle *hints* . . .'

'I'm fully aware of that, Danny . . .'

Danny?!

Kane flinched at Elen's casually abbreviated use of his father's Christian name.

'. . . But when we went into the tiny living-room Dory walked straight over to the fireplace. He said he'd carved his initials there, as a boy . . .'

   '*Inside* the fireplace?'

'No. In the stonework around the side of the chimney breast.'

'Well perhaps he'd already noticed something scratched there?'

'No. It wouldn't have been possible. I mean not from the *angle* . . .'

   'Sorry. Is that . . . ? I'll just . . . Thanks.'

(Sound of small table being cleared off and moved over towards the sofa.)

   'Were his initials there, then?'

'Yes. Well, *no*.'

'Pardon?'

'There *was* a letter, which the girl claimed never to have seen before . . .'

'The letter D?'

'No.'

'An I?'

   'No . . .' Elen cleared her throat, nervously, her voice almost dropping to a whisper. 'A J. A tiny letter J. Dory *claimed* it was an I, but written in the Germanic style. Then after he'd *said* it he kind of . . . he kind of *turned* to me and gave me this . . . this awful *look*.'

'A *look*?'

'Yes. A kind of a . . . a *mocking* look. A *loaded* look.'

'Oh.'

Pause

'Is that dripping driving you mad?'
'Pardon?'
'The tap – the dripping tap?'
'The *tap*? No. *No*. I hadn't actually noticed it.'

Pause

'So you think it was a J, then?'
'Yes. I'm absolutely sure of it.'

Another pause

'Well . . .' Beede rattled what Kane presumed to be a teapot, 'I don't think we should allow ourselves to get too worked up over this. It was probably just a coincidence. He got lucky. He was flying by the seat of his pants . . .'

'But you said the other day . . .' Elen lowered her voice to a whisper again '. . . you said that you were worried about *fwah fwah fwah-wah fmwah-wah-wah* . . .'

Kane almost choked with frustration at his inability to hear her.
'I was just being paranoid,' Beede insisted.
'But things have become so . . . so *fluid* lately. And the meditation's definitely a part of it. He's developed this strange routine with a bandage. He winds it around his head – over his eyes and his nose . . .'

Kane stiffened.
'. . . I looked it up in his Pranayama book. There was a picture. It's called the Six Openings Seal . . .'
'I tried to confront him about the yoga the other night,' Beede interjected, 'after our conversation at the laundry.'

Huh?

Kane raised his eyebrows.
'You met up?' Elen sounded excited. 'You didn't say . . .'
'Only very briefly.'

Pause

'He was concerned that he might've bruised your arms. He said there were bruises but that you'd hotly denied it . . .'

Kane flattened both his palms against the door. His jaw tensed.
'So you talked about the yoga?' she asked (simply letting the other matter pass).
'Absolutely. I mentioned that I had some misgivings, that rather than *improving* matters, his behaviour seemed to be deteriorating . . .'

'And how did he respond?'
'Not well. He seemed very – I don't know – *caught up* in the whole thing. He was even keeping some kind of a diary . . .'
'Yes,' Elen interrupted, 'I often see him scribbling in it.'
'Have you ever managed to take a peek inside?'
'*No!*' Elen sounded shocked. 'It's private. I wouldn't dream of it.'
'Of course. Of *course* . . .'
Beede sounded embarrassed.

Pause

'Anyway,' Beede continued, 'Dory claimed that there was a technique in the Rosen book which his father had taught him as a child. I couldn't really get to grips with it – not off-hand – it was all rather convoluted . . . something to do with . . . with Witnessing, or *being* a Witness . . .'
'I just wish he'd *stop*,' Elen interrupted emphatically.
'Yes. I know you do.'

Pause

'Me too.'

Longer pause
Clinking of teacups

'There was this really *awful* interlude on the beach . . .' Elen finally confided.
'Really?'
'Yes. On Winchelsea Beach. Although the first sign of something odd

was in Dungeness. He disappeared while we were visiting the light-house. He left Fleet and I on the second floor and ran to the very top. I found him outside, on the viewing platform, totally hysterical, hundreds of feet up.'

'Good God,' Beede sounded alarmed, 'you must've been terrified.'
'Yes.'

Silence

Kane scowled, jealously, wondering what signs of tenderness – if any – this silence might contain.

'Was he coherent?' Beede finally asked.
'Almost. He seem obsessed by the power station. He kept telling me that it was in the way. He said it was obscuring the port.'

'Which port?'
'Old Winchelsea.'
'But Winchelsea's a town. It's inland.'
'I know. I said that. He claimed that there was an old town which was washed away during some terrible storm and that they'd moved the port to a hill. He insisted we went to try and find it . . .'
'And did you?'
'Yes.'

'How was he at this point?'
'Surprisingly good, really, all things considered . . .'
'So you went to the port?'

'There *was* no port. We went to the town and he got terribly upset. He ran off again. We eventually found him on the beach. He was wading around in the mud, clowning around in the mud . . .'

'He was very bad?'
'Terrible.'
'So how on earth did you get him back?'
'I didn't. I got into this ridiculous conversation with a local man – a teacher and writer – who lived in this tiny cottage close by. He took a great interest in Fleet. Fleet was being very . . . I don't know . . . difficult . . . *gregarious*. Just letting off steam, I guess. He said he had some books about gifted children which he wanted to give us. He was involved in some government-funded organisation . . .'

'Hang on a minute . . .' Beede sounded incredulous. 'You mean to tell me that in the midst of all this chaos some total stranger approaches you on the beach and starts up an arbitrary conversation about Fleet's *giftedness*?'

'Yes. I suppose it *does* sound a little strange . . .'

'And Dory was rolling around in the mud, meanwhile?'

'Yes.'

'Well how in God's name did you go about explaining that?'

'I didn't. I . . . I just . . .'

'Then you went back to his house?'

Beede seemed astounded.

'It was right next to the beach . . .'

'You went alone?'

'It was complicated. He'd lost his daughter in the Sudan. I couldn't get out of it. He'd gathered together this big box of papers and stuff . . .'

'But what about Dory? Was it safe to leave him?'

'Yes. *Yes*. He'd . . . I don't *know*. It was a difficult situation. Embarrassing. I didn't want to seem rude so I just quickly went to grab this book from him . . .'

'A book or a *box* of books?' Beede demanded.

'Pardon?'

'You said a box, then you said a book. Which was it?'

Silence

'This is exactly what Dory did,' Elen said softly.

'What?'

'He kept asking all these *questions* as though he didn't believe me.'

Kane almost stopped breathing, he was listening so intently.

Silence

'I didn't mean it like that,' Beede backtracked.

'It *does* sound improbable, I know. But it was all completely innocent. It was completely . . .'

'Of *course* it was,' Beede insisted. 'Ignore me. I'm just . . . I'm just fractious, just tired.'

'He's got so paranoid now, so suspicious, that he thinks I'm having an affair, that I'm keeping things hidden from him. When we were arguing on the way home he called me a slut. In front of Fleet. He can't bear being around me. He thinks I'm disgusting . . .'

'*Stop* it!' Beede chastised her, agonised. '*Please*. Dory wouldn't say that. Dory wouldn't *think* that. How *could* he?'

'But it seemed like him, Beede. He started making *fun* of me – repeating things I'd said in this awful voice – this cruel voice – private things, word for word, like it was all just some kind of horrible *joke*, some kind of awful *game*. But I couldn't play along because I didn't know what the *rules* were. I just wanted it to be all right. I just wanted to make it better, and I *couldn't*. . . .'

She broke down.

'I'm so sorry,' Beede's voice was very soft. 'Put that down . . .'

(Clanking of a teacup.)

'Come on, come here . . .'

Silence

Kane now had his full body-weight pressed up against the door. To all intents and purposes Kane *was* the door.

Silence

'How's your shoulder?'

It was Elen speaking. Her voice sounded husky, as if she'd been crying.

'It's fine.'

(Sound of a nose being blown.)

'I just really, *really* want things to go back to how they were before.'

'I know you do. Of course you do.'

'It was *manageable* before.'

'Yes. I know. You've been very brave. Very patient. It's obviously . . .'

Their conversation was suddenly interrupted by a loud clattering sound.

Holy shit!

Kane leapt back. His phone. His stupid *phone* had suddenly begun vibrating against the door.

'What was that?' Beede asked, sharply.

Before Elen could answer – or Kane could gather himself together – the door had swung open.

'Kane,' Beede said.

'Hi!' Kane smiled, flushing to his roots, lifting his hand and waving it, like a fatuous, ceramic Chinese cat.

'What do you *want*?' Beede demanded.

'I'm just heading out,' Kane pointed to the front door, pulling up the collar on his crombie, 'I just thought you should . . . I mean in case you . . .'

Beede was staring at him, like he'd lost his reason.

'Gaffar. That little *chat* . . .' Kane stuttered.

'There's no rush,' Beede said coldly, 'I said later would be fine.'

Kane shrugged. 'Good. *Great*. Then I'll head off.'

He removed his phone from his pocket and glanced down at it.

'Winifred,' he exclaimed, glancing up. But the door was already shut.

TEN

The elusive Reverend Jacobs was eventually located – after a helpful tip-off from a garrulous cleaner – cowering under a desk in the tiny Nurses' Station on an extremely busy Geriatric ward.

'If Sister finds you here, ducks,' Kelly warned him, jabbing fondly at his neat rump with one of her crutches, 'she'll use ya knackers for door-jams.'

'*Kelly!*' the Reverend exclaimed, abruptly lifting his head (and inadvertently smacking it into the desk's small drawer). 'How *delightful* to see you!'

'If he can see you from down there,' Gaffar observed (with typically implacable logistical acuity), **'then he's got eyes in his arse.'**

The Reverend slowly backed his way out (trying his utmost to retain what little remained of his dignity). 'I was actually searching for a *pencil*,' he said.

'Here . . .' Kelly grabbed one from the desk-top.

'I mean I *dropped* one . . . ,' he continued, vaguely. 'Oh . . . *Thanks*. Fantastic. Now I can finish off that pesky *cross*word . . .'

'This is Gaffar,' Kelly said, as Gaffar politely assisted him to his feet, 'I told you all about him, remember?'

'Yes. Absolutely. Charmed to meet you . . . '

The Reverend dusted off his knees, tightened his dressing-gown belt and then offered Gaffar his hand.

'How do you *do*?' he enquired, eyeing Gaffar's bruises somewhat trepidatiously.

'He don't *always* talk like he got a fist up 'is jacksie,' Kelly nudged Gaffar, confidingly, 'just *most* of the time, like.'

Gaffar sniggered. The Reverend shot her a dark look.

'So guess what?' she demanded.

'What?'

'The doc says they're finally gonna send me packin' . . .'

'*Wonderful* news!' the Reverend clasped his hands together, thrilled.

'. . . Which means I can hang down here wiv' *you* all day,' Kelly prattled on blithely, 'readin' the Scriptures an' shit.'

'Oh . . .' The Reverend's joy rapidly dissipated. '*Marvellous*.'

Kelly's phone started ringing (the tone having been recently altered to How Great Thou Art). She took it out and inspected it.

'Mum,' she growled, flashing the screen briefly in Gaffar's direction. 'I ain't answerin'. Linda should be there by eleven, an' I got *bigger* fish to fry . . .'

The Reverend stared at her, disapprovingly.

'God's Will an' all that,' Kelly shrugged, slipping the phone into her pocket.

The Reverend turned. 'I think you'll soon discover,' he told her tartly, leading them both back out on to the ward again, 'that not *everything* you think and feel can simply be attributed to God.'

'Why not?' Kelly demanded, hopping along behind him.

'Because it *can't*. If everything you ever thought and felt could be attributed to God then you would *be* God . . .' he shot her a scathing look, 'and I can hardly imagine The Almighty teaming moon boots and a mini-skirt.'

'*Huh?*'

Kelly inspected her outfit, offended.

The Reverend flounced over to his bed and flopped down on to it.

'So . . .' Kelly gazed around her, inquisitively '. . . they've gone an' stuck you on a ward wiv' a load of pissy, old farts, eh?'

Comic pause

'Well at least *someone* in this shithole's finally got you pegged right!' She elbowed Gaffar in the ribs, snorting. Gaffar winced.

'I don't believe God would've said *that*, for example,' the Reverend snapped.

Gaffar pulled out a chair and helped Kelly to sit down on it.

'So what *would* God say?' Kelly demanded. 'Just tell me an' I'll say it.'

'God would say that he loves all of his subjects equally – young *and* old – although he's *especially* devoted to the sick and the needy . . .'

'*That's* a crock for starters,' Kelly interrupted.

'How so?'

Kelly shrugged. 'Well he either loves everyone the same or he don't.'

'When God created man,' the Reverend's voice took on a preaching tone, 'he granted us a free *will* . . .'

Gaffar picked up a bottle of cologne from the Reverend's bedside table and inspected the label. The lid promptly fell off and rolled under the bed. He bent down to retrieve it.

'. . . so in all the decisions we make,' the Reverend continued, irritably, 'in all the things we *say* and do – God gives us the choice to lean either way: towards good or towards evil . . .'

Gaffar reached blindly under the bed, groped around for a while and then carefully withdrew a stainless-steel chamber pot (unused).

'As *Christians* we use Jesus Christ as our template,' the Reverend glowered at him, 'our *guide* . . . Shove that back under there, will you?'

Gaffar happily obliged him.

'We *familiarise* ourselves with his teachings. We struggle against our baser instincts. We do our best to emulate him . . .'

Gaffar finally located the lid –

'Yah!'

– and held it up, victorious.

The Reverend snatched it from him. 'And in that way we hope – very slowly, very *gradually* – to become better people . . .'

Kelly gazed at him as he spoke with a look of blank incomprehension. He sighed, resignedly. 'I suppose this must all sound rather *pedestrian* . . .' he waved the lid at her, dismissively, 'to a girl like you.'

'You told me you was a *sensitive*,' Kelly maintained stolidly, 'so maybe *I* am too.'

'Charismatic,' he corrected her, replacing the lid on to the cologne bottle, 'I said I was Charismatic with sensitive *leanings* . . .' he sniffed his fingers, fastidiously, then dabbed them on a blanket, 'although I rather regret that now . . .'

Kelly looked shocked. 'But you had all your *visions*, Rev.'

'I was *bored*,' he snapped, 'and just tossing a few ideas around.'

While he spoke, Gaffar idly acquainted himself with some of the Reverend's other grooming products. He inspected a jar of moisturiser.

'Careful – that's expensive,' the Reverend snapped.

Gaffar placed it back down again and picked up an electric razor. He flipped a switch to turn it on, but ended up releasing a small hatch of beard shavings down the front of his jumper instead.

'Urgh!'

The Reverend lay down flat against his pillows and crossed his hands over his chest. 'Like the doctors said,' he continued (barely repressing a smirk at Gaffar's expense), 'my "visions" were probably a side-product of something else . . .'

'*Shame* on you,' Kelly murmured. 'After everything what's happened.' The Reverend shrugged. Gaffar dusted himself off, grimacing. Kelly sat quietly for a while, eyeing the Reverend, balefully. 'So where's your Calvins?' she eventually asked.

'Eh? My *Calvins*?' The Reverend looked briefly disconcerted. '*Uh* . . .' He glanced sideways, shiftily. 'They got broken – last night – in all the chaos.'

'Oh yeah? Where's your *screen,* then?' Kelly gesticulated, impatiently. 'An' why ain't it closed?'

'It's there . . .' the Reverend thumbed over his shoulder, 'I just haven't had a chance to *draw* it yet . . .'

'Gaffar,' Kelly pointed to the Reverend's bedside table, 'check out his top drawer for his sunnies, will ya?'

Gaffar promptly opened the drawer, poked around, and withdrew the Reverend's glasses from inside.

'Ay ay,' Kelly slowly shook her head.

'I said they were *broken* not lost,' the Reverend huffed.

Gaffar tried them on. They seemed perfectly fine.

'Those suit ya, mate . . .' Kelly commended him, 'you look like Ray Liotta in *Goodfellas*, but foreign, an shorter, an wiv'out the zits.' She paused. 'So I guess if they're *broke*, Rev,' she turned and delivered him a saucy wink, 'then you won't mind *Gaff* here takin' 'em off your hands?'

The Reverend scowled. Gaffar removed the glasses and shoved them into his top pocket, delighted. The Reverend harrumphed, rolled on to his side and lay with his back to them. Kelly smiled at him, indulgently. 'Just admit it,' she taunted him, 'you don't *need* those specs no more, *do* ya?'

'Don't be ridiculous,' the Reverend barked. 'Of *course* I do . . .'

'My *arse!*' Kelly grinned. 'An' I'll tell you why not, too. Because from the *moment* we began dietin' together you began to feel *better* . . .'

'*Rubbish* . . .'

'Oh my *days*!'

Kelly slapped her hand, excitedly, on to the Reverend's tensed thigh. 'I just had a *thought*, Rev . . .'

'*What?*' The Reverend's tensed thigh now tensed up still further.

'In your second vision you said how the house collapsed but the man was left standin', yeah?'

The Reverend frowned.

'I mean to say he weren't *hurt* or nothin' . . . ?'

The Reverend continued to frown.

'Well that was *you*, yeah? Everythin' collapsed but you was *fine*. It was meant to be a *sign*, see?'

'I *wasn't* fine!' the Reverend rolled over to face her again, indignant. 'I have a painful line of bruises all the way down my back. The doctor said I was lucky the pole didn't fracture my *spine* . . .'

'Nope.' Kelly shook her head, 'Not *lucky* . . .'

'*What?*'

'Not lucky. He didn't say you was *lucky*, he said it was a *miracle*. Remember?!'

She was grinning again.

The Reverend closed his eyes. He didn't speak. Kelly leaned forward, confidingly. 'I ain't a *fool*, Rev,' she murmured, 'I know you're pissed off wiv' me. It's written all over ya. Far as *you're* concerned I'm just a pest – a dork, a *dill*. I don't know nothin' about nothin'. You just wanna get well rid an' I don't *blame* ya, neither . . .' she paused, 'but what I *also* know – in here . . .' she pointed to her chest, 'is that God's brought us together for a *reason*, yeah . . . ?'

'I don't *care*,' the Reverend said, haughtily.

Silence

'Did you *hear* me?'

More silence

He slowly opened one eye and appraised Kelly with it. She didn't seem in the slightest bit upset or intimidated. She was actually in the middle of sending a text. He opened his other eye and glared at her.

'So what will it take?' he suddenly demanded.

'Huh?'

She glanced up from her phone.

'What do you *want* from me, Kelly?' He threw out his hands, dramatically. 'What do I need to do? What do I need to *say*? That I'm actually an *abysmal* priest? That I'm self-centred? Vain? Lazy? Complacent? An uninspiring orator? That I smoke Cuban cigars and drink too much Advocaat? That I don't care quite as much as I should about the undeserving poor? That I download pornography? That I'm a fat-head and a hypocrite? That my life and my Ministry are a total disaster? Is *that* what you need to hear? Is *that* what it's going to take to get you off my case?'

'*Advocaat?!*' Kelly exchanged horrified glances with Gaffar. 'Are you *serious*? I thought only *grannies* ever necked that crap.'

'Look . . .' The Reverend clenched his hands into fists. 'I *know* you're a good girl – I mean at *some* level. Foul-mouthed, *abrasive*, even, but fundamentally sincere . . .'

'An' you've got a nice bum,' she volunteered (in the spirit of fair exchange), 'for an old codger.'

'. . . but you don't actually know me from *Adam*, do you?' he persisted. 'I mean I'm a *complete* stranger. I could be a psychopath, a fraud, an *imposter* . . .'

'*Sweet!*' Kelly chuckled. 'That's *well* sick! I fuckin' *love* the way your mind works . . .'

'Just *listen* to me,' the Reverend ploughed on, determined to get his point across. 'If you're serious about being a Christian, a *real* Christian, then take my advice and just . . . just . . .' he faltered '. . . just do what E.T. did . . .'

'*Huh?*'

'*Go home!* Join a local congregation. Grieve for your brother. Care for your mother. Reappraise your life. Acquaint yourself with the Bible. Accept Jesus as your personal saviour. Ponder. Consider. *Digest* . . .'

She gazed at him, quizzically.

'I'm perfectly *serious*, Kelly,' he maintained. 'Because if there's one thing I've learned during my time in the Church, it's that faith's not ready-made. It's not convenient. It's not a quarter-pounder with pickled gherkins and extra cheese. Faith is a *slow* meal. A nourishing meal. It's plain and healthy and sensible. A kind of emotional *casserole* . . .'

'Fine,' Kelly butted in, 'I *get* ya.'

'Really?'

'Yeah. I know it ain't gonna be no stroll in the *park* . . .' Kelly conceded '. . . but what I *also* know,' she continued staunchly, 'is that you had those three visions an' *two* already came true. First my bro' died . . .' she held up one finger, 'Then the *ceilin'* fell down . . .' she held up another, 'so what about number three? *Huh?*'

The Reverend collapsed back on to his pillows, covering his face with his hands.

'The visions were *metaphorical*,' he groaned.

'*Balls!*' Kelly rubbished him. 'You wanna know what *I* think?'

The Reverend shook his head. He didn't want to know.

'I think God's tryin'a *tell* you somethin',' she insisted, 'but you're too shit-scared to listen. So he sent *me*, because I ain't. Fact is, he's *here*, Rev. In the air. In this room. All around you. Free will or *no* free will. He's a *livin'* God an' he can do *anythin'* he damn well chooses. He can push a person off a wall, tap 'em on the shoulder, ring 'em on a phone . . .' Kelly grabbed the phone from her lap and held it high, for effect.

The phone rang. They all stared at the phone.

'Hello?' Kelly pressed the phone to her ear.

'*Forgive* me?' Harvey Broad bellowed jovially. 'What the fuck *for*, ya crazy Sort? I'm takin' ya ta bloomin' *Florida*, remember?!'

'What're ya doin'?' Kelly demanded.

'*Doin?* I'm phonin' *you*, ya plum! Little Kelly Broad! My favourite nice!' He paused '. . . *niece*,' he corrected himself.

Kelly's eyes narrowed into slits.

'Sorry to hear about Paul,' he added (almost as an afterthought), 'I just had your old ma on the blower burnin' my bloody *ear* about it, but like I says to her, I says, "Dina, the kid made his *own* choices, yeah? 'Nuff said."'

Kelly grimaced. 'Where *are* ya, Harve?'

'*Where?* Uh . . . I'm on Mill Bank Road, as it happens, on my way to see a client.'

'What for?'

'To wring his scrawny *neck*, darl, for tryin' ta cancel on a job.'

'Then stop right there, Harve,' Kelly instructed him. 'This is *important*, yeah? Pull over. Stay *exactly* where you are, d'ya hear me? I'm signin' myself out, mate . . .' she indicated, impatiently, to Gaffar '. . . and then I'm comin' to save ya.'

634

'I'm rushed off my feet, Win,' he grouched, yanking on the hand-brake and cutting out the engine. 'Can't I call you back later?'

'My head's completely *fucked*, Kane,' Winifred whined. 'I barely even slept. I *really* need to get stoned . . .'

Kane inspected his watch. It wasn't even lunchtime yet.

'Where are you?' he asked.

'London.'

'*London?*' Kane frowned. 'So why the hell ring *me*, then?'

'Because I've got some bad news for Kelly and I needed some advice on how to *break* it to her. I'm still at the bloody *library* . . .'

'What?'

Kane grabbed his cigarettes from his pocket, tapped one out and flipped it into his mouth. He peered anxiously through the window. He was parked at the end of an exclusive cul-de-sac facing a luxury, detached town house in well-tended grounds.

'Andrew Board. The infamous *doctor*. There's a strong possibility that he *isn't* related to her . . .'

'What?'

'I know. I *know*. I mean she was so *excited* about the whole thing.'

'Back up a minute . . .'

Kane was searching for some matches, but instead he found a lighter. He removed it from his pocket and stared down at it, blankly. Then he blinked –

How the hell'd that get there?

It was the red lighter – the Ronson – which he'd handed over in the restaurant, several days before. But it was different. It *felt* different, lying there, in his hand.

'So she forgave you too, huh?' Winnie mused.

'Who did?'

Kane was totally confused.

'*Kelly*. Kelly *Broad*. Your *girlfriend*, remember?'

'*Ex*-girlfriend.' Kane lit his cigarette. 'In fact I'm currently up to my ears in the funeral arrangements for her brother . . .'

'Right now?'

'No. Not right now. Right now I'm going to see a client . . .'

'Well let them wait. This is important. Because what I really need to know,' Winifred continued, 'is whether it's better to *tell* her or not.

I mean the probability of her finding out any other way is minute, and I only came across it in a secondary text . . .'

'Stop . . .'

Kane closed his eyes. 'Just go back to the beginning. I'm all at sea here. Kelly isn't *whose* relative?'

Winifred drew a deep breath. 'Dr Andrew *Board*. The physician. Henry's physician. The bloke who wrote the book about the *Jester* . . .'

Winifred paused. 'Although he *wasn't* actually the king's physician and he probably didn't write the book *either*, if it comes to that . . .'

'So you mean . . .' Kane scowled '. . . you mean the guy who wrote the book which you photocopied for Beede?'

'*Yes!*' Winifred all but exploded.

'I saw Kelly had it when I visited her the other day . . .' Kane muttered, 'which I thought at the time was rather strange . . .'

'She delivered it for me, as a favour,' Winnie butted in, impatiently. 'But beyond that . . .'

'And she thought she was *related*?'

'*Duh!*'

'But on what evidence, exactly?'

'Because her father or her uncle or someone was always going on about how they had this famous relative who was once a physician to royalty. They claimed he wrote a book about building practices in the sixteenth century but she'd thought it was all just bullshit . . .'

'She never mentioned this before,' Kane said, glancing over towards the house.

'Why would she?'

'Why *wouldn't* she?'

'I've been up all night, Kane . . .' Winifred groaned, 'and I'm feeling *really* weird. My head's buzzing. My heart's racing. It's almost like I'm . . .'

'Too many espressos,' Kane interrupted, breezily.

'You can't take drinks into the Rare Books section,' she snapped. 'It's against the rules.'

'The *rules*?!' Kane scoffed. 'Since when did Winifred Shilling submit to the *rules*?!'

'Grow up,' Winifred snarled.

'Hang on a minute . . .' Kane's spine suddenly straightened, 'I *forgive* you,' he grinned. 'Of *course* she did. I got a text – late last night . . .'

'She forgave *everybody*, you moron. She found *God*. Where've you been? Her dead brother sat up and said "bollocks" and she thought it was a *sign* . . .'

'Her dead brother? *Paul?* Paul came back to *life* again?' Kane was astonished.

'No, *stupid. Before* he died. He sat up. He swore. And some lunatic old Reverend – I mean I'm filling in the gaps here – had some kind of a *vision* which predicted that he would . . .'

'Fuck off, Win.'

Kane's grin was starting to slip a little.

'I'm serious. *Ring* her. *Ask* her.'

'Fuck *off*, Win,' he repeated.

'I'm *serious*.'

She sounded serious.

'Let's just cut to the quick here, shall we?' (Kane suddenly felt rather irritated by the whole thing.) 'What is it that you really want?'

'I already *said* what I really want. I want your *advice*, you *idiot*.'

'My advice?'

'Yeah.'

'Well my advice – for what it's worth – is to leave well alone.'

'That's *always* your advice,' Win said tightly. 'And that advice – for your information – is a piece of crap.'

'Thanks.'

'Pleasure.'

Pause

'This is where you hang up,' Kane informed her, inspecting his watch again, 'and I run off to meet my client.'

'You're right . . .'

'Although . . .' he frowned, 'one quick question . . .'

'Fire away.'

'First my dad, then my ex-girlfriend . . . Might there be some strange kind of *pattern* developing here?'

Winnie chuckled, dryly. 'You're barking up the wrong tree.'

'Am I?'

'Oh yeah. Completely.'

'Well if I am, then would you kindly tell me how the hell *you* happen to fit into all of this?'

'*I* fit, *you* fit, we *all* fit,' Winnie snapped. 'That's the whole f-ing *point*.'

'Nope. I'm still not . . .'

'She forgave *me*, too,' Winifred interrupted. 'I got this text late last night . . .'

'How'd she get your number?' (Kane wasn't buying it.)

'From the bloody *photo*copy. Same as you.'

'Oh.'

'And it pissed me off, quite frankly. She'd been holding me responsible for her brother's stupid *glue* habit. You know how I loathe glue . . .'

Kane slowly scratched his chin.

'So you're serious?' he said.

'Deadly.'

'This isn't some ornate wind-up?'

'Bloody *hell*!' Winifred expostulated. 'You actually think I'm capable of inventing this stuff?'

'In your sleep, Win. On your *head*.'

'Fine. Whatever. Think what you will. I don't care.'

As she spoke, a large, green Rover pulled up behind The Blonde and parked. Kane glanced at it, fleetingly, in his rearview mirror.

'So Kelly found God,' he murmured, shaking his head. 'That's ridiculous.'

'Why?'

'I don't know. It just is.'

'She said everything suddenly fitted together, like a puzzle. She claimed we were *all* somehow a part of it. She was completely hyped up.'

'She was probably just stoned. They gave her something to calm her down at the hospital. She was climbing the fucking walls when I spoke to her earlier . . .'

'Well she was perfectly lucid when we chatted at around twelve . . .'

'Oh.'

Pause

'I'm still a little confused,' Kane said.

'But it *is* quite weird – quite confusing – I mean when you actually stop and *think* about it . . .' Winifred persisted.

'What is?'

'The coincidence. She falls off the wall – yeah? – delivering this book to Beede. She breaks her leg. She goes to hospital. She acquires the book again – I'm not entirely sure how. An old Reverend predicts her

638

brother's death. Her brother suddenly dies. She reads the book and realises that she's related to this crazy religious nut, this *monk* . . .'

Pause

   'Sorry? A *monk*?'
'Yeah.'
'But you said he was a doctor.'
'He *was* a doctor – or a *Physic*, as they called them back then – but he was also a monk. *Underneath*. A Carthusian. They're a very strict . . .'
   'Yes,' Kane interrupted her, 'I know who the Carthusians are.'
'They're totally fanatical . . .'
'*Yes*, Win, I *know*.'
'Hair shirts, fasting, the whole kit and caboodle . . .'
   Kane took a long drag on his cigarette. A tall man in a uniform was now climbing from the driver's side of the car behind him. Kane glanced out of his window, casually exhaling, then he froze –

Fuck

It was *Dory*. It was Isidore. His forehead horribly disfigured by this terrible *bruise*.
   Kane quickly sank down in his seat, choking back the smoke.
'Kane? *Hello?*'
Winifred again.
   'Hi.'
Kane suddenly had a huge frog in his throat.
'Kane?'
He coughed into his hand to try and dislodge it.
'Hi,' he croaked, his eyes watering, 'I'm still here . . .'
   'Is there actually any *point* in my talking this through with you?'
'Yeah. *Sure*. I'm just . . .'
He coughed again. Then he sniffed.
'Late for a client,' she finished off, bored.
   Kane watched through streaming eyes as Dory approached the town house, took out a key and unlocked the front door. He'd barely pushed it open, though, when a blonde woman appeared and invited him inside.

Kane pulled himself up straight again, with a grunt, rubbing his face dry with his sleeve.

'Okay,' he said, struggling to gather his thoughts into some semblance of order. 'So just *tell* her, Win. Be straight up with her. That's my advice. Ring her. She'll be fine about it. She's a very sensible – very practical – girl, beneath all that mouth . . .'

'But I wish you could've *heard* her . . .' Winnie interrupted. 'I mean it was incredibly . . . I don't know . . . incredibly *touching*, somehow . . .'

'What was?'

'How happy it made her feel. How delighted she was that her family weren't all bad. She thought it was important – a *sign*, a *portent* . . .'

'But she was wrong. She simply got her wires crossed.'

Silence

'I mean you said this monk guy was a lunatic – a nut – so where's the loss?'

'I didn't say that.'

'Yes you did.'

'No. I said he was a little *flakey*,' Win rapidly rallied to the monk's defence, 'but he was an astonishing character. This seething mass of contradictions. He was released from his vows – as a bishop – after twenty-odd years of strict observance, but he still continued to wear the hair shirt, fasted – the whole deal – right up until his death. He was totally hardcore, in other words. It just transpired that his *real* love, his real *calling* was medicine. He was talented at it, by all accounts. He travelled extensively – all over the world – working as an ambassador for Britain – a diplomat, even a kind of *spy*, on occasion. He wrote some of the earliest known texts in the English language. Stuff about building, astronomy, medicine, *comedy* . . .'

'But I thought you said . . .'

'Yeah. There's some doubt over his authorship of the Scogin book. It may well have been written later and just attributed to him. The Prologue kind of sets out his store – I don't know if you read it – all this stuff about how "honest mirth" preserves health . . . That's *very* Boardian. But the same introduction also claims he was the King's Physic, which he definitely wasn't. He may've attended Margaret – Henry's daughter, once or possibly twice . . . I mean he was a Catholic

– a bishop – he was imprisoned intermittently even *after* he swore the Oath of Conformity. He died in jail – Fleet Prison . . .'

Kane frowned.

'. . . 1550 or thereabouts, although he wasn't locked up for treason. He was imprisoned for maintaining three loose women in his chamber, "for *his* use" – I quote – "and that of the other priests".'

'The old dog,' Kane murmured.

'Yeah. He was a passionate adherent of the *humoral* theory of the body; this idea that the body of a man contains four main *humours* which have to be perfectly combined for good health – blood, phlegm, yellow bile, black bile . . . And then a similar – equally important – combination of the four *elements*: hot, cold, wet, dry . . . The theory originates with Hippocrates. Sounds a little crazy to begin with, I'll admit, but when you sit down and really *think* about it, it's actually quite a cool idea . . . Kind of modern . . . *Holistic*, even . . .'

'Sure.'

Kane wasn't concentrating. He was staring over at the house. 'So what's this guy's name again?'

'Andrew Board. B-o-a-r-d.'

'But that's completely different.'

'I know. That's what Kelly thought. That's why she had her doubts, initially. But I told her how the language was in flux back then. English was only just being established as an official tongue. Nothing was set in stone. How a name *sounded* was just as significant as how it was spelled . . .'

'Board/Broad . . .' Kane tried this on for size. Then his hand shot into the air – quite spontaneously – and hurled his cigarette on to the dash.

'*Shit!*'

'What's wrong?'

'Nothing. I just . . .'

Kane reached out to retrieve it.

'I re-examined the Scogin text this morning,' Winifred blithely chatted on, 'a very early edition, even earlier than the one I photo-copied for Beede . . .'

'*Huh?*'

Kane was dusting flecks of ash from the top of his speedometer.

'John Scogin, the jester . . .'

'John?' He glanced up. '*John* Scogin?'

'Yeah. I was bearing in mind all these academic theories on why it was that Board *hadn't* written the book – and then it suddenly occurred to me, as I worked my way through it, how the story adheres – and in the *weirdest* way – to the Hippocratic theory . . .'

'You've lost me, Win.'

Kane dabbed at his eyes again.

'It's a fascinating business. Kind of like solving a crime. Like unravelling a *mystery* story. All the clues are in the text and your job is simply to sniff them out.'

'I see.'

'I mean it's hardly *rocket* science or anything – my reading's simply based on the loosest possible *literary* interpretation . . .'

'Win?'

'But I think it pays off – in fact it's actually very interesting, really *illuminating* . . .'

'Win?'

'The way I see it – and I'll try and keep this brief – is that John Scogin – simply as a *character* – seems to personify the coming together of all these totally disparate extremes – the same way Board himself does – I mean he's this well-educated guy who advances his path in life by pretending to be a fool – a jester – and thoughout the narrative we see this bizarre opposition between fire and water which – the way *I* choose to interpret them, anyway – kind of represent passion and *reason* – sex and *loyalty* – lust and faith . . .'

'*Win* . . .'

'Just *listen*, Kane,' she snapped, 'and you might actually learn something . . .'

Kane rolled his eyes.

'Early on – yeah? – when Board describes John setting fire to the *barn*, for example . . .'

'Sorry?'

Kane froze.

'The barn. He sets fire to the barn. For me it's one of the standout anecdotes of the entire book. An *awful* story, by modern standards, but presented in the text as simple high jinks – just a joke . . .'

'He sets fire to a barn?'

'Yeah. He sets fire to a barn which he's filled – at his wife's behest – with dozens of pesky beggars from the local area who are waiting patiently inside in the misguided belief that he's going to distribute alms . . .'

Alms

Kane started, involuntarily –

Arms

– then glanced down at his wrist. He'd pushed up his sleeve and was plucking at his scar –

Ow.

He quickly desisted, wincing.
    '. . . but instead he actually locks them in there and he sets the barn on fire . . .'
'What?' Kane was horrified. 'He *burns* them?'
'Sure.'
'Does he kill anyone?'
    'I'm not sure. Boorde doesn't say. The act *itself* is the punch-line, and then afterwards he accuses the beggars of setting fire to the barn themselves, out of pure spite . . .'
'But this isn't a true story, surely?'
    'Oh yeah. Absolutely. Exaggerated a little, perhaps . . .'
'But that's . . .'
'I know. Totally fucked. The *point* is that John has this powerful association – this affinity – with fire. And it's a very *female* vibe, somehow, a very negative, very *sexual* vibe, which is later played out fully in his warring with Elizabeth Woodville and his bizarre – almost neurotic – attacks on her honour . . .'
    'Elizabeth who?'
'The queen. Elizabeth Woodville. Edward IV's wife.'
'So he was jester to the *king*? I mean in real life?'
    'Of course. Who else?' Win tutted, impatiently. 'Keep *up*, Kane. So that's the fire side dealt with – although there's more – *much* more – obviously: his threat to burn down his house in Cheapside as a ruse to get protection money from his neighbours, climbing into an oven and leaving his arse hanging out so he doesn't have to stare Edward

in the face – because he'd been banned from doing so by royal edict
. . . this was shortly after his return from France . . .'

'He went to France?'

'Yeah. He was banished there. But he was incredibly ambitious. He
worked for Louis – the French king – and this uptight bishop who he
alienates by making jokes about his long nose. He's such an idiot. So
arrogant. You kind of have to *admire* it, really. I mean there are no
lengths he won't go to, no lines he won't cross. He's a force of nature,
this Dionysian spirit. This total arsehole. Utterly vicious and amoral.
The absolute personification of misrule . . .'

'Did they ever meet?' Kane wondered.

'Who?'

'Board and this jester, this . . . this *John* character?'

'Uh . . . I've no idea. Scogin would've been much older, but he was
apparently quite long-lived, so there's just an outside chance, I suppose.
And he would've been a legendary figure during his own lifetime. All
the top jesters were. Jesters held this very special place in medieval
culture because the Motley served as a kind of protective armour.
They were pretty much the only people in society who were permitted
to speak their minds freely. They had a kind of intellectual immunity.
This meant that humour could often be a direct route to power, and
these guys knew it, Scogin more than anybody.

'He was definitely at his creative peak during Edward's reign. There
was this astonishing kind of – I don't know – *affinity* between them.
Edward was hugely charismatic. Sensual. Very physically powerful.
Brave. But ultimately degenerate. His main flaw was his love of beauty
– of women, of sex. He was a terrible philanderer, and his wife tolerated it – extremely well, under the circumstances – but John wouldn't
let it go. He was like a cat with an injured bird, he kept on throwing
it in her face, mocking her, deriding her, humiliating her. He put the
king into an impossible position. He forced his hand. It was such an
amazing period in history, so diverse and corrupt and fascinating; the
very end of an age . . . Ends are so much more *interesting* than begin-
nings, don't you think?'

She didn't wait for him to answer.

'So much more *telling* – everything in stasis, everything in *flux*. I mean
think about it this way: John survived the Black Death, he lived on
his wits, he wormed and blagged his way into the top echelons of
society where he would've rubbed shoulders with the likes of the

legendary Jane Shore – the king's famous whore – and the young Richard. He would've been a witness to the murder of those two boys in the tower. And as loyal as he was to Edward, I'm guessing he was a pragmatist at heart, that he may well've served Richard too – which would've taken a *huge* leap, emotionally, *morally* . . . Although huge leaps were apparently very much his *forte* . . .'

'What?'

'He loved to jump. To leap things. It was all part of his act . . .'

'Oh.'

'He may even have survived through to the reign of Henry. He was one of the last of a great breed . . .'

'The last? How d'you mean?'

'Because of the development of the printed word. Books. The growth of the English language is generally believed to have precipitated the end of the jesting profession.'

'Why?'

'People started *reading*. They started entertaining themselves. They became more sophisticated. And what Board actually did was to solidify that process – to actively *encourage* it – both as a writer and as a physic. He condensed all the best known elements of John Scogin's life into a loose narrative. He created one of the first ever joke books. He pinned John down with words, skinned and filleted him, *dissected* him. He made him *tabloid*. He *sold* him. I mean we're talking 150, 200 years before Richardson wrote *Clarissa* – the first, great English novel . . .' she paused, speculatively. 'But that's hardly the point . . .'

'Isn't it?'

'No. Because what's really interesting is the text itself – this all-pervasive yin/yang quality, this literary opposition – as Board describes it – between fire and water. The wet side, the *liquid* side,' Win ran on, 'which is *equally* important – is personified by John's loyalty to the *masculine*, to the king – Edward IV. When he arrives at court he stands under this dripping pipe and pretends he hasn't realised he's getting wet. It's rather stupid, if you ask me, but this prank – which seems to go on for many hours – causes a real stir in court. Eventually it comes to the king's attention and the long and the short of it is that the king employs Scogin as his jester . . .'

'Did Beede mention why it was that he wanted this book?' Kane suddenly enquired.

'Pardon?'

'Beede. Did he ever mention *why*?'

'No. Well, *yes*. He's become totally fascinated by the period. And he has this crazy theory about how the British Renaissance took place – at least in part – because of the evolution of English as a language . . .'

'Sure,' Kane said flatly, 'I heard all about that.'

'There's actually another book which I haven't managed to get a hold of yet called *Tales of the Jesters*. I was chatting to this guy – this comedy journalist – who had his own copy, and he was telling me how Scogin's final request when he died was that he should be buried beneath a waterspout in Westminster Abbey. "I ever liked good drinks," he apparently said. And that's exactly what happened. They buried him there, under this dripping waterspout. But only a handful of years later the king decided to build a new chapel on that spot – so the old jester's bones were just casually unearthed. I don't know where they ended up . . .'

Kane was staring out of his window again, over towards the house. 'That's very interesting,' he said, finally.

'Yeah. I mean this stuff's a fair old hike away from my usual scholastic stamping ground, but since I've been studying the original texts again this morning I've become totally fascinated by the whole thing. Completely hyped-up. Really excited. In Board's book we definitely see the jester ducking and hiding between words. Words are his allies. It's like he's at his most powerful, his most mischievous, when experimenting with the variableness of language. Does that make sense at all?'

Kane didn't bother to answer her.

'Many of the stories are about deceiving and then disappearing, about pulling a fast one and then doing a runner, and the language itself really seems to aid and abet him. Beede's little hypothesis has some validity in that respect . . . In fact I was having a quick look at this book edited by Gamini Salgado which I noticed Beede reading the other week – it's a collection of texts from the mid-sixteenth century – many of them totally contemporaneous with the Scogin book – and one of them in particular by a John Awdeley called *The Fraternity of Vagabonds* is basically a dictionary of the slang of the Elizabethan criminal underclass. This bizarre secret language. It's amazingly weird. Very beautiful, too. Most of it's probably fallacious – just a wild fabrication. But that hardly even matters, really. I mean where do words come from anyway? What is it that gives a word its longevity, its staying power? Who legitimises it? Why? And how? I'm seriously thinking about researching further into this whole area now, creating some kind of spontaneous academic *thesis* around it. Bringing it all right up to date, too, via *patois* – my speciality – musical and urban street-slang, African prison languages . . . Maybe even researching another book.'

Kane snorted, bitterly, 'Beede'll be ecstatic.'
'Yeah . . .' (She didn't take his bait.) 'I mean just this idea that language is constantly changing, that it creates these weird little *loopholes* which allow people of different classes and races and backgrounds to gain ready access to an otherwise inaccessible parent culture . . .'

'So I guess you had your own little epiphany, too, huh?' Kane said. He was almost joking.

Silence

'Uh . . . I hadn't really *thought* about it that way . . .'

Pause

'Yeah. How very *odd*. I guess I did . . .'

Kane frowned. 'I hate to burst your bubble, Win, but didn't you say that Kelly *wasn't* actually related to the Board guy?'
'No. *No,* she probably isn't. Uh . . . At least I've certainly got my doubts . . .'
'So everything *doesn't* fit so snugly, after all . . . ?'
(He struggled not to sound too smug about it.)

'In one of the books I was looking at this morning,' Winnie began rapidly paging through her notes, 'they'd reprinted this totally bizarre attack on Board – who apparently at some point wrote something negative about beards . . .'

'Sorry?'
'Beards.'
'*Beards?*'
'Yeah. About beards – growing beards, wearing beards . . . He thought beards were unhygienic. He hated beards. And this caused quite a stir at the time. Beards were huge back then. Anyhow, I happened across this long kind of "answer poem" to Board's hypothesis –

completely bloody *obscene*, coincidentally – all about the virtues of beards – which includes several side-swipes to what an acknowledged *con*-man Board is, how disreputable, what a *criminal* . . .'

'But how exactly does this relate to Kelly?'

'Hold on. I'm getting to that. Because in the detailed analysis accompanying the text the author of the book – I forget *who*, exactly, but he certainly seems to've had a certain amount vested in upholding the doctor's reputation – says that after much investigation he's discovered that there was actually *another* family of Boards, *also* from East Sussex – which is where the original Board was raised, in Cuckfield, a place called Board Hill . . .'

'Okay . . . *Okay* . . .' Kane was struggling to keep up. 'And this *other* family . . .'

'A really bad lot. Undistinguished. Opportunistic. Constantly cited in local court files . . . But with the same name, from the same area, and so this understandable *confusion* naturally arose . . .'

'Ah. *Now* I get you . . .'

'It just seems . . .' Winifred almost sounded ashamed of her hypothesis, 'I don't know . . . somewhat *probable* . . .'

Kane shook his head. 'Nah . . .' he stubbed out his cigarette, 'I'm not buying it.'

'You aren't?'

'Nope. Because for starters, the original Board, the doctor, was a disreputable bastard himself . . .'

'Well that's hardly fair . . .'

'*Fair?* He was a monk who kept *whores* in his chambers. A Catholic bishop who signed the Oath of Conformity and betrayed his *faith* . . .'

'These were different times, Kane . . .'

'Yeah, yeah. Colours were brighter, smells were stronger. I know all about that. But the guy was a snob. He even lied in print about working for the king . . .'

'But he *didn't*, not necessarily. As I already said, the Scogin book was probably . . .'

'No. You've been banging on for hours now about how certain *clues* in the text strongly indicate that Board *did* write the thing . . .'

'I was just *speculating* . . .'

'It's pure, academic *snobbery*,' Kane scoffed, 'plain and simple. This pathetic need on the part of subsequent intellectuals to protect their own. To try and remove any stain from the great doctor's name . . .'

Winnie was quiet for a while, and then, 'So you *don't* think I should tell her, after all?'

'Come *on*, Win,' Kane exclaimed, growing impatient, 'you're a *historian*, for Christsakes. Work it out for yourself. Anyone who's studied the past in any real detail knows that people will invariably draw their own loaded conclusions, whatever the actual *facts* are. Why should Kelly be any different?'

'I just feel . . .' Winifred paused, thoughtfully. 'This may sound odd – no, it *is* odd – but I just feel strangely *protective* of her – of the story – strangely *grateful* to her . . .'

'Why?'

'I dunno. Because our brief conversation – this stupid conversation – just made everything crystallise, somehow. It brought these arguments, these ideas, these *people* into an extraordinary kind of relief . . . Made them throw all these weird *shadows* inside my head . . .'

'You *seriously* need to get some sleep, Win,' Kane interrupted her.

'Maybe.'

As she was speaking the door to the house suddenly opened and Dory re-emerged. Kane winced (*God*. That awful *bruise* again). Dory slammed the door shut behind him. He was frowning. He seemed to be deeply preoccupied by something. Kane sank down in his seat.

'Look, I've *really* gotta make tracks now,' he murmured.

'Fine,' she sighed. 'See ya,' and cut him off.

Ow.

Kane stared at the phone for a second, then shoved it into his pocket.

Dory, meanwhile, was strolling back down the path and towards his car. He paused for a moment, though, on the pavement. Kane glanced over his shoulder, thinking he'd been spotted. But he hadn't. Dory was actually standing by a lamp-post, reading something. A leaflet or a poster . . . He was scowling. He opened his mouth and spoke – quite emphatically – swore, perhaps, then reached out his hand and tore whatever it was from the post, screwed it up and shoved it into his pocket. He climbed back into his car, started up the engine, revved it, fiercely, then drove off.

Once he'd gone, Kane clambered out of The Blonde and glanced around him. Twenty or so yards away he espied something flapping on another post further along. He walked over – limping slightly – to take a look, standing in front of it for a while, frowning, holding it steady with his hand –

Eh?

It was a hand-made poster about a missing dog. A spaniel. There was a large, colour photograph. And underneath, in neat print, he read: *Missing! Much loved spaniel bitch. Spayed. Lame. 12yrs old. Large reward offered. Any information gratefully received: Garry Spivey, The Saltings, 27 Talley-Ho Road, Stubb's Cross* (followed by a number).

Kane inspected the picture again – a small, slightly bemused smile playing around his lips – then he carefully smoothed it out and retaped the corners (as best he could), before turning and striding out across the frosty lawn towards the house.

ELEVEN

'Woodsmoke . . .' Beede said, returning to the sofa, frowning. 'Do you smell it?'

Elen shook her head.

'Are you sure?'

'No.'

She picked up her cup of tea, her eyes fixed to the carpet, and took a small sip of it.

'He's been behaving very oddly of late,' Beede mused, 'like he's suddenly started revisiting things, re-accessing things . . .' he paused, 'the *past* . . .' then he frowned. 'Although perhaps it's just me. Perhaps it's just *my* perception of his behaviour that's altered. Perhaps it's just some kind of . . . of internal *shift* on my part . . .'

Elen cleared her throat. 'You're worried about him,' she said.

Beede shook his head. 'No. Not at all. Kane's tough, just like his mother was.'

'And you?'

'Pardon?' He seemed surprised by this question.

'Are you tough?'

She stared up at him, intently. He looked away, embarrassed.

'I don't know.'

He frowned.

'I think you are,' she said.

'I don't know,' he repeated flatly, 'I've never really thought about it.'

'So have you tried talking to him?' she wondered, leaning forward and idly tucking her trouser into her boot-top.

'Who?'

Beede blinked. He'd been staring at her neat hand, her slim calves.

'Kane.'

'Kane? Talking to Kane?' Beede almost smiled. 'No. Kane and I don't really . . . that's not really . . .'

He sat back down on the sofa, wincing. 'Talking's not really our style.'

'Why not?'

He shrugged, then winced again.

'You need a massage,' she said, 'to release that knot.'

Beede ignored her.

'It's not that we don't understand each other,' he mused, 'because we do – *too* well, perhaps. There's simply this lack of a common . . . a common *goal*, a common *language* . . . Our moral outlooks don't match up. They barely even overlap . . .' He shrugged. 'It's probably just a generational thing. '

'Then you need to invent one,' she said.

'Pardon?'

'A language. You need to invent one. To improvise a little, to experiment.'

Beede shook his head. 'Kane's my son and I care about him deeply . . .' he paused, 'but increasingly I can't help thinking that there are some things you just *can't* talk about. Issues that shouldn't be discussed. Because to do so would be diminishing,' he paused, scowling, as if he'd thought about this a great deal recently, 'I mean to both of us.'

She stared at him, sympathetically. 'You prefer to keep it all bottled up?'

'Yes.' Beede nodded, irritated. 'There's far too much talking nowadays. Too much pointless self-analysis, too much endless *venting* . . . It's like we're all slowly drowning in this awful glut of *feeling*. We need to become more resilient, more reserved, a little less self-indulgent. How a person behaves is the best possible demonstration of who they are. Not how they *feel*, but how they *act*.'

'The Blitz spirit,' Elen grinned, almost teasing him now. 'How ridiculously old-fashioned you sound.'

'Yes,' Beede said, smiling wryly at himself, 'I'm an old stalwart, an old war-horse, an old partisan.'

Then he winced again.

'Who cares, anyway?' she shrugged. 'So long as you're happy. That's what really counts.'

Happy?

Beede stared at her, blankly, as if astonished by her choice of word.

Elen placed down her teacup, pulled herself to her feet and moved around to the back of the sofa. 'Although I don't really hold with moral absolutes myself,' she mused, 'this idea that certain kinds of

652

behaviour are always completely right or definitely wrong. The best any of us can hope for is to function successfully within the particular constraints that life has imposed upon us.'

Beede shrugged. 'Everybody's different,' he said grudgingly.

'You'll need to remove your jacket,' she told him.

He peered up at her, alarmed. 'Why?'

'For the massage.'

'Good *God*, no.'

He looked away, horrified.

'*No?*' She pretended to be hurt by his rejection of her.

He frowned, embarrassed. 'I mean . . . I mean *no* . . .' (he couldn't think of another word, off-hand) '. . . It wouldn't feel appropriate.'

'*Appropriate*? Don't be ridiculous,' she mocked him. 'It's probably just a trapped nerve. It won't take a minute to sort it out.'

Beede didn't move.

'I trained professionally in Germany. I'm perfectly proficient. Here, let me . . .'

She gently leaned forward and slipped the jacket from his shoulders, folded it and laid it over the back of the couch. Next she reached for his jumper. As she leaned forward again one of her brown plaits fell across his shoulder. Beede started, in terror, as if the brown plait were a snake.

'What are you doing?'

'I'm removing your jumper. It's too bulky . . .' she paused, smiling, 'Stop being such a terrible *baby*, Danny.'

'I'm not,' he said, his colour rising.

She removed his jumper, setting his glasses askew as she pulled it off. He quickly set them straight again.

'Now the shirt,' she said.

'It's very cold in here,' he complained.

'Then I'll turn the heating up,' she said. 'Where's the thermostat?'

'I don't . . .' he scowled, then swallowed down his frustration. 'It's on the wall – behind the door.'

'Fine. Good. Now take that off. *Pronto.*'

She clapped her hands, twice – like a no-nonsense schoolteacher – then walked over to the door, opened the small box there and turned everything up.

'Not too high,' Beede grouched, unbuttoning his shirt and pulling it off, resentfully.

She returned and stood before him, steadily appraising him, in his vest.

He clasped his hands together, struggling to meet her gaze. He felt ridiculous. He hated being stared at.

'There's this slight – almost imperceptible – imbalance,' she said, 'it's evident *here* . . .' she pointed, 'in your shoulders, in the way you're holding yourself.'

She described the shape of him, in the air, with her hands.

'Oh.'

He tried to push his shoulders back, but they were already as far back as they could possibly go.

'It's not your posture,' she emphasised, 'you've got amazing posture for a man of your age.'

'Oh,' he said again, stupidly.

'Wait . . . I'll show you . . .'

She pulled off her jumper – in preparation – and threw it down on to the sofa next to him. Underneath she wore a plain, slim-fitting, long-sleeved vest – in an appealing dove grey colour – and no bra. The soft, brown bulbs of her nipples were partially visible – like two milk chocolate truffles – through the thin, downy fabric. Beede rapidly averted his gaze. Elen walked back around to the rear of him, flexing her hands and her fingers, then leaned forward and carefully locked her arm around his neck. 'Stay very still,' she murmured ominously, her breath tickling his ear. 'Be sure and relax your jaw.'

He felt her small breasts cushioning his head. She seemed very lithe, very strong. He closed his eyes, appalled at her closeness, feeling her other hand slipping under his chin and grasping it, firmly. She paused for a second, inhaled, and then suddenly jerked her arm and her hand – quite violently – in opposite directions. Beede gasped, shocked. There was a loud, cracking sound. He felt a dramatic release of pressure in his throat and upper back.

'There . . .' she stepped away from him again and casually appraised the progress she'd made. 'That's better . . .'

She pushed up her sleeves in a business-like manner, then drew forward again, carefully placed each of her fingers on to different parts of the dome of his skull, and slowly began applying a steady pressure. 'How's that feel? Not too uncomfortable, I hope?'

He felt his eyebrows beginning to melt.

'You trained in Germany?' he asked. His voice sounded slurred.

She began to rotate her fingers, but without moving them, and without any lessening of the pressure.

'I was there for almost a year. Isidore's father was dying. Dory insisted on nursing him himself.'

'I see.'

Beede's eyes suddenly filled with tears.

'This can sometimes makes your eyes water,' she said (although she'd no way of apprehending the effect she was having). 'It's these two fingers here . . .'

She lifted the two fingers in question for a second.

'Were they close?' he asked, blinking rapidly.

'Yes. His father was a lovely man, but rather overbearing. An ideologue. Very stern.'

She relaxed the pressure in her fingers and gently ran her hands though his hair.

'You have wonderful hair,' she said. She leaned down and sniffed it, her plait falling across his shoulder again.

'Isidore never speaks of him,' Beede moved his head forward, swallowing. His mouth was dry.

'Pardon?'

'His father. He never mentions him.'

'No.'

She straightened up again, firmly repositioning his head to the correct angle, and moving her index fingers to his temples, her thumbs to a position behind his ear. Again, more pressure.

'Unclench your hands,' she said.

He promptly unclenched them.

'Good.'

'That was very dutiful of him,' Beede continued vaguely, his eyes scanning the room for any available distractions.

'Pardon?'

'To nurse his father like that.'

'Ah.'

She released the pressure from his temples and then smoothed her fingertips around his jawline, down on to his throat, to the back of his neck and on to his shoulders. She rested them there for a moment, light as two chaffinches.

Beede suddenly shot out of the chair.

'The *cat*,' he exclaimed.

'Cat?' Elen echoed, confused.

'Didn't you hear him? In the bedroom? He's probably anxious to get out.'

'You have a cat?'

'Yes.'

Beede strode through the kitchen to his bedroom. He pushed the door open.

'Manny?'

He peered around him in the gloom. He couldn't see the cat. Not at first. The curtains were still closed and the room seemed different, somehow. Cavernous. Fuzzy. Airless. He closed his eyes and shuddered. He drew a deep breath.

'What kind of a cat?' Elen asked.

Beede started. His eyes sprang open. She was standing directly behind him.

'Oh *look*, a *Siamese* . . .' she moved forward, smiling, before he could answer her. 'He's on the *bed*, all curled up.'

Manny lay in the middle of Beede's counterpane.

'Hello, boy . . .'

She bent forward and put out a hand to stroke him. 'Is he friendly?'

The words had hardly left her mouth before the cat had uncoiled, with a hiss, and had lashed out at her, spitefully, with his claws unsheathed. She gasped and quickly withdrew her hand, instinctively placing it to her lips. The cat sprang from the bed and ran next door, the bell on his throat jangling.

'Did he scratch you?'

Beede was horrified. Elen turned, removed her hand from her lips and offered it to him, like a child.

Beede resisted taking it for a moment, but she continued to hold it out, plaintively.

'Here . . .' his resolve quickly weakened, 'let me see . . .'

He took her hand and inspected it, drawing it close to his face in the half-light, trying his best to be business-like. But the hand was so small and so soft . . .

'He's drawn *blut*,' Beede murmured thickly, his chest tightening as he inhaled the roses on her, then he frowned. 'Blood,' he repeated.

She didn't speak. He continued to inspect her hand, almost hypnotised by it now, following the line of the scratches with his finger like they were the path of a river on a map. She drew a step closer and pressed the back of the injured hand against his cheek. He held the hand there, staring at her, in silence, for what seemed like an age.

'I'm seeing Dory at ten,' he murmured, finally, as if uttering the name alone might save them.

'I have a client to see then,' she said.

Neither of them moved.

'What time is it now?' he wondered.

'I don't know,' she said.

He heard her voice speaking and then echoing, like a trickle of water falling into a deep pool.

'Do you hear that?' he asked, tipping his head slightly towards the sound.

'Yes,' she said, 'I hear it.'

Then he let go of her hand – suddenly – almost like it was some kind of experiment to see if it would stay aloft. If it *could* stay. The hand remained suspended, quite effortlessly, against his skin.

He reached out and took a hold of her two plaits, running his fingers down them as if they were bell-pulls, then his grip changed and tightened. 'Braid,' he murmured softly, thinking of a horse's tail, sensing the gloss and slide of horse-flesh '. . . *Bridle* . . .'

He rapidly twisted the plaits around his knuckles as if they were reins – and yanked them in towards him, cruelly, as if to pull her up short, to bring things to a halt, but this sharp movement had quite the opposite effect. It pulled her still closer. He felt the soft pressure of her body against him. He frowned, confused, his hands dropping to her shoulders. Her own hand flipped around now and her palm caressed his cheek, then slipped down lower, to his mouth where she followed the outline of his parted lips with her index finger. Her touch felt liquid. He felt subsumed in it. He could hardly breathe. He felt dizzy. He closed his eyes.

BOO!

A man leapt out at him; sharply etched, brightly lit, fully dimensional against the heavy black curtain of his eyelids; a lean man with a shaved head, a tattered, yellow coat, an inquisitive stare. Beede gazed back at him, quite amazed.

Who are you? he heard a voice whisper. It was his voice. The man didn't answer, but he smiled.

'Oh *God*,' Beede said. He knew that smile. He peered over his shoulder, panicked, hearing Elen suddenly calling –

'Hello? *Hello?!* John? Is that *you*?'

– her voice a strange, somewhat *disquieting* combination of apprehension and longing.

'What happened?' Laura demanded. 'Was there an accident or something?'

She seemed a little hysterical.

'I've been waiting outside in the car . . .' Kane brushed past her, dismissively, 'just twiddling my thumbs until your other visitor left.'

He strolled through a grand, split-level entrance-hall towards a full-size, oriental-style mirror, caught his reflection in it and drew to an abrupt halt. He stared at himself, confused.

'Oh *bugger* . . .' she was still peering outside, nervously. 'Did you walk across the *lawn*, Kane? I see footprints on the lawn. Never step on a lawn when it's frosty. Didn't you know that? The grass blades snap and the lawn turns brown. Tom's *really* fussy about his lawn. It was only put down last summer . . .'

She turned, slamming the door shut. 'Did you wipe your feet?'

They both stared down at his boots. He hadn't wiped them.

'I need to wash my face,' he said, glancing back into the mirror again, bemused. His skin was blackened with charcoal and his cheeks were streaked with tears.

'Was there a fire?' she asked, trotting along subserviently behind him as he opened a selection of doors in search of a cloakroom. 'Are your hands clean?'

He looked down at his hands. His hands were spotless.

'Tom's incredibly houseproud . . .' she wittered on. 'It's kind of a *show*-home, really. Tom – my brother-in-law – built it himself. He's a contractor. He used to be involved in all these big, *commercial* projects – factories, stations, that kind of thing, but lately he's expanded into housing. Cedar Wood was his first major development, and this is his first attempt at the *luxury* end of the market. He built all the properties on this road . . .'

Kane finally hit pay-dirt. He walked into a magnificently fitted cloak-room, located the sink and tried to turn on the tap. He couldn't get it to work.

'The fittings are all Italian,' Laura said, bustling over and operating it herself, 'they take a little bit of getting used to.'

Kane leaned over and began rinsing his face. Once he was done, he blindly reached out for a towel.

'Not the towel!' Laura all-but squealed, 'They're 100 per cent Egyption cotton. Just use some of *this* . . .'

She quickly unravelled a handful of toilet-roll. Kane took it from her and gingerly dabbed at his face with it. It flaked on to his stubble. He grimaced. Laura immediately moved in to help.

'It's good quality paper,' she assured him, plucking away at his jaw. 'Quilted. It really shouldn't break up so easily . . .'

'This house is crazy,' Kane observed, peering around him, perplexed. 'Kind of too-much, almost.'

'Everything's top of the range,' Laura insisted. 'I think it's a dream home – just beautiful, just *perfect* – but poor Pat really hates it and she actually has to live here . . .'

'Pat?'

'My sister-in-law. She says she's almost afraid to *fart* in case she dents or scratches something . . .'

Kane inspected himself in the mirror above the sink. 'That's better,' he said.

'Would you like some tea?' Laura asked, unable to resist the urge to straighten his collar.

Kane frowned. 'I'm actually in quite a *rush* today, Laura . . .'

Her face crumpled. He sighed, 'Okay. *Sure*. Why not? But just a very quick cup . . .'

She beamed, delighted, and led him back out into the hallway.

'So why are you hanging around here?' he asked.

'No reason,' Laura shrugged, 'I just popped over to feed the cat. Normally they have a professional in to do it – a security guard who also keeps an eye on the other empty properties – but he didn't turn up last night. It's Tom and Pat's Wedding Anniversary – they've gone to Miami for a week. Tom actually has quite a few business interests there . . .'

'How romantic,' Kane interjected, dryly.

'Yes . . .' Laura paused for a moment next to a badly framed photograph on a small table in the hallway.

'Look – that's Pat, there . . .' she pointed. 'She's my best friend as well as my sister-in-law. This was taken in Durham last year when their oldest boy – Max – graduated from university . . .'

'Lovely.'

Kane barely even glanced down.

'*I* took it,' Laura said proudly, 'but then Pat framed it.'

Kane homed in on the photograph again. It consisted of three people sitting companionably around a table in an upmarket restaurant: a middle-aged woman, a young man and an older man who was cheerfully toasting the photographer with a glass of champagne.

'Who's that?' Kane asked, pointing to the older male. 'He seems kind of *familiar* . . .'

He picked up the picture and scrutinised it more closely (knocking a small, slightly incongruous china donkey in the process).

'That's Tom. Tom *Higson* – from Power and Higson Ltd, the contractors?' Laura darted out a quick hand to rescue the donkey. 'He's quite a well-known businessman in the Ashford area.'

Kane stared at the man for a little longer.

'And he's called Tom, you say?'

'Yes. And that's Pat. And that's Maxwell . . .'

She took the photograph back from him and carefully arranged it on the table again.

'*There* . . .'

'So he built this house himself?'

Kane peered around him, ruminatively.

'Yes . . .' she paused. 'I mean . . .' she paused for a second time, somewhat apprehensively, 'I mean *I* helped with some of the fittings – I chose the hardwood floors and the sink and the cabinets in the kitchen . . . Pat's not really *interested* in that kind of thing. Tom's spent a fair bit of time in Saudi. He got a few of his main design ideas from the hotels there . . .'

'There's certainly quite a *palatial* feel to the place,' Kane remarked as they walked through to a huge, well-equipped kitchen where the first thing his eye alighted upon was an ugly, pine mug-tree placed – somewhat conspicuously – in the middle of one of the work-surfaces.

'Well *that's* a classy touch,' he grinned, running his hand over the counter-top.

'It's made from a special kind of marble,' Laura volunteered (getting her wires crossed), 'Greek marble . . . although I can't remember the actual *name* of it . . .'

She went to grab the kettle. Kane removed two mugs from the tree. One was chipped, the other bore the legend: *The World's Best Fisherman*.

'The devil's in the detail, eh?' he joked, carrying them over to the table.

Laura turned as he placed the two mugs down. 'Let's not use *those*,' she protested, 'there's a whole new service . . .'

She opened a cupboard to reveal a smart, white tea set. 'Tom bought it for Pat's birthday. It's from Selfridges. I helped him to choose it.'

'But I like these,' Kane insisted.

Laura snatched up the chipped mug and stared at it, frowning. 'They're Pat's favourites. It's not that she doesn't have any *taste*, as such, it's just that all the things they had before – in the semi – from when the boys were small, and from her parents' old home, somehow look so out of place here. Tom was all for throwing everything away and starting afresh but Pat wouldn't have it. She says she won't live her life like it's an article in some stuck-up *design* magazine . . .'

Laura glanced over at Kane as she spoke, trying to gauge his re-action, plainly still not entirely resolved on this issue herself.

'That's fair enough, I guess,' Kane shrugged.

'Yes.' Laura nodded violently as she plugged in the kettle, 'Yes . . . I mean that's such a typically *male* way of going about things, don't you think?'

'What is?'

'To want to just throw everything out and start afresh . . .'

Kane smirked. '*God*. You should meet my dad – he's the total oppo-site. He never gets rid of anything. He's stuck in a complete time-warp. He lives like a refugee from the late 1950s . . .'

'I *have* met your dad,' Laura observed, testily.

'Oh . . . yeah,' Kane winced, 'of course . . .'

'And he seems very *nice*,' Laura emphasised, her cheeks flushing as she pulled a thick, slightly broken cork stopper from an ugly-looking red jar with TEA written on it and removed two bags from inside.

'Like I said on the phone,' Kane murmured, 'I'm really sorry about Gaffar – he was totally out of line . . .'

A cat came trotting into the kitchen as Kane spoke, its arrival heralded by the jangling of a small bell. Kane glanced over towards it, distractedly. 'He should've been more discreet. I had a stern word with him about it . . .'

The cat was a Siamese. A blue-point.

'No. *No. I'm* the one who should apologise,' Laura sighed. 'I shouldn't have got so upset earlier,' she shrugged, 'it's just a tricky situation, that's all.'

'How so?'

The cat commenced winding itself, somewhat feverishly, around Kane's ankles.

'Well Pat's set up this little *group*, this little *committee*, to try and put pressure on the Council to get this road crossing built . . .'

While Laura spoke Kane subtly tried to push the cat away with his foot, but it was extremely persistent. He glanced down at it, irritably.

'*Wow* . . .' he suddenly exclaimed. 'This cat's just like Beede's. In fact it's almost identical . . .'

Then he frowned.

'It's wearing a bell,' he added, his voice falling strangely flat.

'I know. I just caught Dora – the security guy – putting that on him,' she grumbled. 'I mean he feeds him and keeps an eye on the place when Tom's away, but putting a bell on someone else's cat is taking things a little far, don't you think?'

Kane stared down at the cat again, without comment.

'I really should've said something at the time,' Laura continued, 'but I chickened out.'

'What's his name?' Kane asked.

'Dora. He's German.'

Kane stared at her, blankly.

'Oh – you mean the *cat*. He's called Manny.'

'I see . . .'

Kane nodded, feeling a slight twitching sensation in his foot, like a bad case of pins and needles, or a mild case of cramp.

'It's short for Chairman Mao . . .' she frowned. 'Which I've always thought was rather an *ugly* name for such a sweet, little thing . . .'

Kane smiled, thinly. 'I think it's meant to be a joke,' he explained.

'It's the name of a famous, Chinese dictator . . .'

'Really?' Laura looked amazed. 'How *strange*. A dictator? But what's so funny about that?'

'Nothing, in principle. It's just a play on words . . .'

'But how's that any different . . .' Laura scowled, confused, 'from calling the poor animal Adolf? Or . . . or *Thatcher*?'

'It isn't . . .' Kane glanced back down at the cat again '. . . Although – now you come to mention it – Thatcher's probably quite a *good* name for a cat.'

'Are you serious?'

Laura seemed horrified by the notion.

'So you were telling me about this road crossing thing, this committee . . . ?' Kane tried his best to return to their former subject, but Laura was having none of it.

'I mean if he was so *concerned* about the poor creature he should've turned up last night and *fed* him, don't you think?'

'Uh . . . yes,' Kane nodded. 'Absolutely.'

'And did you notice that awful *bruise*?'

'Pardon?'

'That awful *bruise* he had? On his forehead?'

'No,' Kane lied, 'I didn't.'

'Well it was *huge*. All purple and pink and swollen . . .' she grimaced, gazing down at the cat again. The cat shook himself, vigorously, and his bell jangled accordingly.

'I'm going to take that stupid thing *off*,' she huffed, bending down and snapping her fingers to attract his attention. '*Manny?* Come over here, my love . . .'

No reaction

'Manny, baby, come here, come to Aunty Laura . . .'

The cat continued rubbing himself, lasciviously, up against Kane's calf.

Laura gently clapped her hands together.

'*Hey! Gorgeous!* Remember me? Come on! Come over here!'

The cat sat down and began licking his shoulder.

'Do you like cats, Kane?' Laura asked, finally straightening up.

'No,' Kane admitted, 'not especially.'

'It's strange, but they really seem to *sense* it when a person doesn't like them,' Laura beamed. 'It's a kind of special *power* they have. Cats are *always* drawn to the one person in a room who isn't actually keen on them . . .'

'I'm not sure if it's a special power as such,' Kane demurred, 'I think it's just a body language thing. In cat psychology if you turn your head away then that's a sign of respect. If you stare, a cat interprets that as a show of hostility. Dogs respond in basically the same way . . .'

Laura gazed at him, wide-eyed.

'So why d'you think he stuck the bell on him?' Kane wondered, keen to return to less contentious ground.

'I don't know,' Laura shrugged, 'I just walked into the room and there he was, fastening it on. He said something about it being "better for the bird". He said it was a "warning" for the bird. But I don't think it's really his place to make a decision like that, do you?'

'No,' Kane agreed.

'Which bird, anyway?' she wondered. 'Tom and Pat don't even *have* a bird.'

'I see.'

'*We* have a bird – a parrot – but Manny isn't *my* cat, obviously. And *our* bird lives in a cage.'

'Perhaps he just meant birds in general, wild birds . . .'

'*Wild* birds?' Laura looked frightened. '*Which* wild birds?'

'I mean the wild birds outside, the *garden* birds . . .'

'Oh . . .' Laura considered this for a while and then shook her head. 'But Manny's a house cat. Always has been. Pat's last home was near a main road so she never risked letting him out . . .'

'Maybe his English isn't quite up to scratch,' Kane suggested.

She shrugged. 'Maybe . . .' then turned towards the kettle as it came to the boil. 'I'm actually quite fed up with him, to tell you the truth.'

'The security guy?'

She nodded, grabbing the kettle and pouring boiling water into an old, brown teapot. 'Everybody just loves him around here – Charlie thinks he's *wonderful* – and he and Tom go way back. They worked together on the Channel Tunnel . . .'

Kane watched as Laura stirred the pot and then popped on the lid.

'Sorry . . .' he suddenly said, 'they worked together . . . ?'

'On the tunnel. The *Chunnel*. That's how they first met. But now he's gone and stuck his *oar* in over all this road crossing stuff – insisting on bringing your dad on board because of the influence he apparently has with the Council . . .' she paused, scowling. 'And I'm sure if he hadn't stuck his nose in then Pat might've just dropped the whole thing. I mean Tom knows we're not terribly *keen* on the idea. He tried to have a word with her, but once Pat has a bee in her bonnet . . .'

'Sorry . . .' Kane still wasn't quite satisfied. 'They worked on the tunnel? The Channel Tunnel?'

'Yes.'

Laura walked over to the fridge. It was a huge, American-style fridge. 'Look at the size of this thing!'

She opened the door. 'Isn't it ridiculous?'

She took out some milk, checked the date and then smelled it.

'So Tom helped to build the tunnel?'

'Yes. It was one of his first big contracts – although he was mainly involved in the demolition side of things back then . . .'

'And Isidore?'

Laura glanced over at him, sharply. 'Who?'

'The German?'

'You mean *Dora?*' she shrugged. 'He was probably just a part-time labourer – a student, I think. He came from that place we're joined with . . . *doubled* with . . . That *German* place . . .'

'Bad Munstereifel,' Kane winced as his foot cramped up again, 'we're twinned with them.'

'Twinned? Is that what they like to call it?'

Laura tipped some milk into each of the two mugs and then picked up the teapot. 'I can never actually remember whether it's a sign of bad breeding to put the milk in first,' she smiled, starting to pour.

'So that was how they met, huh?' Kane mused.

'Yes. But then obviously after all those *buildings* burned down . . .'

Laura filled Kane's mug and handed it over. 'Would you like a biscuit?'

'Sorry?'

'A biscuit?'

'The *buildings*? Which buildings?'

'Tom's warehouses. Three different fires. Five, six years ago. It was tragic. An awful blow.'

Kane stared at her, in shock. 'He burned down your brother's warehouses?'

'No, *stupid*!' Laura chortled. 'He was a *fireman*. He put them all *out*. He was quite the hero, in fact . . .'

'Wow.'

Kane watched her – his mind racing – as she began searching through the cupboards for biscuits.

'Biscuits . . . *biscuits* . . .' she murmured, slamming one door after another.

'How about the jar?' Kane suggested.

'What?'

She turned.

'There's a jar, right there, next to the tea jar. It says biscuits on the front of it.'

Laura peered over at the jar.

'Biscuits,' she read, clumsily, as if she'd never actually seen the word written down before. 'Gracious me,' she exclaimed, 'you'd think I'd know that by now. I've eaten biscuits in this kitchen with Pat often enough . . .'

She reached for the jar.

'*Bis*cuits,' she repeated slowly. 'Isn't that a funny, old word?'

'Twice cooked,' Kane responded, almost without thinking, 'from the Latin root *bis* – twice, and *coctus* – cooked. It reached English via the Old French: *biscut*.'

'There's Jaffa Cakes,' Laura said (completely ignoring Kane's inter-jection), 'or a few broken Hob-Nobs at the bottom of a packet.'

'I'm fine,' Kane murmured, scratching his head, confused.

Laura threw the broken Hob-Nobs on to a plate, pinched up some of the crumbs between her fingers and keenly devoured them.

'What I still don't quite understand,' Kane said, 'is why you're so dead set against the whole road crossing thing. I mean if there's an actual *need* . . .'

'It's Charlie,' Laura almost choked on her mouthful. 'He just *hates* the idea.'

'Why?'

'He just . . .' she coughed for a while, her eyes frantically scanning the room, 'he just *does*. He just . . . he just wants to leave all the bad stuff behind us. He just wants to move on.'

She quickly turned away from him, grabbed the teapot again and began filling her own mug.

'And you?'

'Yes. *Yes*. Of course I do.'

Her hand shook as she poured.

'It's just that we've never actually talked about it,' Kane mused.

'About what?'

'About your son's death. In all our conversations you've never really brought it up. Not even in passing . . .'

Laura's hand began shaking even more violently. The tea spilled. She put the teapot down. 'Just look at that!' she exclaimed. 'What an awful mess!'

She walked over to the sink.

'I was the same myself, if it's any consolation,' Kane confessed.

'How d'you mean?'

Laura glanced over her shoulder at him, her colour still high.

'When my mother died. Everybody kept pestering me to talk about my feelings, but I really didn't want to. I couldn't. The truth was that I didn't really *have* any. I was numb. And I guess what I couldn't admit to at the time – even to myself – was that I felt this amazing sense of *relief* – the pain had been so bad towards the end . . .' Kane frowned. 'And then there was all this *other* stuff . . .' he frowned, '*private* stuff . . . *complicated* stuff . . . stuff I just couldn't go into because it would've been a betrayal of her, of the relationship we'd had, of her confidence . . . I dunno. I just clammed up. It was easier that way . . .'

'Exactly,' Laura said, almost too enthusiastically. 'So there you go.' She held a dishcloth under the hot tap and then wrung it out.

'But I suppose I'd had a certain amount of time – in advance – to prepare myself . . .'

As Kane spoke Laura held the cloth under the tap for a second time, then wrung it out again, her movements growing increasingly jerky and uncontrolled. The tap was now running extremely hot. A small cloud of steam began to rise from the sink. Laura held the cloth under for a third time, then she dropped it, gasped in pain, shoved her fingers under her armpit, lowered her chin on to her chest and emitted a huge, choked-up sob.

'Laura?'

Kane strode over to the sink and turned off the tap. 'Are you all right?'

Laura shook her head.

'What's wrong?'

He put a hand on to her shoulder but she shrugged it off, and when she next spoke her voice was uncharacteristically low and hoarse. 'I just didn't *love* him enough, Kane,' she whispered.

'Don't be ridiculous,' Kane reprimanded her, gently squeezing her arm this time. 'Of *course* you did.'

'No.' She shook her head, refusing to make eye contact. 'I was a *bad* mother, and that's all there is to it. I should've looked after him better – *cared* for him better – instead of always thinking about myself.'

'That's just not true,' Kane maintained, aware (at some level) of having bitten off more than he could chew here. 'I'm sure you were a great mother . . .'

'*Really?*' she gazed up at him, her eyes flashing. 'You *think* so, do you?'

'Yes,' Kane nodded.

'Well then *this* might interest you,' she hissed. 'Guess where Ryan's "*great* mother" was when he was lying in hospital, fighting for his life?'

Kane shook his head.

'She was having extra-marital *sex* in a hotel room in Canterbury.'

'I see.'

Kane nodded, stiffly.

'Ryan wasn't killed instantly,' Laura continued, determined to get it all off her chest now. 'He fell in and out of consciousness for *five* hours. He was in hospital for *five* hours, struggling for every breath. But I wasn't there. Nobody could contact me. Nobody knew where I was. My phone was turned off. So Pat sat with him. Pat held his hand. Pat talked to the surgeons. *Pat* was at his side when he died.'

Kane stared at her. He wasn't sure what to say.

'It wasn't the driver's fault,' she insisted. 'It was Ryan's fault. He missed the bus home. He was playing football with his friends. He ended up walking. It was a new road. One of the new A roads. When he crossed he was looking in the wrong direction. It was a stupid mistake. He wasn't careful enough. He just stepped out . . .'

'What about his dad?' Kane asked.

'He was away in Manchester on business,' she glanced up at the ceiling, to try and stop her tears from flowing, 'but he *still* managed to get home over an hour before I did.'

'Did he suspect?' Kane wondered.

Laura looked down, frowning. A tear dripped on to the tiles. She slowly shook her head. 'It's even worse than you think,' she said, trembling.

'How?'

She didn't answer.

'Who was the affair with?'

Again, no answer.

'Was it Tom?' Kane took a wild punt.

She gazed up at him, amazed. 'How did you guess?'

'Are you still with him?' Kane asked.

'No.' She dabbed at her cheeks with her sleeve. 'It only lasted a few months. We were . . .' she sniffed and then put out her hand and rested it, almost reverently, on the marble work-surface.

'Working on the house together,' Kane filled in.

Laura nodded.

'Did Pat ever find out?'

'I don't think so.'

She shook her head, but then she shrugged, confused. 'I mean . . . I mean she knows about the *affairs*. Obviously she does. Because that's just *Tom*. That's who Tom *is* . . .'

Laura turned, grabbed the teapot and quickly filled up her mug. She wasn't shaking so much now. Kane quietly withdrew to his former position. He cradled his own mug in his hands. 'So did you usually meet Ryan from school?' he wondered.

'No.'

'Then the accident would've happened anyway . . .'

'That's not the point,' she snapped.

'Isn't it, though?' Kane persisted. 'You weren't able to say goodbye to your only son. Isn't that a sufficient punishment for whatever you did wrong?'

Laura stared down at the floor, grimly.

Kane adjusted the mug in his hand. The fisherman mug. He stared at it for a second. Then he blinked.

'Do you believe in God, Kane?' Laura suddenly demanded.

'Me?' Kane glanced up again. 'No. Absolutely not.'

'Karma, then?'

'Nope.'

'Well I do. I think God punished me for sleeping with my brother-in-law by taking away my only child.'

'The flipside of a vengeful God,' Kane quickly shot back, 'is eternal life.'

'*So?*'

'So, by your estimation, Ryan must be up in heaven, now.'

Laura gave this some thought.

'I'm not sure . . .' she said.

'You can't have one without the other,' Kane maintained.

'I'm *not sure* . . .' she said again, confused.

'That's the deal,' Kane persisted.

Silence

'I've recently started wondering . . .' Laura cleared her throat, gazing up at the ceiling again, 'if things might feel better – if it might bring some *relief* if I just . . .'

'No,' Kane said, briskly.

She peered over at him, frowning. 'But you don't even . . .'

'Yes I do. You were going to ask whether I thought you should confess.'

Laura grimaced.

'And the answer is no. Definitely not.'

Laura grimaced again.

'Pat probably suspects, anyhow,' Kane maintained, 'Charlie too.'

'You think so?'

Laura covered her mouth with her hand.

'Yes. Because secrets have a way of seeping out. They kind of . . . I don't know . . . *leak*. Maybe that's why Pat's still persisting with the whole road crossing thing, even when she knows you're not entirely happy about it. Maybe that's her way of punishing you.'

'No.' Laura shook her head. 'Pat wouldn't do that. It's not in her nature. She's been so kind to me, so patient. She's my best friend in the whole world . . .'

'*Such* a good friend that you shagged her husband behind her back,' Kane interrupted.

Laura looked hurt.

'The fact is that she might not even realise she's doing it. Her hostility might be unconscious. Yours too, for that matter.'

'Unconscious?' Laura scowled. 'I don't know what that means . . .'

'It means that you can love someone on the surface – very sincerely – but still hate them a little underneath . . .'

'*No!*' Laura was horrified. 'I *couldn't* hate Pat!'

'It's very deep down,' Kane persisted, 'so deep that you may hardly even realise it . . .'

'*No!*' Laura clenched her hands together, distraught. 'That's not possible. How could I hate Pat? She been so *kind* – she's been my *rock* . . .'

'Well I'd hate her in your place,' Kane shrugged. 'I mean how could you *help* yourself? She has her kids, this house, Tom, a clear conscience. She got to be with your son when he died, then to nurse you through your misery. And now she even gets to commemorate Ryan in public by setting up this committee . . .'

'I *love* Pat,' Laura sniffed. 'She's been wonderful . . .'

'Of course you do,' Kane shrugged. 'And I'm sure she loves you, too. It's just that feelings are complicated things. They don't always add up. And in my experience, the truth rarely makes things easier – quite the opposite, in fact.'

He stared down at the mug once more, as though irresistibly drawn to it.

Silence

'So . . .' Kane finally pushed the mug away and grabbed something from his coat pocket. 'Do you still want these?'

He held out a small bag of tablets.

Laura inspected them for a moment, and then slowly shook her head.

'Fine. *Good.*'

He shoved the tablets away again. 'Should I continue to send Gaffar?'

Laura shrugged.

'Tomorrow maybe?' he wheedled. 'The day after? Just to help with the transition?'

'Okay then,' Laura nodded, stiffly. 'If you think it's a good idea . . .'

'I do.'

Kane stood up.

'Thanks for the tea,' he said.

He turned.

'Kane?'

He turned back again.

'*Gaffar* . . .' Laura was twisting her two hands together, like a self-conscious schoolgirl.

671

'Yeah? What about him?'

'Well . . . I mean . . .' she cleared her throat, embarrassed, 'does he actually have . . . *you* know . . . *sex* with *all* your female clients?'

'Uh . . . Wow . . .' Kane frowned. 'Now *there's* a question . . .' Then he smiled. Then he scratched his head for a while, obviously thinking, very carefully, before delivering his answer.

TWELVE

When Beede finally regained consciousness he was standing in the shower, his naked body slumped heavily against the tiles – numb, leaden, inert – like an old, abandoned hog carcass. His hands and his arms – he gazed at them, blankly – were covered in scratches. The scratches were bleeding. His teeth were tightly clenched. His jaw was aching. He slowly relaxed his jaw and his teeth began chattering. He was *freezing*. The water –

Ye Gods!

– was absolutely, bloody *icy*.
   He turned and fumbled at the tap –

Eh?

He wasn't entirely sure how it worked. At first he pulled at it, then he pushed at it, then he gently, *gently* twisted it, his strong brow knotted with concentration.
   Once the water had stopped flowing –

Yah!

– he gradually took stock, peering down, dazedly, at his feet. He felt off-kilter – wobbly, like a toddler. His balance seemed shot.
   As he stared down – his eyes falling dazedly in and out of focus – it slowly began to dawn on him that the base of the shower cubicle was full of water. It was ankle-deep and flowing over on to the bath-room floor. The bathroom floor was actually *awash* . . .
   Beede frowned. He knew that he should be feeling something – anxiety? Fastidiousness? Concern? – and knowing that he should feel these things almost made the feelings flow . . . *Almost*. But then they didn't. They didn't flow. Instead he felt nothing, simply an idle – almost insolent – curiosity.

He shifted his feet (just to see if he could –

Yup . . .)

– and as he moved, still more water tipped out of the cubicle and on to the floor. He watched it surge, fascinated. Riding on the tiny wave he'd created were a series of small, black boats – little, dark canoes, vying with each other to win the race to the bathroom wall. He blinked –

Huh?

– not canoes but feathers. Black feathers. He peered down at his feet again –

Ah . . .

– and discovered that the plughole in the shower cubicle had actually become blocked by them –

Pen . . .

He made an idle scratching motion in the air with his hand –

Penna

– he smiled –

Feder –

He frowned –

Feather

– he shook his head –

Feather

– he shook his head again, dissatisfied. He idly prodded at the feathers

674

with his toe, then he bent over, stiffly, and grabbed at them with his fingers.

Once the blockage was removed – at least partially – the water began to drain out. Beede crouched down and watched it disappear – grinning, delightedly, at the tiny whirlpool he'd created – still clutching the feathers tightly in his hand –

Wah-hoooooooo!

His head slowly rotated, round and around and around and *around* . . .

Wah-hoooooooo!

He found the suck, spin and glug of the water thoroughly absorbing. It was mesmerising. It was beautiful.

Once the water was gone –

Aw!

– he focussed in on the feathers again –

Penna

He began sorting them out, quite methodically, casting aside the smaller ones, before settling, finally, on the longest and strongest of the bunch. He inspected the tip of its quill with an expert eye –

Hmmn . . .

– then dabbed it, matter-of-factly, on to his tongue.
He grimaced.
It was a *black* feather –

Phleagh!

He grimaced again, as if disgusted by the taste of it, but then he stopped grimacing –

Phlegh?

Phleg?
Bhleg?
Bloec?
Blac?

Eh?!

Blac?

Blac?

– he peered down at his arms. They were covered in scratches. The scratches stung a little and they were still bleeding. 'Blac . . .' he murmured, frowning, then tipped the quill of the feather into a little stream of blood . . .

Hmmn

He shook his head –

Enque

Enke

Ink

He scowled, frustrated –

Blac

He shook his head –

Enke

He shook his head –

No . . .
Ruh . . . ?
Eh?

676

He thought quietly for a while. Then –

Reudh?

Ruber?

Rood?

Rud?

Red?

Red?

Blut-red?

Eh?

Blut?

He examined the *blut* on his arms. He inspected the *blut* . . . But every time the concept of the *blut*, the idea of the *blut,* was formalised into a proper form of words, he felt something *hiccough*, he felt something disconnecting, he felt a kind of . . . almost like a . . . a rupture . . . a sudden cutting-off, a terrible, maddening, frustrating *cleft* – a *chink* – between his understanding and his feeling, as if the idea and the emotion had been violently rent. He stood silently for a while – struck dumb, wavering slightly – on the brink of this deep abyss – this intellectual *chasm*.

He couldn't cross it. Not yet. So he stopped trying and stepped jauntily out of the shower cubicle instead. He dropped the feather. He reached for a towel and wrapped it around him. He opened the bathroom door (no problem with the handle) and padded out into the kitchen.

Here the tiles were also soaking. His feet made a series of delightful slapping sounds against them –

Viet-waat-viet-waat-viet-waat . . .

Hah!

He stood and gazed around him. Things seemed different – *very* different – but he didn't know what the differences were, and he wasn't exactly sure how he might be expected to respond to them. He frowned, thoughtfully, his sharp, brown eyes consuming every detail.

All the furniture in the living-room had been shoved – and in some cases, thrown – against the three outer walls. It almost looked as if a small tornado had been at work there. The middle of the room was now completely empty. Beede appraised this new space, inquisitively. Then he smiled . . . Yes. *Good*. He *liked* this new space. It was a *fine* new space . . .

As a mark of his approval he paraded around in the space for a while; he swaggered about in it, he preened and he strutted – kicking up his legs, thrusting out his chest, tossing back his head, both hands resting jauntily on his hips.

During the course of this brief interlude his towel fell off. Beede hurriedly grabbed for something to replace it with, chancing upon the shirt he'd removed earlier (drawing it – with a sense of palpable satisfaction – from the heart of the surrounding chaos) and eagerly pulling it on, but the wrong way around; fastening the top button at the back of his neck so that now (from the front, at least) he exuded a pious – almost a *priestly* – aspect.

He promptly recommenced his theatrics, fully aware, as he pranced, that the cheeks of his arse were fluttering in and out of view as the wings of the shirt flapped cheekily around it. He quickly integrated this into his walk, winking and leering, shaking his hips, thrusting obscenely, the whole, lascivious spectacle culminating, finally, in an extravagant bow (also – by sheer coincidence – a shameless piece of mooning).

As he straightened up (plainly delighted by this brazen display) Beede's head smacked into something –

Eh?!

He glanced skyward, frowning. Suspended directly above him (attached to the electrical cord from the broken light fitment by what looked like a tie or a dressing-gown belt) was the cat. The cat was strung up, tightly, by his neck, like a piece of game that'd been left out to hang.

Beede stood and gazed at the cat, fascinated. The cat wasn't yet dead. He still showed some slight signs of consciousness. His mouth leered and drooled, his eyes blinked, whitely. His back leg twitched.

Beede pulled laboriously on his chin as he appraised the cat. He tapped his foot. He rolled his eyes. He mimed himself thinking, strenuously. Then he stood on his tip-toes and reached up, as if to try and free the unhappy creature, but he was too short to untie the knot, so he turned and peered around him, looking for some kind of physical support.

His eye finally alighted upon a chair (the chair from his desk) which was lying upside down on a messy pile of books. He marched over to inspect the chair. He bent over to pick it up, but as he bent he froze, glanced over his shoulder, grabbed a hold of his two shirt flaps, held them modestly together, and simpered, coyly.

Once he'd finished simpering (once he'd taken it about as far as it could possibly go – then still further) Beede casually released the flaps, stationed his two feet firmly apart and bent over, crudely, to seize the chair. But instead of lifting it effortlessly (as was only to be expected – it wasn't a large chair, after all), Beede discovered himself signally unable to establish a firm grip.

It was almost as if the chair had been oiled. Every time he placed a hand on it the hand slid off – and at great speed, to boot. Yet rather than responding to this challenge sensibly – slowing down, perhaps, or inspecting the chair more closely (locating the *source* of the problem, even) – Beede reacted by launching ever more frenzied attacks on it – throwing himself at the chair with such haste and such violence that each time he made physical contact he flew on to the floor, with a crash: once, twice, five times, ten . . .

Soon he was red-faced, sweating and out of breath. He mimed himself exhausted – panting like a thirsty hound, swiping a heavy arm across his forehead. He peered around him, searching for somewhere to sit and take stock. Naturally he espied the upturned chair. He went and grabbed a hold of it and set it straight. He sat down on it and appeared to relax . . .

Phew!

. . . until three/five/seven seconds later and then –
'*Weeeeeeeeee!*' he slid off the chair, at speed (as if the seat had been lubricated) and landed – *thump* – on the carpet.

He turned to appraise the chair, scratching his head –
'Hmmn.'
– then he yanked himself to his feet and went over to inspect the cat. The cat's foot was barely twitching now, but his eyelids were still fluttering.
'Hmmn.'

Beede went back to try and grab the chair again, brusquely spitting on to his hands and wiping them on his shirt to secure his grip. This time (his body language proclaimed loudly) he really meant business.

He bent over, arms extended, and prepared to lunge, but just as he was lunging, he remembered his shirt. He pulled a bashful expression. He glanced behind him. He observed his naked buttocks. He gasped. He snatched at the shirt flaps, but snatched so vigorously – with both hands, simultaneously – that he ended up performing a compact somersault.

Beede landed, back on his feet, with a resounding thud. He looked astonished, as if he couldn't quite comprehend what'd just happened. Then he calmed himself down. Then he returned to the chair. Then he spat on his hands. Then he slowly bent over. Then he prepared to lunge. Then he remembered his bare arse again. Then he glanced behind him again. Then he gasped. Then he snatched at the shirt flaps. Another dramatic somersault –

Thud!

On this second occasion, however, he somehow managed to land with his hands pinning his shirt tails together – his modesty almost fully intact. He grinned, smugly. Then he dropped the flaps, spat on his palms, rubbed them together and grabbed at the chair like a wrestler commencing a brand-new bout.

This time his hands didn't slip, they held firm, but instead of lifting the chair, the chair seemed to lift *him*.
Beede remained in the air for a few seconds and then was thrown down, sprawling, on to the carpet.

What?!

He gazed at the chair, appalled. Then his face purpled-up with rage. He clambered to his feet and he attacked the chair, savagely. Once again the chair got the better of him. It threw him up – into a lop-sided handstand – and then violently tossed him down.

Beede glared at the chair from his position on the rug. He was now – if it were possible – even angrier than before. Then a cunning thought suddenly occurred to him –

What if . . . ? (his expression seemed to say) . . . What if I were to creep up on it?

To take it unawares?

To launch a secret attack on it *from the rear*?

Ha!

Beede slowly clambered to his knees – trying to remain as inconspicuous as possible – and furtively commenced crawling. Every so often, he'd pause, peer behind him, and place a warning finger to his lips –

Shhhhh!

As he drew closer to the chair his crawling slowed down to almost a snail's pace and the warning finger grew ever more insistent –

Shhhhh!

– until, just as he was perfectly positioned to launch his assault, to spring to his feet, to attack –

Parp!

– he suddenly let rip – discharging a fart of such volume and such ferocity that he was spontaneously launched, like a rocket, over the back of the chair, landing – supported by the seat this time – on his two hands, struggling (even so) to clutch at it – only to be tossed, once again, into a dramatic flick-flack.

On his second hand-spring he managed to inadvertently kick the suspended cat. The cat swung up sharply into the ceiling, hitting it with a stomach-wrenching *smack*. Beede caught him –

Phut!

– (already upright again), on his downward trajectory –

Ta-dah!

The cat was now very still. Beede appraised him, with a poignant sigh. He let go of him. He walked over to fetch the chair. He grabbed it. He carried the chair over to the cat. He clambered on to the chair. He carefully untied the knot around the cat's neck (his expression one of unspeakable tenderness), and then, as the knot came loose, he casually leaned back and allowed the cat to drop, unceremoniously, on to the carpet.

Beede peered down at the cat from his chair, with a shrug. Then he blinked. Then he looked down again, shocked, as if suddenly the floor seemed like it was many miles below him. He grimaced. He gave the distant cat carcass a tentative, little wave (almost as if suggesting that the cat might save *him* this time).

No movement from the cat. Beede grew increasingly alarmed by his high altitude. His knees began to knock. He gnawed on his fingernails. He personified anxiety. And then – in the wink of an eye – he'd back-flipped from the chair and on to the carpet, landing neatly and cleanly, like a seasoned gymnast –

Hah!

He slapped his hands together, smugly (to indicate a job well done) then turned and marched off jauntily towards the bedroom (obviously well-satisfied with the performance he'd given). Half-way to the door, though, the unexpected happened: his knees almost buckled under him –

Argh!

He threw out both arms (to prevent himself from falling) and ground to an abrupt halt. His face creased up in agony. He gazed down at his feet, despairingly. He groaned. He tried to walk again, but he couldn't (his toes were in an awful rictus – curled up like claws – while the arch looked strangely pinched and contracted), the best he could muster was a pathetic hobble.

He glanced around him, looking for some kind of relief. His eye alighted on a mop and broom leaned up against the wall in the corner of the kitchen. He shuffled towards them, grabbed them, upended them, placed the padded/bristled sections under each of his armpits and employed them as a pair of piece-meal crutches. Slowly, stiffly, wincing – quite the oldest man in the planet – he pitched and staggered his way into the bedroom.

Five minutes passed. During this interlude the cat didn't move. When Beede finally re-emerged he was well-spruced and tidily dressed – his hair neatly greased, his shirt buttoned up (in the traditional style), wearing a well-pressed pair of trousers, clean socks and shoes. His shoulder seemed tense – a little stiff – but his gait (in general) seemed relatively normal. He was holding the mop in his hand –

Eh?!

– and wearing an expression of slight confusion.

As he entered the kitchen he drew to a sharp halt. He peered at the floor, at the wet tiles underfoot . . .
'Good *God . . . What . . . ?*'
He inspected the mop again, scowling –

Oh –
Of course . . .

He placed it down on to the tiles and began cleaning up. Once the mop was saturated he looked around – somewhat dazedly – for the special bucket in which to wring it out . . .

Where is it?

He glanced over into the living-room, perplexed. His jaw dropped.

'*Kids . . .*' Kane drawled boredly, slowly pulling past a smart-looking saloon which'd recently been dumped at the entrance to the slip road from the Bad Munstereifel segment of the A2042 (half-on the kerb, half-off it), the door thrown open into oncoming traffic.

'. . . Idiot, fuckin' *joy*riders . . .'.

He drove on, accelerating boldly, casually negotiating one of the voluptuously looping, helter-skelter of curves leading down towards the roundabout while howling along, raucously, to an old Zappa cd –

Don't go where the huskies go!
Don't you eat that yellow snow!

He was still able, nevertheless (and quite miraculously, under the circumstances) to detect something strange (something anomalous, external, *extraneous*) beyond this marvellously impenetrable, aural wall –

A horn?

Kane scowled –

Eh?!

– instinctively covering the brake with his foot and reaching out, blindly, to turn down the music, when –

Fuck!

– he almost hit a man – one-handed. He wrenched at the steering wheel, gasping, to avoid the collision, then wrenched at the wheel again to avoid hitting an old Metro which'd just that second braked and swerved for precisely the same reason –

Bollocks!

He clipped the Metro's back light as he flew past it, hearing a horn repeatedly sounding in time to the music –

My horn . . . ?

(He inspected his hands)

684

Yup

– pulling over just as soon as was feasible –

Speeding . . .
Was I?

– hurling the Merc up on to a grassy verge –

Ouch!
Undercarriage didn't like that much . . .

– as a third car shot by which had somehow succeeded in avoiding a collision –

Jammy swine!

– and so drove on, without stopping.

Kane glanced into his rearview mirror to check on the progress of the car he'd just clipped. It was currently stationary; stalled, at an angle. A woman sat the wheel. His eyes quickly shifted beyond her to confirm something which (instinctively, at gut-level) he already knew –

Isidore?
Is it . . . ?

He sprang from the Merc and ran over to the Metro. Just as he was drawing near, though, the car's engine turned, unexpectedly, and it shot forward (without warning – still in gear, presumably), almost ploughing straight into him –

Jesus!

He leapt out of harm's way as the driver (with an audible squeal) steered herself, clumsily, back into the kerb.

Isidore, meanwhile – about 10 yards behind them – seemed supremely oblivious to the chaos he was generating. He hadn't even looked up. He was inspecting the road, bending over, scowling, scratching his head, clearly deeply preoccupied by something.

Kane winced, horrified, as a fourth car swung past, sounding its horn, only narrowly avoiding Dory, being obliged to swerve for a second time to avoid the Metro, and then –

Balls!

– for a *third* time to avoid him. Kane made eye contact with the driver and casually waved him on –

No problem, my friend –
It's all under control . . .

The driver cussed him, furiously –

Charming!

Kane jogged over to the Metro, slapped his hand on to the roof, bent down and peered in, benignly, through the passenger window – 'You all right in there?'

The car had stalled again. The blonde woman was twisting her keys in the ignition and pumping on the accelerator. She barely even glanced up.

'I'm fine,' she yelled. 'The starter motor's just dodgy. What about *him* . . .'

She indicated behind her, finally making proper eye contact. A *frisson* passed between them, then the engine abruptly sparked and roared into life.

'There's a short, dirt track,' Kane pointed, 'on the left – you should pull off . . .'

She stuck the car into reverse (squinting over her shoulder, spinning the steering wheel, slamming down on the accelerator) and then – zip – nix – *zilch*. It cut out.

'*Shit!*'

A fifth car roared past them, its horn sounding.

Kane ran to the front of the car and immediately began pushing it.

'*Handbrake,*' he yelled.

She took off the handbrake and the car slowly lurched uphill. As soon as it was pointing in the proper direction he jumped aside and the car commenced rolling, unaided, down the slope, although it couldn't build up enough momentum to take the turn in one go, but simply ground to a halt about half-way along, its back-end still jutting out – perilously – on to the tarmac.

Kane quickly jogged down after it, shoving hard from the rear this time, heaving and pushing until it was fully contained within the short, dirt drive, its nose pressed up snugly against a neat, wooden gate. Just the other side of this gate stood a horse and a sheep, companionably observing the unfolding drama with expressions of cheerful resignation.

Kane was panting, exhausted. Two more vehicles roared by – a jeep; a white, Ford van – but neither sounded its horn.

He turned –

Eh?

– and gazed up along the road again. Isidore was gone. He'd vanished. He scratched his head, puzzled.

'Where'd he go?' the woman demanded, clambering from the old Metro and peering around her, spooked.

'I don't know . . .'

Kane suddenly remembered the estate car, abandoned, at the start of the slip road. He put two and two together, 'Remember that Rover?' he pointed. 'Just after the turn-off with its door slung open?'

'What a total, bloody *nutter*,' the girl exclaimed, and then, '*WAH!*' she yelled, jumping violently up and down in a novel (and somewhat startling) attempt to unburden herself of the stress she felt.

Kane stared at her, impassively.

'I met you at the cafe,' he said (once she'd finally stopped bouncing), 'a few days ago . . .'

'Yeah,' she nodded, her mass of blonde curls in a state of chronic disarray now.

'Kane,' he said, offering her his hand.

'Maude,' she said, taking it and squeezing it. Her palms were hot but her fingertips were icy.

'So what d'you think he was looking for?' Kane wondered, glancing up along the road again.

'Who?'

'On the tarmac. He was looking for something . . .'

'I dunno,' she shrugged, helplessly, 'I mean I didn't *see* anything . . .'

He frowned. 'I clipped your back light, didn't I?'

He went to take a proper look.

'It's my mother's car,' she said, grimacing, 'I'm not actually insured to drive it.'

'There's not too much to worry about,' he said, determined to put a brave face on it, 'just a broken light and a tiny dent in the boot . . .'

'How's yours?'

She indicated, nervously, towards The Blonde.

'I dunno. Probably just a scratch on the bumper. She's tough – built like a tank.'

The girl nodded, biting her lip.

'Sure you're all right?' Kane asked, reaching into his pocket for his cigarettes.

'He was crying . . .' she murmured. 'And did you notice that awful *bruise* . . . ?'

'Smoke?'

He offered her the packet. She shook her head, then lifted her hands and began savagely pinning back her stray curls.

'D'you think he'll be okay?' she asked.

Kane propped a Marlboro into the corner of his mouth and then slowly began sauntering along the grass verge. The girl followed, still pinning.

'Will I be liable for the damage to your car?' she asked.

'Nope . . .' he found his lighter and lit the cigarette. 'I hit you, so it's my responsibility . . .'

'It's just that if we get the police involved, or the insurance . . .'

'God forbid,' he inhaled deeply. 'That's the last thing I need. Just get me a quote and I'll happily cover it.'

'Good. Great. Fantastic.'

She seemed considerably cheered by this.

He reached the approximate point on the tarmac where Dory had been standing and stared over at it, intently –

Nothing

'Don't step off the kerb,' she warned him, grabbing on to his arm as he instinctively moved forward.

'No,' he said, glancing down at her hand.

She let go, embarrassed.

688

Kane removed the cigarette from between his lips and casually flicked its ash on to the tarmac. Maude quickly moved away and began inspecting the plastic collar on a small Holly bush nearby.

'They plant these damn things in their *thousands*,' she grumbled, 'but then there's never any proper *after*-care . . .'

'*Jesus*,' Kane mused idly, 'you sound just like my dad . . .'

He glanced at her, sideways, but she was already striding back, purposefully, towards her car. Kane gazed blankly at the road again. Two highly customised Volkswagens sped past (possibly en route to some kind of specialist car show). He shuddered.

After a minute or so Maude returned, pulling on a pair of black, hand-knitted gloves – with a neat line of pale, pink ribbons sewn on to the knuckles – and holding a treacherous-looking Stanley knife between her teeth. She caught Kane's quizzical look. 'My da ha breatht canther,' she lisped. 'I thell the ribbonth for tharity . . .'

She formed her hands into fists and held them out. 'Wou you li one?'

As she spoke a small quantity of spit dribbled down on to her chin. 'Uh . . .'

Before he could answer she was reaching into her pocket to locate him a ribbon. She pulled one out, but it didn't have a pin attached.

'Your dad died of *breast* cancer?'

He winced at the idea.

'He din't *die*,' she removed the knife, shocked (carefully dabbing at her chin with her sleeve). 'He's *fine*. He's in remission . . .' she stared up at him, candidly. 'Men have breasts too, you know.'

'Of course . . .'

Kane reached into his own pocket, scowling, as she continued to try to locate a spare pin.

'No bloody pins,' she muttered.

'It doesn't matter. Just hang it over the button or something . . .'

She did as he'd asked. 'Don't you go and lose it,' she warned him. 'I won't.'

He found a pound coin and handed it to her. She inspected the coin. 'This is Gibraltarian,' she said, and passed it straight back again. 'Oh.'

He inspected the coin himself while Maude calmly released the blade on her knife, moved over to the small Holly bush, and started hacking away at its plastic collar. The collar came off, quite readily.

'*Urgh*,' she muttered, indicating angrily towards a thick gash in the bark. 'See the damage it was doing?'

She tossed the collar aside, enraged, and then moved on – automatically – to the next bush in line.

'Are you allowed to do that?' Kane enquired, almost without thinking –

Allowed?!

'*Allowed?*' Maude shot him a withering glance.

'Is it legal?' he persisted –

Legal?!

'*Legal?*' Another withering stare.

'Sure . . .' Kane stuck to his guns, 'I mean aren't those collars Council property or something?'

'You planning to stage a Citizen's Arrest?' she snorted.

'*No.*'

'You seriously think the *Council* gives a shit?' she sneered. '*Ashford* Council? *Jeez*. Just look around you. When I was a kid this place was a beautiful, rural backwater, and now it's like fucking *Lego-land* . . .'

She shook her head, disgusted, hurling the second collar to the ground.

'Oh come *on*,' Kane scoffed. 'It was hardly as great as all *that* . . .'

She shot him a black look.

Kane gazed along the steep curve of the embankment. There were hundreds of collars surrounding hundreds of small trees and bushes. 'How many are you planning to do?' he asked.

'*Why?*'

She hacked away, furiously, at another collar as he watched on benevolently.

'Your hair's coming loose again . . .' he reached out his hand to gently reposition a tight, bright, blonde ringlet which seemed determined to fall into her eyes as she worked. She pulled back, defensively.

'I'll do as many as I possibly can,' she muttered, flattening out the curl herself and pinning it down. 'See how the collar's cut into the bark?' She indicated, irritably, towards a lop-sided conifer. 'I mean they haven't even been *fitted* properly . . .'

690

Maude kicked at a Gorse bush which'd collapsed under its own weight – 'See that? There's no real *support* . . .' – then her head snapped around and she fell inexplicably silent.

'What's up?' he enquired, after five seconds' grace.

'Shhh!'

She put a finger to her lips.

'What?' he demanded, mystified.

'Didn't you hear it?'

'What?'

'Listen . . .'

They were quiet for a while. Several cars rumbled past.

'You should give me your mobile number,' Kane said, refusing to indulge her any further. 'Then at least we can . . .'

'I don't have a mobile,' she cut in. 'The electromagnetic waves have a devastating impact on avian reproduction.'

'Pardon?'

'Shhhh . . . !' She jerked her head around for a second time '. . .There it goes again . . .' she grinned, taking a couple of tentative steps forward, standing on her tip-toes and peering, excitedly, into the field beyond.

'I didn't hear it,' Kane said, bemused.

'Eee-ooo-ii! Eee-ooo-ii!' she called.

He frowned at her, surprised. She seemed entirely different now (out here, by the road) from the shy girl he'd first encountered at the restaurant. He quietly inspected her face, in profile. She was pretty, but her nose was tiny; too flat and too snub. Her lips were full, though, if somewhat chapped.

'King of the Birds,' she announced, delighted.

'Sorry?'

'King of the Birds,' she repeated, 'the peacock.'

Kane scowled.

'Flannery O'Connor,' she expanded, smugly, '"The King of the Birds". It's the title of an essay she once wrote about keeping peacocks. We studied it at college. It's actually a brilliant piece of writing – very dry, very funny, very clever . . .'

Kane continued to stare at her, speculatively.

'Not much of a reader, *huh*?' she shrugged.

'I know who Flannery O'Connor is,' he asserted.

'Oh yeah?'

She removed a third collar and threw it down (somewhat provocatively) at his feet.

Kane smiled, unperturbed, nudging at the collar with the toe of his boot. As he lifted his foot, however, he felt a sharp dart of pain beneath it, centred on the arch area –

Verruca

He drew a deep breath. 'My late mother was a huge fan of Southern Gothic writing . . .' he observed haltingly (trying to distract himself), 'Carson McCullers? Eudora Welty . . . ?'

Maude nodded.

'In fact she once helped to choreograph a modern dance production of *Wise Blood* . . .'

'*Really?*' Maude looked incredulous.

'Yeah. It had a completely original score, a semi-professional cast, and even a small, live orchestra, composed mainly of students from the London School of Music. It played the Edinburgh Fringe for over a month and then moved down to this tiny theatre in North London for a while . . .' his voice gradually grew more confident as he spoke, his tone more insistent, 'The Intimate Theatre – in Palmer's Green or Winchmore Hill . . . I forget which. I still have the programme somewhere . . .'

He frowned. 'This was 1974, 1975. She took a couple of minor roles herself – an old, blind woman, a gorilla . . .'

He grinned, remembering. 'She actually kept the mask – from the gorilla costume – and I used to mess around in it as a kid . . .' He shook his head, fondly. 'It received blistering reviews,' he winced, 'really venomous. People just weren't ready for it back then. It was all too new, too radical. Mum tried to put a brave face on the whole *débâcle* . . .'

He blinked –

What?!

– '. . . but it totally killed her confidence. She was badly cut-up about it . . .' he shrugged. 'She kept everything – *hoarded* everything – as a reminder, in this special little scrapbook: stage directions, costume designs, material samples, loads of photos and stuff . . .'

Maude was peering up at him as he reminisced, her expression a strange combination of impressed, galled and fearful. Kane stared back at her, helplessly, as if growing increasingly perplexed himself by this extraordinary volume of words which kept tumbling – apparently unbidden – from between his lips.

'I mean this was *way* before O'Connor was widely known in the UK,' he continued (feeling not unlike a frightened parent pursuing a runaway pram down a steep hill). 'I believe the book was first published in the late 1950s . . . I've never really been a great fan of it myself – it's just too stark, too relentless – although I wouldn't have dared tell Mum that – she was completely in love with it . . .'

Enough!

Kane scratched his head, confused –

Just shut up!

'I actually prefer the short stories . . .' his mouth prattled on, unreservedly '. . . *You* know – *Everything that Rises Must Converge*? And the collected letters are just phenomenal . . .'

What?!

'. . . Although I'm struggling to remember the name of them – the *title* . . .'
   Kane paused for a second, to try and ponder the issue, but then –
'. . . I always thought it a rather strange coincidence,' he suddenly babbled on (his eyes darting around him –

The road, the bush, the fence, the sky . . .

– his heart hammering away like a woodpecker in his chest) '. . . that O'Connor died when she was thirty-nine – the exact-same age my mother was when she first attempted suicide . . .'

What?!
Fuck!
Are you insane?!

'. . . Although I suppose that's hardly a coincidence at all. I mean not in the formal sense of the word. More of an . . . an *ee-ron* . . .' he frowned, utterly baffled, as his mouth refused – point-blank – to conform to his brain's bidding, 'an *ee-ron* . . .' he shook his head, 'an . . . an eíron? . . . *iron-i-a?* . . . *i-ron-ee?* Irony? Is that . . . ?'

Shut up!

He quickly covered his mouth with his hand, and then – '*THE HABIT OF BEING!'* he roared (through the small cracks in his fingers), almost tipping over backwards with the sheer force of this ejaculation.
　　Maude's eyes widened, in shock.
'The collected letters,' he explained (steadying himself, dropping the hand, reddening), 'the *title* . . .'

Shut up!

'. . . Although I don't even know if they're still available in print . . .'

Shut up!

'. . . but you could always look them up on the internet, I guess. Get yourself a cheap copy second-hand . . .'

SHUT UP!
SHUT UP!
SHUT UP!

　　At long last, he fell silent –

. . . .

　　Maude continued to gaze up at him, daunted. He stared back at her, his lips firmly clamped together, as if terrified that the swarm of words within him might – at any second – prise them back open and fly free again. Then he blinked.

What?!

His eyes had begun to water –

Balls!

'Sorry . . . *Damn* . . .' He shook his head, confused –

STOP!

'. . . I don't even know why I *said* that . . .'

NO!

– '. . . She wasn't thirty-nine at all. She was older . . .'

Stop!
Please!

'. . . she was *forty*. Forty-one. Forty-two. I mean my *mother* . . .' –

NO!

– '. . . when she . . . when she . . . d-d-d-'
He was suddenly stuttering, uncontrollably, 'd-d-d-*dey* . . . *dey-ja* . . .
dey . . . *dau* . . . *dieg* . . .'

What?!

– '. . . When she d-d . . . when she *d-died*.'
He double-blinked.
   '*Yes*. She was forty-one. When she . . . when she . . .'
He swallowed hard, rotating his cigarette – neurotically – between his
finger and his thumb.
Maude opened her mouth to speak.
   'O'Connor *was* thirty-nine, though,' he interrupted her, firmly, '*that*
wasn't apocryphal . . .'

Apocryphal?

Maude's mouth remained open. She gaped at him.

'From the Greek,' he explained, '*apókruphos* – or . . . or "hidden" – via the Latin. It's . . . it's . . . it's ecclesiastical in origin . . .'

Kane's hands – he realised – were now shaking quite violently. He gazed down at them, astonished.

'*Jesus.*'

He stuck his cigarette into his mouth, inhaled and then coughed. His eyes filled with tears again. He sucked in his cheeks, turning away – appalled.

Silence

'Well there's a definitely a peacock around here somewhere . . .' Maude murmured, turning away herself – with a show of some delicacy – and then launching a concerted attack on her fourth, consecutive bush.

Kane didn't respond. He'd taken out his phone –

Masking behaviour

– and was pretending to check his messages. He rolled down the menu (his fingers clumsy with the cold), barely even focussing on the display, his mind – searching for calm, for *comfort*, perhaps – retreating back to that ludicrously extravagant kitchen where he'd sat and chatted with Laura – just twenty minutes before – his hands tightly cradling a steaming mug of tea –

World's Greatest Fisherman

Then his thoughts regressed still further, to that quiet corner of Beede's dark bedroom, where he'd stood and inspected an all-but identical mug – tagged and displayed in an upturned crate – his nostrils prickling with the pungent scent of cat litter . . .

Eh?

Kane double-blinked. He grimaced. He refocussed. He called up the number for Peta Borough on his phone. He dialled it. The phone rang. He held it, impatiently, to his ear.

'Uh . . .' Maude peered over at him. 'You could always collect those together if you felt like it . . .' she pointed to the abandoned collars. 'It'd save them from blowing into the road. You could form them into some kind of a . . . a *bundle*, maybe . . .'

Kane didn't move –

Nope –
No answer

'I can recycle them for cash,' she continued. 'Not for *much*, obviously . . .'

Still, Kane didn't respond. He was waiting to leave a message – 'Peta? Hi. It's Kane. I must see you. It's urgent. Bye.'

'I have a friend who works on a plantation in North Kent . . .' Maude rattled on, aimlessly.

Kane brusquely shoved his phone away. 'So I should contact you about the car repairs via the French Connection?' he demanded, studiously avoiding eye contact.

'Sure. If you like . . .' Maude bent over and gathered up the collars herself. 'They're far easier to transport when they're tucked up inside each other . . .'

She tried to wrangle them, but without much success.

'It's *cold* out here,' Kane shuddered, drawing on his smoke –
As he inhaled he heard a strange, haunting call – a cry – some way off in the distance. His skin puckered into goose-bumps –

Eh?

'Peacock again,' Maude smiled. 'You *must've* caught it that time?'
'Aren't they meant to be bad luck?'
Kane shivered, paranoid.

'What?' Maude delivered him a scornful look.

He caught her eye and then glanced away, embarrassed. At precisely that moment, a scooter sped past, travelling at an unconscionable speed, its engine chronically over-revved, two people on board, only one of which (the driver) was actually wearing a helmet. The passenger was a girl – a scraggy girl, unsuitably dressed for the freezing weather (in a mini-skirt and tank-top) – wailing (in terror? *Delight?*) as they took the corner. This dramatic spectacle was rendered doubly absurd (or risible, depending on your angle) by the fact that the girl was clutching on to a Bible (as if her life depended on it) while stiffly holding out a severely broken leg, which bounced up and down as they drove, only inches above the tarmac.

'Bloody hell,' Maude exclaimed, her head whipping around.

'What the . . . ?!' Kane gasped, and then, '*Gaffar? GAFFAR?!*'

He ran a couple of steps down the embankment, waving his arms, but they'd already high-tailed it.

'You know them?'

'Uh . . . yeah.'

Kane tugged on his ear-lobe, bemused, still staring blankly down the road as a second vehicle swung by (but at a rather more sedate pace, this time). It was a large, dark-green Rover and Isidore sat at its wheel; ramrod-straight, hatchet-jawed, insanely focussed on the road ahead.

This was all the incentive Kane needed. 'Gotta go,' he threw down his cigarette and turned, instinctively, to follow.

'I hope you don't make a habit of doing that,' Maude clucked, sticking out her foot and extinguishing the stub with the heel of her old hiking boot.

'Think you can get your car to start?' he yelled, over his shoulder.

'Yeah. It'll be the plugs. I'll just dry them off. It'll be . . .'

She grimaced. 'It'll be *fine*,' she sniped.

But he was already well out of ear-shot.

THIRTEEN

'It was KAAAAAANE!' Kelly screamed, repeatedly smacking Gaffar's back with her Bible as they hurtled around the roundabout. 'KAAAAAAAANE!'

'Huh?' Gaffar glanced over his shoulder.

'We gotta STOP!'

Gaffar promptly applied the brakes.

'Not on the fuckin' ROUNDABOUT, you LOON!'

Gaffar accelerated again.

'We're LOST. We need to get back on to the MAIN ROAD . . .' Kelly pointed to the relevant turn-off, but Gaffar had already shot past it.

'BALLS! Harve ain't gonna sit around waitin' all fuckin' DAY, you DICK!'

Kelly took a swipe at his helmet this time. Gaffar ducked to avoid it and the scooter wobbled, precariously.

'WAAAH!'

They took the roundabout again (still wobbling) and somehow managed to exit correctly, circling back up on to the A2070 where they rapidly rejoined the Bad Munstereifel section of the busy dual carriageway.

Kelly took out her mobile and attempted to dial her uncle as they sped along it.

'WHERE NOW?' Gaffar bellowed.

'SHUT UP! I'm just tryin'a ring HARVE to FIND OUT, you PILLOCK!'

They were fast approaching another roundabout.

'I can't get any fuckin' . . . WOAAHH!'

Kelly clung on tightly as they commenced the turn. Then –

'Head STRAIGHT!' she yelled, pointing, 'an' PULL OVER! We need to get . . .'

They exited on to Malcolm Sargent Road.

'STOP!' she yelled. 'STOP!! DOUBLE-QUICK! BY THE VAN!'

Gaffar careered in towards the pavement, braking hard. Kelly jolted

forward on the seat, her forehead smacking into the back of his helmet.
'*OW!*'

As they drew to a halt she leaned over sideways and spewed a neat,
semi-translucent mouthful of bile into the gutter. A man was standing
nearby, taping a poster on to a street light. He turned.

'Little Kelly *Broad*,' he exclaimed, strolling over with a beaming
smile. 'Well here's a turn-up!'

He shoved his hand into his pocket, withdrew a tissue and handed it
to her. Kelly snatched the tissue, thrusting him her Bible, in exchange.
He took it and inspected it, quizzically, as she patted at her mouth,
groaning. She was a pale shade of lilac.

'That must've been some ride, kid,' he observed, shooting Gaffar
a disapproving look.

'Butt *out*, Garry,' Kelly snapped (every inch the stroppy teenager), then,
'How's that?' She peered up at him, owlishly. He gazed down at her,
frowning. Her entire face was streaked in black spider-legs of mascara.

'Uh . . . well you've still got a little bit of . . .' he pointed '. . . *you*
know . . . around the eye area.'

'What?'

'The Panda Effect I think they like to call it.'

'*Mascara?*'

She patted, ineffectually, at her cheeks.

'It's more . . . uh . . . more *general* . . .'

She handed him the tissue, scowling. 'Just wipe it off, then, will
ya?'

'Me?'

He looked alarmed.

'Yeah. Just dab it off. Go on,' she bullied him, 'don't take all *year*
about it.'

'Bloody *hell* . . .'

He spat on the tissue and gently commenced dabbing. Kelly – rather
surprisingly, Gaffar felt – lifted her small chin into the air, and received
his attentions, uncomplainingly, like a small girl having her face cleaned
by an attentive nanny after devouring an over-sized sundae at a fair.

Gaffar pushed up his visor and peered over at the stranger, suspiciously. He was a short, burly, middle-aged man with an unruly mop
of frizzy brown hair (receding a little at the crown), a keen pair of
light-green eyes (fringed by disarmingly long and curly lashes) set in
a rough, wide, distinctly gnomish face.

'This here is Garry Spivey, Gaff,' Kelly informed him.

'*Eh?*'

'My Uncle Harvey's Best Mucker . . .' she grinned.

'*That'd* be the day, Kell.'

Garry rolled his green eyes, long-sufferingly.

Kelly pointed. 'I thought I recognised that clapped-out old van of yours, Gaz. Still too tight to get yourself somethin' proper?'

'If it ain't broke,' Garry shrugged. 'The old girl's still doin' me pretty good service . . .'

'That's an old Dodge, Gaff,' Kelly explained. 'It's Yank-made. Though it's hard to tell through all the layers of *Hammerite* . . .'

Gaffar shrugged.

'Like a fuckin' *tank*, it is,' Kelly expanded. 'Gas-powered, ain't it, Gaz?'

'Yup.'

Kelly shook her head. 'There's a canister-thing in the back, Gaff, an' this tiny, little pipe which feeds through to the motor. Someone ever rams him from behind an' he'll go up like a fuckin' Catherine Wheel.'

Gaffar didn't respond. He watched Garry closely as he dabbed away, tenderly, at Kelly's face with his huge, intensely callused, workman's hands.

'This takes me right back, Kell,' Garry chuckled.

'Oh yeah?'

'Yeah. Remember how I used to pick you up when you was hangin' around outside that Print Works near the Sports Ground with those older kids after school, give you a quick clip around the ear for smokin' weed an' drive you straight home?'

'Drop me off at the end of the street?' Kelly smirked. 'You was a *pest*, Gaz, straight up. Always stickin' your oar in where it wasn't wanted. Ruined my bloody social life, you did. You was worse than my bloody *dad* . . .'

Kelly suddenly faltered, embarrassed, 'I mean . . . I mean not like *that* . . .'

She blushed.

'There was this one time I remember,' Garry prattled on (keen not to dwell on the negative stuff), 'when you had blood all down your top from a nose-bleed some boy had given ya, an' you didn't want your mum to find out, so I took you home an' Stephanie shoved it in the washer . . .'

'How *is* Steph?' Kelly enquired (determined to change the subject). 'I ain't seen her around town in a while.'

'Good,' Garry responded, almost too brightly. '*Very* good, as it happens. Just found out she's expectin' wiv' her new partner. She actually moved up to Stoke last year, to be closer to her sister.'

'*Huh?*' Kelly frowned, confused, then the penny dropped. '*Oh . . . Right*. Well give her my best when you speak to her.'

'Will do, Kell.'

He continued dabbing.

'Nearly done?' she enquired.

'Yeah. Pretty much . . .' Garry drew back to appraise his work. 'So you broke your leg, then?'

'Yeah,' she rolled her eyes, 'fell off a damn *wall*.'

'*Typical!*' he grinned. 'Even as a toddler you was always into everythin'. Fearless, you were. We always used to say you was part-girl, part-chimp.'

'*Fuck* off!'

Kelly lunged at him, and almost toppled from the scooter. Gaffar tensed his legs, with a grunt, to keep it upright.

'*Oi*!' Garry grabbed on to her arm to save her from falling. 'You take care, there . . .'

He frowned. 'Bloody hell. You're *freezin'*, girl . . .'

He placed the Bible and his posters down on to the pavement, pulled off his coat and hung it over her shoulders. 'There you go . . .'

'Thanks, Gaz,' Kelly sniffed. 'You're a cobber.'

She pulled the coat even tighter around her. It was an old, brown leather bomber jacket. It smelled of flaking paint and fresh putty. The lining was in tatters.

'Pretty *attached* to this old thing, are ya?' she grinned, poking her fingers through the decaying fabric.

He shrugged, resignedly. 'I never was much of fashion plate, Kell.'

'*Aw!*' She stuck out her bottom lip, poignantly, then (afraid of seeming too much of a push-over) she winked at him, saucily. 'Although I'm sure you do all right, eh?'

A slightly uncomfortable silence followed.

'So . . .' Kelly cleared her throat, 'you wouldn't happen to know where Mill Bank Road is, would ya?'

'Mill Bank? Yeah. Sure . . .' Garry turned and pointed. 'It ain't far. Just straight down here, left on to Wotton Road, straight on again, left on to Kingsnorth, then right when the road divides. That's Mill Bank.'

'D'ya get that, Gaff?'
   Kelly cuffed Gaffar's shoulder.
'Sure . . .' Gaffar nodded.
'Then let's split.'
   Kelly shook off Garry's coat and returned it to him.
'Nice to catch up, yeah?'
'Yeah . . .'
   Garry frowned, obviously perturbed, as Gaffar revved up the engine.
'You be sure an' look after yourself,' he counselled, 'all right?'
Kelly nodded as Gaffar accelerated, at speed. Then, *'HEY!'* she yelled,
her face partially obscured by a cloud of exhaust smoke.
'What?' Garry yelled back.
'Why not treat yerself to a *NEW COAT*!' she caterwauled.

Two, three, *four* seconds of blind, almost *unfathomable* terror –

WHAT?!
But . . . but HOW ?

– before those trusty, old instincts kicked back into play again –

Austerity childhood
Military training

– and Beede promptly disengaged himself from his wayward emotions,
rolled up his sleeves and got down to work –

Ours is not to reason why,
Ours is but . . .

   The first thing he did was to check for any remaining signs of life
in the cat –

Eyes, gums, nose, throat . . .
Nope.
Chest . . . ?

There were none. The cat was dead. His face (when he turned him over) had set into a strange sneer (where his lip had ridden up against the carpet), and this curious expression –

What's that?
Eh?
Lodged under the tongue . . . ?

A feather?!

– didn't alter once the pressure was off. The whiskers, he noticed, were already starting to stiffen.

He wrapped the animal up in newspaper (like an old-fashioned serving of fish and chips) then placed him, gently, into a biodegradable bin-bag. As he tied a neat knot in the neck, Beede noticed that his knuckles were badly grazed –

Bruised . . .
How'd I . . . ?

– he shook his head and tried to think of something else. The something else he thought of was a kind of . . . of *metaphysical* debate about whether it was actually *better* to try and think of something else . . .

Isn't that what the Yogis do?
Think of something else?
Gently turn away?
When they meditate . . . ?

He frowned –

How about Peta?

His frown deepened –

What would she say?
Would she be secretly impressed?
Would she think I was exhibiting . . .

He snorted, sarcastically –

. . . 'admirable restraint'?

He flared his nostrils –

Or . . . or . . .

He grimaced –

Or just plain cowardice, more like it?

He completed the knot and placed the bag firmly aside (quietly opting to do the same with the debate).

Next, he located the bucket for the mop. It was hidden under the upturned sofa – which he set straight, shoving it back to its former position (although there was no careful measuring this time, just a rough approximation).

His progress was painfully slow. The pain in his shoulder was quite intolerable (the arm on that side was virtually numb now and his grip was growing increasingly weak in the hand).

Once the sofa was rearranged he returned to the kitchen and set about mopping up the wet floor. He gradually noticed that the source of all the water –

What is the source?

– was located elsewhere – in the bathroom – so he opened the door –

Woah!

– and tentatively ventured inside –

Jesus wept!

The floor was awash, and there were more feathers in here – *black* feathers (although no sign of an actual *carcass* to speak of –

Hmmn.
Strange.)

– but the main feature in this room to draw his eye –

Oh dear . . .

– was the blood. There was blood on the tiles. Blood in the sink. Blood dripping down the walls inside the shower cubicle . . . Blood smeared, splattered and daubed . . . not . . . not *huge* amounts (by any means) . . . not . . .

Uh
Dangerous . . .

Beede swallowed, nervously, feeling a tiny chink forming in the brick wall of his composure. But then instead of surrendering to it –

Nope.
Don't.
You won't.

– he corralled his anxiety into the task of cleaning up. This was his *business*, after all. His trade. He was an expert at it. He grabbed hold of a J-cloth and began washing everything down –

Wipe, rinse, wring
Wipe, rinse, wring
Establish a steady rhythm . . .
That's the spirit!

– then he paused, frowning –

Eh?

– staring intently at something –

What's . . . ?

    There was a handprint, on the mirror, above the sink. He inspected it for a second and then glanced down at his own hand. He lifted his own hand up –

Ouch
Hard to . . .
Heavy

– and held it, gingerly, adjacent to the print –

Smaller

The print was considerably smaller. Almost like a . . . a woman's hand. His own hand began to shake. His lower lip started to wobble –

What have I . . . ?

    Then his head spun around –

Huh?!

– drawn by a sharp, repetitive *ringing* sound –

The phone?

    He dropped the cloth, vacated the bathroom, padded rapidly through the kitchen and back into the living-room . . .

Still ringing

He gazed around him, confused –

Where?

– then walked over to the wall where the phone socket was located and saw that a wire was still feeding into it –

But of course it is, you damn fool!

   Beede crouched down and carefully began uncovering the wire . . .

Papers
Bills
Broken plant pot
Soil
Books
Little side-table

Eh?
Good God!
How'd that end up there?!

He pulled a dark, wooden cross from the midst of the chaos – a hand-carved, wooden cross (20 inches long, 12 or so wide) –

Remember?

– part of it (a small part) had been roughly whittled (in a primitive style) and the word MUM scratched in a childish hand across the middle. But the other part? The best part? Painstakingly, even exquis-itely chiselled with a dozen tiny, intricate wild roses, blooming (as if against all the odds) between a dense and tangled thicket of leaves and stems and thorns.
   Beede stared at the cross for a while, almost regretfully, then he placed it down and recommenced his search. The phone – when he found it – was actually hidden under a small wigwam of cushions. He threw them aside and grabbed the receiver –
'Hello?'
   His voice sounded very soft, very low. His voice sounded . . .

Scared?

   'Beede?'

'*Yes?* Hello?'
'Beede, it's me, it's Dory . . .'
   '*Dory?*'
Beede seemed surprised. 'Dory? Are you all right? Is something wrong?
You sound . . .' He paused '. . . different.'

Silence

'Dory? Hello? *Dory?*'
'Where are you?' Dory demanded, somewhat childishly, almost petu-
lantly. 'What are you doing?'
The reception on the line was bad.

Uh . . .

'I'm at *home*, Dory,' Beede scratched his head, 'you've rung me at
home. I'm here, at home, speaking on the phone.'
   'At home?'
Dory seemed confused by this answer.
'Yes.' Beede nodded, frowning. 'At home. At *my* home. But how on
earth did you get this number?'
   'The number? I don't know. It just . . . It just popped into my head.
The same way it did – *you* know – before . . .'
'*Before?*'
Now it was Beede's turn to sound confused.
   'It doesn't matter,' Dory said. 'The important thing is that you need
to come, and you need to come *soon*.'
Beede thought he heard a car horn sounding, in the background. It
was followed by a nasty crackle of static on the line. He winced.
'Dory? Are you still with me?'

Silence

'Dory?'
'Yes?'
'Where are you?'
'Where?'
'Yes.'

'Uh . . . I'm in the little room. *You* know . . . The little, metal room which likes to move around. I'm sitting in the middle of the little, metal room.'

'Right. *Okay*. You're in the *car*. You're driving somewhere in the *car* . . .'

'Yes,' Dory sounded pleased, proud, almost, 'that's *exactly* what I'm doing.'

'And do you know where you're heading?'

'Heading?'

'Yes. In the car. Do you know where you're going?'

'In the car? I'm going *heim*, of course.'

'*Heim*?'

'*Ja*.'

'You're going *heim*?'

'*Ja*.'

'Right. *Right* . . .'

Beede inspected his watch. 'I was meant to meet you there, wasn't I, at ten? I'm afraid I got a little . . . uh . . . *caught up* in something . . .'

'Well you really need to come,' Dory reiterated, quite matter-of-factly, 'because he's here, Beede.'

'Sorry?' Beede frowned.

'He's *here*. He's right here.'

'Who is?' Beede's throat suddenly contracted.

'*He* is. *Him*. The . . . the . . . *you* know . . . the . . . the d-d-d-d . . .' Dory began to stutter.

Beede closed his eyes. 'You've *seen* him?' he whispered.

'He's *here*, Beede, and he's being very . . . very *strong* . . . very . . .' Dory cleared his throat. 'I honestly don't know how much longer I can hold him off for.'

'Right . . .' Beede struggled to calm his nerves. 'Okay. And did he happen to mention what he wants?'

'Yes. Absolutely. He says he wants to speak with you. In fact he told me this number. He recited it to me. He said he wants to *see* you.'

Pause

'Beede?'

'Yes?'

710

'I think he's intending to do something bad. In fact I'm not sure if he hasn't already done it. He seems very d-d-d-'

'Dark,' Beede said, standing up, abruptly, almost lifting the entire body of the phone into the air on its tangled wire. 'Then I must come,' he murmured.

'Yes . . .' Dory sounded a little distracted. 'He says we must go *ho* . . .'

'Home?'

'Yes. *No*. Not like in home, like in . . . in *hot* – *ho* – like in hot or . . . or cot . . .'

'*Hot?*' Beede was immediately concerned. 'Did he mention *fire* at all? Because you must be on your guard, Dory. D'you hear me? You *must* be on your guard. Just be sure and keep away from . . .'

'No, not *hot*,' Dory maintained stolidly, 'not hot: *hoch* . . . He means *hoch*.'

Eh?

'*Hoch* . . . ?' Beede slowly mulled this over, then, 'Oh . . . Of *course*. Hoch. Hoch, as in . . . as in "high"?'

'Yes. That's it. On the roof. The *roef*. He wants to go up on the *roef*. He doesn't want to be hot. He wants to be . . . to be *hoch*. On the *roef*.'

'Which roof, Dory?'

Beede suddenly visualised a huge expanse of roof – an infinite expanse – covered in antique, red tiles. And he saw a hand – *his* hand – reaching out towards them. He also saw the sky –

So blue!
Beautiful!
Look at that!

– and he saw a turret. And then he felt –

What?!

– this vast, this black and intoxicating wave of *rage* engulfing him . . .

Urgh!

He shook himself –

Enough!

   'My *roef*,' Dory repeated (Beede hadn't actually heard him the first time).
'Why?' Beede's voice was pitched very soft and low again. It was almost a growl.
'Pardon?'
   'Why does he want you to go on to the roof, Dory?'
'Why? Because he says there's something we need to *do* up there.'
'So you've been *talking*?' Beede felt his anger rising – he felt it *climbing*, scampering –

Higher and higher

– on mean, painful, little feet – he felt it . . . he felt it *barking* inside of him . . .

Roof!
Roof!
Roof!

He was a fierce dog, scratching away, keenly, at the door of its rage –

Roof!

– waiting for release.
   'What do you mean, Beede?'
Dory sounded bewildered.
'You've been *discussing* these things together?' Beede demanded (quite unable to help himself).
'Yes. *No*. I'm . . . I'm not sure . . .'
   'For how *long*, exactly?'
Beede's cheeks were crimson. His upper lip was shiny with perspiration.
   'I'm not . . .' Dory stuttered '. . . I don't . . .'
'Weeks, is it? Months? *Tell* me!'
'I can't . . . I'm not . . .'

712

'My *God*, how you must've *laughed*!' Beede snarled. 'How funny this all must've seemed. What a spectacular *joke*!'

'A joke?'

'Yes. *Yes* . . .' Beede was livid now, *betrayed*. 'So you've been changing my furniture around, eh? The *rug*? Did you swap the rug? And the kettle? The *bed*? Is Elen in on it too?'

'You're confusing me, Beede,' Dory interrupted, 'I don't have a clue what you're talking about. I don't even know whether . . .' he paused. 'Did you call me or did I call you?'

Beede blinked. The wave smoothly withdrew. Quick as a breath, his anger retreated. He shook his head, confused.

'Beede?!' Dory sounded terrified.

'You phoned,' he said tiredly, 'you called me.'

'Really?'

'Yes.'

'But *why*?'

'Because you said . . . you said you needed my help.'

'Did I?'

'Yes.'

Silence

'Oh God,' Dory groaned (as if suddenly remembering). 'He's been whispering things, Beede. I've told him to go away. I've pushed him away – with the yoga, the Pranayama, I've tried to block him out. But it's almost had the opposite effect. It's brought him even closer. And now he keeps telling me all this . . . all this *stuff* . . .'

'What kind of stuff?'

Beede gnawed on his lower lip.

'Things about you. About Elen. The boy. He calls Elen the most terrible, the most *unforgivable* . . .'

'What does he say about me?' Beede interrupted, coldly.

'About you? Strange things. Stupid things. He keeps telling me that you made your own key. He keeps repeating it. He keeps going on and on and on and *on* . . . I mean at first I didn't *understand* – he speaks differently to us. He kept repeating the word *kay* and I just couldn't . . . but then he said *lūk* . . . then *loch* . . .and I knew he meant lock. Like a lock and a key. A *key* . . .'

'He seems rather confused,' Beede snapped, 'rather *incoherent*.'
'Yes.' Dory sounded forlorn.

Pause

'So I suppose . . .' he sighed, 'I suppose we'll just be waiting for you on the *roef*, then.'
'No,' Beede butted in, 'that's not a good idea. It sounds too dangerous.'
   'But he . . .' Dory's voice was dreamy, now, and quite resigned, '. . . he simply *insists*, Beede.'
'Then you should be strong with him. You should refuse him.'
'I know,' Dory yawned, tiredly.
   'Try and stay lively,' Beede said. 'Buy yourself a coffee. Or eat a bar of chocolate. Conserve your energy.'
'Yes.'
Dory yawned again.
   'You need to stay awake, Dory. You're driving. If you're going to fall asleep then you must pull over.'
'I know. I *know*. I already did. I pulled over earlier. But I don't have too far to go now . . .'
   'Then just keep on talking,' Beede said. 'Tell me where you are. Tell me where you're going.'
'I'm going . . .'

Pause

'Dory?'
'Yes?'
'Tell me where you're going.'
'I'm going . . . I'm going on the . . . I've got . . .'
'Then tell me where you've *been* . . . Tell me about your morning. Did you drop Fleet off at school yet?'

Pause

'Fleet?' Dory sounded very vague.
'Your son, remember?'
   Beede was gripping the phone so tightly now that the receiver was almost cutting into his ear.

'Dory?'

He automatically switched hands (and ears) to relieve the pressure.

'Damn!'

His grip failed. He dropped the receiver.

'Damn!'

He swooped down, wincing, to retrieve it.

'Dory?'

Silence

'Dory? Hello? I'm sorry about that. I just dropped the . . .'

Silence

'Hello?'

Silence

'Hello?'

Silence

Beede peered down at the phone, confused. He shook the receiver. He stared into it. He gazed over towards the wall. The phone was unplugged.

He blinked –

Eh?

He blinked again –

But how long . . . ?

Then slowly, very cautiously, he peeked over his shoulder.

FOURTEEN

Tenterden. He'd planned to head for Tenterden –

Peta –
Peta Borough –
The f-forger . . .
The f-fabricāre . . .
She's definitely the k-k-kay, here

– but when he drew up at the roundabout –

Eh?

– the Rover was just one car ahead of him –

Kay?

– so he calmly proceeded to follow –

F-f-fabric-what?!

– almost without thinking – ignoring the first turn-off (for Canterbury
and Willesborough), the second turn-off – *his* turn-off – (for Hastings,
Lydd and Hamstreet), indicating at the third (Cedar Wood) and slowly
pulling on to the brand-new (still only partially completed) access-
route into the estate beyond.

At first – fearful of blowing his cover – he tried to maintain a
certain distance between his Merc and the Rover, but Dory's progress
was so gradual, so erratic, so halting –

Brake –
Accelerate –
Brake –

Accelerate . . .

What the hell is he playing at?

– that it was about as much as Kane could do not to plough straight into the back of him.

　He promptly solved the problem by casually over-taking; furtively observing – as he roared past – that Dory appeared to be deeply embroiled in a telephone conversation –

Yeah?
Well that certainly explains a lot . . .

　Three short minutes later and The Blonde was neatly slotted into the driveway of a vacant property (just two doors along from Dory's home address) with Kane hunched down low in the driver's seat, both eyes glued to his side-mirror. Twenty long seconds ticked by –

Shit . . .
Was this completely the wrong call?

– and then –

Ha!

– just as he'd anticipated, Dory pulled into the street, kangarooed his way along it, and brought the Rover to a juddering halt at the end of the very driveway on which Kane himself was parked.

Eh?!

　Kane immediately began to panic –

Why'd he do that?

– crouching down still further –

Has the swine blocked me in?

– uncertain where to look, taut, agonised, all his senses on red alert, when –

YAAARGH!

– his phone began shuddering inside his coat pocket –

Jesus Christ!

He almost leapt out of his skin –

Fuck!

He grabbed a hold of it, turned it off, hurled it, furiously, on to the back seat –

There!

– then sat, staring down at his tightly clenched hands, barely even daring to draw breath.
    Ten seconds –
Twenty –
Thirty –
Forty –
    Kane slowly lifted his chin and peeked into his side-mirror –

Diddly-squat

Just the back bumper

He glanced over to his left, but the mirror on that side –

Damn!

– had been knocked flat (by his earlier collision, he presumed), so all that was currently reflected back at him was the crown of his own, terrified head –

Huh?

718

He blinked –

Am I thinning out a little on top, there?

He gently patted his hair. Then he blinked again –

Now just hang on a . . .

He covered his face with both hands –

FUUUUCK!
WHAT IN GOD'S NAME AM I DOING HERE?

Kane remained in this position for a further full minute, then he dropped his hands and began hunting around inside his coat pockets for the small, polythene bag of tablets which he'd recently offered to Laura. He couldn't find them. He noticed a small hole in the lining and poked his finger through it. His search became increasingly frantic . . .

Fuck, fuck, fuck . . .

He found his cigarettes and pulled them out, hoping to unearth the spare spliff which he generally kept for emergencies in the bottom of the packet. He opened the box and peered into it –

Nope

– then threw it, disgusted, on to the passenger seat.
   He closed his eyes and tried to deepen his breathing –

Okay, okay . . .
Just tell him . . .

His eyes flew open –

Yeah!
Say you've come to look at the house –
Say you're waiting for an Estate Agent . . .

Say the Estate Agent's running late . . .

– he quickly glanced into his mirror again –

Nada

– then slowly twisted around in his seat, straightened his spine and peeked over his head-rest (like a startled chad, or a timorous prairie dog scanning the dry, mid-western plains for a skulking predator).

Dory (it transpired) was still snugly ensconced in his car, apparently oblivious to everything around him. Kane squinted –

Eh . . . ?

– He was leaning over the steering wheel and seemed to be scrawling something, frantically, into a small, black note-book –

The diary?

Kane recalled the earlier conversation between Elen and his father while scratching away at his arm –

Bloody fleas . . .

– his eyes still fixed on Dory, who continued to scribble –

His written confession, perhaps?
'He was pestering my wife, so I cornered him in a neighbour's driveway and then . . .'

Huh?

Kane's attention was momentarily distracted by the smallest, slightest, most *insidious* of tapping sounds. He abruptly stopped what he was doing, tipped his head and listened. The sounds persisted –

Tap-tap, tap-tap-tap –

Huh?

720

Kane turned, with a grimace, and immediately recoiled –

YAH!

Standing directly in front of him – only a yard away, at best – was a bird –

Starling?

– the same pesky, black bird (he was certain) which'd attacked him, unprovoked, several days earlier.

It was perched on the Merc's bonnet, pecking away, determinedly, at one of the small, rubber discs – the washer – which helped to secure the Merc's windscreen-wipers to its chassis.

Kane glared at the bird. The bird paused for a moment and stared straight back at him (with a single, mean, yellow-rimmed eye). It was so close that he could see the magnificent, iridescent sheen on its feathers, the constellation of white dots speckling its plumage, the slight, blueish tinge at the corner of its beak, and then – as it turned (to recommence its violent assault on the washer) – its tail made passing contact with the windscreen and he was privileged to observe the tiniest, the *daintiest* of grease-stains left behind on the glass –

Urgh!

Kane threw out his hand, revolted, determined to scare it off, but the bird didn't move. It wouldn't budge. It seemed fearless.

Urgh!

He continued to inspect it with a mixture of fascination and abhorrence, soon noticing that – for all its apparent vitality – there seemed to be something inescapably *awry* with the creature. He looked closer and saw a sticky patch of soft down at the base of the bird's chest (consistent with a puncture wound or bite, perhaps) and a dribble of shiny, partially dried blood running down one scraggy leg. The tail also seemed thinner than it might be – tatty – wonky – lop-sided.

Even so, the bird still made short work of the rubber washer (tossing it aside within six or seven seconds) before calmly hopping forward to start jabbing away at the neat, black rubber trim around the Merc's tinted windscreen.

Kane expostulated, furiously, throwing out his hand again, but before he could make actual, physical contact with the glass, the bird had crouched down – with an angry squawk – and had taken wing – heading off – like a dark bullet – towards the scaffolding two doors along.

Huh?

Kane slowly twisted around and peered over his head-rest –

Shit!

It was Dory. Dory had finally stopped writing and had climbed out of his Rover. Kane ducked down, having observed (through the Rover's still partially opened door) that he'd placed his diary on to the dashboard – directly behind the steering wheel – where a sharp gust of wind snatched at the pages, making them flutter, wildly, *whitely*, like the damp wings of a newly hatched moth.

Kane heard the door slam shut, closed his eyes –

Pretend to be asleep, yeah?
Why not?

– and steeled himself for a confrontation of some kind. He waited, listening out for the heavy thud of Dory's footsteps on the cement driveway.

He did hear footsteps (eventually) but they certainly weren't on the driveway. They were faint at first, then grew still fainter. Kane opened his eyes again –

Now what?

He drew a deep breath (almost irritated by the delay), twisted around and peeked over the head-rest. Dory was currently standing some distance away (in the middle of the street), staring over towards his own home, a thoughtful frown creasing his forehead. He was holding something rolled-up in his hand which he carelessly shoved into his back pocket . . .

Kane squinted –

The Missing Dog poster?

He quickly sank down in his seat (still following Dory's progress – almost obsessively – in his side-mirror) as the German turned and strolled back towards the Rover again, yanked open the boot, leaned down, scrabbled around inside it for a while and then withdrew holding –

Oh shit!

– a large, metal tool of some kind –

Spanner?
Wrench?

Dory slammed the boot shut and paused for a second –

Not the car!
Please, God –
Anything but The Blonde!

– then turned and headed purposefully back down the road, drawing to a sharp halt in front of his home and calmly appraising the front of the property – his head at a slight angle, a speculative look on his face – before marching determinedly across the pavement, on to the lawn and directly out of Kane's immediate sightline.

Kane cursed the annoyingly lustrous evergreen bush growing directly to his left which meant that for the next few minutes the only real clues he could accrue as to Dory's activities were those of a strictly audible nature.

From what he could tell, Dory appeared to be engaging directly with the scaffolding ('Shoring it up,' he mused, 'I guess . . .'), and from the sheer volume of the resulting clamour, he was undertaking this task with considerable enthusiasm.

After several more minutes of idle speculation, the suspense grew too much for him and Kane hauled himself over, clumsily, on to the back seat –

Ouch!

– fishing out his mobile from under his thigh, observing how Dory was almost half-way up the scaffolding now (and climbing ever higher) as the dark bird – Kane shuddered – darted all around him; *pestering* him; squawking, flapping its wings and bouncing from metal bar to metal bar like some kind of crazed, avian supervisor.

Kane reduced the volume on his phone and quickly checked his messages. One from Dina –

Where's Kelly? Why ain't she answerin' her mobile? If you see the little minx, tell 'er Linda's home. Tell 'er Linda wants a quick word with 'er . . .

– and four more from angry clients, impatiently awaiting their deliveries –

Nothing from Gaffar –
Nothing from Peta –

Kane shoved his phone away again, scowling, plainly frustrated by his own lack of professionalism –

You really need to . . .
Uh . . .

He peered through the back window to see if it would be possible to reverse the Merc from the driveway without tangling with the Rover –

Nope

Luckily there was next to no proper planting in the adjacent patch of garden – just a brown, slightly frozen lawn (no gate, no fence). Kane calculated that – if the worst came to the worst – it'd be perfectly possible to reverse the Merc across it, over the pavement and down on to the road again without causing too much conspicuous damage.

As he made this calculation his eye was drawn – almost irresistibly – to the diary on the Rover's dashboard. Its pages were still rotating –

Hmmn . . .

Air conditioning left on?

Kane grimaced, grabbed for the hem of his old crombie and began inching his way around it with his finger and thumb –

Where'd my stuff get to?
Is it lost in the lining?

– but he couldn't feel anything and soon grew restive –

Need a smoke . . .

– so snatched his cigarettes from the front seat and lit one, then lay down flat on his back and gazed over towards his quarry, speculatively –

Nope.
It's no good . . .
I just gotta . . .

He shoved his cigarette into the corner of his mouth, rolled on to his belly, felt for the door handle and slowly released it –

Click

As he pushed it open a cruel blast of winter air hit him square in the face. He closed his eyes for a moment (as if secretly hoping that it might jolt him back to his senses) –

Nah-ah

– then slowly, carefully, he slid out of the Merc, crouched down on to his hands and knees and began crawling, awkwardly, along the driveway. He was initially shielded from Dory's sight – at least partially – by the Merc's square chassis, but once he'd reached the bumper it became abundantly clear that the actual gap between the two vehicles was quite a considerable one – 5 or 6 feet, at least – with every inch of them in plain view.

Kane peeked around the Merc's heavy rump and up towards Dory.

Lucky for him, Dory still seemed fully preoccupied with the scaffolding, so Kane snatched his opportunity and scrambled over towards the Rover, rising to his knees when he reached the driver's door and peering in through the window to check out the alarm system –

Deactivated . . .
I think.

The black jotter continued to flap seductively on the dash. Kane applied his hand gently to the door handle, squeezed, heard the mechanism disengage, grinned, pulled the door open and leaned into the car to grab the book.

As he leaned, a small portion of ash from the tip of his cigarette dropped on to the seat.

Bollocks

Kane quickly swiped it off with his hand – knocking it down on to the tarmac. As he swiped he sensed a vague shift in the atmosphere around him – a strange, almost indefinable sensation – as if the wind had changed direction, or the sun had passed – very briefly – behind a cloud. He frowned, glancing nervously over his shoulder –

Nothing

– then shrugged and straightened up –

Oh shit

He froze.

Perched on the steering wheel, directly in front of him, was the bird.

Kane stared at the bird. The bird scratched itself, vigorously (patently unconcerned by Kane's close proximity), spraying an extraordinary quantity of fluff and skin-flakes into the surrounding ether.

Kane flinched, revolted. The bird responded with a sharp sneeze, then shook out its remaining feathers and hunkered down (for the long haul, it seemed), its neck neatly disappearing into the black feather boa of its shoulders.

'What do you want?' Kane whispered.
The bird opened and closed its beak a few times, but without making a sound.
'You're guarding the diary, eh?' Kane mused, noticing how the bird's third eye-lid kept passing slowly across the eye, in between blinks. 'Well, whether you like it or not,' he continued bolshily (screwing his courage to the sticking place), 'I'm still gonna *take* the damn thing . . .'

He reached out to grab the book and the bird instantly took wing. He cringed (automatically anticipating a physical assault of some kind) but the bird swooped gracefully over his head and out through the door, without so much as a sound.

No actual, physical assault as such – no – but he *did* feel . . .

Uh . . . ?

– He definitely felt . . .
Kane glanced down at his crombie –

Jeeesus!

The bird had shat across his shoulder. Prodigiously.

You filthy little . . .

Kane reached up, snatched the diary, stuck it under his arm, carefully closed the Rover's door –

Quietly . . .

Quietly . . .

– and scuttled back to the Merc, pulling off his crombie before clambering inside, unearthing an old tissue from under the seat and scraping off the worst of the mess with it –

Urgh!

He became so engrossed in this task that several seconds had elapsed (at least) before it finally dawned on him that the racket from the scaffolding had temporarily abated. He glanced over towards the house, alarmed. Dory was high up in the structure now, standing bolt upright, his hand shading his eyes (like a mariner in a crow's nest searching for dry land).

Kane hurled himself down flat on to the back seat, covering himself with his crombie (struggling to hold his cigarette away from the coat's fabric), thanking his lucky stars for the Merc's tinted windows.

After thirty or so seconds he peeked out. Dory was inspecting his watch and frowning, as if to imply (Kane imagined) that he might be awaiting someone's late arrival. Then he turned and calmly returned to work again.

Kane remained supine, quietly watching Dory's progress as he finished off his cigarette. He was certainly impressed by the German's dynamism, although still rather cynical about how much of an actual impact Dory's frenzied repairs were having on the structure, overall. The scaffolding – as a whole – seemed increasingly unstable; so much so, in fact, that when at one point Dory straightened up and glanced around him (alerted by a distant sound, perhaps) the entire edifice seemed to wobble and Dory was obliged to grab on to the guttering (part of which came away in his hand) to stop himself from losing his balance and plummeting to the ground.

Kane sat up, shocked, almost preparing to leap from the car – 'And do what?' he asked himself, scowling. '*Help?*'

He stubbed out his cigarette and lay back down again just in time to apprehend the lunatic German clambering on to the actual roof and scrabbling along the tiles like some kind of crazed, alpine goat, apparently heading for one of the two small, pitched promontories which jutted out – like a pair of frog's eyes – above a couple of the upstairs windows. Sure enough, when Dory reached the first of these, he hauled himself on to it, slinging his leg over (as if mounting a horse), sitting jauntily astride it and gazing around him; the king of all he surveyed.

Kane glanced down at the jotter, frowning. He opened it up, randomly –

Wow . . .

Dory's writing was inconceivably tiny and ludicrously neat, so much so that he'd managed to compress three lines of script between each of the printed lines on the page.

'Day 23' – Kane read – 'I am trying to concentrate on the inner ear. I am drawing the channels of the ear together. They are certainly "soft and deep" now (as Rosen suggests). Svatmarama claims that after only two weeks' practice it is possible to hear subtle sounds in the "yoga ear". I am hearing these sounds. I have not heard clouds (or horns, for that matter), but I did hear bells, the sound of the sea and the buzz of a fly. With the sea comes nausea. With the bells? A sense of excitement, a longing, a strong pull . . . And the fly? I don't know . . . A cruel mix of things. Boredom? Dread? Frustration? Fear?

Rosen says that indolence is one of the biggest obstacles for any serious student of this particular discipline. My fly is certainly indolent. It makes me doubt. It distracts me. I follow it around inside my mind. It wears me down. It exhausts me. This feeling is apparently familiar to the yogis. They have a special name for it. They refer to it as "Tamas" . . .'

Kane's eye moved a little further down the page: 'I watched a real fly the other day,' he read, 'rotating in a crazy circle underneath the light fitment in the kitchen (attracted – no doubt – by the bowl of dried dog food which Elen always insists on leaving out). It moved in a most hypnotic manner – two, maybe three circles in quick succession (just under a foot in diameter) then a dramatic drop. Two circles, three, then a drop. This "dance" went on for almost seven minutes, without pause. From what I could tell, there seemed to be no earthly point to it.

'Elen once told me that we humans actually share some of the same DNA as a fly. She read it in a copy of the New Scientist which she found hanging around in the surgery (she said). We came from the same place, originally (she claimed), crawled from the same swamps. At first I thought this might just be yet another of her pointless fabrications, but increasingly I am convinced by it.

'The fly inside my head is not an appealing proposition. It is an erratic fly. A dirty fly. A persistent fly. It pesters and molests me. But through practice I am learning to deal with it. Through practice, I am learning to embrace what horrifies me most about it. I now see, through practice, that in many ways I am the fly, that we have an identical energy . . .'

Kane grimaced. He turned to another page: '. . . because if it can now be scientifically proven that water has a memory,' he read, 'then why not the blood? Why not the bones and the hair and the muscles?

My practice allows me to accept the idea that "I" am nothing more than a random accumulation of sense-impressions, hastily tied together like a bundle of firewood. I see that the whole world dwells within me, passes through me. I am a million voices, crying out, all at once . . .'

Kane turned several pages on: *'I always tried to ignore it (him) before. I forced it away, I pushed it aside (I just cut out, blanked out . . .), but my practice is gradually removing all those boundaries (slowly but surely – one at a time). Now there's almost a conversation, a dialogue, what you might call "an exchange", of sorts . . . The Witness seems to actively encourage this new "relationship". It counsels me to embrace this . . . this . . . What is it? What do I call it? My fear? My punishment? My affliction? My cross? Does it matter? Does it even need a name?*

'Both Elen and Beede are determined to make me stop (of course). Elen, because she is obsessed by it (him) and how can she possibly hope to continue their degraded (degrading) flirtation while I stand close by and calmly apprehend?'

Kane frowned, pulled himself up into a sitting position and slowly re-read this last paragraph. He shook his head, perplexed.

'And Beede?' he soon continued. *'Because it serves his "purpose" to keep the two of us apart. And she has bewitched him, of course. She has brought him to heel. She has "reached out". She has invaded him. She has inhabited him in much the same way that "it" inhabits me. And how could she not? It's such a convincing act, after all. Poor, sweet Elen! So quiet, so modest, so loyal, so sensible. And all in the face of such terrible adversity! How wonderfully accepting she is! How marvellously resigned! How infinitely patient and sympathetic and understanding!*

'(The whore playing the martyr? What a joke! What a travesty!)'

A small gap in the text followed, and then, *'Travesty: trans – over + vestire – to dress.*

'I still sometimes find myself using words which I can't understand.'

Kane scratched his head. He turned over.

The following page was empty except for one short paragraph which'd subsequently been crossed out. Kane pulled the diary up closer to his face –

'But what if HE is the fly?' Kane slowly deciphered. *'What if Elen pushed this thought on to a hook and then dropped it, like bait,*

inside my head? And what if I am feeding on the bait, gorging on it, without even realising what's hidden within? What then? Will all hope be gone?'

Kane pulled away, confused. He turned several pages on: '. . . because it wasn't fated,' he read, '(I know that now), it isn't meaningful. It's just arbitrary. It's pure coincidence. There were holes, gaps, rough edges, and this "energy" simply inhabited them for a while, clung on to them. But I am filling these holes with a different kind of energy now. I am filling these holes with light. I am letting go of all the chatter (citta). I am filing down the rough edges. I am becoming smooth. Discovering that the boy isn't mine – that I am, in some senses, his – was a struggle at first, but increasingly I realise that it has made this entire process so much easier. I have not given in, no, but I feel myself giving up. I am finally floating free of all earthly ties. I am quietly rising above all the confusion, the anger.
'Let it (him) find refuge elsewhere. Or let it stay. I no longer care.'

Kane's eye ran down the page a way to a section of the text which had been written entirely in stark capitals: '. . . I DO NOT HAVE AN AGENDA HERE! I DO NOT HAVE AN AGENDA! THEY ALL DO – EVEN THE BUILDER!!! BUT I DO NOT. THERE IS NO AGENDA. I AM SIMPLY THE CHANNEL, THE BODY, THE VESSEL . . . NO! NO!! STOP!!! CALM DOWN! MUST NOT LET THIS IDEA THAT THEY HAVE A PLAN, THAT THEY ARE PLANNING . . . MUST NOT LET THIS IDEA . . . NOT HELPFUL. MUSTN'T KEEP TURNING THIS WHOLE THING IN ON ITSELF – LOOKING FOR ORDER WHERE THERE IS NONE. CAN'T. MUST MEDITATE. BREATHE. MUST BREATHE. OR JUST . . . JUST RUN . . . JUST ESCAPE.'

Kane's eye lifted to the paragraph directly above this section: 'Beede said the coffee was fine, even though I had poured five sachets of sugar into it. A test! HE FAILED! (Or was it just pity? Does he pity me? Is that how low we've sunk?) I explained about The Witness, the Pranayama, and he pretended that he knew nothing about it, even though I know he has a copy of the book on his table at home. Elen accuses me of paranoia, but these are important clues, surely?'

Kane turned several pages on, to one of the final entries:
'. . . so very tired. If I can't just blank it out (NO! MUSTN'T SAY THAT – THAT'S NOT WHAT I'M DOING AT ALL! IT WAS HIM!!! HE MADE ME THINK THAT!) then the facts will just keep on piling up and eventually they'll start to obliterate . . . No. Am confused. The past keeps on piling up. Yes. But that's only normal, surely? Sometimes I wonder

if I am the only one who sees it, if I am the only one who sees the same tree – the same old book, the same wall, the same piece of road – as thousands of eyes have seen it before, and who feels the weight, the terrible weight – the actual weight – of all this apprehension. As if I am the only one who feels history, who sees the storm of pure emotion raging away behind everything. The buzz and clash of the atom. This awful friction. This urge to truth. This urge to destruction. This urge to vengeance. Oh God! Where does it flow from? Why? For what?! And how much longer can I possibly be expected to hold it all back?'

Kane's chin suddenly shot up as a vehicle pulled on to the road and drove along it, at speed. He watched through the back windscreen as it roared past, mounted the pavement and squealed to a sharp halt directly in front of Dory's home. The vehicle in question was vaguely familiar to Kane – an extravagantly customised 4x4 Toyota Hi Lux. The driver's door flew open and out sprang Harvey Broad –

Ah . . .

– still talking animatedly on his phone – 'I already *told* you the address, Kell,' he said, 'just keep ya bloomin' *wig* on, will ya?'

Harvey strutted confidently down the garden path (oblivious to everything bar his conversation) but was soon obliged to interrupt his call as one tile – two tiles, three, four – began smashing on to the ground in a savage arc around him.

Kane peered up at the roof, shocked –

Dory?
Was that . . . ?

Dory sat there, hands neatly clasped, smiling quietly, as before.

'What the *fuck*?!' the builder exclaimed, leaping back, almost dropping his phone.

Kane saw Dory's mouth move, in response, but he was unable to work out what the German was saying, so he took hold of the door handle, gently squeezed it, and pushed it open by a couple of sly inches.

'You did that on purpose!' the builder was bellowing. 'That's *assault*. I swear to God! I'm callin' the police! You're fuckin' *barkin'*, you are!'

732

'Isn't it quite extraordinary,' Dory chuckled, grinning down benignly at Harvey from his vantage point on the rooftop, 'that on the *very* day I terminate your contract you finally get around to gracing us with a visit?'

'You're *barkin'*!' Harvey repeated. 'Lester says you think I'm havin' an affair with your missus . . .'

Kane's eyes widened.

Dory stopped smiling. 'Lester's lying,' he snapped.

'*Bollocks!*' Harvey snarled, darting forward and placing a tentative hand on the scaffolding (as if half considering scrambling straight up it). 'Lester wouldn't lie. Not to me. Not about somethin' like that.'

'Take care, there,' Dory warned him, 'the scaffolding's quite unstable. My builder's a complete imbecile . . .' He shrugged, regretfully. 'That's why I had to sack him.'

Harvey stepped back again, enraged. 'I want my bloody money,' he snarled. 'I ain't leavin' here till I get it. You owe me six an' a half grand – an' that's just for materials . . .'

'Well you're in for a *very* long wait, my friend,' Dory grinned, removing three tiles from the roof behind him, tossing them into the air, and proceeding to juggle with them.

Kane's jaw slackened, in awe, as he watched this artful performance from the car.

'Well *here's* the thing,' Harvey hissed (refusing to be impressed), 'either you fork up the first instalment, *pronto*, or I'm gonna *double* the overall amount by suing your tight, Kraut arse for wrongful dismissal.'

Dory gave this threat a few seconds' consideration, and then, '*Arse*,' he suddenly exclaimed, 'accidentally' dropping the first tile. '*Ars-us* . . .' he expanded, dropping the second, '*Arsio*,' he chortled, dropping the third.

'*Oi! Oi!*' Harvey leapt back, startled, as the tiles rained down around him. 'Are you off your bleedin' *head*?'

'*Ardēre*,' Dory ran on, completely ignoring him.

'To *burn*,' Kane murmured. Then he did a sharp double-take –

Eh?!

Dory clapped his hands together, delightedly, emitting a strange, high-pitched giggle.

'What the fuck are you *on*?' Harvey demanded, plainly somewhat shaken by this extraordinary display. 'Lester *said* you was a fruit-loop, an' he weren't far wrong, neither . . .'

Kane peered up at Dory, to gauge his reaction. He blinked. Dory suddenly seemed . . . uh . . . *different*. Tighter. More intense, more . . . more *compressed*, somehow.

'While we're on the subject of Lester,' Dory observed sardonically, 'and this *fine* relationship you both share, I don't suppose he happened to mention that I've been subsidising his money each week, in private, just to bring it up to the level of a Minimum Wage?'

'What?'

Harvey seemed thrown off his stride by this piece of information.

'I've been subsidising his money,' Dory repeated. 'So how'd you fancy sharing *that* with an independent tribunal?'

'But I pay the kid a small fortune,' Harvey exclaimed, hurt.

'The sad truth about Lester,' Dory confided, 'is that if he'd spent even a *fraction* of the time actually working that he spent telling tales on you, he could've single-handedly rebuilt our home by now . . .' he paused. 'Although that's probably just wishful thinking on my part,' he conceded, 'your average five-year-old probably understands more about basic construction techniques than that Cabbage-head does.'

'*BOLLOCKS!*' Harvey exploded, leaping forward again, grabbing a hold of the scaffolding and shaking it, violently (as if the scaffolding was a pear tree and Dory the ripened fruit hanging tantalisingly in its boughs). '*MY SON AIN'T NO CABBAGE-HEAD!* COME DOWN *HERE* AN' *SAY THAT*! I *DARE* YA!'

'Your *son*?!'

Now it was Dory's turn to look astonished. Harvey took a quick step back, panicked, as the scaffolding shifted a mite more readily under his influence than he might've expected it to.

'But you never said he was your *son* . . .' Dory babbled.

'Well I never said he *weren't*, neither,' Harvey shrugged. And then – seconds later – '*Ha!*' he chortled. 'Seems like that sneaky, little twat's been havin' the best of *both* of us!'

A proud grin slowly enveloped his face. 'Lester *Broad*!' he cackled. 'Who'd've thought the little turd had it *in* 'im, eh?'

Dory didn't respond, he simply reached into his back pocket, withdrew something, unfolded it, and stared at it, morosely.

'What's that?' Harvey asked, his mood quite restored.

Dory held up the Missing Dog poster. 'Recognise this, by any chance?' he asked.

Harvey barely even glanced at it.

'Nope.'

'Well have another look,' Dory suggested.

Harvey squinted up into the grey sky. 'It's gonna rain,' he sniffed, wincing as a stray drop landed on the pristine fabric of his puffer jacket. 'You must be freezin' your bags off up there. Why don't you come down an' we'll deal with this situation like two proper *gents*, eh?'

'This is a picture of Michelle,' Dory said, still holding up the poster, refusing to be railroaded.

'*Who?*'

Harvey dusted the raindrop from his jacket.

'This is Michelle,' Dory repeated. 'This is a photograph of our spaniel, Michelle.'

'*Yeah?*' Harvey rolled his eyes, indulgently. '*Aw* . . . How *cute.*'

'Although she isn't actually *our* spaniel,' Dory expanded, 'as I'm sure you already know.'

'You're off your rocker, mate,' Harvey scoffed.

'She's actually . . .' Dory peered down at the poster, 'according to the information printed here – she's actually the property of a Mr Garry Spivey.'

Harvey stiffened at the mere mention of his rival's name. '*Who?*' (This was more of a challenge than an enquiry.)

'A Priori,' Dory leaned forward, with a grin (taking up the challenge, quite happily). 'First in the book, apparently.'

'If you *must* know,' Harvey suddenly blustered, 'I *didn't* try it on with your wife – she ain't really my *type* – but that sure as hell didn't stop her from tryin' it on wiv *me*, though. Keen as *mustard*, she was . . .'

Huh?!

Kane's grip tightened on the door handle.

'It took quite a while, I admit,' Dory continued, perfectly unflustered, 'but then I suddenly *remembered* . . .'

'What the fuck are you goin' on about?' Harvey demanded.

'I remembered how I knew you, Harvey. I remembered where we first met.'

Harvey scowled, suspicious. 'How d'ya mean?'

'We worked together.'

'*Bullshit!*'

Harvey's reaction was instantaneous. 'That's *baloney*!'

'Yes we did,' Dory insisted. 'Years ago. Very briefly. I was an exchange-student, earning some extra cash during my summer holi-days. And you were older, temping – just for a week or so. We were guarding the same site together. In Newington.'

'*Nah*. You got it all wrong, mate,' Harvey tried his best to fob the German off. But he was starting to look uneasy.

'I don't think so. It suddenly all came flooding back. I remember it very clearly, in fact, because it was the same week that consignment of tiles went missing.'

'*What?*'

'The tiles. Antique tiles. Tiles from the old mill. They went missing. And I was held partially responsible . . .'

'Really?' Harvey seemed delighted by this news. 'Get the boot, did ya?'

'No. I mean *yes*. I mean I was very lucky. My boss – *our* boss – Tom Higson, was extremely reasonable about the whole thing . . .'

'Yeah,' Harvey sniggered, 'very good of 'im, weren't it?'

'So you *do* remember, then?' Dory cut in.

'Nope.'

'Well I was sacked from the job, officially,' Dory explained. 'TML forced Higson's hand. But then he still kept me on with the firm; moved me to a different project – the Park Street Sainsbury's. They were expanding it at the time . . .'

'So what's the big problem?' Harvey demanded.

'There isn't one,' Dory shrugged, 'I just remembered you, that's all. I just remembered your face. I remembered that night – how you came to ask for my help after a group of protestors broke into your section of the site . . .'

Dory smiled, dreamily. 'Although when we actually went down there – to take a proper look – we couldn't find any evidence of a break-in, because the cruel irony was – as I'm sure you already knew – the *real* break-in was going on elsewhere . . .'

Harvey glanced off, sideways. He didn't comment.

'. . . but I kept my mouth shut,' Dory shrugged, 'I took the brunt of it. If I remember correctly you weren't long out of prison and expecting your first child . . .'

A long silence followed, punctuated by the gentle pitter-patter of rain.

'So . . .' Dory eventually broke the silence between them, 'the fates have finally seen fit to draw us back together.' He held his hands up to the sky, catching the raindrops on his open palms. 'And for some, strange reason,' he grimaced, 'you just couldn't resist the idea of mugging me for a second time.'

Harvey scowled. He didn't speak.

Dory sighed, almost forlorn now. 'But that's where you made your fatal mistake. You got too cocky, too smug. And somewhere along the line you forgot the single, most important rule of Cheat's Law . . .' Dory shook the rain from his hands and leaned forward, his voice almost dropping to a whisper . . .

Over in his car, Kane rapidly suspended his breath, determined to hear:

'Never kid a kidder.'

Eh?
Was that . . . ?

Kane grimaced, frustrated, not sure if he'd . . .

Did he just . . . ?

And then –
'HAAAAAARVEY!'
Kane's head snapped around as a scooter roared on to the road, at break-neck speed –

Kelly?

'HAAAARVEY!' Kelly was screaming, her arms gesticulating wildly. 'LOOOOK OWWWWT!!'

Harvey turned – confused – taking a single, tiny, almost *mincing* step towards her, as the air around him suddenly resounded with a most deafening clamour.

FIFTEEN

'He had three visions – *three* of 'em – all different . . .' Kelly's speech was garbled, her wide, brown eyes were bulging from their sockets, her hands were flying around, 'and the first one was about *Paul*, see? Which came true. And then the second one was about the *roof* fallin' down . . .'

She paused, scowling. 'No, I mean the second one . . .'

'Just take it easy,' Beede murmured, patting her on the shoulder, then pulling off his crash helmet and resting it, carefully, on the seat of his old Douglas, 'you're probably still in shock.'

'. . . The second one was about a *house* fallin' down, but then after the ceilin' collapsed – last night, on the ward . . .'

'Ah yes . . .' Beede smiled at her, sagely, 'I think I may've caught wind of that incident on the hospital grapevine . . .'

'Yeah, well I thought that was *it*, see?' Kelly interrupted. 'I thought that was the vision come true, cuz the Rev weren't actually *hurt* or nothin' . . .'

'Hang on a minute,' Beede frowned, concerned, 'a doctor *has* formally discharged you?'

'*What?*'

'From the hospital? You have been discharged? Formally discharged?' he paused. 'And while we're at it – should you really be resting so much weight on your bad leg yet?'

Kelly gazed down at her plaster-cast. 'Uh . . . Yeah . . .' she slowly shook her head, and then – quite out of the blue – 'Oh my *God*!' she gasped, panic-stricken.

'What's wrong?' Beede asked, alarmed.

'I've only gone an' lost the bloody *Bible*!'

Kelly patted frantically at her skirt pockets (on the improbable tip that the volume in question might've been miraculously condensed, reduced and then secreted inside one of them). Next she peered down the front of her skimpy top.

'*Shit!*' she scratched her head, confused. 'What the hell did I do with it?'

'So your uncle wasn't hurt?'

Beede tried to refocus her.

'Huh?'

'Your uncle?'

'My uncle? You mean *Harve*?! Nah. I mean *yeah* . . .' Kelly glanced around her, slightly paranoid. 'I told him to stay put. He rang me an' I just . . . I had this *feelin'*. It came over me really, really *strong* while I was talkin' to the Rev . . . But then we got lost – me an' Gaff – on the way over to . . .'

She fell quiet for a moment, chewed on her lower lip (with an expression of intense concentration) and then, 'That's *it*!' Her face broke into a beatific smile. 'Garry's got it! I gave the Bible to *Garry*! I got him to hold on to it for me while I was . . . an' then I . . .' She silently re-enacted the scene in her head.

'So when you finally arrived here,' Beede pushed on, regardless, 'your uncle was just standing there – perfectly alone – in the middle of the garden?'

He indicated towards the scene of unalloyed carnage which had once happily passed as Elen's front lawn.

'Uh . . .' Kelly scratched at her head again. 'Yeah. *Yeah*. He was just standin' there, an' we was comin' down the road . . .' she pointed '. . . on the scooter . . .'

Beede automatically followed the line of her finger. As he gazed down the street he detected a slight movement from within a parked car just two doors down. He focussed in on it. The car was a beige Mercedes. He frowned.

'And then I just . . .' Kelly drew a long, shuddering breath, 'I just . . . I had this *feelin'* again, kind of like a . . .' she grimaced, slightly bashful '. . . like an *orgasm*, really. But not . . . Not *dirty* or nothin' . . .' she shrugged, *'you* know. So I just called out – at the top of my lungs. I just *screamed*. I went *HAAAARVEEEEY!'*

Beede cringed at the undiluted volume of her recollection.

'I see.'

He dragged his eyes away from the Mercedes and turned back to face her. 'I see . . . And then the scaffolding . . .'

'Yeah. It fell. *KA-BOOM!'*

'Gracious.' Beede reached up a tentative hand to massage his aching shoulder. 'Well that certainly sounds quite . . . That must've been extremely . . .'

'He took a tiny step towards me,' Kelly continued, 'as I yelled. Just one, tiny, little step, yeah? An' the metal bars fell every side of him – *CRASH!* – with only millimetres to spare. Didn't hurt a single hair on his head, though. It was a miracle. Took him a full five minutes to climb his way out of there – I was goin' nuts all the while, obviously, 'cos if we hadn't turned up when we did, if I hadn't screamed, if he hadn't taken that tiny, little step, he'd've been a goner, for sure. No doubt about it.'

'He was incredibly lucky,' Beede confirmed.

'It weren't *luck*,' Kelly snapped. 'It was an Act of God. Like I already told you . . .'

'Whatever it was,' Beede said, 'your uncle was extremely . . .'

He paused for a second, unwilling to use the word 'lucky' again (toying with the word 'fortunate' instead).

'Your hand's all knackered,' Kelly mused.

'Pardon?'

'Your hand.'

He inspected it himself.

'Uh . . . *Oh*. Yes.'

'An' you've got . . .' she pointed, 'all these *marks*. On your lip, on your neck. An' a couple more – over there – on the side of your . . .'

Beede moved his hand to his neck.

'*Scratches*. On your cheek. Not . . .' she impatiently repositioned his hand for him '. . . on the other side.'

'I was *uh* . . .' Beede cleared his throat and then glanced around him, looking for a quick get-out. 'Should your uncle really be doing that?'

Harvey was attempting to reverse his Toyota from under a section of the collapsed scaffolding (with the able assistance of Gaffar who was providing directions from the road).

'Dunno,' Kelly shrugged.

'Good *Lord!*' Beede exclaimed (pulling an old, cashmere scarf from his coat pocket and winding it, rapidly, around his throat). 'Gaffar looks like he's been in the wars . . .'

'Urgh . . .' Kelly growled. '*Scrappin'*, more'n likely. In some filthy *gamblin'* den or other. He went to Readin' last night – supposedly to sit wiv' Paul – an' that's how the little chancer came back.'

As Kelly spoke, her conversation was neatly punctuated by her uncle's repeated honking of the Toyota's horn. When the honking stopped it was followed by a loud and ferocious string of expletives.

Kelly chuckled, indulgently. 'He *loves* that stupid car. He nearly pissed his damn *pants* when he saw the windscreen was smashed . . .' Kelly snorted. 'I honestly think he'd've rather the scaffoldin'd landed on *him*. Silly sod.'

As if on cue, Harvey popped his head out of the passenger window. 'There ain't no point in all your *blabbin'*,' he harangued the Kurd, 'if I can't understand a bloomin' *word* of it. Speak in English, mate. *Ing-leesh*. In English we say *left* . . .' he waved his left hand, 'an' we say *right* . . .' he waved his right. 'Ya followin'?'

He scowled over towards his niece. 'Where'd you pick up these retards?' he asked. 'Is there a special *store* or somethin'?'

Beede took a quick step forward. 'Uh . . . Excuse me? Hello . . . ?' He waved. '. . . Mr Broad?'

Harvey began to withdraw.

'*HAAARVE!*' Kelly bellowed. 'The old boy's tryin'a *speak* to ya!'

'Huh?'

Harvey paused for a second (looking Beede up and down, irritably).

'I just wondered whether it might not be a good idea,' Beede cautiously suggested, 'to wait for *professional* help before attempting to move that?'

'*Professional?!*' Harvey spluttered, enraged. 'What d'ya *mean*, "professional"?! I *am* a professional, you idiotic *turd*.'

He disappeared from view again. Ten seconds later he accelerated forward. The Toyota wouldn't budge, so Harvey accelerated harder – then still harder – until a plume of smoke began pouring from the exhaust.

Gaffar yelled and gesticulated wildly over the roar of the engine. A terrible, creaking noise issued forth (followed by a loud crash, followed by the brutal sound of tearing metal), and then suddenly the vehicle jerked forward, casting off its heavy wig of scaffolding (like a care-worn barrister after his final day in court).

The assembled party watched on, in astonishment, as the Toyota shot down the street, free at last, but completely stripped of its upper half.

Gaffar strolled over to Kelly, with a shrug. 'Your uncle's a monkey's arse,' he said.

'Think he's all right?' Kelly wondered, as Harvey performed a high-speed u-turn and then roared back past them (chin held aloft, refusing all eye contact), driving doggedly on (and away) as if nothing was remotely wrong.

They stood together, in silence, heads cocked, listening to the Toyota's over-revved engine negotiating a path through the remainder of the estate.

'*Well* . . .' Beede shrugged, once an atmosphere of quiet had finally been restored.

'Would you ever?' Kelly murmured.

Gaffar slowly shook his head and then sucked on his tongue, ruminatively.

'I s'pose *we'd* better be puttin' our skates on, Gaff,' Kelly finally broke the silence, proper, 'an' head back to Malcolm Sargent Road. I forgot the stupid *Bible*,' she explained. 'I left it wiv' Gaz. The Rev'll go nuts if we return wiv'out it.'

'Oh. Okay. *Sure*.'

Gaffar walked over to where he'd parked the scooter, pulled on his helmet, kicked the scooter from its stand and pushed it towards them. He helped Kelly on board and then climbed on in front of her.

'Are you certain that's a good idea?' Beede asked, horrified.

Gaffar started the engine and revved it up. Kelly grabbed on to his waist. Then –

'Hold up a sec,' she said, noticing the brown envelope still protruding from Gaffar's back pocket. 'This is yours, ain't it?'

She pulled the envelope free and passed it to Beede with an apologetic grin. Beede took it, confused.

'The bloke what wrote that's actually my great-great-great-grandad,' she swanked (almost – Beede felt – by way of an excuse), then, '*Tally-ho!*' she slapped Gaffar on the shoulder and off they sped.

Beede inspected the envelope (his eyes watering slightly from the scooter's emissions), then he winced, reached up his hand to his neck again and massaged it, distractedly, while glancing over at the house. He took a couple of halting steps towards it, then quickly changed his mind and limped slowly down the road towards the parked Mercedes instead.

On reaching the car, he peered in through the window and saw (much as he'd suspected) that Kane was lying, flat-out on the back seat, covered in his grey crombie.

'Kane?'

Beede knocked on the window –

No response

Beede tried the door, found it unlocked, and pulled it open.

'Kane?'

Kane didn't budge.

Beede reached out his hand and yanked off the coat. Kane lay there, perfectly still, his eyes closed.

'*Kane?*' he repeated, an edge of concern entering his voice. He gave his son a peremptory shake.

At last Kane stirred. He yawned, then he stretched himself, then he opened his eyes and stared around him, dopily, finally focussing in on his father. His eyes widened, in surprise.

'*Beede?*'

'What on earth are you playing at?' Beede demanded, not taken in for a second by Kane's pathetic little act.

'Uh . . .' Kane pulled himself into a sitting position. 'Sorry,' he blinked, 'I must've just nodded off. I was waiting for an Estate Agent . . .'

He inspected his watch.

'She's actually very late . . .'

He picked up his phone, with a scowl, to check his messages.

'An Estate Agent?' Beede scoffed. 'Why?'

'Why?' Kane glanced up. 'Because I wanted to take a quick look around . . .'

He pointed towards the house.

'Don't be ridiculous,' Beede snapped. 'You already have a perfectly good home.'

'As an investment,' Kane persisted, staring back down at his phone, 'to rent out.'

'You're parked in,' Beede informed him.

'Am I?'

Kane glanced over his shoulder.

'Yes. And that's Dory's car.'

'Is it?'

'*Yes*. Yes, Kane. It is.'

Beede's tone was bordering on the vitriolic.

Kane reached for his cigarettes.

'Hang on a minute . . .' Beede's sharp eyes had alighted upon Isidore's diary. 'What's this?'

He scooped up the black jotter from the back seat, then winced at the intense pain this quick movement afforded him.

Kane lit his cigarette, irritated.

'Is your shoulder still bad?' he asked.

'No.'

Beede threw the envelope down (his one hand was so weak now that he found it almost impossible to manage both objects in conjunction).

Kane gave the envelope – then his father – a searching look before reaching into his coat pocket. 'You're obviously still in pain,' he observed, 'and I can give you something to relieve it . . .' he felt around for his stash, 'but you should definitely see a doctor at some point . . .'

'It's fine,' Beede snapped, '*I'm* fine. I don't need your pills . . .' then he paused, churlishly. 'No. *No.* What I mean to say, Kane, is that I don't *want* your pills.'

Kane withdrew his hand. 'Don't mince your words, eh?' he smiled, obviously hurt, but trying to make light of it.

'I won't,' Beede growled. 'There's already been far too much of that.'

'Really?' Kane looked intrigued. 'From whom?'

'From me, of course.'

'From *you*?'

Kane almost laughed out loud.

'*Yes.*'

Beede was indignant.

'*Wow* . . .'

Kane slowly shook his head, amused, as he inhaled on his cigarette.

'You still haven't answered my question,' Beede continued (infuriated – as always – by his son's trademark combination of charm and cynicism).

'Didn't I?' Kane shrugged, vaguely.

'No.'

Kane inspected his phone again.

'Would you put that infernal thing *down,*' Beede snarled, 'and just try and be straight with me for once?' He brandished the diary like a Methodist minister preaching fire and brimstone from his roadside pulpit.

Kane refused to put his phone down. It was actually turned off, but he continued to stare at it. 'The diary was in the Rover, on the dash,' he murmured sullenly, 'and he'd parked me in, so I just . . .'

'You stole it?'

'I borrowed it.'

'*Why?*' Beede demanded. 'And no more of that ridiculous clap-trap about . . .'

'Okay then,' Kane butted in, turning to face Beede, full-on, 'I'll tell you why, shall I? I'll tell you *exactly* why. I'm here because I followed him, and I stole his diary because – to put it plainly – I think he's a lunatic and I was intrigued to know what he'd been writing in it.'

'What did you discover?' Beede asked.

'That he's crazy. That he's losing his mind. That he's totally paranoid . . .'

'Really?' Beede smiled, superciliously. 'And who are you to make that kind of assessment?'

'Pardon?'

'Who are *you* to stand in judgement on a man like Dory? A decent, respectable, hard-working . . .'

'He's *crazy*,' Kane interrupted, his temper rising. 'I almost ran him down, earlier. He was just standing in the road, like a zombie . . .'

'When?' Beede demanded. 'How?'

'About half an hour ago. I was negotiating a sharp bend . . .'

'Where?'

'Just north of here . . .'

'Why?'

Kane frowned.

'I mean what exactly were you up to?'

'*Up* to?'

'Yes.'

'I was making a delivery,' Kane answered haughtily, 'to a client, if you must know.'

'To Elen?'

'What?'

Kane stared at Beede, bewildered. 'Why on earth would I be making a delivery to her?'

'Why wouldn't you be?'

'Because she isn't one of my clients, for one thing, and for another, she was actually with *you* all morning.'

Beede slowly processed the infallible logic of this statement. 'Of course,' he said, tightly, 'so you were making a delivery. Fine. Then what?'

'I was negotiating a sharp bend, I heard a horn sounding, I covered my brake, and the next thing I knew, I was swerving to avoid a man – *him*, Dory – standing in the middle of the road.'

'What was he doing?' Beede wondered.

'Nothing. Just standing there, staring down at the tarmac. I swerved to avoid him – like I said – then I swerved to avoid a Metro which'd just done the same thing. I lightly clipped the back of it. There was a woman driver . . .'

'But Isidore was unhurt?'

'He was extremely lucky . . .'

'And he was just standing there, you say? Looking down at the road?'

'Yes. And crying. I think he was crying. He was obviously deeply upset about something . . .'

'About what?'

Kane threw up his hands. 'How the hell should I know?'

'You didn't speak to him?'

'No. There wasn't time. The Metro was obstructing the road and she couldn't get it re-started, so I . . .'

'Was *she* hurt?'

'No – not so far as I'm aware. And by the time I looked around again, he'd vanished.'

'I see.'

Beede looked perplexed.

'Although a few minutes later,' Kane continued, 'he swept past in his Rover, like nothing had happened. He didn't even glance over.'

'So then you followed him?'

'Yes. *No*. I didn't plan to – not to begin with – but his driving was so bad – so erratic – that I just thought it might be safer . . .'

'Purely in the spirit of *altruism*, eh?' Beede scoffed.

'Yes. Why not?' Kane enquired, piqued.

Beede didn't respond. He stared down at the black jotter. 'Well you had no right to steal his diary,' he said.

'In a perfect world,' Kane conceded, 'you'd probably have a point, but he's out of control. He's a danger to himself and to the people around him . . .' he paused. 'I mean what about poor Elen? All those awful bruises on her forearms?'

'Poor *Elen*?!' Beede parroted, scornfully, then he glanced down, surreptitiously, at his badly grazed knuckles. 'Did she *say* Dory was responsible for those?'

'No. Not in so many words . . .' Kane shrugged. 'But then she's prob-ably just protecting him – in the same way that you are . . .'

'I'm not protecting him at all,' Beede insisted, 'and contrary to what you might think, I'm perfectly well-acquainted with how strange – even dangerous – some of Dory's behaviour can be. But I've known him for a long time now, and while he may have a few problems – some serious, long-term health issues – underneath all the mess – all the confusion – he's still a decent, gentle, highly intelligent . . .'

'How about you?' Kane suddenly butted in.

'Pardon?'

'How about *your* problems?'

'*My* problems?' Beede was thrown off-kilter. 'What problems?'

'Well you're £38,000 in debt, for starters.'

Beede didn't flinch. 'And?'

'And you're in love with his wife.'

'*Rubbish!*' Beede hissed, his cheeks reddening. 'Dory is my *friend*. Elen is my *friend*. I'm just helping them through a rough patch . . .'

'Purely in the spirit of *altruism*, of course,' Kane grinned.

'I should've known I could depend on you,' Beede sneered, 'to put some kind of vulgar slant on it.'

Kane said nothing. He just continued to smile.

'This strikes me as a rather good example,' Beede continued, obvi-ously riled, 'of the pot calling the kettle black.'

Kane's grin grew still wider.

'What you seem incapable of realising,' Beede snapped (finally losing his cool), 'is that you're meddling in things here which are none of your damn *business* . . .'

'But they *are* my business,' Kane interrupted.

'How?'

'They became my business when you stole drugs from me – to give to *her*, presumably . . . Or did you steal them for him? I don't know. I don't really even care. What I *do* care about is the fact that you let Kelly take the rap for it. That was shabby. If you'd wanted drugs you should've just asked. I would've handed them over, quite happily.'

'Well here's a turn-up,' Beede snorted, 'me receiving a lecture from *you* on moral probity.'

'Amazing, isn't it?' Kane smiled (refusing to let his father wind him up). 'And while you're in the mood to exchange idle aphorisms . . .'

Beede stared at his son, unblinking.

'The road to hell is paved with good intentions.'

'Oh really?' Beede smirked. 'And you'd know all about that, I suppose?'

Kane nodded, with feeling. 'Absolutely.'

Beede rolled his eyes. 'Well I'll take that under advisement, if you don't mind.'

'Dory may be your friend,' Kane persisted (determined to get his point across), 'but he's still a *bona-fide* fruitcake. And while it's perfectly understandable that you should want to help him – to protect him, to shield him from the harsh realities of everyday life – there comes a point beyond which that kind of interference – that help – is actually counter-productive; you only end up making matters worse . . .'

'No,' Beede refused to yield, 'you don't know what you're talking about.'

'Don't I?' Kane stared at his father, thoughtfully. 'Why? Because I lack the relevant *experience*, perhaps? Because you never really cared for *me* in that way?'

Beede looked confused.

'Okay,' Kane stubbed out his cigarette. 'What if I told you that it wasn't just an accident that the scaffolding collapsed?'

Beede was silent.

'What if I told you that Dory was perching on the roof and that he pushed it down?'

'I'd say you'd taken leave of your senses,' Beede declared.

'I sat here and I *watched* him, Beede.'

'Well I spoke to Kelly,' Beede maintained, 'and she said Harvey was all alone . . .'

'Dory was on the roof. He pushed the scaffolding down.'

'And you *saw* that? You actually *saw* him do that?'

'Yes.' Kane nodded, then he paused. 'Or as good as . . . I mean I turned away for a split second when the scooter pulled on to the road. Kelly was making such a *racket* . . .'

Beede gave a derisory snort.

'He'd planned it all out in advance,' Kane back-pedalled, furiously. 'It was *obvious*. Just look where he parked his *car*, for Christsakes . . .'

Kane turned and pointed.

Beede turned himself to inspect the Rover.

'That doesn't prove a thing. The scaffolding was always unstable . . .'

'I sat and I *watched* him, Beede,' Kane refused to be gainsaid, 'I was *right here*. I watched him parking his car, I watched him climb out of his car and remove some kind of heavy wrench – or spanner – from inside the boot, I watched him stare over at the house for a while and then stroll over to the scaffolding and begin hammering away at it . . .'

'He was tightening it up,' Beede shrugged. 'He was shoring it up.'

'Yeah. That's exactly what I thought to begin with. But the more he bashed away at it, the more unstable the whole structure grew, to the extent that he was actually forced to grab on to the roof at one point to save himself from falling . . .'

Beede stared down at Kane, scowling. He said nothing.

'He kept inspecting his watch, as if he was waiting for someone.'

'He was waiting for me. I was late . . .'

'Then perhaps he was intending to kill *you*,' Kane volunteered (although not entirely seriously).

'Don't be ridiculous,' Beede exclaimed (visibly spooked by this idea).

'And here's another thing,' Kane continued, emboldened by his father's fearful look, 'there was a history of bad blood between them . . .'

'Between whom?'

'Between him and Harvey Broad.'

'Well what does that prove?' Beede scoffed. 'Everybody hates Harvey Broad. He's an incorrigible crook . . .'

'No. This was serious. This was *personal*. This was the continuation of an argument that'd started some twenty-odd *years* ago when they were both working together on the Channel Tunnel. It seems that Dory was actually there – in person – when those tiles were stolen. He was working as a guard. In fact they both were – him *and* Harvey. I heard them arguing about it . . .' he paused, thoughtfully. 'Although maybe you already knew that . . .'

'Which tiles?'

Beede seemed bewildered.

'*Which* tiles?!' Kane taunted. 'Oh come *on*! The tiles. The *antique* tiles. The tiles you got so steamed-up about. The tiles from the old mill.'

Beede stared at him, blankly. 'You remember that?'

'*Remember?!*' Kane cackled, indignantly. 'You seriously think I wouldn't *remember*? The fucking *tiles*? The antique, fucking *tiles*?! Of *course* I remember!'

Beede looked stunned. 'But you were so young . . .'

'How could I possibly forget?' Kane demanded. 'How could I forget what it *did* to you? How it totally messed you up? How you let it eat away at you. How you let it . . .' he struggled, momentarily, to find the right word, 'how you allowed it to . . . to . . .' he clenched his hands into fists, 'to completely *eviscerate* you?'

'No.' Beede shook his head. 'That's not true . . .'

'Yes it *is*!'

Kane suddenly realised that he was shaking, that his eyes were full of tears.

'How could I *not* remember?' he yelled, furious at himself.

'How?! When it *changed* everything? When it ruined *everything*?'

Silence

'I didn't realise . . .' Beede finally murmured, shocked.

'No . . .' Kane shook his head. 'Me neither.'

'Well I'm sorry,' Beede said, 'I'm very sorry.'

His father suddenly looked haggard – *old,* Kane thought. But instead of feeling sorry for him, instead of wanting to reach out to him, to *help* him, Kane felt a strange, warm sensation in his stomach, a kind of *glow,* a deep feeling of contentment, as if seeing his father so horribly diminished was – in some sick, subterranean way – profoundly empowering to him.

'Perhaps you should call Elen?' he volunteered, proffering Beede his phone. 'And tell her what's been going on?'

'Yes,' Beede answered, vaguely, 'maybe later.'

'Later? You don't think she needs to know now?'

Beede frowned.

'You don't think she needs to know *now*?' Kane repeated (an edge of hysteria re-entering his voice).

'It's very complicated,' Beede murmured. 'It's a complicated situation . . .'

'Yeah,' Kane snapped, frustrated, 'so you persist in saying . . .'

'It just has to be . . .' Beede scowled, 'it just has to be *handled* . . .'

'Handled?'

'Yes.'

'Then perhaps *I* should tell her,' Kane suggested, 'if you feel like you're too embroiled in the whole thing? Do you happen to know her work number, offhand?'

Beede didn't answer. He stared down the road, deep in thought, then he turned back to his son again, impetuously. 'I've never made a habit of ordering you around, have I?' he asked.

Kane frowned, disconcerted. 'Uh . . .' he thought for a minute, 'No. I guess not. I mean not in so many *words* . . .'

'I've never nagged at you, tried to manipulate you, bullied you into decisions that you didn't feel comfortable with . . . In fact I *pride* myself on it. I've always encouraged you to make your own choices, your own mistakes . . .'

'Sure – and then oozed disapproval,' Kane smirked, 'or – better still – *disappointment*, from a sensible distance.'

Beede looked hurt. 'I'm sorry you see it that way.'

'I don't,' Kane jumped in, 'I was just . . .' he shrugged.

'Well here's the nub of the matter,' Beede quickly moved on, 'I've never made a habit of asking you for anything – not directly, not outright – but if there was *one* thing, one special favour – father to son – that I needed to ask from you, one request, one heartfelt appeal . . .'

'What?' Kane demanded.

'Stay away from her.'

'Who?'

'You *know* who.'

'*Why?*' Kane was outraged.

'For no other reason than that I've asked you to,' Beede said. 'Because I care about you. And because I care about Dory.'

Kane was quiet for a while, and then, 'What if I can't?' he said.

'I know you can,' Beede countered. 'You can do anything you set your mind to. You're young. You're strong.'

'Then what if I just don't *want* to?'

Beede closed his eyes. 'She's inhabiting you,' he muttered, 'she's *invading* you. It's all very subtle, very artful. You may not even fully realise – you may think it's all happening on *your* initiative – but trust me, it isn't. This is her talent, Kane, it's what she *does* . . .'

'*Inhabiting* me?' Kane scoffed.

'Yes.'

'Did she inhabit *you*?' he asked, suddenly jealous.

'Yes . . .' Beede shrugged. 'I'm not sure. Perhaps . . .'

'But isn't that just *love*?' Kane demanded. 'Aren't you just in love with her?'

'No. *No* . . .' Beede seemed horrified. 'Absolutely not.'

'But isn't that what love's all *about*?' Kane persisted. 'Isn't it always an invasion of sorts? Isn't that why people like to say that their hearts have been conquered or . . . or taken prisoner, or overwhelmed?'

'No.' Beede shook his head. 'This is different. This isn't love. It's just a strange kind of . . . of *congruity*. She looks for a weakness . . .'

Kane flinched. Beede couldn't help but notice. 'That was a poor choice of word . . .' he paused for a second, flustered. 'Let me put it *this* way: in your particular case, for example, she knows that you have an amazing capacity to care, this deep reservoir . . .'

'*Do* I?' Kane butted in, surprised.

'Yes. *Yes*. Because of your mother. She senses this feeling of *hurt* within you, this . . . this vulnerability . . .'

'No,' Kane shook his head, 'you're wrong. I *didn't* have an infinite capacity. Quite the opposite, in fact. I actually had a very *limited* capacity . . .'

'Okay,' Beede shrugged. 'Then perhaps – at some level – she's *feeding* on that knowledge, on the guilt you may well feel as a consequence of it . . .'

Kane stared at his father, suspiciously. 'You can't have it all ways,' he said, and then, a few seconds later, 'You seem *different*,' he murmured cruelly, '*smaller*, less . . . less . . .' he wanted to say *square*, but suddenly, for some inexplicable reason, he was struggling to separate his words from each other, 'less-es-*esquare*,' he finally stuttered, and then, 'es-es-es*quire* . . .' he tried to correct himself.

Beede stared back at him, frowning.

'I *feel* smaller,' he said, 'I don't really know why . . .' he gazed down at his knuckles. 'It's like everything suddenly closed in on me – caved in on me. I started thinking about the past,' he sighed, his face full of regret, 'and then, pretty soon, it was *all* I could think of . . .'

Kane said nothing.

Beede smiled, tiredly. 'There must be something you could prescribe me for that,' he joked. 'A pill of some kind?'

Kane scowled.

'Here . . .' Beede threw down the diary, 'put this back where you found it.'

Then he turned, without another word, and headed off towards the house.

Kane glanced down at the seat and noticed the envelope.
'You forgot this . . .' he murmured, picking it up, but Beede was already dodging his way through the scaffolding, grappling with the side-gate and disappearing from sight.

Dory was sitting, cross-legged, on the carpet, staring into the bulb of an old-fashioned standard lamp.
'Isn't this just *wonderful*?' he murmured. 'The way it goes on and then off, on and then off?'
He reached out his finger and touched the bright bulb with it.
'Ow!'
The bulb was burning hot.
'How are you feeling?' Beede wondered (speaking quietly, softly, keen not to alarm him).
'Good,' Dory said, smiling, still gazing into the lamp, 'better than ever, in fact.'
'I'm sorry about the scaffolding,' Beede said, 'I came in through the back . . .'
Dory didn't seem to hear him.
'I noticed that you have a dog,' Beede said, indicating over his shoulder, 'a dog in a box.'
'Pardon?'
Dory frowned.
'A little *dog*. A little spaniel. Sitting inside a box – a large, cardboard box – in the kitchen.'
'Oh. Yes.' Dory nodded, indifferent. 'Michelle.'
'She was crying.'

No response

'She seems a little . . . uh . . . *distressed*.'
'Who?'

753

Dory glanced up. He almost did a double-take. 'Beede!' he sprang to his feet, bounded forward and grasped him, warmly, by the hand.

Beede frowned, confused. 'Who did you think I was?'

Dory shook his hand, vigorously.

'I don't know,' he grinned, shrugging, 'just a voice, a small voice in my head.'

'You're hearing voices, now?' Beede asked, concerned.

'Good *God*, no!' Dory guffawed. 'I just thought *you* were a voice . . .' he paused, '*the* voice . . .' he paused again, 'a voice . . .'

'Oh.'

Beede frowned.

Dory dropped Beede's hand and turned to face the table, then he took a small step back and tensed himself.

'What are you doing?' Beede asked.

'I'm going to jump it,' Dory said.

'Jump the table?'

'Yes!' Dory grinned.

'But I don't think there's quite enough *room*, Dory,' Beede cautioned him.

'Really?'

'No. It's just a little . . . a little cramped in here for all that.'

'Oh.' Dory relaxed again.

They both stared, in silence, at the matchstick cathedral.

'La Berbie,' Dory muttered dreamily.

'I'm sorry about the scaffolding,' Beede repeated, glancing nervously towards the window.

'Are you?' Dory smiled.

'Yes.'

Beede pointed to the lamp. 'Maybe you should turn that off?' he suggested.

'What?'

'The lamp.'

'The lamp?'

'Yes. It looks rather hot.'

Dory peered over at the lamp. It was precariously balanced on a couple of cushions.

'That damn *boy*,' he muttered furiously, striding over towards it, 'I keep *telling* him not to move it, but he simply won't *listen* . . .'

'Fleet?' Beede asked.

'He throws shadows with it.'

Dory knelt down in front of the lamp, as if intending to lift it from the cushions and turn it off, but instead he twisted his hands together and threw a shadow of his own.

'Look who's here!' he chuckled, peering at Beede, mischievously, over his shoulder.

Beede took a couple of steps forward to try and see what Dory was doing. He blinked.

He saw a bird. A small, black bird, shivering miserably against the skirting-board.

'*Aw!*' Dory murmured softly, cocking his head, poignantly. 'But he doesn't look *well*, does he?'

The bird opened its beak to squawk, but nothing came out.

'We can't *hear* you, my little friend!' Dory cooed.

Beede turned away, disturbed.

'So is that *your* dog, Dory?' he asked, keen to distract the German. 'Is it new? I haven't seen it here before.'

'The dog?'

Dory scowled. He dropped his hands. Then something seemed to click back into place inside his head.

'God, *yes* . . . the dog.' He sprang up. 'I have to return the dog.'

He barged past Beede and darted down the hallway. 'I'd forgotten all about that. I'm in a ridiculous hurry. I really *must* . . .'

Beede followed him into the kitchen.

'I was packing everything together,' Dory said, scratching his head. He peered into the box. 'I've got her cart, her litter tray, her lead, her water bowl . . .' he scowled. 'What else?'

His eye alighted on her food bowl.

'Her food bowl . . .' he went over to grab it. 'Would you mind having a quick look in the fridge, Beede? See if there's a can of dog meat in there?'

Beede walked over to the fridge and opened the door. Inside he saw a half-eaten tray of dog meat, neatly sealed inside a plastic bag. He removed it. He closed the fridge. He paused. Still inside the tray was a spoon, an old teaspoon. He peered at it, closely –

Hospital Issue

He blinked.

'Okay,' Dory was saying, 'that's it. I think we have just about every-thing . . .'

He began hunting around for his car keys.

'I need my keys . . .' he murmured.

'You're going to drive?' Beede asked, horrified.

'Yes.'

Dory reached into his back pocket and pulled out a piece of paper. He unfolded it. It was a Missing Dog poster.

'This is the address,' he said, pointing.

'Perhaps I might come with you?' Beede asked, passing over the tray of food.

'Really?'

Dory placed the food into the box.

'Yes. Just for the ride.'

'Are you *sure*?' Dory looked confused. 'I mean it won't be terribly . . .'

'Yes. You just seem a little . . . uh . . . a little *tired*. I thought you might appreciate the company.'

Dory frowned as he straightened up.

'Your keys are on the table . . .' Beede pointed.

Dory turned, spotted his keys and grabbed them. He peered around him.

'Did you turn off that lamp?' Beede asked. 'The lamp in the dining-room?'

'No.'

Dory threw him the keys, but Beede was unable to catch them. His responses were way too slow. He bent down to retrieve them, wincing, as Dory sprinted off to the dining-room. When he arrived there he saw that the lamp had actually fallen, that it was lying, bulb-down, on the carpet. His nostrils twitched at the slight aroma of singeing fibre.

He quickly crouched down next to it. But instead of picking it up, he manipulated his hands in front of the small remaining segment of emerging light and threw a quick shadow with them.

Flames. Tiny flames, flickering against the wall.

Next he threw the injured bird, cowering, terrified. Then back to the flames again.

He chuckled.

'Dory?'

He heard Beede's voice, calling from the kitchen, 'Are you all right in there?'

Dory coughed, waving his hand in front of him to try and dissipate the encroaching cloud of dense, foul-smelling smoke.

'Fine,' he said. '*Great*. Just coming.'

SIXTEEN

Kane snatched a magazine from the top of an unsteady pile in the surgery's cramped – and rather unprepossessing – reception area, then quickly took his seat. He rested the magazine on his lap, pulled out his phone, turned it on, saw that he had over sixty messages, shuddered, turned it off again, and then shoved it back, hastily, into his pocket.

He wondered if he'd be allowed to smoke. He looked around for a sign –

Nothing

– then he looked around for an ashtray, and his eye alighted on a sign –

No Smoking

He scowled and peered down at the magazine. It was a copy of *The Wound* –

Eh?!

– a specialist, nursing publication. He opened it up, randomly –

JEEESUS!

– and then promptly slapped it shut. He felt ridiculously jittery –

Why?

He closed his eyes for a second –

Guilt?

'Would I even be here,' he wondered, 'if he hadn't expressly asked me *not* to?'

Answer –
(In words of only one syllable . . . ?)
Uh . . .
Hell, yeah.

'Beede?'
Kane almost jumped out of his skin –
'*Kane?* Kane Beede?'
His eyes flew open.

The receptionist was pointing, encouragingly, towards the angular, open-plan stairwell. 'First floor,' she informed him (with a brisk smile), 'second door on your left.'

Kane threw down *The Wound* and bounded upstairs (moving as quickly as he possibly could without breaking into a sprint). On reaching the designated door he clenched his hand into a fist and prepared to knock, but then paused for a second, his eye settling on a neatly typed card (slotted inside a small, metal frame which was screwed into the wood).

He drew closer:

ELEN GRASS
Chiropodist

he read –

Grass?

He unclenched his fist and lightly touched the card. As he applied a slight pressure to it, the card shifted. He pushed his finger to the right and the card shifted still further. Soon it was out of the frame altogether and resting in his palm. He smiled, closed his hand around it, and slipped it, softly, into his coat pocket. He drew a deep breath, then he knocked.

'Come in.'

Kane entered the room with as much confidence as he could muster but was then immediately confounded by the ludicrous *size* of it. It was minuscule – a large cupboard, at best – barely 6 foot in width. Much of the space was taken up by a large, red, leather chair (centrally positioned), a grey, metal bookshelf-cum-desk-cum-supplies cabinet (pushed up against the left-hand-side wall), a couple of open cardboard boxes (partly hidden behind the chair) and a small sink (in the back, right-hand corner) which was barely even broad enough to support a medicated soap dispenser and a thick wad of paper towels (which had been propped up, lop-sidedly, behind the tap).

Elen had her back to him. There was a tiny window (behind the chair) and she was standing, facing it, speaking on the phone – 'Fine,' she said, abruptly, 'then put him through . . .'

She gestured an impatient welcome over her shoulder (without turning) and indicated for Kane to take a seat. Her hair was loose, he noticed, hanging in a dark, shiny sheet down her back. She was wearing a thigh-length white overall (her black trousers and boots poking out underneath) with a disposable, plastic apron tied over the top.

Kane gently closed the door behind him and then did as she'd requested. He sat (it was his only real option – there was insufficient room to do anything else).

'You'd better take off your coat,' she murmured, covering the phone's mouthpiece with her fingers, 'and hang it up behind the door, there. I won't be a minute . . .' she paused, then cleared her throat, nervously. 'Sorry about this . . .' she added, 'I wasn't actually . . . *Hello? Charles? Yes, hello, yes,* it's Elen . . .'

She sounded slightly breathless, Kane noticed; agitated – excited. He stood up, removed his crombie and debated where to hang it. There were two pegs behind the door; Elen's soft, black jacket was hung on one of them; the other supported a worryingly familiar-looking Sainsbury's bag –

Urgh.
Hawk

Kane opted to place his coat over the top of Elen's. The mere act of eclipsing her pliant, soft, black garment with his own (much heavier, much stronger) afforded him a secret thrill. He stood facing the door for a moment, delicately tweaking the grey fabric (to ensure that her jacket was entirely obliterated), then caught himself in the act –

God –
Just sit down,

760

You pervert

He turned, a little sheepish, and retook his seat.

'No . . . *no*, not at *all*,' Elen chatted away quietly, her voice barely even audible above the gentle creak of the building's antiquated heating system, 'in fact I really wanted to say . . .'
She paused again '. . . Exactly . . . Yes. Me too.'

She fiddled with the tie on her plastic apron. 'I'd love to, but I'm actually with a *client* right now . . .'

Client?

Kane was traumatised.
'. . . if you could possibly just . . .'

A client?
Is that . . . ?

'. . . yes . . . just hold on for a . . .'
   'Kane?'
Kane lifted his head, sharply. 'What?'

'Remove your boot and your sock and I'll be with you in a moment.'

Oh.

Kane stared down at his foot, blankly.
   'Hello? Charles . . . ?'

But I wasn't . . .

He frowned.
   'Yes . . .' Elen's voice was – if possible – even lower now. 'Well, podiatry is actually the American . . .'
Small chuckle
'Yes.'
Pause.
'No. *No* . . .'

Slightly more serious.

'. . . although I'm sorry to have to say that your blanket didn't quite survive yesterday's adventure . . .'

Pause.

'That's extremely kind of you. I hope the mess wasn't . . . ?'

Elen bit her lip.

'Well that's something, at least . . .'

She peered down at her feet, modestly.

'*Thank* you!'

Shy laugh.

As Kane listened to Elen's conversation –

Who the hell is she talking to?

– he gradually became aware of a kind of dislocated drone –

Blanket?

He glanced up, somewhat listlessly –

Adventure?

– and saw a fly – a common house-fly –

Mess?
What kind of mess, exactly?

– rotating, senselessly, beneath the screw-in light fitment –

Is she actually flirting with this guy?

As Kane trailed the fly's progress with his eye –

One circle, two circles, three circles . . .
Drop!
One circle, two circles . . .

– his sullen reverie was suddenly interrupted by an unexpectedly intimate physical sensation –

762

Eh?!

His head jerked around –

Wah?

It was Elen – Elen's hand –

Her graceful hand

– gently adjusting the collar on his shirt. Kane closed his eyes for a second. He almost stopped breathing. Once the adjustment had been made, her hand –

Her lovely hand

– rested softly on his shoulder.

   'No. *No.* I insist on replacing it . . .' Elen chatted away, amiably.
Pause.
Rather more determinedly, 'No, Charles, I really *must* . . .'
Long, slightly awkward silence.
   Kane opened his eyes and glanced up at the light-fitment (almost insanely attuned to the weight of her fingers). He watched the fly, passively, feeling himself vibrating, internally, as if his intestines were being powered by a small battery –

> *'I now see,*
>   *through practice,*   *that in many*
>   *ways I am the fly,*
>   *that we have an identical energy . . .'*

He blinked.
   'Yes . . .' Elen murmured, 'I did, too.'
Pause.

One circle, two circles . . .

'Not at all. It was . . . I was . . . I was just incredibly *flattered*.'

Flattered?!

Kane stiffened –

How?
Why?

   As if responding to Kane's unease, Elen applied a comforting pressure to his shoulder, then lifted her hand and casually tucked a long,
stray, blond wisp of his fringe behind his ear. Kane felt his ear heat
up. He felt it glow.
   'Your boot . . .'
She was leaning towards him again, whispering. Kane blinked.
He could feel her breath on his cheek. He automatically moved
forward –

Stay, you fool!

– and began to remove it.
   'No, sorry, that was . . .'
Great amusement '. . . *Exactly!*'
   Elen turned towards the window again. An extremely long silence
followed, and then, 'What an amazingly generous offer!'
Pause.
'I honestly . . .'
Delighted laugh '. . . I really don't know what to say.'
Pause.
'No. *No*. Don't be silly. Not at all.'
Pause.
'I'm sure Fleet would just . . .'
Pause.
'He'd absolutely *love* it.'
   Kane brusquely tucked his sock inside his boot, then inspected his
bare foot. He felt uneasy at the sight of it –

Bare/Raw/Nude

– but wasn't entirely sure why he should feel this way. It wasn't a *terrible* foot, all things considered (he appraised it, dispassionately), although it didn't look quite . . . there was something . . . *uh* . . .

His mind turned, briefly, to his mother's feet – her magnificently messed-up dancer's feet, her scarred and brutalised dancer's toes – and then to his earliest memories of Elen –

ELEN GRASS
Chiropodist

– down on her knees, tending to them.

A powerful, erotic charge coursed through him –

Oh God –
Not . . .

He glanced into his lap, chewing on his lower lip, his eyebrows rising. He tucked his hands between his legs and tried to think of something else –

Anything

He gazed up at the fly again –

One circle, two circles, three . . .

– then he smiled, pensively (as if struck by a divine insight) –

Play
It's just playing –
Surely?

'The human mind,' an officious voice promptly informed him, 'can only disengage itself from the magic circle of play by turning towards the ultimate.'

Huh?

'I read the first few chapters late last night,' Elen murmured, 'and it was so sad – so beautifully written – I could hardly bear to put it down . . .'

Kane turned – still eager for distraction – towards Elen's small, grey, metal desk. He carefully appraised it. The surface-area was chaotic. There were piles of papers – order forms, patient files, receipts – three pairs of scissors, two boxes of disposable gloves, a tray of sharp-looking silver implements –

Yik

– a large, open, plastic, screw-top jar of sterilising fluid, a book –

?

– its cover partly concealed by a terrifying black and white photo-graph of a young boy who had fallen prey to a severe case of 'Hammer' toe.

'Absolutely . . .' Elen was still smiling as she spoke. A very long pause followed, hemmed in by another soft laugh.

Kane squinted at the book's spine: *The Lily of Darfur*, he read, then –

Urgh
But of course . . .

– he almost snorted, out loud.

'Okay. Sure. I definitely will. And thank you.'
Pause.
'No. I really *mean* that. I wouldn't just . . .'
Pause.
'I know. '
Pause.
'I know. Thank you.'

Kane leaned back in the chair again. He slowly shook his head. He flexed his foot. Behind him he heard the splash of running water –

Tap?

He half-turned, surprised that the phone conversation had come to

766

an end. Elen was drying her hands, fastidiously, on a paper towel.

'Right,' she said, tossing the towel into a flip-top bin which was neatly stationed beneath the sink, 'let's have a proper look at this foot of yours, shall we?'

Kane leaned forward, anxiously. 'I didn't actually . . .' he started off. Then he stopped, appalled.

Elen was pulling up a tiny stool and perching on it, grabbing a hold of his foot and lifting it, confidently, on to her lap. Her hair was casually tied back now, away from her face, revealing the early stages of a black eye (a bloodshot white, a puffed-up eye-lid), and a nostril (on that same side) which was also inflamed, bruised and daubed (deep inside) with tiny remnants of dried blood.

'Ah-*ha* . . .' she chuckled, immediately honing in on the problem area. 'Well here's the culprit . . .'

She glanced up. 'It's tucked in underneath the arch, which is fairly unusual for a wart – you generally find them forming on the pressure points . . .'

She carefully inspected the rest of the foot. 'No secondary growths,' she murmured, 'which is great . . .'

As she spoke she pulled on each of his toes (keenly inspecting the gaps in between them). He tensed up. He remembered his mother playing a similar game with him as a boy –

> *This little piggy went to market*
> *This little piggy stayed at home*
> *This little piggy had –*

'Warts are such fascinating things,' she was saying. 'And really quite mysterious. Their aetiology can often be extremely baffling. Some vascular growths are caused by trauma, others are simply viral – although even then they're pretty amazing: their incubation periods can extend anywhere up to twenty months – that's the best part of two *years* . . .'

She reached out and grabbed a tiny scalpel from a tray on her desk, then readjusted Kane's heel on her lap –

Don't think about her lap

– drew in close –

Don't think about her mouth

– and scratched away at Kane's foot with it. He felt nothing, right up until the point when he felt something –

Ouch!

His knee stiffened.
'Did you feel that?'
She gazed up at him, concerned, her scalpel held gracefully aloft.
'No. *No.* It's fine. I'm just . . .' he scowled, 'a little ticklish, I guess.'
'Ah . . .' she nodded and returned to her work. He remained hypnotised by her injuries. The nostril, especially. He wondered what it would feel like if he touched it with his tongue –

Would it taste of iron?
Salt?
Would it sting?

'Okay,' she leaned back, decisively, ready to make her assessment. 'So we can freeze it out, or we can burn it out. The choice is entirely yours.'
Kane dragged his eyes away from her nostril –

Go on –
Ask . . .

'How did you . . . *uh* . . .' he swallowed, nervously, 'treat Beede's?' he wondered.

Coward

He could've sworn he saw Elen wince – just slightly – at the mention of Beede's name – but then she looked up at him with a frank smile.
'We tried both techniques,' she explained, 'but your father's wart was very persistent. It didn't respond particularly well to either method.'
'Oh,' Kane frowned, discouraged.
'His was an exceptional case, though,' she insisted.

Go on –
Just . . .

'So how did . . . *uh* . . .' Kane forged on, doggedly. 'How did you
. . . uh . . . get rid of it in the end?'

Gutless

'In the end?' Elen hesitated. 'In the end we just charmed it away.'
'You charmed it?' Kane was surprised.
'Yes.'
   She inspected his foot again. 'You have lovely feet,' she said, 'thin
feet, very graceful, just like your mother's. Although hers were typical
dancer's feet . . . incredibly muscular. Extremely . . .' she frowned,
searching for an appropriate word '. . . extremely *characterful*.
Covered in old corns and bunions – a total mess – do you remember?'
   Kane stared at her, blankly –

The word . . .

He grimaced –

What was that word he'd used?
That strange word?
Con-con-con . . . ?

   'Kane?' she repeated. 'Your mother's feet – do you remember?'

'She looks for a weakness . . .'

'Kane?'

'. . . She senses this feeling of hurt within you, this . . . this . . .'

   Kane blinked. 'Well perhaps you could charm mine away,' he volunteered.
Elen gave this suggestion a moment's consideration and then, 'Okay,'
she shrugged, 'I suppose we could always give it a whirl . . .'
   She placed down his foot, stood up, dropped her scalpel into the

bottle of sterilising fluid, pulled aside her apron and her overall then shoved her hand into her trouser pocket. She felt around for a while before withdrawing a ten pence piece. She inspected it, thoughtfully, then closed her eyes and squeezed the coin, tightly, inside her fist.

Kane peered up at her –

She's so beautiful
I could just lean over – right now – and . . . and . . .

He puckered his lips –

. . . hitta

He started –

Hit-ta

'Hold out your hand,' she said, opening her eyes.
Kane didn't respond at first. He was still in a daze – ·

Hit-her . . .
Hit her

– because he suddenly had a clear memory of *exactly* that – of hitting her –

No!

Of hitting Elen –

No!

– and of taking a *deliberate* pleasure in it. They were in a wet room. A *white* room. They were alone together . . .

And he knew – he was certain – that this was what she expected – what she *wanted* – that there was a long history between them, a well-established protocol.

But she was messing around with it – with him – and he didn't like it. 'Don't take my son,' she was pleading, 'I'll do anything you ask – *anything* – if you'll just leave the boy alone.'

'But you *always* do anything I ask,' he reasoned, implacably.

'Kane? Your hand,' Elen repeated.

Kane blinked. 'Oh . . .'

He held out his hand and she pressed the coin into his palm, folding his fingers around it like an aunt giving a child some money for their birthday.

'There,' she said softly, 'I've bought the wart from you,' she smiled 'and now it will disappear.'

Kane gazed down at his hand, bewildered –

Con . . . con . . . con . . .

– then he slowly opened his hand and he inspected the coin.

'Is that it?' he asked, flatly.

'Why?' she grinned, pulling back. 'D'you think it's worth more? D'you think I've undervalued it?'

Kane didn't answer. He continued to inspect the coin –

Con . . . con . . . congruity?

'The traditional amount is a penny,' she was explaining.

Kane stared up into her bruised face –

That two things are in sync?
In parallel?

He drew a deep breath, 'So how . . . ?'

His foot spasmed –

Jeesus!

– 'So how much did you pay Beede for his?' he winced.

'Beede?' Elen seemed surprised by this question, as if the idea of buying a wart from Beede was quite preposterous. 'Good *God*, no,' she chuckled, walking back over to the sink, 'I didn't *buy* Beede's wart. You couldn't *buy* a wart from Beede . . .'

Con . . . con . . . congruity?
Con . . . con . . . congruent?

  Kane's brain began buzzing –

Con . . . con . . . congruere –

It hiccoughed –

Ruere . . .

He blinked –

To fall?
Ruere . . . to ru- to ru- to . . . to ruin?

  Kane frowned. He turned. 'But I don't understand . . .' he muttered.
'Don't understand what?' she asked, pumping some soap on to her
palm from the dispenser.
'I don't understand what the difference is . . .'

To fall

To ruin

'. . . I mean between *us* – between me and Beede . . .'
  Elen reached out her hand to turn on the tap and in that same
instant Kane was flung, unceremoniously, back into that cold, white
room – that wet room – and she was clawing, terrified, at his neck,
his cheek, and he was swiping her away from him, laughing, because
it was, it was –

Funny!
Her fear –
Hilarious!
Delicious!

– then suddenly he was in another place – a darker place – but it
was still the same memory, the same transaction, the same *idea* –

and he was tying her to a bench. And she was screaming. She was furious. And he was applying a gentle blade to her. There was a doctor. There was a servant. They were bleeding her together. They were letting blood. They were definitely in cah . . . *ah . . . ahh . . .ahhh!* . . . .*Caaa-HOOTS!*

Kane sneezed himself back into the red, leather chair again. He stared down at the coin, his nose prickling, his eyes tearing-up, shocked.

'Bless you,' she said. And then: 'I suppose I just thought it might be a little too straightforward for him,' she murmured, 'a little obvious – a little *crude*, even . . .'

What?!

'But not for me?'
Kane glanced up, livid.

'I didn't mean it like that,' Elen back-pedalled, 'it's more of a *generational* thing,' she tore off her apron, 'Beede's very old-fashioned.'
Kane gazed down at the coin again –

Coin –
Cuneus –
Kunte –
Cunt

– he shuddered.

'And the problem with his foot was much more severe,' Elen tried her best to mollify him as she screwed the apron into a tight ball and dropped it into the bin, 'much more serious.'

'Is it because of my line of work?' Kane demanded, paranoid. 'Is it because I'm a dealer?'
Elen didn't answer him. A small strand of her hair had become caught around one of the buttons on her overall and she was struggling to disentangle it.

'Does that just make you automatically assume,' Kane continued, furious, 'that I'm the kind of person who thinks pretty much *anything* can be bought and sold?'
Elen freed her hair then unbuttoned her overall, pulled it off and folded it up. It was almost as if she hadn't heard him.

Kane turned the coin over in his hand. He felt cheap – dirty – paid off. 'You think I'm fickle . . .' he murmured, 'feckless, *superficial* – just like *he* does. . .'

Still, no response.

He twisted around in his chair. 'Elen?'

Her name felt odd on his tongue as he spoke it – like a dirty thought; like a swearword.

Elen was placing her carefully folded overall into one of the open cardboard boxes behind the chair. She straightened up. 'You can put your boot back on again now,' she told him, turning to inspect her reflection in the small mirror above the sink, 'the treatment's over.'

Kane leaned forward and grabbed his boot –

Boat

'So how did you finally get rid of it?' he murmured, shoving his foot back into it –

Boat

– then feeling himself pitch, unexpectedly, to the right –

Wooah

'Pardon?'

Kane pressed his lips together for a moment, feeling unstable, slightly nauseous, clinging on to the chair's arm for support.

'Beede's w-wart,' he stuttered.

'I used a rather more traditional technique,' Elen explained, apparently oblivious, 'involving an Ash tree and a pin. You push the pin into the tree, then into the wart, then back into the tree again . . .'

'And that's it?'

Kane struggled to focus.

'Pretty much. I mean you say a few words . . .'

'What do you say?' he gasped.

'Uh . . . You say . . .' she frowned, arranging her hair over the bruised side of her face, 'you say, "Ashen tree, Ashen tree, please take these warts from me . . ."'

'Ash,' Kane murmured, drawing a deep breath and then grabbing for his laces and pulling them stiff. He glanced up as he pulled and saw a huge sail tightening behind him. The wind that blew into it – a hot wind, a dry wind – filled the sail with a deafening clamour, a thunderous babble –

Asche, it howled, *aska*, *arere*, *ardere*, *ardour*, *arson* . . .

– he saw words clashing and merging and collapsing and rotating. He saw chaos – an infinity of teeth, tongues, mouths, breath. He saw a storm of confusion. And he was holding the line hard, and the words kept on filling it, and the vessel kept on ploughing – relentlessly – through the water . . .

Then the shoe-lace snapped, under pressure –

What?!

Kane gazed down at the lace, dazedly.

'Do you need some help with that?' Elen was kneeling down in front of him, smiling. But she wasn't smiling *at* him, she was smiling beyond him. She was smiling over his shoulder, at someone behind him. He leaned back, terrified, then gazed up at the light fitment –

The fly
Where is it?

– searching for the fly. '*But what if HE is the fly?*' a quiet voice whispered.

Eh?

He quickly looked down again, aghast.

Elen had taken a hold of his laces and was retying his boot.

'You're not fickle at all,' she was murmuring. 'You're kind and sweet and brave and incredibly loyal.'

She tied a tight double-bow then reached out her hand and caressed his chin with it. He saw compassion in her eyes, empathy, *sympathy* – and he felt himself sinking into it, helplessly – deliriously – into the tenderness of her touch, into her kindness, into her *pity*, but just as he was falling into it, collapsing into it – there was a hard, sharp knock –

'Elen?'

What?

Kane was jolted back to consciousness –

Where?

– and he was surrounded by smoke. He jerked forward, automatically, starting to choke, longing to cough, but he felt a pair of strong hands on his shoulders, at his throat –

I can't . . .

'It's all so very *sudden*, Elen,' a voice was murmuring, a male voice, plainly distraught. 'What brought on this decision? I thought you liked it here. I thought you were *happy* at the practice . . .'

Just let me . . .
Oh God . . .
Must . . .

'Yes. I do. I *am* . . .'
(Elen's voice, answering.)
'. . . I suppose it was just something I'd been mulling over for a while . . .'
Her voice faded a little –

Can't . . .
Just have to . . .

'Good *gracious*!' the voice responded (also quieter now). 'What on earth have you done to your nose?'

Must get . . .
Must just . . .

'Oh God,' Elen sounded embarrassed, 'does it look terrible? I didn't have time to . . . It's all been so . . .'

'Is it broken do you think?'

Kane struggled for all he was worth – writhing, gasping, kicking – until the the hands finally slipped, somewhat regretfully, from his shoulders.

'I was down on my knees in the kitchen, cleaning up a small puddle which the spaniel had left behind the door . . .'

Kane fell forward, panting, his hands clutching at his throat. He blinked repeatedly. The smoke gradually thinned out.

'. . . and then Fleet came barrelling in . . .'

Kane peered around him, bewildered. The door to the treatment room was almost shut, but through a smallish chink he could see a man – an oldish, benevolent-seeming individual – standing in the hallway. He was wearing a white coat. He was tenderly inspecting Elen's face.

'. . . The edge of the frame caught my eye, then my nose hit the handle. It was ridiculous. And poor Fleet was so distraught – inconsolable. He's just at that age where they throw themselves into everything with such enthusiasm, such *violence* . . .'

Kane lurched to his feet.

'I must go,' he murmured, half to himself. He lunged for his coat but his focus was shot and he grabbed hold of the Sainsbury's bag instead. He stared down at it, bemused. Elen must've heard him get up. She peered around the door. 'Are you heading off?' she asked, and then, 'Oh good – so you found the bag . . . ?'

'Yeah . . .' Kane nodded, watching, in amazement, as her words marched on past him like a tiny army of leaf-cutter ants, 'Yeah. My . . . uh . . . My *bat* . . . uh . . . my *beit* . . . *bite* . . .'

He exercised his jaw for a moment, 'my *boat* . . .'

He ducked – '*Fuck!*' – as a sudden spurt of ocean spray came hurtling towards him, then grabbed for his coat, shoved rapidly past her, stumbled out into the hallway and headed for the stairwell. His feet felt . . . he looked down, horrified . . . they felt *tiny*, yet curiously painful and unwieldy – like he was walking on hooves, on pegs, on stilts. He approached the stairs, carefully – still holding the bag, his coat, clutching on to the coin as if his life depended on it – leaning his full weight against the banister as he staggered down.

'Will you settle your account?' the receptionist asked as he teetered past her.

'What?'

Kane paused.

'Will you settle your account?'
'Uh . . .'
Kane shrugged.

'Mrs Grass is leaving us. Didn't she tell you?'

Wow . . .

Kane stared at her, agog, as more ants marched on by.
　'Yes.'
Kane frowned.
'No . . .'
He shook his head.
　'Are you all right?' the receptionist asked. 'You seem a little . . .'
'My feet are very smell,' Kane informed her. Then he frowned 'I mean
smel . . . smal . . . I mean *small*. They're very *small* now.'
He blinked.

Did I actually just say that?

'Thank you,' he said, 'I must *gaa* . . .'
He shook his head. '*Gaaaaa* . . .'
　His mouth was yawning at her, insanely. He snapped it shut. He
swallowed. 'I mean *gaa-n* . . .' he said '. . . gone . . . I mean *go*. I
must . . .'
He smiled, self-deprecatingly. 'On my small feet. I must *gaa* on my
smell . . . on my tiny . . .'
　He pointed. He slung his coat over his shoulder. He staggered from
the surgery.
Outside, on the pavement, he gazed around him, blankly. It was
freezing cold. He shivered. He tried to pull on his coat, but the bag
and the coin seemed to actively disable him –

Just get rid of them

　He peered down into the gutter and saw a storm drain nearby. He
casually flipped the coin into it –

Chink!

Plop!

Yeah –
And fuck you, too

– then inspected the bag, irritably. He glanced up. Directly opposite him stood a neat row of suburban houses, and just beyond those: a wide, clear sky interspersed with welcome flashes of winter green. Kane smiled –

The cemetery

– he recalled Elen mentioning – in passing, the previous evening – how it might be a suitable location for burying the kite –

Fine . . .

He turned left (the cemetery's main entrance was on the Canterbury Road – where he'd parked his car), but then thought better of it and turned right instead (following a secret route which he still vaguely remembered from the scant adventures of his Ashford boyhood). He rapidly eclipsed the row of houses, skirted the Mace Industrial Estate and found himself on a small, overgrown pathway which meandered along the cemetery's tall back wall.

The wall was old, brick-built and rose to a height of around 7 feet. Kane cleaved to it faithfully – for 12 yards or so – until he reached a particular point – a familiar point – where the ground had shifted and the masonry above was cracked and jagged. He stopped – with a wide smile of recognition – hurled his coat over the top, placed the bag's handle between his teeth and scrambled his way up.

He swung his leg over. Beyond him lay a beautiful, frost-tinged expanse of well-tended, freely undulating grass dotted with a sparse collection of headstones (some large and grand, others much smaller, many lying flat) all interspersed with a rich abundance of mature trees and bushes. Over to his right, a neat path jinked its way through a dramatically topiarised group of ornamental Yews.

He peered down. Directly below him was a giant compost heap –

Ah!

He clambered to his feet –

Whoops!

– wobbling precariously at first, but then steeling his nerve, lifting his chin, puffing out his chest, holding up his arms and leaping into thin air – wildly, without inhibition –
Waaargh!
– landing on the heap, spread-eagled – with a soggy *thumph* – and collapsing into the rotting leaves and weeds and grass cuttings, guffawing lustily, a small cloud of steam ascending around him. He inhaled the heady, dank aroma of slowly rotting matter. He shoved his face right into it – he *bit* into it – groaning his delight as a million bugs sighed and creaked inside the shifting walls of the dark insect city below. He suddenly felt alive – free – unencumbered – ecstatic.

Several minutes passed. Kane lay flat on his belly – blissfully supine. Then slowly but surely his hands contracted and his fingers began to scrabble, to clutch, to *dig*. Pretty soon he was tunnelling into the heap with a sense of real gusto, each handful he ejected growing warmer and moister and denser and steamier.

The deeper he dug, the more frenzied his efforts grew. Before too much longer he was literally *clawing* at the heap – like a frenzied badger – flushed, abandoned, panting, intoxicated – a spectacular arc of muck and soil flying around him.

'Excuse me?'

Eh?

Kane paused.

'Excuse me?'

Eh?

Kane rose to his knees. Directly below him, on the ground – holding a rake and pushing a wheelbarrow – stood a gardener. Kane appraised the gardener imperiously. 'Excuse you?' he echoed haughtily, wiping an impatient arm across his dripping brow. 'But why *should* I, when you don't offend me in the slightest part?'

The gardener stared back up at Kane, nonplussed.

'Would you mind telling me what you're doing here?' he demanded.

'*Hmmn* . . .' Kane considered this question, thoughtfully. 'I would mind telling you,' he confided, 'although if you *must* know,' he peered down at himself, 'I'm kneeling – and sweating – and breathing – and *talking* . . .'

Kane lifted a muddy paw to his lips. 'In fact I'm talking to *you*. I can feel my mouth moving . . .' he dropped his hand, with a bright smile, 'but now I must dig.'

He recommenced digging.

The gardener – a wiry man in his mid-fifties – scratched nervously at his neck.

'What are you digging *for*?' he asked.

Kane stopped digging.

'I'm digging to make a hole,' he explained patiently.

'What *for*?'

'Not four,' Kane demurred, shaking his head (a shower of bugs and dirt cascading around him).

'*Huh*?'

'Not *four*. I'm not digging *four* holes. I'm only digging one. One hole will suffice. But it must be a whole hole and not just a measly *half* . . .'

'Well you're going to have to stop it,' the gardener interrupted him.

Kane considered this for a second. 'But what shall I stop it *with*?' he asked. 'And how might I stop a hole which isn't even yet dug?'

He paused for a moment before adding, with a shrug, 'Surely every hole must simply stop itself?'

'Okay. *Okay* . . .' the gardener's patience was wearing thin. 'Either you get out of that heap voluntarily or I'm calling for back-up and we'll drag you out.'

'I'm not *in* a heap,' Kane giggled, 'I'm *on* a heap.'

As he spoke his attention was briefly diverted by a slight movement near his knee. He glanced down and saw – much to his joy – that he'd uncovered a hedgehog. The tiny beast was curled up, hibernating, inside a compact, straw-lined nest. Kane drew in close to it (sticking his muddy rump into the air like a playful hound). He drew so close that his nose was only millimetres from it, so close that he could sense the fleas scuttling through its quills, the salt and grit on its skin, the tickle of its breath, even the blackberry seeds plugging the gaps in its teeth.

He sighed, enchanted, released a cacophonous fart –

Heh!

– then closed his eyes and remembered . . .

Yes

– blackberrying with his mother as a small child – reaching his tender arms, fearlessly, into those treacherous bushes, plucking gently at the plump, ripe fruits with his purple-stained fingers, pushing them greedily between his lips or gathering them together in a disparate assortment of plastic ice-cream tubs . . .

Raspberry Ripple –
Neopolitan –
Mint-Choc-Chip –

He sighed again, wistfully. He smiled. And then –

Huh?!

– he froze –

But what in God's name . . . ?

Kane's eyes flew open. He straightened himself up, traumatised –

Did I just . . . ?

'Is this your coat?'
The gardener was holding out Kane's crombie. Kane realised that he was absolutely covered in muck.
'Uh . . . yes.'
He made a pathetic attempt to slap the soil from his hands. 'And I actually had a . . . a *bag* . . . A white, polythene . . .'

The gardener scouted around him. 'What did you have in it?'

'Nothing,' Kane responded, perhaps a touch too keenly.

'Just . . . just rubbish . . .'

'It's here,' the gardener interrupted, 'I have it.'

He retrieved the bag from the foot of the heap.

'Will you . . . *uh* . . . Would you mind passing it up to me?' Kane wondered, reaching out a tentative hand.

'Why?' the gardener asked, suddenly suspicious. 'What are you planning to do with it?'

'I just want to bury the contents.'

The gardener appeared signally unimpressed by this idea.

'You can't just bury things in the compost heap,' he said.

'Or somewhere else,' Kane volunteered, obligingly, 'anywhere . . .'

'Is it a pet?'

Kane shook his head.

'Because you can't simply turn up here, without warning, and expect to bury things, willy-nilly . . .'

'It's not a pet, it's just something I found.' Kane leaned over and gently shifted a few handfuls of leaf-mould back on top of the hedgehog to shield it from the cold.

The gardener was peering inside the bag now. He scowled, exasperated. 'You can't possibly bury this here,' he said.

'Well what else am I meant to do with it?' Kane asked.

'I don't know – take it home again,' the gardener shrugged, 'donate it to Oxfam or something.'

'Donate it to *Oxfam*?' Kane snorted. 'Are you crazy?'

The gardener delivered him a straight look.

'But I can't take it home,' Kane muttered, starting to shiver as his sweat turned cold. 'It's disgusting. Couldn't I just . . .'

He pointed '. . . you know . . . drop it off somewhere? Behind a hedge? In a quiet corner?'

The gardener casually inspected the sticky nimbus of spider's webs decorating Kane's hair.

'I want you to climb down from that heap,' he announced, matter-of-factly, 'take back this coat and this bag, and then accompany me on a short walk to the front entrance gate.'

'*Fine*,' Kane grimaced. 'Have it your way . . .'

He yanked up his trousers and then set about engineering his cautious descent. He felt hollow, disconsolate.

The gardener offered him a helping hand but Kane sullenly ignored it.

'Look,' the gardener took pity on him, 'you're obviously feeling the cold . . .' he lifted the bag, helpfully, as Kane clumsily slid down –

Ow!
OW!

– '. . . so why don't you just put this thing *on*, eh?'
'And how do you suggest I do that?' Kane demanded, planting his two feet back firmly –

Thank God

– on *terra firma*.

'It's very simple,' the gardener humoured him, 'you just pull it on over your head . . .'
Kane scowled at him, incredulous, then saw – much to his surprise – that the gardener was actually holding out a freshly laundered jumper.

'I can slip the book into your coat pocket if you like,' the gardener continued, removing a book from the bag.

'Book?' Kane reached out his hand.
The gardener passed it over. Kane took it and frowned down at it. It was a non-fiction paperback entitled *The Dressing Station* by Jonathan Kaplan – a South African surgeon – which detailed, in grisly detail, Kaplan's work as a 'medical vagabond' in some of the world's most treacherous trouble-spots.

Kane opened the book up. Inside it Elen had written, 'Medical vagabond? Sound familiar?' followed by two kisses. And underneath those, in a bracket, 'Carpenter? *Nah*. Always secretly thought you had a surgeon's hands . . .'

'Is something the matter?' the gardener asked.
Kane didn't respond. The gardener gently took the book from him and handed him his jumper. 'Put this on,' he said.
Kane did as he was told.

'Now your coat . . .'
The gardener passed Kane his crombie. Again, Kane obliged him, but

as he fastened a couple of the buttons he noticed that the pink ribbon Maude had given him had gone. He glanced towards the ground and saw it lying in some tall grass close by. He bent down to retrieve it, then held it tightly, protectively, in his hand.

Once Kane was properly dressed again the gardener shoved the Kaplan book into the crombie's pocket and they slowly began the walk to the front gate together. Kane idly inspected the trees as they strolled along, the pink ribbon now looped loosely around his thumb.

'Is that an Ash?' he asked, after a minute or so's silence, indicating towards an Elm.

'Nope. We only have one Ash . . .' the gardener pointed. 'It's over there . . .'

Kane stopped.

'Could I have a closer look at it?'

The gardener frowned.

'Please?'

Kane gazed over at him, appealingly.

'You have a special interest in trees, eh?' the gardener enquired. Kane nodded. 'So how do you go about identifying it?' he wondered, heading off towards it, at speed.

'That's easy,' the gardener followed him without complaint. 'In winter, by the hard, black buds, set either side of its twigs and in late summer and autumn by its keys . . .'

'Keys?' Kane echoed.

'Yeah. Special seeds – like flat, cream-coloured tadpoles – or little skittles . . .'

'Keys?' Kane repeated. 'Why do they call them that?'

'Because in the very old days they used to resemble the actual keys that people used for their locks.'

'Key,' Kane mused, dreamily, 'kay . . .'

He shook his head. He mind turned to Peta.

'Here we are . . .'

They drew close to the tree. It was a handsome specimen – 60 or 70 foot high. The gardener patted the trunk, fondly. 'They thrive on calcium,' he said.

'Chalk . . .' Kane interjected.

'Yeah. Limestone. So they're a good all-rounder. Fast growing. Live about 150-odd years – not nearly so long as some of the old, churchyard Yews, but they produce a fine, strong wood, very tough. Great wood for hammer and axe handles, great for oars or hockey sticks. A marvellous, traditional British timber.'

Kane slowly circled the tree, inspecting the neat meshwork of ribs in its attractive grey bark. He circled the tree a second time and was almost losing heart when his eye alighted on something – something very tiny – sticking out of the trunk. A pin.

'Ready to head off yet?' the gardener asked, impatiently stamping his feet against the cold.

'Sure.'

Kane reached out his hand and extracted the pin. He held it between his fingers for a second, thoughtfully, then he removed Maude's small, pink ribbon from his thumb and attached it, with a careless smirk, to his lapel.

SEVENTEEN

The Saltings was a large, well-kept, modern bungalow set on a generous parcel of land (although built inexplicably close to the road) which projected itself – from a distance, at least – as a perfectly uncontentious and coherent whole, but which was actually – from close quarters – plainly nothing more than the sum of its well-executed parts (a series of extensions, add-ons, lean-tos, conservatories and sheds): not so much a house as a perplexing amalgam of sudden whims, capricious fancies and afterthoughts.

On pulling through the large, wrought-iron gates (left casually open) and into the stark, smoothly concreted courtyard beyond, Beede was unable to work out which piece – if any – of the visible structure might be considered 'original'.

It came as no surprise, he mused (as the car drew to a neat halt), that the property was owned by a family of builders, although he was curious to observe the unusually large number of solar energy panels on the roof and the fact that all the doors were constructed extra-wide (with neat, wooden ramps and strong guide-rails attached); leading him to the inevitable conclusion – and quite correctly, as it turned out – that either one or more of the inhabitants might be wheelchair-bound.

The short drive over to The Saltings had been (much to Beede's intense relief) both easy and uncontentious. Dory's behaviour had been good, his conversation lucid, and his motor-skills (in both senses of the word) little short of peerless.

'Did you think to phone in advance?' Beede enquired, as Dory turned off the engine, unfastened his seat-belt and gazed over towards the house.

'Uh . . . No, I didn't, actually . . .' he admitted, a tinge of regret seeping into his voice.

'Well hopefully someone'll be home,' Beede shrugged, 'I'm pretty sure I saw a light on . . .'

He opened his door and began to climb out, but as he stepped free of the vehicle, he felt a sudden, sharp, extraordinarily painful shooting sensation in his left leg, as if the very marrow from his bones was being extracted through a hole in the base of his foot. He gasped, shocked, clinging on to the door for support.

'Beede?'

Dory was staring over at him, concerned.

Beede tried to catch his breath.

'I'm fine,' he insisted. 'It's nothing, just . . .' he closed his eyes for a moment, 'just a cramp. I must've been sitting at the wrong angle . . .'

As he spoke, one of several doors leading from the property flew open and a handsome, diminutive yet generously proportioned woman (in late middle age) with a mop of tightly permed, heavily gelled, dyed-black hair came tripping down the ramp towards them. She was sporting a sumptuous, fuchsia-pink velour tracksuit, a pair of purple-feather stiletto-heeled slippers and a saucy apron emblazoned with the cartoon-style bikini-clad form of a much younger female.

Just as she was stepping down on to the concrete, however, a large, scruffy van pulled into the courtyard – swerving sharply to avoid Dory's Rover – and had barely drawn to a stand-still before a small, intensely genial, wide-faced man had jumped out from the driver's side. Beede could immediately tell that the pair were related – mother and son, perhaps.

'I thought you was the meat-man!' the woman called over to Beede, placing her hands on to her hips and appraising him intently. 'But you *ain't* the bloomin' meat-man, *are* ya?'

'Uh . . . no . . . Sorry, we . . .'

Beede turned to Dory to furnish an explanation.

'We're actually looking for a Mr Spivey, a Mr *Garry* Spivey,' Dory said.

'That'll be me, then, Guv,' Garry stepped up to him, holding out his hand.

'You'll have to excuse my old mum,' he confided (loud enough to be clearly overhead by everyone). 'She has the most *ridiculous* crush on our local butcher . . .'

'*Oi!*' she bellowed. 'Less of that!'

'Like a big, teenage *girl*, she is,' Garry expanded, with a gentle grin. 'Leave her alone for twenty minutes an' the next thing you know she'll've bought half a cow.'

'It weren't a cow!' his mother clucked, outraged. 'It was a soddin' *pig*, an' you didn't need askin' twice to polish those lovely chops off, did ya?'

Garry smirked, unyielding.

'Well I'm very pleased to meet you both,' Isidore shook Garry's hand (plainly slightly taken aback by this high-octane familial exchange). 'My name is Isidore, and this is my friend . . .'

'We've met before, I reckon,' Garry interrupted him, nodding towards Beede.

'Yes. I think I knew your father,' Beede said. 'Alisdair Spivey? We worked together on Dr Wilk's Hall, when they turned it into the Ashford Museum. He was one of the most conscientious builders I ever met. His restoration work was second to none . . .'

'That's Dad, all right,' Garry grinned, 'a perfectionist to the bone.'

The black-haired woman snorted (as if she'd suffered herself at the hands of A. Spivey's perfectionism). 'Got that from 'is nanna, he did,' she interjected. 'That cheeky, old mare'd send back the scones at the Savoy, she would.'

Garry smiled at his mother, nodding fondly, then returned his full attention to Isidore. 'So what can I do for you?' he wondered.

'Well it's probably more a question of . . .' Dory opened the Rover's back door and reached inside. He withdrew holding a traumatised Michelle. The spaniel was shaking violently and its hind-quarters were – not untypically – drenched in urine.

Dory held it out, fastidiously, so as not to get any mess on his clothes. A short, stunned silence followed, and then –

'Bloody *hell*, Mum, would you feast your eyes on *that* . . . ?' Garry Spivey exclaimed, but his words were completely obliterated by a hysterical screech from his mother, who came running around the car (the heels of her slippers pounding out a rousing flamenco on the concrete), her arms outstretched, wailing like the chief mourner at a funeral.

'It's my *Molly!* Oh my *God!* I don't *believe* it! It's my beautiful Molly! My gorgeous, beautiful Molly-Dolly!'

She grabbed the dog from Dory's grap and pressed her, violently, against her expansive bosom. 'Don't just stand there gawpin', Gaz,' she squawked, 'run an' fetch *Nan*, double-quick!'

Garry didn't need asking twice, he dashed into the house.

'Oh my dear, sweet Lord!' Mrs Spivey crooned. 'I don't *believe* it!

Nanna's little baby come home at last. How's my little Molly, eh? How's my little angel been doin' all the while?'

As she spoke, Mrs Spivey rained a million passionate kisses down on to the spaniel's domed crown. The spaniel yawned, nervously.

Dory (visibly alarmed by this unstopped swell of feminine emotion), reached into the car to remove the large, cardboard box of Michelle's possessions.

'Oh my God!' Mrs Spivey screamed. 'He's got your little *cart*, Molly! Just look at that!'

Mrs Spivey showed the dog its cart.

Beede noticed – with some alarm – that Michelle was actually urinating again. A steady stream of warm, yellow liquid ran down Mrs Spivey's plastic apron, cascaded off her veloured knees and finished up in the fluff of her slippers.

'Uh . . . I think she might be . . .' Beede started.

'I know,' Mrs Spivey cooed, 'but I don't give a *hoot*, do I, my dear-love? She's home, ain't she? My little baby-cuddles is *home*, an' that's all I care about.'

Garry re-emerged from the house, pushing what Beede initially took to be a severely disabled child, but what was actually (he realised, on closer inspection) an extremely tiny, frail and elderly woman propped up in a wheelchair. He carefully manoeuvred her across the courtyard, around the car and drew her to a firm halt in front of his mother.

The woman – Nanna Spivey – was so old that she had hardly any teeth or skin or hair. She looked like a fractious newt or a newly born kitten. The veins in her temples and on her hands were the same shade of blue as willow-pattern china.

'*Look*, Nanna, *look!* See what I've got here!' Mrs Spivey exclaimed, holding out the spaniel.

Nanna Spivey didn't look. In fact she barely seemed to apprehend that she was actually being spoken to. She stared at the ground, her chin hanging down on to her chest, her head wobbling around as if she had no functioning muscles in her neck or throat.

'*Wot's gowin' awwn?*' she finally croaked.

'Nanna,' Garry gently intervened. 'Up here, *look* . . .'

He lifted Nanna's chin and supported it with his fingers.

Nanna gazed up towards the dog, blankly.

'*Wot's gowin' awwn?*' she repeated.

'It's little *Molly*, you silly mare!' Mrs Spivey exclaimed. 'It's your lovely Molly come back home again!'

Nanna Spivey gazed at the dog, vaguely, no sign of recognition in her dun-coloured eyes.

Garry smiled over at Isidore. 'She's 102 years old,' he said, 'so she works on a slightly different time-scale to the rest of us.'

He turned to his mother. 'Why not put Molly on Nanna's lap?' he suggested.

Mrs Spivey leaned forward and gently placed the dripping spaniel on to Nanna Spivey's wasted thighs. Nanna Spivey leapt back, as if alarmed, then looked down at the dog, blinking and confused.

'I'm afraid she might be a little *wet* . . .' Isidore began explaining.

'*Shhhh!*' Mrs Spivey raised a preremptory hand. 'She's fine. Let's just wait and see what Nanna *does*, shall we?'

They all stared at Nanna. Nanna stared down at the dog.

The dog sat patiently on Nanna's lap, staring, dazedly, into the middle distance.

Then suddenly, without warning, the old woman gasped. Her arms stiffened. She looked up towards her granddaughter, blinking.

'That's your lovely *Molly*, Nanna, come home again, see?' Mrs Spivey whispered softly. 'That's your little baby Molly come back home.'

The old woman's mouth slowly fell open and a tiny, high-pitched whine emerged from her throat.

Garry crouched down in front of her.

'D'you want me to take her back again, Nan?' he asked softly. 'Is she a bit too much weight for those poor, old legs of yours?'

Several huge tears began rolling down the old woman's cheeks. Her nose was running freely. She shivered, uncontrollably, while the dog (possibly for the first time in Dory's experience of her) appeared perfectly calm and at its ease.

Garry reached out to take the dog, but Nanna's arms jerked protectively around it.

'My beautiful Molly!' she rasped, 'come home to her Nanna! It's my beautiful Molly come home!'

Mrs Spivey quickly turned away, overcome with emotion. Garry gently stroked the top of the old woman's hand.

'That's right, Nanna. It's your Molly. She's home. This kind gentleman brought her back for ya. Would you like to thank him, Nanna? Say thank you? D'you think that might be a nice idea?'

Nanna peered over towards the registration plates on Garry's van. 'Thank you.' Her voice was barely audible, just a hoarse whisper. 'You brought me my Molly back, Gawd bless ya.'

'It's a pleasure,' Isidore murmured, gazing over towards the registration plates himself, 'an absolute pleasure.'

Mrs Spivey turned back around again (having finally regained some control over the powerful ebb and flow of her emotions). She dabbed at her eyes with her sleeve. 'You've made an old woman very happy,' she sniffed.

'An' Nanna's pretty, bloody chuffed, too, eh, Mum?' Garry quipped.

Mrs Spivey leaned forward and delivered Garry a playful slap (he hollered, good-naturedly) then stationed herself, resignedly, behind Nanna's chair. 'I suppose I'd better take the old love back indoors again before she catches her death out here.'

Isidore nodded (obviously relieved at the thought of Nanna's departure). 'Bye then, Nanna,' he said.

'*Wot's gowin' awwn?*' Nanna demanded, gazing down at the dog.

'Molly's done a little widdle, Nanna,' Mrs Spivey murmured gently, beginning to manoeuvre Nanna away from the group, 'but we'll soon clear it up, eh?'

As she steered Nanna back towards the house she delivered Beede a covert wink over her fuchsia-pink shoulder. Beede smiled, sympathetically (naturally presuming that some kind of tiny midge – or random speck of dirt – had flown into the poor woman's eye).

'You should come inside yourselves,' Garry exclaimed, obviously keen for the celebrations to continue, 'an' we can discuss the reward over a nice, hot cuppa . . .'

Isidore glanced – rather fearfully – in the general direction of the retreating pair. 'We should probably head off,' he said, 'and I don't want any reward. I'm just happy that Michelle . . .' he faltered, 'I mean Moll . . .'

He frowned '. . . Moll . . .' He shook his head, confused.

As if sensing a potential problem, Beede rapidly hobbled around the car to join the two of them. 'I see you've got an impressive collection of solar panels on your roof, there, Garry,' he observed (providing Dory with a brief reprieve in which to try and gather his thoughts together).

'That's my passion,' Garry smiled, somewhat ruefully. 'I make those myself.'

'Really?' Beede was intrigued.

'Yeah. I did a course on environmental engineerin' with the OU before Dad passed. I really got into it. When I'm not on the job I spend every wakin' moment locked up in my workshop tinkerin' away on some crazy project or other . . .'

'And do you manage to integrate what you learned into your day-to-day building practice at all?' Beede wondered.

'Chance'd be a fine thing,' Garry chuckled.

'Not too many forward-thinkers on the environmental ticket in the Ashford area, eh?' Beede mused.

'Ten, twenty years down the line an' it'll probably all be different,' Garry reasoned. 'But these things take a while to percolate . . .' he sighed, 'I only hope it ain't too late by then.'

Beede nodded, soberly.

After a brief pause, Garry turned back to Isidore again. 'So I've been dyin' to ask ya,' he confided, 'how'd you actually find her?'

'Pardon?'

Isidore's attention was momentarily distracted by the distant wail of a fire engine siren.

'Molly,' Garry persisted. 'How'd you . . . ?'

'*Oh*. Uh . . . She just turned up,' Isidore explained, 'at my home . . .'

'What?' Garry seemed baffled. 'Under her own steam?'

'Good *God*, no . . .' Isidore scoffed at the very idea.

'Because she initially went missin' from my van,' Garry expanded. 'Someone prised open the window . . .'

'Well it's a rather complicated story,' Isidore confessed, 'but the long and the short of it is that I've had a certain Harvey Broad doing some renovation work on my home . . .'

'Oh yeah?' Garry frowned. 'So how's that pannin' out?'

'I sacked him this morning.'

'Ah.'

Garry didn't seem especially shocked by this news.

'Anyhow, I think his son – Lester – must've brought the dog around to begin with, and then my young son – Fleet – grew very attached to the poor creature . . .'

'Hang on,' Garry interrupted. 'So you're sayin' you think *Lester* might've stole the dog?'

'Or Harvey, and then entrusted it to Lester to look after . . .'

'Harvey bloody *Broad*,' Garry growled, 'I should've bloomin' *known*.'

'I saw the poster this morning,' Isidore continued, 'and then the coin suddenly dropped.'

He paused.

'Although I suppose there's no actual *proof* . . .'

'Harvey bloody *Broad*,' Garry repeated, obviously furious. 'When my mum finds out she'll do her bloomin' *nut* . . .'

'If it's any consolation,' Isidore added, 'shortly after I sacked him this morning, the scaffolding on the front of the house collapsed and almost wrote off his Toyota . . .'

'You know what the worst part is?' Garry demanded (not mollified in the slightest by the Toyota anecdote).

Isidore shook his head.

'The worst part is that he's a good builder. When he puts in the effort, he's a solid builder. He actually started off in an apprenticeship wiv' my dad. In fact when I was a kid I just loved the fella. He was like the older brother I never had,' Garry shrugged. 'But then the rot gradually set in. He just got bored of *tryin'*, somehow. It reached the point that he'd rather spend twice the amount of effort *avoidin'* a job . . .'

'You're not telling me anything that I'm not already painfully aware of,' Dory grimaced.

'I don't suppose,' Beede suddenly interjected, half-turning towards Isidore, 'now Harvey's out of the picture, Garry's got his dog back and you're in desperate need of a new contractor . . .'

Garry and Isidore stared at each other, slightly startled (like two women wearing identical dresses at a cocktail party).

'Truth is,' Garry volunteered, 'I've been cuttin' back on my work commitments in recent months in the hope of doin' some travellin' abroad . . .'

'That's absolutely *fine*,' Dory insisted, keen not to press the matter. 'Don't give it a second thought . . .'

'. . . But now that I've *got* the time set aside,' Garry continued, wryly, 'I don't really have the first clue where I wanna go or what the hell I plan to do wiv' myself when I actually *get* there,' he grinned. 'Pathetic, ain't it? So if you're keen on the idea, then I'd be more than happy to take a look at the job . . .'

'What's that word the Arabs use to describe situations like this?' Beede interjected (delighted by his own involvement in this happy scenario). '*Kismet*?'

Garry inspected his watch. 'I'll just grab a sandwich, change my jacket . . .' he gently fingered the lining of his leather coat, 'an' then head straight on over. Give you a quick quote. Can't say better than that now, can I?'

Beede turned to the German, smiling, but was surprised to notice that Dory didn't seem quite as enthralled by these developments as he might've expected. He appeared jittery and distracted.

'Just scribble down your address for me . . .' Garry pulled a pencil from behind his ear.

'Sure . . .' Dory suddenly snapped to attention. 'Let me . . .'

He felt around inside his jacket pocket for a scrap of paper, eventually locating a scrunched-up piece of packaging, unfolding it and turning it over to write on the back.

Beede's smile evaporated.

Garry passed Dory the pencil.

'Bell,' Beede murmured quietly, almost to himself.

'Come again?' Garry interjected.

'Bell,' Beede repeated, 'it's a fascinating noun with virtually no relatives in the European languages . . .'

He watched closely as Dory carefully printed out his address.

'. . . Although apparently there was an ancient verb in Old English,' he continued, raising a hand to his shoulder and massaging it, clumsily, 'related to the baying call made by a hound or . . . or a stag . . .' Beede paused, his face contorting, 'of which . . . of which "bellow",' he finally concluded, hoarsely, 'is a direct descendant.'

'Well I never!' Garry exclaimed (without the slightest idea as to what Beede was banging on about).

Dory completed the address and handed it over. Then he turned to Beede with a cheerful smile. 'So, ready to head off, now?' he wondered.

EIGHTEEN

Kane took out his kays –

KEYS, Goddammit!

(He shook his head –

STOP this now!
ENOUGH!!)

– inserted them into the lock, then paused for a second and stared down, frowning, at his outstretched hands –

Surgeon's hands?

He snorted, derisively –

Nah . . .

– although they were certainly *attractive* hands (tapering hands, rather graceful). They were strong hands –

No bones about it –

But *surgeon's* hands?!

Is she crazy?

He removed the book Elen had given him from his coat pocket and carefully inspected it. It looked like a fascinating book – gory, visceral, thoughtful, challenging – a worthwhile book –

Worthwhile?!

Kane shook his head, grimacing, then quickly re-read the synopsis on the inside cover, his eye halting, irresistibly, on the words 'medical vagabond'. He turned to Elen's dedication and gazed at it, blankly, then sighed, slapped the book shut and roughly shoved it back into his coat pocket. He unlocked the door and pushed it open.

'*Gaffar?*' he yelled, stepping into the hallway. 'You home yet?' There was a letter lying on the mat. He picked it up. There was no name or address on it –

Junk

'*Gaffar?*' he yelled, slamming the door shut and tearing the letter open. 'You back?'

Nothing

He peered towards Beede's flat. The door was slightly ajar. He walked over to it. 'Beede?'
He knocked.

Nothing

He removed the contents from the envelope. Inside it was a folded-up piece of paper, and when he unfurled it, a car key dropped into his hand –

Huh?!

'Beede?'
He pushed the door open, still staring at the key. He flattened the paper it'd been folded up in and turned it over –

Nothing
Although . . .

He frowned, looking closer . . .

Isn't there something . . . ?

A vague . . . ?
A kind of . . . ?

He moved over towards the window to try and inspect the paper in a better light, but as he moved it gradually began to dawn on him that there was something very different, something very . . .

Wrong

He glanced around him –

JEESUS!

His jaw dropped. The room looked like some kind of explosive device had recently gone off in it.
'Beede?'
He suddenly had a vision of his father lying dead (or injured) in another room. He panicked – *'Beede?'* – and ran into the kitchen, then the bedroom –
'Dad?'
The bedroom was dark. The bed was a mess. He stared, uneasily, at the rumpled counterpane.
'Dad?'
He ran into the bathroom. The floor was soaking. And there were tiny traces of . . .
He peered at the walls –

What?
Blood?!

Kane returned to the living-room and gazed around him, horrified –

Is anything . . . ?
Was he . . . ?

He scowled –

Could this conceivably be . . . ?

He ran to the door –
'GAFFAR!'
– then sprinted upstairs.

His own flat looked exactly the same as when he'd left it that morning. He stood in the middle of his sitting-room for a moment, struggling to catch his breath, then promptly headed off to find his stash. He found it, undisturbed, and shoved it – all of it – into his coat pockets before sprinting back downstairs again and standing in the open doorway to Beede's flat, his eyes ransacking the room for clues – evidence – ideas – *anything* . . .

Kane suddenly froze –

Oh my . . .

– then he slowly began moving – as if hypnotised – towards the sofa. Propped up, carelessly – lop-sidedly – against the arm, was a cross; a large, beautifully carved wooden cross –

Can that . . . ?
Is that . . . ?

He knelt down to inspect it, his eyes lingering (to begin with) on the terrible, naive lettering in the mid-section before moving, ineluctably, to the marvellous profusion of exquisitely carved wild roses on the outer reaches.

Kane gazed at the cross, in silence, for several minutes. 'But why . . . ?' he finally murmured, scratching his head, confused.

He peered around the room again –

Where's the fucking cat?

He glanced up at the light-fitment –

Is that broken, too?

– then became aware, once more, of the letter in his hand. The key –

Peta . . .

He sprang to his feet and walked over to the window. Outside he saw The Blonde (parked – rather haphazardly – over by the front gate) and sitting neatly – unobtrusively – in The Blonde's habitual parking space? A mysterious, black Lada with darkened windows –

Now what did she call it again?

Kane frowned –

The Commissar?

He stared down at the key. He inspected the envelope –

Nope

– then he held the plain piece of paper back up to the light.
When he looked at it carefully, at a particular angle, he was sure he could see . . .
He turned and strode over to the mess of books, furniture and papers against the opposite wall. He fell to his knees, took a pinch of soil from an up-ended plantpot and applied it, very gently, to a small section of the paper. As he rubbed, a tiny line of letters and digits came into relief. Kane walked back to the window and held the paper up to the light again –

II Corinthians XII. IX

?!

He stared around the room –

Bible?

– then began hunting through the debris –

Hopeless

His mind turned to Kelly (waving at him from her scooter – Bible clutched in her hand – a couple of hours earlier). He grabbed his phone and dialled her number –

No answer

As it rang, he stared over at the cross again, with a shudder. Kelly's voicemail clicked in. He cut it off and texted her instead:

*2 Corinthians 12.9
K.*

A couple of minutes later – on his way out to the car – he quickly checked his reflection in the hallway mirror, then paused, shocked, and drew in closer. He looked odd – faded, haggard, *spooked* – as if he'd just seen a ghost. Or perhaps – even worse than that –

Much worse –
Much scarier . . .

– as if he was actually the ghost *himself* (a transient ghoul, a fugitive spectre), drifting – aimless and confused – through a bold, clearly defined world of private jokes, cast-iron alibis and irrefutable facts.

Dory was speaking to him, but Beede couldn't actually focus on what he was saying because –

Pain

– it had recently begun to rain and the sound of the paindrops –

Raindrops

– hitting the Rover's roof had generated this strange counter-conversation inside his head –

> A Master of Art is not worth a fart,
> Except he be in schools,
> A batchelour of Law, is not worth a straw . . .

The sound of the pain –

Rain

– was soon eclipsed by the wailing siren of a fire engine. They were turning off the A2042 (on to the steeply curving slip road beyond) when the engine drew abreast of them, its blue light flashing. Dory rapidly slowed down and allowed it to pass. He muttered something, but Beede didn't quite catch it because he was gazing, dazedly, out of the window, where his eye was momentarily arrested by a pretty, young, blonde girl who was methodically removing the plastic collars from the trees and the bushes at the top of the embankment.

The girl straightened up as the fire engine passed and their eyes made brief contact. He blinked. She blinked. He was certain that he'd seen her before, but he couldn't say where, exactly. He also knew (in that same moment) that –

> A Master of Art is not worth . . .

– her father was in recovery from breast cancer, that her mother was going to be very angry indeed –

Too angry,
Silly moo . . .

– about the dent in the car, that she had an irrational fear of small spaces, that she hated the taste of uncooked tomatoes (but virtually lived on ketchup), that she fervently regretted not taking A-level Japanese (or Spanish, or Arabic), that when she was thirty-two she would develop diabetes during her second pregnancy, that this child would subsequently inherit a slight heart-murmur (from her grandfather on her mother's side), that her first child (a daughter), would become a leading expert in the field of post-traumatic stress, that the boy with the whispering heart would become a keyboard player in an unsuccessful pop band, but would then write a tune (in his late forties) – a short jingle – which would eventually be adopted to spearhead a ten-year campaign to sell the world's most successful brand of sugar-free, fat-free, dairy-free chocolate . . .

Dory accelerated off again. He quickly built up speed.

. . . But most important of all, Beede saw that this girl – this damp, diligent, blonde girl with her savagely pinned-back curly hair – would loyally support her husband through medical school, and that when he eventually graduated they would travel to Uganda together (and do great work there), then on to the Congo, then on to the Sudan – to Darfur – where he would soon become embroiled in a tragic, sexual liaison with a talented engineer called Eva Jane Bartlett (who had helped to design, build and fund a small hospital he was working at), that he would be shot – and fatally wounded – by her estranged husband, a famous local brigand, and that . . .

Isidore suddenly slammed his foot down.
Beede heard a loud squeal of tyres, then felt a nasty, searing pain across his shoulder –

Seat-belt

– as the car jolted to a sharp halt.

Beede turned to stare at Dory. Dory was gazing into the road wearing a look of mute astonishment. Beede turned to look into the road himself –

Good God!

Standing there, in majestic profile (its tail covering a full two-thirds of the total width of the tarmac): a magnificent peacock –

What?!

Dory honked his horn, glancing, terrified, into his rearview mirror – 'I have a bad feeling about this . . .' he was muttering, unfastening his seat-belt, 'a really strong sense of *déjà* . . .'
The bird lifted its beak and stared haughtily towards the car, then it

swung around, and in one, sublime movement it lifted its tail and fanned it out.

Beede's mouth fell open. Dory began to scrabble (sightlessly) at his door handle.

'No, *wait*. Let me . . .'

Beede unfastened his own seat-belt and leapt from the car. He hobbled towards the bird. The blare of the fire engine was still wailing in his ears ('Must be the strange acoustics,' he reasoned, 'on this part of the road . . .').

'Okay, big fella,' he murmured, 'get out of the way now. Quick-smart . . .'

The bird turned to face him, shaking out its feathers. Through Beede's rain-splattered lenses the peacock was a gorgeous, blue-green blur, a shimmering, technicolour waterfall, a faultless jewel. It cocked its crested head and eyed him, archly.

'You're going to end up as cat food if you don't move pretty smartly . . .'

Beede tried to hustle the bird backwards, towards the grass verge. The peacock immediately took offence. It squawked, furiously, then turned, panicked, to reveal a slightly bare (and somewhat dingy) back-end, supported by pair of surprisingly long and muscular legs.

Beede shoo'd him swiftly forward, but as he moved he felt something crunching under the soles of his shoes. He glanced down –

What is that?

Grit?
No –
Seed . . . ?
Tiny ears of . . . ?

In ten seconds, at best, the indignant bird was safely stationed on the embankment.

'You'd better drive off,' Beede yelled, waving Dory onwards, 'I'll . . .'

That moment, a second fire engine came careering around the bend, its siren blaring, and smashed straight into the back of Dory's Rover.

Dory hadn't yet refastened his seat-belt. As the engine made contact he flew forward – wearing a look of slight bewilderment – into the steering wheel, then up, and over, and into the front windscreen. The windscreen cracked and then Dory slumped back.

But that wasn't the end of it. Because he'd barely touched the seat again before another vehicle – a car – shunted into the back of the fire engine, then another car behind that, then a van, then another car, then another van, and each time a new vehicle made contact, this cruel, metal snake, this ravenous, steel gecko devoured a few extra metres of the road.

Beede glanced down. The bird had turned on its heel and had run for cover. Only a single, bright feather remained, pinned under his foot. Beede bent down to grab it (because what could he . . . ? There was nothing . . . Because he couldn't . . .).

As he bent over he felt a heavy weight (a *familiar* weight) on his shoulder, and calmly realised – in that instant – that he probably wasn't going to be able to straighten back up.

The small courtyard was deserted. No geese – no turkeys – no dogs – no armed, hatchet-faced, Northumbrian housemaids in bizarre, wooden clogs.

Kane parked The Commissar and sat quietly for a while (gently strumming his fingers against the dash), then he clambered out and took a quick walk around. The farm machinery was gone. He tried the doors on a couple of the barns –

Locked

– then walked over to the cottage. The curtains had been taken down. He peered inside. All the furniture had been removed.

He stared up at the tiles on the roof. He slowly shook his head, then reached into his pocket and took out his cigarettes. He propped one between his lips and then tried to find his lighter, but couldn't.

It had started to rain. He returned to the car and climbed back inside it, then slowly and methodically emptied his pockets. He removed ten or fifteen packets of tablets, his phone, Elen's book, the rolled-up brown envelope that Beede had left earlier. He threw each object – one by one – on to the passenger seat. Still, no lighter.

He peered around the interior of The Commissar. He opened the dash –

Registration documents

– then felt inside all the side pouches and under the seats.

Kane snorted with frustration, clambered out of the car and went to look in the boot. He opened it up –

Please –
Not a . . .

– but the boot was empty, except for a plastic bag crammed full of rubbish, its handles neatly tied together.

Kane stared at the bag. He lifted it out. He looked around for a trashcan. There was an old metal bin in the far corner of the farm-yard, its lid weighed down with a rock. He carried the bag over there. He removed the rock and then the lid. The bin was empty. He prepared to toss the bag into it, but then something suddenly struck him and he thought better of it. He carried the bag back over to the car, climbed inside, untied the knot, opened it up and slowly sifted through the contents.

Inside the bag there were sweet wrappers, biscuit wrappers, orange peel, a couple of scrunched-up old newspapers, five empty cigar boxes, a clutch of receipts (for newspapers, sweets, cigars), several empty coffee cups, about twenty used scratchcards –

What?

Kane shook his head, disapprovingly.

Approximately half-way down he struck gold –

Yes!

A lighter – an old *bic*. He grabbed it and struck it –

Nothing

He struck it again and a tiny flame emerged. He pushed his smoke between his lips and struck it for a third time –

Nothing

– then a fourth. This time it sparked and he shoved his cigarette into it, puffing maniacally –

Yes . . .
Yes . . .
No

Balls!

    Kane tossed the lighter aside and recommenced his search. He winced as his hand made unwitting contact with a couple of old apple cores, then delved in still deeper –

Crisp packet
Crisp packet
Peanuts
Peanut
Crisp packet

– pulling out what he took to be a card of matches –

Yes!

– only to realise that it was actually two further scratchcards folded up together. He hissed under his breath, then noticed – with some surprise – that one of these two £5 cards hadn't even been scratched yet. He snorted, threw them back into the bag and felt around some more until his hands discovered –

Wonder of wonders!

– another lighter. He yanked it out so enthusiastically that he tipped the bag over –

Fuck!

– and almost half of its contents fell on to his lap –

Urgh!

  He struck the lighter –

Nothing

He struck it again –

Yes!

– and shoved his cigarette – inhaling frantically – into the puny flame. The cigarette took –

Thank God

  Kane closed his eyes and savoured it for a moment, then opened them up, crammed all the rubbish back into the bag, retied the handles, leapt out of the car, ran over to the dustbin and tossed it in. He replaced the lid. He replaced the rock –

There

– then returned to the car.
  He sat in his seat, frowning, thinking, puffing on his cigarette. Every so often he inspected his hands –

Surgeon's hands?
Eh?!
Fuck off!

When the cigarette was almost done he stubbed it out and grabbed his phone. He switched it on –

174 messages

He quickly turned it off again. He cast the phone aside. He leaned over and picked up Beede's brown envelope. He opened it. He pulled out the batch of photocopied papers. He stared at them, frowning. He turned to a random page and squinted at the badly reproduced script. His frown deepened. He turned to another page, then another, then another.

Kane closed his eyes, leaned forward and rested his forehead on the steering wheel, then he pulled himself together, tossed the papers on to the passenger seat, started up the engine and performed a careful three-point turn. He drove out of Peta's smallholding, back on to Barnfield, on to Ox Lane, on to Silver Hill and the Ashford Road. As he drove, a police car, an ambulance and two fire engines overtook him. Then the traffic slowed down. Then it stopped.

NINETEEN

Kelly was sitting at a bus-stop on a virtually grid-locked Malcolm Sargent Road, gazing poignantly at her phone.

'Enjoyin' the view, Kell?' a cheery voice enquired from a short distance behind her.

She didn't even look over.

'Fuck off,' she snapped, 'for the *thousandth* bloomin' time, just *Fuck. Right. Off.*'

'Well that ain't a very Christian way to react,' Garry exclaimed, shocked.

'*Huh?*'

Kelly's head spun around.

The jovial builder was removing a Missing Dog poster from a nearby lamp-post.

Kelly almost fell from her seat. 'We was just comin' ta find ya, Gaz,' she tried to struggle up (but couldn't quite manage it), 'then the damn scooter ran out of juice an' we got stuck here. Gaffar's meant ta be pushin' it to the nearest garage, but I reckon he must've done a *bunk* or somethin'. He's been gone over an hour . . .'

'Everythin's totally grid-locked,' Garry explained. 'I was meant to be headin' over to Cedar Wood but I couldn't get through, so I nipped round here instead . . .' he shrugged, 'an' *now* look at it – bumper to bloody bumper.'

'You've changed your coat,' Kelly observed, surprised.

'Uh . . . yeah.'

Garry's cheeks flushed.

'That sports jacket looks good on ya,' Kelly mused, 'I always said you scrubbed up all right . . .'

'I just got my dog back, as it happens,' Garry interrupted, keen to change the subject.

'Did ya?'

'Nan's over the moon,' he grinned.

'*Aw*,' Kelly cooed, 'I always *loved* your old nanna . . .'

She paused. 'I always wished she was *my* nanna . . .' she paused again. 'Although you can keep the dog, mate. That dog is fuckin' *rank* . . .'

Garry looked hurt.

Kelly quickly turned away. 'These two arseholes in a car was really givin' me some gyp earlier,' she muttered (as if hoping to justify her inexcusable brashness). 'I tried to turn the other cheek an' all that, but I ain't too good at it yet . . .' she grimaced. 'In truth, Gaz, I don't know if I'm really cut out for all this Christian palaver.'

'Well I suppose Christians've always had a history of persecution, Kell,' Garry volunteered helpfully.

'Ya reckon?'

'Sure. Didn't you ever see *Gladiator*?'

'Yeah.' Kelly nodded, 'I had the hots for Joaquin Phoenix.'

'Well Russell Crowe was actually the Christian in that.'

'Russell Crowe was?'

'Absolutely.'

Kelly gave this some consideration. 'So what about you, Gaz?'

'What about me?'

'Are you a Christian?'

'Uh . . .' Gaz shrugged, 'I ain't much of a church-goer, Kell, but I like to think I'm a Christian man – by nature – if that amounts to anythin' . . .' he paused. 'You know, Love thy neighbour . . . Do unto others *etcetera* . . .'

They stared at each other.

'If you don't mind my sayin',' Garry confided, 'you're lookin' a little the worse for wear.'

'Paul died,' Kelly murmured poignantly, 'I've just been sittin' here, all on my tod, tryin'a get it straight in my head, like.'

Garry came to sit down next to her. 'I was real sorry when I found out, Kell,' he murmured, lacing his hands together and staring off, morosely, into the traffic. 'I had a lot of time for that boy. I mean Jase an' Linda could happily go *hang*,' he shrugged, 'but you an' Paul, well, that was an entirely different matter . . .'

'I weren't there for him, Gaz,' Kelly lowered her head, ashamed, 'none of us were.'

'Oi!' Garry gently reprimanded her. 'You did what you could, Kell. You had your own shit to deal with, remember?'

Kelly didn't respond.

He reached out and placed a comforting arm around her shoulders. 'Paul always took everythin' so much to heart,' he murmured. 'He was such a sensitive little bugger. Not the sharpest knife in the drawer – not by any means – but he weren't stupid, neither. He just felt things more deeply than your average bloke, an' the only way he thought he could cope was to blank it all out . . .'

Kelly nodded. A single tear dropped on to her lap.

They were quiet for a while.

'So who told ya?' Kelly finally asked. 'About Paul, I mean?'

'One of the nurses rang.'

Kelly frowned. She pulled away slightly. Garry dropped his arm, circumspectly.

'*Which* nurses?'

'From the hospital in Readin',' he elucidated. 'They were a terrific bunch. Nothin' was too much trouble for that lot . . .'

'So you went up to visit?' Kelly demanded.

'Sure. Every few weeks,' he shrugged. 'I've got an old school pal in Chertsey so it weren't no big deal.'

Kelly stared up at him, intently. 'You're solid gold, you are, Gaz,' she announced.

Garry looked away, embarrassed. Kelly sniffed and then dabbed at her nose with the back of her hand.

'Maybe you should come an' sit in the Dodge for a while,' Garry suggested. 'The heatin' ain't up to much but it's cold as a witch's tit out here.'

'Nah. I'm fine,' Kelly insisted, 'I don't wanna hold you up.'

'You *ain't* holdin' me up,' Garry grinned, exasperated. 'In case you haven't noticed, I'm stuck in a 10-mile fuckin' *traffic* jam, you silly mare.'

Kelly shot him a sharp look, then immediately relented, and held out her hand. 'Just like old times, eh?' she muttered as he pulled her up.

They staggered over to the Dodge together. It took several minutes to manoeuvre her inside.

Once she was settled, Garry turned on the engine and switched the heating up.

Kelly cleared her throat. 'There's somethin' I gotta tell ya,' she confided, 'now I've turned over a new leaf an' all that . . .'

'Oh yeah?'

Garry was trying to hunt down a spare blanket in the back.

'Remember that bloody nose I got?'

'Yup.'

'Well it weren't actually *blood*, as it happens. It was half a tin of tomato soup.'

Garry stopped his search, shocked. 'Are you serious?'

'Straight up. I was just a stupid, little skank, Gaz. I only did it to try'n grab your attention. '

'But why, Kell?' Garry asked, saddened. 'You already had my attention, so far as I can recall.'

'I guess I just wanted more of it,' Kelly shrugged.

Garry slowly sat back down again. 'Well I truly regret givin' that kid a sound thrashin' now,' he murmured.

Kelly's eyes widened. '*No way!*'

Garry maintained his aggrieved air for a couple of seconds longer, then chortled, delightedly, at her shocked expression.

'Oh come *on*. That's hardly my style, Kell!' he snorted.

'You runty *bastard*,' she punched him on the shoulder.

Her phone suddenly bleeped.

'Text,' she said, grabbing hold of it. She accessed her menu, delighted. 'This weren't even *workin'* five minutes ago . . .'

Garry rubbed his arm where she'd hit him. 'You pack a mean punch,' he said, 'for such a skinny scrap.'

'It's from Kane,' Kelly mused, still inspecting her phone, 'an' it says . . .' she frowned, 'it says *2 Corinthians 12.9*.'

She glanced up, confused. 'So what the hell's *that* s'posed ta mean?'

Garry glanced over at her phone. 'I dunno. It's a Biblical quote, I guess . . .'

'Where's my Bible, Gaz?' Kelly demanded.

'It's in the glove compartment . . .'

Garry pointed. Kelly leaned forward, with difficulty, to try and pull it open, but the lock was jammed, and she couldn't get sufficient purchase to wrench it loose.

'It won't . . .'

Garry leaned across Kelly's lap and yanked it open himself, but as he leaned, the pencil behind his ear slipped out and fell down between her knees.

'Your pencil, Gaz,' she muttered.

'Oh.' Garry straightened up, gazing down at her bare thighs, startled.

'*Ouch*,' Kelly squeaked, wriggling. 'It's fallen in between . . .'

She tried to retrieve it.

'*Ouch*,' she repeated, 'it's pokin' into my . . .'

She placed her hands either side of her legs and lifted her bottom into the air. The pencil dropped down on to the seat below.

'Would you mind just . . . ?' Kelly asked.

Garry tentatively slipped his hand underneath her and grabbed for the pencil, but before he could remove it, Kelly had sat back down again.

'*Hmmn*. Lovely warm knuckles,' she mused.

Garry rapidly yanked his hand out, horrified.

'Well I bet that's about as much excitement as your pencil's seen in a while,' she sniggered.

Garry didn't respond, he just leaned over and grabbed her Bible from the glove compartment.

'There you go . . .'

He handed it to her with an abrupt nod.

She took the Bible from him and quickly flipped it open. The pages automatically parted at the place where she'd stored her AIDS orphans article from *Maire Claire*.

'Bloody *hell*,' she suddenly gasped.

'What?'

'Just take a look at *that* . . .'

She held up the book to him.

Garry frowned.

'I tore this article from a magazine, right?' she explained. 'An' I just shoved it into the Bible to keep it safe, yeah? Then Kane texts me with this quote – God only knows why – and guess where it turns out I'd stuck the article?'

'Where?' Garry asked (already guessing the answer).

'Pushed between the *very* page . . .'

'Uh . . . The very *next* page,' Garry corrected her, inspecting it.

'The very *next* page . . .' Kelly echoed (still equally impressed). She removed the article and silently entrusted it to Garry's care, then slowly ran her finger down the verses.

'Here it is,' she said, finally, '2 Corinthians, Chapter twelve, Verse nine . . .'

She cleared her throat: '*And he said unto me, My grace is sufficient for thee: for my strength is made perfect in weakness.*'

She frowned, then read it out again, '*And he said unto me . . .*'

Garry held the article loosely in his hand as he listened to her. His eye rested on it, idly, as she read. But it wasn't actually the AIDS orphans article he was staring at. It was the article on the flip-side of the page, an article about a charity dedicated to bringing solar power to Africa.

Most poor, African households (the article said) were dependent on Calor Gas for their day-to-day power needs, and this was not only ruinously expensive (thereby increasing the cycle of poverty) but environmentally unsound. The only rational way to approach energy provision in the third world (the article continued) was to exploit their greatest natural resource: the sun. By fitting solar panels to people's homes, not only could all their energy needs be fulfilled (and virtually free of charge), but the environmental impact would be all but negligible . . .

'A bit complicated, *huh*?' Kelly scowled.

'I think what it means,' Garry reasoned, 'is that you don't necessarily have to be some kind of a saint to be a good Christian. It's sayin' that you can sometimes learn more when you're weak – or when you fail – because the experience of failin' at somethin' is what makes you into a better person . . .'

'*Wow*.'

Kelly gazed over at him, full of admiration. 'You always did have an amazin' way of puttin' things . . .' she murmured.

Garry shrugged. Kelly continued to stare at him, her cheeks slightly flushed. 'An' I'm really sorry about before,' she added.

'About what?'

'About sittin' on your hand back then. An' about punchin' your arm. An' about callin' you a runt. I was just – *you* know – havin' a bit of fun.'

Garry cleared his throat, nervously. 'Don't stress yourself out about it.'

Kelly continued to stare at him. 'I'll tell you somethin' for nothin', Gaz,' she said, finally.

'What?' he peered at her, long-ways.

'If it turns out that all this crazy stuff that's been happenin' to me lately was just so much pie in the sky, yeah? – just a shower of shit – then I won't actually care. Because at the end of the day I'll just be really chuffed – really *stoked* – that I've bumped into you again.'

'But I never went anywhere, Kell,' Garry maintained.

'I know that,' Kelly smiled.

Garry looked down at the article, but he didn't focus in on it.

'I'm thirty-two years old,' he eventually murmured.

'So what?' Kelly scoffed. 'I don't give a flyin' fig what age you are.'

Garry folded the article in half and tried to pass it back to her.

'An' I certainly hope,' she observed, haughtily lifting her small chin, 'that you'll afford me the same courtesy.'

'Yeah, well . . .'

Garry didn't sound too sure on this point.

Kelly finally took the article from him, placed it back into her Bible and slapped the Bible shut.

'Pals?' she asked, offering him her outstretched palm.

'So d'you reckon that heating's workin' yet?' Garry suddenly enquired, leaning over to peer – with an almost bewildering intensity – into the nearest air vent.

After sitting – completely stationary – for fifteen or so minutes, Kane had been unable to resist snatching up the set of photocopied sheets again. He was especially taken by the anecdote about the fleas ('You should have taken every flea by the neck, and then they would gape, and then you should have cast a little of the powder into every flea's mouth, and lo you would have killed them'). It was the same anecdote – he was certain – that the young boy Fleet had told him. But where the boy might've actually *heard* it (when the document in his hands was almost 400 years old and only readily avaliable from the British Library) was anybody's guess.

There was other stuff, too. Stuff he'd come across himself, stuff he'd experienced first hand – the chapter in which John Scogin was banished – for persistently tormenting the queen – and strictly commanded never to set foot on British soil again (and he'd promptly responded – with typical hubris – by journeying to France, filling his shoes with French soil, then returning, in triumph, and smartly informing the enraged king that he wasn't actually contravening the rules of his exile – the soil that he stood on was *French* after all).

There was a story about a pair of goose wings (John tied them – Icarus-like – to his shoulders, pretending he was going to launch himself from a high tower), and the story in which he bled his wife, by force (under the foot, arm and tongue) after she dared to criticise him to a neighbour. And finally, of course, there was the cruel story which Winnie had taken such interest in – where Scogin had set fire . . .

Kane was suddenly flashed by the van behind him –

Eh?

He glanced up. The long queue of traffic in front had recently inched forward while he'd been engrossed in his reading. Kane harrumphed, took off his handbrake, accelerated, and slowly made up the distance.

He returned to the document . . . Yeah – setting fire to the *barn*. John had been living in Oxford at the time, and his wife had complained to him about the pushy, local vagrants . . .

The van behind honked its horn. Kane started and peered up. The car directly in front of him (a new Volkswagen) had just crept forward by a total distance of approximately 3 measly feet. Kane wound down his window – with some effort (the car had manual winders) – stuck out his hand into the frosty, afternoon air and showed the bolshy driver his middle finger –

So fuck you, too –
Idiot.

The car honked its horn again.

Kane gritted his teeth. He slapped the steering wheel. He gazed into his rearview mirror, cursing under his breath. Then –

Screw it

– he caved. He lifted the handbrake and moved the car gently forward –

There!

Happy now?

The car flashed him –

Yeah. I should think so, too.

Kane glanced into his side-mirror, then back down at his reading matter –

The barn . . .

He began to read. He stopped reading. He closed his eyes –

Now just hang on one . . .

He opened his eyes and peered into his side-mirror –

Cigar

The driver of the van behind was smoking a cigar. And he was –

No, she . . .
Her

– she was holding it regally aloft, her dainty hand neatly encased in a soft, white glove.

Kane laughed to himself, wryly. He slowly shook his head. Then he jumped out of the car and strolled over to the van.
'I have a train to catch, Kane,' Peta informed him with a caustic look. 'So if you could just bring yourself to actually *concentrate* . . .'
'Are you leaving for good?' he demanded.
'For the better, I hope,' she responded smartly.
'Was it a sudden decision?'
'I suppose all decisions are,' she mused, 'when you finally make them.'
He frowned at her.
'So how are you warming to The Commissar?' she wondered.
'Pretty well,' he conceded. 'Although the handling . . .'

'*Urgh*, the handling,' Peta interrupted him, scandalised, 'quite *shocking*, isn't it? So clunky and unyielding . . .'

'Although I love the stickers on the back,' Kane admitted, 'the Jamaican flag was a master-stroke.'

'I thought you might give the car to your friend,' Peta told him. 'Did you find the registration documents in the glove box?'

'My friend?'

'Yes. Your crazy friend. The friend who worships peacocks.'

'Sorry?' Kane frowned. 'Do I actually have a friend like that?'

'Yes. You know . . . the Kurd. The one who's terrified of salad.'

'*Gaffar?*'

'That's him. Gaffar. I thought you could give it to Gaffar. I thought it might quite suit him.'

'Or perhaps I could give it to Beede,' Kane volunteered.

'Oh really?' Peta didn't seem especially taken by the idea. 'But d'you think it's entirely Beede's *style*?'

She raised a single, perfectly etched brow at him, then took a puff on her cigar.

'I suppose he could always sell it,' Kane suggested, 'and use it to pay off some of the interest on his huge debt.'

Peta turned to look at him in mock-surprise. 'Beede's hugely in debt?'

'Beede's problem,' Kane cordially informed her, 'is that he's developed this strange, little habit. It involves paying a professional forger to duplicate random objects . . .'

'An artist,' Peta interrupted.

'What?'

'He's been paying an *artist*, not a forger.'

She paused for a moment. 'Do you think it might be a good idea,' she abruptly changed the subject, 'to turn the engine off?'

'Pardon?'

'The Commissar . . .' she pointed. 'You appear to have left the engine running.'

Kane peered over at the car (his expression one of studied indifference). 'So what happened to *your* friend?' he wondered.

'*My* friend?'

'Yes. Your friend with the incomprehensible accent. The woman you claimed to have – now what was the word you used . . . ?' He deliberated for a moment. 'Ah yes, *collected*.'

'You mean Ann?'

'Was that her name?'

'Still is,' she said, tartly.

'So how many other people do you have?' Kane enquired.

'Have? In what *sense*?'

'Well a collection can never be just *one*, can it?'

Peta merely smiled at this.

'Did you collect Beede I wonder?' Kane continued, silkily. 'Did you collect *Dory*, perhaps?'

'Did I collect *you*?' Peta asked, with a smirk. She offered him a puff on her cigar, but he refused.

'So let me get this straight . . .' Kane continued.

'Don't you just adore this song?' Peta interrupted him. She reached into the van and turned up the volume on her scruffy, old cassette player. A cacophonous horn cut through the icy air around him.

Kane scowled. 'Who is it?'

'It's *Bird*, you ignorant boy . . .' she leaned in again and turned it up still louder. 'Charlie Parker. "Steeplechase". It's based on the chords from "I Got Rhythm". Miles is in the mix there too, somewhere . . .'

She tapped her cigar ash, rhythmically, on to the tarmac. 'This was actually one of the first recordings Bird made after seven months in Camarillo Sanatorium. Before that he'd been living like a tramp, in a garage, subsisting on charity handouts. He'd developed schizophrenia . . .' she shrugged. 'Although the booze was his real problem . . .'

She took another puff on her cigar, then coughed and tapped at her chest, impatiently.

'When he finally came out,' she continued, her eyes watering slightly, 'he got a regular gig at the Hi De Ho Club, and apparently, each night, before he'd even blow a note, he'd sink eight double whiskies, back-to-back.'

She leaned in and adjusted the volume again.

'Miles left shortly after they recorded this session. They say Charlie never got over it. Miles was like his adopted son . . .'

They both listened to the music for a while, in silence.

'Anyhow,' Peta frowned (changing the subject, on a whim), 'it was all totally above board. There was nothing remotely dubious in it.'

'Sorry?'

Kane was still thinking about Miles and Charlie.

'The work I did for Beede. I charged him, per hour, at my standard rate. If he'd been anyone else I'd've charged him double – the work itself was soul-destroying; stupid, pointless, *incredibly* tedious . . .'

'Did you ever think to ask why?' Kane asked.

'Why what?'

'Why he wanted you to duplicate those objects?'

'Of course not,' she snapped, 'I already *told* you, it isn't my place to ask questions like that. It wouldn't be polite.'

'*Polite?*' Kane snorted. 'Maybe you just didn't bother asking because you didn't actually need to. You'd hired a detective. You already knew . . .'

'Oh really?' Peta delivered him a droll look. 'And what did I *know*, exactly?'

'That it was all part of some kind of crazy vendetta against Tom Higson.'

'Why?'

'Because Higson was behind the theft of those tiles from the old mill, and to pay him back Beede resolved to duplicate his life. To turn everything he touched – everything he cared about – into a lie . . .'

'But it wasn't just a straightforward duplication,' Peta expanded, helpfully, 'I was instructed to build a tiny fault into each piece. Something to help generate this indefinable sense of unease . . .'

'Did he say that was why?'

Kane was shocked.

'He didn't need to. It was obvious.'

'Okay,' Kane scowled, 'so here's the part I don't get . . .'

He reached out and took Peta's cigar from her, then inhaled on it, deeply. 'What I can't understand,' he exhaled, then passed the cigar back, 'is why he came to you, when you were the very person Higson had stolen the tiles for.'

Peta inhaled on the cigar herself. She didn't speak.

'I guess you must've wanted me to know . . .' Kane reasoned.

'The photo in the barn,' Peta interrupted wistfully, 'a bit of a give-away, huh?'

Kane nodded.

'What can I say?' she smirked. 'I just love to dance on the razor's edge.'

'But what you still haven't explained,' Kane persisted, 'is why Beede came to *you* . . .'

'That's simple,' she shrugged, 'because I'm the best.'

'But didn't he know about your involvement? Didn't he have the slightest inkling?'

'*Ah*. The million dollar question,' Peta sighed. 'Did he or didn't he?' Kane was quiet for a while, and then, 'Beede's hardly famed for his great sense of humour,' he mused, 'but is it remotely possible that he might've commissioned you as . . . I dunno . . . almost as some weird kind of *joke*?'

'Don't think it hasn't dawned on me,' Peta grimaced. 'My passion – my *reason* – is to celebrate beauty . . .'

'But Beede transformed you into the queen of the ceramic donkey, the chipped coffee pot, the *mug*-tree . . .'

Kane sniggered. 'Perhaps the *real* mug here . . .'

'Was me. Yeah,' Peta growled. '*Hilarious*.'

'But if you suspected as much up front,' Kane frowned, 'then why didn't you simply turn him down – refuse the job?'

Peta gave this question some serious consideration.

'I suppose because I was intrigued – at least to begin with . . . amused, tantalised, *seduced*. And maybe there was a small element of guilt . . .'

'*Guilty?*' Kane chortled. '*You?!*'

'And I wanted to keep an eye on him,' Peta persisted, 'I wanted to see how it might play out. I wanted to . . .'

'*Collect* him?'

'No. *Protect* him, if you must know. From himself, in the main.'

'*Wow*,' Kane slowly shook his head. 'Well you've certainly done one *helluva* job.'

Peta shot him a sour look. Kane glanced over at the traffic. There was now a space in front of the Lada of about 10 or 12 feet.

'So what did you make of the scheme?' he wondered, turning back.

'Beede's scheme?' Peta rolled her eyes. 'What do you *think* I thought? It was ludicrous. It was idiotic. I couldn't make head or tail of it . . . I mean Tom's a law unto himself. He's brash. He's totally unsentimental. He lacks integrity. He lacks *empathy*. What could *Tom* be expected to understand about the *essence* of a thing? The *heart* of a thing?'

She paused. 'Although Pat – Tom's poor *wife* . . .'

'But you went ahead with it, just the same . . .'

'*Uh* . . .' Peta inspected the glowing tip of her cigar, 'well, *yes* and no . . .'

She tried to repress a smirk.

Kane frowned. 'You duplicated the objects . . .'

'Absolutely,' she nodded, 'I did a grand job. In fact I did *such* a grand job . . .'

Peta pondered something for a while. 'Are you much of a poker player, Kane?' she wondered.

'Sure. I play the odd hand . . .'

'Then you'll be familiar with the concept of a double-bluff?'

Kane nodded, slowly.

'Well let's just say,' Peta grinned, 'that if there *was* a joke played, then I wasn't the only victim of it.'

Kane stared at her, bemused. Then the coin dropped. 'You swapped the things *back*?'

She shrugged, coyly.

'But . . .' Kane scratched his head, confused. 'When? *How?*'

'*Urgh,*' she waved her hand, airily. 'Let's not get into all of that. It wasn't *difficult*, trust me . . .'

'But he paid you forty grand,' Kane was horrified. 'Money he obviously didn't have. He paid you in good faith . . .'

'Good *faith*?' Peta chuckled. 'Just listen to yourself! What's happening to you, Kane?' She reached out and tousled his hair. 'How *sweet* you suddenly sound . . .'

Kane glowered at her.

'Anyway,' she confided (in the kind of voice you might use when counselling an idealistic child about why it was fine for his parents to lie about the existence of Father Christmas), 'I think you'll find that these things generally have a strange way of working themselves out.'

'Do they?' Kane wasn't buying it. 'How, exactly?'

'The way I'm seeing it,' Peta shrugged, 'forty grand is a small price to pay to get your only son back.'

Kane scowled.

'So what about Dory?' he demanded, keen to move on. 'How did he fit into the whole thing? Did he help Dad? Did he betray him?'

'Oh *please* don't make me trawl through all this, Kane,' Peta groaned, 'I've got a train to catch. And life's too short. Just enjoy the *mystery*. Take from the situation what you *need*. Be selective. Pick and mix. You're usually so talented at that.'

'But I saw Dory in your cottage,' Kane wouldn't let it drop, 'and I know you said you'd hired a private detective. That's what Dory does, isn't it? I also know that he's cunning, that he's fucked up. That he hung a bell on Beede's cat. Or Higson's cat. Or whoever the hell's cat it actually was . . .'

'A bell?' Peta seemed astonished.

'I know that Dory was actually there when the tiles were stolen, that he was on the scene during the burning down of Higson's warehouses, that he had some kind of a grudge against Harvey, something that possibly even went back way beyond . . .'

'Are you sure you shouldn't turn the engine off?' Peta was peering over towards The Commissar again. 'In my experience . . .'

'Screw the car,' Kane interrupted her. 'Stop evading the issue. Just tell me the truth, for once . . .'

Peta suddenly burst out laughing. 'The truth? Are you serious?'

'Yes.'

Kane was indignant.

'The *truth*,' Peta informed him, baldly, 'is just a series of disparate ideas which briefly congeal and then slowly fall apart again . . .'

'No,' Kane shook his head, 'I'm not buying that. What's been going on feels really . . . really *coherent*, as if . . . as if everything's secretly hooking up into this extraordinary . . . I dunno . . . this extraordinary *jigsaw*, like there's a superior, guiding *logic* of some kind . . .'

'The truth,' Peta smiled, 'is that there is no truth. Life is just a series of coincidences, accidents and random urges which we carefully forge – for our own, sick reasons – into a convenient design. Everything is arbitrary. Only art exists to make the arbitrary congeal. Not memory or God or love, even. Only *art*. The truth is simply an idea, a structure which we employ – in very small doses – to render life bearable. It's just a convenient mechanism, Kane, that's all.'

'I've *seen* things,' Kane doggedly maintained, 'I've experienced things . . . *crazy* things. I've felt this energy, this sense of . . . of *connectedness* . . .'

'Just chemicals,' she pointed to his head. 'Up here. Too much coffee. Too many hormones. Too much sugar . . .'

'But other people have felt it, too . . .'

'Then a kind of joint hysteria . . .'

'No.' Kane shook his head.

'We're all raised to think we're so special,' Peta scoffed, 'that all our experiences are so important, so meaningful, so *particular*, so individual. But if you look at the work of the confidence trickster, the magician, the psychic – even the *priest*, for that matter – what they depend on – how they *function* – is to play on the universality of human experience, on how bland, how predictable, how *homogenous* we all really are . . .'

'But what if I've discovered things – or seen things – which are completely beyond my range of possible experience. Stuff about the past. Stuff about . . .'

'You were telling yourself a story. You were weaving a spell. You were making all the parts fit. You were feeding into a general energy, a universal energy. You were probably adhering to a basic archetype – a "first model" as the Ancient Greeks would have it – something like . . .' she shrugged, 'he's threatened by his father, he loved his mother, he's terrified of death . . . or maybe something more intellectual, more esoteric like . . . I don't know . . . like the idea of this disparity between fire and water,' she pulled a moronic face, 'or the absurd idea that language has these *gaps* in it and that lives can somehow just tumble through . . .'

'That was Beede's idea,' Kane interrupted her. 'You said it was a good idea before. You *liked* it.'

'Nah. I probably just said what I needed to,' she shrugged, 'so we'd both end up here.'

Kane took a step back from her. 'You're a class act,' he smiled, 'I'll give you that.'

'You seriously believe *I'm* behind all this?' Peta grinned. 'You honestly think that I have the energy – the *means* – to bring this all together? That I'm some kind of a conduit? Some kind of . . .'

'But why not?' Kane demanded. 'It's your story too, isn't it?'

'I'm flattered,' Peta chuckled, 'touched, even.' She paused. 'And perhaps I was an unwitting midwife to something,' she conceded, 'but if I was, then it was something that was already born. Because everything already exists. It's all there for the taking. But we never actually take it all. We just choose the little bits we need to further our agenda. And why shouldn't we? Because it doesn't serve our purpose to see the whole picture. And the parts that we do see? The parts that we do discover? They're often the same parts. And how we keep it fresh is that we constantly re-create them, then conveniently forget them, then suddenly rediscover them anew, own them anew . . .'

'Maybe,' Kane said. He didn't seem entirely convinced.

'It was never about the tiles, Kane,' Peta sighed. 'It was only ever about Beede and what he felt. Or maybe – more to the point – what he *couldn't* feel.'

'Perhaps you underestimate him,' Kane maintained. 'Perhaps Beede actually knew something – all along – that you didn't.'

Peta merely shrugged. She glanced down at her watch, then looked up. 'The Commissar is just about to overheat,' she announced.

Kane peered over towards the car. He saw a tiny plume of steam ascending from the bonnet.

'Balls,' he cursed.

'Just as the traffic starts to shift,' she groaned. 'Would you believe it?'

She leaned down and grabbed something from the van's front passenger seat. It was a large bottle of water. She handed it to him. 'He'll take twenty minutes to cool down,' she said, 'and give it five, at least, before you risk unscrewing the radiator cap.'

Kane took the bottle and started walking, backwards, towards the car. 'I'm not finished with you,' he yelled.

'Yes you are.'

She switched on her indicator, and slowly overtook. Kane was reaching – anxiously – into the steaming engine as the van drew past. He glanced up. He saw her lips moving. He heard her mutter something – a parting shot. And it was either, 'Take care not to burn your hands' or 'Take care of your *surgeon's* hands . . .' Either one or the other. He couldn't tell which. But after she'd spoken, he saw her head tip back, and he could've sworn he heard a sharp, cruel cackle – a chuckle, a *chortle* – as if she'd actually just said something totally hysterical.

TWENTY

'Beede?' Dory was muttering. 'Beede? *Beede?* Are you still with me?'
Beede was sitting on a bench in a stationary ambulance, clutching on
to the feather as if his life depended on it. Dory was lying on a stretcher
beside him. He was bleeding heavily. His shattered head had been
fitted with some kind of padded helmet and he'd been heavily sedated.

'Dory?' Beede leaned over towards him. 'It's Beede. I'm here. I'm
right beside you.'
He tried to grab Dory's hand, but his free arm was too heavy to lift.
He shuffled a little further forward instead, wincing as he moved. One
of the two ambulancemen gave him a warning look but Beede ignored
him.

'Dory?' he repeated. 'I'm here, I'm right here. I'm not going
anywhere, I promise.'
Dory's blue eyes fluttered open. 'Is he gone, Beede?' he gasped. 'Is
it finally done with?'
Beede considered this question, carefully. 'Yes,' he said, glancing nerv-
ously over his shoulder, 'I'm sure he is. I'm sure it must be.'
'Oh thank God,' Dory panted, smiling. 'Oh thank . . .'
Then his eyes suddenly widened. 'Sm . . . *smoke* . . .' he coughed.
His voice sounded hoarse again.

The second ambulanceman gave Dory some oxygen. 'Just try and
stay still,' he advised him. 'We'll soon be on our way . . .'
He glanced over at Beede. 'There's a terrible traffic jam,' he explained,
'because of a huge fire on one of the local estates. An entire street
went up, apparently.'

Dory tried to knock his oxygen mask away. 'What's happening?'
he gasped. He tried to lift his arms, to sit up, but they were strapped
down too tightly.
'You're in an ambulance, Dory,' Beede told him. 'You're going to
hospital. You're going to be . . .'
The ambulance jolted forward. Its siren began wailing. Beede winced
again.

'But I need to . . .' Dory's eyes were starting, his temples were pulsing. 'I *must* . . .'

'Calm down,' Beede tried his best to soothe him, 'just calm down and . . .'

'*Stop* . . . I need to . . . to . . .'

Dory gazed, in desperation, towards the ambulance's back windows. 'I need to *stop* . . . '

'Try and stay still,' the second ambulanceman repeated. 'You're in shock. Try not to move your head around too much . . . '

Beede glanced towards the windows himself.

'*No*. I *must* . . . I *can't* . . .' Dory continued to struggle.

'We may need to sedate him further,' the first ambulanceman murmured to his partner.

'Can we really risk that?' his partner murmured back.

'*Tür*,' Dory suddenly wheezed, his hands struggling with the straps that bound him, 'can't . . . can't . . . *tür*.'

'Do you know what he's saying?' the first ambulanceman asked Beede.

'He's saying . . . *uh* . . . tür,' Beede interpreted, slightly panicked. 'I think that's German for . . . for door . . . although . . .' he frowned, confused, 'although *tier* . . . it could be *tier*. That means an animal, or . . . or – more formally speaking – a *breathing* thing . . .'

Dory was hurling himself around so violently now that some of the straps which bound him were beginning to loosen up.

'He's incredibly strong,' the first ambulanceman muttered, battling to re-tighten them. His partner replaced the oxygen mask over Dory's face. Dory tried to knock it off. He was frantic. His voice echoed away, hollowly, inside of it.

'In . . . in some other Indo-European languages,' Beede suddenly began to speak again, 'in . . . in Lithuanian and Church Slavonic, for example, there are variants on the word which mean "gasp" or . . . or "breath". They come to us via the pre-historic . . .'

Beede paused. He stared, in horror, at Dory's contorted face. Dory was still shouting. His eyes were bulging.

'*TÜR*,' he was screaming, '*BEEDE! BEEDE! TÜR!*'

'Perhaps you should take that thing off,' Beede exclaimed, shifting even further forward, 'he needs to be able to speak freely. He needs to be able to . . . to *communicate* . . .'

The ambulanceman was trying to inject a further dose of sedative into Dory's arm. 'Just stay back,' he told Beede sharply. 'If you actually want to *help* your friend then just . . .'

He struggled to hold Dory's arm still. His partner was physically restraining Dory's head.

'TUUUUR!' Dory screamed. 'NO!'

He began to experience some kind of seizure. He was foaming at the mouth. His eyes were rolling back in his head. His fists were clenched. A series of mechanical alarms started to go off.

Beede stood up. The pain he felt as he did so was really quite unimaginable.

'This must be the end,' he thought, 'this can't continue.' He felt a strange sense of relief, almost of satisfaction.

'Sit down!' the ambulanceman yelled.

'I'm going to the *door*, Dory,' Beede informed his friend, staggering around a little as the speeding ambulance raced along. 'I'm going to the *tür*! The *door*. See? I can *hear* you, Dory, *see*? I can *understand*. *Look!* I'm going to the door . . . I'm standing by the . . . the *d-d-deur* . . . '

He blinked.

Huh?

Dory's quivering body suddenly relaxed. His strong arms went limp. The alarms continued to sound.

'Oh *shit*,' the first ambulanceman said.

Beede frowned. He stared down at the German, confused. He raised a shaking hand to his neck. He felt a terrible pain there, an intense pain, like a blow, almost a *kick*. Then his eyes widened. He took a quick step back.

A man stood before him – a small, mean, dark man – with both arms outstretched. He was smiling. He was moving forward. There was something cruel, something almost *sinister* . . .

'Oh my *God*,' Beede murmured, 'but of . . . of *course* . . . the *tür*, the . . . the *door* . . . *That's* what he . . . '

He quickly glanced behind him. The doors flew open. He held on to the feather. He carried the feather with him.

It took exactly twenty minutes for the car to cool down again. During this time Kane loaded his stash into his pockets, shoved the book and the photocopied sheets into the glove compartment, tried to light a cigarette, but he couldn't find the . . .

The fucking lighter –
What is it with these fucking lighters?

He peered down the side of the driver's seat –

Nope

He peered down the side of the passenger seat –

Nope
Although . . .

He frowned. He squeezed his hand down the thin gap –

Ouch

– he winced (he'd managed to acquire a small steam burn on his palm) and retrieved –

Jesus H!
A bloody scratchcard!

It was the un-used scratchcard which he'd thrown away earlier –

Must've dropped out . . .

Kane stared at it, morosely. Then he stared at his cigarette. Then he stared over at his phone. He threw the cigarette on to the dash. He grabbed his phone. He turned it on –

219 messages
Fuck.

He dropped the phone into his lap and re-inspected the scratchcard. He rubbed at it, idly, with his thumbnail –

One
Two
Three
Four . . .

Eh?

He picked up his phone again. He drew a deep breath. He rang Gaffar.
'Gaffar?'
'*Yah?*'
Gaffar sounded severely short of puff.
   'What are you doing?'
'Push this stupid bike.'
'The scooter?'
'Yah.'
   'Where are you?'
'Uh . . . I dunno. My bike is not petrol.'
   'You ran out of gas?'
'Yah.'
'And you don't know where you are?'
'Uh . . .'

Silence

'. . . no.'
   'Is there a signpost?'
'Uh . . .'
'Is there anyone around you could ask?'

'Sure, is plenty car. Is uh . . . is all stop here.'

'A traffic jam, huh?'

'Uh . . . yeah.'

'Well just knock on the window of the nearest vehicle and hand them your phone. I'll do the rest.'

'Serious?'

'Sure. Just knock on a window and . . .'

Long silence

'Hello?'

'Hi. Did some Kurdish dude just hand you this phone?'

'Yeah.'

'That's great. Would you mind telling me where you are?'

'Where *I* am?'

'Yeah. He's lost. I'm trying to find out his exact location.'

'Well I'm stuck in a traffic jam. I'm just waiting at the roundabout for the Hamstreet turn-off. Cedar Farm's to my right . . .'

'That's great,' Kane butted in. 'Thanks. Could you pass him back the phone?'

Pause

'Gaffar?'

Silence

'Gaffar?'

Silence

'GAFFAR?'

'Yah?'

Gaffar sounded a little distracted.

'What's happening?'

'I dunno. Is this . . . uh . . . this *sound*.'

'A sound? What kind of a sound?'

'Is uh . . .' he inhaled, and then, *'Eee-ooo-iiii Eee-ooo-iii.'*

'Fuck.'

Kane pulled the phone away from his ear.

'Is bird,' Gaffar expanded. 'Is big tail bird.'

'Can you see it?'

'No.'

'Oh.'

Pause

'Well I'm about 2 miles down the road,' Kane continued, 'so if you just stay where you are, I should be with you in about ten minutes. I've got some work I need you to help me with . . .'

He paused, 'And I've got you a new car.'

'Yah?' Gaffar sounded intrigued. 'Whas?'

'It's a Lada.'

'Fuck off!'

'Seriously. It's a Lada. A Lada Estate. Black. Fat wheels. Crazy suspension. From Jamaica.'

'Fuck *off*.'

Kane chuckled, 'Yup.'

He prepared to hang up, but before he did, 'And guess what else?' he said, his smile slowly fading.

'What?' Gaffar asked (still pondering the Lada).

'I just won forty grand on a scratchcard . . .'

Kane inspected the scratchcard as he spoke, with a scowl.

'*Lucky*, huh?'

Maude had approximately 150 trees still to do. She was exhausted, and she had a painful splinter in her finger, but she kept on hacking away at the collars. She was determined to get the job done, come hell or high water.

'Hello again.'

She glanced up. It was Kane. He was leaning out of a black Lada.

'What are you doing back here?' she growled.

'I'm looking for my friend,' Kane said. 'He's short, dark, Kurdish – doesn't speak much English . . .'

Maude shook her head.

'He was pushing a scooter. He said he'd be waiting for me down at the roundabout. I found the scooter dumped by the road there, but he'd vanished, so I'm just driving the whole circuit in the vain hope . . .'

Maude was inspecting her finger. She seemed upset.

'It's been crazy around here,' she observed.

'There was a huge fire on the estate, apparently,' Kane said. 'You can see the plume of smoke for miles . . .'

'There was a crash on the slip road,' Maude interrupted him, 'in almost the exact spot where you hit me, earlier. It was a ten-car pile-up. This fire engine slammed into the back of . . .'

'Did you see it?'

'No. But I heard it. I ran down there. There was a pregnant woman. She was trapped inside her car. She was panicking. She thought she was losing her baby. I had to stand there and wait with her. Hold her hand. All these other people around me were crying out for help, bleeding, staggering from their vehicles . . .'

'*Jesus.*'

Kane sprang from the Lada. 'What on earth are you still doing here? You must be in shock. Get into the car. Let me drive you home . . .'

'And I've got this . . . this *stupid* . . . ' Maude pointed, enraged '. . . this *splinter* in my finger . . .'

She yanked off her glove.

Kane drew in closer. He gently took her hand. 'That isn't actually too bad,' he told her, 'I can probably just . . . '

He squeezed the splinter – hard – under his thumbnail.

'*Owwww!*' she bellowed.

He jerked back, alarmed.

'I already *tried* that,' she whimpered, 'I need a pin to dig it out with, but I don't . . .'

'Hold on a second . . .' Kane smiled. He removed the pink charity ribbon from his lapel.

'I have one,' he said, showing it to her.

She inspected the pin, mollified.

'What's that special word the Arabs always use . . . ?' Kane murmured, taking hold of her hand again, then gently applying the pin to her fingertip. He pushed it in, very carefully, and five seconds later, the splinter was out.

'There you go,' he said, brushing it on to his own fingertip. 'See? It was only very tiny . . .'

'Thanks.'

She smiled up at him. 'That didn't hurt at all.'

Kane placed the pink ribbon against his lapel and tried to pin it back into place again, but as he applied pressure to it, the pin – for no reason that he could fathom – suddenly snapped in half.

He grimaced, hung the ribbon over his button and dropped the two tiny fragments into the grass.

Maude, meanwhile, had returned to her task.

'God, you're tenacious,' he said, almost admiringly.

She didn't respond.

'Not too many left now,' he continued, peering down along the embankment.

'You'd better head off and find your friend,' she suggested.

'Yeah.'

Kane turned to go. He took a couple of steps towards the car, then he paused and turned back again. 'Let me do the last few,' he said.

'I'm fine,' she insisted.

'No, go on. I'd be happy to . . .' he paused. 'I'd *like* to.'

He put out his hand for the Stanley knife.

'It's pretty blunt,' she warned him.

Kane took the knife, bent over, and removed five collars in quick succession.

'Easy,' he said.

She snorted.

'So you're a student?' he asked.

'Yeah.'

He removed another three collars.

'What of?'

'English, Economics and Political Theory, although I'm pretty crap on the financial side of things . . .'

'And what do you plan to do with those?'

'You mean when I graduate?' She shrugged. 'Become a teacher, I suppose.'

835

Kane removed a further two collars.

'So what do *you* do?' she wondered.

'Huh?' he scowled. 'How d'you mean?'

'Well I've seen you in the French Connection . . .'
She gave him a significant look.

'Oh . . .' Kane slowly straightened up. 'Uh . . .'
He gave his response some careful consideration. 'Well, I suppose I'm what you might call a vagabond,' he answered finally.

Maude glanced over at him, mystified.

'A kind of . . . of *medical* vagabond,' he expanded, before casually delivering her his most disarming smile.

The Darkmans lay in wait. He knew it would only be a matter of time before one of the two men came. Gaffar was the first to arrive. He was limping. He'd developed a blister on his heel from his new, leather boots. He was searching for the bird, but all he found was a stray feather by the edge of the road.

As he bent down to inspect it Gaffar noticed that there were shards of broken glass everywhere. And traces of blood. And there was corn on the tarmac – tiny, crushed ears of corn.

He approached the feather with caution (he had no intention of picking it up), but then he spotted The Darkmans – from the corner of his eye – moving stealthily towards it.

'No,' Gaffar said firmly, reaching down and grabbing it for himself, 'it's mine.'

He clutched the feather, tightly, in his hand. He claimed it as his own. He *annexed* it.

The Darkmans prowled around him, foiled, enraged, fascinated. And as The Darkmans prowled, Gaffar's mind was suddenly transported back to Hasankeyf. He was just a boy, sitting by the banks of the Tigris River, dreaming of the cool caves, of the magnificent obelisk, of the old, stone archway. Then – without warning – everything was submerged. Gaffar saw himself drowning. He saw his life slowly washing away from him (his family, his dreams, his home, even his tongue).

He felt a moment's sharp anxiety – a sense of suffocating panic – but then he quickly turned away from it. He kicked hard with his feet and swam up to the surface. He drew a long, deep breath –

Haaaaaaah!

The Darkmans crouched down and appraised Gaffar intently. He held out his hand for the feather. He pretended to be sad. He pretended to be broken. He dabbed at his eyes. He shivered like a kicked puppy.

Nope. Gaffar shook his head. But as he watched The Darkmans' pathetic act, Gaffar's mind was suddenly transported back to Diyarbakir; the Town of the Black Walls. And he was standing, barefoot, in the dirt, his hands clenched into fists. And he was fighting a losing battle to keep his insides in and the outside out. Then, half-way through the battle, he turned, with a gasp (the taste of blood on his lips), and he saw his poor mother standing behind him, on the sidelines: abandoned, disappointed, alone.

Gaffar winced. He felt a moment of profound self-loathing, but then he sprang forward and he delivered it a swift, sharp upper-cut. He kicked it. He winded it. He hurled it down.

The Darkmans slowly rose to his feet. He scratched his chin, thoughtfully. Then he pulled himself up to his full height, placed his hands on to his hips, opened his mouth and *demanded* the feather. His voice crashed through the air like rolling thunder.

Gaffar tipped his head and he listened. And as he listened, his mind was suddenly transported back to a place that he'd never seen before; a place of his father's ancestors, a place called Sinjar. He saw his people farming in peace there. He saw them caring for their livestock, delivering their lambs, waiting patiently for the summer rains. He saw them praying. He saw white turbans, clean robes and joyous devotion. He smelled incense burning. It was a lovely vision, but it quickly faded. Then everything was overturned. He saw chaos, he saw movement, he saw poverty, he saw persecution, and in the midst of all of this he saw his father, alone, in the Sheikhallah Bazaar. He saw the light. He saw the dream. He saw the whale. He saw the lie.

Gaffar scowled. He felt a moment of despair, of profound desolation, but instead of giving in to it, he shoved his hand into his pocket and he felt for his five die. He rattled them in his palm. He removed them from his pocket and showed them to The Darkmans, proudly –

See?
I make my own history

The Darkmans pricked up his ears. He stood to attention. He seemed intrigued, even delighted. He took a small, halting step forward.

Gaffar watched The Darkmans' uncertain approach through bright yet slightly hooded eyes. He chucked quietly to himself, and the chuckle echoed down deep inside of him (it reverberated against the walls of that bottomless well within, that place where the women came to gossip, where the children played, where the mythical peacock loved to perch).

Then, without further ado, Gaffar smiled, extended a gracious hand, and with the legendary ease and beneficence for which his ancient tribe were duly famed, he cordially invited The Darkmans to a game. He even went so far as to promise him the first throw.